He Wanted to End Her Tortured Past—of Shame and Outrage.

"Oh, Daniel, tell me. Am I ruined? Will any man want me now?"

He stroked her long black hair and ran his hand down her back. "Oh darlin', darlin'. Any man would want you. You couldn't help what happened to you. It wasn't your fault."

"But—"

"Glenna, darlin', all men aren't like that. Believe me they aren't. I don't want you to be afraid because of what that perverted beast did. Promise me—promise me you'll forget what happened."

And she was in his arms and he was kissing her, deeply, passionately. The sweetness and longing and hunger seemed to devour her, and she clung to his soft lips long past breathing. She felt his hand on her breast. When his fingers softly stroked her nipple a new sensation joined the sweet havoc his lips were creating. She felt herself sinking into a warm abyss of surrender.

Elizabeth Bright

Reap the Wild Harvest

PUBLISHED BY POCKET BOOKS NEW YORK

A POCKET BOOKS/RICHARD GALLEN *Original* publication

POCKET BOOKS, a Simon & Schuster division of
GULF & WESTERN CORPORATION
1230 Avenue of the Americas, New York, N.Y. 10020

ISBN: 0-671-83233-6

First Pocket Books printing November, 1979

10 9 8 7 6 5 4 3 2 1

Trademarks registered in the United States and other countries.

Printed in the U.S.A.

BOOK ONE
Glenna

1

Glenna O'Reilly loved the cliffs. They ran for miles along the southern coast of County Cork, rising at some points nearly three hundred feet above the North Atlantic. She loved to walk the path atop the cliffs, enraptured by the smells of heather and gorse and the caress of the wind against her skirt. It was always windy on the cliffs, and the surf pounding against the rocks below made its own music, a deep bass melody accompanied by the strident descant calls of the gulls.

It was a rare day for Ireland in September. There was hardly a cloud in the sky, which seemed to extend endlessly until it finally joined the sea. It was as if the sea and sky had embraced and were one, erasing even the horizon in their pleasure with the sun and the warm south wind.

But this day in 1829 Glenna did not dawdle to enjoy the beauty of the cliffs. She raced from her father's farm. She was late. For a time she didn't think she'd be able to get away. Then, in mid-afternoon, she had used a pretext of checking the cows which grazed along the cliffs. Now, breathlessly, she arrived at the lean-to built to shelter the herd from the harsh winter storms.

"Oh, Liam, I didn't think I could make it."

Liam O'Connell said not a word but swept her into

his arms and devoured her mouth with his kisses. And she gave herself to the sweetness, but only for a moment. Pushing him away she said, "Wait. Let me catch my breath."

She was seventeen, almost eighteen and in the full bloom of her maidenhood, with long, lustrous hair, so black and shining it resembled polished onyx, eyes the color of flawless sapphire, and a generous mouth now crimson from his kisses. But it was her complexion that gave her true beauty. Her skin was extraordinarily fair, almost pure white with scarcely a hint of color. At moments like this when she was excited, it seemed to shine with an inner luminescence.

"I cannot resist you, Glenna."

She tilted her head back as she laughed at him. "What did you say, Liam?"

It was how she teased him. Liam was born and raised a Cork man and spoke as all Cork men do, very rapidly, slurring all the syllables together so any utterance sounded like one long, unintelligible word. Glenna was born and raised in Dublin and was very proud of her speech. As her father loved to say, "The best English in the world is spoken in Dublin." He always insisted that Glenna speak correctly, even though they now lived in Cork.

Liam sighed and tried to speak more slowly and carefully, although with only small success. "I said I love to kiss you." And he did, pulling her tight against him, enjoying the pressure of her breasts against his chest.

Again she pushed him away. "And I still haven't caught my breath," but she said it rapidly, mimicking his Cork accent.

Liam O'Connell was twenty-four and Irish to the core. His hair was dark and so wavy it was almost curly. His eyes were blue and his complexion fair, except for his red cheeks which glowed like ripe apples when touched by wind or cold. Glenna was glad she didn't have the Irish cheeks. She thought it unsightly. She had embarrassed Liam by laughing at his speech. She would hate to have her cheeks glow everytime she was embarrassed.

To make it up to him, she tried to kiss him lightly. She intended just to brush his lips, but he again grabbed her, pulled her hard against him and smothered her lips with his. She felt the flatness of him against her and the hard muscles of his back. His kisses were sweet and his passion exciting. She felt a stirring deep inside. "Oh, Liam," she said, tearing her mouth from his.

She leaned back against the rough stone of the lean-to, trying to control what was happening to her. Her lips were slightly parted and her eyes wide, unblinking. He came at her again, his lips hot, drenching hers, his strong arms pulling her ever tighter, arching her backwards, his loins with his hardness pressing against her. Again she tore her lips away. "No, Liam. No."

He released her then and kissed her forehead and her hair and her ears, and buried his mouth in her throat. As he did so, his fumbling fingers undid the buttons of her bodice and in a moment she felt his hand on her left breast. He was gentle, but the rough callouses of his hand caused incredible sensation. "Liam, no . . . please, no." But he didn't stop. He bent his head and his lips consumed the nipple. His tongue and teeth circled and teased it and she felt her body speckled with sensation. Despite herself she moaned and held his head against her. In a moment she moved her shoulders and guided his mouth to her other breast. She leaned against the stone, her body weak with the torment of pleasure.

But he went too far. His right hand left her breast and reached to pull up her skirt. She was unaware of what he was doing until his hand touched her bare thighs.

"No! Absolutely not!" She hissed it at him and pushed him away so hard he lurched to the middle of the lean-to. "Liam O'Connell, I told you. I won't do that. I am not a trollop. I'm not a tavern wench. I've already gone too far with you. But I'll be a virgin as a bride."

His cheeks burning, he let out a stream of almost incomprehensible speech. "But Glenna, you know I love you. I want to marry you."

"Marry? And live where? And on what?" Her head was raised in scorn, her eyes bright with anger. "You'll never get your father's farm. He'll never let you have it. And even if he does, I won't marry you. I'll not be a farmer's wife."

Suddenly she realized her bodice was open, her breasts exposed, and began to button it.

"Don't cover yourself, Glenna. You know how much I love your breasts."

She stopped her fingers and looked at him, then smiled coquettishly. "Do you now?"

"I do, Glenna, I do. There is no skin like yours. You are so soft and smooth—like silk."

"Whenever did you feel silk?"

His cheeks flared again. "Don't make fun of me, Glenna. I know I'm a country boy and you're a Dublin girl, but—"

He looked so contrite, so like a little boy being punished that Glenna felt a return of pity for him. "You like my breasts, do you?"

"Oh, Glenna, there are none like yours."

"And you know all about that, do you?"

Again he was crushed. "Oh, Glenna, please—"

She interrupted him with her laughter. "My goodness, you are sensitive, Liam O'Connell. Come here."

He came to stand in front of her. She took his hand and guided it to her breast. "I like what you do to me, Liam, but if you ever try to touch me anywhere else, I'll confess you to the priest and he'll forbid my ever seeing you again. This is too much sin for him already."

A moan escaped his lips and he bent his mouth to her nipple. She held his head close and looked down at him, feeling a wonder of sensation, but also a deeper feeling she scarcely understood. Like a baby at his mother's breast. Is this how a mother feels? Or is it the intimacy, the sharing of private places between a man and a woman? He has private places. She had never seen a man naked. She wondered what he must look like. Someday. Soon, maybe, but not with Liam. He loved her, she knew. He made her feel good, very beautiful, very feminine, very desirable. His kisses were sweet. She loved what he was doing to her. But no more. She could not marry a farmer, live in Cork forever, and surrender her life and youth and beauty to cow dung and chickens. Then she emptied her mind and surrendered her body to the havoc of sensation his mouth was creating.

He knelt on the earth floor before her and buried his face in her opulent breasts. Again and again, in a ceaseless circular motion, he revolved his face over the flowered nipples, his eyes and nose and mouth and cheeks. She felt the rough edge of his whiskers and it sent streaks of sensation through her whole body. Continually he did it, first one breast and then the other. With his hands he pressed the mounds together until the nipples were mere inches apart, then levied on her a torment of kisses as he rapidly swept his mouth from nipple to nipple. "Oh, Liam," she moaned. She felt herself grow weak. Sparks seemed to be arcing throughout her body. Behind her closed eyelids, everything seemed speckled and bright, full of sparks and lights and popping sounds.

She knew she was surrendering and she didn't want to. But she seemed powerless to forbid what he was doing to her. In a last effort, she opened her eyes and tried to concentrate on the reality around her. She saw the dirty lean-to, the sunshine, the gorse bushes, the cows grazing contentedly nearby. Still she felt the sensations and heard the popping sounds. She shook her head to try to clear it. The popping sounds continued.

She pushed his head away. "Liam, what's that noise?"

He tried to move back toward her, but she wouldn't let him. "I hear nothing, Glenna."

"Yes, yes. Listen." She strained her hearing and for a moment heard only the wind. Then the sound returned, pop . . . pop. A hesitation, then another pop.

"Don't you hear it?"

"Yes, I hear it." He rose to his feet and looked out of the lean-to.

"Well what is it?"

He frowned and shook his head. "It sounds like gunfire, muskets going off." He saw the fear and horror registering in her face. "Don't worry about it. Probably just some hunters."

Glenna knew better. Her father was a wanted man. Brian O'Reilly had been a leader of the revolt in County Dublin. The English had put a price on his head. He and Glenna had fled Dublin and come here to the end of the earth to hide out. For three years, they had posed as farmers, grubbing out a minuscule living on this worthless land near the sea. Both had begun to think the English had forgotten about them. They had even talked of returning to Dublin. Now she too recognized the sounds as musket fire and was filled with horror. Had the hated English found her father? "Oh, my God," she cried and ran from the lean-to, Liam O'Connell racing after her.

Her long skirt billowing behind her, she ran desperately across the cliffs toward home a half mile or more away. From the lean-to, the path meandered through thick gorse up a long slope. Her chest hurting for air, she forced herself to dash upwards as fast as she could. Her skirt caught on brambles and ripped, but she was unaware of it.

At the top of the rise, she ran, faster now, across a plateau perhaps a hundred yards long. Father. It couldn't be her father. But the ever louder sounds of gunfire borne by the wind told her it was. Then, from the plateau she saw a cloud of black and gray smoke rising ahead of her. "God, no," she screamed.

Totally winded, Glenna stopped at the edge of the cliff. Her father's farm lay below her at sea level. A small stream had made a natural gorge on its way to the sea and the tiny farmhouse was beside the stream. She saw the redcoats, perhaps a dozen or twenty in a skirmish line before the house, firing at it. There were other redcoats on horseback. Even as she watched, one of the men on horseback galloped up carrying a torch and set fire to the thatched roof of the house. The barn was already burning. She saw a puff of smoke from the front window of the house. Father was firing back at them. "No, father, no," she screamed and started to run down the slope. But Liam O'Connell had caught up with her. He grabbed her arms and held her. "No, Glenna, no. Stay away."

Glenna tore herself free from him and, screaming, her skirts flying, she ran and stumbled down the slope toward her father. Halfway there, she saw the door of the house open and her father, his brilliant red hair gleaming in the sun, stumble out carrying a pistol. He seemed to be coughing and gasping for air. "Father, father," she screamed as she ran, but no one seemed to hear her or know she was there. Brian O'Reilly raised the pistol. She heard it fire and saw the puff of smoke from its barrel. A redcoat on a horse screamed and tumbled from his mount.

Running with all her might, Glenna was almost to her father when she heard a loud noise and felt a hot wind near her cheek. Suddenly, just as she was mere steps from him, her father, her beloved father, clutched his chest. An expression of horror and fear mingled with his recognition of her. He seemed to be trying to say something to her, but his knees buckled under him and no sound came out. She reached him in time to keep him from falling. But her father, her only relative in the world, was dead in her arms. His blood poured from his wound and on to her dress. She called out to him over and over, stroked his head and wet his cheek with her tears, but none of it would bring him back to her.

Then rough hands pulled her away from him, and he fell to the ground.

"What 'ave we 'ere?"

Through her tears Glenna looked with horror into the smirking face of a redcoat. She saw his gaze fixed upon the open bodice of her dress. She had forgotten to button it.

Almost in one gesture, he dropped his musket and ripped open her dress with both hands. "Migod, lads, see 'is. 'Ese Irish lassies are tasty morsels. Look at 'em tits, would ya?"

Liam O'Connell had followed Glenna down the slope, but more cautiously, hoping to avoid trouble with the English. But when he saw the soldier rip open Glenna's dress, a cry of rage rose from his throat and he hurled himself forward. He grabbed the redcoat and threw him to the ground. Quickly, he put his arm around Glenna to protect her. But it was of no use. Two other soldiers pulled him away from her. He struggled with them, but only briefly. One of the officers on horseback rode up and ended his young life. The sharp sabre cut through his neck at the shoulder. Liam O'Connell stood there a moment, disbelief on his face. His hand went up to try to stop the gusher of blood from his wound, but he fell before it moved halfway.

Glenna watched in horror, both hands covering her mouth.

A soldier kicked the corpse of Liam O'Connell. "These Irish are all alike," he said. "They'll never learn to fight."

The redcoat who had ripped her dress was now back on his feet, leering at her. "But the women. Such big tits. Such skin." He reached out to touch her breast. She backed away from him. "Come on, lassie. I won't 'urt you—not too much anyway." He laughed and jumped forward, grabbing her. With his free hand, he ripped off the rest of her dress, her petticoat and undergarments. He held her totally naked in front of him. "By the Lord, you is a ripe one." Quickly he tripped her and forced her to the ground. "Finders is first," he said as he forced her thighs apart and fumbled with his britches. In horror, Glenna watched a red and purple rod appear in his hand. "You'll like 'is one, lassie," he said, grinning. She felt his weight atop her and saw his ghoulish face blot out the sun. She felt something hard and hot pushing against her. He was trying to put that thing in her, she realized with terror. She tried to struggle, but his weight was too much. "Lie quiet, me lassie. Enjoy." The hard rod pushed harder against her.

Suddenly she heard horse's hoofs and the sound of a gunshot. "Get him off of her," a voice barked, and the weight was quickly gone from her. She saw an officer on horseback, his pistol pointed skyward. "Grover, I'll have you flogged for this. This is the King's Guard, not a whorehouse." Then she saw him look down at her. His eyes widened. What was that look on his face? Then she realized she was naked, lying as she had been left, legs wide apart, knees bent. Quickly, she scampered to her feet. But she was naked. There was little she could do for herself.

The man on horseback laughed. "I must say, Grover, you have excellent taste. Too excellent for scum like you. I should imagine his Lordship will want to—" He laughed again. "—interrogate this prisoner." He holstered his pistol and turned his mount. "Sergeant, get rid of those bodies and march the men back to the barracks. Billings, give that wench a blanket to cover herself, then bring her to me."

A rough, gray horseblanket was tossed at her. Gratefully, she unfolded it and covered herself. Then rough hands pulled at her. "I'm not going anywhere," she screamed. "My father's dead." She struggled against the hands. The blanket fell away from her shoulders.

"Tie up the wench."

Glenna felt her hands forced behind her and the bite of rope into her wrists. The blanket was again tossed around her shoulders and she was lifted upwards and on to the horse in front of the rider. His foot kicked the animal's flanks and they galloped off in pursuit of the first officer.

2

The ride was wild and the wind created by the speeding horse bent Glenna's raven hair nearly straight back. It stretched past the ear of the man named Billings who held her captive. Even on such a warm afternoon, the wind chilled her body where the blanket opened down her front.

Yet, no amount of wind was enough to dry the tears which coursed down her cheeks. Her father was dead, shot down like a dog as he tried to defend his home. Brian O'Reilly had been a gentleman. He had never hurt anyone. Oh, he hated the British. He fought for Irish freedom. But he was not a violent man. He had gone to Trinity College in Dublin. He was a scholar, a man who read and wrote, trying to tell the Irish of their history and their birthright. Now he lay in a pool of his own blood.

He was the only parent she had. Her mother had died giving birth to her. Brian O'Reilly had raised her alone. And such a good father, warm, loving, patient. In a country where girls were considered fit only to bear children, he read to her and taught her. "You should develop your mind, child. Ireland will need the best of all its citizens." The cursed English. She would see her father's murderer hang. She promised herself that.

And poor Liam. Thinking of him, new tears flooded her cheeks. Poor, sweet Liam. He had loved her. He had tried to protect her. And now he was dead. Was everyone she knew and loved going to die?

The ride went on for a long time and Glenna's sorrows and tears consumed most of it. But eventually the chill of her body, the pain of sitting the horse entrapped within Billings' arms as he held the reins, forced her to think of herself. Where was she? Where was she being taken? What was going to happen to her? The man on the horse ahead had said something about a Lordship wanting to question her. About what? She knew nothing of her father's activities. She'd asked, but he'd said it was better she not know. He'd refused to tell her anything. Men occasionally visited the farmhouse at night, but she hadn't known any of them and had not been allowed to eavesdrop. She had not cared about revolution. That was the foolishness of men. Now she wished she'd listened. One way or another she'd avenge her father's death.

The pain from sitting the horse was mounting. If she could only move a little. She tried, but Billings tightened his arms against her and told her not to move. She tried to forget the pain by concentrating on the cold which had seized her. She was shivering. If only she could close the blanket. But her hands—suddenly she was aware of the numbness in her hands. The rope was much too tight.

"The rope is too tight," she shouted against the wind. "My hands are numb."

"I'm not stopping till he does. We're almost there."

"Where?"

"You'll find out."

Wherever she was being taken, she was arriving in a fine state. She was naked except for her shoes. Lord God, what were they going to do with her? She

remembered the shame on the ground in front of her
house. That beast had tried to rape her. She shivered
with revulsion as much as from the cold and forced her
mind away from that ugly thing that vile man had tried
to put inside her. Never would she let any man do that
to her. It was her body. Hers alone. She would never
let another man touch her. Fleetingly, she remembered
the pleasure Liam had brought her in the lean-to. It
seemed centuries ago, although it couldn't have been
an hour. Poor Liam. Fresh tears ran down her cheeks.

Glenna did not realize it, but she was being taken to
the headquarters of James Charles Winslow, seventh
Earl of Wormley. King George IV, acting on the
instruction of his prime minister, Arthur Wellesley, had
appointed him military commander of Ireland with
express orders to end the civil insurrection among the
Irish by rounding up and eliminating the troublemak-
ers. Fresh troops had been made available to him. Lord
Winslow, eager to gain favor with the government and
mindful of a promise of Irish lands as a reward, had
gone about his tasks with brutal energy. He had
hounded the leaders, real or imagined, of the Irish
revolt either into hiding or, more commonly, to the
gallows. Dublin and the counties to the north had taken
several months. He was now ridding Cork and the
south of the seeds of rebellion. These Irish peasants
had to be taught a lesson, however harsh. It was for
their own good. There would not be another America
in Ireland. He would personally see to that.

The seventh Earl of Wormley had set up his headquarters in considerable luxury at Three Oaks, the
estate of a distant cousin, near Cobh, the principal
southern seaport of Ireland. Glenna might have recognized Cobh—she and her father had landed there by
ship from Dublin—but she was brought overland from
the southeast and did not see the harbor. All she knew
was that they galloped up a long tree-shaded drive and
stopped before a huge stone mansion. It was easily the
largest house she had ever seen. She was pulled roughly

from the lathered animal and pushed toward the door by Billings. Stumbling though she was, she was still grateful at last to stand.

The door was opened by a liveried footman, and she was pushed inside to stand beside Billings while the other officer went off to a room at the left. She wanted to ask Billings to please pull the blanket tighter around her, but she was afraid to speak. Instead, she looked at the foyer. She had never seen anything so fine, all marble and polished wood and gilt-framed mirrors. The marble staircase was the grandest thing she had ever seen, unless it was the chandelier of Waterford crystal that seemed to fill the ceiling above her. From her left she heard voices.

"It has been a pleasure talking to you, Morgan. I'm quite sure we'll be doing business together—your country and mine." To Glenna, the voice was very British with the rounded tones of the upper class. A gentleman's voice, obviously.

"I'm glad to hear it." This was a low voice with an accent she had never heard before. It was neither Irish nor English, yet there was a softness and lilt and sonorousness to it.

"I'm having a little party for my officers tonight. Must keep up morale in this godforsaken place. Would you like to attend?"

There was a pause, then the English voice, sharper now with more command in it, said, "Yes, captain."

"I'm sorry to interrupt, your lordship."

"Quite all right, captain. We were—oh, yes, Daniel Morgan, Captain Gordon. Mr. Morgan is an American here on business. Captain Gordon, as you surmise, is one of my officers."

There were mumbled greetings.

"You have a report, captain?"

"Yes, your lordship. We found the scoundrel O'Reilly. Unfortunately, he resisted and we had to kill him. I'm sorry. I know you wanted him taken prisoner."

"What do you mean, you had to kill him." There was annoyance in his voice.

"We tried to burn him out, your lordship. But he came out shooting. He killed one man and would have gotten another. We had to shoot him."

There was a sigh of resignation. "It would have been useful to learn what trouble he was brewing. But I'm sure you did your best. It will save hanging him."

"Thank you, your lordship."

"Very well, captain. I'll see you this evening. As I said, Morgan—"

"Pardon me, your lordship, but there is something else."

"Yes."

"We do have a prisoner. O'Reilly's daughter. I thought she might tell us what we want to know."

"Good thinking, captain. What have you done with her?"

"I brought her here, your lordship."

"Here?" To Glenna, the word sounded like a rasp.

"Yes, your lordship. She is a comely wench and I thought—"

Laughter. "Sometimes you think too much, captain. Well, bring her in. It might amuse Morgan here. These Irish can be interesting sometimes."

In a moment Gordon appeared in the doorway of the foyer and motioned to Billings to bring her. Glenna, aware of her nakedness under the blanket, tried to hold back. She could not use her hands, but she planted her feet and refused to move. Billings dragged and pushed her forward. At the doorway he gave a particularly hard shove and she stumbled into the room. As she did so the blanket fell away.

She saw two men standing before a fireplace in what appeared to be a study or library. She was aware of shelves of books. One man was dressed in an elegant frock coat of dark green velvet shaped to his waist with well-tailored tails falling behind to his knees. His trousers were of a striped material and heavily embroidered near the waist. She supposed it to be the height of fashion, but to her he appeared foppish. He was in his late twenties, perhaps thirty, short, thin and with the strangest eyes she had ever seen. They were a very pale blue; indeed they were virtually colorless. The other man, taller with broad shoulders, wore a brown suit with a long coat of coarse heavy material. He had dark, curly hair and vivid blue eyes, the color of an autumn sky. Both men looked at her in amazement. Then she saw the taller man look away. He seemed embarrassed. The other man, his lordship she assumed, continued to look up and down her body. His gaze was most direct. She felt her whole body flush with shame.

His lips parted into a thin smile. It seemed a sneer to Glenna. "What have we here, captain?"

"This is O'Reilly's daughter, your lordship. I'm afraid one of the men ripped off her clothing trying to rape her. I'm having him punished."

Winslow laughed. "I hope not too severely. Some temptations are just too great." He thought himself amusing and laughed again.

"We had no other clothing for her." He bent to pick up the blanket to drape around Glenna.

"Don't bother, captain. I'm sure the fire will keep her warm." Slowly he strode toward her, his hands folded behind his back. He seemed to be trying to make himself taller, not unlike a strutting peacock. He strode to one side of her and then the other, peering intently. "Sometimes these Irish wenches are quite remarkable. Don't you agree, Morgan?"

She glanced at the other man. He still was not looking at her. There seemed to be a look of pain on his face.

Slowly Winslow reached out and touched her breast. "Quite remarkable, indeed." He gave a quick hard pinch to her nipple. Despite herself Glenna cried out in pain. "So you do have a voice. Tell us your name, then."

Glenna stared at him in hate. She would not speak.

"I asked for your name." He then pinched her other nipple, much harder this time. But Glenna was ready and endured in silence.

"I believe she is known as Glenna, your lordship. Glenna O'Reilly."

"Thank you, captain. You are well informed, as a good officer should be." Slowly he continued his walk around her. She felt him touch her buttocks, then felt another hard pinch. She could barely contain a squeal.

"My, my, a lovely, lovely thing. Such skin. A lot of these Irish are very fair. It makes a strange combination, dark hair, blue eyes and very fair skin." He laughed. "If only they weren't Irish. Don't you agree, Morgan?"

With some heat Morgan, a slight flush to his face, said, "Really, your lordship. I hardly think this is called for."

"You don't?" There was a simpering, sneering quality to his voice.

"I do not indeed."

"Ah, yes. You colonists—I mean you Americans are an egalitarian bunch. I keep forgetting that. But then you never had to deal with the Irish. A stubborn, quite nasty lot. They have a habit of killing our soldiers. But perhaps you are right, Morgan. This lovely thing wouldn't harm anyone, would she? How do you suggest I get her to tell me about her father's—er, associates?"

"I'd start by giving her the blanket to cover herself."

Winslow smiled at Morgan, but dutifully took the blanket from Gordon and draped it around her shoulders.

"See, Morgan, I'm quite a humanitarian at heart." He then spoke to Glenna, a sneering unctuousness in his voice. "Now, Glenna my dear, I want you to listen to me. I am Lord Winslow, the Earl of Wormley. I am the military commander of Ireland. The King has sent me here to bring peace to this part of his realm. I'm sure you'd like that, wouldn't you? Peace, goodwill to men, all that sort of thing?"

She said nothing, but continued to look at him. She felt only hatred. This was the man who had killed her father and poor Liam. The soldiers were acting on his orders.

"I thought you'd agree. You will help the cause of peace if you will just tell me the names of some of your father's associates. You will do that, won't you?"

Still she said nothing, only glared at him as her hatred intensified.

"I think it might be wise for you to speak, my dear."

Glenna spat at him. Winslow ducked and the spittle missed him. His bland eyes narrowed and hardened and Glenna suddenly felt a chill course through her.

He stepped back out of range. "I fear, Morgan, your ideas may not be working too well. But enough—for now. Gentlemen, take her away. You know where."

Quickly, much too quickly to realize what was happening to her, Glenna was pulled from the room and hustled through the kitchen and pantry. Wedged between the two officers, she was pushed and dragged up a series of long narrow stairways. Twice she stumbled and skinned her shins. Up and up they ran her until she stood before a heavy wooden door. Gordon turned a key and pushed her inside. The two men followed her, looking around.

"I wonder what he does with them here?"

"Best not to wonder about some things, Billings. Let's go." Both officers turned to leave, then Gordon, remembering, said, "You won't be needing that," and snatched the blanket from her shoulders.

Glenna stood there in bewilderment. Unable to move or protest, she saw the door shut and heard the key turn in the heavy lock. Suddenly, she began to shiver uncontrollably. Her whole body shook. She had never felt so cold in her life. Why couldn't they have left the blanket? And her hands were still tied behind her. The numbness was worsening. Why couldn't they have untied her?

She looked around the room. How strange. Abso-

lutely bare, just unpainted plaster walls rising up all
around her. From the slant of the ceiling she could tell
it must be some sort of garret room. Very high, perhaps
twelve or fifteen feet above her was a long, narrow
window letting in some light, and it was fading fast. She
wondered what time it must be. From the light, it must
be after seven. Mother of God, what a day. She looked
around the room again. No way out but the door.
Nothing to climb on to reach the window. What was she
going to do? What was going to happen to her? What
sort of place was this? No rugs, no furniture, nothing.
A cell, that's what it was. A place to lock her up. A
bare room, six or eight feet square. Lord, she was cold.
What comfort that blanket had been.

Shivering, she sat in the corner against the wall and
pulled her knees up to her chest. It afforded some
warmth, but she continued to shiver. How cold she
was. But not as cold as father. Poor father, cold, dead
in some scooped-out grave, no one to pray for him, no
one to intercede for him. Silently, only her lips moving,
she began to pray for his soul and for Liam O'Connell's, too. She said her Hail Mary's, wishing she had her
rosary, then asked the Blessed Virgin to intercede for
both men, to give them the warmth and peace of
heaven.

Soon she herself felt warm, terribly warm, though
she still shivered. She realized she was sweating and
shivering at the same time. Fever. Chills and fever. She
couldn't be getting sick. Not now. She couldn't.
Huddling in the corner, alternately freezing and sweating, numbness creeping into her wrists, she repeated
her Hail Mary's over and over until, her head resting on
her knees, she fell into a fitful sleep.

Winslow paced the floor of his bedroom suite in some
agitation. The Irish girl had excited him terribly. Never
had he seen such a body. Such skin, so soft, so thin, so
white. And shining. She almost seemed to have an
inner light. And the tiny waist and the full breasts with

their pink flowers and the hard round bauble at the end. And the thighs, slender and white reaching to her womanhood framed in black. He felt his excitement. He knew he wanted her. Perhaps this remarkable girl would be the one. Yes. . . .

Never had he actually penetrated a woman. He knew that if he didn't soon, he would be the last Earl of Wormley. He had tried so many times. In a high state of excitement he had come to them, certain this would be the time. Yet, something always happened. She said something or did something and he couldn't. There was to him something terribly humiliating in the sex act, being naked, his organs exposed for ridicule, the knowledge he was dependent on the woman, that without her he was helpless. It was his pride, he knew. He had to control everyone, use them, dominate them, make them cower before him. And where was his power with a woman? He never felt he was dominating them. He had no capacity to overpower them physically. Always he was left with shame and ridicule. He could see it in their eyes. He knew they whispered about him to others, damn them. It had been a long time since he had even tried.

But this girl. How she stirred him. Maybe with her. Then, if he did it the first time, there might be others. He could marry, produce an heir. Yes, maybe with this wench. He'd win her to him, be courteous to her, give her elegant clothes. Surely she'd be grateful. She'd never seen anyone so grand as he. Yes, she'd be in awe of him, then perhaps. . . . Yes, maybe this Irish girl.

Irish. That was the rub. Oh, how he loathed these people, poor, dirty, always quarreling and fighting. He'd never be able to consummate his desire with an Irish girl, not even one as appealing as this one. Hadn't she spat at him? The dirty pig. No, never with her.

Then his frown slowly turned into a smile. No reason to waste the girl, though. Some fun was still to be had. And she needed a lesson. And he knew just what to teach her. He began to giggle involuntarily in excite-

ment and anticipation. With trembling fingers he began
to undo his jacket and vest.

Glenna awoke with a start at the sound of the lock
grating in the door latch. While she slept it had grown
quite dark and the light from the candle carried into her
cell blinded her. She closed her eyes against the light
and lowered her head behind her knees. She heard the
door being closed and locked.

"Don't pretend to be asleep, my dear. If you aren't
awake, you soon will be." It was the voice of Lord
Winslow.

Then she both heard a sharp crack and felt a stinging
stab of fire across her shoulder, side and thigh. She
cried out in pain and opened her eyes. In horror she
saw several red welts, already filling with blood,
stretching across her leg. As she turned to look at her
back, she screamed again and bloody streaks appeared
across her breasts. "God no!" she screamed and
pushed herself erect in the corner.

"I thought that might awaken you."

What she saw filled her with terror. In the light of a
candle set on the floor and casting gigantic, eerie
shadows on the walls and ceiling, she saw Winslow. He
wore an outlandish getup entirely of shiny brown
leather, boots rising above his knees, a loin cloth
between his legs, a short vest open at the front and tied
with leather thongs, and long black gloves. On his face
was a hideous beaked mask, also of leather, that made
him resemble a ghastly animal, a dog, a wolf. Only his
voice and cold blue eyes revealed who he truly was. In
his hand he carried a short whip of thongs attached to a
heavy stick. He was raising it even as she saw him.
Again it crashed down on her, like fire, searing her left
shoulder and breast. She screamed and tried to run, but
the whip stung her waist and hip. She pushed herself
into the corner to try to escape it. With her hands tied
behind her, she was defenseless.

"Very sensible, my dear." His voice was strange, hard, cruel, controlled, yet extremely excited. "There is nowhere for you to run." Again and again the whip streaked down on her, raking her, stinging her, lacerating her back and thighs and buttocks. And each time the whip bit into and bloodied her flesh, he shouted: "Who were your father's friends?" Crack! "Who? Just tell me who?" Crack!

The lash seemed to take Glenna's breath away each time it fell, yet she was still able to scream as the whip seared her. Finally, he stopped and she slid back to the floor, sobbing in pain. Her whole body was a mass of bloody welts. It felt on fire.

"Tell me," he hissed, "or there will not be one shred of your pretty skin left." The lash ripped her again with particular savagery.

Finally she was able to stammer, "I-I can't. M-my father n-never s-said. I—I d-don't know."

He lashed her again and she screamed again. The whip had struck her face, narrowly missing her eyes.

She huddled on her side in the corner, her knees raised into the fetal position to protect her face and chest. Repeatedly she felt the lash tear into her side and legs and her arms still behind her. "Tell me, tell me," he screamed.

Then he was pulling her, his left hand grabbing her foot, turning her over while he lashed at her with the whip. She fought him, pushing and kicking with her feet, but it only seemed to worsen his frenzy. She tore her foot from his grasp and again covered herself with her knees. "I'll have you, damn you, I'll have you," he shrieked, flailing with the whip. Then he threw it down and lunged at her. She turned to meet him with her feet and shoved at him. He lurched backwards and lunged at her again. He seized both her knees and tried to force them apart. In his frenzy he had surprising strength, and Glenna felt her thighs giving way. She heard him panting and grunting and cursing as he struggled with her. Then, in the next instant, he stamped his foot down on her left knee and shoved with all his might against her right. She first heard a sickening popping sound, then felt a tearing in her groin, followed by a stab of acute pain. She cried out in agony as his weight crashed down atop her.

3

Daniel Morgan had not wanted to stay at Three Oaks. He had taken an instant dislike to Winslow. Indeed, he abhorred everything about the man, his wealth, his title, his arrogance. More, he instinctively sensed a broad streak of cruelty in him. An inherent malevolence seemed to lie behind those blue eyes. The strangest eyes. Morgan felt he was looking at two holes in the head of the British nobleman.

But this long trip had taught Morgan not to judge but to accept. He was on an unofficial mission for Andrew Jackson, president of the United States. He had a job to do. He was there to make friends—not judge the character of those he must deal with.

He remembered Jackson's instructions vividly. "Old Hickory" had summoned him shortly after his election, even before his inauguration. "I have an important mission for you, Daniel. There are others I might send, but I think this is a job for you."

Morgan had been awed. He had the greatest respect for Jackson. The aging soldier with the long, sad face had always been his hero. He believed that if Andrew

Jackson asked him to walk on water, he'd stride boldly from shore.

"This is going to be the greatest country in the world, but only if we have people. This is a vast land. We have resources we don't even know exist. Our future lies untapped because we have no one to find our wealth, develop it and exploit it. We need people, strong people, to work the land and the mines and the factories. Oh yes, the factories. They'll be coming soon. We'll make England an also-ran one day. We'll exceed England and France, indeed all of Europe. We'll be the most powerful nation on earth—but only if we have more people who want to work and share in our great untapped wealth. And I don't mean slaves. We don't need men driven to labor with the whip. We need free, strong, willing men and women. And we need them right now. Ever hear of a railroad? They're going to pull wagons on rails. It's going to work. I believe in it. The whole country, east and west will be united. Why, right now the people of Baltimore are raising money to build a railroad over the mountains to Ohio. Think of it. People and goods traveling overland to Ohio in a matter of a few days."

Morgan had expressed his amazement.

"It's just what this country needs. A fast, all-weather means of transportation. But it won't come unless we have workers. Somebody has to put down those rails. We need *people* to work. Do you understand?"

Morgan said he did.

"Europe is teeming with people, good people, but poor, oppressed, longing for the freedom and opportunity of America. We need them here. We need them right away to help build this railroad. And we will have them. They will come. I want you to go to Europe as my personal but unofficial representative. I want you to go to England and France, Holland and Germany and Scandanavia. I want you to gain permission for us to send recruiters to sign up people, whole families of people, and bring them to the United States to work.

We have lots of room. We can take all the good hard workers we can get."

And so for months Morgan had toured the capitals of Northern Europe gaining the permissions Jackson sought. European kings and their ministers figured America was insane to want their rifraff, but were nonetheless thoroughly pleased at the prospect of being rid of them. Ireland had not been on his itinerary originally, but in London he had learned that the Emerald Isle teemed with eight million people, too many to be fed. He had met with Winslow to discuss recruiting procedures. Like so many others, Winslow had leaped at the chance to ameliorate his problem by simply shipping out malcontents.

"I can't imagine what you want these Irish for," Winslow had said. "You'll find them stubborn and quarrelsome. But if you want them, you can have them by the boatload." There had been scorn in his laugh.

Morgan had intended to return to his ship that night. His mission was over. The ship had cargo to unload in Lisbon and Madiera, then he would be heading home. He was weary of travel and sick of condescension such as Winslow displayed. Then the girl—Glenna, Glenna O'Reilly—had been brought in. In dismay and disgust, Morgan had witnessed Winslow's humiliation of her.

Now he paced his room at Three Oaks. He shouldn't get involved, he knew. What Winslow did in his official capacity was his business. Andrew Jackson had not sent him to create international incidents. He was to make friends and further the interests of the President of the United States. Yet . . .

He couldn't forget the girl. He had never seen such raven hair and full lips. Her glorious figure and that skin, such skin. There was a fragility and delicacy to her, and she was so young, so obviously innocent and vulnerable. He had seen the terror in her eyes, yet also her defiance, her pride. Such a girl. What man could resist her? Not Winslow, surely. Morgan had seen his lust, his cruelty. Parading around her as if she were cattle on auction. He had seen similar events in the slave markets at home. He had hated it then, and he loathed what he had seen in this house.

Morgan tried again to tell himself not to interfere. And why was he? Because the girl was beautiful? He was not a child. He was thirty-two. He'd had many beautiful women and would have many more. Why bother with this one? He shouldn't. But he knew he would. Somehow he had to get her out of that house. Winslow was an evil man. The girl was in danger. He had to get her out of there.

To where? What would he do with her? Morgan had no plan, merely a half-formed idea of taking her on the ship with him to America. What if she didn't want to come? He had no right to force her. But he couldn't leave her here, not with Winslow. Morgan thought of what he might do to her. Glenna wouldn't stand a chance.

How would he get her out of there? Morgan didn't know. But he realized he had already crossed the point of decision. Whether he should or not, get her out of that house he would.

Even as he witnessed her degradation in the library, Morgan had taken the first steps to try to rescue her. When she was removed, Morgan said, "I'll accept your kind invitation to spend the night. I'd like to meet some of your officers."

"Very good. I think you'll have a good time. The company of men is always stimulating."

Winslow had summoned a servant to show him to his room, saying he had something to attend to.

Now, Morgan paced his room, waiting for dark. Damn, it got dark so late in these latitudes. There was nothing to do but wait. With dark, he could steal out to the stables and get the horse he had hired ready if it were needed. With dark, he could search the house. He'd find her. She had to be somewhere. Then, maybe, perhaps, with luck, he could take her out and ride off to the ship.

For Morgan, the party was both ghastly and interminable. There were perhaps two dozen officers in attendance, all quite drunk, gorging themselves on food and wine. Winslow had appeared, rather late, and in excellent spirits. He seemed much more confident than in the afternoon, very relaxed, having a good time. Yet, he had never seemed to Morgan more arrogant, more supercilious, more condescending toward his officers and his American guest.

"I toast the colonies—oh, excuse me, Mr. Morgan—your country."

Morgan tried to smile and acknowledge the toast.

As the party wore on, Morgan realized that maybe it was affording him a chance. Everyone was quite drunk. Perhaps he could slip out, get Glenna and leave. Yes, why not? His heart pounding in anticipation, he waited. Then, as the officers, egged on by Winslow, began a boisterous song, Morgan slipped out of the hall. He waited outside the door for a moment. If they came for him, he could always pretend to be looking for the toilet. But there were only the sounds of the raucous song. He hadn't been missed.

Where could she be? He had tried to study the house as he was shown to his room, but that had given him little clue. He tried to think. If Glenna was hidden in the back of the house near the kitchen, he had no chance. It would be full of servants. He could not possibly take her out that way. He had to hope she was upstairs. Quickly he crossed the foyer and bounded up the great stairs three at a time. He paused on the second floor. His room was to the right. If she were hidden there, he would have heard her or seen some glimpse of her. She had to be further up. He bounded up the stairs to the third floor. As quickly, yet as silently as possible, he ran from room to room, opening doors. Most were unoccupied and all were empty. Damn. Where could they have taken her?

Think, man, think. He tried to visualize the house as he had ridden up to it. A huge place, fifty rooms certainly. He was on the third floor. There were no more stairs, yet the mansion seemed higher than that. There had to be an attic. That's where she was. But how to get to it? He looked around. No stairs leading upward. Yet, there had to be.

Then he remembered. One door in the center of the hall had been locked. That could be the staircase. He ran back to it and pulled the knob. It wouldn't open. For a moment he thought of breaking down the door. But it would make too much noise. There just had to be a key somewhere. Winslow.

Recklessly, he bounded down the stairs to the second floor and entered Winslow's suite. He ran from room to room. He had to have left the key here—either that or there was no hope. Frantically he searched. Then he found it, in a small inlaid box atop a chest. It had to be the key to the attic. It just had to be.

In four strides he was at the door to Winslow's room. He jerked it open, then quickly closed it. Two of Winslow's officers were below, crossing the foyer. They hadn't seen or heard him. Thank God. He waited a moment. Got to hurry. No time to lose. The party must be breaking up.

Urgently, still trying to be quiet, he slipped out the door and up the stairs to the third floor. He fumbled with the key in the lock. It couldn't be the wrong key. It just couldn't. Then the lock turned. He opened the door on a staircase. He swore. It was nearly pitch black. He needed light. Quickly, he picked up a candelabra from a table in the hall, then mounted the steep stairs.

It took only a minute or two, although it seemed much longer, to find Glenna's cell. He knew it as soon as he saw it. Thank God, there was a key in the lock. He turned it and opened the door on a sight that sickened him. On the floor, unconscious, lay Glenna. Her whole body seemed to be a mass of dried blood. Between her legs lay a pool of blood already turning black.

He moved beside her and set the candelabra on the floor. Poor child. What had he done to her? He touched her forehead. My God, she was on fire with fever. His hand awakened her. She opened her mouth as if to scream, but he placed his hand over her mouth before any sound came out.

"Don't scream. It's Daniel Morgan. I've come to get you out of here."

She looked at him, her eyes glazed. He wasn't sure she recognized him.

"We've got to hurry. And be as quiet as possible. Not a sound, you hear?"

As fast as he could, he reached for his knife and cut the thongs at her wrists. He helped her to a sitting position and rubbed her wrists. All the while he whispered to her. "Mother in heaven, what has he done to you? But it'll be all right now. I'll get you out of here." He took off his coat and put it around her shoulders. "Sorry, darlin', but it's all I got. I didn't think of a blanket."

Tears were streaming down her cheeks. Barely audibly, she moaned, "He hurt me. He hurt me so."

He helped her to her feet. "It's all right now. We just got to get out of here." He tried to lead her toward the door, but she didn't seem able to move. "Oh, God, you can't walk." He bent to pick her up in his arms. She moaned in pain. "This'll hurt, darlin', but we have no choice."

Holding her in his arms like a baby, he carried her out of the room, across the attic and down the stairs to the third floor, guided by the light from below. In the brighter main part of the house, he moved more quickly to the second floor and started down the main staircase. When he was halfway down to the foyer and the front door, Winslow and three of his officers emerged from the left.

"What are you doing?"

Morgan reacted with fear, and the fear made him angry. "I'm taking this child out of here, you god-damned beast."

"Oh, no you're not."

It all happened in an instant. Morgan threw Glenna over his left shoulder like she was a sack of potatoes, and ran down the remaining stairs for the front door.

"Stop him! Seize them," Winslow shouted. But the officers, quite drunk, were slow to react. They might have stopped Morgan on the stairs, but they missed their chance. They all reached the front door. Morgan, strengthened by rage, aimed a blow at the first redcoat. He fell backwards into the other two officers. All fell down. In the confusion Morgan opened the door and ran outside toward his horse. Still carrying Glenna over his shoulder, he had mounted and sent the animal racing down the drive before he even saw another figure reach the door.

4

For a long time, Glenna could not tell dreams from reality. She dreamed of being hot, as though standing in fire. In these dreams she had terrible images of fire and pain. Later, she dreamed of cooling waters and other times of being bathed like a baby and gently rocked in a cradle. This dream seemed to last the longest, and she enjoyed the gentle swaying, back and forth, back and forth in a warm breeze.

Consciousness came slowly. Eyes closed, she began to realize that she truly was swaying. It was not a dream. It was so wonderful and she fell back asleep. When she awakened, and opened her eyes, she saw rafters and paneling of dark wood. Where was she? Yes, she was swaying. Everything was swaying. She closed her eyes, then opened them again. Nothing had changed.

She turned her head and saw she was in a ship's cabin. A lantern burned near the ceiling. She was on a ship. Then she saw a man, a tall man, slumped in a chair, his legs out-stretched, his head off to one side, asleep. She gazed at him a moment. The dark curly hair, the angular chin looked familiar. Then she could keep her eyes open no longer and fell back asleep.

When she awoke again and opened her eyes, nothing had changed. She was in a bunk, a beautifully warm and soft bed. She turned her head to look at the figure sleeping in the chair. Who was he? She knew him from somewhere. She tried to turn in the bed. A sharp pain stabbed at her groin. All the memories of her agony in the garret came flooding back to her. She moaned in pain and started to cry out. They were still after her.

The moan awakened Morgan. He jumped from the chair and went to her and put his hand on her shoulder beneath the blankets. "Lie still. Don't try to move."

She looked at him wide-eyed. He was not Winslow. "Who are you?" Her voice was only a whisper.

"I'm Daniel Morgan." He smiled down at her. "I took you out of that place. You don't remember?"

Still confused, she looked at him. How beautiful he was. "Where am I?"

"You are at sea aboard the *Chesapeake*, a schooner out of Baltimore. You are all right now. Just go back to sleep."

There was something so soothing about the voice. She felt so warm and lovely she couldn't seem to keep her eyes open. She tried, but his cool hand closed lids. "Sleep," and she did.

She did not awaken of her own accord the next time, but was aroused by a hand gently stroking her forehead. "Would you like some broth? You need some nourishment to get back your strength." A hand raised her head and she felt a spoon at her lips. Hot liquid coursed down her throat. It was delicious and she sipped hungrily at the spoon.

"I think that's enough. Not too much at first."

Her head was placed gently back on the pillow. The hot broth did wonders for her. She could already feel her strength returning. "Who are you?"

He smiled. "I told you. Daniel Morgan. I met you at—at Three Oaks."

Then she remembered. The man in the library.

"I couldn't leave you there. I found you and carried you out. I didn't know where to take you. I brought you here."

"A ship?"

"Yes."

"And where are we?"

"On the high seas, bound for Lisbon, then the Madeira Islands and America. I'm sorry. I had no choice but to bring you here."

None of what he said had much meaning for her. "How long have I been . . . been—"

"Three, almost four days. You were a very sick girl. I thought you were a gonner." He put his hand on her forehead. "Your fever has broken. You'll be all right now."

Suddenly, memories of what Winslow had done to her came rushing back. She tried to move her legs and felt a sharp stab of pain.

"Lie still. You have torn ligaments in your—your legs. You need to mend. I think I should make the bandage tighter."

She remembered the whip and felt for her body. But she was wearing some warm, soft garment. "You—you—"

He smiled, but in embarrassment. "This is but a small schooner, miss. We have no ship's surgeon. You needed looking after. There was no one else." His voice trailed off and he whispered, "I'm sorry."

Then it made sense to her, her dreams of being

bathed and rocking in a cradle. She felt a wave of shame and embarrassment.

"I would not harm you. But you needed someone to administer to you. In fact, you should be bathed again."

"Not by you," she said. "Not by any man. I'll do it myself."

"As you wish."

He left the cabin and returned with a basin of warm water and a cloth, placing both on a chair beside her bed.

"If you'll leave me, sir, I'll administer to myself."

He smiled again. "As you wish, but I'll not leave you. I'll turn my back, but I don't think you'll be able to manage this."

He strode across the tiny cabin and looked out the porthole.

Glenna folded back the blankets. She wore some kind of soft shirt, a man's shirt. This man had seen her naked, dressed her. She felt both embarrassment and anger. But as she reached to pull up the shirt, pain stabbed at her and she cried out. She tried again and the pain was greater.

"Please, Glenna. I can't stand to have you in pain. I took care of you when you didn't know it. Does it matter so much now?"

After a third sharp pain, she collapsed on the bed. "I certainly can't do it myself."

He went to her and gently raised her hips and pulled the nightshirt up her waist and over her head. She lay there naked, her body a mass of welts and scabs. "Very nasty," he said, "but they're getting better. You'll heal very nicely."

He dipped the soft cloth in the water and began to bathe her wounds gently and pat her dry with an absorbent towel, first the welts on her cheek, then her shoulders, breasts, waist and hips. He rolled her gently toward him and laved her back, making tut-tutting sounds as he did so. She wore some kind of bandage, much like a diaper, wound between her thighs and around her hips. He unwound it until she was fully naked and began to wash her inner thighs. "I'm sorry," he said, "but it has to be done." And he began to wash her most private places. "You were hurt badly here," he said, but he did not look her in the eye. He seemed to be very businesslike, disinterested, much like a doctor.

When he had finished with the water, he began to apply an ointment to all the welts and cuts, very gently, his hands cool against her skin. She felt a sensation of healing and coolness over her body, then something else, a warmth, a tingle as his fingers kneaded the ointment into the welts across her nipples and into her lower abdomen and thighs. When his fingers gently parted her vulva and administered to her torn, most sensitive flesh, she felt a sharp sensation and remembered Liam in the lean-to. She heard Morgan swear. "The beast. What he did to you." He said no more.

He reached for a section of clean cloth. She recognized it as sail. "The medical book says you should be bound tightly." Gently, but expertly, he began to wind the strip of cloth in a figure eight around her inner thighs and across her hips. Instantly she felt the pain lessen.

"Is that too tight?"

"No. Tighter, I think."

He unwound it a little, then pulled it tighter. Miraculously, the pain almost disappeared. She sighed and told him so. He finished in a moment, then helped her back into what had been his nightshirt and pulled the cover back over her.

"Now that wasn't too bad, was it?"

She shook her head against the pillow, but smiled as she did so. She felt herself unable to speak because of the wonder of it all. This man, this wonderful man, had done the most private, personal things to her, yet so gently, so caringly, so sensitive to her feelings. She decided he must be an angel.

She continued to sleep on and off for another day or so. In her periods of wakefulness, almost as pleasant as sleeping, he fed and bathed her. She felt she had no secrets from him, nor did she want any. Her strength returned rapidly and, when bound tightly, she was able to sit up and then to take a few halting steps, leaning on him, to relieve herself in the corner behind a curtain he had rigged for her. There was no privacy to speak of, yet she lost all sense of embarrassment with him.

"I'm sorry, but I have to sleep here," he said. "This is a small ship and there is no other cabin. Besides, I don't think you can look after yourself just yet."

"I understand. It's all right." Actually, she knew she didn't want him to leave. "I must be inconveniencing you terribly." She glanced at the hard pallet on the floor. "Have you had any sleep since I came aboard?"

"Enough, enough."

He brought her a dress. "I'm afraid we have no women's attire on board. The sailmaker tried his hand with a couple of my shirts." He held up a white garment.

"Why, it's lovely."

"Hardly that. We'll get you some proper clothes when we get to Lisbon."

"It even has ruffles." She picked up the dress and fingered the rough-sewn frills at the hem. "He even made a ruffle for the throat."

Morgan laughed. "Don't give him too much credit. That came with the shirt."

After he had bathed her, he helped her put it on and stand up. The sailmaker's dress fitted her better than she had thought possible, accentuating her tiny waist, although the shoulders were still quite large. "Why, it's lovely," she said again.

He looked at her, then flushed just a little in embarrassment. "No, I think it is you who is lovely."

She smiled. "Thank you, sir. I think I need to be told that."

They talked a lot. He told her of his home. "Maryland is a small state, but the most beautiful, I think. My father's plantation is in what we call Southern Maryland on the west side of the Chesapeake Bay. Our house lies on a hill overlooking the Patuxent River. It is a small river, but wide. So beautiful. I think it the most beautiful river in the world."

She smiled at the light that came into his eyes.

"What is your place called?"

"Aurial. We have a brightly colored bird, all orange and black, associated with Baltimore. It is called the oriole. My great-grandfather named our plantation after the bird, but spelled it differently."

"And what do you grow there?"

"Tobacco, mostly. I think we grow the finest tobacco in the world. I'm smoking some now. It's strong flavored, yet mild. Do you like it?"

She liked it when he lit up his pipe. It seemed such a masculine thing to do. Her father had smoked a pipe. "Oh yes, I love the aroma."

"I miss home," he said, wistfulness in his voice. "I haven't been home much in recent years and I long to return." Then he told her of his life. He had been fifteen when the British attacked Fort McHenry, seized Baltimore and razed Washington. He had fought with the defending troops, then made his way to the west, ultimately joining the forces of Andrew Jackson. He had fought with him at New Orleans. Glenna both saw and heard his worship of Jackson. "He is a strong man, a man of sensitivity and of property, an aristocrat really. But he is also a man of the people. He has brought a new revolution to America. He is finishing what was started in 1776. Yet, he is doing it peacefully, under the Constitution."

Glenna didn't understand what he meant, but she loved the way he spoke of it.

And he told her of his mission to Europe and what had brought him to Three Oaks in Cobh.

"I'm glad you were there," she said.

He looked at her a moment. "And I too," he said.

She hesitated. "Why did you save me?"

"Because . . . because . . ." He seemed at a loss for words. "Because you were so young—so helpless, so vulnerable." He paused, unsure of what more to say. "Because . . . because you were the most beautiful girl I had ever seen. Because I feared something terrible was going to happen to you, and I couldn't allow it to." He swore. "But I did. I was too late. But, God, I could not come before."

He seemed very distressed. She had to comfort him. "I know, I know. It wasn't your fault. It couldn't be helped."

That night as she lay in bed listening to him toss and turn on the floor, she thought of his words. You were the most beautiful girl I had ever seen. She silently said them over and over to herself and a flush pervaded her body as when she had had the fever.

5

During the next several days, the circumstances of the small cabin made a certain amount of intimacy inevitable. He told her when he had to dress and undress. She turned her face away so as not to look at him. She didn't really want to, but she was afraid to have him see that she was looking.

She did watch him shave. He stood before a small mirror, stripped to the waist. She admired the quick sure strokes of his razor, the way he arched his neck and bent his arm to slide the blade across his throat.

But mostly her eyes devoured the hard, firm muscles of his arms and shoulders and chest. She saw his slender waist, the muscles moving rhythmically in his back. She thought him beautiful—and then she had to look away. He must not see her blushing.

She heard the sound of the razor sloshing in the basin and of water being splashed on his face.

"Do you need me to help bathe you today?"

She knew she was capable of doing it herself, at least all but her back. Besides her wounds were healing rapidly and she wasn't sure she needed the daily treatment. "Please," she said, her voice very soft.

Still without his shirt, he emptied his shaving basin, poured in fresh warm water and brought it to her bed. She raised herself and he helped her off with the nightshirt. As he gently bathed her, she saw and smelled the nearness of him. It was all she could do to refrain from touching his smooth skin. *You were the most beautiful girl I had ever seen.* Did he still think so? She knew she was healing. Did he still think so?

"You are healing beautifully." His voice sounded strangely husky. "I don't believe you'll scar at all."

She said nothing. She was afraid of the sound of her own voice.

When he removed the bandage and tenderly touched her most private places, she winced.

"Did I hurt you? I'm sorry."

"No, it's all right," she said quickly. She could feel his hands trembling as he touched her. She looked at him. He kept his eyes averted from hers. She feasted on his hands and arms, his naked shoulders. Then she saw the bulge in his trousers.

He seemed to hurry the administration of the ointment, but was careful to rebind her tightly. As he did, he spoke, "Glenna, I have no right to ask, and if you don't answer I'll understand, but what happened to you that day?"

"The whole day?"

"I'd like to know anything you want to tell me."

She hesitated for a time, still enjoying his hands on

her, then began. She told of being on the cliffs with Liam O'Connell, omitting only the details of what they had been doing, and of hearing the gunshots and of running to see her father murdered, poor Liam, too. She told of having her dress ripped off and of the wild ride to Three Oaks. "You were there when I was brought in."

"I remember." She hesitated and he saw pain registering on her face. "You don't have to go on."

"I know, but I think I need to—to tell it all."

Haltingly, with tears welling in her eyes, she told of Winslow entering the cell dressed in his outlandish costume and whipping her. Then, sobbing, she told of what he had done. Morgan kept trying to stop her, saying over and over not to remember, that it wasn't important, but she went on, blurting it all out.

"And he kept whipping me and then he forced . . . my legs . . . apart . . . and. . . ."

She almost collapsed again from the memory of it. Unmindful of her nakedness, he swept her into his arms and cradled her against his chest, murmuring to her as though she were a baby. "Oh, darlin', darlin', it's all right, it's all right. You're safe now. No harm will come to you ever again, I promise."

She cried against his bare chest. "Oh, Daniel," she managed to say, "he hurt me so."

"If only I'd come earlier."

"Thank God you came when you did. I think he intended to kill me. He can't have people know what he's really like."

"I know, I know." Then he began to swear, calling Winslow every vile name he could. "I swear by all that's holy that beast shall pay for this."

Suddenly she pulled away from him and sat up. "He'll pay all right, but not by you, Daniel Morgan. He did this to *me*. I don't know how or where or when, but I'll make him pay. I'll make him suffer as he did me. I swear by the Mother of God."

"Yes, yes."

"Do you believe me?" There was a terrible fierceness to her voice.

"Yes, I believe—but don't fret now."

Then she threw her arms around him, crushing her breasts against his chest. "Oh, Daniel, tell me. Am I ruined? Will any man want me now?"

He stroked her long black hair and ran his hand down her back. "Oh, darlin', darlin'. Any man would want you."

"But now . . . after—"

"Yes, now, anytime, forever. You couldn't help what happened to you. It wasn't your fault."

"But—"

He pushed her away from him, his hands on her shoulders, and looked into her eyes. "Glenna, darlin', all men aren't like that. Believe me they aren't. I don't want you to be afraid because of what that perverted beast did. Promise me—promise me you'll forget what happened."

And she looked back at him. Very seriously she said, "Daniel, I won't forget, but I won't be afraid—" she smiled at him "—if all men are like you."

And she was in his arms and he was kissing her, deeply, passionately. The sweetness and longing and hunger seemed to devour her, and she clung to his soft lips long past breathing. She felt his hand on her breast. When his fingers softly stroked her nipple a new sensation joined the sweet havoc his lips were creating. She felt herself sinking into a warm abyss of surrender.

Then he pulled himself away. "Darlin', darlin', I love you so. But we can't. Your injury."

"Please, please." She was barely able to speak. "I'm all right now."

He was panting, too. "No, you're not. You're just beginning to get well."

Her eyes half closed with passion, she moaned, "Oh, Danny, is there nothing we can do?"

"There is." And he took her back in his arms.

He kissed her eyes and her ears and her throat and

said over and over how beautiful she was. "I love you, Glenna. I can't help it. I love you." And as his lips and tongue found her nipples, she moaned her pleasure and cradled his head as if he were an anchor that kept her from floating away on a sea of sensation. "Oh, my love, my love," she moaned.

In time he told her to lie down and close her eyes. He lifted her hips and unwound her bindings. Tenderly, he parted her thighs. "Does that hurt, darlin'?"

"No, no."

Then she felt his head between her thighs and the hot ice of his lips and tongue upon her, gently, yet stabbing her with desire.

"My God, Danny, my God!"

The wonder of it all. Was it possible? Involuntarily she moved her hips, but he told her to lie still. His hands reached up and stroked her nipples and she cried out with heightened pleasure.

It seemed to come a very long way, a tension building inside her, like a wave far from shore. As his lips and tongue tormented her, the wave would move towards shore, then recede. Then a new, bigger wave would form from the sea of tension and come closer and closer. Over and over it happened, rising, receding, closer and closer, larger and heavier, receding each time. "Oh, Lord," she moaned. Her half-closed eyes opened and widened. She looked down at his face buried between her legs and met his uplifted gaze. But only briefly. She felt herself about to break with some terrible tension. Then a giant wave crashed down upon her and she cried out, "Oh my God, my God!"

Afterwards, he remained where he was, gently laving her with his tongue and stroking her thighs and abdomen.

She was finally able to speak—lazily, in delicious exhaustion. "Daniel Morgan, what I did—is that what I'm supposed to do?"

He raised his head. "Yes."

She reached down, took his arm and guided him to

the bed beside her. When he held her in his arms, she sighed, "Oh-h, it was so wonderful. I didn't know it was possible."

He kissed her gently. "It will be better—when you are well."

She smiled at him. "It couldn't be."

"It will be, you'll see."

She buried her face in the crook of his arm. "Then I'll hurry and get well."

Still passionate, he brushed her cheek and ear and neck with repeated kisses. "Oh, darlin'," he said, "it was so good to please you."

She stopped his kisses and turned her face to look at him. "Was it truly?"

"Oh, yes, to know you are pleasing someone else— even though you don't quite know what they feel—it's like a . . . a . . ." He was at a loss for the right word.

"Like a mystery?"

"Yes."

"You're part of some great mystery you can never solve."

"Yes."

She moaned a little from the remembrance of pleasure. "Oh, Daniel, it was a very . . . very intimate thing you did."

"Yes."

"It's like there are no secrets between us—except for the mystery."

He bent and kissed her lips. "I love you, darlin', more than I ever thought possible."

"Yes, yes." She didn't want it to stop. She asked him, "Isn't there something I should do for you?"

"No, it's—"

"But I want to." She sat up, her legs bent together under her. "I want to know the mystery, too." As she began to unfasten his trousers, she said, "There shall be no secrets between us. Always remember that." Then his manhood stood erect, hard before her.

"Glenna, I—"

"Sh-h." She ran her hands over his groin and thighs and felt the heat as her fingers encircled his throbbing hardness.

He moaned but remained insistent in protest. "Glenna, I don't think you—"

"Be still. This is my mystery." Gently, she explored with her fingers; gently she began to move her encircling hand up and down.

"Glenna, you—"

She felt him harden and pulsate and heard him moan, "No."

She turned her head and saw the passionate yearning in his half-closed eyes, despite his protest. Then she returned to his rigid member on her hand, continuing to stroke it as she stared at it with fascination. Her desire was sudden and irresistible. She bent swiftly and took it on her mouth, doing now with her lips and tongue what she had done with her hand. Abruptly she felt his body stiffen and heard him gasp. Moment by wondrous moment, she kept moving her head up and down, hearing both his breath quicken and her own heart pound.

Suddenly he gasped a warning, "Not in—"

She understood and lifted her head in time to see a stream arc from him. A great well of it seemed to pulsate from him, again and again. "My goodness," she exclaimed. "Heavens!" Her eyes gleamed at the sight. Then she looked at him and saw his face contorted as with pain. "Daniel, did I hurt you?" The pulsing ended. His convulsions stopped and his whole body relaxed. "Oh, Danny, if I hurt you . . ."

He finally smiled. "Silly darlin', you didn't hurt me."

"You liked it?"

He pulled her down beside him to lie with her head against his shoulder.

"I'll like it better when you're well."

She kissed his chest. "Then I shall mend quickly."

They were silent for a time. Then he said, "Why did you do that to me? I thought after . . . after what—"

"I know. I thought about it. I was afraid at first. But I

believed it when you said not all men are alike and I shouldn't be afraid. I didn't want to be afraid. I thought maybe it would . . . sort of wipe out part of what happened."

"And?"

"I promise to listen to you more often. Such a mystery."

They lay in silence together for a time. Then very softly she said, "You made an awful mess on the bed, Daniel. Your trousers are ruined."

"I suspect so." He laughed. "But it was in a good cause."

And she laughed, too, and hugged his chest tightly. "Oh, darlin', I don't ever want there to be anyone else but you."

"There better not be."

She smiled and thought he sounded like a husband.

6

That afternoon he carried her up to the deck. The air was wonderfully fresh after the cabin and the sun deliciously hot. It was never this hot in Ireland. The azure sea and white sails straining in the breeze thrilled her. Sitting with Morgan nearby, she felt ecstatically happy.

Captain Ian MacDoul came up and spoke with her. "I'm glad to see you are feeling better, lassie. This sun is the best thing for you. It'll have you fixed up in no time." MacDoul was a huge, merry Scotsman in his early thirties with green sparkling eyes and a full beard and head of hair, all a brilliant red. She thought, except for the name, he could have been Irish.

She told him what a fine ship he had.

"She's a good sailer, all right—but one day soon, we'll have ships that'll sail like the wind itself. They'll make the *Chesapeake* here seem to be standin' still."

"And I'm sure you'll be the captain of one."

"'Tis my fondest dream, lassie."

The sun bore into her, warming her body, and she found out that what Cap'n Mac, as his crew called him, had said was true. She could feel the heat healing her groin. She asked Morgan to walk with her. He protested, but she whispered, "I thought you wanted me to heal fast." So they began to stroll the deck, slowly at first, then more easily. She relished the walks. She enjoyed being beside Morgan and touching him and she enjoyed hearing words of encouragement from the deckhands.

There were days of bliss on shore for Glenna. That night she and Morgan accepted the captain's invitation to a superb dinner enhanced further by the charming attention paid to her by the ship's officers. They applauded lustily when on invitation she sang a few Irish songs bespeaking her love for her country. The captain asked if she perchance played whist. "I do, sir. My father was an excellent player and taught me." She made a friend of MacDoul for life that night.

It was much the same for two more days and nights—sun, dinners with wine, whist and love. Many times Glenna awoke in rapture to feel herself nestled in Morgan's arms. The bunk was small and they had to lie mostly on their sides, his knees bent to match hers, his manhood often hard against her as he slept. His strong arms were around her, cradling her breasts. She was certain she had never known such happiness.

On the third day they sailed into Lisbon, the most breathtakingly beautiful harbor Glenna had ever seen. She stared in wonderment and almost cried as their ship sailed slowly up the Tagus River to drop anchor beneath the magnificent cliffs. All around her, the Portuguese city lay white and massive and sparkling with brilliant colors reflected back into the still, sunlit harbor waters. She could spend weeks, she felt, just looking at this harbor's beauty.

Almost immediately, Morgan left for shore and returned within an hour with a dressmaker, a tiny, fussy man with a small mustache. When Glenna realized she was going to have to undress for a fitting, she insisted on seeing Morgan alone. The dressmaker was hustled outside for a moment.

"I can't undress." Her voice was frantic.

"Why not? I understand it's done all the time."

"I just can't. Look at me. He'll know."

"No, he won't. Your stripes are practically healed. You're beautiful."

"But this." She made a motion toward her hips.

"Oh, I forgot." Quickly he lifted her skirt and unwound her bandage. "Now just stand. Don't try to walk."

When he let the little dressmaker in, he said for Glenna's benefit, for he knew the Portuguese could not understand a word of English, "Mrs. Morgan was shipwrecked on her passage from America. She lost all her luggage." She smiled gratefully at him.

Morgan waited on deck. When the dressmaker finally came out, he was jabbering in Portuguese and making excited, complementary gestures about Glenna's beauty. Morgan nodded; he knew about Glenna's beauty even if he couldn't understand a word the man was saying. With a gesture promising a generous bonus, he arranged to have the first of the dresses delivered the next afternoon.

Next day the dressmaker returned, accompanied by his wares and an entourage of two women and a dandyish young man. Morgan was hustled out of the cabin. He figured their procedures might take some time, so he went ashore and had an ale in a dockside tavern. When he returned there was still no sign Glenna was ready. Pacing the deck, he waited and he waited.

Finally, near nightfall, the dressmaker, puffed with pride, appeared and summoned him. Morgan entered the cabin to be astounded by Glenna's loveliness. Her hair had been piled atop her head with curls falling behind. Her gown was blue, precisely matching her eyes. It was in the empire style, with a high waist that hung in a narrow skirt of soft folds to the floor. The bodice was tiny, almost too tiny to Morgan, for half her breasts were exposed, separated by deep cleavage. Another woman might have looked brazen in this bodice, but because of Glenna's extreme petiteness, the fragility of her face and neck, shoulders and arms, the soft luminescence of her skin, the effect was of demureness and delicacy.

Glenna had awaited his entrance, with mingled feelings. She was tired from the fitting, enraptured with the gown and afraid Morgan would disapprove of it. Then she saw the expression in his eyes and all doubts fled. "You like it, don't you?" she said happily.

"I do," he said quietly. "I like it very much."

She looked down at her front. "Is it too daring?"

"Yes, much too." Then he smiled, "But I like it." He went to her and kissed her lightly, not wanting to make a display in front of the others.

The dressmaker, beaming, was holding up some jewelry and making gestures. Morgan gathered he was to buy them. He nodded assent. Clucking his approval, the dressmaker fastened a sparkling necklace to her throat, matching her pendant earrings.

Glenna squealed with delight as she touched them. "Diamonds Daniel. You shouldn't."

"And why not?"

"They cost a fortune."

"So my father and I will plant an extra acre of tobacco next year."

Alone with her at last, Morgan said, "Darlin', there has never been anyone so beautiful."

She laughed lightly. "Not me, darling. It's the magic of that little man. Such a lovely dress. Do you have any idea how much a girl dreams of wearing a gown like this?"

Slowly she pirouetted in front of him, making the skirt dance at her ankles. Suddenly he remembered and picked up her binding.

"Not that, Daniel. You'll ruin my dress."

"Better the dress than you. Now up with your skirt."

Making an exaggerated pout, she obeyed and stood still as he bound her. "It'll show. Everything will be ruined."

"No, it won't. Stand still."

She had to admit the support eased the pain, realizing only then that it had been mounting. And when she dropped the skirt, it didn't show. He made her sit while he changed into his dress suit. Again she admired and was excited by his lean body. As he donned his jacket over his ruffled shirt, she said, "Where are we going?"

"To dinner. It's supposed to be a grand place."

"I'm already jealous."

"Of what?"

"Of you. You're going to be the most handsome man there."

He laughed and pulled her to her feet. "Would I ruin anything if I kissed you?"

"Probably." And she was in his arms, her breasts crushed into his chest, their lips bound in passion.

He broke away. "I think we better go before—"

"Yes, I think maybe."

The restaurant was indeed elegant, filled with red velvet curtains and matching chairs, lighted with crystal chandeliers. Glenna felt she was making an entrance. Conversation stopped and all eyes turned to her as the *maitre d'* led them to their table.

When they were seated and looking at the menu, Morgan said, "You're right. Everyone *is* looking at me."

She smiled at him. "I think maybe you can put a poor Irish farm girl in such a dress, but I'm not sure you can have her act right in it."

"And I thought it was we Americans who were supposed to be savages." He shook his head and laughed over the leering attention being paid her. But he was proud. "Relax. You look exquisite and act it."

When they had ordered and were alone, he said, "I mean it. You look born for a place like this. I think you are something other than a poor Irish farm girl. You have a secret."

She smiled. "Hardly with you. No, I have no secret I'm aware of. I was not born to the purple."

The waiter brought the wine, after which Morgan persisted. He did not mean to pry but he was curious. "It's difficult to see you learnin' courtly manners on a farm."

She told him of her father, then feeling a sadness come over her. "He was the most wonderful man. Even in County Cork he insisted we were Dubliners. He read to me and insisted I read. We always had books. He loved poetry. And he insisted on manners. I always had to be a lady with him."

"And your mother?"

"She died when I was born. I never knew her. My father raised me." She paused, remembering, and smiling at the memory. "He loved music. I remember when I was—I must have been twelve, I think. He took me to a concert. The orchestra played Handel, Mozart and a new piece by that young German composer, Beethoven. I was enchanted. I adored every second of it."

And he was enchanted with her. "I think you will always be surrounded by music."

Glenna smiled at him, feeling a rash of affection for this man who was bringing to life a part of her nature all but buried in the tortures of a few days before. Such a change in so short a time. Who would have believed it possible? She was loving Daniel Morgan more and more.

They stayed late at the restaurant, listening to the music. Featured were some husky-voiced singers performing sad, mournful songs in rhythms Glenna had never heard before. Morgan said he understood it was called *fado* singing, an art peculiar to Portugal.

She even danced a little, although he protested she shouldn't.

It was long past midnight when they returned to the ship and closed the cabin door. They stood just inside and kissed passionately. She was ecstatically happy. She'd had the most wonderful evening of her life—a time so simply enjoyable, so free from care, that her heart brimmed with desire to make more of it.

"Oh, Daniel, Daniel . . . I want you so," she moaned. "Oh, Danny, can we . . . tonight?"

His hot kisses on her mouth stopped. "No."

"I'm well enough, darling, I am."

"No."

"If I can stand for hours for a fitting and walk to a restaurant and even dance, I am well enough to be made love to."

"No."

"Please, Danny. We haven't wiped away everything . . . but everything that happened. I promise to tell you if you hurt me."

Naked in bed beside him, she succumbed to his passion—the exquisite torment of his mouth and touch, then to the wondrous lovemaking, his hard body thrusting on hers, that he had promised they would have together. She kept moaning with the rapture of it as she pushed her hips hard up against him. "Oh, Danny, Danny, God, you feel so good." He did not move for a moment and she felt the tension rise, a great wave far from shore. Again he thrust into her, first slowly and gently, then harder. Closer and closer came the wave, higher and higher. And then, all too quickly, it broke over her and she cried out with the joy of release. "Danny boy, Danny boy, darling, oh darling, darling." She felt her head roll from side to side and tears roll down her cheeks.

He lay still atop her. "You're so wonderful," he said, huskily.

"Oh, Danny, I'm so glad, so happy. How can anything be so awful one time, so wonderful the next?"

He smiled at her. "I think it's called love."

"Oh, Danny, I do love you. With all my heart." She could still feel him inside her, filling her. She asked him, in real awe, "Is it always like this?"

"Only for us."

She held him tight and felt the passion of his kiss, then realized he was still hard within her. In alarm she said, "Didn't you—"

"No."

"Why not? Am I doing something wrong?"

He smiled at her. "Not hardly. You're doing something terribly wonderful."

"But how?"

"Darlin', I'm thirty-two. I've had other women. You must know that. But never one like you. I've never held off like this before. It is . . . it is like torture, exquisite torture. And to have you . . . I love you, Glenna."

He looked deeply into her eyes. Almost imperceptibly, his body began to move in hers once more. She moaned, "Darling, again, yes, again . . . Oh, Lord!" She wrapped her legs around him to ride with him on whatever course he took. Harder and harder he thrust, ever more powerfully, until with a final lunge he cried out his own eruption within her, and she too exploded under him in a monumental prolongation of her pleasure.

Afterwards, she lay languidly in his arms.

"Daniel Morgan, I—I think I adore you."

"And I you, darlin'. You will make the most wonderful mistress of Aurial."

She raised her head and smiled. "Is that a proposal?"

"Don't tell me you're surprised."

"Oh, darling, when will we get there? When will we be married?"

"Soon."

"I can't wait."

"We can be married here, now, by the captain."

"No, I want a proper wedding, by a priest, in a church." She saw that church in Maryland on her mind's eye, even heard its bells ring. Her eyes glowed. Her cup filled with happiness.

They had six more precious days in Lisbon, on the third evening of which they went to a dinner and ball at the American Embassy. The engraved invitation came by messenger. "Mr. Daniel Morgan is invited to attend . . ." His identity had become known in Lisbon. Her husband-to-be, Glenna noted, was a man of importance.

The little dressmaker outdid himself. The snug gown he fitted to her for this function was of black satin, a most unusual color for a maiden so young and therefore all the more eye-catching, Glenna was cinched into a whalebone corset. The effect was to present her with a most tiny waist and slender hips, while pushing her bust up and enlarging it. Her breasts were covered by just a few strips of lace. She felt virtually naked and gasped at herself in the mirror.

"I can't wear this," she said when Daniel entered.

He smiled at her.

"I'm about to be a married woman. I don't need this."

"True."

"I'll wear the other gown. It's shocking enough."

He hardly heard her, so rapt in admiration was he. The fussy little dressmaker had to be a genius. He said, "You've never looked lovelier."

"But I'm a spectacle."

He smiled at her. "Indeed you are."

At dinner she sat next to the British ambassador, Lord Oliver Penwood, a short, obese man in his sixties, obviously suffering from gout. He had a massive head, nearly bald, and an aura of urbanity and imperiousness. Early in the dinner, he and the other men discussed the Barbary pirates and the difficulties the British were having in subduing them. "They are a vile lot and stubborn," he said, "but we'll get them yet."

"If the French don't beat you to it," came a rejoinder from across the table.

"Ah yes, that is always possible."

As the evening wore on and the wine glasses were incessantly filled, Lord Penwood became somewhat tipsy and increasingly attentive to Glenna. Shorter than she, he seemed unable to take his eyes from her decolletage.

"I must say, my dear, such beauty as yours does us English proud."

"I told you, milord, I am not English, but Irish."

"Ah yes, Irish. Well, that is practically English. I declare you English for this evening."

Glenna bristled. How like the English to appropriate everything they wanted! But she said nothing. No point in causing trouble.

"Where is your home in Ireland?"

She hesitated. She had to be careful. "I was born in Dublin, milord."

"Ah yes, Dublin. Attractive city."

"Thank you, milord. I think so, too."

"Then you must know some of our people there. Lord Winslow perhaps?"

Glenna felt both anger and fear at the mere mention of the name. With visible effort she tried to control herself.

"I asked if you know Lord Winslow."

She didn't know why, but she replied, "No, I don't believe I do."

"Splendid chap. Doing a good job I hear. A hard man, but no more than is required, I suppose."

Glenna said nothing for a moment as she wrestled with the torrent of emotions within her. She glanced across the table and saw the concern in Morgan's eyes.

Just looking at him, calmed her and in the back of her mind a thought, still mostly intuition, began to form. "This Lord Winslow. What sort of person is he?" She smiled at Penwood and leaned toward him. His eyes devoured her cleavage.

"My dear," he said in a moment, "I hardly know the man."

She leaned a little more toward him. "But you know of him."

"Ah yes, to be sure." Perhaps it was the wine or his fascination with her, but he said too much. "Winslow is very ambitious. He is a favorite of the King and I suspect fancies himself the next prime minister."

"Really."

"Only time will tell about that, however. Winslow has made many enemies. And I hear his finances are not all they might be. He has lost a good bit in some rather—well, unfortunate investments."

"How regrettable."

Then Morgan interrupted from across the table and the conversation passed on to other topics. But Glenna smiled to herself. She couldn't imagine how it might ever be useful, but she knew she had learned a little about the man she knew to be her adversary.

The ship sailed out of Lisbon. Glenna felt a twinge of sadness at leaving yet she was eager to get on, too—to become the Mrs. Morgan that arrival in America would bring. As the ship sailed for the last stop at Funchal in the Madeiras off the coast of Africa, Captain MacDoul again invited them to dinner and whist. He lavished compliments on Glenna's new wardrobe and spoke to her with a kind of affectionate slyness.

"You look especially happy, lassie. Far more so than when you first came aboard."

She beamed at Morgan. "I am that, Cap'n Mac, I am that."

MacDoul looked from one to the other and smiled. He had not spoken to Glenna of any personal feelings he might have had toward her, yet Glenna thought she saw a hint of resignation in his eyes.

Over whist MacDoul told her he hoped she was a good sailor. "The gauge is falling. I think we are in for a bit of weather."

"With you at the helm, Cap'n Mac, I'm sure we can sail anywhere."

The weather did turn bad, very bad, that same night. A hurricane approached them, huge, menacing, blown by freak circumstances far off usual course of hurricanes to the east. But Glenna and Morgan were unmindful. They went to their cabin, and above the howling wind and loud protests of the rigging she made him tell her again and again about Aurial and what life would be like for them there.

They clutched each other in bed as the ship tossed and rolled. "It is a bad storm," she said after awhile. She shivered. She couldn't help herself.

He held her tight. "It is, but no harm can befall us now. I refuse to permit it." And they made love, passionately, timing their hungered motions to the roll of the ship. Both thought it a most marvelous thing to do on such a night.

7

The bunk was pitifully small for the two of them and that night Morgan slept only spasmodically. The ship rolled violently as the storm began howling with more and more fury. He dug his left shoulder into the mattress and braced his foot against the side, cradling Glenna in his arms so she could sleep. To hold her still against the swaying, he had both his arms around her, her breasts overflowing his hands. He tried to concentrate on the marvel of this girl he had found, rescued, nursed back to health and come to adore. Once or-twice in his contentment he almost fell asleep, but each time the *Chesapeake*, responding to wave and wind, lurched him awake.

He felt her turn in his arms and speak against his ear. "It is going to end, isn't it?"

He had been on several short voyages along the east coast of the United States and on this trip for the President he had been at sea for months. Never had he experienced weather as bad as this. "Just a little gale, darlin'," he lied. "Nothing to worry about. Go back to sleep." He kissed her cheek for reassurance.

She did not believe him. She had a terrible foreboding which even his strong arms could not erase. Just then the ship pitched sharply and it was all Morgan could do to keep them in the bunk.

"Shouldn't we get up, do something?" she said.

"No. Just go to sleep."

She tried, but couldn't. She was now wide awake, supremely conscious of every motion of the ship, every howl of wind and rigging, every creak and groan of the straining planking. In time she said, "I'm afraid, Daniel."

He couldn't hear her. "What?"

She repeated herself, nearly shouting, although her lips almost brushed his ear. And he too raised his voice in answering. "I told you. I'll let nothing happen to you—to us." He braced them against another roll of the ship. Then, as the *Chesapeake* righted herself, he said, "Darlin', I do love you."

She heard and snuggled against him. "And I you, Daniel." She felt his hand squeezing between their bodies, and she moved away slightly to enjoy his touch upon her breast. In response she reached down with both her hands and held him. She raised her head to kiss him. As their lips touched, the ship lurched and they nearly went to the deck. Both laughed as she held on to him to keep him in the bunk. Shortly afterwards they got up and dressed in their warmest clothes.

They were just in time for there came a loud pounding at the door. Morgan answered it, shouting something to a sailor. He came back and told Glenna. "They need all hands to man the pumps. I'm going to help."

"I can help, too."

"No, you best stay here."

"I will not. I'm a young, strong girl."

He protested, but gave in.

Ian MacDoul had heard old sailors speak of "killer" hurricanes but had chalked them up as fanciful yarns. The two previous hurricanes he had weathered had been bad enough. No wooden ship seemed built to withstand the mountainous seas and savage wind that had torn at his sails and timber. That he had ridden them out both times had amazed him.

MacDoul remembered those other hurricanes as savage, brief affairs. This one recalled to his mind the "killer" legend. Perhaps it was real.

Near midnight the seas began to rise, mounting and mounting through the night, and now near dawn the center of the storm had not yet attacked them. He feared for the *Chesapeake*. How much more of this she could take he could not guess. She was a sturdy ship, but far from new. It had been too long since the planking and masts had been replaced. The vessel needed to be recaulked. He tried to remain confident of his ship. A captain had to do that. But he wasn't and the doubt lapsed into nagging worry, then fear. He began driving his men to lash the rigging even tighter and prepare the ship for the worst. At dawn, as he sensed the worst was approaching, he tried to comfort himself that all that could be done had been done. He had set the sea anchor to keep the schooner headed into the wind. The men were lashed to the wheel which was itself tied to keep the straining rudder always into the wind.

As dawn came, late, faint and reluctant, the sight of his predicament filled him with dread. His ship was a tiny cork amid mountainous seas. The *Chesapeake* at times flew through the air, only to drop suddenly into a trough, hitting hard, barely righting herself before a new wave bore down. And through it all an incredibly fierce wind tore at the ship. It was as if Neptune himself was offended that such a tiny thing dared to enter his domain and was determined to rid himself of her by blowing her away.

During his break from the pumps, Morgan made his way to the deck. The scene appalled the American. It took all his strength to hold on and not be blown overboard. Instantly wet to the skin from both the torrents of rain and the breaking waves, he inched his way toward MacDoul, then touched his arm and shouted at him. MacDoul had no awareness of Morgan until he was grabbed, nor could he hear what Morgan shouted. His voice was simply blown away. MacDoul only shook his head and motioned for Morgan to return below.

Glenna, meanwhile, was doing everything she could below—spelling men at the pumps, otherwise bringing them cold coffee and soggy hardtack from a galley all but awash with the surging sea. For the men returning from the deck watch, she was an angel of mercy. When Hansen, the boatswain, came below, his arm broken in a fall, she created a makeshift splint, then tore up her petticoat to fashion a bandage and sling.

The center of the storm struck at about eight o'clock with a sudden shriek of the wind. On deck, MacDoul saw the mainmast crack. He screamed an order for it to be lashed, losing a sailor to wind and sea as the task was laboriouly done. But the mast held, MacDoul breathed a cautious sigh as it remained upright against the monster gale.

They passed through the edge of the eye, a wall of rolling black clouds stood off to the starboard while the ship itself was bathed in sunlight and calm blue skies. But the lull—an incredible sight to those on deck, lasted only brief minutes. Ahead lay the hurricane's back side, and, true to its nature, it swirled clockwise. When the savage winds now struck from the west, the cracked mainmast snapped off like a matchstick, crashing into the deck with a mass of spars and rigging. The wreckage dragged into the sea. It created a huge sea anchor, and the ship's deadliest peril, for it was now turned starboard against the wind. A giant wave crashed down, nearly foundering the vessel. The next or the one after would surely capsize it if the rigging were not cut away.

The pumps were abandoned as all hands raced on deck with knives and axes. Glenna, among them, had her breath almost blown away. Then the wind took her skirts like a sail and flung her on the deck, only the railing keeping her from going into the sea. On her hands and knees she was clutching at the railing with both arms when, in fright, she saw another huge wave mount. It broke over the ship like a blue-green avalanche. She screamed as she saw the little sailmaker, the one who had made her first dress, swept overboard like a leaf in a fall wind. She heard him scream from across the void.

The men with the axes watched in stupefaction. Then, reacting to MacDoul, they redoubled their hacking at the wreckage. Another wave broke over then, but this one was a godsend, for it stripped the last of the wreckage and took it out to sea. Slowly the *Chesapeake* righted herself and turned gradually back into the wind. They had not capsized. The demasted ship still had a chance.

The storm blew through the entire day, but with gradually diminishing fury. The *Chesapeake* remained afloat, more driftwood than sailing vessel, still in perilous shape. During the evening and into the night,

MacDoul drove the exhausted crew to man the pumps and patch timbers with oakum. For a time it seemed the water would win and the ship sink, but near morning the tide had turned and the water in the hull had begun to recede.

The morning broke sunny and hot under an azure sky. It was as if there had been no storm at all, and they had imagined the nightmare of the day before. Still, MacDoul would allow no rest, driving one and all to erect a jury mast and raise every speck of sail they could. He was ferocious in his commands, thundering at his men to do more than they could, faster than was humanly possible.

Morgan went to him to protest, insisting the men needed some rest.

"I think I know best, Dan'l," the red-bearded captain said sharply. "You and your lassie may rest, but I do only what must be done." Then he looked at Morgan a moment. When he spoke again his voice was softer. "I am sorry, my friend. You and the lassie have done more than your share. I mean no offense."

"I understand, Mac. No offense taken. But surely a hot meal and a little rest would speed the work in the long run."

"Perhaps you are right, but I cannot take the chance. When we have this rigging up and can make a little headway, there will be plenty of time to rest."

Morgan tried to smile. "It's your ship, but may I ask why the rush?"

MacDoul looked away and sighed, then turned back to the Marylander. "All right, I'll tell you—but I suggest you keep it to yourself. Panic among the crew will be of no help just now. Above all, I think your lassie should not be alarmed. First thing this morning, I took the reading by sextant. The storm has blown us far to the east. We are perilously close to the coast of Africa. In fact my guess is that it is not much beyond the horizon."

"So? Why not make repairs in some friendly port?"

MacDoul looked around to make sure they were not being overheard and even then lowered his voice. "My friend, there are *no* friendly ports. Over there lies the coast of Barbary, so named because the Romans considered the inhabitants barbarians. And the Romans were right. They *are* barbarians—murderers, cutthroats and pirates. I'm sure the heathen have already put to sea in search of disabled ships. We will be easy pickings. So now you see why I want to get out of here as fast as we can?"

"Barbary pirates? I thought they were in the Mediterranean. This is the Atlantic."

"The so-called Barbary pirates, or what's left of them, are in the Mediterranean. But there are pirates in these waters, too. They used to be called Saliemen. The English called them Sea Rovers. By any name they are a lot we don't need." MacDoul turned his back on Morgan and began to bark orders to his men to work faster.

Morgan went back below to help man the pumps. There he found Glenna. She smiled bravely at him, but he could tell she was near to dropping from fatigue. Her dress was torn and still heavy from her drenching the day before.

"Darlin', you've done enough. To bed with you."

"No, no, I'm all right." But she wasn't. Morgan saw her sway. She was on the edge of fainting.

In one motion, Morgan caught her as she fell. She did not protest as he carried her to their cabin and deposited her in their bunk. He removed her wet clothing and covered her. Of all this Glenna was unaware. She was asleep the instant her head touched the pillow.

MacDoul's fears were realized just at dusk when the last slanting rays of the sun reflected off a sail on the horizon to the northeast.

"Pirates?" Morgan asked.

"I don't know. It is wise to fear so, however."

Both peered at the sail. When the sailor aloft cried, "Sail ho," MacDoul motioned to him to be silent.

"What can we do?"

"Hope. We can hope they have not seen us against the sun. We can hope night falls quickly. We can hope we get away in the darkness."

Morgan remained on deck long after dark, straining to see a following ship, but he saw only the stars and the phosphorescent sea.

He felt MacDoul at his side. "There is no use in our worrying tonight, Dan'l. I suggest you and your lassie put some of our fare in your stomachs, poor as it is, then get what sleep you can. The morning will bear what evils or joys it may."

Morgan knew it was good advice. He ate a few bites of salt beef and biscuits, for no fires were lit again that night, then went below. He was bone weary. His beloved Glenna was still sleeping. Quietly, he stripped off his clothes and crawled in beside her. He felt her move in the darkness and heard her moan with pleasure as his arms surrounded her. She did not awaken. His mind barely recorded that fact when he was into a deep sleep himself, the deepest since they had begun sharing this diminutive bunk.

At dawn the next day, the sea was clean of sails and MacDoul both sighed his relief and smiled his elation. When an eager Morgan appeared shortly after the sun was up, MacDoul accepted his congratulations.

"I changed course several times in the night. Perhaps it worked."

"I'm sure it did, captain. I'm sure of it."

A frown marred the Scotsman's face. "I hope you're right. This may be the longest day of our lives."

The tip of a sail, like an augur of evil, appeared on the horizon at midmorning, then grew ever larger as it tracked the crippled schooner.

"Could you be wrong? Are you sure it's a pirate

ship?" Morgan asked. He was answered by a shrug from the captain.

An hour later the full ship was visible as it overtook them from the northeast. MacDoul peered at it through his glass, frowning and muttering. "I fear we're in for it."

"May I see?"

MacDoul gave him the glass and Morgan raised it to his eye. After a moment he said, "What a strange ship, high at the bow and stern, low to the water at midships. And there is just one big sail."

"It's called a xebeck. It's the usual type of Moorish ship."

Morgan peered through the glass once more. "It doesn't look very formidable."

"It isn't—if we were a man of war."

"Is it fast?"

"Not really. We'd outrun it easily if we had our full sail." MacDoul swore. "Damn that storm."

Morgan lowered the glass, a look of determination on his face. "Well, we'll give them a good fight."

MacDoul smiled sardonically. "Will we? If you look again you'll see the xebeck already has her guns run out. There are three at the bow and three at the stern, six or eight pounders I should judge. There are six more on the starboard, twelve in all. Exactly how much of a fight do you figure to make against that?"

Through the glass Morgan saw what MacDoul had described. "Yes, I see them."

"They'll blow us right out of the water."

Morgan looked a moment longer, the hopelessness of their situation beginning to register with him. "What do they want?"

"The ship, the cargo, all of us."

"Us? What do they want with us?"

"From what I hear, people are of the greatest value of all."

"What d'you mean?"

"If we're lucky, we will be held for ransom. Not too

many years ago the American government paid over two million in ransom. I'm afraid it will cost a penny before you ever see Maryland again."

"All right. I'll pay ransom—although I hate to. That is no problem." He watched MacDoul shrug. "You said if we were lucky. What if we are unlucky?"

MacDoul said, "I hear they practice slavery. It is not a good life, I understand."

Morgan's anger flared. "By God, they'll not. Where are these people from? What country?"

"Barbary. Some call it Morocco. By any name it's a wild, heathen place, I'm told."

"Oh yes, Morocco. I remember now." He looked aloft at the rigging. "I see you're flying the stars and stripes. Good. These people will remember our spanking of them in 1805. Commodore Preble and Stephen Decatur did their job well. We haven't paid tribute to these devils since."

"But they may not remember it kindly."

"And we've had a treaty with the Sultan of Morocco since '24, I believe. Yes, we have a consulate in Tangier. We'll demand to be taken there."

"I doubt if these pirates care very much about diplomatic niceties."

Morgan's outlook was brightening. "Wait, I remember hearing in London that the Swedes, I think—yes, the Swedes, or maybe the Dutch—bombarded the Moorish port of Larouche. It's along the coast here somewhere."

"Yes, south of Tangier."

"There you have it. The Swedes taught the Moorish pirates a lesson. They cannot have forgotten it. Only a year ago they lost a half dozen pirate ships to a real man of war. And with what Decatur did, I think they'll back off."

MacDoul paused, trying to follow Morgan's line of reasoning. "So what are you proposing?"

"That we bluff it out. I'm a personal emissary of President Jackson. I have papers to prove it. I shall

demand safe conduct to the American consulate in
Tangier, as well as full repairs for this vessel, or they
shall answer to President Jackson personally."

MacDoul listened, then turned away to look at the
now much larger approaching ship. He could see the
guns with his naked eye. "All right, Dan'l. It may work
for you, even for me, my crew and this ship. But there
is a problem."

"Yes."

"Your lassie. These Arabs, so I hear, have a great
fondness for Western women for their harems. As
bonnie a lassie as your Glenna will be much prized."

Morgan's face paled. "They wouldn't dare!"

"I hope you're right. But I would take no chances, if
I were you."

"Can't we hide her? Below decks, maybe."

"We can, but there is sure to be a thorough search.
She will be found."

Morgan thought a moment, panic growing within
him. "I have it. We'll hide her among the crew. We'll
put her in men's clothing. She can hide her hair in a hat.
We'll even cut it short if we have to."

MacDoul made a gesture of disdain. "No, Dan'l.
Under the best of circumstances the crew will be
separated from us and treated badly. She will be
discovered, believe me she will, then you will be able to
do nothing to save her."

Morgan sighed. "Yes, of course, you're right." He
paused, trying to think. "I'll not let them touch her,
Mac. We've got to do something."

"Yes."

Both men watched the xebeck draw ever closer.
Finally, MacDoul spoke. "We're running out of time.
Your idea for the diplomatic bluff is our only chance.
We'll have to include your lassie in it. Tell them she is
your wife and you are returning to America. Have her
dress as befits the wife of an emissary. You'll have to
demand safe conduct for you both."

"Yes, it'll have to work."

"Indeed it will. You'd better hurry and get her

ready." As Morgan turned to go below, MacDoul said, "If I were you, I'd have her wear something as unattractive as possible. They may be less interested in her if she is ugly."

Despite his agitation, Morgan smiled, "I submit making her ugly will be the most difficult task of all."

8

Glenna was awake when Morgan entered the cabin. She had been lying there, delicious amid the sheets, remembering when she first awoke on this ship to see her lover slumped in the chair. How much had happened. What happiness she had found. She reached below the sheet and discovered her nakedness. He had undressed her and put her to bed. The thought thrilled her. What a divine man. How lucky she was to have him. Mrs. Daniel Morgan, mistress of Aurial.

Her joy disappeared as Morgan entered the cabin. She hadn't known him long, but she instinctively sensed trouble. Perhaps it was the light-hearted manner he often used to disguise his concern. He used it now.

He came to her and kissed her lightly. "Well, sleepy head, don't you think it's time to get up?"

She smiled but kept eyeing him wonderingly. "I must have slept hours and hours."

"If you lie here much longer, you'll have slept the clock around—twice. I'm afraid you'll get bedsores."

She sensed he was hurring her. He even took her hand and pulled her to a sitting position.

"What's wrong, Daniel?" she said quietly.

"Nothing, nothing. We're just about to have some visitors, that's all. You need to get dressed."

"Visitors?"

"Yes. A ship will be alongside soon. We need to greet them properly."

"What kind of ship?"

He lied and she knew it. "I'm not sure. Still too far away. Probably it wants to offer us assistance."

She slid out of the bunk and stood before him. She did not know whether to confront his lie or not.

He had gone to the closet and was poking among her gowns. "I think you should wear something warm and—well, concealing." He laughed nervously. "Don't want to excite sailors too much."

She hesitated. That was definitely not like the Daniel she knew, "Daniel, there is trouble."

"No, no trouble. I just—"

"Darling, be honest with me. You're trying to protect me. Please don't. I can face—together with you—whatever comes. But I have a right to know."

He hesitated.

"Please."

He sighed his discomfort, then quickly told her of the pirate ship, leaving out his fears regarding slavery and the position of women in the heretic nation. "I'm sure we'll be able to negotiate with them," he said. "I'm an emissary of President Jackson. They wouldn't dare harm us."

She tried to smile reassuringly. "I'm sure you're right, dear. So you want me to dress as befits the wife of a diplomat." Her smile broadened. "If you'll leave, I'll do the best I can. I'm sure Cap'n Mac needs you more than I."

Her wardrobe was small, consisting only of the few gowns made for her in Lisbon. Standing before the closet, she pulled aside the blue gown and the shameless black dress. They would never do. In fact there was nothing that would do. She was young and in the full bloom of her beauty. The little dressmaker, enamored of her figure, had made her a collection of gowns to show it off. If only she had an old trunk, a proper wardrobe.

In desperation, she chose an afternoon dress of dark green wool. When she put it on, she realized it too did not entirely suit the purpose, being extremely low-cut in front. The dress, however, came with a short cape. She quickly covered her shoulders with it and tied it neatly at her throat.

There. It would do. It would have to do. She stood at the mirror a while longer and worked with her hands.

The girl who appeared on deck a few minutes later was swaddled in folds of green cloth. Her lustrous hair was pulled back tight and wound into a bun at her neck. She wore no makeup other than an excess of powder which dulled and gave a pasty cast to her skin. A large hat came low over her eyes. From a distance she was not striking, but when she came up to Morgan and MacDoul both realized the disguise was far from perfect. Beneath the shade of the hat, her sapphire eyes shone with excitement, and her youthful figure could not be concealed.

"Is it all right?" she asked.

They hesitated.

"It's the best I could do."

Morgan roused himself. "You're fine, dear."

Quickly, he explained their situation. MacDoul had done the best he could to make a show of force. The *Chesapeake's* crew was armed with muskets, pistols, a few with sabres. Glenna saw that Morgan carried a sword in his right hand. He looked dashing. Then she saw the xebeck's cannon mouths growing ever larger across the water and saw the apprehension frozen like scars on the crew's faces. Her heart sank. They were no match for the pirate ship.

MacDoul peered across the water. He saw the xebeck's gun crews clustered around their weapons and another group of figures on the bridge looking at them, grinning and motioning. "They want us to heave to," he said.

"Shall we?"

"Not until we have to."

"Maybe they're just looking us over and will leave," Morgan said.

It was not to be, the two ships sailed along, the Moslem vessel to the starboard and rear. Then Glenna saw a puff of smoke followed by a loud report from a cannon. All eyes turned to watch the splash and skip of the ball across the bow.

MacDoul appraised the cannon shot realistically. "That's it," he said with resignation, then ordered his men to drop sail and prepare to heave to. But even as they moved a second shot crossed the bow nearer and more menacingly.

It all happened with terrifying swiftness. As the *Chesapeake* lost headway, the xebeck seemed to sweep down on them like a falcon, bumping into the side. Bandanna'd pirates swung on ropes from their rigging and dropped to the deck of the schooner, while grappling hooks and spikes bound the sides of the crafts together. In what seemed only seconds, the peaceful deck of the *Chesapeake* was alive with screaming, bearded men brandishing weapons, their eyes burning. More from fright and surprise than by design, a *Chesapeake* sailor raised his musket and fired. A pirate dropped in his tracks. Other shots rang out. The sailor stood there, then clutched his chest and crumpled to the deck, dead.

Morgan never had a chance to raise his sword. The blade was quickly knocked from his grasp. He, Glenna and MacDoul were surrounded by a dozen leering men, their swarthy skin glistening with sweat. As one, they stepped toward them with dirks raised and Glenna screamed, certain she was about to die.

A loud voice stopped the pirates' advance. Glenna did not understand the words, but recognized the effect. She saw a man in a red uniform step along the railing and hop to the deck of the *Chesapeake*. He had the evilest face she had ever seen—hard, cruel eyes, thin lips, a short beard around the mouth, a livid scar on the left cheekbone. The uniform was makeshift. The man carried a sabre and used it as a wand to wave his men away. When they backed off, a crooked smile spread on his lips, and he lowered his blade.

"*Americano, sí?*"

Glenna, Morgan, MacDoul, all remained silent.

"Americano—yes."

Morgan found his voice. "Yes, we are Americans."

The pirates's smile broadened. "*Sí, sí, Americano muy bueno. Parlez vous francais? ¿Habla español?*" Greeted with silence, he put a finger on his bruised lower lips. "You speak French? Spanish?"

Morgan said, "We speak English."

Another grin. "Ah, *sí, inglés*. I speak *inglés* too."

Morgan sensed the danger behind the man's ostentatious display of his ignorance. He was short, a full head shorter than himself. He obviously took great pride in his uniform. Morgan recognized the red coat as British, the britches as French, the cocked hat probably Spanish—all pirates' loot. His smiling and bowing and gesturing with his sword—all bravado. In a man-to-man fight he would be a coward. On a deck jammed with his henchmen, he was a conqueror.

The sword touched Morgan's chest. "*Capitán?*" the pirate asked.

It seemed strange to Morgan to hear a Moorish pirate speaking Spanish until he remembered the northern part of Morocco had been conquered by Spain. Many of the Moorish pirates must be of Spanish descent.

"I am the captain." MacDoul stepped forward towering over the Moor. "I demand that you leave my ship this instance and permit us to continue our voyage. I warn you of dire consequences if you proceed with this piracy."

The smiling and nodding and bowing of the Arab

indicated he hadn't understood a word MacDoul said. Again he pointed his sabre at Morgan. *"Quién?"*

"I am Daniel Morgan. I am the personal emissary of President Jackson, President of the United States of America."

The pirate's nodding increased. *"Sí, sí, emissario, El Presidente, Estados Unidos. Comprendo."*

Morgan felt emboldened. "I demand safe conduct for my party to the American consulate in Tangier."

The pirate shook his head. "Tangier?"

Morgan restrained his impatience. "Yes, Tangiers." He was not sure of his Spanish and paused. *"Consulato."*

Again a proliferation of nodding. *"Ah, sí, diplomático. Bueno.* Good. *Señorita?"* He seemed to notice Glenna for the first time.

Morgan tightened his arm around Glenna's shoulder. "This is my wife."

The pirate seemed to try to say the word "wife."

Morgan said, *"Señora."*

"Sí, sí, señora." The Moor's nodding and smiles indicated his comprehension. He raised his sabre and tipped Glenna's hat, already askew from her rough handling. *"Muy bonita,"* he exclaimed, staring at her intently. His gaze traveled down her bodice, the narrow waist below the folds of the cape, then returned to her face. He looked boldly into her eyes. *"Monísima,"* he said softly, *"monísima."*

Then he turned away abruptly, waved his sword and barked orders in Arabic. The results were immediate, Morgan, MacDoul and Glenna were pushed, shoved and hauled over the railings and into the deep deck well of the xebeck. Within minutes, the lashings were cut and the pirate ship sailed majestically away, leaving dirk-armed men behind to coax the prize ship and its crew into port.

Glenna had been terrified. The events on the deck had lasted only minutes, all but immobilizing her with their suddenness and violence. The shooting of the unfortunate sailor had flooded her mind with visions of the bullet hole in her father's chest. The naked blade in the hand of the strutting man in his ridiculous uniform had recalled cutting down of Liam O'Connell. Past and present mingling in her mind had led her to expect still more horrors for herself. She expected to be seized, her clothes torn off and thrown to the ground. When rough hands shoved and lifted her into the xebeck, she was unable even to scream. Then, when she came to her senses and her voice filled her throat, she realized the arm around her shoulder was Daniel's and he was trying to comfort her. She collapsed against his chest, sobbing.

9

The ship sailed east-by-northeast all that evening and night. MacDoul, making his calculations from the stars, knew they were headed for Africa's Barbary coast and so informed Morgan. The knowledge gave them scant ease.

Morgan tried to comfort Glenna. No bedding was offered them. They stood, then sat and finally sprawled on the aft deck. The night turned cold and Glenna shivered despite her cape and scarf. Morgan gave her his jacket. She slept fitfully on the hard deck, her head on Morgan's thigh.

The morning sun was blisteringly hot. By midday the deck, shielded by the high stern, was a breezeless oven. Glenna sweltered in her wool dress. She longed to remove the cape and scarf, but understood she must not and so endured. They had no food and a mere mouthful of water apiece. MacDoul understood why. The pirates had weathered the storm in port, then rushed out to gather in stray ships, not taking time to provision their vessel.

All day they baked in the heat. Twice Morgan went to the Moor to explain anew that he was a presidential emissary from *"Las Estado Unidos,"* receiving bows and smiles and other acknowledgements. Morgan felt his actions futile, but, in private, MacDoul encouraged him. "It may cost you more in ransom, but at least they may consider ransom seriously. It may be the only chance Glenna has."

Cap'n Mac, kept looking for land signs. By mid-afternoon he saw seagulls, then, at dusk, the dim blueish loom of Africa on the distant horizon. The greenish-purplish mountains that appeared an hour later were almost welcome. The ship continued towards them for a couple more hours. Then, well after dark, MacDoul observed its change to a more northerly course.

MacDoul and Morgan sat on the deck in the dark, talking in whispers. Morgan held Glenna in his arms, trying not to move his aching arms unnecessarily and awaken her. "Where are we headed, Mac?" he asked.

"North mostly, along the coast. If it were light I think we would see the coast very near, maybe only a few hundred yards away. These vessels sail best in coastal waters. Did you see the construction, the wide bottom and shallow draft? This big sail doesn't need sea wind—it can pick up and move on a sniff."

"North along the coast. What do you think it means?"

Mac hesitated in the darkness. "I don't know. I can't read their minds."

"Could they be taking us to Tangier?"

Again a period of silence. "I don't know. Maybe."

"You must have some idea."

"From our last position and the direction of sail, I'd

guess we are in a latitude south of Rabàt. It's a seaport on the Atlantic coast. But we could be south of Casablanca, another port to the south. I just don't know."

MacDoul hesitated a long time, then went on. "They could be taking us to Tangier, Daniel, but my guess is not. I think it best we hope for the best and prepare for the worst. Just north of Rabat is Sali. Sali is the traditional lair of pirates in these waters. It is said to be an impregnable fortress. They might go further north to Larouche—if the shelling by the Swedes hasn't scared them away from there."

Morgan said nothing. He felt the gentle swaying of the ship and heard the whine of the ropes against the rigging. Glenna stirred in his arms. He held her more tightly and heard a gentle sigh, followed by her regular breathing.

MacDoul watched the consternation on his face.

"God, I don't know what these heathen will do, Dan'l. We are certainly going in the right direction for Tangier. I tell myself the ransom money must be more valuable to them than our bodies as slaves. I pray that I am right."

The sun rose precipitously. MacDoul, who had not slept, peered bleary-eyed at the shore. He could make out long stretches of surf rolling into sandy beaches. Behind were shallow bluffs and occasional dunes. Still further back were tufts of grass and a few trees. How close in they were. Yet he still did not know precisely where they were—aside from its vegetation, the land was featureless. Nor did Glenna and Morgan have any hope of recognizing the location. Glenna tried to take comfort simply in the sight of land. But she was afraid.

Near midday a sail appeared off to the northwest. The pirates' lookout aloft saw it before the captives and scurried down to set the crew off in a flurry of activity. MacDoul saw them trying to set every speck of sail they could.

Glenna and Morgan watched with mounting excitement. The wisp of white seemed to hang tantalizingly on the horizon, then, as the sun rose, grew larger. "He's spotted us," MacDoul said. "He wants to investigate." The sail, now heading landward, grew closer, then split into a series of sails, all filled with the sharp sea breeze. MacDoul watched intently, wishing he had his glass. Morgan transferred his attention to the pirate crew. Their agitation revealed unmistakably that it was not a friendly sail.

The second ship rapidly closed, for it was heading directly landward to intercept the xebeck. "It's a British frigate," MacDoul pronounced, delight brightening his voice. "What a beauty she is! She'll sail rings around this tub." Indeed, the frigate seemed to come on with tremendous speed. The pirate captain, his red coat discarded in the heat, waved his arms and shouted unintelligible words as if to move his ship more rapidly by will alone. "She's British," MacDoul kept shouting. "A British frigate!"

"We're saved," Morgan shouted. "We're saved!" He cheered at the top of his lungs and hugged Glenna, swinging her off her feet in his excitement. Glenna cheered too. Together with the other captive sailors, they jumped up and down and waved encouragement to the British man of war.

MacDoul did not check. After his initial outburst, he studied the frigate and what would happen in the next few minutes became all-to-clear to him.

Morgan glanced at his friend and read the grim expression in his face. "What's the matter, Mac?"

MacDoul shook his head. "The frigate draws too much water, Daniel. It will have to turn soon or be beached."

His words were almost instantly prophetic. The frigate tacked to take a course parallel to the xebeck while still several hundred yards away. Then it reduced sail to remain abreast of the pirate ship.

"See. She cannot come in here. These rascals can

hug the coast till nightfall, then try to slip away. We are anything but saved yet."

Glenna and Morgan watched the British vessel, the safety it offered so near and yet so far. "Is there nothing they can do?" Morgan asked, his hopes dimming.

His answer came from a telltale puff of smoke from the man of war, followed by the delayed report of a cannon. They looked to the xebeck's bow and saw the multiple splashes of the skipping ball. A second boom was heard and another ball created a fountain ahead, but closer this time.

"She can blow this ship out of the water," Morgan said with renewed fervor.

"Yes," MacDoul agreed.

But his word was nearly lost in the deafening roar of the batteries on the pirate ship, the rasp and heavy rattle of guns recoiling on their carriages. The acrid smoke stung their eyes. Above the din of reloading and shouted orders, Morgan screamed, "My God, they're going to take on the frigate!"

The experienced MacDoul remained calm and observant. He knew the xebeck was outgunned and could be outsailed by the frigate. The Arabs had to know this too. Returning fire had to be a delaying tactic. He turned away from the battle and looked toward shore. Lord, they were close in. It seemed to him he could almost reach out and touch the beach. Then why return the fire, risking damage and death? Why not simply beach the ship and take off overland? Some would get away even if Marines off the frigate followed. MacDoul was puzzled.

A second ball from the frigate pounded into the xebeck, sending a shower of deadly splinters that felled members of a forward gun crew. The shrieks of the dead and dying rose above the din of battle.

Again MacDoul looked toward shore. Suddenly, he saw the explanation for the pirates' delay. Mounted horsemen in billowing white robes, their swords and muskets glinting in the sun, raced along the beach. The British would not dare attack such a force.

No sooner had MacDoul touched Morgan's shoulder and pointed toward shore than the xebeck veered sharply to starboard. Glenna and Morgan saw the sandy beach rise ahead of them with terrifying rapidity. For just an instant Glenna saw a panorama of heavy surf; then the boat struck the shore. She would have been thrown against the bulkhead except that Morgan grabbed her waist and the railing at the same time. Both were thrown off their feet, but his hold on the rail kept them both from injury.

The pirates, brandishing weapons, shouting and cursing, both fear and defiance in their eyes, pushed them over the railing and into the water, leaping in after them.

Glenna was a good swimmer. In the summer she had bathed almost daily along the rocks off their home in County Cork. She was thus used to surf. But now she struggled. The heavy folds of her wool dress and cape were like an anchor dragging her toward the bottom. Morgan tried to take her hand, but she pulled away and struck out toward shore with her best strokes. She made headway, but it was tiring. The skirt weighed her down. She could feel her strength ebbing, her lungs aching for air. She knew she could not go much further. There had to be bottom soon. The shore seemed so close.

She stood up, feeling the sand just below her toes. She sank below water, bent her knees and thrust forward and upward, filling her lungs with air as she broke to the surface. The beach was rising sharply. Soon she would be there. Up, down, up, down. Then she could not rise. Her upward thrust twisted her backward into the surf, almost filling her lungs with water. She bent forward and looked below. Her skirt was caught in a branch of submerged log. She grabbed the fabric with both hands and pulled. Nothing budged.

Again she pulled and felt the fabric rip. Her lungs were already beginning to ache. She pulled hard and the fabric tore a little more, enough for her head to just break water. She gasped for air.

She had to get loose. With fresh air in her lungs she again bent below the surface and tore at her skirt. Then she saw Morgan beside her, diving at the offending garment. She saw his strong arms grab the fabric and pull with all his might. She gained more distance, floating up again to gulp air. On the surface she saw Morgan rise beside her, his mouth open sucking in air. Together they dove below. She saw him rip at the skirt, but the hem was caught in the branch and no amount of force would free it.

They came to the surface, breathed and dove again. She saw his motions and understood. She tore off the cape and ripped open her dress. Gratefully, she struggled free of it and swam toward shore.

Moments later, Morgan guiding her, she struggled through the heavy surf, falling and scraping her knees, to collapse on the beach coughing and sputtering. In a moment she was able to stand and instantly became aware of a rider on horseback, his swarthy face sheathed in flowing white, staring at her. She registered the lust in his eyes, then looked down at herself self-consciously. She had lost her dress and petticoats. She wore only her chemise and pantaloons and was aware of her breasts nearly bursting that garment as she tried to catch her breath. Instinctively she covered her front. The rider stared a moment longer then reared his horse and galloped toward others struggling ashore.

Aided by Morgan, Glenna stumbled further inland to where the sand was dry, soft and deep beneath her feet. It was an immense beach stretching nearly as far as the eye could see, and wide, rising slowly toward dunes and sand grass on a bluff nearly a hundred yards away. So vast was the beach it seemed to dwarf the survivors of the pirate ship and the troop of mounted men. She turned to look back to sea. The xebeck, quite distant now, rocked in the swells pounding toward shore. In the distance the frigate was still firing, but ineffectually. In a moment the cannonading stopped. There was an eerie silence, broken only by the calls of gulls. Then she saw a glint of metal and patches of red appearing over the side of the frigate.

"By God," Morgan said, "they're coming ashore to attack." He shouted his joy at the thought of rescue.

A musket went off nearby, a futile gesture of defiance from the mounted men on shore. Turning toward the sound, Glenna saw one of the men on horseback, apparently the leader, the one who had stared at her, gesturing broadly as he talked with the soggy and bedraggled pirate captain. Their motions were furious and occasionally, borne by the wind, she could hear words in the tongue she didn't understand. The captain kept pointing at them, then to the left, the north. The horseman also pointed at them, but also to the east across the beach. The charade went on for several moments, then was apparently completed with shrugs of resignation on the part of the captain.

The horseman motioned to his men and several galloped at full speed toward her and Morgan, reigning their mounts only a yard or two away. Sand from the hoofs stung her skin. Several riders quickly dismounted and seized Morgan, pulling him away, leaving Glenna standing there alone. She felt as though she were in suspended animation, the whole scene dreadfully familiar to her. Then the leader kicked his horse. It pranced forward. The rider leaned down and Glenna felt herself being lifted into the saddle.

A scream erupted from Morgan's throat. He tore free of his captors and ran toward Glenna and the man who held her. "No, by God, no!" he shouted. "You'll not have her!" He made perhaps a dozen steps. The leader turned his horse, then a shot rang out. Morgan struggled forward another step, then fell to his knees. He tried to rise, then collapsed to his knees again. In a vision of hell, Glenna saw the torment on his face and the spreading spot of blood on his shirt.

She screamed. "No, no, don't hurt him."

MacDoul saved Morgan's life. Breaking free, he rushed to Daniel and kept him from plunging on to be killed. The white-robed rider, clutching Glenna, seemed to view the whole scene with disinterest. He nudged his horse and rode off at full gallop toward the east, with Glenna held close to him, other riders following.

Part II

bareback and the wind whipping hair into her mouth, but she paid no heed to the discomfort. People were everything. She had no idea where she was or how long

10

Mulay Abd al-Rahman II, Sultan of Morocco, made a scoop of his hand and lazily splashed some of the warm water on his chest and bulging paunch. He was fifty-two but seemed older, a victim of his own excesses complicated by worsening rheumatism and the tertiary syphillis which would eventually provide him a horrible death. But it was the pains in his joints which worried him the most. No matter the cares of state, he insisted on enjoying his warm mineral bath twice a day. It reduced his aches, at least for awhile.

Again he splashed water on his arms and shoulders. "It feels good, does it not, Haddad?" He spoke in classical Arabic, the language of the Koran.

"Indeed, sire." Rashid al-Haddad, younger, taller, stronger, his body trim and hard from a soldier's life, did not feel the need for a mineral bath. He might have enjoyed it, however, had he not felt so completely uncomfortable to be sharing his sovereign's private bath. Rashid did not like to view the Sultan naked. It was embarassing to see his knobby legs and the rolls of fat around his middle. There was nothing imperious about him so exposed and Rashid tried to avert his eyes from him as much as he could. Still, there was a necessity to appear relaxed and enjoying the great

...im. Bathing with the sultan, no
... breathe a word of it to anyone.

... ately unimpressed with his ruler's
... nonetheless suitably awed by his style
... ...ace in Fez, the royal capital of Morocco,
was ... ...ment to extravagance—spacious, filled with
founta... and flowers, a sea with precious mosaics,
much of it in gold leaf. Rashid had never dreamed of
such luxury. Abd al-Rahman II had enough servants
currying to his every whim and comfort to win a small
battle against the French. This bath alone was big
enough to cleanse a troop of men, yet it was for the
exclusive use of the Sultan. The water was warmed to a
precise temperature, the steam rising from it in the
cooler air of the cavernous room. Sunlight angled
sharply through latticed windows near the ceiling,
dancing and sparkling on the blue-green waters of the
bath, then making moving reflections on the bright
mosaics of the walls and columns. For Rashid it was
luxury undreamed of.

The Sultan, supreme ruler of this kingdom, had
political concerns. He was in the eighth year of his reign
and matters were not going at all well. The French had
attacked neighboring Algiers just a few weeks ago.
They had blockaded the city, bombarded it, then taken
it, sending their legions throughout all of Algeria. He
wouldn't have believed it possible. The lair of the
Barbary Corsairs lost to the French! The Corsairs had
been legends even when he was a boy, the fiercest
fighters known to man, the terror of the seas. They had
made them all wealthy with their booty. Now they were
gone, lost to the French infidels. He couldn't believe it.
Would he be next? As sure as Allah, he could feel the
French licking their chops over the fertile fields of
Morocco. They would not have them. He would fight to
the last. While he lived, infidels would not rule
Morocco.

But he was weak. This, too, he had to face. He had

spent a fortune outfitting privateers. Though the world called them pirates, they were secretly his royal navy. But such a navy. Six vessels had been lost in the bombardment of Larouche. Just days ago another vessel had been lost, driven aground by a British frigate. Such incompetence. He was surrounded by fools.

He glanced at his companion. He felt envious of him in a way. Rashid's body was lean and hard, his stomach flat. In his youth he had looked like that. Damn this rheumatism. The soldier's life made a man out of you. You rode like the wind, the horse an extension of your own body. Yes, he envied this man. He also needed him, and the reason he needed him looked at him right now. Those blue eyes, bright, vivid amid his fair skin. This man was part Berber. That ancestry plus his skill as a soldier had led al-Rahman to elevate Haddad over the soft, jaded court favorites to Pasha of Marrakesh. Perhaps this man would have success, where so many others had failed, in gaining the allegiance of those rebellious Berber tribes in the south. Without the Berbers—by Allah, they were horsemen—he would have no chance against the French.

"Tell me again, Haddad. Was it your mother who was Berber?"

"No, sire, my grandmother."

"Ah yes, but it will be sufficient for your task, I trust."

"I am sure of it, sire. I have maintained my family ties. The Berbers will abide me, then come to trust me."

The Sultan shook his head sadly. "I pray to Allah it is so. The rebellion in the south must end."

Rashid felt the need to be tactful. "I'm sure they do not rebel against you personally, sire." He hesitated, searching for the correct words. Offending the sultan was the last thing he wanted to do. "It is just that the Berbers are most independent. They think of themselves as free men. The great desert is their home. Knowing they can always escape there makes it—well, difficult for them to accept authority."

"How well I know."

"But they are good men, sire, the best horsemen, the most courageous fighters in the world. And they have the Faith, as you know."

"Praise be to Allah for that." Again he splashed himself with water. "I'm giving you the widest possible authority in your new post, Haddad. I'm sure you'll use it wisely."

"I'm overwhelmed by your confidence, sire."

"I am suggesting that you not try to overwhelm them with force. That has been tried so many times. I'm hoping your grandmother's blood in your veins will enable you to win them to our will."

"It is my fervent hope, sire."

The Sultan stood up, pushing himself out of the water with difficulty. He shook himself, a bit like a fat dog, making the water fly from his body. "Then it is settled." He stepped out of the water and quickly donned a soft wool *djellaba*, Rashid did the same. "When will you leave for Marrakesh?"

"Immediately, sire."

The Sultan laughed. "There is no need for that. A soldier from the field needs a day or two of relaxation. Come."

He strode to a darkened corner of the bath, behind a silk screen, and bent his head to peer through a small slit in the stone. He remained thus for several minutes, his tongue constantly wetting his lips. Rashid stood behind him, mystified, uncomfortable.

When the Sultan stood up, he smiled broadly. "The ladies in their bath. It may interest you. Perhaps one will take your fancy."

Rashid appeared as though struck. To peek into the Sultan's harem was unthinkable. Men had been drawn and quartered for even attempting it.

"Go, have a look."

Rashid was nearly speechless. "Sire, I—"

"Go. I command you."

Still disbelieving, Rashid stood there a moment longer, then recovered his voice. "You do me great honor, sire."

He bent at the waist and peered through the slot on a vision of carnal delight. Through the rectangular tunnel, he saw a brightly lit room, all gold and ivory. Perhaps a dozen or fifteen young maidens, all quite naked, were laughing and splashing in vivid blue water. A lovely fountain was at the center. Rashid thought it paradise, but he knew better than to do more than glance at it. He backed away and stood up. "Thank you, sire. Most lovely."

The Sultan laughed and put his hand on his shoulder. "Don't be timid, Haddad. Find one you like. I want to make you a gift."

"Oh, sire, I couldn't."

Again a royal laugh. "But you will. A soldier from the field needs his reward. And a pasha needs his harem. I insist. Which do you like?" Al-Rahman was serious in this. Such a gift was guaranteed to cement the loyalty of this Berber. Beside, he had ordered his favorites held back from the bath. One of those left would not be missed. "Make a choice."

Rashid again bent to the peephole. Paradise is what it was. It was an honor to have a daughter in the Sultan's harem, and he knew the most beautiful and richest girls in the land were sent to this place. But he also knew better than to select one. He forced himself to not even think of it. Then from the back of the bath a new girl appeared, accompanied by two hags in black. They shoved her into the pool, pulling a robe from her shoulders as they did so. She stood there in the knee-deep water. Rashid gasped in astonishment. The girl's hair, black and shining, fell to her shoulders. Her skin, now wet and gleaming, was the whitest, most lustrous he had ever seen, fairer even than ivory. She was obviously angry and upset; her magnificent breasts, bursting with a pink flower at the end, rose with her breathing. Her black triangle was most luxuriant. Rashid felt his mouth go dry with lust. Never had he seen such a woman.

"There must be one you like, Haddad. Oh yes, I hear I have a new one, some infidel off a shipwreck, a *nasarah,* I believe. I have not seen her myself. Perhaps she would interest you."

Rashid had no intention of requesting any one of them. If he was to receive the gift, it must be his sovereign's. Courtesy required no less. But he had to say something, and the Sultan's comment gave him an opportunity. "Which one is new, sire?" It was simply a question, not a request.

"Let me see." As Rashid quickly backed away, the Sultan took his place. A quick perusal located the newest maiden, and he gasped his astonishment. Such a woman! By Allah, he would not give away such a prize. But almost as quickly he changed his mind. Anything to gain peace in the south. Such a gift would surely make this Berber his most dutiful servant. "I see her," he said. "Quite lovely. You are a lucky man, Haddad. It I were a bit younger I'd be more than envious of you. But, alas, I'm not the man I used to be."

Rashid stammered. "But, but—sire, I can't accept. You can't—"

"Don't be silly. She's yours—and a most splendid beginning on your own household. I'll have her prepared for you tonight."

Despite herself, Glenna enjoyed the bath. The water was heavenly, and it felt so good to cleanse her skin and wash her hair. There had to be foot-deep dust on her after the endless ride on horseback. She lay in the water, feeling it circulate over her, laving her skin. What a luxury to be clean.

But the water could not relax her mind. She knew

where she was. In a harem. Mother of God, a harem. She didn't know where or whose, but by the looks of the place he had to be someone rich and important. And she knew what happened in harems. By God, no, not to her. She would kill anyone who tried to touch her. And, failing in that, she would kill herself, although as a devout Catholic the mere thought of suicide and eternal damnation would ordinarily have been unthinkable to her.

She had screamed as they rode away with her. Helpless, there had been nothing else to do, and she had screamed and screamed, her lungs bursting out her agony. And when she could scream no more, she had wept, there on the speeding horse. She was helpless to stop the tears. Amidst them, she had cried out, "Mother of God, why?" All she loved in the world dead, taken from her, her father, Daniel, sweet, precious, loving Daniel whose strength was her strength, shot down like some animal as he tried to come to her. The vision of him, the crimson spot on his shirt, blotted out her memory of her father and of Liam O'Connell and she wept and wept.

The ride had been wildly fast, a full gallop to leave the coast far behind. But she had paid no heed to where they were or even the direction they traveled. All she knew was that it was near night fall and she was shoved into a strange-looking tent of some striped material. There were curtains inside and pillows, and she had fallen on them, crying and sobbing until sheer fatigue brought sleep. When she awoke, she didn't know how long later, there was a candle in the tent and a platter of food. She suddenly realized she was weak with hunger. With the storm and the capture and shipwreck, it had been days since she'd eaten. Part of her wanted to accept nothing from these people, but her hunger won out. She picked up the platter. There was nothing to eat with, no spoon or knife, no utensil of any kind. The food seemed to be some kind of yellowish meal, called *cous cous,* which was like dried mush. It was moistened with a spicy broth and was covered with chunks of lamb, cabbage, carrots and onions. In her hunger, she ate with her fingers, as she would learn the Arabs did. It was delicious and she ate ravenously.

The food brought back her strength. She realized that in her near-starvation she had been unable to think clearly. Daniel was not dead. The scene at the beach came clearly to her now. The spot of blood had been at Daniel's left shoulder. He had tried to rise again to come to her and would have had not Cap'n Mac stopped him. Thank God for that. If he had made one more step, he would have been killed. Daniel was not dead, merely wounded. He would get well and somehow come to save her. She was as sure of that as of life itself.

Save her. Where was she? For the first time she took stock of her position. She was in some kind of elegant tent in Morocco. She tried to remember. It had been late afternoon on the beach. They had stopped at nightfall, but they couldn't have taken her more than twenty or thirty miles. Yes, inland. The sun had been at their back. She could still escape, make her way to the coast, find Daniel. They couldn't have taken him far.

Cautiously, as quietly as possible, she padded toward the front of the tent and pulled back the flap to peek out. There were two men right in front, their backs to her, standing guard. She retreated inside and went to the back of the tent. Pulling aside the curtain and kneeling, she tried to pull out a stake. She tugged with all her might, but could not budge it. And there was not room to crawl under. She stood up and looked around for a knife, something to slit the tent. There was nothing. She might as well be behind bars.

She returned to the cushions and sat down. What were they going to do with her? Then she knew. That man on the horse, the one who'd kidnapped her. She'd kill him if he tried to touch her. She'd kill anyone. She sat there, afraid, expectant, waiting to do battle. But no one came. In time her resolve weakened into sleepiness. She was so tired. And before she knew it she was asleep. Her last conscious thought was to wonder if those guards out front were to keep her in or to keep people out. She never did decide on an answer.

She awoke shortly after dawn the next morning. To her fright, the flap opened and the leader stepped inside. He looked at her a moment. What were his eyes saying? But he purposely avoided looking down at her body. Rather, he handed her some clothes, indicating she was to put them on, turned on his heel and left. She unfolded the garment, a wool robe, very loose and concealing. Gratefully, she donned it. And there was a long white piece of fabric resembling a scarf. She didn't know what to do with it.

When she stepped out of the tent, he was waiting for her. He looked at her with disapproval, took the scarf from her hand and wound it loosely around her head and face so that only her eyes were exposed. Half smiling, he now nodded. Glenna was aghast. She felt smothered and reached to remove the wrap. He stopped her, gesturing that she was to wear it.

They rode in a reduced party of four all day. When Glenna was shoved atop her horse, she felt a surge of excitement. With her own mount, she would be able to get away, simply ride from them, back to Daniel and safety. This hope was soon dashed. She was not given the reins. Her horse was led. She determined to escape the first chance she got. Indeed, the word "escape" resounded in her mind along with the sound of the horses' hoofs.

It was not as hard a ride as the previous day, but steady, making good time while saving the horses. By noon she was weary. By nightfall every bone in her body ached, and she fell into an exhausted sleep. They rode through rolling green country along roads largely lined with trees. Nearby she could see occasional copses of trees and farmers working in the fields. No one seemed to pay attention to them.

After a night alone in her tent, she was awakened early. The ride continued through gradually steeper country. In the distance she could see mountain peaks, some snow-capped. Yet, as attractive as the landscape was, there was a monotony to it, which increased weariness as well as her sense of uncertainty as to where she was. Shortly after midday they climbed a rise and paused to look down upon a large walled city near a river. The walls enclosed a large number of buildings, many of them high and domed. In the center was a castle, seemingly trying to reach the sky. In other circumstances she would have considered it a beautiful sight. Now, it seemed merely forbidding to her, a city turned inward behind its walls.

In less than an hour they rode through a massive gate, then through a cobblestone street which led almost immediately downward. They seemed to ride down and down a gradual slope. The street was so narrow that two horses could barely pass abreast. Everywhere was a mass of animals and people, men in their long *djellabas*, knots of veiled women in dark, flowing *haiks* and hooded *bernous*, donkeys carrying incredibly heavy burdens. Glenna saw men pushing handcarts, herds of sheep and goats, thousands of barking dogs, and beggars, many of them blind, by the score. All seemed to be crying and shouting, braying and barking all at once. As the horses slowed to get through the crowds, she felt overwhelmed first by the noise, then dizzied by odors of putred excrement, spices, incense, tobacco, wood.

Down and down they rode through streets lined with stalls. At intersections she could see other, similar streets. The city was maze-like. They passed whole blocks of shops selling nothing but brass or pottery, meat or vegetables, clothing or incense. Glenna could hear animals being slaughtered nearby. Her senses assaulted and all but numbed by the unfamiliar, she wanted to scream. Where were they taking her? What was going to happen to her?

At the bottom they passed a mosque filled with men prostrate in prayer. Then the street climbed, up and up, until they reached the castle, where Glenna was pulled from her horse, shoved through a gate, a doorway, a passageway—until, finally, she was in the Sultan's harem.

In a large, gilded room, filled with flowers, diminutive trees and fountains, she saw nothing but women. Most were young, some no older than fourteen or fifteen. They seemed happy, laughing as they played games. Most were dark-haired, sloe-eyed Arabs with dark complexions. A few women Glenna guessed were Europeans. She even noticed a couple of fair-skinned, blonde Nordic girls. They seemed better-dressed, almost haughty. But her passage through this room was too rapid for her to form more than a fleeting impression.

She was taken to still another room and disrobed. She resisted, but two women in black had her in charge now and both were experienced and strong. The scarf was unwound, then the robe taken off over her head. The two women stared for a moment at her chemise and pantaloons, then stripped them from her. When she was fully naked, they looked at her and made noises deep in their throats. Glenna could not tell whether the noises meant approval or disapproval. A black robe was thrown around her shoulders. She was taken down other passageways, through a doorway, and then pushed into a pool. It was at this point that Glenna began to feel her will to resist weakening. She felt the lulling effect of the pool's warm water. She lay on her back propped up on her elbows, and felt the water seemingly wash the pain away from her joints and relieve the ache in her muscles.

She was allowed to remain in the pool a long time. Finally, the old women motioned to her. She ignored them at first, but finally went along. She was led back to her room and locked in. She told herself with some determination that surely she could escape from two such old hags, but once alone she began to see the futility of an escape attempt at that time. The window was barred. Through the bars she could see the city lying far below. She was high in the palace. And the door was locked.

She examined her room—cell, really, though it had gilt walls and was draped in silk. There was a mat in the corner surrounded by silk cushions. Lord, she was tired. The bath had relaxed her. She knew much of the fight was out of her. She would escape tomorrow—or the next day. She arranged the pillows into a sort of bed and was soon fast asleep, dreaming of a cabin on a tiny ship and a man who loved her more than she had ever dreamed possible.

11

Glenna awoke suddenly, reluctant to surrender her dream, and only dimly conscious of her strange surroundings. The two women in black had returned. One offered her a cup of tea, holding it to her lips. Groggy but thirsty, she drank it. It was hot, spicy, warming to her throat and stomach; indeed, it was delicious. The cup was tilted deeper to her lips. She drank fully. Such strange tea. She wondered what it was.

She sat up and, seeing the pot extended toward her,

held out the cup to be refilled. She drank again. She was so thirsty and the warming fluid was so delicious. She turned to look at the window. Dark outside. Night. The light in the room came from candles. The second woman went out and came back with warm bread, cold chicken and a bowl of fruit. Glenna ate hungrily. She was starved. As she ate, the women, many gaps in their teeth, nodded and smiled their approval. She spoke to them, but they made only strange sounds she did not understand.

Glenna pushed away the remainder of the food and, still cross-legged on the cushions, stretched. She felt warm and sleepy. Not exactly sleepy. She realized she was wide awake but felt languid, relaxed, at ease with herself. She had not a care in the world. She smiled at the women and they smiled back. They aren't too ugly, she thought. In fact, they were rather attractive in a matronly way. Or they looked like nuns; she wasn't sure. If only she could talk to them. She saw them nodding at her and laughing, softly, knowingly. And she heard herself laughing, too. How nice.

They helped her to her feet and removed her robe. She stood naked before them. She was not at all embarrassed. Quite the contrary. She was proud. She saw them touch her breasts, buttocks and thighs, their eyes bright, their lips parted in gapped smiles, their heads bobbing. They thought her pretty. How good of them to think so. Her nipples hardened.

She was offered more tea and she accepted. Her pillows were rearranged and she was bidden to lie down. How exquisitely comfortable and luxurious she felt. She felt she was sinking into her feather bed back in Ireland, and now she was almost positive the two women were nuns. They knelt beside her. A delightful cold liquid ointment was poured on her skin; then heavenly odors filled her nostrils. The most exquisite perfume. What was it?

She did not ask the question aloud. The women began to rub the ointment into her skin and Glenna surrendered to their expert massage. Over and over they kneaded her flesh, adding salves, more ointments and oils, each with its own exotic fragrance. They neglected no speck of her, reaching to her thighs, her calves, even her toes. The massage went on for the longest time and Glenna never wanted it to stop. The whole room seemed filled with aromas, and her own tingling tides of sensation.

Soon they brought her a different liquid to drink, which was sharp and acrid. She felt deep inside her that she should not like it, but drank and liked it nevertheless. What was it? Was it wine? Almost instantly a tremendous warmth spread through her body, followed by a sense of awareness more acute than she had ever known. Her body had a life of its own. Her vision was extraordinarily clear, her perception heightened and rarified. She saw the nodding, smiling women, the yellow drapes of the room, the orange cushions, all with tremendous clarity, sharpness and focus. And it was so beautiful, all so lovely! Her body! Every touch sent shivers of delight coursing through her, as the women's hands returned to play upon her skin, rubbing, stroking, massaging the oils and perfumes into her arms and shoulders, breasts, thighs, all of her. She felt her legs being parted. The caressing hands reached between them. She didn't object. She loved the sensation. She wanted to enclose the furnace within her.

Then they stopped and she opened her eyes to see a tray of little vermillion bottles. Such a pretty color. They stroked the palms of her hands and the soles of her feet with the color. They were painting her red. How fabulous! Then a hand came near her face and she saw a hint of blackened fingers just before she closed her eyes. A gentle stroking of her eyelids and a soft touch on her lips sent sparks like lightning through her. Gently she was pulled to her feet. She looked down at herself. Her skin was glistening, the light from the candles flickering off her breasts and oil-rubbed thighs.

A mirror was held before her. The heavy black out on her lids intensified her sapphire eyes into the deepest blue and made them larger than she had ever seen them. Her lips were bright red. A spot of color in her cheeks heightened the whiteness of her skin. How remarkable. She had never looked so grand.

Next, the women flashed golden jewelry before her. She saw the light glint and leap from the surfaces and knew she had never seen anything so lovely. Golden pins went into her hair. More and more gold appeared and sparkled in their hands. Necklace upon necklace went around her throat, ropes of gold that covered her chest and hung between her breasts. Gold bands were fastened to her arms, then more and more to her wrists and ankles until she jangled when she moved. What lovely music she made! So much jewelry! They put rings on her fingers, her toes. Then she saw in their hands the largest piece of gold of all. She squealed with pleasure and turned so they could fasten to her hips an apron of gold. As she pirouetted, she saw and heard its golden bangles fly about her, adding to the music of her other jewelry. She laughed with delight at the sounds she made.

Lastly, they gowned her in a kaftan of the sheerest, most diaphanous silk shimmering with golden threads. She exclaimed her joy that she was to wear it, then eagerly let them help her into it and fasten it down her front. Over her head went a veil of the same sheer silk. Their cackles of approval seemed most appropriate. It was, Glenna thought, to be a delightful costume party. Wait until Daniel saw her dressed so.

Basking in her giddy warmth, Glenna was taken from her room and led down a darkened hall. The stones felt cold on her feet, but oh, so wonderful. She had never felt so alive, so beautiful, so much a woman. And she was making music as she walked, beautiful tinkling music. She was so happy, so eager. What a wonderful party it would be.

They paused and a door opened. She went inside. The light was not bright, but so acute were her senses that she was momentarily blinded. She shielded her eyes, hearing the music from her wrist as she moved. Then she opened her eyes. She was in a dream room—a golden room with golden drapes and golden cushions to form a lovely bed. And the odors. What appeared to be incense burned in the corner, filling the room with wisps of blue-gray smoke. She gasped at the marvel of it all.

But the best was yet to be.

Glenna peered and saw a man reclining on the golden cushions. He was wearing a golden tunic and his blue eyes were bright and eager. She knew that expression.

"Daniel," she exclaimed. "You're here! How did you get here?"

He did not answer.

"I'm so glad you are. Do you like my dress? Isn't it the loveliest thing you ever saw? And all this gold."

Still he didn't answer.

Why didn't he answer? Then Glenna heard strange, rhythmic music. She looked to her left and saw three old men, a drum, a sort of fife, a strange stringed instrument. Then she saw the old men's eyes. They were blind. Three blind musicians. How sad that they couldn't see her lovely dress. The music grew louder, more rhythmic, more compelling. It seemed to sink into her body with a driving force. Why didn't Daniel speak to her? She'd make him speak to her.

Slowly she began to sway with the rhythm, back and forth on her red-soled feet, her red-palmed hands at her sides. The music seemed to fill the room, the drum beating incessantly in her ears. Her swaying became more pronounced. She felt her arms raising, her hands clasped above her. The sensation of her oiled arms slipping and sliding against each other sent spears of warmth through her. And her legs began to move, her inner thighs sliding against each other as her hips revolved. Why were they doing that? But the thought was lost in the sudden aching desire that overcame her.

The music became louder and faster. She pirouetted. She wanted to see the lovely ropes of bangles flash around her. But they didn't. Where were they? The gown. It was in the way. She began to unfasten that lovely gown, her body swaying back and forth, back and forth. In a moment, bending to her ankles, she undid the last of the kaftan and let it fall to the floor. She stood erect, arching her back, thrusting her breasts forward.

"There. What do you think of me now, Daniel Morgan? I'll make you talk to me."

Slowly, knees bent, arms curving above her, she began to weave her hips. Faster and faster she went, the arc of their movement ever enlarging. Now she saw the chains of bangles flying round her waist and thighs, glinting, sparkling as they caught the light. She could make them fly higher and higher. See, see. With the chains at their peak, she stopped abruptly and let them wrap around her waist, laughing as they whipped her skin. She bent over and saw her necklaces hanging straight down before her. She shook her shoulders. See, she could make music that way, too. She shook her shoulders once, twice. Yes, such music. She raised herself and began to shake her torso, shake, shake, as hard as she could.

"Louder, faster," she called. The music seemed to obey her and she answered the mounting rhythm, her whole body quivering and shaking, her hips pulsing to the beat. The beat shortened, quickened. She bent her knees and arched backwards, deeper and deeper, her body in a quivering paroxysm of frenzied movements.

The music, building to a thundering climax, suddenly stopped. Glenna straightened her arched body. The silence was as deafening as the music had been a moment before. She saw the musicians stand and file out of the room.

"Don't go," she said. "I want to dance."

Daniel arose from the cushions. How handsome he looked. But why didn't he speak? He handed her a golden cup. Yes. She was so thirsty. She raised it to her lips and drank. Again that sharp, acrid taste. No matter. She drank. And again she felt the heat in her body, almost searing her from the inside out.

"Do you like my dress?" she said, then looked down at herself. Where was her beautiful dress? What happened to it? Why didn't he speak to her? Why was he just standing there hot-eyed? Why wasn't he taking her in his arms?

She dropped the cup and threw herself at him. "Oh, darling, darling, my Danny, my Danny." She felt his strong arms, his hands at her breasts. How wonderful to be in love. She stepped back from him. "This silly veil," she said and pulled it off. Again she melted into his arms. "Darling, you have a beard. When did you grow a beard? But I love you however you are."

She felt him lifting her. He carried her to the golden cushions. She moaned with pleasure and spread her legs, never before so eager for him. She saw him fumbling with his tunic. "Hurry, Daniel, hurry. Please hurry." Then he came to her. Never had her skin been so alive to his touch. Never had it thrilled her so. Her entire body ached for him.

"Please, please," she moaned. With anticipation of pure pleasure, she saw him rise above her, then felt his weight crash down upon her. Her insides filled to bursting. Never had it been like this. She seemed disembodied, floating on an endless sea of ecstasy. What was that noise? What *was* that noise? Someone screaming. Who would be screaming? For a moment she thought it was herself, screaming with joy as she rocked her hips beneath him. She lost all track of time. The world stretched to infinity. Suddenly she felt him leave her and gasped in alarm. But then she felt herself being lifted up and turned and that too was a thrill. She opened her eyes. What was that below her? Gold. A sea of gold. No, gold fabric. She was on her hands and knees, looking down at gold damask. She remembered. The cushions. She felt hands on her breasts from behind, kneading her, stroking her. Thrills coursed through her. She felt hands on her hips, holding her hard. Then she heard a scream—a tremendous scream. Was it pleasure or pain? Was that her voice?

Deep in her mind something told her to resist. Something was wrong. But as that thought struggled to enter her mind, she felt a powerful thrust between her parted legs. She was being entered, filled up, but in a way she never had pain before. More screaming. Why didn't it stop? Deeper went the thrusts from behind. Consciousness, reality came closer. Something was wrong. Something nagged at her but was lost in this new burst of sensation. Was it pain, was it pleasure? Was that herself groaning, aching, yet hungry for still deeper thrusts? Or was it herself screaming? She tried to focus. What was it? Daniel with a beard. He had never had a beard. How did Daniel get here? If only the screaming and the aching and the unbearable pleasure would stop she could think. There had to be answers.

Her hips were held tighter. She felt Daniel's chest on her back. A heavy, quick sobbing came from him. His breath was hot on her neck. There was a tremendous pounding in her heart as, uncontrollably, she jutted her buttocks backward to meet the suddenly increased pressure of his hot, hard thrusts.

The screaming—it was coming from him, from Daniel!

Glenna gasped in delicious agony as a mighty eruption flooded her insides.

For a moment, she remained still, on her hands and knees. Then, herself sated, she turned her head around lazily and looked into the closed-eyed face of the man still astride her.

She saw more clearly now. The drugs or her lust or both having run their course, she saw the man and knew he was not Daniel.

In her heart, Glenna knew she was lost.

12

Rashid al-Haddad had heard tales of the exotic splendors of the Sultan's harem. He had hardly believed them. And in his wildest imaginings he had never expected to experience them. Yet, it had happened.

He lay deep in his cushions, still naked, too satiated to rise and cover himself. His head ached. Those surely were powerful aphrodisiacs they had given him. He smiled from remembered pleasure. Never had he enjoyed it so much—a laugh escaped his lips—or so often. He knew, how well he knew, he would never have been so powerful without the drug. But who was complaining.

He could remember everything. Such a woman. He had never dreamed such a woman existed. Such skin, shining, so smooth, so luxuriantly soft. And perfumed. That had seized him. And that dance she did. It had aroused a torrent in him and he had been torn between watching her, those pulsating hips, the flying breasts, and his desire for her. Finally he had sent the musicians away. Allah be praised, he had done everything to her, everything he had ever thought of doing or imagined being done, and she had loved it, screaming for more. Impossible, yet it had happened.

He wondered where she was from. He didn't recognize her language. What was that strange word she kept repeating? *Dan-yull.* He shrugged. It was meaningless to him. She spoke with her body. He laughed. And such a language! Yet, it would be nice to speak with her a little. One couldn't expect everything, even in the Sultan's palace. Smiling, he remembered when he had mounted her from the rear. Always wanted to do that. And her screams of pleasure. Still, he knew it was the aphrodisiac. He wondered what she would be like without it. Perhaps one day he would find out. She was his, always. The Sultan had given her to him. He would take her to Marrakesh. There could be many such nights, many, many. And he would not always need the aphrodisiac. He had heard that women, having once experienced such pleasure, were grateful and came willingly, naturally, eager, even unbidden. That thought aroused him. He would delay his departure another day as the Sultan urged. He needed his rest. He laughed aloud at that. He needed this woman again. Abruptly he arose, donned a robe and clapped his hands. When the servant appeared, he left orders for the woman to be brought again that night.

Glenna struggled for consciousness against the combined effects of the hallucinogens, the aphrodisiac and the sleeping potions they had forced down her throat after she was carried fully exhausted from the golden room. At first her sleep had been heavy, dreamless, as though she had entered some black void. Consciousness came only for a few seconds and only partially. She was aware of her whole body aching and terrible pain in her groin. She fell back asleep and now dreamed horridly of being in the cabin on the ship and Daniel, cruel and demanding, doing terrible things to her.

She slept through most of the day, half awakening for periods of confused and painful consciousness. During these times she struggled to discover herself and where she was. She opened her eyes, saw light through the golden bars, the yellow and orange of the room and remembered. She was in her cell in the harem. The harem! She closed her eyes and opened them again, turning her head. On a small table beside her was a small pot, wisps of smoke wafting toward her. That was the "incense" she smelled. It was not incense but Kif, the form of hashish native to Morocco, and it was already taking effect.

Then, with a rush the events of the night before flooded her mind with terrible clarity.

That had fooled her. What had she done? How could she have thought it Daniel? They must have tricked her. Yes, the tea, that foul liquid they made her drink. Who was the man? Who *was* he?

She fell back against the pillows sobbing bitter tears of self-loathing. How could she have done it? She had made the most obscene erotic love to a stranger. She had done and allowed to have done to her acts which she had never even imagined. And she had been a willing partner. She had wanted it and loved it. What had happened to her? Would Daniel ever forgive her? Oh God, would Daniel ever love her again? New tears flooded out of her.

The women came into the room, smiling, bobbing their heads as they cackled at her. This girl was the talk of the harem. Not only had she been chosen on her first night, but she was chosen to return again. Simply incredible. The harem was filled with girls who had never been chosen. Indeed, most women were virgins. The two hags had lived with the old Sultan and now the new one all their lives and they were as virginal as nuns. Many came to the harem, but only few were chosen. The sultan liked the strange ones, the blondes, lavishing gifts and favors on them. But not one of them had been selected two nights in a row. All this would lead to great jealousy, great trouble in the harem. But there was no choice but to obey.

Unthinking, Glenna accepted the cup of tea offered her. Her thirst overpowered her caution, which was already weakened by the Kif. She allowed herself to be helped to her feet and into a robe, then led to the bath.

She was aware of the pain in her groin and a slight limp as she walked. She entered the water willingly and felt the warmth lave her body, caressing her skin, healing her aching muscles. She remained there a long time, until nightfall. It was heavenly.

She was taken back to the cell and fed. She was ravenous and the food seemed to restore her strength. But also thirsty, she drank several cups of the delicious tea. It was much as the night before, the anointing with perfumed oils, the deep massage of her skin, ecstatic display of jewelry and fine silk. The jewelry was silver this time, masses of it, brighter and more blinding than the gold. Her wrists and ankles jangled with it. A short tunic, a sort of harness of silver bangles, was affixed to her, covering her shoulders and chest but leaving her breasts entirely exposed. Again she thought it beautiful. The silver apron at her hips led not to bangles this time but to sheer silk pantaloons of the palest blue, bound at her ankles.

She drank the bitter liquid, unable to stop herself, and felt the same excruciating awareness of senses, the same overwhelming sexual desire. But it was all different somehow. When she was taken to the golden room, there was no music, no lascivious dance. He virtually lunged at her, ripping away her wisps of clothing and the tunic so laboriously arrayed only moments before. And he took her, ferociously, even savagely, again and again, forcing her body into exotically depraved positions and propelling her into many orgasms, one upon another. He seemed to pause only to drink more liquid, force it down her throat and pour it on her body. Through it all Glenna was not deceived. She knew what was happening to her. Above all she knew this man was not Daniel. She was merely helpless to prevent this violence from being done to her.

The next day Glenna had the greatest difficulty orienting herself. First came the awareness of great pain throughout her body, then the dreams of being at sea. Daniel flitted in and out of the dreams, at times evil and cruel, then again loving and considerate. Each time her consciousness tried to surface, she was again aware of the feeling of being at sea. She could even hear the creak and rumble of the rigging. She could feel the rocking and swaying. This dream continued, through repeated periods of near wakefulness. She finally opened her eyes and saw blue sky. Where were the gilded bars? And the air. It was so fresh.

At last, slowly, as though from a great distance, full consciousness came to her. She was swaying and rocking, but she was not at sea. She opened her eyes and saw she was in some kind of cart or wagon. She sat up, saw trees and grassy land rolling slowly by. She turned and saw up front a driver and team of horses. Stretching ahead and behind were horsemen in white robes and turbans similar to those worn by the men who had seized her at the seashore. An entourage, some kind of caravan. She squinted at the sun. They were heading south.

She felt a hand on her shoulder. One of the hags who had served her in the harem motioned her to lie down. Glenna obeyed, for neither the ache in her body or the last dregs of the drugs had left her. She was given some fruit and bread and a cup of liquid. Now thoroughly conscious and cautious, she held back her thirst long enough to taste it before swallowing. Water, clear, cool water.

The ride in the wagon continued. With the food and water, the last of the drugs gradually left Glenna. She was fully awake now and thinking clearly. Where was she? Where was she being taken? What was going to happen to her now? She sat up. As the front of the caravan rounded a bend in the dirt road, she saw a man on horseback leading it. He wore a blue turban. She recognized him as the man from the golden room. Emotion surged through her—fear, hatred, shame and although not admitting to it, a twinge of desire. Bitterly, she vowed to make him pay for what he had done to her. Mother of God, he would pay as no man had ever paid.

She turned and looked to the rear. A mere half-dozen horsemen. Perhaps she could jump from the cart, escape, find Daniel. But she considered this impossible. She would never get away from horsemen. She would have to wait, bide her time, seek the chance to steal a horse and then escape.

The hag offered her more water and Glenna accepted gratefully. She had to regain her strength, prepare herself for whatever happened. She looked down at herself. She was swaddled in a white robe with a hood over her head. And she was veiled. She remembered the encampment the first night she was captured. No one had looked at her then. The captain of the troops had insisted she cover her face. Yes. She was a member of the harem being taken some place. This slow pace was a procession. She was a harem girl being moved. Where? Some new harem? Not if she could help it. Never again would she be used. She remembered the spicy tea, the bitter fluid. Not again. She would not be violated again.

At sunset the caravan stopped and made a luxurious camp. She alighted from the wagon and stood near it, the hag at her side. She saw the leader in his blue turban rein his horse near her and look at her. Who was this man who had so used and mis-used her? He seemed important. She saw the hag avert her eyes from him and bow. Glenna did not. She looked him straight in the eye. They were bright blue flames and she saw a twisted smile rise on his lips. Hatred welled within her.

Glenna entered an ornate tent with the woman. Obviously she was her servant, charged with looking after her. Glenna saw the interior, the silken drapes, the piles of cushions for a bed, the guards at the entrance. A portable harem. That's what it was.

She ate and drank, but only water. Guardedly, she waited for him to enter the tent at any moment. She lay awake a long time, but he did not come and she gratefully slept, undrugged and undisturbed. She did not know he had gone off to be an honored guest in the town of Khenifra and was enjoying other pleasures.

The next day the procession moved on. Glenna had little to do but look at the countryside. They wound along a narrow, rushing stream of white water, its banks lush and green, through mountains higher even than those Glenna had seen in Ireland. They were the Middle Atlas Mountains jutting through the midsection of Morocco. The river valley, quite wide in places, was surrounded by blunt peaks, a few already covered with a skiff of snow. She thought it wild and beautiful, a remembrance of home, but she was too fearful, too on guard to enjoy it.

They camped again that night. She saw him—who was he?—close up once, handsome, arrogant, obviously in command. When she entered her tent, she was sure this was the night he would come to her or send for her. But again nothing happened. She was surprised, but hardly saddened. She did not know that Rashid al-Haddad had again been feted, this time in Kasba Tadla.

The next day was again bright. Glenna felt the increasing heat of the sun as they made their way south, but, as she noted, more toward the southeast. Soon they left the mountains behind and entered flatter country, more parched. By early afternoon, she recognized she was passing through desert. The green fields had given way to small dunes of sand, much gravel and great quantities of bushy plants, resembling gorse, heather and sage. The stream, now smaller, ran gently beside them, providing the only green within her eyesight. The sun began to be unmerciful. She felt sweat prickling her skin beneath her robe. She longed to remove it and feel the air, but knew that was both impossible and unwise. In time, she came to realize the heavy robe had a cooling effect.

Again as before, they camped near nightfall. Amid the bustle of tentmaking, the feeding and watering of horses, she saw him. He raced near her, reining his mount at the last moment, creating a cloud of dust. She saw his eyes, blue, shining. She read the lust in them. Yes, this night he would want her.

She tried to create a plan. In fact, she had thought of little else during the endless monotony of the ride in the wagon. But she could not make one. She didn't know what would happen. Would he come to her? Or send for her? How could she make a plan if she didn't know what to plan for? All she could do was vow that he would never have her again. She would not be fooled and used any more. And—the thought filled her with excitement and anticipation—if she got a chance she would escape. As she entered her tent, she noted where the horses were tied. Perhaps, maybe, possibly, dear Mother of God, a way to escape would present itself.

Almost as soon as she entered her tent, she knew she had guessed right. The hag did not prepare food. Rather she heated water. She poured perfumed oils in the brimming basin. Compliantly, Glenna disrobed and allowed herself to be bathed, even enjoying the luxury of the aromatic water. It was hardly the baths at the sultan's palace, but nonetheless welcome.

She was offered tea. She recognized the spicy aroma and took a mouthful. But she pointed to a corner, distracted the hag and spat the tea on the sand. With satisfaction she watched the fluid disappear. When the hag turned back to her, she was raising an empty cup to her lips. Glenna endured the annointing, forcing herself to concentrate on the pleasures of the massage, ignoring, or trying to, the repugnance of the aromatic oils and the presence of the hag's hands on her private places. She remembered thinking once how marvelous this was. How could she have? Twice more she managed to throw away the tea, and when the acrid liquid was offered to her, she distracted the hag by knocking over a vial of oil. The aphrodisiac disappeared into the sand.

The portable harem was not as well-equipped as the Sultan's. Her jewelry was only a few strands of colored beads, but the kaftan of soft silk was gossamer thin. Over that went a heavier kaftan of blue silk brocade. At least, Glenna thought, her nakedness was covered.

She was led out of the tent by the hag. Glenna had an impression of the coolness of the night. She saw a sky of black velvet dotted with diamonds of stars. She heard a horse neigh nearby and remembered the location. Off to the left not far away ' she saw campfires, men clustered around them. As she was led off to the largest, most ornate tent, she was conscious of heads raised to look at her. She was sure she heard laughter.

Rashid al-Haddad had stayed away from her for two days. He had been filled with himself, his new importance as Pasha of Marrakesh, the fetes in the towns, the trip south through increasingly hostile country. He knew full well that horsemen could rise out of those hills and sweep his tiny force from the face of the earth. And well they might. But he was not arriving as a conqueror, but as a peacemaker. The Sultan had given express orders for that. As the outreaches of the desert approached, he became increasingly cautious and worried.

But no Berber horsemen appeared. He was passing into the Plain of Rehamna uneventfully. Surely word had spread of his coming and the manner of his coming. He would arrive in Marrakesh, grandson of a Berber woman, new royal governor. If not welcomed, he would be tolerated. He understood these people enough for that.

He felt more relaxed in this knowledge. All was going well. As the day wore on, his thoughts turned to the woman in the wagon. Who was she? Now, twice enraptured, she surely would come to him willingly. If not, he would have her anyway he could. Against the saddle, he felt the heat in his loins. He left word for her to be prepared. With anticipation, he remembered the delights of her body, her screams echoing in his ears. It would be good if she made much noise. The men would hear. Tales would be told. It would be a good beginning. He decided to have her dine with him. It would make a long evening better, sweeter, if he stretched it out. What else was there to do in the desert, anyway?

Obediently, Glenna entered the tent, noticing the absence of guards at the entrance. She had thought her tent sumptuous, but his was more so, with drapes of gold and silver fabrics, a small mountain of cushions, gleaming dishes of gold and brass arranged on tables.

Glenna knew she should bow and scrape, be obsequious, shrink from his presence. But that was foreign to her nature. She looked at him levelly, her blue eyes meeting squarely his blue eyes. But she sat when bidden, servants puffing up cushions behind her. She was offered tea, the same, hot, spicy tea. She accepted, held it in her hand while he drained his cup. A moment later she found a way to dispose of it on the sand. She allowed her cup to be refilled, but she did not drink. He did. She saw it acting in his eyes. They grew hotter, more insistent, blue flames arcing over to her. She felt his gaze on her body and was glad for the heavy kaftan.

More tea was served and *cous cous*. She ate hungrily, but drink she would not. There was music in the corner of the tent, but not so wild and lascivious as before. Merely a single stringed instrument, strange, discordant to her ears. He spoke to her, smiling as he did so. She did not understand a word. He made a gesture, pointing to himself. She listened carefully to the sounds. Rashid al-Haddad. She decided it must be his name. He pointed at her. She said, "Glenna, Glenna O'Reilly." He tried the sounds, almost saying it correctly, and smiled and nodded approval. He wanted to be friends. She would be friends with the devil first. More tea was served. Again she got rid of it. Fruit came, oranges, pomegranates, a strange juicy, yellow fruit she did not recognize but ate hungrily.

He clapped his hands and motioned the musician out of the room. In the silence, he rose and came to where she sat, extending a hand to help her rise. Warily she did so. He reached for her. She recoiled, but his hands followed her. Then she realized he wanted to remove the brocade kaftan. She held his hands, the skin soft and cool beneath hers. She couldn't. This was her only protection. He was insistent. She looked around, desperate. She had practically nothing on underneath. Then she saw a knife at his waist, a small dagger with an ivory handle. That. Yes. She had to get it. But not now. There was no way yet. She ceased her protest and herself undid the ties to the kaftan, sliding it from her shoulders. In shame she stood there as his eyes feasted on her body beneath the gossamer material.

He motioned for her to sit. She did and he sat opposite her. He offered her tea which she refused. He lifted a bowl of fruit toward her. She refused again. He helped himself to an orange, deftly peeled it and ate, the juicy fruit wetting his lips. He drank more tea and she saw its effects.

In her loathing for him, she had to admit he wasn't unattractive. Another time, another place, without all that had happened, if she were properly attired . . . but it was not so. She had determined to kill him. Mother of God, she was going to commit murder.

Glenna looked down at his rich tunic of silver brocade. He thought she was admiring him. She was looking for the dagger, plotting how to get it to plunge into his heart. Perhaps when he took her in his arms, maybe then she could grab the dagger. She looked at him, a drop of tinted juice on his lips. She watched another wedge of orange being inserted between them. He was not ready. She sensed Arab men did not want their women to be forward. What could she do but bide her time?

She saw his eyes travel downward to look at her barely concealed breasts. Yes, he liked that and that was the way. She had been sitting crosslegged on the cushions. Slowly, she pushed herself erect. Raising her arms above her head, she began to sway back and forth in an imitation of the dance she had done under the influence of the drugs. Without the music it was difficult, but she twirled on her toes, slowly, seductively, and when she again faced him she saw the heat in his eyes and knew it was working. Around and around she whirled, revolving her hips and shaking her shoulders, bending at the waist, straightening up, arching backwards, all to a silent rhythm.

She went to him picked up the kaftan he had taken from her and made an arc around him, passing her breasts, covered, then uncovered, near his face. She let the filmy material ensnare his face and she heard his hot gasps of pleasure. He reached for her, but she darted away, using the kaftan as a veil. She came near him and again he reached for her, but she escaped another time. Then he caught her, ensnaring her waist, his two hands almost reaching around her, so tiny was she. He lifted her up and she arched her back away from him. He leaned forward and smothered his face in her breasts. She heard him moan.

Deliberately she relaxed, letting him do as he wished. She felt his hot mouth and tongue at her nipples. He was bent to her as she stood before him. She peered down the length of his back and saw the dagger, its silver and ivory handle glinting against the black leather sheath. She heard him moan as his face passed from breast to breast. She pressed harder against him, but not in passion. Her arm was extended, but the dagger was tantalizingly out of reach. She pressed her breast deeper into his open mouth and heard him moan as her fingertips felt the cold handle. She too cried out in pleasure, but it was the pleasure of knowing she had won. The handle filled her hand. The sheath offered only slight resistance and she raised the knife. His scream rent the silence as the dagger plunged into his back and he fell away from her.

She closed up the kaftan and ran from the tent. She

was aware of voices, cries of consternation, the pounding of feet. She ran as fast as she could, toes biting into the sand, donning the kaftan as she ran. She saw the horses, dim shadows against the velvet sky, the whites of their eyes picking up the light from distant fires. She fumbled for the retaining rope, found a tether, and quickly untied it. She bent below the rope, pulled back the halter and, leaping with all her might, mounted the back of the animal. She turned it sharply and galloped away madly into the night.

13

Without realizing it, Glenna had chosen Rashid's horse, a huge Arabian stallion, so large and strong and swift she had difficulty controlling it. And in her fright, she didn't really try, letting the animal have its head. All she wanted was to get away, as far and as fast as she could. The horse, sensing her fright and urgency, delighted to have less weight than it had been carrying, eager to run after days of slow prancing, raced at full speed southwest along the road they had been traveling.

In the darkness, Glenna was unmindful of all but the wind bending her hair and the thunder of the hoofs—that and the exultation of escape. She was riding bareback and the animal's spine bit into her cruelly, but she paid no heed to the discomfort. Escape was everything. She had no idea where she was or how long they raced. Escape, escape. The words were a litany in her ears. When the horse, tired and winded, began to slow, she dug her bare heels into its flanks to spur it on.

Later, when the horse, truly tired, slowed to a canter, then a walk, refusing to obey her urgings, she reined it in. She listened for following hoofs, but heard nothing but the wind. But she would not be deceived. She kept urging the horse, which periodically obeyed her by stretching into a trot. The animal was tired. She could feel the lather on its flanks beneath her bare legs. And suddenly she knew she was tired, too. By dawn she was hardly able to sit the horse. Its slow pace kept rocking her to sleep. Once or twice she almost fell off.

The sharply angled rays of the sun, breaking over the mountains behind her, warmed her. Drowsiness intensified and she nodded off constantly. She had to rest, get some sleep. Then she was shocked momentarily awake by a realization of danger. How could she have been so stupid? She was still on the road. She had never attempted to reckon herself with the stars, but the rising sun clearly indicated she was traveling southwest. To where? Where did the road lead? She had to get off of it. Someone would come. She would be found. All would be lost. She reined the horse to a stop and turned to look back at the sun. In what direction should she go? She tried to think. Upon leaving the coast, she had ridden into the sun in the morning, east. She needed to go west to reach the sea. Then what? She didn't know, but Daniel had been in the west on the coast. Her only chance of rescue lay in reaching the sea.

She turned her mount sharply to the right, off the road, and into the desert. She dug in her heels and spurred the lathered animal to trot a few steps away from the road. But it quickly returned to the tired walk. She tried to remember the map of the coast of Africa she had seen in MacDoul's cabin. Africa curved sharply to the southeast. She needed to go more north than west. She turned the horse a few degrees to the right and continued the measured pace.

In time she could no longer see the road she had left and that gave her some sense of safety. But the safety brought a return of her fatigue. Repeatedly she shook her head, trying to stay awake. But it was a losing battle and she knew it. The sun quickly passed from warm to hot. Hatless on the fringes of the Sahara, she could feel herself growing dizzy. She had to find some shade, take a nap. It would be better to travel by night. And she needed water. Her throat was parched and she knew the horse must be nearly dead from lack of water.

Ahead she saw a small bluff and under it shade from the morning sun. She reined the horse in that direction and in a few minutes gratefully slid from its back. She was hardly able to stand. Walking was painful. Her groin, her whole body ached. But she forced herself to move deeper into the shade and tether the horse by placing the reins under a rock. No one would see them deep in the shade. She looked at the sorry horse. Its once black coat was nearly white from dried lather. She should rub him down, but she knew she didn't have the strength.

"Sorry, old boy," she muttered. "I suspect we are both a mess. And there's no water. But at least we can rest."

She looked for a place to sleep. Suddenly she realized she wasn't standing on sand, but gravel, sharp, dun-colored, stretching as far as she could see, shimmering in the bright sun. But beneath the bluff was a patch of sand. It was there she lay, barely noting its softness before she was fast asleep.

In her fatigue and dizziness, Glenna had not reckoned with the passage of the sun. As it rose in the sky, her spot of shade gradually shrank. The horse was the first to stand out, and the riderless animal was like a beacon in the naked plain. Glenna did not awaken as Kemal Khadooj, driving his tiny herd of sheep and goats, approached and stood over her.

He was in his forties, but looked much older, his face wrinkled, darkened to the texture of old leather by constant exposure to the sun. He wore a dirty *kibr* of vertical black and white stripes that reached to his sandals. On his head was a filthy, dark gray turban. In all his life he had never expected to see the sight before him, a girl, a young woman asleep in the vast, arid plain of Rehamna that stretched for miles, mostly barren, before Marrakesh. He grubbed out a meager living, keeping his herd alive in the summer and fall until the winter rains again gave life to the sparse grasses which survived in this inhospitable place.

He looked down at her disbelievingly and shook his head. Perhaps the sun was getting to him. No, it was a girl all right. He saw her rich brocade kaftan. Never had he seen anything so fine. She must be rich. He saw her fair skin and the long black hair cradling her cheeks. She was very beautiful, this girl, whoever she was. But she did not belong in the desert. How did she get here? He looked back at the horse. A fine animal, a very fine animal, but ridden hard, very fast for a long time. This girl must have ridden through the desert at night. And alone. He found that truly unbelievable, yet there she was.

He nudged her with his foot and heard her moan. He nudged her again, harder, and she sat up quickly, startled, afraid, her blue eyes wide and shining. She screamed something at him. He did not understand what she said. And in that instant he knew she was an infidel. How had she gotten here?

But as that question was framed in his mind, she jumped to her feet and began to run, screaming and stumbling over the gravel. He caught her easily, but she fought him, kicking, pummeling him with her fists. This he thought funny and exciting, his nearly toothless gums exposed as he laughed. He had both her wrists now. She tried to struggle but was powerless in his grasp. He forced both her hands behind her, bending her backwards, and grasped both her wrists in his left hand. With his right he ripped open the kaftan, gasping at what was revealed. Never had he seen such skin, such a body. He saw the gossamer material, such fine silk, and the jewelry, and he understood. She was an infidel and a harem girl. She had escaped somehow, stolen this horse and ridden hard at night to reach this place.

Glenna was terrified. This blackened, filthy man, leering at her with his toothless smile, the foul smell of his shepherd's clothing and his breath, as he panted, almost gagged her. She knew what he was going to do. She saw the lust in his brown eyes. And he did, and she was powerless to prevent it. He threw her on the gravel and, pinioning her hands, raped her under the brilliant sun. Her screams were as nothing, lost in the vast reaches of sand and gravel, as he pounded into her again and again.

There began for Glenna a living hell. She felt less than human, some kind of animal. Indeed, the horse was treated better than she, fed, watered, curried until its coat regained its brilliance. She was kept mostly tied, her wrists often, sometimes her ankles, not infrequently both. Sometimes he tethered her like one of his animals, a long rope fastened to her ankles so she could not run away. She had very little covering, for the kaftan was virtually in tatters, and she nearly froze in the frigid nights. By day the sun beat down, blistering, making her head spin and her vision swim. She huddled in the filthy, stench-filled tent to escape it. Without that protection for her head she would have died, she knew. And there were times when she longed for death, most especially when he came at her in lust, his foul mouth upon her, his *djellaba* raised, falling upon her to pound his evil rod into her. He seemed insatiable, raping her several times a day.

Leaving her tied and tethered, he would go off for a few hours with the herd. Many times she hoped he would not come back, be lost, killed in the wilderness. But he always returned, bounding at her with renewed energy. Worst of all was the degradation he inflicted on her. She truly thought him deranged, for he treated her as though she were some kind of living toy, a doll to be played with. He kept her largely naked, feasting his eyes on her, rubbing her skin, making strange guttural sounds as he did so, playing with her, pinching her all over until she was covered with black and blue marks, poking his fingers into her. For her it was worse even than the rape.

He gave her water and little food. She was being kept alive, for what she did not know, but she was weakening. All this was a losing battle. She must find a way to get away from him. But how? And how long would she have the strength to run away. She lost all track of time. How many days had this nightmare gone on?

In the times she was free of the revolting, degrading agonies he inflicted upon her, she tried to sustain herself by thinking of Daniel. Would she ever see him again? Would he want her if she ever did? Was he still alive? Had he died of some terrible infection in his wound? Bitter tears of fright and longing ran down her cheeks. And she tried to think of Ireland, cool, green Ireland, the cliffs beside the sea, the breeze whipping her skirts. But even these remembrances seemed to fade in the inferno of heat and under the lechery of the man who held her captive.

Kemal Khadooj wrestled with his problem for ten days. On one hand he wanted to keep her. He had found her, hadn't he? And the horse? Both his by right of possession. It was as if he had found a gold coin in the desert. He would pick that up and put it in his pocket and spend it as he wished. What the difference with this woman and the horse? Never had he dreamed of such a woman, the fair skin, the blue eyes, the softest skin. The mere thought of her made his loins ache. And he could have her anytime he wanted. And he did, because she was his, an infidel slave. He felt like a mighty sheik. She had been in someone's harem. Now she was his harem. He reveled in his sense of power.

Kemal had never married. He was too poor even to be considered fit for the women of the village. He had wandered alone out here in the plain, sheep and goats for companions. He had hardly even had a woman. He smiled his toothless grin. But look at him now. No man he had ever known had possessed such a woman. And she was his. He had found her. He would keep her always.

But other thoughts nagged at him, particularly after he had satiated himself in her. He could not hide her forever. She would be seen and he would be found out. She would be taken away and he would have nothing. She belonged to someone rich and powerful, he was sure of that. He would want her back. They were probably searching for her now. The Plain of Rehamna was large, but not that large. He would be found, punished. He would be accused of stealing her and the horse. His hands would be cut off. The Koran decreed such punishment for thieves. The thought of the punishment caused Kemal to shake with fear.

He knew he should try to find out where she belonged and return her. He could claim a reward. But where did she belong? He had no idea and he could not talk to her to find out. He did not understand her infidel tongue.

As the days wore on, extending past a week to nearly two, a plan came to him. Why should he surrender what he had found for just a couple of coins? A girl like her was worth a fortune in the slave markets of Marrakesh. Between her and the horse he would be rich for life. They were worth more in a second than all the sheep he would ever graze and sell in his whole lifetime. But what would he do with the money? Would money ever buy him a woman like this? He wanted to keep her. He would keep her.

Kemal wrestled with the problem, weighing his lust against his greed. He wavered, unable to decide. Ultimately, the fear of having his hands cut off tipped the scales toward greed. He would take her to Marrakesh and sell her. But first, he would have his fill, enough of this woman to last the rest of his life. He went at her with a savagery and urgency that burst all bounds. Glenna, who had hoped familiarity would offer her surcease from his demands—how many times could he want her, after all—was horrified, then numbed. She wished for death and began to think seriously of suicide, the unthinkable thought for a Catholic girl.

14

It took only a day and a little more to reach Marrakesh. Glenna had not dreamed she was so close to a civilized place, if it was civilized. But it was a day and a half of torment for her. He dressed her in the only thing he had, his spare *kibr*, filthy and stinking, and wrapped her hair in a nearly rotten turban. It at least offered protection from the sun. Thus, she became an imitation of him. From a distance they looked like two Berber shepherds driving the flock to market—or they would have except he was on horseback. While he rode, he kept her tethered with a long rope around her neck. That left her hands and feet free to obey his motions to drive the sheep.

By nightfall Glenna was near exhaustion. Her bare feet were cut and bleeding from the sharp gravel. Her whole body ached and her strength had almost ebbed from her. Even that did not save her. He raped her repeatedly that night, numbing her body, until she finally passed out.

In any other circumstances Glenna might have been enchanted by the sight which gradually arose out of the desert, the rose red city of Marrakesh, although she did not yet know that name. It began as little bumps and figures in the shimmering sand, seemingly more mirage than real. Then as Glenna drew closer, the golden dome of the Kutubia mosque, its gleaming minaret rising two hundred feet above the desert floor, came into view. Behind were the massive, snowcapped peaks of the high Atlas mountains. Had Glenna not been frightened and exhausted, she would have thrilled at the blue skies, mountains, the golden dome rising above rose walls and houses of the city. The next morning when she was awakened and saw the first rays of the sun strike the city, she had the impression of the rose bursting into bloom and for a moment felt it must be a magical place.

They camped a few miles from the city, although in the plain it appeared they were much closer. He hobbled the sheep, then dragged her inside his square tent, bound her hand and foot and for the first time gagged her so she could not scream. She heard him ride away on the horse. She lay in the stifling tent all day, her hands and feet numb and aching, nearly choking on the filthy rag he had shoved in her mouth. For a time she hoped someone might come by, peer in the tent, find her and rescue her. But after all she had been through, she knew there would be no advantage in rescue by another of these desert herdsmen. There was nothing to do but lie there. Once or twice she mercifully dozed off.

In late afternoon, he returned. She saw triumph and anticipation in his face. He seemed happy. He untied her, although he maintained the gag, and to her horror raped her one last time with prolonged, ultimate lunges of particular ferocity. Unable to scream, unable to endure, she passed out, but even that did not stop him.

Near dark, they began the trek into the city and it was long past nightfall when they arrived. Glenna, gagged and tethered, but not bound, could see almost nothing. She had the impression of buildings and of walking across a wide, open place, a sort of immense plaza or square, then down narrow streets to stop before a door. In a moment she was taken into a brightly lit, if sparsely furnished room. A fat man in an ornate black and white *djellaba* stood there peering at her intently.

Abdallah al-Kallid knew who she was or at least strongly suspected. News had traveled fast. The new pasha, Rashid al-Haddad, was making his triumphal march toward Marrakesh when he had accidentally fallen on his daggar. He was severely wounded and died in great pain days later. That was the official word. With that report came the rumor which amused one and all. The pasha had actually been stabbed by his harem girl, a lovely, fair-skinned infidel, who had escaped by stealing the pasha's own horse, no less. Tongues had done nothing but wag for days and all Marrakesh laughed at the reports of the pasha's amorous debacle.

When the miserable herdsman had appeared earlier that day to offer an infidel woman for sale, Abdallah had known instantly. He had taken one look at the horse, a powerful stallion worthy of royalty, and had guessed the truth. Abdallah's first impulse had been not to consider the matter. The pasha's men were looking everywhere for the girl. He shuddered to think what would happen to him if she were found in his possession. Then he thought a little more. If the girl was as beautiful as they said, then it would be a shame to have her merely put to death. A fair-skinned, blue-eyed woman could bring a great price in Marrakesh. Even now Mulay Mohammed Ibrahim was mounting a caravan of European slaves for barter in the south. If this girl—he smiled at the thought—this stabber of pashas was as wild and beautiful as they said, she would be worth a great price. He could keep her hidden, then quietly arrange the sale to Mulay Ibrahim. She would be out of Marrakesh before anyone saw her. And so, pretending reluctance and disinterest, Abdallah agreed to see the girl that night.

Glenna, when brought before him, was anything but a great beauty. Her face—he could see it was a woman in man's clothing—was red and blotchy, the work of sand fleas, dirty and streaked with dried tears. And she stank. Did she stink! He ripped off the filthy turban and saw her hair fall down her back. Yes, long black hair, now matted and grimy. This was the girl all right. He drew his knife—scaring Glenna as she saw the blade move toward her—and slit her putrid *djellaba* down the front, letting it fall to the floor. He kicked the stinking thing into the corner and looked at the naked girl before him.

Never had he seen a girl in such a sorry state; grimy, unwashed, dried semen caked on her legs, her body a mass of bruises. This herdsman had used her cruelly. Anger welled within Abdallah at what had been done to this person. She might be an infidel, but that was no reason to treat anyone that way. He saw that she was pitifully thin. Her ribs showed like on a hungry dog. He must not even have fed her. And she was weak from hunger. He could tell she was dizzy and in her frightened eyes, despite their heavenly blueness, he saw that she had been defeated by all that had been done to her.

Yet, through all the dirt and abuse, he saw that she was a great beauty. Her long, curved limbs, her tiny waist were apparent. Her breasts fairly leaped at him and he felt lust rise in himself. More full, rounded breasts he had never seen, and he had bought and sold many an infidel woman. Yes, she was a beauty and she was the one sought by the pasha. He would have to hide her carefully. Then, with a bath, some food and proper treatment, Mulay Ibrahim would pay a high price for her.

None of this he revealed to Kemal. Rather, he referred over and over to the terrible condition she was in. If he hadn't mistreated her so, perhaps she would be

worth more. They haggled a long time—no Arab could
properly buy and sell without some ceremonial
bargaining—then Abdallah dug into his purse and gave
the herdsman a fraction of her true worth. It was still
more money than Kemal had ever dreamed of possessing. He would not have it long. The next afternoon
when he tried to sell the stallion, he was spotted by
soldiers. When he ran in terror, they shot and killed
him.

Glenna stood there through the inspection, too
weak, tired and dizzy to be capable of much more than
numbness. The appearance of the knife had frightened
her, arousing her just the once, but she could not resist.
She had not the strength. She saw the lust in the fat
man's eyes, but after all that had happened to her, even
that produced little alarm. Anything had to be better
than the herdsman.

She did not understand a word they were saying, yet
somehow she knew what was happening. The argument, the pointing at her and the touching of her meant
she was being sold. And when the money changed
hands, she knew. *Sold!* She was a slave being sold for
money like a pig or cow. In as much as she was capable
of any feeling, she felt revulsion, dismay that this was
happening to her.

To her disbelief, she was treated well. When the
herdsman left, the fat man clapped his hands. Two
women appeared, wrapped her in a robe and led her
away to a bath. She cried from the pleasure of warm
water on her soiled, violated body. Then she was fed.
She recognized the food as cous cous. There was an
immense platter of it, although she was able to eat only
a little of it. Then she was put to bed on soft cushions.

She mostly slept for the next several days. She was
aware of being awakened frequently for food. Her
owner seemed to be begging her to eat, forcing more
food on her than she wanted. And she did eat and
consequently felt her strength returning, her wasted
body filling out. There was a luxurious daily bath and

perfumes for her skin and much brushing of her hair. It soon recovered its brilliant onyx luster.

She enjoyed the treatment. It was in fact heaven after the hell on the desert, but she was not fooled. She was being fattened and groomed for resale. She didn't know how she knew, but she knew. The only unpleasantness was the daily inspection. Once each afternoon Abdallah came into her room. The women undressed her and she was forced to stand there naked while he walked around her, examining her as though she were some prize bull at a judging. He issued unintelligible orders to the women, the result being more food and more grooming. She also saw the approval in his eyes as he looked at her and, more, the lust. Nightly she expected him to come to her, but he never did. Abdallah al-Kallid was too good a businessman to risk spoiling valuable merchandise.

On the eighth day she was annointed. The warm, perfumed oils were rubbed into her skin until she glistened as she had at the Sultan's palace. Shiny brass jewelry was affixed to her ankles, wrists and throat. Not a lot of it, but some articles of decoration. She was sure she was being prepared for the fat man's pleasure. A warm kaftan was held out for her and she was led into the room she had first entered with the herdsman. She saw a second man there and understood. She was being offered for sale.

The man with Abdallah was seated, obviously a person to be deferred to. He looked aristocratic, with pale skin, piercing green eyes, and a pointed, short cropped gray beard. He looked to Glenna to be in his fifties. He wore an elegant wool djellaba of broad black and white stripes and a tarboosh on his head that gave him an almost regal appearance. As the two men talked, obviously about her, Abdallah seemed to defer to his visitor, smiling and bowing frequently. This was to be her new master.

When the robe was taken from her and she stood there in her shining nakedness, she saw the surprise, then the quick rush of lust as the old man's gaze traveled down her body, dwelling on her breasts, then her thighs. Glenna was nearly well physically, and her anger, shame at what was happening to her, her pride, her determination to somehow escape all returned to her. As she felt this man's cold eyes on her, she wanted to leap at him, scratch him to blindness, but something deep inside her restrained her. This was not the time. She had endured so much worse, she could endure this.

Abdallah took the old man's arm, inviting him to closer inspection. Slowly and with great dignity Mohammed Ibrahim arose. The beauty of this girl stunned him. A prize worthy of a Sultan, which he knew she had been. Yet, he was not about to be victimized. Standing his most erect, although that still made him shorter, he went to her. He pulled down her chin and looked at her teeth. He nodded approval, fine teeth, very white. He saw no empty places. He looked up her nostrils and closely at her eyes, then pulled her hair gently to see if it was real. Such hair. He touched her skin, her arm, shoulder, then boldly her breast. Too much oil. These people were always oiled to make them appear healthy. With the sleeve of his djellaba he wiped vigorously at her breasts, enjoying their pressure against his arm, until her skin was dry. Then he felt her with his fingers. Allah be praised, such softness. And her skin truly was so white and clear. He bent closer to examine her breasts. She had been mistreated. He could see faint bruises. Oh well, she would heal in time. He ran his hands along her thighs and between them till the soft, luxuriant hair stroked his fingers. He pinched her gently and saw her jump. Yes, very good. He wiped off her derriere and ran his hand over that. Yes, a truly magnificent woman.

The bargaining began and continued for a long time as Glenna stood there, naked, mortified. She knew what they were doing, but not what they were saying about her. Abdallah was praising his possession, Ibrahim complaining of the bruises and her status as a fugitive. It was most dangerous for anyone who owned her. Abdallah replied that once she was taken out of Marrakesh, there would be no difficulty.

Ultimately the price was agreed upon. Glenna saw that her grinning, bowing ex-master had accepted a purse far larger and heavier than he had given the herdsman. She had brought a good price and that thought was bitter in her mind. She would get even. She would get away. Over and over she vowed that.

15

Two women came into her room at Abdallah's near dark. They disdainfully discarded the clothes Glenna wore and dressed her in garments they had brought. They were harem clothes, or so Glenna thought of them, filmy, gossamer silk. But unlike the attire at the Sultan's palace, she was more modestly covered. She had a bodice of blue beads and sequins that covered her breasts, and pantaloons which covered her hips and derriere, although her legs were exposed. Glenna was grateful for the modesty, but still fearful of why she was being so dressed.

Over this costume went a haik of white wool. Her head, and most of her face were wound in scarves. As this was occurring, Glenna's hope flared. Both women were older than she, a full head shorter. She could easily overpower them once they were out in the street. But the thought nagged at her not to try it. She had learned, bitterly learned, the lesson of premature

flight. Still, this was a city. Surely she would not
encounter another cruel herdsman. Someone would
help her, surely. And she owed it to herself, to
Daniel—Oh, Daniel, where are you, my love?—to try
to escape. The issue was settled as she was led out the
door. Two heavily armed men, scimitars glinting at
their waists, fell in step behind them. She was going
nowhere. Strangely, she felt relieved.

Again she saw Marrakesh after dark, a few torches,
hung on the sides of buildings, making eerie light. She
saw narrow streets, then the same huge square she had
crossed before. She was led to a large, imposing
building, through an arched doorway and up several
flights of stairs.

The harem she entered begged comparison to the
delights of the sultan's palace. It was much smaller, a
single room of modest size, nearly barren and utilitarian with small cell like rooms leading off it. She saw
several girls, dressed much like her, sitting on cushions
or standing. She stood there a moment looking at the
girls. One, short, very scrawny and pale with dark hair,
stood up and spoke to her. Glenna did not understand.
Before she could react, she was led off to the left by the
women and taken to one of the small cells and her haik
removed. The women departed silently. The room was
nearly barren, with stone walls and a barred window.
By candlelight she saw two piles of cushions for beds.

"God in heaven, don't tell me you're English."

The sound of her native tongue stunned Glenna, so
long had it been since she had heard it. Her immediate
reaction was disbelief.

"My God, do you speak English?"

Glenna whirled. It was the same girl who had spoken
to her before. She stood in the doorway, her brown
eyes wide, an expression of astonishment on her face.

"Oh, yes, yes," she cried, and the two women,
strangers till that instant, rushed into each other's arms,
hugging and crying. They held each other a moment,
then stood apart, a cascade of grateful English welling
out of them. Then they both laughed. Each tried to let

the other speak. After two false attempts, Glenna was able to be silent enough to hear the lovely music of the other's voice.

"I didn't think I'd ever hear English again. I'm Anne Townsend. I'm from Guilford in Surrey."

Glenna's inborn hatred for the English flared for just an instant, but was lost in the wondrous, exquisite pleasure of being able to speak and hear in her native tongue. Neither Glenna nor Anne slept much that night. They sat in the cell—by accident they shared it—and talked and talked, telling all about themselves and how they got there, tears running down their cheeks as they recounted their own experiences and heard the horrors visited upon the other. Just being able to speak of it all to a sympathetic person who had shared similar fates was a balm to their aching souls.

Anne Townsend was twenty-six years old, but looked far older. She had been sickly all her life, much given to colds and bronchitis. The chilly, rainy English winters almost killed her several times. When she left England a year previously, she already knew she had consumption. One of her reasons for accepting the position in Egypt was her belief the dry climate would cure her. She had never made it. Since her capture by Barbary Corsairs, she had experienced an incessant array of cold, drafty dwellings. Her consumption had worsened. Even as she poured out her tale to Glenna, she coughed frequently. At twenty-six, there were already gray streaks in her hair. She knew she could not survive much longer.

Anne was the only daughter of an English vicar, Emanuel Townsend. Her mother had died in giving birth to her, and Anne had been raised by her father, a tall, rail-thin, prematurely gray man of Celtic stock, gentle, loving and dirt poor as only vicars of small English parishes can be. But the Reverend Townsend was a scholarly man. His principal joy, other than his God, his Christ, his flock and his daughter, was his books. He read them constantly and imparted to his sickly daughter a similar love of books. She read and studied voraciously.

Because she was so sickly, her father was able to hold her back from formal schooling. Instead, he gave her a far-ranging classical education. She learned Latin and Greek fluently. She had a natural gift for language. French, Spanish, German came easily to her and she read the classics in those tongues. She had a smattering of Italian, it was so similar to Latin, after all, and a good bit of Spanish. She even knew a little Russian.

Only one course lay open to a frail woman of good breeding, much erudition, but humble connections. She trained for a career as governess and tutor. In her early twenties, she took day jobs with prominent families in the Guilford area, earning praise for her scholarliness and her patience as a teacher. When the dreaded tuberculosis seized her, both she and her father knew she had to find a warm, dry climate. When an opportunity developed in Egypt, she applied. The British ambassador needed a governess and tutor for his children, knowledge of Arabic essential. With her gift for language, Anne took a cram course in classical Arabic, Muslem history and Arab culture. She applied and was accepted. Reluctantly, tearfully, she sailed from Southampton for Alexandria.

Her ship was captured by the Corsairs and her personal hell began. She was raped at once, repeatedly and almost incessantly for days. She believed every man in the crew had his turn at her.

"If I looked like you—you are so lovely, so desirable," she said to Glenna, "I might have become a favorite of one. He might have wanted me, protected me. But looking like I do, I was of no importance. They tossed me from man to man like so much baggage." Tears streamed down Glenna's cheeks as she heard her new friend's terrible tale.

Anne had ultimately ended up in the harem of Fetic al-Qatar, the Sultan of Algiers. Relief had come to her there, for she was not very pretty. When the French bombarded and invaded Algiers—she gave Glenna vivid impressions of her joy at seeing the French men of war pounding shells into the Arab city—she had been taken into the desert along with other members of the harem. They had escaped, rather al-Qatar had escaped, from Algiers into Morocco, where he was taken under the protection of Sultan Abd al-Rahman. The harem had been too big to be maintained. Qatar had sold off his less desirable women, including the neglected Anne Townsend. She had been traded and sold a half dozen times and was now in Marrakesh.

Together the two women rejoiced in their language, tears of sorrow and joy coursing their cheeks. Glenna told her of the raid on her father's house, his death, her beating in Ireland, Daniel—oh how she told her of Daniel—the heavenly days in Lisbon, the pirates and all that had transpired.

"Who did you say whipped you?"

"Lord Winslow."

"Good heavens, not him. I know him—at least I know of him. He is the Earl of Wormley. That's very near Guilford. Everyone knows of him. He has an evil, wicked reputation. He has disgraced his family name. His own brother, unfortunately younger, will not speak to him. My dear, I had no idea he was that wicked. Tell me again what he did."

Glenna repeated the story, hearing the delicious sounds of consternation and disapproval of the evil Winslow.

"He has squandered his inheritance. He gambles heavily, I hear. But I did not know he was so evil, so cruel. He *whipped* you. Like an *animal*. My dear, may God forgive him." And she took Glenna in her arms, crying with her, patting her like a baby in comfort for the offense. Both were emotionally drained by the reliving of their experiences. They fell asleep in each other's arms, grateful for their growing friendship.

When Glenna awoke the next morning, she felt the first happiness she had known in a long time. She was grateful to have a friend, someone to talk to, to share her fears and shame with, someone for her to comfort and be comforted by. Her love for the English girl grew rapidly.

Most importantly, Glenna learned a great deal about where she was and what had happened to her. She learned that she had been in Fez, the royal capital, and had been in the sultan's harem.

"What is a sultan?" Glenna asked.

"He is the ruler of Morocco, sort of like a king, but not like our English kings. The sultan is an absolute ruler. His word is law in everything. In one way or another all the wealth of Morocco is his. And he is said to be fabulously wealthy." Anne laughed. "For you to be in his harem was a great honor."

"One I could have done without." Glenna said the words sharply, her bitterness revealed in her voice.

"Nonetheless, every father in Morocco would sell his soul to have his daughter selected for the sultan's harem."

"Not I. It was a nightmare." She hesitated. "But who was the man who . . . who . . . "

"The Sultan?"

"I don't know. Perhaps it was. He was a young man, very strong."

"Young? It seems to me I heard the Sultan was an older man."

"And he had piercing blue eyes. I remember his eyes. That is what fooled me, I think, and that potion they gave me. I thought he was Daniel and I—" Tears welled in her eyes and she was unable to finish.

"Blue eyes you say? Then it was not the Sultan."

"How do you know?"

Anne sighed. "It is a little hard to explain, but I'll try." She smiled. "We don't have much else to do, do we? There are two races of people in Morocco, the Berbers and the Arabs. The Berbers were here first. In fact, they are an ancient people and no one knows where they came from. They are fair skinned and blue eyed. Some are even blond. All that is known is that they were here in Roman times. The word *berber* comes from the Roman word for barbarian and that is how the Romans thought of them. They were never able to conquer the Berbers. They are proud, independent and fierce fighters. All the Romans could do was drive them south into the desert and keep them there.

"Several hundred years after the Romans, the Arabs came. They were basically an Asiatic people, darker skinned, black haired and brown eyed. They came from the east in successive waves, conquering Morocco, even Spain as you know, converting all to the Moslem religion. They won the Berbers over to Islam, or largely so, but they were never able to subjugate the Berbers any more than the Romans had. The Berbers remained desert people. They controlled the south, still proud, independent and fierce. The Arabs remained in control in the north. The sultan would always be Arab, dark haired and brown eyed. A blue eyed man would be a Berber. He could not possibly have been the sultan."

"Then who was he?"

"I don't know."

"Well, whoever he was he is now dead."

Anne remembered hearing the story of the dead pasha. So this was the girl. Nearly speechless, Anne could only say, "You didn't"

"Yes, I stabbed him. That night in his tent, I grabbed his dagger and plunged it into his back. I ran, stole a horse and got away."

"My dear, you didn't!"

Glenna spoke fiercely, her eyes bright. "I did. I'm proud of it. I did no wrong. God will forgive me."

"That's not what I mean. They'll hunt you down. I'm surprised they haven't killed you already."

Glenna saw the worry in her eyes and suddenly realized the danger she was in. "I suppose they do want vengeance. Then why am I here? That fat man who bought me could have turned me over to them. This man who now owns me could do the same." Then she exclaimed, "Do you think he will? Is that what is to happen to me?"

"No, I think not. If that was going to happen it would have by now."

"But why not?"

Anne smiled. "Surely you know."

"I know nothing."

"Just look at yourself, dear. You are so beautiful. I have never seen anyone so beautiful. Your skin is the color of new fallen snow. Your figure would excite any man. Surely by now you know the effect you have on men."

Glenna covered her face with her hands and cried bitterly, "I know, I know. Oh, what they've done to me. I hate this body. I hate the way I look."

"You shouldn't. You'd be dead by now if you looked any less. If I had stabbed my master, stolen a horse and run away, I'd be long in my grave. I'd have been turned over to him for the reward. I'd have been made an example to others. The manner of my death is not very nice to even contemplate. But you . . . Look at yourself and consider yourself most fortunate. You have been saved by your snowy skin and your voluptuous body. You are too valuable to be allowed to die. And that is why you're here, still alive."

"How can you call me fortunate? That herdsman in the desert. The terrible things he did to me."

"Yes, but he saved your life. He hid you. If the pasha's men had found you—my dear, it would have been far worse."

"Oh Anne, what is going to happen to me now, to us? I don't even know where I am. What is this city?"

"You are in the fabled city of Marrakesh, gateway to the Sahara, the great desert. This is the legendary Oasis city, the terminal point for all the desert caravans, the pride of all the nomadic tribes." She smiled wanly. "We should consider ourselves fortunate, I suppose.

Few Europeans and hardly any women ever get to see Marrakesh." Both women scoffed bitterly at the notion they were fortunate.

Her voice almost a whisper, Glenna asked, "What do you think will happen to us?"

"I don't know exactly. We are slaves, infidel to them, and as women lower than the animals they tend. Our only value is our bodies—and the work we may be able to perform."

"Will we remain here?" She made a gesture. "In this . . . this harem?"

"No. They are planning to take us over those mountains—they are called the Atlas mountains, some of the highest in the world—and into the desert beyond. I don't know exactly what will happen, but we will be sold. If we survive the trip across the desert, we will be sold again and again. If we are lucky, we may end up in some rich man's harem." Her voice was low as she spoke, mirroring her fear.

After a time Glenna spoke. "And if we are unlucky?"

Anne smiled wanly. "I don't know. Someone very much like your herdsman, I suspect."

Glenna gasped her horror. "No, I can't, I won't."

"I'm afraid you will. What choice do either of us have. You particularly. There is a price on your head, I'm sure."

"But Anne—"

"There are no buts, darling. This has happened to thousands of women. They are captured by corsairs or seized in raids on coastal towns. That happened to the three Spanish girls that are here now. And one of them is only twelve. Only twelve! And what she has gone through already! She and her sisters were gentle girls from a good family. Don't you see. Tens of thousands of women have just disappeared. They are seized, taken into the desert where they vanish, never to be seen or heard of again."

"No!"

"Yes. We have been unlucky. It has happened to us." Tears ran down her cheeks. "We will never see our loved ones again. I will not see my father. You will not see your Daniel. Accept it."

"I can't accept it. I won't. Never!"

"I'm sorry for that. The Moslem religion, so I've read, gives a very low state to women. One thing saves them—fatalism. Their God, Allah they call him, is all powerful. Everything that happens is Allah's will. There is no point in striving against Allah's will. Just accept what Allah has willed."

"And wait for death?"

"Yes." The English girl paused while a spasm of coughing seized her. "For me that will come quickly, I think."

Glenna put her arms around her. "No, I will not let it happen. Somehow I'll find a way to keep us both alive." She saw Anne smile as she comforted her, but also saw the resigned disbelief in her eyes.

16

Glenna could think only of escape. Even as she and Anne engaged in their most pleasant activity, recalling home and endlessly recounting its pleasures, part of Glenna's mind dwelled on the need to escape. She would not be a slave. She would not be driven into the desert like an animal to disappear from the face of the earth. She would not. Nor would her friend. She would find a way for them both to escape. But how? The problem consumed all of her thoughts part of the time, and some of her thoughts all of the time. It never left her.

Her first decision was that she needed to know the language. "Teach me Arabic," she said to Anne.

"Oh, darling, I don't think you want to learn."

"But I do. You are so fortunate to know what is being said, to know where you are, what is going to happen."

"No, I think not. It is terrible to know what is going to happen."

"You're wrong, very wrong. It is far worse to be ignorant of what is happening. I never knew if I was to be killed that very moment. I could never plan for anything, prepare myself. Everything was strange and a total surprise. I wasted my energy when I didn't need to, and I was unable to cope when I needed to. Believe me, it is far better to know what is going to happen."

And so Glenna began to learn Arabic from her friend. She asked her words, phrases, sentences. "What is the word for that? How do you say this in Arabic? What are they saying?" She forced herself to listen to every snatch of Arabic she could hear, even those emanating from the street below their window. She willed her mind to remember the strange words and phrases. She bent her tongue to their repetition.

"There isn't enough time, Glenna. It is a difficult language. You can't learn it in a couple of days."

"So I won't learn it. I'll learn a word, a sentence. I may need it. It may save my life, it may save both our lives. I must learn."

Glenna pursued the matter of escape relentlessly, questioning Anne for any scrap of useful information.

"Where are we exactly?"

"I told you. We are in Marrakesh."

"I know that, but where in Marrakesh?"

Anne took her to the window. From four flights up

they looked down on the immense square she had twice crossed in the night.

"It is called Djemaa-el-Fna. I suppose it is the most famous square in all of Islam. Here meet the caravans from north and south to trade and re-outfit. The nomads come here from the desert driving their herds of sheep and goats for sale. There are slave markets, human beings bartered like animals. We are lucky to have been spared that. And it is the amusement place for the whole desert." She pointed across the square. "There. Those men in white."

Glenna saw a troop of dark-skinned men attired in loose fitting, flowing garments of white, whirling in some kind of feverish dance.

"They are the Dervishes, the whirling Dervishes, as they are called. And over there to their left, see the snake charmers."

Glenna peered. Yes she saw the snake charmers.

"And the jugglers and the dancers. You see, the Djemaa-el-Fna is a sort of combination market place, gathering place, amusement center, the mecca for all from the desert and all who would enter the desert. It really is a fabulous place. And over there to the north is the fabulous souk of Marrakesh, the great market place. Oh, I do wish I'd seen it just once. You can buy anything or everything there. There are thousands of tiny stalls selling everything. You bargain. You never pay the asked price. Oh, I wish I could see it."

Glenna did not share her friend's excitement. She knew now she had passed through the souk in Fez. She remembered the gagging smells and the crush of humanity. And, as she looked down on the giant square, she saw not a romantic, exotic place, but an opportunity for escape. If she and Anne could once find a way to enter that square they could be lost in all those people. No one would notice them, such was the welter of strange costumes and people.

"This place we're in, how many ways out are there?"

Anne only half heard her in her fascination for the panorama of Arab life below her. "What did you say?"

"I asked if there is more than one way out of here?"

"Oh yes, the city has many gates. Fez seemed to be turned inward behind its great wall. Marrakesh is an open city welcoming the world."

Glenna was slightly irritated. "I don't mean the city. This harem."

The English woman turned from the window to look at her. "You don't mean you're still thinking of getting away?"

"Is there more than one entrance?"

And Anne showed a twinge of irritation, also. "No. I told you. There is only one way in, one way out. All men, save the master, are forbidden to even look inside. The door is guarded day and night. There is no escape, Glenna, none at all—except. . . . "

"I know. Don't say it again." Then she smiled at her friend, dissipating her irritation by doing so. "This 'master,' as you call him." She said the word sarcastically. No man would be her master. "Who is he? What sort of man is he?"

"His name is Mohammed Ibrahim. He is a sheik, a powerful one, and an important slave trader. He has collected us over a period of weeks, two French women, those poor Spanish girls, you and I. He will start south with us shortly. We will be traded. He will return with blacks. Another day they will be offered for sale out there in the Djemaa-el-Fna."

"Will he send for me?"

"You mean?"

"Yes."

Anne looked as though she were going to cry. "Yes. Tonight, in fact. I overheard the women say you have been summoned."

Glenna inwardly shrank. Fear gripped her.

"I'm sorry."

She recovered quickly. "You needn't be sorry. I'm getting used to it."

Anne smiled her wan, little smile and touched her arm to comfort her. But all she said was, "Yes."

"He's rather old, but I suppose nonetheless, he'll—"

"I don't know. He is a strange man."

"Did he send for you?"

"Yes."

"What did he do?"

Anne laughed lightly, but there was a tone of bitterness to it. "Nothing—at least not what I expected. He never touched me. He invited me to dine with him and we talked. He spoke to me in Arabic, the only language he knows. He said I had not fooled him. He knew I understood the language. He had seen the reaction, the understanding in my eyes. That's all we did, talk. It went on for hours. In many ways it was the most remarkable conversation I've ever had. He asked me about my country, our form of government, our way of life. And he compared it to his, finding his ways superior, of course. He asked where I had learned Arabic, and about my background, and seemed amazed to find that a woman could have an education. We talked a long time about Islam, Morocco, the Arab way of life. He seemed convinced one day the Arabs would again be the most powerful people in the world. I learned a great deal from him. Above all, I learned that he is the cruelest man I have ever known."

Glenna was aghast. "How can you say he was cruel? He never touched you."

"No, he never touched my body, but he touched my mind. He talked to me, learned all about me, expressed admiration for my education, my willingness to learn, my gift for language. It seemed to affect him deeply that a woman such as I could exist."

"But how was he cruel?"

"Because I was sent back here. I am still a slave. I will still be borne into the desert and sentenced to a life of hell. He thinks I'm a remarkable woman, I know he does. But that doesn't matter. I am still chattel, little more than nothing, a seminal vessel, a slave." Tears filled her eyes. "And to be so treated, after he knows who and what I am, is the ultimate cruelty, I do believe."

Glenna took her friend into her arms and comforted her. Against her ear, she said, "And me? What will he do to me?"

"I don't know. I think his cruelties are cleverly designed. He seeks to destroy the mind of his slaves before he sells them. I don't know what he will do to you. It should be interesting to find out." She smiled. "Oh, I don't mean that the way it sounded."

"I know."

"He can hardly talk to you. I'm sure he'll think of something unique."

"My body?"

"Somehow I should imagine so." She smiled. "I told you how beautiful you are. You have a powerful effect on men."

"Will he use potions, drugs—like the other."

"I don't know. If he does offer them, you should take them, don't you think? Isn't it better that way?"

"No. It is less painful, to be sure, but I will not be degraded. I will not be made to want someone I detest."

Anne smiled at her. "You know best."

"Besides, I want to be fully conscious. Somehow, someway, I will find a way to get us out of here, perhaps this very night."

"Glenna, there is no way. We are two helpless women. We have no weapons, no means."

Glenna's eyes grew cold, but deep within they burned with determination. "But I do have a weapon. You say men desire me. All right, I will use this body, their desire as my weapon. They will have me anyway. I will do what must be done to find a way to escape. I will not perish in the desert. I will not be a slave to any man. I will find a way out of here." She bent her hands to her breasts, cupping them and lifting them up. "If this is all I have to use, then that is what I must use."

"Oh, Glenna, please—"

"No, Anne, don't try to stop me. I love you. You have brought me the only happy moments I've had since Daniel. But I am not like you. I will not give up and wait for death. I will fight with my last breath. Can't you understand that I must?"

Her friend smiled. "Yes, I understand better than you think. It's the Irish in you. Such fighters you are. I admire it." She coughed again. "I just wish I had the strength."

"You do. I'll help you. I'll find a way for both of us to get out of here. It can't be too far to the sea. We'll get out of here, find a horse and ride to the sea."

Again Anne smiled at her indulgently, the sort of smile an indulgent mother gives to a foolish child reciting her daydreams. "Believe, if you must, but it's impossible. Utterly impossible."

"So it's impossible, but we will try."

"And get into worse trouble? Mohammed Ibrahim at least has some semblance of civilization. Neither of us know what beasts lie out there."

Glenna shuddered. "I know, believe me I know. But I have learned one thing in all this. Take each moment as it comes. Seize the opportunity. Let the future take care of itself."

Anne Townsend shook her head ruefully at her friend.

As Glenna was bathed and perfumed that night, her emotions were in torment. On one hand she recoiled at the thought of the old man, his hands on her, what he might try to do to her. The mere thought of it made her want to vomit. But on the other hand, she was excited. She had killed a young strong pasha. Surely this old man would be less difficult. As the time approached, the excitement, her determination won out. Her skin seemed to glow as much from anticipation as from the oils rubbed into her.

Anne sensed her friend's thoughts. "Please, Glenna, don't try anything."

"I will if I can. Believe me I will. And you be ready to run. Don't fall asleep, no matter how late I am in coming for you. And try to find us some clothes to wear on the street. When we are all bundled up they'll never find us."

Anne was still shaking her head in protest as Glenna was led away to her master's chamber.

17

Mohammed Ibrahim made it a custom to have all the women slaves before they were taken into the desert and sold. To the extent he thought about it at all. He considered it simply his due, part of his investment and profit. Thus, it was with mounting excitement that he anticipated the night with his newest acquisition. He had vivid memories of her shining body and soft skin when he bought her. He had deliberately stayed away from her to let his juices mount. He was not as young as he used to be and knew it.

Yes, he was getting old. This would be his last caravan into the desert. When he returned, he would retire and enjoy the wealth he had accumulated. Not bad for a former camel driver. He had done well in the slave trade. How many bodies had he bought and sold. The count had been lost soon after he had begun it. He could single out in his mind only a very few of the women slaves to remember, but deep inside he knew this latest, the last in a long line, would stay with him forever. In his mind's eye, he dwelt on the delicious curve of her breasts, the upturned nipples like jewels—yes, full red rubies.

Perhaps he should not sell this one. He would need comforts in his old age. A small harem to amuse him. This girl would make a jewel in any harem. And she was his. He had paid a high price for her. Then he remembered the price on her head. Most dangerous to keep her. But he could keep her hidden. With the pasha dead, memories of her would fade quickly. She was a wild one, determined to escape. And she had killed the pasha. A most dangerous one to have around. He would have to be careful—until she was tamed. And tamed she would be. All the wild ones were soon tamed. He had no fear of that.

Glenna, trembling with both fear and excitement, was led out of the small, spartan harem. She wore a voluminous robe and a heavy veil, but underneath nothing but the usual jewelry of figured brass. Her awareness of her own nakedness intensified both her conflicting emotions.

The heavy barred door to the harem was opened in response to the gentle rapping of one of the women. As bidden, Glenna stepped out into a narrow passageway made of rough stone. She saw the guard beside the door. He was a large man, one of the larger Arabs she had seen. He wore a sort of tunic and pantaloons. A scimitar was in his belt. She recognized him as one of the men who had brought her to this place. He had his eyes averted rather than look upon a member of his master's harem.

It was only a step or two across the passageway to another door. Obviously, the man guarded both doors. One of the women rapped gently. A word came from beyond the door, it was opened and Glenna felt herself being pushed inside.

It was a large room quite opulently furnished with pastel curtains and an immense, nearly priceless Persian rug. It felt warm and soft to Glenna's feet after the cold stones of the passageway. As befitted a rich trader, Mohammed Ibrahim had acquired valuable possessions, gold and silver, porcelain and crystal, tables and cabinets of teak, mahogany and other rich woods. But Glenna took scant notice of the valuable objects. What she saw was the usual pile of ornate cushions and amidst them the old man in a robe of soft, white wool. He looked much older than she remembered. She saw the deep wrinkles around his eyes, the sagging flesh on his neck. She took particular notice of his hands. The skin was brown and as dry and shiny as leather. He had protected his face from the sun in the desert, but not his hands which held the reins of his camel.

Her mind was in turmoil. Fear gripped at her and physical revulsion of him nauseated her. These feelings competed for control of her mind with a whirl of makeshift plans. Above all sounded the single word, *escape, escape, escape.* She had figured this adventure would go much as it had with Rashid. She'd force herself to entice this old man with some indecent dance, grab his dagger, use it and run. She had been enacting such a scene in her mind all afternoon and had steeled herself to go through with it. But none of it would work, she now knew, and with her plan's abandonment came confusion and uncertainty. There was the guard at the door. How could she ever get by him? And the old man wore no tunic. He had no dagger. Mother of God, what was she to do?

She saw him smile at her and beckon for her to sit beside him. She remained where she stood, looking at him dumbly. He poured tea from a brass jug into a porcelain cup and motioned it was for her. Still she did nothing. He spoke to her, softly, gently, smiling as he did so. Earlier Glenna had hoped to catch a word or two she had learned from Anne. Now, in her agitation she did not understand a single sound.

In a moment he arose from the cushions and came to her. He stood before her, almost half a head shorter, smiling through his salt and pepper beard. Again he spoke to her in the soft, fatherly voice and raised his hand. She had recoiled at the movement, then when she saw his intention, she allowed him to remove her veil, an unnatural encumbrance to her. She saw the look in his eyes as he gazed at her.

He made no other move to touch her, except to take her arm and gently guide her to the cushions next to him. She sat down, her legs tucked under her and he sat beside her crosslegged. He offered her the cup of tea and she took it, but she had no intention of drinking it. She knew all about harem tea. She would only pretend. She raised it to her lips and smelled. Tentatively, she took a tiny sip. It was the ordinary mint tea served with meals. He wasn't trying to drug her.

He kept talking to her, smiling as he did so, acting almost fatherly. Tentatively, she smiled back at him and he nodded his approval. Could he understand English? Anne had said they spoke in classical Arabic. One way to find out. "Do you speak English?" she asked and saw him nod his head and smile again. That didn't tell her anything.

Smiling sweetly, her voice low and huskily musical, she said, "You are a spineless dog of a slave trader." Again he smiled and nodded and said something to her in Arabic, seemingly very pleased that she was talking to him. He didn't know English. Again she smiled as she spoke, "You are a beast, less than a snake, the lowest form of animal life. You abduct women and children, use them for your own pleasure, then sell them into unspeakable slavery. I hate you and I will kill you if I get a chance. I will go to hell before I'll see you live to ruin another life." His approval of all she said was abundantly evident. And he spoke to her, offering more tea as he did so.

Glenna was greatly amused by the conversation. Smiling coquettishly, she said all the hateful things she could to him and won only his seeming pleasure in her words. The act of forming words, the paradox of smiling as she said hateful things, seemed to clear the whirl in her brain. She was beginning to be able to

think, and a plan began to form in her mind. He offered
her some small cakes, and she accepted one. It was very
sweet, rich with nuts and dates, and flavored with anise.
She took a second bite, which pleased him immensely.
A regular English tea with a lecherous slave trader, she
thought. Smiling her best, she said, "What am I going
to kill you with?" She began to look around the room.
He thought she was admiring his quarters. He began to
point out some things to her and speak of them fondly.
Then, reaching for a second cake, she saw it right
before her. Yes, it would do nicely.

Her plan was now alive in her mind, fully formed,
taking control of her every action. She felt her heart
beat faster and her whole body warm with excitement.
It would work. She'd make it work.

Mohammed Ibrahim could not possibly have been
more pleased. Why this girl was little more than an
innocent child, so sweet and lovely and, yes, affectionate. He could tell she was starved for affection and a
guiding hand. No wonder. She was far from home in a
strange land. The young pasha had obviously been too
impatient and brash. Most young men were. He must
have come at her, frightened her. It was surely his own
fault that she attacked him. Young infidels like this
need a little time and reassurance, a gift or two as a
reward. Handled right, as a young colt should be
handled, they can be trained—he smiled at the
thought—to perform admirably. And such training
takes the patience of an older man.

He saw her looking around the room and asked her if
she would like to see his things. He saw her smile
sweetly. Such a lovely girl. Perhaps he would have
someone teach her Arabic so he could converse with
her. He arose and motioning that he intended to show
her his collection, he extended his hand to help her up.
She obliged, and as she rose he saw a flash of white
thigh. Yes, patience was a virtue.

Slowly, taking her arm from time to time, he gave
her a tour of the room, taking time to explain to her an

African tribal mask from near the Niger. He could see the horrible visage frightened her, so, smiling, he explained that it was to scare away evil spirits. Fondly, he touched his things, gold and silver bowls, exquisite figures of ivory, teakwood chests with secret compartments to hide gold. He encouraged her to touch the objects, too, and saw her smiling approval. He was warmed by that. They stopped at a gleaming brass medallion, perhaps four feet across and he pointed out the delicate art work sculptured upon it. That seemed to spark recognition in her. She touched the necklace at her throat, opening her robe a little for him to see it. She meant to say, he knew, that it was similar to the medallion. He knew full well it was, but he reached gently to her throat and lifted the necklace away from her skin as though to inspect it. With his eyes, he expressed some doubt, and she opened her robe a bit more for him to inspect more of the jewelry. He bent more closely, lifting another section of the brass. The soft, smoothness of her skin sent tingles through his fingers and he felt the effects in his loins. But he did nothing other than remove his hand and indicate with many nods and smiles that, yes, her necklace was similar.

He took her arm and they moved on to a large vase filled with beautiful and rare feathers from the jungles of Guinea. He heard her squeal with pleasure as she saw them. He urged her to touch them and she did with delight, lifting them one by one to exclaim how beautiful they were. When she held a brilliant blue one, he took the hand that held it and indicated it was hers, a small gift for one so lovely. He heard her sounds of pleasure, and he tried to indicate that the plume matched the color of her eyes. Impulsively, she bent to him and brushed his cheek with her lips, adding immeasurably to the excitement he felt. Then, straightening up, she tried to affix the feather to her hair, but the plume was too heavy and fell to the rug. Quickly she picked it up. All these actions had loosened her robe and he saw the delicious inner curve of her breasts. Unable to resist, he gently raised his hands and slid the robe from her milky shoulders. In that instant, he made up his mind. He would not sell this girl. She was too precious for other hands to touch. And he would keep the other English girl, the one who spoke Arabic, as her companion and teacher.

Glenna had gone along with it all. At one point, she had thought of doing the sort of dance she had done for the pasha, but somehow she recognized that this older man was not so full of fire. He had his own ways—although the result would be the same, she knew. And it would be the same result as with the pasha. She would see to that. As he showed her his collection, she had smiled and nodded approval, while continuing to call him unspeakable names in English. When she showed him the necklace, she had been sure it would come then. When he gave her the feather, she went through a charade. She had to do it. There was no other way. Anything for escape.

When he lowered her robe, she made no protest. Rather, she lowered her arms, so the robe could fall gently from her. She saw his eyes bright with wonder. Flirtatiously, she lifted the blue plume to cover her breasts and, taking another feather from the vase, covered her own rich plumage. She saw these actions only inflamed him more. Very slowly, he moved her hands and took the feathers from them. Gently he began to stroke her with the blue plume, delicately caressing her breasts. He extended the feather through her armpit and gently pulled it out, then back and forth over her nipples and across her waist and hips and between her thighs. He raised the other feather and tormented her with both of them.

She felt her nipples harden and flower and speckles of sensation rise between her thighs. Damn him, damn him! But there was nothing she could do it she was to carry out her plan. But damn him. He raised the feather and gently touched her face, caressing her cheeks and making her lips tingle with sensation. Damn him, damn him. He was creating desire in her despite herself. He was arousing her and proving to her she could be made to want a man she detested. And that knowledge shocked her. Then in an instant she recognized what Anne had said. This was the cruelty this man had selected to inflict upon her. And, like Anne before her, she was feeling her pride in herself slip away. Yes, he was the cruelist man she had ever known. Despite herself, she felt her breath quicken. Yes, a cruel, cruel man.

She took his hands and removed the feathers from them, then allowed herself to be led to the bed of cushions. She reclined and waited for him to remove his robe. She caught a glimpse of ghastly white and loose flesh before she looked away. She heard him panting, and when his face came over hers, she saw the excited look in his eyes. As he tried to come on top of her, she moved away at the last instant, twisting and pushing until she was on her side and he was on his back on the cushions.

Quickly, she squirmed to her knees beside him and, bending, teased his face with her breasts. She heard his sounds of delight as his hands and mouth found her. For a moment she panicked that he might hold her, but she pushed his hands away and continued to tease him with her breasts, up and down and around his face. On each upward movement, she reached backward with her right hand, waving it frantically for a moment over the table behind her. Down again and around, then up. Where was it? It had been so close. Down again and around, then up. She felt the metal. Yes, she had it. Down a final time, then away from his face. She saw the look of wild passion in his eyes, as her hand closed over the neck of the heavy brass teapot. As she arced it above him, she saw a fleeting expression of consternation in his eyes just before she crashed it down on his head as hard as she could.

She jumped to her feet ready to hit him again. But

she saw he was out. In her inexperience in such matters, she figured him dead from the blow.

Now the guard. Quickly she ran to the door, opened it and saw his startled amazement as he saw her nakedness. Frantically, she motioned him to come. But he stayed at his post across the passageway, and her words to him in English had no effect. Desperately, she opened the door wide so he could see. Finally, he took his eyes off of her, saw his master passed out on the cushions and understood. A cry escaped his lips and he rushed to the stricken Mohammed Ibrahim. Glenna followed. As he bent over the slave trader, she raised the brass pot and clubbed it down hard on the back of his head. The guard fell against Mohammed Ibrahim, then slid off him to the floor.

Glenna remained only a moment to see that he did not move, then dashed across the passageway and quietly opened the door to the harem. In her bare feet, she ran to the cubicle she shared with Anne Townsend. "Come on," she said, "let's get out of here."

The English girl sat up from her bed, her eyes wide. "What've you done?"

"I hit both of them on the head with a heavy pot. I think they're dead. C'mon, we can get away."

"Who?"

"Mohammed Ibrahim and the guard. They're dead. Will you please hurry?" As she spoke she pulled her startled, disbelieving friend to her feet. "Did you get the clothes?"

"Oh, Glenna, this is so foolish. We'll never get away."

"Yes, we will. Where're the clothes?"

"We won't stand a chance."

"And we won't have a chance if we stay here. Where are—" She saw the pile of garments and quickly picked them up, thrusting some toward Anne. "Hurry. We've got to hurry."

It seemed to Glenna it took forever to don the unfamiliar clothes and wrap their heads and faces in the manner of Arab women. And Anne was no help, for her reluctance slowed her movements. Repeatedly Glenna urged her to hurry.

Finally, when they were dressed, Glenna tried to pull her after her, but Anne planted her feet and refused to budge. "Glenna, this is impossible. We'll both die—believe me."

"I won't believe you. They'll never find us after dark on the streets and tomorrow we'll mingle with the crowds. We'll find a horse and ride for the coast. We'll find someway to escape when we get there."

Anne shook her head and tried to protest, but a savage jerk from Glenna pulled her toward the door.

They hesitated at the door to their cell. All was quiet. Motioning for Anne to both be quiet and to follow, Glenna tiptoed through the harem on unfamiliar sandals. She opened the door to the passageway and both stood there uncertain which way to go. Then Glenna remembered. The stairs to the street were to the right. Holding Anne's hand, they moved almost silently down the passage.

They had taken only a few steps, when they heard a ferocious bellow behind them. It froze Glenna with fear. When she turned to look, the guard was standing in the passageway, still groggy and holding the back of his head. Glenna and Anne tried to run, but in a few bounding leaps he reached them. He snatched up them both, one under each arm, ignoring their screams, and carried them back into Mohammed Ibrahim's bedroom. They were stood on their feet and held firmly by the guard.

Glenna saw the slave trader, still naked, sitting there on the cushions, holding the side of his head. In a moment he looked at her, an expression of pure malevolence in his eyes. Instinctively, Glenna recoiled from the hatred she saw there.

In a moment, he spoke in Arabic, slowly, the words biting into her even if she did not understand. Anne did understand and gasped at what she heard. The slave trader said, "When I am through with you, you will pray, both of you pray, that Allah will be merciful and bring you death."

The two were taken from the room. Early the next morning they were placed on horses and led away to the southeast. As the sun rose hot and shimmering, Glenna saw through the haze the massive snowcapped peaks of the Atlas Mountains looming ahead. She could not help but shudder.

18

Daniel Morgan could take no joy in the miraculous return of the *Chesapeake* and his own gradual recovery from his wound. The ship was moored in the busy harbor at Tangier, and he was resting in his cabin, the same cabin he had shared so blissfully with Glenna. It was to him now hateful quarters, but there was nowhere else for him to occupy on the ship.

In the cabin with him was MacDoul, his friend of many hardships, and Cornelius Downing, the American consulate at Tangier. He was an obese man in his late fifties, a fringe of gray hair around his bald pate, sweating profusely in his too-tight suit. For Downing all this was terribly unpleasant. There simply was no way to be tactful about it. But this man, this Morgan, was a known friend of President Jackson. He had to do as he wished. A word from Morgan and his career could be ruined.

Daniel was angry and distraught, which made his

heart beat faster and his still healing wound throb. The pain only increased his impatience at the interview.

"I'm sorry, Mr. Morgan, we have not yet located your friend."

It had been the same every day for days. "She is not my friend. She is my fiancée."

"I'm sorry, your fiancée. You have to understand. We are doing all we can, but it is difficult. This is a strange country. They cannot be hurried. Everything requires a bribe." Downing waved his hand across his face to indicate his dismay at his working conditions.

Morgan sighed. "I don't understand why you have nothing new to report. You told me days ago she was taken to—what is the name of that city?"

"Fez. It is the capital. She was taken to the sultan's—er, palace."

Morgan swore. "Mr. Downing, your phony attempts at so-called discretion are something less than useful. You may think whatever nasty thoughts you wish, but I do not share them. Miss O'Reilly was taken to the sultan's harem. Is that correct?"

"Yes, sir, precisely correct." He hesitated, wiping his forehead, pate and neck with a handkerchief. "You have to understand, Mr. Morgan. These people will not admit to sanctioning piracy. They will not admit to kidnapping and slavery. The sultan will not even admit he has such a decadent institution as a harem—at least not to Europeans, not to us. It is all very difficult."

"I don't care how difficult it is. I want you to find her. You told me—how many days ago was that?—that she had been sold or given to some pasha."

"Yes, one Rashid al-Haddad, newly appointed royal govenor in Marrakesh."

"And that is in the south?"

"That's correct, several days ride to the south."

"And in the desert?"

"The edge of the desert to be precise. It is necessary to cross the Atlas Mountains before reaching the true desert."

"And she never arrived?"

"That is precisely correct. She never arrived in Marrakesh. She has disappeared."

Morgan raised his voice, fairly shouting at the diplomat. "She can't have disappeared. Find her."

Downing virtually quivered. "We're doing all we can, sir."

"It isn't enough," Morgan thundered. "Find her." Then he sank back in his chair, his shoulder truly hurting now.

Downing saw his pain. Grateful to change the subject, he asked, "Is there anything I can do? Would you like the doctor again?"

"No, I'm all right—or I will be when you find Miss O'Reilly."

Downing hesitated. "There is one thing, Mr. Morgan. It is a rumor only. I find it most hard to believe."

"For God's sake what? I thought you had nothing to report."

"It is practically nothing, sir. My secretary, whom I dispatched to Fez, received information that a woman stabbed the pasha and rode off on his horse. I hardly think it true and it seems unlikely—"

Morgan laughed, his first genuine laugh in days. "It's true. That's my Glenna. If that bastard tried to touch her, she'd run him through." Again his laugh filled the tiny cabin. "Glenna's alive, I know it. She's somewhere. By God, we'll find her." He rose to his feet, filled with excitement. "If she got away from him, where would she have gone?"

"I don't know. It's hard to say. She could have gone back to Fez. She could have gone on to Marrakesh. Both seem extremely unlikely."

"I don't care what's unlikely. I care about Miss O'Reilly. Send a man to Marrakesh. Find out what you can."

"To Marrakesh, sir?" His face registered his astonishment.

"Yes, to that blasted Marrakesh, wherever it is. President Jackson would want you to do no less, believe me."

When Downing left the cabin, Morgan collapsed into a chair in pain. MacDoul who had remained silent during the interview said, "So you think your lassie is alive."

"I'm sure of it, Mac, absolutely sure of it. This is the first good news we've had in days. We'll find her, I'm sure of it."

MacDoul went to him. "It'll do no good if you're in your grave. I suggest you try that bunk for awhile before your wound opens again."

Morgan did as he was told, stretching out in the bunk. When MacDoul left him alone, his mind wandered back over all that had happened.

Morgan had knelt on the sand beside the sea, feeling not the pain of the musket ball in his shoulder, but dismay that his beloved Glenna was seized and carried away. He struggled in MacDoul's grasp and cursed his friend for not letting him go after Glenna. Finally, the pain in his shoulder became too much and he collapsed to the sand in agony. "Why, Mac, why won't you let me go to her?"

MacDoul bent over him. "Because, Dan'l, if you'd taken one more step the heathen would've killed you. And what good would come o' that. We'll find your lassie, Dan'l, believe me we will." The Scot raised his head and looked out to sea. "By God," he cried, "we'll get her quicker than you think. Them redcoats is comin' like the wind."

The firefight on the beach was short and lively. The pirate captain made a show of bravado, ordering his men to fire on the fast approaching long boat and cutter dispatched by the frigate. But he and his men had few weapons after struggling through the surf and none could stand up to the guns of the warship. Puffs of smoke rose from the ship and moments later geysers of sand ripped into the shore. MacDoul saw the doubt and panic in the eyes of the pirates.

The issue was settled when the longboat, closest to shore, opened fire with its dreaded carronade, spraying the beach with musket balls and jagged pieces of metal. A little higher aim and the pirates would be decimated. This they knew and with cries of panic turned and fled across the beach, away from the merciless carronade. The pirate captain remained a moment, shouting after his men. Then he turned and looked at Morgan and MacDoul, hatred in his eyes. He raised his pistol and aimed it for them. MacDoul stood frozen for a moment in time, helpless to defend himself. He would remember that fraction of a second as though it were a still life painting. Then the second shot from the longboat struck the pirate full on. Riddled with metal, he was dead before he hit the sand, his pistol unfired in his hand.

The English marines came ashore quickly and raced up the sand in pursuit of the pirates who had already disappeared over the grassy bluff. One man, obviously an officer, strode up to MacDoul and the prostrate Morgan. "I'm First Lieutenant Simmons, sir, of His Majesty's Frigate *Seagull*."

MacDoul smiled and shook his hand. "And mighty glad we are to see you, too."

Morgan roused himself from the sand, "If only you'd been quicker," he cried. "They've taken my fiancée. We must find her and get her back."

There followed a confused conversation with the lieutenant asking who was taken, by whom and where, MacDoul attempting to explain, and both constantly being interrupted by Morgan's frantic appeals for the British to hurry up and go after Glenna.

It took several attempts for MacDoul to shush Morgan long enough to explain what had happened. When Simmons finally understood, he spoke quietly but firmly to Morgan. "I'm sorry, sir. But we have no chance to catch men on horseback. I cannot risk marines on a hopeless foray into hostile country."

Morgan stood there dumbfounded, tears streaming down his cheeks, nearly passed out from pain. "But you must. She's my fiancée. You can't just let her—"

"I'm sorry, sir," Simmons said, "but there is nothing else I can do. Right now I think we'd best have the surgeon look at your wound."

Morgan stood there a moment, his head whirling, his vision swimming, then sank slowly to the sand. When he awoke, he was in a cabin aboard the frigate which was already under full sail.

As he knew his friend would want him to, MacDoul took up with the captain, Robert Carr-Jones, the matter of trying to find Glenna. MacDoul expected a sympathetic refusal and got it. Had he been the frigate captain he would have done the same.

"I'll tell you what, though," Carr-Jones said, a smile breaking his wind-weathered face, "with a little luck I may be able to get your ship back for you."

MacDoul brightened immediately. "Do you think you can, sir?"

"I don't know, but my guess is they'll take her to Sali, the usual pirate lair a bit further up the coast." He pointed to the northeast. "Maybe we can intercept her there."

As soon as the Marines and their boats were aboard, the *Seagull* set sail and with a fresh wind made good time, reaching the intercept point just at nightfall. MacDoul spent a largely sleepless night trying to comfort Morgan and worrying about whether the pirates would sail the *Chesapeake* past them during the night.

For two days the frigate tacked a patrol between Rabat and Sali, all lookouts posted. MacDoul worried incessantly that his ship would not be found and that Carr-Jones would soon give up the patrol. On the third morning, he leaped for joy at the cry of "Sail Ho!" It was the schooner. The small prize crew had a notion to make a fight of it, firing a musket or two, but quickly surrendered when the British carronades were pointed at them.

By midday, MacDoul was back on his own ship, repeating over and over his grateful thanks to the

British captain. An offer was made to accompany the schooner to a safe port, but MacDoul insisted he could make it with his jury rig.

Morgan was delirious all during the search for and recovery of the *Chesapeake,* frequently calling out for Glenna as the fever racked him. When the fever finally broke, he awoke confused, then saw MacDoul. After hearing his friend's happy explanation of the recovery of the ship, Morgan begged him to return ot the beach to look for Glenna.

MacDoul did as he wished, and for two days cruised the shores north of Casablanca where the pirate ship had gone aground. But MacDoul would not put men ashore for a futile search. He and his men kept the eyeglass constantly on the shore, hoping against hope for a glimpse of a lonely figure waving to them from shore. MacDoul even carried Morgan on deck to look for himself. He, too, saw nothing.

"Dan'l, my friend. I'll do anything for you, for the lassie, but—"

Morgan said nothing, but slowly, sadly, forlornly nodded his head. MacDoul, with equal sadness, ordered a course for Tangier.

When he awoke from his sleep, Morgan forced himself out of the bunk and on deck. All around him were the sights and ships of the busy North African port. In the distance, above the white city, he could see the round masses of the Rif Mountains. Another time it might have been beautiful.

"How's the shoulder, Dan'l?"

"It's all right. How's your ship?"

MacDoul understood. His friend believed he could sail someplace and find Glenna, and he was impatient to be off. Repairs to the ship were essential to anything they might do, any opportunity that might arise. "The hull is caulked," he said, "as sound as a squawling baby. And the new mast is in place. But proper spars and sails are as hard to find in this heathen port as a drink of whiskey in church. But never you mind. When word comes, we'll be ready."

Quietly, Morgan echoed the optimism. "I'm sure of it."

"And we'll find your lassie. Take my word for it. We'll not leave this heathen land till we do." But privately he thought—or until there is no hope left.

19

Glenna's horse, its reins tied to the pack ponies in front, was driven at a steady canter through most of the morning. She felt her whole body was shaking apart as she gripped the saddle to keep from falling off. Having her hands tied in front of her added greatly to her discomfort.

The caravan consisted of several dozen—she was unable to count them all—riders, pack horses and a variety of asses, all heavily laden. The riders were few; she, Anne Townsend, the five other harem women, who had it easier because they were not bound, Mohammed Ibrahim, the guard she had struck and several other men managing the caravan. They moved swiftly and steadily across the last of the Plain of Rehamna toward the Atlas massif looming ever larger ahead.

The mountains filled her with dread and she could not even bear to try to imagine what lay beyond. If only she had hit the old man and the guard harder. If only she had made sure they were dead. If only Anne had not been so reluctant, although she could not bring herself to blame her friend for their failure to escape. If only they had gotten away. If only. . . . These words drummed into her head for miles, a rhythm accompanying the incessant pounding of the horses' hoofs on the packed gravel. In time, this refrain gave way to worries about where she was going, what was going to happen to her. Soon, these thoughts were lost in the general ache which permeated her body. Occasionally she could turn and look back at Anne. She could see how much she suffered, too.

The pace slowed a little as the trail began to rise into the foothills of the Atlases, picking up occasionally as more level ground was reached. At midday the caravan stopped and Glenna gratefully slid from the saddle, almost unable to walk at first. She was given a cup of water, hardly enough to quench her thirst, and some rice balls and a few bites of dried lamb. After the Arabs had prostrated themselves in prayer to the east, all remounted and headed south into the mountains.

By nightfall they were in the high Atlases, a terrifying terrain of jagged peaks, deep gorges, sheer cliffs and maddened, white water rapids. There was snow above them and sometimes ice on the trail, as the horses and donkeys slowly picked their way upward. The worst for Glenna was the cold. It was bitter to her after the heat of Marrakesh. She was sure her bare toes in her sandals would freeze. She lifted them, one after the other, under her robe for what warmth it offered. She shivered constantly and longed for the heat.

They camped in the open, high in the mountains with light snow on the ground around them. She and Anne were thrust into a tiny tent of goat hides, given inadequate food, but most blessedly a cup of tea which warmed their frigid innards. Huddling together for warmth, Glenna and Anne lay down, trying to sleep under a goatskin provided them. But it was not to be. The tent flap opened, a man entered and Glenna was pulled out into the cold air. She was pushed and pulled across snow covered ground then shoved inside a larger, more luxurious tent. It was warmed by a pair of glowing braziers and Glenna was grateful for that.

Mohammed Ibrahim stood there alone, his face cold and implacable. The gentle, smiling man of the night before was nowhere in evidence. Glenna had been expecting to be summoned. She believed she could somehow explain to him that she had meant him no harm, but only wanted to escape. Deep in her mind she knew that wasn't true. She had intended him harm, but she had to escape, didn't she? God would not want her to be a slave, used, abused. Standing there, her eyes met his. Colder eyes she had rarely seen and fear gripped her. Bravely she tried to smile at him. She opened her mouth and in English, her only tongue, tried to tell him she was sorry.

His reply was to raise his right hand bearing a short, heavy stick and point to the bed of cushions. Glenna stood there, riveted with fear. No, he wouldn't, he couldn't. It took him only two strides to reach her, flailing her with the stick. The blows fell on her shoulders, back and legs, hard, brutal, and she screamed. He struck her only a half dozen times, but it seemed much more to Glenna. Then she was pushed down on the cushions. He raped her, hard, savagely, mercilessly.

Glenna was taken back to her tent and shoved inside to discover that Anne had been visited, too, by the guard. She lay there used, exhausted, her body racked with spasms of coughing. Not a word passed between them as, their faces wet with tears, they clutched each other in their arms, finally falling asleep.

It took several days—Glenna was already losing track of time—to cross the high passes in the mountains. During them Christmas passed, unnoticed, unobserved as her birthday had been earlier. They were similar days, up and down steep trails, beside roaring streams, along mountain ledges over which the frightened horses and donkeys had to be driven with sticks and shouts. Only the women were allowed to ride. For Glenna, they were days of bitter, unrelenting cold, terror of the heights and narrow passages, meager food and the revolting nightly abuse in the tent of her master. About the only improvement in her existence was that her hands were no longer bound, for there was no possible chance of escape now. She also learned to avoid the stick in the slave trader's hands by submitting quickly if hardly willingly to him. Occasionally he hit her naked body for the joy of it.

Glenna's chief concern was not herself, but Anne. The English woman was deteriorating rapidly. She had caught cold and shivered constantly, her body racked with spasms of coughing. As they huddled at night, Glenna tried to warm her with her own body. By the third night, Glenna could tell she was alternating between chills and fevers. The nightly visit by the guard—Glenna had learned his name was Youssef—ravaged Anne, leaving her weakened more each day, her tiny store of strength slowly ebbing away. Glenna tried to do all she could for her friend, lending her some clothes, offering her her own cup of tea. She even sought out the smirking Youssef, trying to convey to him with motions that she would sleep with him if he would only leave Anne along. She saw his smirk widen and his head nod in approval.

That night in the slave trader's tent was pure hardship, for Glenna knew that she not only had to endure him, but do it again with Youssef. But she steeled herself. Anything to help Anne. The guard was there as, tired and sore, she returned to the tent. As she lay down and felt his weight atop her, she realized with horror that he had already raped Anne and was merely taking a second helping. She cried out and pushed against him. But she was helpless. Her struggles only made him like it the more.

Gradually, they came down out of the mountains and into the desert. The sun grew warm, then hot and

Glenna felt first comfort and then great discomfort under her heavy burnou. She pulled her hood and scarves around her face to keep the sun from blistering her. She hoped the warmth would cure Anne's cold. She did improve, but she still coughed heavily and had attacks of fever.

They passed through country of breathtaking beauty. In the distance all round them were the snow capped peaks of the Atlas Mountains, rising out of the mist and haze to scrub the azure sky. In the nearer distance were long stretches of flat topped buttes of rust red rock. Some rose hundreds of feet above the desert floor. And the desert itself, flat or gently swelling, was of gray gravel atop yellow sand and red dust, strewn with gray rocks and stunted brown bushes. It was a panorama of color reaching endlessly into the distance.

Most beautiful of all was the River (or Wadi) Draa, as Anne identified it to her, along which the trail wound. It was not wide as rivers go, but it contained an abundance of water, melted from the snows of the Atlases high above. The river was sometimes languid, other times racing over rocks. As it flowed, it created a long, slender oasis in the desert, a rich, lush, green ribbon through the desolate sand and gravel. Never had Glenna seen such intensive farming. High above were stately palm trees, yielding dates and palm wine. The leaves were woven into ropes and mats, and eventually the trees provided wood. Below the palms, fruit trees were grown, yielding oranges and apples and pears. On the ground every inch of soil was terraced and used to till vegetables, grain and forage.

Behind this ribbon of green were occasional family farmhouses unlike anything Glenna or Anne had ever seen. They were fortresses, three and four story rust red walls, virtually windowless, keeping out the world. The caravan would stop for the horses to drink from the river while water bags were filled. Fruit and forage and other provisions would be purchased, but not once did the Arab traders enter a Berber fortress. Glenna caught only occasional glimpses of fair skinned people, obviously much more handsome and open than the Arabs. The women were not veiled and they, like the men, wore colorful costumes with much jewelry and ornamentation.

The caravan stopped for a day at the prosperous town of Quarzazate, a most beautiful sight in the desert, with rose red houses beside the green river, laced overhead with graceful palm trees. Glenna ate many oranges, believing it had to be the most delicious food on earth. Despite her weakness, Anne wanted to visit the town, but she and Glenna were camped outside and their tent kept under careful watch. They remained bundled in their bedoin garb, although Glenna longed to bathe in the river and feel the fresh air on her skin. Both women knew they were taken for Arabs. Neither wanted to think of what might happen if they were discovered to be *nasara,* Christians.

The caravan wound on toward the southeast, following the Draa. The terrain changed subtly. The snow capped mountains and red bluffs became more infrequent and distant, the land flatter and drier, the river narrower and the accompanying fields smaller and less lush.

The pace of travel had quickened out of the mountains, and the ride was terribly wearing to Glenna. Each time she dismounted she had great difficulty walking. The sun was merciless during the day, and she could feel her head spinning and her vision swimming. She often had to hold on to remain on her mount. Strangely to her, the heat of the day was followed by sharp cold as the sun went down, leaving her and Anne to shiver under their inadequate covers.

Glenna sensed Anne's continued deterioration under the onslaught of heat and cold. Yet, Glenna took comfort in the fact Mohammed Ibrahim did not send for her so often. Two and even three nights would go by without his attack upon her. Not so, Youssef. He was insatiable nightly, although he did begin to mostly leave Anne alone in his enjoyment of her. For that she tried to be grateful. When the burley Arab left each night, no words were spoken between the women. Indeed, the private ordeal of their bodies was never discussed, not once. But Anne would take Glenna in her shrunken arms, wipe her tears, and with tender solicitude express her gratitude to her suffering sister.

In a few days they came to the tiny oasis town of Zagora and camped outside. The river, not much more than a trickle now, turned sharply off to the east, only a thin row of palms marking its passage into the distance. Straight ahead to the south lay a visage that filled Glenna with dread such as she had never known was possible, a flat, unbroken plain of sand, rock, gravel and dust, all red and orange and yellow, stretching as far as the eye could see. No feature rose out of it, no mountain, no tree, scarcely any vegetation, nothing but emptiness, haze and swirls of sand and dust. Her whole being sank at the realization that she was to be taken there.

She hoped for awhile that it might not be so, but all the signs of her future lay before her. Zagora was a vast encampment, full of tents, a milieu of Arab, Berber and other strangely dressed men she did not know. And camels, thousands of them. This was a staging place for the caravans into the desert, Anne told her, having overheard men speaking, but Glenna had already guessed it.

There seemed to be a great deal of aimless activity. Actually a great deal of trading was going on. The horses and donkeys were sent back over the mountains with goods that would be sold in Marrakesh and eventually all over Europe, America and the known world. Camels were acquired and provisions purchased for the long trek into the desert.

Glenna and Anne knew little of this, for they were kept mostly in their tent, sweltering though it was, out of sight of camel drivers, traders and others who passed their area. Only at night were they allowed outside for a breath of air. Security was extremely tight with a guard, frequently Youssef, constantly at the entrance to their tent. Glenna knew that if she made any move to escape—escape to where?—she would be bound and gagged. So she kept quiet.

From snatches of conversation overheard by Anne, both learned they had been separated from the other five members of the harem. The French and Spanish women were traded to men traveling east from Zagora. With the French in control of northern Algiers, the usual white slave routes had been closed. The white women were being taken overland, across the desert, eventually to reach the Mediterranean at Tunis or Tripoli, perhaps all the way to the Nile and the Red Sea. They would end up, if they survived the journey, in harems in Arabia, Turkey, Persia, even India, lost souls who disappeared from the face of the earth.

When Anne explained this to her, Glenna almost cried with sorrow for the women, although she had never gotten to know them very well. She was kept from tears by her own concern. "What's going to happen to us."

Her voice barely above a whisper, Anne answered, "They're taking us to Timbuktu."

"Timbuktu? Where is that?"

"Across the desert, far to the south."

"God, God, no. What happens to us then?"

Anne shook her head sadly. "I don't know." Her sadness was genuine, but she was lieing. She had heard, indeed she had known even before they left Marrakesh. But it was an end too horrible to contemplate and she could not bring herself to tell Glenna. It was better that she not know, better that she survive each day in hopes for the next. No one could live in knowledge of such a future. And her sadness was entirely for Glenna. Anne knew she would not survive the journey. That vast wasteland out there would be her burial place. Glenna might survive. She seemed to have a tremendous will to live. But in her heart Anne knew it would be better for Glenna to lie in a sandy grave, too.

20

The world maps of the 1830's, even those of much later in the century, showed a great blank space for the Sahara desert. It was a region almost entirely unexplored by Europeans, a vast arid area stretching from the Red Sea on the east to the Atlantic on the west, from the Atlas Mountains on the north to. . . . There was no bottom to the unexplored land on the south. Almost the whole of Central Africa was unknown. Only the pear-like shape had been mapped. Only a few coastal areas of the continent had been visited by white Christians.

Europeans knew there was an immense desert south of the Mediterranean coastline of Africa, but few non-Moslems had entered it and almost no one had lived to return to tell about it. This vast desert, nearly as large as the United States, was perhaps the most inhospitable place on earth, a cruel, vicious land that seemed determined to drive all human occupancy from it. Temperatures frequently rose to 150 degrees Fahrenheit during the day, then dropped below freezing. Winds sometimes reached hurricane force, driving sand before it that would rip the skin off exposed flesh.

There were immense regions of flat emptiness and others of sand dunes reaching hundreds of feet in the air and slowly engulfing all that lay before them. The most precious commodity was water, found in a few scattered wells and oases, some two hundred miles apart. Water was priceless. No amount of money would buy it.

Yet, this inhospitable land was not unoccupied. It was home to some of the most ferocious tribes on earth, mostly nomadic, the Shamba, the Berabiches, the Reguibat, and most feared of all the dreaded Taureg. All were marauders, preying on all who entered their domain.

Despite all the obstacles, the Sahara was a roadway for highly profitable commerce. Here the goods of Europe, Asia and Africa met and changed hands. From Europe came silk, bolts of cotton cloth, knives and swords of fine steel, tobacco, paper, copper, tin, glass beads and mirrors, needles, tar, guns and ammunition, a bewildering variety of manufactured goods. From the east came tea, spices, sugar. These were exchanged in Timbuktu and other trading centers south of the desert for the wealth of Africa, ivory, animal skins, ostrich plumes and other feathers, rare woods, spices and rare scents, dried meat and fruit, incense, indigo, seeds, leather whips and bags, and other products exotic to the rest of the world. These products, borne on immense camel caravans sometimes numbering tens of thousands of animals, were of such value that their price made the perils of the journey worthwhile.

In the 1830s, even the fantastic profits in such items as ivory and feathers paled beside the money to be made from three trading items, gold, salt, and slaves. The world hungered for gold and slaves, the people of black Africa for salt. They changed hands in the desert. The slaves came from the savannahs and jungles of Africa, borne north through Marrakesh and Fez to Tangier and Lisbon, eventually reaching the West Indies and America. The salt came from deep in the desert at Taudeni, perhaps the most hellish spot on earth, mined in blocks from just below the surface in insufferable heat by black slaves whom the Arabs condemned to living deaths, the only mercy being its quickness in arriving.

In the 1830s, the slave trade was beginning to diminish, for the Portuguese, British, Dutch and Americans were establishing "factories" off the west coast of Africa to capture and bear away the slaves for the New World. But Mohammed Ibrahim set forth across the desert in the expectation of amassing great wealth in this his last trip. He carried with him the usual trade goods, of great value surely, but also a white female slave of incalculable value. He knew just where to trade her. The only issue was for how much. It was wisdom for him to keep her alive on the journey. She was the valuable one with her fair skin and blue eyes. If the other sickly one lived, so much the better.

Glenna had known terror and pain, at the hands of Winslow in his garret, the pirates on the ship, most especially the herdsman in the Plain of Rehamna. The trek over the mountains had seemed undiluted hardship. But none of this prepared her for the trip across the great Sahara. Even as they remained in the encampment in Zagora, her dread mounted. As the preparations began and the pack camels were loaded and strung together, nose and tail, in four long files, her dread reached the point of panic. But there was no escape and she knew it. She must somehow endure, somehow survive what lay ahead.

The days in the encampment at Zagora had passed slowly. Forced to remain inside her tent during daylight, she had nothing to do, nothing to read to occupy her mind. So she slept frequently if fitfully in the sweltering tent, flies nagging at her constantly. She found comfort in the fact Mohammed Ibrahim did not send for her, nor did Youssef come to her tent. She did not ask why, merely accepted the fact gratefully.

Anne slept a great deal and Glenna was thankful for

that, although she would have liked more of her company. Glenna hoped the hot dry air and the chance to rest would improve her friend's health. And it seemed to. Her cold left her, but a dry, hacking cough persisted. Glenna plied her with as much water, fruits and other foods as she could. Anne's strength improved, she remained in a greatly weakened condition.

On the third day at Zagora, a young man appeared at the flap of the tent. He looked to be about fourteen or fifteen, rather short but lean and lively, with a deeply tanned face, curly black hair and a smile at the ready. He brought a generous quantity of dates, nuts and fruit and chattered as he gave them, his white teeth flashing often. Glenna was learning Arabic, but she was unable to keep up with the boy. Anne listened and once or twice laughed. It was the first time Glenna had heard her laugh in days.

After the boy bounded out of the tent, Anne explained. "His name is Hassam and he is to look after us on the journey. Mohammed Ibrahim has personally charged him to take care of us and see no harm befalls us."

"Really. What were you laughing at?"

The English girl smiled. "Just him, I guess. There isn't much to laugh at around here, is there? He's just such a good natured boy. It's hard to resist him. He says that when this journey is finished—it will be his first trip—he'll be the greatest camel driver since the Prophet Mohammed himself. That struck me as funny somehow."

Hassam did look after them, making tea for them, bringing the welcome fruit, but even he mostly ignored them. Several more days passed slowly, then Hassam came, struck their tent and led them to their camels. It was the strangest animal Glenna had ever seen, long gangly neck and legs, a high hump in the middle. It seemed impossible to imagine anyone riding it. And the camel's personality, unlike the horse, seemed haughty, irritable, stubborn, disdainful, unruly, devoid of affection. She never developed a liking for the camel, though she tried, nor it for her.

"Hassam explained to me why camels act this way," Anne said. "Before he died the Prophet whispered the hundredth and final praise of Allah in the camel's ear. They know something humans don't and have had no use for man since."

The camel was made to squat on the ground, legs tucked under it. A mat of palm fronds was placed on its back to the rear of the hump, then a wooden saddle, called *arahla*, tied in place. The saddle resembled a sort of bucket, open to the front with flaring sides and back. There was a sort of cross at the front as a pommel. A sheepskin was tossed over the base of the saddle and the camel boy motioned for her to mount. Seeing she didn't know how, Hassam showed her. Then she tried. Taking hold of the pommel with her right hand, she stepped on the camel's folded foreleg with her left foot, then with her right stepped up, turning to drop into the saddle. She did it awkwardly the first time but eventually got the hang of it.

As the camel lurched to its feet, hindlegs first, Glenna had to hold on tight to keep from being thrown off. Then as they began to move toward their place in the caravan and head into the desert, Glenna felt nausea rise in her from the swaying motion of the animal. It had a strange, dragging gait, placing each hind foot down a fraction of a second before each front foot, first on one side, then the other. It seemed to her as if the two sides of the animal had minds of their own and had somehow been stuck together to make this strange method of conveyance. The result was a swaying motion high atop her perch that gnarled her stomach.

Riding beside her, Anne smiled weakly and said, "I've heard the camel called the ship of the desert. I can see why."

Yes, Glenna thought, it was like the motion of a ship. She had never been seasick. She was a good sailor. The nausea went away immediately and she became a reasonably expert, if never comfortable camel rider.

The camel shuffled along slowly, maintaining a steady pace of three and a half miles an hour, roughly a moderate walking pace for a man. With a full day's march with frequent halts and a midday stop, the caravan could make about twenty miles. But with the stops to water the animals at oases and pasture them on bits of forlorn vegetation that were found, the caravan averaged only about ten or eleven miles a day. With nearly a thousand miles of desert to cross, it was to be a journey of three months. It was now January.

Zagora quickly disappeared behind them and Glenna felt herself dropped into an endless orange, yellow, tan void. There were no features to catch the eye, no mountains, streams or trees, just an infinite nothingness. The few bushes seemed dead, the occasional rocks lifeless. This impression of death was greatly intensified by the array of skeletons strewn along the trail. They were mostly camel bones, sun bleached neck bones stretched on the ground, the heads staring at her with empty sockets. The sight of them filled her with dread and she was sure she saw human skeletons, too.

As far as she could see in all directions, it was flat, a gently undulating sea of sand and gravel, variously red, orange, yellow, black, white and gray in color. It was an immeasurable emptiness, made the more so because it was deathly still. The soft pads of the camel's feet made only a slight swishing sound. The wind without trees was nearly soundless. Only the voices of the camel drivers urging on their beasts broke the incredible stillness, and as the days wore on even these became stilled. The result of it all, the vastness which seemed to swallow up and shrink the caravan which she had once thought so huge, the emptiness, the stillness, was mind-bending to Glenna, the most frightening experience of her life. She was nowhere, going nowhere, caught in a hopeless void of emptiness. This she knew had to be purgatory on earth. And she silently prayed for release of her body from this earthly purgatory as hard as she had prayed for release of her father's soul from the spiritual purgatory.

As was the custom, the caravan departed in the afternoon and camped at night after the passage of only a few miles. This was sort of a shakedown march, a chance to uncover problems, loads which needed snugged or shifted, problem animals and the like. It also gave the camel drivers, guides and others an opportunity to get into the rhythm of the caravan without becoming too tired.

Glenna was surprised to discover that she and Anne were the only ones to ride all the time. All the others, including Mohammed Ibrahim, walked at least part of the day, usually in the afternoon, to rest the camels. It was to be a long journey and a dead camel was of no use to anyone. Hassam sometimes walked beside her and Anne, proud of his responsibilities, and other times ran and skipped between the files of camels, aiding the drivers with their charges.

The desert brought Glenna one other most blessed surcease. No sexual demands were made upon her. For a time she couldn't understand it, welcome though it was. Then she understood. A strange kind of democracy existed among these nomads. Since all shared the savage perils of the journey, they also shared what sustained them. Each man, the women too, received the same water ration, the same food. Rank bore no privileges in the desert. And that applied to her body. Since she and Anne were the only women, Mohammed Ibrahim and Youssef could not possess what was denied to others. If they did, chaos would occur among the drivers. So, she was declared off limits to all. She and Anne were guarded just to make sure this was the case. Nonetheless, she frequently saw Youssef looking at her hot-eyed.

Glenna quickly had her doubts that riding was an advantage over walking. The sheepskin over the wooden saddle offered scant padding. Glenna's thighs and derriere became sore, chafed and blistered. She kept moving her legs to a variety of positions, crossing them on the left and then on the right side of the camel, but these movements only offered a different type of discomfort. Her whole body ached from sitting the camel and the constant effort to remain on the animal as it swayed across the desert.

As Glenna had stood before her tent at Zagora looking out over that featureless plain to the south, she had tried to imagine what the journey would be like. She was sure it would be hot. She was not disappointed in this. The sun beat down mercilessly out of a cloudless sky, heating the sand and gravel until it would blister human skin on contact. And it was blinding. The air seemed so clear, so thin and the sun's rays penetrated sharply, like tiny arrows shot from heaven to pierce the skin and eyes. The shadows of the camels, her own body, were the blackest and sharpest she had ever seen as they moved tortuously across the endless expanse.

Glenna tried to protect every speck of her skin. She wore men's baggy trousers, provided by Hassam, under her bernou, letting them hang until they covered even her toes. She kept her fingers hidden beneath the cloth as she held the reins. She covered her whole head, hair, forehead, mouth and nose, even pulling the scarf down as a sort of visor as they rode into the sun. This permitted her to see only the camel and the gravel as it passed beneath, but it prevented her from going blind in the glare. Nonetheless, she quickly became dizzy and would have fallen off the camel had not Hassam been there to catch her. He gave her a turban and showed both her and Anne how to wind it. Quickly Glenna discovered that when wound around the head, the turban had a cooling effect. The turban could be wound innumerable ways, piled on the front, top, sides or back to face the sun from whatever direction it came, and the end of the binding could be pulled across her face for protection.

The first night and many afterwards, as the sun went

down she heard what sounded like gunfire reverberating across the desert. She was startled and afraid the first time she heard it. But it was not gunfire, merely rocks splitting as they passed from hot to cold. Glenna and Anne huddled in their tent each night, warming each other with their bodies. And as they arose in the mornings, they frequently found the water in the goatskin bags had frozen. Hot and cold, the great desert was a study in extremes, offering moderation to no one who entered it.

The wind. It was a rare day it didn't blow. Changing directions at will, raging at her back, then an hour later at her face. It could be bitter cold, then change to smotheringly hot. At times it would be like a gentle if annoying breeze, cooling her, then a moment later, gusting like a tempest, it would almost blow her out of the saddle, lifting sand and dust into swirls and skiffs, sending them like hordes of stinging insects against her body. For a few minutes, perhaps an hour or two, the sand would be driven through the air like a yellow-gray snowstorm, hazing over the sun and reducing visibility so she could hardly see Anne riding beside her.

By midday of the second day, she had discovered the worst enemy of all, however—thirst. In the hottest part of the day, under the blazing sun and the dehydrating wind, she was first consumed with thirst, then nearly maddened by it. Never had she wanted anything in her life as much as a glass of clear, cool water. Thirst consumed her and she moved her cracking lips and parched mouth in anticipation of what was not forthcoming. In the lonely, silent emptiness, as the camel sailed her across the endless yellow sea, she found herself dreaming of water, buckets of it, whole rivers and lakes. Her mind drifted off and she was standing naked under a waterfall, opening her mouth to drink and drink the cooling liquid. And when she roused herself and opened her eyes, to her wonder she saw a lake, a beautiful blue-gray lake shimmering and shining just ahead of her. She cried out with joy and relief. But when the camel, its soft padded feet swishing the sand, reached the lake, it was only more sand. She had heard Anne speak of it. A mirage. Thereafter, tormented and weak from thirst, she was to pass through the greatest desert on earth, a non-existent lake constantly shimmering in front of her eyes.

Glenna discovered very quickly that thirst was the Sahara's most devastating weapon against the intruder. There was water in the desert—a little. Some rain fell, for there is no spot on earth that at least some rain does not fall. Rain can be a great menace in the Sahara, coming down in torrents sometimes, usually in January and February, creating flash floods which cascade down the dry river beds, called wadis, and sweep away the homes built beside them. So hard does it rain sometimes that the mud homes of oases dwellers literally melt into the sand. And when it rains, the desert blooms with flowers, some of them capable of sprouting, growing, blooming and going to seed in mere hours—and some seeds are capable of lying fallow under the blazing sun for a decade waiting for a drop of water to bring them to life. Some shrubs have roots one hundred feet long to sustain them during the heat and drought.

But rain in the Sahara is a coquette, flirting, granting favors, then withholding them. There are places where it may not rain for years on end, especially in the Western Sahara, where Glenna was now crossing.

The tribes who dwell in the desert believe, then as well as now, that the desert is really a great inland ocean with water buried far beneath the surface. The dunes act as slow motion waves. There are fish in the desert. Fossils of fish abound, to be sure, but there are also real, live fish. When the wadis fill, the fish appear and can be caught. When the wadis dry, no one knows where the fish go. Nearly every well has a catfish or two swimming in it.

The underground water surfaces occasionally as wells. Some have existed for centuries. Others appear for a day, a few months or years, then disappear. Some wells occur in clusters, creating a string of oases marked by palm trees, some pasture, a little tilled ground and the mud homes of more or less permanent inhabitants. Other wells are scattered. Some can be reached only after a trek of two hundred miles over barren earth, a supreme test for humans and animals. One such area is the Tanezrouft, where Glenna's caravan was heading.

What life there is in the Sahara, plant, animal and human, is sustained by a limited, exceedingly hard to find commodity, water. It is priceless. No amount of gold, jewels or money can buy a single drop of it, such is the law of the desert. To steal it from another is a crime worthy of death. To waste it is a sin.

The caravan carried water in goatskin bags and it was their most precious possession, even more valuable than the camels or the humans. A strict ration was imposed on all, Mohammed Ibrahim, Glenna, Anne, everyone. At this stage of the journey, where watering holes could be reached every two or three days, the water ration was a cup in the morning and a cup at night. There was no deviation in this, no exception. All would be thirsty, but all would survive. Indeed, humans could exist on less water and would, if by chance the caravan missed the next well or, Allah forbid, it had gone dry. And there was only water to drink. It could not be used to wash, as Glenna quickly discovered. The nomads, she soon saw, scoured themselves with clean sand. She came to do that, too.

The rigid rationing posed a fearful problem for Glenna. The evening after the first full day, Glenna hungrily drained the cup of water brought to her and Anne by Hassam. It seemed such a paltry, inadequate amount. But that night as she held the shivering feverish Anne, Glenna knew some way had to be found to get her friend more water. In her illness, she could not withstand the rigors of this trip sustained on two cups of water a day and a few bites of dried meat and rice balls offered as food.

The next day in her halting Arabic she asked Hassam for extra water for Anne. He shook his head vigorously. Glenna tried to explain with motions and pidgin Arabic that Anne was sick and would die unless there was more water for her. Hassam refused. She begged him, tears rising in her eyes. Still he refused. There was absolutely no way for the law of the ration to be altered. He tried to make it up to her with smiles and a little jig in the sand, but there was no way he could produce more water for Anne.

They came to the first watering hole on the third day. The camels, fed little and watered not at all, became excited and quickened their pace as they smelled water, then could not be restrained from dashing toward it and burying their noses in the liquid. Glenna jumped down and helped Anne do the same. As soon as they could, they, too, buried their faces in the water. It was black and brackish, vile smelling and worse tasting, but neither woman felt she had ever encountered any substance so delicious.

As both learned by nightfall, it had been an immense mistake. The nomads were immune to it, but the European women succumbed to a terrible dysentery which riled their stomachs and brought violent diarrhea, greatly adding to their weakness and dehydration. They remained at the watering hole a day, during which Glenna and Anne were ill. When the time came to leave, both could hardly mount. As they swayed over the desert, Glenna saw that as bad as she was, Anne was infinitely worse, barely able to remain atop the camel.

That night was the first of many nights that Glenna began to give half her own water and food to her friend. Unused to the desert and the discipline of thirst, sick herself, Glenna suffered horribly, more in need of water than anyone in the caravan. But she was determined to somehow keep Anne alive. The thought of being alone in the desert without Anne was more terrifying to Glenna than her own thirst and growing weakness.

And so they passed southward, endless days passing into monotonous dreary weeks. They came across more watering holes, a section of small sand dunes, a few knolls, a dry wadi to be crossed. But it was the same dreary sameness of heat, thirst, cold and stinging wind. The sand and gravel seemed to unravel beneath the camel's hoofs like an endless moving carpet. In her weakness and thirst, a sort of lassitude overcame Glenna, a despairing sadness, leaving her unable even to think of water, home or Daniel. She could rouse herself only to worry about Anne and cater to her as best she could. She came to care more about her friend's life than her own.

She became an automaton, numb, unfeeling except for Anne, almost totally apathetic. When one day a huge dust storm arose, racing black and menacing across the earth like a black forest fire, she hardly noticed. Even when the air went almost black as night and the sun was reduced to a pale yellow ball, she couldn't bring herself to care until she heard Anne coughing incessantly against the dust which choked and smothered them. Glenna tried to rouse herself to help her friend, but what could she do?

Anne grew steadily weaker despite all that Glenna tried to do for her. Her color was ghostly pale and her spasms of coughing seemed to remove what shreds of strength she had. Many days she merely slept in the saddle, holding on, being lurched awake in time to keep from falling off.

Then disaster struck. Sand devils were a common sight, the wind swirling the sand into little twisting funnels which danced across the surface. A stronger wind could make a bigger funnel, but Glenna had considered them harmless. When the giant funnel, driven by gale force wind, leaped into existence and struck the caravan, it created havoc, breaking the tie ropes and scattering the camels. Glenna and Anne were thrown to the ground. The saddles were ripped from the camels, mats and other paraphernalia thrown through the air. It was over in a minute and Glenna, sore and bruised, was able to get to her feet. Anne could not rise.

Glenna bent over her. She was knocked senseless. She soon regained consciousness, but still could not rise to more than a sitting position. Glenna felt her legs. Neither was broken, but she was obviously seriously sprained. Hopelessly, Glenna cried out her fury and frustration, as the men on order from Mohammed Ibrahim lifted Anne to the camel's back and tied her in place.

The pitiless trek wore on, day after merciless day, like some painful funeral procession across an infinite waste. Thin, weak and faint herself, Glenna mustered what strength she had to try to care as best she could for Anne. Her head swimming with vertigo, her body crying from thirst, Glenna would somehow at night rouse herself to try to cheer her companion. She'd force herself to remember Ireland and tell her tales of green fields and running streams and what it would be like when they returned home. Over and over she'd tell her of Daniel, his strength, his gentleness, his love for her and how wonderful it was to be loved and how grand it would be when they were in each other's arms. And she described to her, over and over, her mouth so dry she could hardly speak, Daniel's home in Maryland, Aurial, as he had described it to her. And through it all, Anne would smile weakly in appreciation. Her mind, once so glorious in its innate curiosity, was breaking under her suffering reality. More and more, she lived in the past, her mind losing the capacity to identify the present. Glenna's tales were often the only touchstone of reality in her waning existence.

And when at last Anne fell asleep, her frail, wasted body snuggled in her arms, Glenna would pray for her. "Blessed Mother of God, do not let her die. Please do not take her. I can't go on if I lose her. She must live, she must."

21

Daniel Morgan's mounting impatience gradually gave way to seething rage, as the *Chesapeake* languished, days blending into weeks, in the harbor at Tangier. The repairs were agonizingly slow. The only thing that kept Daniel from pouring his rage out on his friend MacDoul was the knowledge that they couldn't leave, for he still had no word of Glenna.

Less fortunate than MacDoul was Cornelius Downing, the quaking, perspiring American consul. Morgan forced him to come to the ship each day, and each day he had nothing to report.

"You are the official representative of the United States government," Morgan said for the unnumbered time. "What do you mean you cannot learn anything? My fiancée could not have been swallowed up in this land. She is somewhere. Anything better than gross incompetence would find her."

﹒ And for an equally unnumbered time, Downing would endeavor to explain. "Mr. Morgan, this is an unfriendly country, a most hostile one in fact. It is a Moslem nation. You might say these people are fanatically Moslem. They do not like Christians. To them—" He tried to laugh a little, but it came out a sort of throaty hiss. "—the only good Christian is a dead Christian. The sultan does not like Christians and wants as little to do with them as possible. A few nations, the United States included, are permitted, by sufferance I might say, to have consuls here for the purpose of promoting trade. But we are severely limited in what we can do or say. Our travel is extremely limited. I have tried and tried to gain permission for my secretary to travel to Marrakesh as you wish, but it is impossible."

"I told you to send him anyway."

Downing was as aghast at the suggestion now as the first time he heard it. "It would be a sentence of death, Mr. Morgan. I cannot permit it."

"But it's all right with you if my fiancée receives such a sentence." His voice was cold, bitter.

Downing wiped his brow with a trembling hand. "I want no such thing, Mr. Morgan."

"Sometimes I wonder."

As he should have much sooner, Morgan ultimately gave up on Downing and his timidity and sought out the British Consul, who said, "It pains me to say it, but the most knowledgeable person about this Godforsaken country is my colleague, M. LeCompte, the French consul. If anyone can help you, which I doubt, it will be he. I'm sorry, but this is the best I can do for you."

Morgan went ashore for an audience with LeCompte, a tall, slender man with a wide, very waxed mustache, the ends of which he twisted in his fingers almost constantly. When Morgan saw his manner, his hopes sank. Such a man was not what he needed to find Glenna.

LeCompte sat slumped in his chair, toying with his mustache, his bony legs crossed like useless appendages, listening through an interpreter to Morgan's tale. Every so often he would say, "mm," as Morgan did his best to relate all that had happened and all he knew.

At last LeCompte aroused himself from his chair, walked to the window, looked out for a few moments on the teeming city below, then spoke to Morgan. As translated, he said, "Mr. Morgan, I am very sorry for you, but far more sorry for your fiancée, Miss O'Reilly. I regret to say hers is a far too common experience. Even now, I myself, as well as our officials in the recently conquered province of Algeria, have a long list of my own countrymen we are searching for. The British, Spanish, Italian and many other countries doubtlessly have similar lists. Need I tell you it is very difficult and almost entirely hopeless?"

"No."

He walked toward Morgan and stood over him. "My best advice, my dear fellow, is to return to America. You will grieve awhile—" He made a broad gesture with his outstretched fingers. "—but time heals all."

Morgan looked the Frenchman square in the eye. Very slowly and somberly, he said, "I cannot. I will not."

LeCompte held his gaze a moment, then turned away. "I see," he said.

"Twice in both our lifetimes, M. LeCompte, our countries have fought side by side for liberty and justice. There is a special bond between our nations, our people. I wish now to exercise that special friendship."

LeCompte turned to look at him, his eyes squinting as he sized up his visitor. "It will cost you money, monsieur, many thousands of francs."

"Anything."

"And I can promise you no results. Indeed, I can promise you that the end product of our efforts is most likely to be no more than you know now."

"I will try anything."

For the first time, a smile spread the thin lips of the French diplomat. "This Miss O'Reilly must be a remarkable woman to have earned such devotion."

Morgan gave as complete a description of Glenna as he could, tears scalding his eyes as he remembered her, then left, having been advised to return in ten days. In ten days he was told to return in five. Morgan's impatience, having once had some speck of hope, mounted exponentially, until even MacDoul avoided his presence. Morgan began to believe, then was convinced, LeCompte was a fraud. He had merely taken his purse. This was not true. LeCompte siphoned off only part of the money for himself, the rest he spread among informers and Moroccan officials.

On the fifteenth day, Morgan again returned to the residence of the French consul. He was offered a glass of sherry. All he wanted was to get on with it, but he restrained his impatience enough to exercise his manners by accepting and sipping a glass.

At last the Frenchman addressed the subject. "I have some news. It is not very valuable, I fear, but at least it will confirm some of what you already know. Your Miss O'Reilly—er someone fitting her description— was taken directly to the sultan's harem in Fez. She must indeed be very beautiful to have that happen. It is a high honor."

Morgan waved his hand impatiently. "Go on."

"Apparently without ever seeing her, the sultan gave her to one Rashid al-Haddad, a rising young officer in the royal guards. This young officer had just been named pasha of Marrakesh."

"What's a pasha?"

"A sort of governor of a province, an official representative of the sultan. Such posts are normally given to royal kin, but this Rashid al-Haddad was chosen because he had Berber ancestry and the sultan is having a great deal of trouble gaining sovereignty over the rather rebellious Berbers. So, the sultan, apparently to cement the loyalty of his subordinate, gave him one of his harem girls. It is not unheard of, but it truly is a high honor in this land."

"And that was Glenna." Morgan tried to keep his outrage from his voice, but he was not very successful in the effort.

LeCompte nodded affirmatively. "A day or two elapsed, I believe, then she accompanied him as a member of his entourage toward Marrakesh. The young pasha never arrived." The Frenchman shook his head. "There seems no doubt that your Miss O'Reilly killed the pasha by plunging a dagger into his back. Your fiancée seems to be quite a person."

Morgan listened to all this with impatience, for this much he already knew. "Go on, please. What else did you learn?"

"Not much, I'm afraid—and it cost a great deal of your money to learn even that. The pasha's men, quite understandably, made a vigorous search for Miss O'Reilly, assuming it was she all along. We do know, or strongly suspect, they never found her. I've never been to Marrakesh, few Europeans have, and I do not know the countryside, but apparently she was sequestered by some type of herdsman, then taken to Marrakesh. She was purchased by one Abdallah al-Kallid, who admitted that fact only after enough money was offered to him. He says he was good to her, then sold her to a notorious slave trader named Mohammed Ibrahim. Near the end of December he was seen to head south with a party of women. It must be assumed your Miss O'Reilly was among them."

"South to where?"

"Over the Atlas Mountains and into the desert, I assume. It is the usual thing. In any event, that is where the trail ends. I am sorry. I can go no further in finding her."

"But—"

"There are no buts, Mr. Morgan. I understand and admire your regard for this young woman. It is most romantic. But sometimes the head must rule the heart. The Sahara region is virtually unknown, an enormous, unexplored area. Only a few Europeans have ever entered it, and almost none have returned to tell of it. The desert is the size of a whole continent. It is a wasteland inhabited by some of the most ferocious people on earth. They want nothing quite so much as to kill any Christian who sets foot in their domain.

Nonetheless, you must have heard of the most remarkable feat of my countryman, M. René Caillié."

"I'm afraid not."

"Why he was the first man to reach the fabled city of Timbuktu and return. It happened in '28, a little over a year ago, his return I mean. He was a young man, penniless, most ill-prepared, but he possesses stunning courage and typical French ingenuity. Alone, armed only with an incredible story of being a Moslem who had been held captive by Christians in Egypt, he landed on the African coast and went inland through the jungle, up the Niger River, eventually reaching Timbuktu from the south and west. Almost dead of disease, when he got there. He stayed awhile in Timbuktu—nothing like it was imagined all these years—then headed north across the desert in a caravan. He endured the most incredible suffering, but held on to reach this very building in Tangier when my predecessor was here. Quite a tale. He discovered that an English soldier, a Major Gordon Laing had reached the fabled city a year or two before by crossing the desert alone from Tripoli in the northeast. His was quite a feat, too, but Laing was killed shortly after leaving Timbuktu. Anyway the whole area seems to be opening up to we Europeans at last. Where one man goes, others can follow."

Morgan had listened to this tale with great impatience. But common courtesy dictated that he suffer through LeCompte's pride in his countryman. At last, though, he was able to speak. "All right, I understand you cannot learn anything more about Glenna, but you must have some idea, some thought, some speculation."

LeCompte tried a weak smile, twisting his mustache as he did so. "I would say only a guess. There is a market for white women, particularly attractive ones in harems. The usual thing used to be for them to be taken by sea or along the coast from Algiers. But since my country destroyed the Corsairs and occupied Algiers, this route has become too perilous. We suspect the women are being taken across the desert."

"Where?"

"Again only a guess, Egypt, Arabia, Turkey, Persia, India, even beyond, wherever harems are maintained." He paused and looked at Morgan most directly. "You must understand, monsieur, these women are never heard from again. All this is supposition. We have not a shred of proof."

Morgan felt as though he had been struck. "You are saying you don't know where she is. She could be taken anywhere."

"I am sorry, but it is so. If you wish to continue your search for her, you have the whole world in which to do so."

Despair lay upon Morgan like a great weight. He sat in his chair, head bowed, struggling to hold back tears which burned his eyes.

"Would you like more sherry, M. Morgan?" The American made no reply, but glasses were poured for him, the interpreter and Lecompte.

After a period of uncomfortable silence, Morgan had a thought which aroused him. "I know my fiancée. She is a fighter. If she escaped once, she will again."

LeComptc shook his head and extended his arms, showing his disbelief. "In the desert, M. Morgan?"

"All right, not in the desert. When she crosses it and reaches her destination."

"Alas, where is that? You are no better off in your search than before."

Morgan had to admit the truth in that. Again he sank into gloomy despair, his mind desperately trying to find some glimmer of hope.

"I'm sorry, M. Morgan, I wish I could bear gladder tidings."

Morgan said nothing for several moments, then he sat upright in his chair and looked the French consul in the eye. "You advised me to use my head, not my heart. That is good advice. It is past time I did so. I ask you to understand that I am an American. We Americans are not so fatalistic as Europeans. We find it most difficult to admit defeat, to give up, to say anything is hopeless. I cannot and I will not. There must be some way to find her."

LeCompte shrugged. "As you wish."

Morgan tried to think, but failing in that he did the next best thing. He simply talked. "You said the last man known to have Glenna was this slave trader. What was his name again?"

"Mohammed Ibrahim."

"Yes. Tell me about him."

Another shrug. "What is there to tell? I don't know him. I only got the name—at a great price I might say."

"I don't mean him necessarily. What is a slave trader?"

LeCompte acted as though he were indulging a silly child. "A slave trader is a slave trader, he deals in human slaves. As an American you must know a great deal about slavery."

"Unfortunately that is so. But this is Morocco, not Maryland. How does this slave trade operate here?"

"Across the desert. From information brought back by Caillié, Timbuktu is the great slave trading center. Blacks are brought from the jungle, traded to the Arabs at Timbuktu for glass beads and God knows what else, then the slaves—or those who survive—are brought north across the desert to Marrakesh, Fez, this very city. Many end up in your country."

"Then it is black slaves in which he deals."

"Of course."

"Then why did he have Glenna—Miss O'Reilly?"

"For the same purpose. The trade goes both ways. White European women are in demand."

"In the jungle?"

LeCompte laughed. "I hardly think that. I told you, the women are most likely taken east across the desert to Egypt and points beyond."

"I heard that, but—" Morgan's voice was becoming

more agitated. "But this Mohammed fellow is accustomed to going to Timbuktu or whatever it is called. He doesn't go to Egypt."

Again LeCompte humored Morgan. "*He* doesn't, perhaps, but others do. A trade is a simple matter."

"Perhaps, most likely. Forgive me, M. LeCompte, but I submit you don't know."

"That's true, of course."

"Suppose he took her on to this Timbuktu."

"Why on earth would he?"

"I don't know. I don't even know why he would want her in the first place."

LeCompte laughed. "That's easy. She's beautiful and she's valuable as trade."

Quite excited now, Morgan burst on. "Suppose, just suppose, he took her on to Timbuktu. I know, it doesn't make sense, but what in all this does make sense? Where is this Timbuktu?"

All this was ridiculous folly to LeCompte, but he had no choice but to go along. He went to a large globe, beckoning Morgan to follow. "It isn't on here, of course. No one knew exactly where the place was until very recently." He pointed with the tip of a quill pen. "There. I would say Timbuktu is approximately there, just below the desert."

"Why that's practically on the west coast of Africa."

LeCompte laughed loudly. These ingenuous Americans, he thought. "My good man, this is a small map of a very large continent. That spot I showed you is several hundred, maybe a thousand miles from the coast, through some of the densest jungles in the world."

"If Glenna is taken to Timbuktu and if she escaped, she would head for the coast somewhere along there. She would hardly go the other direction—to the east."

"If, if, if, monsieur. If the sun rose in the west we would all have two heads."

But there was no stopping Morgan. The joy of even the slenderest hope shone in his eyes. "And that is the difference between you and me, sir. You say it is impossible. I say it is possible. I thank you. The money I gave you was well spent. You have given me hope, a place to begin looking. As soon as my ship can be made ready, I'm leaving for the West Coast of Africa. That's where I lost her. That's where I'll find her."

LeCompte shook his head, staring at Morgan like he did indeed have two heads.

22

All that morning it had been deathly still and exceedingly clear, both rare in the Sahara. The sky, bearing its infernal lamp, had been a deep blue, meeting the far distant horizon to create a clearly demarked line, as though drawn by an artist. Even in her weakened condition, with ennui and boredom covering her like a shroud as the endless miles passed beneath the camel's feet, Glenna could appreciate that it was an unusual day.

If she had been more alert and more knowledgeable of the desert, she would have seen signs that all was not well, the subtle agitation of the camels, the near perfect silence of the driyers, the fear in their eyes. The stillness and quiet, much greater than usual, gave the whole procession an eerie, unnatural cast.

The storm struck suddenly in early afternoon, coming out of the east like a giant fist rising from the desert. The first gust almost knocked Glenna from the saddle.

A moment later the sand came, nearly horizontal with the earth, a pelting brownish fury that lashed at her like myriad tiny knives, biting even through her clothing, turning the world a brownish, yellowish green. It was as if someone had thrown a bucket of sand hard, directly into her face.

Her camel stopped instinctively and turned his hindside to the wind, then squatted and Glenna climbed down. Her bernou and turban were almost blown away. Then she felt hands grabbing her. It was Hassam, barely able to stand himself, pushing her to the ground. The camel had lain flat on his side, and Hassam pushed Glenna to the ground to lie on her stomach in the lee of the camel. This afforded a little protection from the sand. He pulled the skirt of her bernou over her head. She lay there a moment, hearing the terrifying shriek of the wind and the grating sound of the driven sand striking the earth. Hell could be no worse.

Then she remembered Anne. Raising her head, she saw Hassam struggling to untie her from the squatting camel, which was trying desperately to roll over for its own protection. Glenna jumped up, and driven by fierce wind and sand, her garments almost torn from her body, she struggled across the sand against the wind. It took every ounce of her strength to reach her friend, then to stand there fumbling with the knots. It was an agonizing effort, but finally Anne was released and placed behind the camel. Glenna then prostrated herself beside Anne, her arm around her for protection, and covered both of them with their skirts.

The storm raged all afternoon and long past dark, whipping and slashing at the figures huddled on the ground. It was as if the great Sahara was determined to provide final proof that this was no place for mortals. What thirst and heat, disease and mind-breaking boredom could not accomplish, this great sandstorm surely could.

Glenna lay behind the camel, hugging Anne, frightened, aching, hardly able to find breath amid the torrents of sand. Because Anne was between her and the camel's back, she was not as protected. She could feel the sand pelting down on her and its weight as it collected around her. She was going to be buried alive in the desert. She was sure of that. But even that would be surcease from this hellish storm.

Some sandstorms blow for days in the Sahara. This one blew itself out before daybreak, ending almost as abruptly as it had begun. Glenna had fallen fitfully asleep. But she was awakened by the silence, deep all around after the howls of the wind. She had been dreaming of Daniel. The weight on her back seemed to be him. Why was he lying on her back? Then full consciousness came, the desert, sand, Anne next to her. The wind had stopped. The storm was over. With effort she pulled her skirt from her head and struggled to her feet. It was a clear night. The Southern Cross hung low in the sky, visible against the pale, waning moon. In the dim light, Glenna saw other figures moving about, camels getting to their feet, Hassam running toward her. After so long in the desert she understood when he asked if she were all right. She said yes. And yes again when he commented on what a bad storm it had been. Her knowledge of Arabic was increasing.

Both looked down at Anne. She hadn't moved. Best she sleep, Glenna thought. But an uneasiness grabbed at her and she knelt beside her friend, removing her skirt from her head to give her more air. Anne did not awaken, but lay there, alone on her stomach, her face against the sand, for the camel had risen and wandered off. Glenna hated to awaken her, but her uneasiness, mounting now to fear made her touch her shoulder. Anne did not move. She touched her cheek. It was cold.

There were no tears in Glenna. Her prolonged thirst and dehydration had drained her of them. She could only sigh deeply. "Oh no, God, please not" were the words she uttered. Then she knew that was wrong. She was thinking only of herself. At last Anne, her long ordeal ended, could sleep and breathe the clear, cool air of heaven. Kneeling, clasping her hands in prayer, she thanked God for his mercy and asked Mary, the Mother of God, to speed her friend to eternal happiness.

By early light and with Hassam's help, she dug a shallow grave and placed Anne's body in it. She uttered more prayers and helped to cover the body with sand. She looked around for some sticks, but there were none. So, she fashioned a makeshift cross of rocks she collected. Hassam seemed agitated as he watched her do this. He kept telling her no, but she paid no attention to him. Then, as she mounted her camel for the day's march, she saw one of the drivers run over and knock down the cross. There could be no Christian graves in this Moslem desert. Glenna cried out in protest, but it was useless. Anne Townsend would lie in an unmarked grave in this hellish wasteland. Then she remembered the glorious Southern Cross that blazed aloft each night. It could mark Anne's grave. No one would ever have a finer tombstone.

Late that night they came to the Taodeni salt pits, remaining there several days while the camels were pastured. They filled their bellies with water until they were bloated, for the next well to the south was a minimum of five days away. If they were delayed, none would survive the march. No longer having to share her ration with Anne, Glenna had more water to drink, but the liquid at Taodeni was so brackish and full of salt and minerals she could barely force it down. The principal effect was to increase her chronic thirst and worsen her dysentery. If she had thought of herself, she would have seen she was now thinner than she had ever been in her life, her ribs and other bones protruding. Her strength was almost as non-existent as her will to live.

The salt at Taodeni lay just below the surface of the

sand, rather easily accessible. It was chopped out in rectangular blocks by near naked slaves who had been swept from the savannahs and jungles to work in this most hellish place on earth. The slaves labored in the pits, under a broiling sun, sweat gleaming on their ebony skin, their bare feet ulcerated from the salt and brine, breathing acrid air filled with an unearthly stench. Their only mercy was the shortness of their existence, for no human being could stand the conditions very long.*

The caravan, now enlarged with more camels bearing salt, headed south into the Tanezrouft, one of the worst areas of the Sahara, an immense, waterless plain, roasted by the southerly sun, absolutely arid, featureless. The water ration for the caravan was reduced to a single cup a day. The camels got neither food nor water and many died along the way. Vultures circled high overhead, waiting to strip their bones to whiten in the sun. The wide path across the unbroken expanse, five hundred miles to Timbuktu from Taodeni, was littered with bones as a graveyard.

Glenna had not realized that at Taodeni she was only halfway across the desert. Indeed, she realized very little, for she was numb with grief, loneliness, boredom, weakness, pain and fatigue. She went through each day as an automaton, unmindful of its passage, unseeing, unknowing in order to be unfeeling. Her spirit was broken, her will to live gone. She no longer thought of enduring or of survival. She merely existed.

Thus, when Youssef, breaking the code of the desert, entered her tent the second night out of Taodeni, she reacted only very little. It had been so long since demands had been made upon her that she had almost forgotten. In her apathetic state, surprise was the most

---

*These conditions, little improved, persisted in modern times. Observers witnessed these conditions in the 1960s. The blacks who toil in the mines, now much deeper, must work with their feet in brine. They nominally are not slaves any longer, but are paid in a small portion of the salt they dig. The salt is still carried by camel caravans to the south.

emotion she could feel. But then, as he crawled atop her and tried to enter her, some instinct stirred in her and she struggled with him. But her weakness made it an unequal battle. He quickly pinioned her arms and his weight atop her made the feeble movements of her hips and legs futile. But when he entered her, hard, roughly, she cried out in pain. Again and again he rammed into her, grunting as he did so.

Then his weight was lifted from her. She opened her eyes and saw Mohammed Ibrahim, anger in his eyes, holding a surprised Youssef. His former guard was jerked roughly out the flap of the tent. Not a word had been spoken.

The next morning as the caravan mounted and headed south, Glenna looked back to see the forlorn figure of Youssef standing at the former campsite. He had been cast out alone, on foot, a hundred miles from any water as punishment. Despite her hatred for the man who had abused her, she shuddered and felt a wave of pity for him.

The whole procession passed through the desert, sad, mournful, largely silent, an infinitesimally small speck on a sea of waste that was being consumed at the rate of three and a half miles an hour under the padded hoofs of hungry, thirsty, slowly dying camels. It went on for weeks, day in, day out, cruel in its heat, thirst and stultifying boredom.

Only once was she aroused from her lassitude, and even then not very much. A group of riders, perhaps forty in all, seemed to rise out of the desert late one afternoon, tall men atop huge riding camels. The caravan stopped and Glenna studied them closely. They seemed to be blue men. Their robes and turbans were of bright indigo blue and across their faces was a heavy blue veil. The eyes and bits of skin showing above the mask seemed to be blue, too. They were the dreaded Taureg, the most ferocious and feared of the desert tribes. They were white men of origins lost to antiquity. The blue cast to their skin came from the dyes in their clothing. Glenna had never seen any men so fierce looking. They were all enshrouded and faceless, but heavily armed, a dagger attached to an arm, a broadsword tied to their backs, a sharp spear in their hand.

Mohammed Ibrahim turned his camel to go talk to them. He seemed to be bowing to them. This Glenna could understand, for despite their fierce appearance, these blue men had a noble, even regal bearing as they sat high atop their camels. Then she saw that the pommels on the saddles were in the form of a cross. How strange.

Mohammed Ibrahim seemed to talk to them only a few minutes, then he shouted orders. Quickly a large number of camels carrying salt, more than fifty of them, were cut out of the caravan, and the Taureg, not even bothering to nod, led them off into the desert. Mohammed Ibrahim had paid tribute to gain safe passage for his caravan. It was nearly always so, and he reckoned the tribute in his cost of doing business. As he motioned the caravan forward, he knew the Taureg would be waiting for him again on his return journey. He shrugged. It couldn't be helped. After that, no event other than the gradual deterioration of a despondent Glenna, marked the slow weeks as the caravan inched its way southward.

Timbuktu had once been the capital of the great Songhai nation, a flourishing city, rich with commerce. It had contained a great university and was a seat of learning when Europe languished in its middle ages. But the great black Songhai empire had dwindled and disappeared mysteriously. Timbuktu had hung on as a trading center, supported by salt and slaves largely, but was already declining further. Most slaves were not being taken aboard ships off the coast. In 1830, the population of Timbuktu had shrunk to twelve thousand or less, although with the caravans to and from the desert there could still be much activity. The city lay hot, dusty, pitiful, a shadow of its former self on the southern edge of the Sahara. If Glenna even saw any of this, none of it registered on her mind. She was incapable of reacting to anything.

Mohammed Ibrahim, weary himself, going largely on pride and greed, had brought her to trade her. This would be his last caravan and he intended to make it a rich one. But the girl, he knew, had barely survived the journey. She would hardly bring a great price in her present condition. So, like a cattle man, a sheepherder and, indeed, like a slave trader, he set out to fatten her up.

Glenna was taken to a house in Timbuktu and placed in the hands of two black women slaves. She was given all the cool, clean water she could drink, all the food she could eat, bathed, dressed in clean clothes. Mostly however she slept. She remained grief stricken, despairing, but her young body responded to the care lavished upon her. Her flesh filled out and strength returned to her body. And her body began to control her mind, bringing her out of her depression for longer periods each day. She began to be aware of what was happening to her. She was able, for example, to feel gratitude for the food and water and rest, the roof which kept out the baking sun and cooled her.

As her health and awareness improved, she began to register annoyance at the infestation of insects in Timbuktu. In Ireland, she had hardly ever encountered a mosquito. Now there were swarms of them from the nearby Niger River, and biting flies and ticks which burrowed into her skin. She bundled up, trying to leave no portion of her skin exposed.

Physically, Glenna began to resemble her old self. Her mental outlook, her toughness of spirit lagged well behind, however, until the day early in the third week of her stay in Timbuktu that Mohammed Ibrahim came to her as she was being bathed. Her anger blazed at the intrusion, the first real emotion she had felt in weeks. She saw him looking at her naked body, appraising her, and she felt shame amid her anger.

To the Negro slaves, one older and fat, the other a young girl in her teens, perhaps a daughter, he said, "The nazara is much improved. You have done well." Looking in her eyes, he said, still speaking to the women, "It is too bad to waste food on such as she, but it is necessary." Then his eyes glinted and his lips spread in a thin, cruel smile. "So the nazara has learned some Arabic. Will Allah's wonders never cease."

Glenna said nothing, determined not to let him be sure she understood.

"Don't be silly, woman. I can tell you understand me. And that is Allah's blessing, for I wish you to know something. I am sorry you endured so much suffering on the journey here. I am sorry your friend, the English nazara, died. She was a remarkable woman. But you left me no choice. That night in my apartment—you remember of course—I liked you. I had decided to keep you and your friend. She could teach you Arabic. It would have been a pleasant life for you, if perhaps a little confining. When you attacked me, it was Allah's will that I punish you."

Glenna heard and understood. His words were like a physical blow. In her determination to escape, she had inadvertantly caused such suffering for Anne and her death. And Anne had known, too, and forgiven her. For the first time in weeks, tears appeared in her eyes, for herself, for what she had done to Anne.

Finally she spoke in halting Arabic, for she understood better than she talked. "What are you going to do to me?"

Again the thin smile, this time with triumph in his eyes. "I knew the nazara could speak. As I told your friend that night, you will come to wish for Allah's mercy to bring you the grave your friend now lies in."

The coldness in his voice, the cruelty, the relish with which he uttered it, chilled Glenna. She felt herself shiver. But she managed to speak. "What are you going to do to me?"

"You are my slave—no, less than a slave. You are a

nazara. Like all slaves, you will be sold." She saw his gaze travel down her body. "But you are nonetheless a most remarkable slave. You will bring a high price. You will make me rich for life."

"What do you mean?"

"You will find out shortly." He turned on his heel and left her.

The next day Glenna was fed well, given plenty of water, bathed, her skin oiled till it shone, but unlike previous days she was dressed in only a sort of short loincloth of beads. Other beads were placed around her neck, wrists and ankles. Then, so attired she was offered for inspection. To her horror, the slave trader brought to her room delegations of black men, some dressed in Arab costumes, others in scanty attire of beads and bones and feathers, their faces and bodies garishly painted. Some of the faces were horribly scarred, like someone had cut designs in them with a knife, which indeed had been done. When first she saw these jungle men, Glenna screamed in horror and tried to run, but on a word from Mohammed Ibrahim, she was caught and held by the slave women, forced to stand there as the jungle natives looked at her, grinning, speaking rapidly among themselves, occasionally laughing. Glenna closed her eyes. She could not bear to look at their faces, the horrid look in their eyes. Never had she seen such an expression. Then she truly screamed. They were touching her. She opened her eyes and saw the black hands on her body, her thighs, her breasts, touching her, rubbing their hands over her, making excited sounds, nodding their heads. Glenna felt a wave of nausea sweep over her.

Then, suddenly, she knew, Oh, God forbid, she knew. He was going to sell her to them. And as that thought came to her, she fainted. She was revived and made to stand erect again for the inspection to continue. Fingers were poked into her mouth and ears, her vagina and rectum, all accompanied by low sounds of approval. Her eyes were forced open so the sapphire irises could be studied. Her hair was stroked and pulled.

There were at least three similar delegations that day, a prolongation of degradation and revulsion that left her, when she was alone in her locked room that night, retching over and over, wild with fear and horror. She ran against the door, trying to break it. She shook the bars on the tiny window with all her might. She banged her head against the walls, then in her frenzy tried even to scratch and mutilate her own body. It lasted only a minute, for she was quickly bound hand and foot to stop it all. Helpless, with no physical outlet for her horror and revulsion, she could only lie there weeping and sobbing, occasionally screaming until exhaustion brought sleep.

She awoke some hours later when it was still dark. She was first aware of her limbs aching from her bonds, then of her whole body aching. When she tried to turn to a new position, this seemed to take a supreme effort. And she was hot, so hot. Her room was like an oven. Had they taken her back into the desert? She tried to orient herself. No, she was still in her room. But why was it so hot? Then, she knew. Fever. She was on fire with fever.

Malaria, the plague which made West Africa the white man's curse, had come to her. When she had been forced to stand nearly naked for the disgusting inspection, mosquitos had bit her at will. But in her horror at what was being done to her, she had not noticed them. In truth, these were not the mosquitos which infected her. That had occurred some days earlier in a single sting from a female anopheles mosquito. Her exposure of the day before had only helped to spread the disease.

The next morning Mohammed Ibrahim found her scalded with fever, unconscious and delirious. He cursed his bad luck. He had hoped for the best offer for her. He would have to accept the best of those made yesterday—and quickly. And it was a good offer. Within two days, he had collected a ransom in gold, ivory and slaves and headed north toward home. The Taureg were waiting for him two days south of Tao-deni. The tribute they demanded was too much for Mohammed Ibrahim. He became angry, quarreled and refused to pay. Thus, his last caravan ended in the white heat of the Tanezrouft. While vultures circled overhead, the high price paid for Glenna was carried off by the Taureg. Under their blue veils, they were smiling.

23

Because of her illness, Glenna had only the most flitting memory of the next several days. She remembered being lifted up on some kind of litter and being borne, day after day, on the shoulders of running men. She recalled a bitter, evil tasting liquid being forced down her throat, but not much else. She lost all track of where she was or even what direction she was being taken. All that remained were fleeting impressions of savannahs of high grass dotted with thorn trees, then country rising into mountains and increasing vegetation. She was a very sick girl, lost in West Africa.

Glenna was purchased by the Shinome tribe and carried, half dead, for many days toward the southwest to their home in the mountainous equatorial rain forests of what was then known as Guinea. They did save her life, for the bitter liquid they gave her was derived from the dried bark of the cinchona tree. Much later, the rest of the world would call it quinine and recognize it as both a curative and preventative of malaria.

The Shinome were a small tribe of superior hunters and fierce warriors forced only within the last generation out of a stone age culture by the burgeoning slave trade. For many generations, far longer than any of them could remember, the Shinome had lived in the jungle. It had been their home, food supply and protection. But with the demand for slaves to work the salt mines of Taodeni and the sugar and cotton plantations of America, their way of life had undergone sharp change. The slave traders and their agents (called factors) had long since deflowered the thriving African cultures by taking away the finest young men and women. Tribe had been set against tribe in a search for more and more slaves, and the carnage which resulted had spread far afield to the most remote regions, even to the territory of the Shinome. They had been forced to trade for the means to defend themselves, metal swords, knives and spears. Ivory, gold, feathers and other goods had been used, but eventually the fierce Shinome had themselves dealt in captured slaves.

Still, it was a losing game for them. Their own young men and women were disappearing, sold as slaves to the white men in the desert or those lying off the shore in great ships. For all their new steel weapons, for all their fierce bravery, the Shinome were unable to stand against these white men. They were invincible demons. So recently out of the stone age, thrust into a world they neither understood or condoned, the Shinome sought aid wherever they could. The witch doctors, their best efforts proving ineffective, concluded in their superstition that something in the pale, lifeless color of the white man's skin must be the secret of his strength and invincibility. Surely, some potion, some magic could be derived to protect the Shinome warriors from the increasingly numerous attacks upon them. That belief led to the extravagant purchase of Glenna O'Reilly.

She did not know the bitter fluid saved her life. She knew only, as consciousness fully returned, that her fever had gone, leaving her terribly weak. She knew too that she was being carried quite rapidly on a litter through heavy forest by a group of black men. They were rather small in stature, scantily dressed, their faces and bodies horribly mutilated by long beaded scars arranged into individual patterns. The leader, running ahead as the men took turns carrying her, wore a headdress of brilliant feathers and a terrible, brightly painted mask which covered his whole face to his chest. The men, except those shouldering the litter, carried long, metal tipped spears. They had knives slung to their waists.

The procession would stop at night. She would be fed fruit and berries, strips of meat unlike anything she had ever eaten. She was guarded, but no man molested her, indeed even spoke or hardly looked at her. For this she was grateful, for she was still as naked as when the slave trader had first shown her to these men. The food and water gradually brought back her strength, but she was still too weak to do more than register what was going on. Any sort of escape was impossible. She could only try to endure and control her fear and panic. What was going to happen to her? She tried to avoid imagining.

The forest seemed to grow thicker, darker and gloomier as the days passed. The insects were a scourge and the screeches and howls from the jungle, particularly at night, were terrifying to her. Gradually the undergrowth thickened to the point where it seemed impossible for the defile, now moving slowly, to pass. But it did until ultimately Glenna was borne into a semi-clearing. She saw huts of thatch and vines and leaves which seemed to melt into the jungle, and a great crowd of people, men, women and children, all in various degrees of nakedness. Many, particularly the children, seemed to have greatly distended bellies, although the younger men looked lean and hard.

The crowd was excited as she approached, then grew more silent as she was carried through their midst. Sitting on the litter, her eyes wide with fear, she saw the scarred faces of these people, their intense curiosity, even awe expressed in their eyes, their lips moving in unuttered sounds.

She was carried to the front of what seemed to be a larger hut. Then, amid a tumult of cries from the crowd, her litter was raised on the outstretched arms of the four bearers. Taken by surprise, she sat on the litter, high above the cheering crowd. There seemed to be some word they were saying, but she could not understand it. Precipitously, the litter was lowered to the ground and she was pulled to her feet. As she stood there, largely naked, the cheering was reduced to murmurs. She felt like some kind of spectacle and longed for clothes to put on. Furtively, she glanced around for some way to escape. There was none. The crush of people was too great.

Then to her right, the crowd suddenly parted to form an aisle down which strode a group of men, the foremost of which seemed neither young nor old to Glenna. He was tall and powerfully built, his body naked to the waist. His headdress, the mass of scars, the ornate garment of feathers and bone at his waist, as well as his bearing and the respect the others showed him, indicated he was the chief. Solemnly he came up to her and looked her directly in the eyes. She seemed held by his, yet she was unable to read any expression in them. Then he looked at her body. Still no reaction. Slowly he walked around her, out of her vision. To Glenna it was Lord Winslow in his study, inspecting her. Humiliation and anger flooded over her.

Then she saw that the aisle made for the chief was still open. Abruptly, impetuously, she bolted through it, running as fast as she could. Startled faces blurred past her, but all she could really see was the open space at the end of the aisle. She was almost there. Indeed, in their surprise the natives moved away to make room for her, lest she run into them. Then she was free of the crowd and into the clearing. Ahead was the jungle and escape, and she tried to run even faster. Behind, she heard a loud roar from the crowd. Still she ran—until they caught her at the edge of the jungle and brought her kicking and screaming back to stand before the chief. She stood there, her chest heaving, her eyes wide with defiance, struggling against the hands which held her arms, lunging, trying to get away. The crowd was roaring, but she was only dimly aware of it.

The chief raised his hand and the crowd quieted. He continued to look at her, solemnly, his eyes expressionless, as if nothing had happened. Glenna struggled, but to no avail. And in her frenzy she did the only thing left to her. She spat at him. The spittle ran down his shoulder, but it had no effect on him.

In a moment, he reached out and touched her sweating skin, her shoulder, then her breast, her hip. He did it again, walking to her other side. He seemed to look at his hand a moment, then feel his own fingers. He raised his hand and a smile split his face and a great roar rose as a single voice from the crowd. All rushed forward and there were hundreds of hands upon her, touching, stroking, pinching, pulling, poking her every orifice. Glenna screamed, but to no avail.

Again the chief shouted a command and the hands left her, the crowd retreating as abruptly as it had surged forward. The chief solemnly went up to her and touched her again. He turned to the witch doctor standing nearby behind his hideous mask and nodded, again with great dignity. An immense roar rent the air and Glenna felt herself being seized by the wrists and ankles. Before she realized what was happening, she was thrown on her back on the ground. As thongs were wound around her wrists and ankles, she suddenly knew. She tried to struggle, but it was useless effort. In an instant four stakes were pounded into the soil and she was tied spreadeagled to them.

In horror, unable even to scream, she saw the chief

stand over her like a black giant. He raised his spear above her in his right hand, point downward, and Glenna knew she was to die. After surviving so much it was to end for her in this forsaken place. He held the spear high above him for a moment. Glenna saw it shaking in his hand, the sun glint off the metal tip, then closed her eyes as the point plunged downward. She felt nothing, but heard a thud. She opened her eyes, her heart nearly bursting with fright, and saw the spear impaled in the ground beside her leg.

The came a greater horror. The chief seemed to leap into the air and down atop her, a great cry leaving his mouth as he did so. And a second savage cry escaped him, drowning Glenna's own scream, as he plunged into her with a force that almost seemed to tear her bound ankles from their sockets. Again and again he plunged into her, his cries of triumph bellowing in her ear, drowning out the roars from the crowd, until with a mighty shriek he finished. Glenna lay there, pain arcing through her body. It was as if she had been horribly beaten. Through half-closed eyelids, everything above her at a sharp angle, she saw the chief leap to his feet in triumph, brandishing the spear while the crowd roared its approval. Then she saw him hand the spear to another man. She saw it raised in a new hand and heard it thud into the ground beside her.

Time, reality, pain, suffering, even her humanity ceased to exist for Glenna. All that seemed real to her was the repeated thud of the spear into the ground beside her. She passed out several times, and in between there was only the sound of the spear striking the ground. Her flesh became separate from her mind, and both were numb. She felt herself floating in some great emptiness, a gray void, timeless, painless, without thought or sensation, marked only by thud . . . thud . . . thud. . . .

She was awakened when her hands and feet were untied and she was pulled erect. Unable even to stand, she was dragged to a tree and bound again, her hands behind her circling the bark. Her head was raised from her chest and water poured between her cracked lips. She opened her eyes and saw it was women administering to her. She again had the sensation of many hands upon her and voices. Somehow, as her head again slumped to her chest, she had the sensation it was morning. She was given no food, but the liquid poured down her throat was changed to a stimulant. Despite herself, Glenna came awake and alert, but with that came sharp stabs of pain through her body and equally painful memories of what had happened to her.

She remained there through much of the day, the sun beating down on her between the trees, insects swarming around her. Her fatigue and suffering kept overpowering the stimulant and she passed out frequently. New stimulants kept being forced into her and during the periods of alertness, she saw that some kind of feast was being prepared. She saw wild pigs, lambs and chickens being roasted, piles of fruit and vegetables being collected. She knew she was hungry, but that was an almost unnoticed discomfort amid the greater torments of her flesh.

She also saw that some kind of games were being held. The youths of the tribe were holding contests, running, jumping, wrestling, spear throwing. One youth, bigger, stronger, more arrogant and full of pride, seemed to win most events. But this fact was of no interest to Glenna, just an observation. In her mind, during those periods of forced alertness, she accepted calmly, gratefully, her eminent death. She prayed to the Blessed Virgin with all the intensity and ardor she could muster, and she felt the nearness of Her, a closeness which was like a balm to her pain. Grateful, tears of inner joy streaming down her cheeks, she prayed in thanks to Her for Her mercy, for Her love, for Her forgiveness.

Thus, when Glenna was finally cut down and again tied to the pegs in the ground, she felt in a state of exultation. The end was near. She would soon be with

the Mother of God and see Her Blessed Face. She was
aware of the tall youth, the arrogant one, standing
above her, shrieking as he plunged the spear into the
ground beside her. She was aware of the roars of the
crowd and of the pain inflicted upon her body, but she
held to her feeling of closeness to the Virgin. Her lips
moved constantly in prayer, releasing her mind from
her body, as the spear thudded into the ground again
and again, thrust in accordance with a ranking produced by the games. But Glenna knew none of it. She
was aware she had reached a state of grace and the joy
of that knowledge exceeded anything she had ever
experienced. It seemed to her that she could even see
the Blessed Virgin, attired in shining robes more
brilliant even than the sun, reaching out to her with
both arms, gathering her in to comfort and love her.
Glenna cried aloud from the joy of it and wished she
could see Her face. Oh, how she wished she could see
Her face. And then it seemed to her she could hear the
voice of the Blessed Virgin whispering softly against
her ear, saying, "I sorry, Missy. I come later, save
you."

24

Glenna's first awareness when she opened
her eyes was that it was pitch dark above and all around
her. Then she was conscious of a hand on her face
gently shaking her head as she lay on the ground. Next

came a whispered voice, "Wake up, Missy, please wake up." She turned her head trying to see who was there. But she seemed more to sense than see a figure kneeling beside her. Again the whispers, "Be quiet, Missy, mos' quiet you ever been."

She felt hands at her right wrist and its sudden, blissful release. Hands rubbed it briefly to restore circulation. Then her left wrist and both ankles, then a hand around her shoulders helping her to sit up and a cup of cool water held against her lips, being tilted as she drank thirstily. And the voice, barely audible saying, "Gotta hurry, Missy. Gotta be mos' quiet."

She felt herself being pulled to her feet. Pain stabbed into her thighs and groin and she gasped in agony to stifle the scream that filled her lungs. "I can't walk," she managed to whisper.

"I carry you, Missy. We gotta hurry."

She still could not see more than an outline of the figure beside her. He seemed a good bit shorter than her, yet she felt herself being folded over his left shoulder and being carried away. He seemed to carry her a long distance. She heard him panting as he struggled under her weight. He stopped from time to time, to stand her up and rest. "We almost there, Missy," she heard him gasp. Finally, she smelled a damp, musty odor and heard the gentle lap of water against a bank. She heard the splash of his feet in water and felt herself being lifted up and laid into some sort of boat. She felt the sides with her hands. A canoe. Then she felt the craft lurch as he climbed in and pushed the canoe away from shore.

All the rest of the night he paddled. She could hear the slap of the oar, his panting from his exertions. And they seemed to be moving so rapidly. Had to be going downstream. Through the jungle, she realized. Above her she could see a path of stars through the trees and around her the terrifying night cries of the rain forest.

Toward morning, when only the first tinge of light was showing in the sky, he turned the canoe toward shore. Only the faintest graying of the darkness had begun as he carried her ashore, then pulled the canoe on to the land. In a moment he had located a particularly dense thicket and carried her into it, laying her on the ground. Through a tiny slit in the leaves, she saw him return to the canoe, cover it with leaves and branches, then return to her, carrying a bag of some kind of hide over his shoulder. Kneeling beside her, he opened it. "We safe here. Nobody find. You eat, then you sleep. We travel at dark." She devoured some fruit and dried meat, then, despite her curiosity about who this was, she fell into an exhausted sleep.

She awoke some hours later. She was aware it was daylight, but momentarily confused as to where she was. Then she saw the black youth. He had cut her loose, brought her here in a canoe. She sat up. He immediately leaped to his feet, went to the bag and produced more food for her. "Eat, Missy," he said. "You need strength."

She accepted the food but said, "Do you have any water?"

She saw a flash of white between his lips as he darted back to the bag. "Oh yes, Missy, plenty good clean water. You drink all you want."

He handed her a flask made out of some type of skin. She tilted it above her head and squirted the water down her throat, swallowing rapidly. When she finished, she sat there looking at him above her. He was young, but how young she couldn't say, fourteen, perhaps fifteen or sixteen. He was dressed as the others in the village and his skin was nearly jet black, yet he was strangely handsome, with alert brown eyes and clear, unscarred skin. She saw that he smiled in embarrassment under her gaze, flashing many white teeth as he did so. "You eat now, Miss. Be strong."

She lifted a fruit, one she did not know, and took a bite. As she did so, she said, "Who're you?"

An expression of pain crossed his face. He looked

away from her, then impulsively knelt on the ground in front of her. He looked down at the ground, unable to look her in the face as he spoke, "I sorry, Missy, real sorry. I no wanna touch you. Believe me I no wanna. But I have to. No one trust me, not chief, not witch doctor, no one. I-I have to prove . . . to prove, I. . . . Missy, I sorry, but I have to. Only way to save you."

She remembered and understood. The voice in her ear. She had thought it the Blessed Mother. He was one of those. . . . He had. . . . She shuddered, revulsion and nausea rising in her.

"I had to, Missy, I just had to. I no wanna. But—"

He was near tears from shame and remorse. She did not understand what he meant by saying he had to, but something in his manner reached out to her. His remorse could only be geniune. Her voice barely above a whisper she said, "It's all right. I don't remember you. There . . . there were . . . so many. . . ."

And then he raised his head, looking at her, tears in his eyes, words tumbling out in a torrent from his mouth. "I sorry, Missy, sorry for all Shinome. Not their fault. Witch doctor bad man, real bad man. He tell chief white woman make warriors brave, strong like white man. If have white woman, no Shinome ever captured, ever die. We use white man's medicine, we no fear white man. I know wrong. I know no good. But what can I do? I just boy. They no trust me."

Again he looked at the ground. "When you came, I saw you beautiful. I hear you scream. I know you English. Me like English. I decide to save you. But first, I must prove I real Shinome, true Shinome. They no trust me. I had to. . . ."

"Yes, I think I understand. Except why didn't they trust you?"

Still looking away from her, he said, "When boy, I captured by slavers, taken to place beside sea. Many of us there, in chains, waiting to go on boat. Terrible things happen, Missy, terrible things. But I too young for boat. I live in fort. Many English there. I run and fetch. I good boy. They treat me nice. I learn English pretty good there."

"Yes, your English is pretty good. How long did you live there?"

"No know. Long time though."

"How old are you?"

Still not looking at her, he shrugged his shoulders. "No know. Fifteen, maybe sixteen."

"How did you get here?"

"Much sickness in fort. Many English die. Rest leave. All gone. I big now. Know I be put on boat, so I run away. Take many days, but I find my way back to Shinome. They welcome me as son, but no trust me because I live with white man so long. I sorry, Missy, but have to prove—"

"I know you're sorry. I understand. You needn't say it again." She saw him kneeling there, head bowed, not uttering a word now. "They were going to kill me, weren't they?"

"Yes. Witch doctor say make potion of white skin, drink, give strength like iron coat. Guns no harm."

Despite herself, Glenna shivered. "Well I thank you for saving my life. I owe you everything." Still he sat there, head down. "Please look at me. Please." Finally, he raised his head, a look of gross pain in his eyes. "I mean it. You saved my life. How can I thank you?" He said nothing, but kept his eyes riveted on hers a second, then again dropped his head. Then she looked down at her own nakedness and understood. "I see," she said.

"I sorry, Missy, no have dress."

For the first time in a long time, she was amused. A small laugh escaped her. Imagine being naked in the jungle with an embarrassed native boy. "Well, we'll have to do something, won't we? If you'll get some of those larger leaves, maybe we can make a dress."

Quickly he jumped up and gathered an armful of large, green leaves. Using a length of vine, they fashioned a sort of covering for her breasts, and he helped tie it securely to her. "Now, that's better," she said, smiling. "Maybe you'll be able to look at me—as soon as we make a skirt."

In similar fashion a skirt was made, but when she stood to put it on, sharp pains stabbed at her thighs and groin. Her old injury. She would never be able to walk. But she remembered the bindings Daniel had made for her. Perhaps it would work again. She instructed the boy and together they fashioned a sort of mat of leaves and vines. While he turned his back, she wound it around her groin as tightly as she could, again feeling the blessed relief from pain. She even managed a step or two. Putting on the skirt they had previously made, she said, "How's this?"

The boy turned around. His eyes brightened and a wide grin spread his cheeks. "Very nice, Missy. Almost a real dress."

She saw him almost dance with pleasure, all his embarrassment with her leaving him. "I don't know your name."

"Me? I Joe." And he said it with great pride.

They remained hidden in the thicket until well past sunset when it was again dark. Then they boarded the canoe and headed downstream with Glenna strong enough to add a little speed by paddling some. Again they pulled ashore before daylight and hid in the heavy foliage.

It was none too soon, for shortly after daybreak several canoes filled with natives swept downstream past them. They watched, hardly even daring to breathe. "Shinome?" Glenna asked.

"No, not Shinome. They no find us now."

"Who were they?"

He shook his head. "No know. No want to know."

"Could they be friendly?"

Joe shrugged. "No friend here no more. Everybody 'fraid of slavers. Everybody want to make everyone else slave, so no be slave themselves. We hide. I no want to be slave."

And she understood. "Yes." Then she realized she was white, not black. "They wouldn't make a slave of me. I could protect you."

"No, Missy. Many tribes worse than Shinome. You captured, you be traded for slaves for white man. No good for you, Missy."

And Glenna shuddered, knowing full well what he meant. "What are we going to do?"

"Maybe lucky and reach coast, hide. When ship comes, you go to captain. You safe then."

"But what about you? You can come on the ship, too. I'll tell them you saved my life."

His smile was bitter. "Sure, you tell real nice, but they make slave of me. Make slave of anyone. Slavers no good. No trust slavers—never."

"What'll you do? You can't go back to the Shinome."

"No. No go home no more. I stay on coast, hide. Maybe English come back."

And then Glenna realized what a sacrifice Joe had made for her. He had risked his life to save her. He had given up his home forever to help her escape. And in so doing, he had condemned himself to a life of hiding to escape slavery. The only real slavery she had seen was in the Taodeni salt pits. She shuddered, not able to think of him in that hell hole.

He was looking through the foliage to the river. "We move quick tonight. Rains come soon."

"Rain?"

"Yes, much rain, much, much rain, all time rain. Bad for you, Missy."

And they did move quickly that night and for several nights thereafter. As they hid by daylight, Glenna saw that the river was growing ever wider and the foliage, unfortunately, sparser. A morning or two they were lucky to locate a patch of concealing brush. And traffic on the river increased. Hardly a daylight hour passed without boats going up and down stream. "Slavers, Missy. We be mos' careful now."

They were not to escape the rain. The black and purple clouds moved in quickly, opened up and dumped a torrent of rain on them. It rained all day and all that night as they continued downstream. Glenna, unprotected in her dress of leaves, was drenched repeatedly and shivered constantly. So hard did it rain, she had to give up rowing to bail the boat. At times hers was almost a losing effort against sinking. Wet all the time, sleeping on the wet ground, she felt her fever return. But she said nothing to Joe, for she was determined to keep on with the journey, reach the sea and somehow escape.

Twice they had narrow escapes. Once during a heavy squall a party of canoes headed for shore directly toward them. Glenna and Joe held their breath as the boats came closer. Then, mercifully, the rain let up and the canoes changed course to continue downstream. The second time it was a land party, black men carrying rifles, leading a party of bedraggled people in chains. They passed within a few feet of where Glenna and Joe huddled, so close only the rattle of the chains kept their heartbeats from being heard.

Finally the morning came when Joe said, "Most dangerous part now, Missy. River no good no more, only marsh, heavy grass. Boat get lost. No good for us. We walk from now on."

"All right. I can walk." She smiled, trying to prove to Joe that she was all right. But she had her doubts. The fever raged in her. She was weak, frequently dizzy. How long she could go on foot, she didn't know.

"We rest today. We rest tonight. Tomorrow we walk, reach coast before nightfall."

"In daylight!"

"Yes. Get lost at night."

"We'll be found."

He shrugged. "Maybe. Pray for much rain. Maybe no one see us then."

And it did rain, all that day and all that night. But Glenna, huddled under some protective leaves, got little sleep because of the rain, insufferable dampness and the fever which baked her from the inside out.

At the first graying of the morning they struck out overland. As she had prayed, the rains fell heavily, creating a gray murkiness which would shield them from view of all but nearby persons. To keep hidden, they remained off any traveled path and stuck to marshy ground where reeds and high grass offered some shelter. By mid-morning they had to leave this shelter and cross a grassy area dotted with only a few trees. But the rains came down to shield them. Still the trek was a hardship for Glenna. She controlled her dizziness by concentrating on placing one foot in front of the other, to somehow continue on. She knew she was slowing down Joe terribly, but he would not leave her side.

Ahead, across the grassy plain, Glenna saw a line of trees. "There," she gasped. "We'll be safe there."

"Yes."

She tried to hurry, his arm around her for support, but the distance seemed to grow greater, not shorter. Then, in a perversity of nature, the rains began to let up. In a few more steps it had stopped entirely. Within a minute the sun shone bright and hot through a patch in the clouds. "Oh, God, no," she wailed and tried to run for the trees. Joe pushed and dragged her forward. It seemed an eternity until she collapsed under the protective shade as winded and spent as she had ever been in her life.

She lay there a long time, the cool earth against her face, smelling the pungent pine needles. Pines. How long since she had smelled the pines of Ireland? Then she smelled something else, an unbelievable aroma. Ecstatic, she sat up. "I smell the sea, Joe, I smell the sea."

He was smiling, too. "Yes, Missy. Through these trees, then some grass and sand is the sea. We safe now, Missy. We hide till dark, maybe see ship."

Glenna leaned against the trunk of the tree and

closed her eyes, sucking in great gulps of the fragrance of the sea. How wonderful. How long since she'd smelled the sea? How long since she'd walked the cliffs of home smelling the sea, listening to the thunder of the surf and the shrieks of gulls? How long? Unconsciousness settled over her, gently, like a soft veil.

"Wake up, Missy, look."

She aroused herself and through the vaporous vision of fever looked to where he pointed. She saw nothing at first, then swimming in front of her eyes, were tiny moving figures in the plain they had just crossed. It meant nothing to her at first, for unconsciousness still struggled for control. Then blinking, she tried to focus and *saw*. "Oh, God no. They saw us. They're coming for us."

Joe huddled down beside her. "Maybe not, Missy. Maybe they no see."

Blinking, through eyes filled with tears, she saw he was wrong. The figures grew larger. She saw them point and wave, then the sound of voices. They were so close to escape. They couldn't be captured now, not after all she had gone through. Bitter tears welled out of her eyes. It wasn't fair. Oh God, it wasn't fair.

Joe was pulling her to her feet. "We hide, Missy. They no find us."

Quickly he led her deeper into the thin strip of woods. Much of it had been cut for timber. There seemed scant cover for them.

"There," he said, "we hide under log."

He dragged her to it and pushed her down, wedging her underneath amid the rotting bark. Glenna lay there, her face against the wet ground, fever boiling her brains, struggling against the unconsciousness which kept descending on her. It was as if she were in a surf. A wave would roll over her and she would black out. Then will for survival would force a feverish consciousness upon her only to be lost as another wave of blackness bore down on her. Again she fought it. She could hear footsteps and voices. Then another wave.

She never awoke this time. Some spark of consciousness told her she was dreaming as the voices, drawing closer, seemed to make sense. "I tell you, I saw a black man and a white woman. They're here some place." Helpless, wedged under a rotting log, too sick and feverish to resist any longer, she surrendered to the blackness enveloping her.

Joe lay there, his head just below her feet, wrestling with what to do. He heard the voices and knew they were close. He listened a moment.

"I know what I saw."

"All right, we'll have a look, but this is just another wild goose chase."

Joe wavered between his instinct to hide and his admiration for the English who once had saved him from slavery. Minutes dragged by. The voices grew more distant. Faintly, he heard, "I was so damned sure I saw something, Mac."

"Well, you didn't."

Indecision gripped Joe a moment longer, then he scampered from beneath the log, shouting and waving. "Over here, Mister English. Over here." The two white men and their party of blacks were near the clearing. They didn't hear him. Joe had committed himself. He shouted more loudly. One of the white men turned.

Something was pulling at her arm, hurting her. Something was wedged against her and she was being hurt as it rubbed against her skin. Then she was being pulled to her feet. She opened her eyes and vaporous in front of her was a man. More unconscious than awake, she knew only that she had been captured again. Instinctively, with her last ounce of energy, she screamed and kicked and flailed with her fists. But to no avail. Arms went round her and held her fast. Spent, she could resist no longer. She kept hearing a voice saying something to her, but she did not understand, but it was a gentle voice, a familiar voice. She managed to raise her head and open her eyes. A face swam in front of her. She closed her eyes and opened them. Still she could not focus. She shook her head and there for an instant was a face. Recognition crept up to her. "Daniel?" she said.

She would later have no remembrance of his saying, "Oh, Glenna, my darling, my darling. At last I've found you."

Part III

25

Glenna looked and felt radiant. And with good reason, she thought. It wasn't every day that she was invited to the White House to have dinner with the President of the United States. She didn't pretend to understand this system of government, although Daniel had tried many times to explain it to her. All she knew was that this President Jackson was a very important man, something like a king, and Daniel worshipped him. He must think very highly of Daniel, too, to invite him to dinner.

She sat before a large mirror in her dressing room, applying another touch of powder to her flushed cheeks. The flush had worried her at first. Did it signal the return of another bout of the fever as had happened so often since her escape from Africa? But she felt well. No, it was not the fever. She was flushed with excitement. She saw herself in the mirror smiling. How well she might be excited tonight.

A new worry. Her gown was in the height of fashion, off the shoulder, the neckline a sort of V with flaring sides. Most women wore them, but on her somehow it came out less demure. She saw the rounded tops of her breasts and a deep valley between. Was it too daring to wear to the White House? Daniel said the President was very democratic. A rich man himself, he had been elected by the common men of the western frontiers. He favored them and disliked the pretentious snobbery of the rich easterners. Perhaps the color was wrong, white with a pattern of tiny rosebuds.

She felt hands, cool and tingly on her shoulders, and glanced up to see Daniel, smiling at her in the mirror. He looked so handsome in his black suit and ruffled shirt.

"Almost ready, Mrs. Morgan?"

The very sound of the words thrilled her. Mrs. Morgan. For a long time, she had doubted it would ever happen, oh how she had doubted. But it had, and the three short weeks of their marriage had been ecstatically happy for her.

"How lovely to be Mrs. Morgan. I shall never tire of hearing it said."

"You better not. And speaking of lovely—that's exactly what you are."

She turned from the mirror to look at him. "Are you sure, Daniel? This dress—is it all right?"

"It's lovely, you're lovely."

She stood up and tried rather futilely to pull the bodice up higher. "It's not too—you know. . . ."

"It's not too anything. C'mon, we'll be late."

After she had picked up her cloak, he escorted her out of the bedroom suite, along the upper hall and down the staircase to the foyer. And that was part of her happiness, too, this house, how grand, how lovely, so perfect in all ways. And now it was her home. There were times such as this when she felt she ought to pinch herself.

Joe was waiting for her and Daniel by the doorway. He had grown in the months at Aurial and filled out and he looked very fine in his red uniform. When he came to Aurial with Glenna, he had known nothing about horses and livery, but he had worked and studied hard, for there was in his eyes no possibility of his mistress riding with anyone but him. Indeed, he made it clear that no one else would care for Glenna. Thus, he was a very busy man, alternating between coachman and butler, groom and servant. But he would have it no other way.

"You have the brougham?" Morgan asked.

"Yessir, all polished and ready."

Glenna smiled at him. Among his other amazing accomplishments had been his improved English. She had an idea he had worked very hard at it.

"You look handsome in your uniform."

"Thank you, m'am." Then a broad, impish grin spread his cheeks and he said, "You pretty, too, Missy."

While Glenna laughed, Daniel shook his head. Sometimes this young Joe took too many liberties, but he had to admit he was comfortingly loyal to his wife. He knew this black boy she had rescued from slavery would walk the fires of hell to keep her from harm and that was good to know when he was away from Aurial. And he was bright, a quick learner. He was already becoming an expert with the horses.

Daniel helped his wife into her heavy cloak, for it was early January, quite cold in southern Maryland. They stepped outside and into the brougham. Joe climbed to his seat in front and flicking the whip, set the matched team, eager to move after standing in the cold, into a spirited canter.

Glenna snuggled against Daniel, slid her arm under his and clasped his gloved hand in hers.

"Cold, dear?"

"No, I'm snug."

In their contentment, there seemed nothing to talk about, so Glenna leaned her head against his shoulder, listening for a time to the steady rhythm made by the horses and the wheels of the carriage. And, as so often happens between two people in love, his thoughts turned to the same direction as hers.

Even he had long since stopped trying to figure why he persisted in his search for Glenna. For weeks, so many he had lost count, although MacDoul hadn't, they had prowled the West Coast of Africa, stopping any ship to seek information, sending landing parties ashore at every likely spot to ask questions and leave money and promises of more if any shred of information was forthcoming. But there had been nothing, not a word. A white woman in the jungle. Ridiculous. Unthinkable.

When the rains came in June, Daniel's mind told him that it was hopeless. He knew he was straining MacDoul's patience. He knew how eager he was to get on with some real sailing and make some money with the ship. But Daniel had been unable to let go. Just one more day, one more inlet.

When he'd seen her in the clearing and then lost her, he had become convinced that his eyes had played tricks on him. He had seen what he wanted to see. Then that black boy had stood up and shouted to them. Thank God for that.

The girl he had pulled from under the log was a mere shadow of the girl he had known, loved and sought. She was as thin as a ghost, scratched, bleeding, covered with sores from insect bites, burning up and crazed with fever. He wasn't even sure she had recognized him before she passed out.

They hustled her aboard the *Chesapeake* and put her in the bunk in his cabin. Again he was to nurse her back to health, but this time he had grave doubts of his success. She was literally burning up. She seemed to be sinking, for she lacked the strength to combat her illness. In increasing panic, he realized he might have found her only to have her die.

It was Joe who again saved her life. Morgan had paid scant attention to him. He had just come along on board. It was MacDoul who looked after him, heard his story and knew what he'd done. And it was MacDoul who finally insisted on bringing the boy to the cabin where Glenna lay dying. Tears streaming down his black cheeks, Joe had insisted the jungle men had a medicine for the fever. He begged Morgan and MacDoul to turn the ship around. He would find medicine for the missy. He had saved her once and he would again if they would only let him.

In desperation, willing to try anything, the ship returned to Africa, anchoring where a patch of jungle was visible. Joe had gone ashore with MacDoul and returned with cinchona bark. He had personally dried it and mixed the bitter fluid. Glenna's recovery had begun at that point, although she had remained weak and suffered recurring attacks of fever for many months.

When her fever had broken and Glenna had opened her eyes to see Daniel slumped in the chair, asleep as so long before, her first thought was that she was in heaven. And at that instant, so attuned was he even to the sound of her breathing, he awoke, sat up and saw her eyes open.

"Oh, my Glenna," he said.

"Daniel, is it really you?"

And he rushed to spread his arms around her and smother her face with kisses. "My darling, my darling, thank God you're all right."

It was not possible, she knew, for any human being to be more attentive, thoughtful and caring than he was during that voyage to Maryland. He catered to her constantly, forcing more food and liquids down her than she could possibly swallow, taking her on deck for the sun, talking to her, reading to her, laughing with her, telling her constantly how much he loved her and how glad he was he'd found her again. The others joined in, Cap'n Mac, the sailors, bringing her little presents, doting on her constantly. She felt wrapped in a cocoon of love which was, she knew, rapidly blotting out her painful memories.

They had landed at Baltimore, a large and beautiful city to her, topped by a high monument on a hill. It was the first monument erected to George Washington, Daniel told her. He had taken her by carriage to Aurial. The sight of it took her breath away. The plantation sat on the point of a triangular piece of land where the broad Patuxent River met the wide mount of Short Creek. The house sat on high ground on the west shore overlooking water on three sides. The main house looked huge to Glenna, built of stone and brick—built to last Daniel had said—painted white with a wide veranda graced with three-story wooden columns along the front. A little distance from the house were barns, sheds, stables and other buildings, for Aurial was a working plantation, worked by free men, not slaves. Glenna had been so glad for that and so proud that it was Daniel's greatest pride. A white fence surrounded the whole estate, running for what seemed miles along the mail road. With the plentiful trees and wide green lawns, the carefully tended flowers and fields, Aurial seemed a fairy tale to Glenna.

She had expressed her delight over and over—much to *his* delight. And with pride he had shown her the house and loved every second of her pleasure. It was a large house, built for many people, spacious, yet homey, a home to be lived in as a home. Glenna had exclaimed over the furnishings, some of which had been brought over from England by Morgan ancestors almost two centuries before.

That evening, as on many evenings to come, Daniel escorted Glenna outside to sit on the veranda. It seemed to her it must be the peace of heaven, the quiet enlivened only by the songs of birds, the rustle of leaves and the gentle lap of the rivers as they swept their stately course to join in front of the house.

"That's the Baltimore Oriole's song," he said.

"For whom Aurial was named—if misspelled," Glenna said, smiling. "How lovely it is." She saw the trees, maples and elms mostly, reaching almost to the water's edge, and the small boat dock, and the opposite shore of the Patuxent, already beginning to purple in the sunset. "It's all so lovely, darling. It must be the most beautiful spot for a home in the world."

Daniel laughed. "At least Kingston would agree with you."

"Who's Kingston?"

"Bradford Kingston, my neighbor, back up the road along Short Creek. He has never forgiven my forebears for getting to this spot ahead of his. I sometimes think he'd sell his soul to get hold of Aurial."

"He sounds menacing."

There was a scoffing tone to Daniel's reply. "Hardly. We manage to get along as neighbors, although there's no particular love lost between us. He doesn't care for me because I own Aurial, and I don't care for him because he owns slaves. Other than that we get along fine."

Morgan's return to Aurial had been marred by the news of his father's death during his long absence. The necessary mourning, plus Glenna's recurring bouts of fever had forced a delay in their wedding until just before Christmas, 1830, more than four months after her arrival at Aurial.

Glenna had not told Daniel everything that happened. She told him of the pasha, the herdsman, Mohammed Ibrahim and Youssef and of the Shinome tribe and of her pain and suffering, but not all they had done to her. She had been kept from it by her shame, the painfulness of the memories and her certain conviction Daniel would not want a woman as used and soiled as she. If he had asked, she would not have lied. She would have found some way to tell him. But, mercifully, he did not ask. Rather, he conveyed to her with his arms and his lips, his tender concern, that all her suffering was behind her and that all he cared about was her return to him.

Still, he did not try to make love to her. For a time, she was grateful. She simply was not ready for that with anyone. And she understood his legitimate grief over his father, his remorse that he had not been there when

his father needed him. And, too, his solicitousness told
her of his worries about her weakness and recurring
fevers.

With time, however, these reasons began to wear
thin. She wondered if they weren't excuses. In moments of depression, particularly when she could feel a
relapse of the malaria coming on, she wondered if he
really loved her. Or was he marrying her out of pity, a
feeling that he ought to? Was he in love with the
memory of the love they had once had? Worse was her
nearly incessant fear that Daniel, indeed no decent
man, could want a woman who had been soiled as she
had. As her wedding day approached, she was in a state
of near panic.

Theirs was a small, but lovely wedding in the great
living room at Aurial. The huge fire burned warmly.
The room was brightly lit with candles and filled with
flowers. She wore a white gown of silk and lace and was
given away by a beaming Cap'n Mac, who also acted as
best man to Daniel, while the happy crew of the
Chesapeake joined a few neighbors in the audience. As
she knelt beside Daniel to hear the priest's prayers, she
had for just a moment felt something akin to the state
of grace in the jungle. Silently, her lips barely moving,
she had given her personal thanks to the Blessed Virgin
who had saved her.

The wedding dinner had been generous and fun,
replete with banter and boisterous tales of pirates and
rescues. Glenna had participated, dancing with nearly
all, and had enjoyed it, yet the party had seemed an
eternity, fear clutching at her like a steel claw. In truth,
MacDoul, ever sensitive under his heartiness, had
gathered up his men and left to continue the rousting
elsewhere shortly after ten o'clock. The other guests
departed soon afterwards. The servants, importuned by
Joe, scurried to clean up quickly.

By eleven they were alone. Quietly, he poured two
glasses of champagne and gave one to her. Standing by
the fire in this house they both loved, he toasted their

love and their marriage. Then he toasted her as the new mistress of Aurial, the best and most beautiful of all. He had kissed her then, warmly, passionately and she had felt the desire rise within her. But he had kissed her many times, and she had felt desire many times. What did *he* feel? Why hadn't he touched her? Was this all a sham on his part?

They went upstairs then, each to their separate but adjoining suites. She took off her wedding dress and folded it neatly to be put away, then donned a gown, white in color, of sheer silk and lace. She went to her mirror and brushed her already shining hair waiting for him to come. She saw her reflection in the mirror and knew she was beautiful. She had regained her figure. Her complexion shone with the inner luminescence of old. She saw her breasts straining against the thin fabric, the touch of pink amid the lace. She would excite him, she knew. She knew all about exciting men, she thought bitterly, all about lust. But would he want *her,* Glenna O'Reilly, now Glenna Morgan, really, truly her, as a person? Would he love her as he once had? As she brushed and brushed her hair, the sinking feeling in the pit of her stomach gave its own answer to her questions.

He came to her finally, dressed in a dark blue robe. He carried two glasses of champagne. Why all this wine? He was just trying to put it off as long as possible. She set down her brush and accepted the glass, smiling as she did so, then looked down at it, twisting the stem within her fingers, using it as an excuse to avoid looking at him.

"Glenna. . . ." His voice sounded strangely forced, hoarse, as though it were difficult to speak. He cleared his throat nervously. "Glenna, once before I helped to wash away your pain and memories, and I want to again, more than anything I've ever wanted in my life. But it was so easy then. We were alone in a small cabin on a tiny ship in a great ocean. I bathed your wounds and put salve on them to heal you. What happened between us was so natural, so inevitable. I really don't know how it happened. It just did—and I lived a long time in the memory of that."

She heard the earnestness in his voice and raised her head to look at him, his face swimming through her tearful vision. He looked so serious, so like a little boy making a confession of wrongdoing.

He looked down at his feet. "It is not the same now. I don't know what to do. I feel strange, stiff—" He raised his head and smiled ruefully at her. "—like a groom is supposed to feel, I guess."

And Glenna smiled, too, through her tears.

"But I do love you, Glenna. You are so beautiful, it wounds me to look at you. I want you, Glenna. I've always wanted you. I sailed that Goddamn coast beyond all sanity because I was unwilling to give you up. I want you, Glenna. I want you. I don't care or want to know about others. None of that matters. I want you, just you, only you, forever you."

She stood there a moment, looking at him, tears coursing down her cheeks, throat aching, feeling the last of her pain and suffering and fear peeling away from her forever. Then, as the sobs reached her, she was in his arms, his mouth on hers, salty with her tears. She couldn't stop crying. She just couldn't. The tears came out of her like some inexhaustible well, as he removed her gown and caressed her and said over and over how beautiful she was and how much he desired her, even as he buried his face, wet with her tears, in her breasts. And she cried, all the torturous months of suffering coming as streams from beneath her eyelids, as he carried her to the bed and loved her and loved her and loved her. And she cried as he caressed her over and over, and cried as her own desire for him rose, and cried with joy as he gently entered her and she knew she was still a whole woman, and sobbed out her ecstasy as her passion exploded within her, even as his did for her.

She continued to cry long afterwards, as he held her in his arms, patting and caressing her, their flesh intertwined, his hers and hers his. Finally, she was able to speak. "Daniel Morgan, when you said you wanted to wash away all that had happened, I didn't think it would be with my own tears."

Now, snuggled against him in the carriage taking them to Washington, she heard him ask, "Happy, dear?"

She raised her head and smiled at him. "Does an Oriole sing?"

He laughed and put his arm around her. Again she listened to the music of the horse and carriage, feeling, enjoying, relishing her peace and happiness.

"Glenna, I need to say something to you. I hope you'll understand."

He sounded very serious. "Try me."

"You know nothing that happened to you matters an iota to me. You do know that, don't you?"

"Yes."

"But there are people, I'm sorry to say, who will misunderstand. There are gossips, many of them, who thrive on scandal. President Jackson was a victim of their evil tongues. He married his beloved Rachel, then a question arose about her previous marriage. He remarried her to have everything legal. Forty years later, the gossips brought up that incident, accusing her of adultery. She overheard the remarks as she was shopping for her inaugural gown. It upset her so she died shortly thereafter, never living to see her husband become President. Old Hickory was and is heartbroken. He loved her so much. He still carries her picture in a locket over his heart. He hates gossips and so do I."

"Yes." But in truth, she did not understand what he was getting at.

"And you know there is slavery in America—that damnable institution. It will destroy us some day. We have the most inhuman form of slavery in the world, for we hardly treat the slaves even as human beings. To be black in our white society is to be almost sub-human.

Coming from Ireland, I don't think you understand the depths of racial prejudice in this country."

"Yes, dear, but what are you trying to say."

He hesitated. "All right. I'm trying to say I don't think you should tell anyone, not the President, not our friends, no one about what happened to you."

She laughed. "Is that it? You needn't worry. I hardly want to even think about it, let alone discuss it."

It was as if he hadn't heard her. "I realize you must say something. Just tell people you were kidnapped by pirates, taken across the desert and escaped. Tell them about the camels and the sand, but leave the rest out."

"I'd like to leave all that out, too."

"Above all, don't tell them about the sultan's harem and the jungle tribe. That could lead to trouble."

Glenna, who thought him very silly to worry, said, "Darling, have no fear. I just can't imagine whom I'd ever want to tell it to."

"It's just that these gossips, these slanderers are so terrible. The less they know the better. I wouldn't want your reputation besmirched. I wouldn't want you hurt by these clattering tongues."

Glenna patted his chest and again thought him very silly. "Yes dear. Don't worry."

"Look what they're doing to poor Peggy Eaton. Just ghastly, I tell you. I've met her. She's a lovely, charming woman, full of life and vitality. But the tongues are wagging just because she grew up in a tavern. I've been there, the Franklin House, a most respectable place. President Jackson himself stayed there. Peggy O'Neale was her maiden name and she was friendly and vivacious. She used to sing and dance to entertain the customers. She was a marvelous mimic. I saw nothing wrong with it."

"Did you say Peggy O'Neale? Was she Irish?"

"Yes, as a matter of fact. Almost as lovely as my Irish girl," he said, feeling her snuggle deeper against his shoulder. "Well, all the talk started. It was claimed she was dispensing more than amusements to the guests, but there never was a word of proof of it. It got worse after she married. Her husband was some kind of sailor, away a lot. She became friendly with Jackson and his best friend, John Henry Eaton, his fellow senator from Tennessee. My, did the tongues wag. When her husband died at sea, Jackson insisted Eaton marry Peggy O'Neale. It seems to be a happy marriage, quite a delightful one.

"But, oh, the scandal. The so-called better ladies of Washington refuse to accept her. Mrs. Calhoun, the Vice President's wife, refuses to speak to her. Emily Donelson, the president's niece and official hostess, won't have her in the White House. All Washington is up in arms over her, snubbing her constantly."

"That's terrible dear."

"Well, Old Hickory is showing them. He's getting even for what they did to his Rachel. He not only has appointed John Eaton his Secretary of War, but he's insisted on having Peggy to the White House and even sat her on his right at official dinners. How's that for showing them?"

Glenna only half listened to Daniel's story. She loved hearing his voice and loved his tales of the White House and official Washington, but something he said reminded her of her suspicion that she was pregnant. The thought of it filled her with happiness, particularly when she realized how fortunate she was not to have it happen when. . . . She couldn't even finish the thought, so horrible was it to contemplate. Involuntarily, she shuddered.

"Are you cold dear?"

"No, I'm fine."

Yes, she had been lucky. The child would be Daniel's perhaps conceived on their wedding night. How wonderful to have had it happen then. It was still too early to tell for certain. Against the fabric of his coat she smiled to herself. Wouldn't he be surprised and delighted when she told him. But not yet. She'd wait a little while longer.

26

In January, 1831, Washington, D.C. was anything but the most attractive city in the United States. Indeed, built on marshy soil beside the Potomac River on land given jointly by Maryland and Virginia, Washington probably ranked as the least livable capital in the civilized world. It was hot and mosquito infested in summer, isolated and lonely the whole year around. No wonder a French diplomat lamented, "My God! What have I done to be condemned to reside in such a city!"

In its first half century of independence, the United States had made progress toward building a suitable national capital, but not nearly enough. There had been long wrangles over obtaining the land and agreeing on suitable designs for the city and its principal buildings. Progress had been severely retarded when the British sacked the capital in 1814, gutting the White House by fire and damaging the Capitol. Congress appropriated money for improvements, but often in a most niggardly fashion. All this reflected the national ambivalence, as Americans were torn between their desire for an attractive national capital and their fear of engaging in pretentiousness which smacked of monarchy.

The Washington Glenna and Daniel drove through that evening had not a single paved street and no sanitation at all. Even in winter the whole place stank and in summer it was so rank as to be unbearable. The principal landmark was the Capitol. It had just recently been completed more or less along the design of William Thornton. There were two wings, one for the Senate, another for the House of Representatives. For years, wooden planking had joined these two structures. Then in the late 1820s, a connecting portion had been built to house the Supreme Court and other offices. Atop it was a low dome, which in later hands would become the lovely rotunda of the Capitol. But in 1831, the structure merely had possibilities.

In front of the Capitol was an eyesore, the terminum of a canal hopefully but mistakenly built to carry traffic from Ohio and the West to the Potomac River. There was little traffic on it and the good citizens of Washington used it as a garbage dump, adding greatly to the miasma of odors and the various infestations. The main street was Pennsylvania Avenue. It was wide and potentially grand, but then it was fronted with a motley array of nondescript buildings, behind which stretched the "hidden city" of Washington, huts and hovels in which the black population lived.

At the other end of Pennsylvania Avenue from the Capitol was the Executive Mansion, its official name then. This was an attempt to avoid the unpleasant, very non-republican former name of "Presidential Palace." Most people simply called it the "White House" after its color. Much smaller than it would eventually become, although still far too grand and pretentious for the eyes of many citizens, it was a squarish structure with a columned portico in front. A low section called the south portico had recently been added.

The structure sat amid largely untilled land. It was surrounded by a small kingdom of shacks and outhouses, and a long railing where Treasury Department employees tethered their horses. The White House was devoid of plumbing and furnished with extreme paucity. Congress appropriated funds most sparingly and none at all if the occupant was of the wrong political party, as Jackson's predecessor John Quincy Adams had been. Most Presidents moved in some of their own furnishings and brought their own servants. Jackson was no different in doing this.

In her excitement and because it was after dark when she arrived, Glenna received a much more favorable impression of the White House. She saw only a large house, which it was, with large rooms warmed by numerous roaring fires and lit by a forest of candles.

Glenna was met by Emily Tennessee Donelson, niece of Rachel Jackson, whom the President had selected as his official hostess. She was then twenty-two, but looked even younger, blonde, lovely and charming. She was the mother of two children. Her husband, Daniel Donelson, was secretary to the President.

Andrew and Rachel Jackson had never had children, perhaps the great regret of his life. They adopted a son, Andrew Jackson, Jr., a handsome, gregarious young man on whom Jackson doted. But then he doted on nearly everyone who was young. During his tenure, partially in his loneliness and grief for his wife, he filled the White House with a host of nieces and nephews, an incredible number of whom were named Andrew Jackson something or other, and their friends. With their dates and romances, weddings and births, the White House was a festive place, full of young laughter, dancing and parties, most of which were financed by Jackson himself. He adored children, spoiling them unmercifully. As President he was often irascible, stubborn and imperious. His enemies called him "King Andrew." But among the young people who flocked to the White House, he was kindly, benevolent old "Uncle Andrew."

When Glenna first saw him, he was sitting by a roasting fire, a child on each knee, three others at his feet, reading a bedtime story. "Uncle Andrew will be with you in a moment," Emily said, smiling. "Nothing will keep him from his bedtime stories."

Glenna felt sure she had never seen anything so charming, and waited patiently until the story was finished and he had kissed the youngsters and sent them off with their mothers. The man who arose from the chair and greeted her was tall, six-one at least, and looked taller because he was so exceedingly lank. He wore a black suit, indeed always did, with a ruffled shirt and high collar, and a black armband to signify his mourning for his wife. He was nearly sixty-three years old and looked every moment of it with his thin, pinched face, deep wrinkles and shock of gray hair. His most prominent features were the high forehead, the proud beak of a nose, and deep blue, hooded eyes that seemed to reflect all his moods more quickly than any mannerisms or words. As he came up to her and took her hand in greeting, holding in his own cool hand overlong, patting it gently, she was aware of his powerful, magnetic presence. She was drawn to him, rendered quite in awe, a common experience of those who met him daily, let alone for the first time.

Jackson, the strong, imperious President, the Indian fighter, the general, celebrated duelist, the opponent of the National Bank and the South Carolina nullifiers, the man who told the Supreme Court to enforce its own orders, the President who threw the "rascals" of the "Virginia Dynasty" out of the White House and brought in the common people to stand on brocade settees with their muddy shoes at his inaugural and stood all of Washington on its ear by giving jobs to his supporters, was at heart a hopeless romantic. He had been so all his life, beginning with his courtship of Rachel and his efforts to help her divorce her first husband. In the White House he was an indefatigible matchmaker. He loved nothing quite so much as a pretty woman, unless it was the chance to defend her honor, as he had done with Peggy O'Neale Eaton.

"My dear," he said, patting her hand still. "I'm dumbfounded. I had no idea you were this beautiful. No wonder young Daniel here stayed away so long to search for you."

Glenna glowed, the color rising in her cheeks. "Thank you, Mr. President."

He leaned forward to whisper conspiratorially. "We have had some pretty young ladies here, but—don't breathe a word of it—you have got to be the prettiest ever."

Glenna smiled and could not keep from giggling. "Mr. President, what can I say?"

"You can begin by calling me Uncle Andrew. Mr. President is for the Whigs and my other opponents. Then you can come over here, sit down and tell me all about your incredible adventures—or should I say misadventures."

She was seated across from him by the fire, Daniel standing behind her. Rather quickly and with considerable brevity she told of her capture and the trip across the desert, her escape and fortunate rescue by Daniel.

"You are too modest, Mrs. Morgan. May I call you Glenna?"

"Yes, please."

"I think you are too modest. I have been in the wilderness myself. I think perhaps I have an idea how much you must have suffered. Three months across the great desert. You are a very courageous woman, Glenna."

His eyes seemed to bore into her and she felt uncomfortable. At a loss for words for a moment, she finally was able to say, "I think very lucky, also." And smiling, she reached up and patted Daniel's hand on the chair behind her.

"Ah yes, newlyweds, I almost forgot. Allow me to congratulate you both." He looked up at Daniel, smiling. "I have an idea it is you, young man, who is the lucky one."

"I couldn't agree with you more, sir."

They were summoned to dinner, sitting at a large table, the proverbial groaning board, covered with ham and fish, chicken, turkey and roasts. It was a family dinner with two dozen young relatives and friends chattering away. Glenna thought it a wonderful, warm, homey meal. The President sat her at his right and insisted she tell him all about the fabled city of

Timbuktu. He asked many questions and exclaimed to others what a remarkable thing it was to have visited it. If Glenna had ever enjoyed herself more, she couldn't think of when.

After a prolonged dinner, during which wine was served to the young ladies, stronger spirits to the men, the President escorted Glenna and Daniel to his private study, a small masculine room dominated by a large cluttered desk and warmed by a fire. After remarks about the room and glasses of sherry among the three of them, Jackson sat behind the desk near the fire and became serious.

"I have asked you both to join me here. Ordinarily, you and I would discuss this Daniel, but having met your lovely wife—and it does warm these old bones to meet such a lovely, courageous woman—I have decided she should join us. You don't mind do you, Daniel?"

"Of course not, sir."

"I have an idea that too often we men think this is a man's world. We tend too often to leave women out of men's affairs. And that is a mistake, I am thinking. We men have too often made a mess of things. Perhaps if we listened to the ladies more . . . Do you agree, Daniel?"

"I haven't thought of it exactly, sir, but as you say—" He hesitated. "The woman's point of view can only be useful."

Jackson laughed. "When you have been married longer, you'll be able to say that with more conviction. I hesitate to think how many times I would have made a fool of myself if Rachel hadn't helped me think better of it." He set his glass down on the desk, leaned back and folded his hands across his chest. "Ever hear of Texas, Daniel?"

"Of course, sir, the Mexican province."

Jackson nodded his head slowly. "Yes, the Mexican province, smack up against our Southern borders. It is an empire, Daniel, larger than all of France, and rich, incredibly rich, with fine soil, abundant forests, deer and buffalo as far as the eye can see, and only God knows what other resources. It is also becoming a problem. Unfortunately, the French never annexed Texas, so it was not part of that Louisiana Purchase Jefferson made. And wasn't that a great act by a good President? Texas remained part of New Spain and then Mexico."

"And you believe it should be part of the United States."

"It would be nice, Daniel, I'll admit that. Someday this country will stretch from sea to sea. I'm sure of that. Our people are already reaching into the Oregon territory. 'Course that is largely unclaimed land. But frontiersmen, trappers and farmers are already reaching into Upper California and New Mexico. And, of course, Texas. Our people are eager for expansion. I don't think you or I or anyone else can keep them cooped up east of the Mississippi.

"I see trouble ahead with Mexico. My secretary of state, Martin Van Buren, has made sort of informal soundings about our purchase of Texas. They won't hear of it. They want to keep Texas, although they don't want to do much in the way of governing it. The Mexicans profess to worry about American expansion, yet they turned around in '23 and gave Stephen F. Austin the privilege of settling three hundred American families on some of the richest soil in Texas. The number of settlers has now grown to several thousand people. Austin runs it like a proprietary colony and damn well. It's better run than most of the governments in our western states. He gives nominal allegiance to Mexico, but lies a lot to conceal the slavery practiced there, which is illegal in Mexico. In simple language, the Americans are beginning to chafe under Mexican rule. There's a lot of trouble brewing, I'm sure, and the last thing we need right now is a war with Mexico over Texas or anything else. What worries me the most is this. Some real firebrands, Sam Houston, the Bowie brothers, Davy Crockett, are making noises about going to Texas to liberate it. I like Sam Houston. He was one of the best generals who ever fought under me. But when he gets a notion about something, he doesn't give too much thought to the difficulties he causes other people. I'm afraid he wants Texas to be part of the United States and doesn't care a hoot how it happens."

Daniel listened attentively, wondering what all this had to do with him. Glenna was completely puzzled.

"I guess you're wondering what all this is leading up to. Daniel, I want you to go to Texas as my personal representative, talk to people, look over the situation, find out what is going on and more importantly what is most likely to happen in the near future, then report back to me."

Daniel heard the words with both dismay at what was being asked and pride that he had been offered the assignment.

"I know what I ask, Daniel. Believe me you can refuse if you think best. You were away over a year. You have your place in Maryland to run. You've just married this lovely lady and I can't blame you for wanting to enjoy that."

Morgan hesitated, then stammered, "I-I don't know what to say."

Jackson smiled. "I figured you wouldn't, which is why I asked this little lady to join us. Mrs. Morgan, would you be willing to part with your husband long enough to do a little chore for me?"

Glenna was looking down at her hands. The idea of Daniel leaving her again filled her with fear. She already had a dull ache just thinking about it. But she raised her head and said, "Mr. President, I mean, Uncle Andrew, how long would he be gone?"

"We'll send him down there by fast boat. I should think a few weeks should do it, not over three months. He'll be back in plenty of time to see the azaleas bloom at Aurial."

"Will it be dangerous for him?"

Jackson smiled, "Spoken like a good wife. No,

hardly at all. It's civilized country down there. He's in more danger walking across Pennsylvania Avenue, what with all these horse carriages."

"Why me?" Daniel asked. "Is there no one else to send?"

"Sure, but no one as good. I can't send anyone connected with the state department or the military. The Mexicans will read something hostile into it. The truth is, Daniel, I can't think of anyone as able as you or whom I can trust as well as you."

Daniel hesitated. "I would do anything you ask, sir, you know that. But Glenna caught some kind of fever, malaria I think, in Africa. She has these recurring attacks. I don't think I—"

"I'll be all right, Daniel. I'm much better, really."

There was silence for a few moments. Glenna heard the sound of a clock ticking above the mantle.

"I don't want to force you in any way, son."

Glenna knew both men waited for her to speak. She hesitated. She didn't want him to go. What would she do without him? She couldn't agree. But when she spoke she said none of this. "Daniel, if this is important and the President needs you, I think you should go. Three months isn't very long, after all, and I'll be quite all right."

Morgan looked at her a moment, then turned to the President. "Then I guess it's settled. I imagine you want me to leave right away."

"Yes, tomorrow if you can arrange it. And you, my dear, I want you to come live here in the White House while he's gone. You'll be a most delightful addition and I'll be able to look after you properly."

Glenna was flattered by the invitation, but refused. "I can't, Mr.—Uncle Andrew. My place is at Aurial. I want to be there."

"As you wish, but I intend to have you over here as often as possible. Such loveliness as yours shouldn't be hidden from view."

On the way home in the carriage, Glenna felt

strangely cold and huddled inside Daniel's arm. They rode in silence awhile, both full of their own thoughts. Finally Morgan said, "I don't want to leave you for a minute, Glenna. I should have refused."

"No, you did the right thing." She said the words, but they did not bear enough conviction to ease the growing ache she felt.

When they reached Aurial and were in their bedroom, Glenna in a light blue gown, sitting before the mirror brushing her hair, Morgan came to stand behind her. Looking at her reflection, she at his, he said, "I love you, Glenna. I don't know how I'm going to be able to leave you."

"Yes." It seemed to be all she was able to say.

Slowly he reached down and untied the bodice of her nightdress. It slid away from her shoulders into folds on the stool and carpet. He put his hands on her shoulders, then bent to kiss her neck. "There is no skin like yours, Glenna. I'll die for wanting to touch it."

"Yes." In the mirror she saw his gaze upon her breasts, the marvel and desire in his eyes. "They're yours alone, Daniel."

"Oh, darling." He reached down and covered her breasts with his hands, then cupped them from below, their fullness spilling over his fingers. "I love your breasts. I'll not be able to stay long from them." Slowly, he began to revolve his index finger over and around her flowered nipples, shooting sensation through her. She closed her eyes a moment, then opened them to see what pleasures her body felt.

"Daniel."

"Yes, my love."

"I want us to make love better and longer than we ever have before. I want it to be better than either of us ever thought possible. I want us to love and love and love. . . ."

She felt the upward pressure on her breasts and she rose in obedience. As she stepped around the stool, his hands encircling her waist, she quickly undid his robe and melted into his arms. Their kiss was long, soft, deep, passionate, lasting a long time. Breathless, she stood back from him, then smiled up at him, wonder shining in her eyes, then stroked his chest gently with her hand. "I love your body, too," she said, "more than you can know." She caressed his waist and then bent to her knees before him, her arms encircling him, the flatness of his back giving way to gentle curves beneath her hands. Her arms around him, holding him tight, she said, "After this night you'll never even notice those Mexican ladies."

"I do so like a jealous woman."

They spent the night at the well of love, dipping deep, pouring out, filling up. The first gray streaks of light were in the sky before they allowed sleep to come for two exhausted bodies.

27

Glenna was militant about remaining busy at Aurial, not wanting idleness to make her lonely for Daniel and cause the days to go by so slowly. She repotted every plant in the house and greenhouse and on warm days dug in the rose garden. She redecorated two rooms and made important revisions to improve the kitchen service. With Joe at her side, she visited the homes of every worker on the plantation, bringing small gifts of flowers for the women, cookies and candies for the children. Each day, except when it rained or snowed, she rode the spirited horse Daniel had given her and which she had named "Cork" after her home in Ireland.

In the evening she forced herself to read history and other books about her adopted country to learn more about it. And she wrote Daniel, almost nightly, not knowing if he would ever receive the letters. She now knew with certainty she was with child and rejoiced in that. She was tempted to write the news to Daniel, but thought better of it. He would only worry about her, and she was fine, truly fine.

In the third week she received an engraved invitation from the Executive Mansion inviting her ten days hence to a formal state dinner. On the back, in his kinky scrawl, President Jackson had written: "The affairs of state have regrettably forced me to neglect my promise to look after you. I hope you will attend. A lot of uppity diplomats will be there, and I want them to see what beautiful women we have in this country." She smiled in remembrance of the kindly man who had written that. Then she turned the card over to read: "Your presence is requested at a dinner honoring His Majesty King William IV's special Emissary Lord Oliver Penwood." Then she remembered. She knew him. The funny little man with the gout in Lisbon. Imagine his being here. Yes, she would go. Daniel would want her to.

Driven by Joe, she spent a day in Baltimore shopping for a dress and two more days with her maid Jessie, the one she knew Joe was making eyes at, altering it. The dress was made of a lovely blue silk taffeta and that is why she bought it, but aside from the waist being too large for her, the dress was too fussy with lace and bows. Fashion or no fashion, she liked her gowns to be simple. But after she'd removed it, Glenna saw that the lace on the bodice had a purpose. When she tried it on, she saw that half her breasts were exposed beside a deep cleavage.

"This will never do," she said to Jessie, trying in vain to pull up the neckline.

Jessie was only sixteen, but she had been born free to

free parents, and had lived in the security of Aurial all her life. There was nothing silly or obsequious about her. Glenna had noticed from the first a capableness, a maturity, a dependability to her. And she was pretty, with lovely brown skin, full soft lips and a slender figure of a young girl.

"I think it'll do just fine, Miss Glenna."

"Never, Jessie. It might be fine in Paris or London, but it'll never do in Washington."

"Oh, Miss Glenna, I do so wish I had your figure."

Glenna studied herself in the mirror, greatly upset for she had ruined the dress. "I'm not sure I like it very much right now."

"Please, Miss Glenna, wear the dress. It is so lovely. It'll do you a lot of good." She giggled a little. "I suspect old Washington will never be the same afterwards."

"That's what I'm afraid of." She continued to frown as she studied her reflection. Then she saw the invitation on the vanity. She picked it up and read the President's message again. He wanted to show off his beautiful women to Lord Penwood. She had seen him glance at her neckline approvingly that day at the White House. She smiled. Yes, this dress was what he had in mind. And so the decision of what to wear was made.

The affair at the White House was not a formal sit down banquet. Too many guests had been invited for that. It was a reception with food served buffet style. President Jackson and Lord Penwood received guests in the Blue Room and there was dancing in the East Room. "Uncle Andrew" greeted her effusively, saying he certainly could understand why Daniel had not wanted to accept his assignment. Bending forward, he whispered in her ear, "Your gown is just what I had in mind. I see that along with being beautiful and courageous, you can read an old man's mind."

"I fear it is too much."

"Of course it is. Shock these old biddies and

dowagers to death. Do 'em good. Give 'em something else to talk about."

After the receiving line disbanded, he insisted on taking her on his arm and introducing her to one and all, Vice President John C. Calhoun, Secretary of State Van Buren, Senators Henry Clay and Daniel Webster, many others. That night she met most of the great men in America and danced with several of them. She was ecstatic with happiness. If only Daniel were with her.

In the receiving line, she asked Lord Penwood if he remembered her. He looked at her closely, puzzlement on his face, then his gaze traveled briefly to her bosom. "Oh, yes, Lisbon wasn't it. I'm afraid I can't remember your name."

She gave her married name. "I'm Mrs. Daniel Morgan."

"Oh yes, I remember him, tall man, very well set up. And your name was—"

"Glenna. Glenna O'Reilly."

"Of course. You were from Ireland. We talked about Dublin, didn't we? How on earth did you get here?"

"It's a long story, milord."

"As soon as this bloody business is over, I want to hear every word of it. I shan't let you leave until you do."

And so, later in the evening, she sat on a divan telling Lord Penwood her story. "You don't mean it, Mrs. Morgan. You actually escaped from the Barbary pirates. I never heard of such a thing."

"Well, only for a little while. You see I was recaptured." She then told him of the caravan trip across the desert and of, as she put it, "making her way" through the jungle to the coast where her beloved Daniel found her.

"How extraordinary. I can scarcely believe it. You actually went to Timbuktu and made your way here. Utterly fantastic. Do you realize that as far as I know only one man has ever been to Timbuktu and back. A Frenchman, I believe. Can't remember his name. He was more dead than alive, I heard. Major Gordon Laing, an incredibly courageous fellow, had actually made it to Timbuktu, but was killed after leaving it. It is absolutely unbelievable that you, a beautiful young woman—" For the hundredth time, he looked down at her cleavage. "—could have made such a journey."

"I assure you it's true."

He laughed. "I'm not doubting you, Mrs. Morgan. It's just—well, you must appreciate my profound amazement. You must have suffered horribly."

Glenna bit her lip. Just remembering was causing her pain. "Yes," was all she said. In a moment, she thrust back the memories and smiled. "I wonder if you would do me a favor, Lord Penwood."

"Anything, my dear."

"I was not alone in the desert, at least for half the time. I had a companion a—to put it frankly, a fellow slave. She was English, Anne Townsend." Glenna's eyes filled with tears just remembering her, and she had difficulty speaking. "She was young and beautiful . . . a scholar. She actually spoke Arabic. She was the daughter of a clergyman living near Guilford, a Reverend Emanuel Townsend. She had studied to be a tutor and governess and was on her way to a post with the British ambassador in Egypt when she was captured by corsairs. She suffered horribly before and after we met in Marrakesh." Tears were openly running down Glenna's cheeks now. "She was the kindest, gentlest, most loving person I've ever known. I loved her deeply and when she died in the desert, I grieved for her terribly. I didn't see how I could go on without her." A sob ended her ability to speak.

Solicitous, Penwood handed her his handkerchief. "My dear, please. You mustn't go on. You are too upset."

Glenna dabbed at her eyes and in a minute regained her composure. Smiling wanly, she said, "I'm sorry. I do so hate tearful women."

"But your tears are for good reason."

"Yes, I think so. The favor I want to ask is this. Could you possibly locate Reverend Townsend and tell him of his daughter—she was his only child. Tell him how courageous and good she was to the end. Tell him that she is buried somewhere in the vast region of the desert. Tell him that I did my best to give her a Christian burial in an awful, heathen land."

"My dear, please—"

"And tell him that her grave is marked by the Southern Cross in the night sky. . . ." Glenna broke down and wept, unable to say more.

"My dear, my dear. . . ." Penwood patted her hand and made low, cooing sounds in an effort to comfort her.

In a minute or two, Glenna was able to compose herself and try to smile. Wiping her eyes, she said, "I must look ghastly now."

Penwood, relieved to have her crying over, laughed. "How many women would love to look as ghastly as you." Eager to change the subject to keep her from more tears, he said, "What I don't understand is how you escaped from Timbuktu. Surely you didn't go wandering through the jungles alone."

Still dabbing at her cheeks with a wet handkerchief, Glenna said, "No. The Arabs sold me to a jungle tribe, the Shinome, ghastly, beastly savages deep in the jungle. They held me prisoner, intending to kill me, cook me I guess, and make some potion of me which they believed would make them immune to white men's bullets."

"How extraordinary!"

"Yes, isn't it."

"How did you get away?"

"A young member of the tribe had lived for awhile with English missionaries on the coast. He helped me to escape and led me through the jungle to the coast, where my fiancé Mr. Morgan found me. The black boy is today my devoted servant."

Penwood was looking at her open-mouthed. "I am speechless my dear woman. This is the most extraordinary story I've ever heard. It simply astounds me."

Glenna smiled. "But it's all over now. I'm safe at Aurial, my husband's home in Maryland. I am befriended by President Jackson. I am even with my husband's child. I am the luckiest, happiest woman in the world."

"And without doubt the most beautiful and courageous."

They chatted for awhile and he asked about Aurial and her life there. She described the estate in glowing terms, and he said how much he would like to visit it sometime.

Before she could issue an invitation, he interrupted. "Say, I believe there is someone else you'll want to know. Seems to me we talked about him in Lisbon that time."

Glenna followed his gaze to a man standing across the room near the punchbowl. Her eyes widened in shock and disbelief.

"Shall I call him over?"

"No, never, please, please."

"Whatever you say, my dear. It's just that it's Lord Winslow. You said in Lisbon you didn't know him. I thought perhaps—"

"No, I don't care to meet him." She was struggling to gain her composure. She had seen Winslow look at her, but in passing. As their eyes met briefly, she saw no sign of recognition in them. Why should he recognize her? Why should he expect her to be here?

Then she heard Penwood droning on. "As you know, I don't care much for the chap myself. He's—"

"What's he doing in Washington?"

"Nothing official, I can assure you. He's quite out of favor with the court these days. Makes a bloody botch of everything he puts his mind to. I'm not sure why he's here. I believe he has something to do with railroads. Yes, I think he's representing some group in London that wants to invest in this new-fangled method of transportation you Americans are building."

Glenna left the reception soon after that and headed home. Winslow hadn't recognized her. It was better that he not be given a chance to.

28

Glenna was wrong. Winslow had recognized her. It had taken only a second or two—awareness that there was a beautiful woman, the sense of familiarity, the knowledge he knew her and finally memories of events in Three Oaks back in Ireland.

Close on the heels of the recognition came dismay, then fear. How had she gotten here, a ragtag Irish peasant girl now poised and elegant in the Presidential Palace in the United States? It wasn't possible. It couldn't be. For a moment he wavered. Perhaps he was wrong. Many Irish girls had black hair, blue eyes and fair complexions. But the issue had been decided when their eyes met across the room. He was careful to make a mask of his face, concentrating on the vacant, bored expression which was so useful among British upper classes. But behind the mask, he knew for certain it was her. And in the fleeting instant their eyes met, she left no doubt she recognized him. Her mouth came open and her eyes widened. These Irish wenches had no poise.

From the corner of his eye he watched her talking to that old fool Penwood. He saw her crying, the old fool patting her hand and consoling her. What were they talking about? Was she telling him about Ireland? God forbid. It couldn't be. He was in enough trouble already. There had been an outcry in the House of Commons about him. Liberal members had denounced him personally for his excessive cruelty in Ireland. One member had even cited the murder of Brian O'Reilly, saying a moderate force in Irish politics had been needlessly, stupidly, ruthlessly killed. Winslow had been recalled. He had denied the charges, for there was no proof against him. But he had remained suspect and had been relieved of his command.

Now, here, an ocean away was the girl who could provide the proof. He should have killed her when he had her in the garret. But how did he know that stupid American—what was his name?—would rescue her. She was a menace. If she told Penwood of what he had done, the news would be carried back to London almost immediately. He would be ruined. Fear gripped at his entrails.

He watched her leave the White House reception, much too precipitously. Who was she now? Hardly Brian O'Reilly's daughter. He had seen her being squired around by the President. He was fawning over her like she was his personal pet. So anyone would want her attention, but this was the White House and there she was with the President. He swore under his breath. She should have been killed when he had the chance. Winslow asked someone who she was. Mrs. Glenna Morgan. Then he remembered. The American had been Daniel Morgan, special envoy from President Jackson. Winslow swore again as an escape valve for the fear which gripped him.

He spent the next day in panic, pacing the floor of his hotel room, worrying about his problem and what to do. In the afternoon he rented a horse, asked directions and rode out to Aurial. He didn't ride up to it, but remained at a distance, looking at it a long time. The wench had married well. There could be no doubt she was in a position to do him great harm. Riding back to Washington, he knew he had to talk to Penwood. He had to find out what she had told him. And he had to find a way to neutralize this girl and whatever she might do or say.

Luck was with him. He saw Penwood that very night at a reception for him given by the Senate Foreign Relations Committee. Winslow forced himself to be patient, watching the old fool down glass after glass of wine and brandy. He would soon be tipsy, his tongue loosened. Late in the evening he went up to his fellow English peer.

"My dear Penwood, are you having a good time?"

The gouty old man belched slightly under his breath. "Oh, Winslow. Yes, indeed. These Americans are most hospitable."

Winslow smiled, his thin lips spreading, but no teeth showing. "So I've observed. Why only last night you were in the company of a most beautiful lady at the Presidential Palace."

Penwood, somewhat befuddled by drink, seemed confused. "Last night?"

"Don't you remember? You talked for a long time to a lovely black haired young woman?"

"Oh, yes, yes, Mrs. Morgan. Utterly charming."

Winslow knew the time had come to press him. "I couldn't help but notice she seemed very upset about something."

"As well she might. She told the most extraordinary story. Seems she was captured by pirates and sold into slavery in Barbary. Ended up in the sultan's palace, no less. She escaped, but was captured again, taken across the great Sahara to Timbuktu, if you can imagine, then sold to a jungle tribe. Most extraordinary."

"Indeed."

"She only escaped from there because one of the natives had once been befriended by some English missionaries. He led her through the jungle to safety. The fellow, once a savage, is now her devoted servant. Hard to believe, but I'm convinced it's true. The lady would hardly make it up."

"To be sure. And, as you say, it is not hard to see

why she was upset about it." He hesitated, uncertain how far to press Penwood. "Did she tell you anything else?"

"Of course. There was a great deal more to the story. She was most upset about an English woman who had been her companion. She died in the desert. Mrs. Morgan asked me to get word to her father, a vicar in Surrey. I fully intend to do that."

"Did she tell you anything about her . . . her background?"

"What is there to tell? She's Irish, I believe. Grew up in Dublin."

Winslow was inwardly elated. She had said nothing. Penwood knew nothing. But his face was a mask as he said only, "I see."

"You were in Ireland. Did you know her there?"

Winslow forced a smile. "To my regret, no. She is most attractive."

"Yes, she is that. Her husband has prominence in this country. She should do well here. Funny thing though. I seem to remember mentioning your name when I first met her in Lisbon. That was before all her adventures in Africa. Last night I intended to call you over to introduce you. She seemed upset and asked me not to."

"Entirely my loss, Lord Penwood. Perhaps she was tired or ill. I noticed she left the party rather abruptly."

"True. Doubtlessly that is the explanation."

Even as he talked to Penwood, a plan came to Winslow's mind. Instantly he knew it was right, in fact, terrific. She had not yet told Penwood of events in Ireland. But she would, inevitably she would. He had to so discredit her that anything she said would not be believed. And Penwood, the half drunken old fool, had given him the means to discredit her. Yes, indeed, he had.

Winslow, nursing his own drinks, waited close to an hour before Penwood, quite tipsy and on the verge of making a spectacle of himself, left. It was difficult for Winslow to be patient. He passed up several opportunities to act, but he knew it was best if Penwood were not present. He wanted none of this traced back to him.

He went up to two ladies, one of whom he recognized as having been at the White House party the previous night. Both women were middled aged. To him their calico gowns were ghastly, almost peasant costumes. Indeed, they looked like two middle aged farm wives trying to be elegant.

"Excuse me, ladies," he said, smiling and bowing. "I don't mean to interrupt, but I am most curious about this punch. It is most interesting. Would you happen to know the recipe?"

The taller, grayer of the women laughed. "I'm afraid I don't, but whatever it is, I'm sure it is generously doused with Tennessee whiskey. Much too strong for me, I'm afraid."

"Yes, it does have tang, but it is still delicious." He bowed again. "Forgive me, I should introduce myself. I'm James Charles Winslow. This is my first visit to America. I find it fascinating." He purposely avoided his title, knowing the egalitarian tendencies of Americans.

"Indeed! Such an honor to meet you," the older woman said. "I am Agnes Booth and my friend here is Janice Caldwell. Our husbands are Senators. They're around here some place."

"It is I who am honored to meet such charming wives of such distinguished citizens."

More pleasantries were exchanged. He told them of his interest in the new American railroad and answered the inevitable questions about how he liked America.

"Yes, indeed, I find your country most interesting. I've met the most fascinating people. Why just last night I heard the most fabulous story from Mrs. Morgan. I believe you were there, Mrs. Booth. You remember her, the lovely woman with black hair."

Mrs. Booth, the wife of the senator from Vermont, sucked in her breath. "Indeed, I do." She turned to her friend from Delaware. "She wore a scandalous gown,

Janice. Positively indecent, most revealing. I would not be caught dead in it in private, let alone in the Executive Mansion."

Mrs. Caldwell smiled. "Perhaps she has more to reveal than you and I, Agnes."

"She tells the most extraordinary story. Seems she was captured by pirates off Africa, then lived for a time in the harem of the Sultan of Morocco."

The ladies looked as though they had been struck. In unison they exclaimed, "Did you say harem?"

Winslow smiled. "So I understand. And that's not all, she was taken across the desert and sold to a tribe of blacks. She lived in the jungle with them for quite some time. Sort of a white goddess, I suppose." With delight, he saw the expressions of shock on the faces of his listeners. "I'm sure she didn't want to be there. Who would? But she became friendly with one of the natives. He helped her escape and is now her *devoted* servant. Quite remarkable story, wouldn't you say?"

Winslow never said another word about the subject the rest of the evening. He knew he didn't have to. In a half hour the whole room was abuzz with the delicious tidbit of gossip.

Glenna had tested her own feelings about Winslow. She had been shocked to see him again and that feeling had quickly given way to an intermingling of fear, anger, outrage and shame. But in the next few days she was happy to realize she had lost her desire for vengeance against him. She was merely glad he had not recognized her, for she knew all she wanted was to put the whole unhappy episode behind her and live contentedly at Aurial as the wife of Daniel Morgan, mother of his child. When would he come home so she could tell him? His occasional letters were loving, but gave no hint of his return.

During February, she twice received handwritten invitations from President Jackson, but refused both times. She had gathered from what Lord Penwood had said that Winslow was to be in Washington only a brief time on business. It was best to remain at Aurial until he left and not risk unpleasantness. There would be plenty of time to visit Uncle Andrew when Daniel returned. Besides, the fever had returned. It was only a mild temperature, but she was trying to ward off a more serious attack by getting plenty of rest.

It was in the first week of March, one of those warm early spring days which occur in Maryland, that an open carriage drove up the drive at Aurial and stopped. An attractive woman in her late twenties alighted. Beneath her bonnet, Glenna could see black hair, parted in the middle and combed straight down to frame her face and cover her ears. She had a generous mouth and large green eyes that were the liveliest and merriest Glenna had ever seen.

"I have wanted to meet you for such a long time," the woman said, smiling as she sort of bounced up the steps toward Glenna. "I have despaired of your ever coming to Washington, so I decided to come out here to see you for myself. Hope you don't mind. I'm Peggy Eaton."

Glenna extended her hand and smiled, while inwardly struggling with the name. Then she remembered, Peggy O'Neale Eaton, the scandalous wife of the Secretary of War whom Daniel had told her about. "I don't mind at all," she said. "I'm delighted to meet you. Won't you come in."

As Glenna escorted her guest into the house, there were predictable exclamations over its beauty. They sat in the small parlor, now bright and sunny, done in yellows during Glenna's recent bout of redecorating. "Would you like some tea? Lemonade, perhaps."

"Lemonade would be fine, dear. It really is a warm day, not that I mind after that horrible winter. Yes, I'd like some lemonade." She laughed, rather heartily. "And if you have some gin to put in it, I wouldn't mind that either."

Glenna gave the order to Jessie, specifying just plain lemonade for herself.

"I have to say it, my dear. You are every bit as lovely

as I've heard. Just stunning. There really is something about the Irish girls, isn't there?"

Glenna smiled. "That's right, you're Irish, too. Where from?"

"I was born in this country, but my father was from County Wicklowe."

There followed a lengthy discussion of Irish origins and Irish place names, during which the lemonade, one with gin, was served. Glenna found her friendly, jolly and ebullient, but was not really drawn to her. She could not quite put her finger on it, but there was a frankness, a toughness, even a touch of crass to her which Glenna found difficult to accept. Perhaps it was her years as a tavern maid which made her so.

"All I can say is that we Irish girls have to stick together."

Glenna was puzzled but said nothing.

"Yes, indeed, the old busybodies in Washington are giving us both a going over. Myself, I'm used to it. I don't give a hoot what they say or think. But I thought you might need a little cheering up. To be frank, President Jackson asked me to come over to see you, not that I wasn't eager myself."

Glenna's puzzlement deepened. "I'm afraid I don't understand."

"My dear, you must have heard all the talk."

"What talk? I don't know what you mean?"

"Good heavens, you mean you haven't heard? Where have you been?"

"I've been here, at Aurial, where I belong. What are you talking about?"

"That's what I'm talking about—the talk. All of Washington is agog with gossip about you. The old busybodies are telling the silliest, most absurd stories about your living in some sultan's harem and with some jungle tribe in Africa." She laughed. "As I hear it, they've even gotten you sleeping with your black servant who rescued you."

The blood drained from Glenna's face. Her hands

covered her open mouth in an involuntary gesture of surprise and shock. "Oh God, no!"

Peggy Eaton prattled on, unmindful of the effects of her words. "I don't believe a word of it, myself. Believe me, I know all about these Washington gossips. The stories they've told about me. I've learned to go about my business and pay them no mind. In fact, I sort of get a kick out of showing up and seeing their disapproval." Again she laughed and mimicked one of the gossips talking about her. "But I thought you might need a little moral support, so that's why I'm here."

Glenna had little memory of the rest of the visit. She hardly heard another word the woman said. As abruptly as courtesy permitted, she got Peggy Eaton back into her carriage and on the way back to Washington.

"You just keep your chin up, my dear. For my part, I'm going to tell everyone what a lovely, gentle person you are. You're a real lady."

"Yes, thank you."

How had it happened? How had it happened? Alone at last in the house, she asked herself that over and over. Then she remembered. Lord Penwood. She had told him about Anne Townsend, asked him to contact her father. She had been very upset. She had said too much. Oh God, no! How could she have? How could Lord Penwood have told anyone? How cruel of him. She was disgraced. Daniel was ruined, simply ruined. And it was all her fault. He had warned her. Oh God, what was she going to do?

The next days were a torment of worry, fear, tears and despair. She was unable to sleep or eat. She paced the floor almost constantly, weeping, her mind a tumult of remorse and panic. Jessie scolded her. "You gotta eat, Miss Glenna. You gotta rest. You'll be sick if you don't." Glenna was inconsolable.

Three days later, as she still frantically paced her room, Joe brought word that Lord Penwood had come calling.

"Oh God, no. I don't ever want to see him."

"He said he couldn't blame you if you didn't want to see him, but he said he was begging you to accept his forgiveness. He said something about a big mistake. He said he's going back to England. He wants you to know how sorry he is before he leaves."

Glenna sighed. Yes, it had probably been a mistake. He doubtlessly had not realized the harm he was doing. Again she sighed. "Tell him I'll be there in a moment."

She washed her face and powdered it heavily, but the talcum was inadequate to improve her gaunt appearance and red-rimmed eyes. Slowly, holding on to the banister to steady herself, for the sleeplessness and mounting fever had weakened her, she descended to the parlor. Lord Penwood had refused a seat, despite the discomfort in his gouty foot. He looked solemn, quite distressed in fact.

"You do me an honor I do not deserve in receiving me, madam. I truly did not expect you to. Few women would have the kindness, the generosity of spirit to do so. You are one of the most remarkable and courageous women I have ever known. You are more a lady, believe me, than many of those who bear the title in my country. I have, however unwittingly, caused you great harm. I could not live with myself if I did not muster the courage to come here and at least attempt to express to you my profound regrets for what I have done. I can only beg you to forgive a doddering old fool."

Glenna heard him out, her seemingly inexhaustible supply of tears again rising in her eyes. But she fought them, unwilling to cry anymore. "My regrets are for my husband, milord, a fine, honorable man to whose name I have brought disgrace while he is away in the service of the President."

"You have done nothing, madam. It is I who have brought you and your husband disgrace—I and that cad Winslow."

"Winslow?"

"Yes, an evil man and no gentleman. I could weep for what is happening to my countrymen."

"What did Winslow have to do with it?"

She saw him wince. "Would you allow me to sit? I fear my gout is—"

"Of course." She sat in a small rocker by the window, thus enabling him to take a place on the gold damask divan.

"I realized, of course, the sensitive nature of the confidences you did me the honor of telling me that evening in the Presidential Palace. Believe me, I have mentioned not one word of them to a soul—except one man. And that is how I know he is the root of this evil done to you. The next night after we talked, I went to a reception given by some senators. I fear I am not used to the stronger spirits you serve in this country. I became—I might as well admit it. I became more than tipsy. I was intoxicated. Thus, when Winslow came up to me and asked about you, my tongue was loosened and I regrettably, oh how regrettably, mentioned some of your experiences. As near as I can learn, Winslow, the cad, began telling the story that very night, exaggerating it, coloring it to demean your courageous acts. No tongue has been silent since." He shook his head solemnly. "And it is all my fault."

"No, milord, I was indiscreet. My husband warned me of just this, urging me to say little or nothing of my experiences. I disobeyed him. He is the one who must suffer."

"And it is I who was indiscreet. Of all the people to have told—Winslow."

"Yes. Lord Winslow has reason to want to harm me."

Penwood looked at her sharply. "Pray what is that? I thought you didn't know him."

"I lied to you about that. I did know him. My father is, or was, Brian O'Reilly. You English put a price on his head because he was a patriot and loved Ireland. We were forced to leave Dublin and hide out in County Cork. Winslow found us and sent troops, who killed my father. They also killed Liam O'Connell, a friend who tried to defend me. An attempt was made to rape me on the spot. But officers stopped that act and took me—I was quite naked—to Three Oaks, Winslow's headquarters. He inflicted indignities upon me in front of the man who was to become my husband. I was locked in a garret. He came to me, whipped me savagely, then raped me. Mr. Morgan came that night and took me out of the house to his ship. We stopped at Lisbon where I first met you. On the way to America, we were captured by the pirates. The rest you know."

Penwood's face registered his amazement. "My God, child!"

"I had never intended to tell anyone of my experiences, shall we call them, with Lord Winslow. He apparently feared I would. Hearing what you have told me, I have no doubt he stirred up this gossip about me to ruin my reputation so nothing I might say would be believed." She pursed her lips in resignation. "In that he has been entirely too successful."

"By God, madam, when I return to London the whole world shall know of him."

"I'm afraid it is much too late for that to be of any benefit to my husband or myself."

29

Winslow held the note in his hand, reading again the words of doom: "You, sir, are a cowardly cad. If I were younger, I would summon you to a field of honor. But I promise you I will do the next best thing. When I reach London, I will see that you are personally ruined. It will be a trifling punishment for what you have done to a fine young woman." It was signed "Penwood."

Yes, Penwood could ruin him. He could hear the talk in London, the debate in Commons. "Mr. Prime Minister, would you tell us if all your ministers whip and rape young women as part of the administration of your government's policies?" He would be a laughing-stock. His career was finished. He wouldn't even be able to show his face.

And that Irish wench had done it, damn her soul in hell. She would pay. Oh Lord, would she pay. He would personally choke the life out of her. He would hack her to pieces. He would rip the skin off her alive. He would cut out that tongue which had ruined him. In his fury, he broke up his hotel room, smashing lamps and mirrors, ripping curtains, overturning furniture. Exhausted, his chest heaving for air, he leaned against the doorway. She would die. He would kill her.

Yet, such was Winslow that even in his fury and fatigue, his mind was still functioning. He could not kill her himself. He was an alien in this Godforsaken country. He would be hanged for murder. But there had to be a way to kill her, some method that could not be tied to him. But what? He would think of it. That he knew, as surely as he knew the Irish bitch had not long to live.

The problem consumed him. He slept very little, his mind alive with ideas, all of which were rejected as soon as they occurred. Two nights later, as he was returning from a solitary meal, his mind filled with foolish schemes of how he could kill her and not be charged with murder, his taxi stopped at the edge of a large crowd in the street. It was some kind of demon-stration. There seemed to be a hundred or more men, many carrying torches, shouting angrily in support of some individual who harangued them in a loud voice. Winslow was annoyed at first at the delay, then began to listen.

"They don't think we know nothin'. Know-nothin's is what they call us. Well, we know a lot. We know there ain't no jobs, no food on our tables, no roofs over our head."

This brought loud cheers of support from the crowd.

"And we know why. Because the jobs are going to the damn Irish and Germans and Swedes, immigrants, ferriners, Godless Papists. Hell, the damn niggers got more jobs than we do."

More cheers.

"Who's building the railroads? You and me? Real Americans, honest men who fought and died for this country? Not on your life. I'll tell you who."

As one voice the crowd shouted, "Who?"

"Goddamn Irish Papists, that's who. Ferriners. Immigrants. Niggers. Are we going to stand here and starve while Papists and niggers get our jobs?"

A tremendous bellowed "No" erupted from the crowd.

"Are we going to get what's rightfully ours as Americans?"

"Yes!"

"Are we going to fight for what is ours?"

"Yes!"

"Are we going to get rid of Andy Jackson and the good for nothing Papists he brought here?"

"Yes!" The roar from a hundred throats was deafening.

A bright gleam came to Winslow's eyes, signalling an idea that excited him. Quickly he alighted from the cab and paid off the driver. He hung around the edge of the crowd for a half hour or so. When it began to break up, he pushed forward to grab the arm of the man he had heard speaking. "Excuse me, my good man," he said, doffing his hat. "May I have a word with you?"

"Who're you? A Goddamned Papist?" The man's voice was hoarse from shouting, but his eyes were bright with excitement and hatred.

Winslow smiled condescendingly. "Hardly, my good fellow. I'm as devout a Protestant as you. And I have some information I think might interest you—you and your justifiable cause."

"You don't look like one of us, you and them fine clothes. You got nothin' to say I wanna hear."

"My friend, I have listened to you for an hour. You strike me as a man who knows a great deal. If you will let me, I propose to make you even more knowledgeable."

The man's name was Stacey Bennett and he was a rising leader in what eventually would come to be known as the "Know Nothing" movement. At that moment, however, he was dumbfounded by this man and his language, little of which he understood. "You're a Goddamned limey," he said.

"That I am and I fear I can't help it. But I can help you. I can, for instance, tell you who is responsible for bringing these Papists here to build the railroad."

"Nah," Bennett said, shoving Winslow away. "I already know who it is, Andy Jackson."

"No, my friend. Another man who lives not very far from here is the one who went to Ireland for Jackson and recruited the very workers who're stealing your jobs."

"And who might that be?"

Winslow clapped him on the back. "Let's have a pint and I'll tell you all about it."

Bennett was dry and the thought of a free pint appealing. "And who be you?"

"My name, my good friend, is Jim Winslow." He was already learning the uses of American familiarity.

Over a pint and a second and a third at the Bull 'n Whip, Winslow told his man of Daniel Morgan. "I was there myself. I saw him recruit the workers for the railroad. Morgan is a Papist himself. And he married a Papist, an Irish girl. You heard of her. She's the shameless one who sleeps with her nigger servant."

The pints were doing their work. Bennett was aghast and then enraged to think he was out of work while people such as this took the bread out of his mouth.

"That's what they're doing—taking the bread right

out of your mouth and feeding it to niggers and Papists."

Bennett let out a sound closely akin to a growl. "Where be this Morgan and his nigger lovin' hussy?"

"They live not twenty miles from here."

Another growl. "God. To think. All this time and I never knew."

"And now you know. You ought to show them. You and your men ought to take those torches and burn them out. Show them who really runs this country."

Glenna knew she could cry no more. She had disgraced Daniel and there was only one thing for her to do. She must go away, someplace where no one knew her and she would never be found. Daniel would come back and she would be gone. He loved her, she knew. He would grieve for awhile, but soon he would be able to start a new and better life. People would forget. They would again speak well of him, say he hadn't known what sort of woman he had married. He would regain his reputation. She thought of the child she carried. If he never saw the child, he wouldn't love it. And she would raise the child to always speak well of his father.

Slowly she began to do the most difficult thing in her life, take a pen and paper and write to Daniel. He would receive it somewhere in Texas, wherever that was, long after she was gone.

"Dearest Daniel," she began. "I love you as I have always loved you, but I have disobeyed you and brought disgrace to myself, ruin to you." She saw the words swimming as she penned them. She was sure she wasn't crying. She couldn't cry anymore. Then why were the words so uneven and moving before her eyes? "I have done an unforgiveable thing. In telling Lord Penwood about Anne Townsend, I also told him. . . ." She went on to relate, in watery words, the whole story, including Winslow's actions. "I know he meant to harm me, but it makes no difference. It is I who was foolish and gave him the weapon to hurt me. But it is you who is hurt the most. There is nothing else for me to do but go away, far away so you can't ever find me, and leave you to rebuild your life and reputation."

Her throat ached as she wrote and her eyes burned, but she refused to cry. Slowly, with great difficulty—why couldn't she focus?—she began a new paragraph. "I have not told you because I did not want you to worry about me. I have been carrying your child for nearly three months. I am sure it will be a son. I will see that he grows up to love and respect his father, as I do." She gasped and cried out as she wrote the last words. Quickly she signed it, "My love always, Glenna," sealed and addressed the envelope care of Stephen Austin in Texas.

She held the envelope in her hand. Yes, it was the right thing to do. She must give it to Joe immediately to take to Baltimore so it would catch the next boat. She arose from her chair and took two steps toward the door. The envelope slipped from her fingers. "Oh, my letter," she said. As she bent over to pick it up, a wave of dizziness washed over her and she collapsed to the floor, blackness engulfing her.

Jessie heard her fall and rushed to her, Joe close behind. "Lord in heaven, she's burning up," Jessie cried. Together she and Joe carried her to the bed.

Winslow wished, as he had wished for few things in his life, that he had a company of the King's Guard under his command. It would be so much easier to dispatch a mounted troop and be rid of the Irish wench forever. But he had no command, and he was an alien in a country still none too friendly toward Englishmen. He had to make do with what he had at hand, and what he had were fools. To him, Stacey Bennett was the dumbest, most disgusting human being he had ever seen.

Yet, standing on the fringes of the crowd two nights

later, Winslow had to admit Bennett had a certain talent as a rabble rouser. His simple-minded logic could stir crowds, which had increased each night. "Murderer, that's what he is," Bennett bawled. "He's murdering our youngins, takin' the food out o' their mouths and lettin' 'em starve to death. Morgan is a murderer, I tell you, a murderin' Papist. Does he wonder where his next meal is comin' from?"

"No!" The crowd was thunderous in its response.

"Does he go hungry?"

Again a roared "no" from the crowd.

"You're damn right he don't. He lives out there high and mighty on his big estate with his niggers and his nigger lovin' wife."

Winslow was delighted with the references to Glenna.

"We gotta rid this country o' such people. We gotta get rid o' the uppity rich. We gotta get rid o' the Papists. We gotta get rid o' the ferriners that steal our jobs and those what brought 'em here. We gotta get rid o' nigger-lovin' women. We gotta give this country back to the decent, hard workin' folk."

Winslow loved it and had a certain grudging respect for Bennett's skills at oratory, but he wasn't fooled. He could stir up a crowd, but he couldn't lead it to action. A proper English mob would have long since marched off and burned out the Morgans. He quickly saw what needed to be done.

For the next several nights, he prowled the lower class taverns of Washington, studying the patrons and asking questions of barkeeps. "I'm looking for a big strong fellow to do a job for me."

"What sort of job?"

Winslow smiled. "The sort of job that needs a big, strong chap who doesn't ask too many questions and isn't afraid of a little trouble."

More often than not the answer would be, "You want Big Jud Purdy."

"Where might I find Mr. Purdy?"

"Mr. Purdy is it? He's too mean to ever be a mister. You'll find him at the Plowhorse, most likely."

The Plowhorse, paradoxically located near the riverfront, was sleazy, dank, littered with sawdust, rank with the odors of urine and vomit. Winslow had to steel himself even to enter it. He sat in a corner and ordered a pint of ale. There was a loud, boisterous group at the bar. Several of the tables were graced with drunks already passed out.

When the barmaid, a deeply pockmarked and clearly syphillitic woman in her thirties, brought his ale he inquired for Purdy.

"That's him over there." She pointed to the bar. "The biggest one."

He was indeed a giant of a man, well over six feet tall, with massive shoulders, bulging arms and a distended belly from too much ale. He must weigh twenty stones, Winslow thought. He could see a mass of black hair to his shoulders, but not Purdy's face which was hidden in the shadow of a wide brimmed hat. He did single out his voice, deeper and louder than the others.

"Would you see that Mr. Purdy and his friends all have a fresh pint. And ask Mr. Purdy if he would do me the honor of joining me when he has an opportunity."

The barmaid snickered. She had never heard such talk, but she complied.

A few minutes later, Purdy approached Winslow's table, towering over him. "You got somethin' to say to me?"

Winslow felt a crick in his neck from looking up at him. "I would like to speak to you, yes. I have a proposition for you."

"What kind o' proposition?" The voice was mean, hostile, suspicious.

"One you'll like, I'm sure. If you'll sit down, I'll tell it to you."

Purdy looked at him a moment. Winslow could see

his face now, bright black eyes under bushy brows, a wide slit for a mouth and an astonishing scar, purple and angry, running from his left ear almost to his mouth. It was a face of evil, but rather than being frightened, Winslow was delighted.

Purdy raised his leg over the back of the chair and sat down opposite the Englishman. "Let's have it."

Instinct told Winslow that this was not a man to fool around with. He had best get at it directly. Clearing his throat, he spoke, his voice little above a whisper. "There is a man who has done me great harm. I would like him burnt out, him and his wife killed."

Purdy didn't even blink. "What man?"

"His name is Morgan, Daniel Morgan. I will of course pay you handsomely."

"Where's he at?"

"He lives about twenty miles from here on the west shore of the Patuxent River. Aurial is the name of his place."

"All right. How much?"

Winslow was astonished. "You aren't going to ask why I want him killed."

"Ain't no matter to me. How much?"

Winslow suddenly realized he didn't know the going rate for this sort of thing. "What's it worth to you?" He saw the big man look him up and down and the glint of greed enter his eye.

"Five hundred."

Winslow's impulse was to agree to any price, but he knew he had to bargain if he was to control this man. He reached into his breast pocket and extracted his wallet. Counting quickly, he laid a stack of money on the table. "I'll give you two hundred now, two hundred when the job is finished." He saw the look in Purdy's eye harden, then give way to uncertainty. He looked at the money on the table, hesitated a moment, then picked it up and folded it into his shirt pocket.

"When you want it done?"

"The sooner the better."

For the first time Purdy smiled, revealing yellow

teeth. He started to rise. "Me and my boys'll get 'er done tonight."

"No. I have a plan I want you to carry out. There is a crowd down the street. It is led by a man named Bennett."

"That pipsqueak. I can pinch his head off with one hand."

Winslow smiled. "I've no doubt of that. But Bennett has a certain usefulness as an orator. It is important that this look like an angry mob burnt out Morgan. I want you and your bully fellows to join that crowd tomorrow night. I want you to do what Bennett can't. Lead that mob into action. Burn out Morgan."

Purdy smiled again. "That's easy. But we'll need horses."

Winslow looked at his man. He was big enough and cruel and ugly. He had no doubt that Purdy could with a word lead Bennett's mob off to the Morgan place. But what would he do when he got there? If any problems arose, did he have the brains to deal with them? And even as his mind formed the question, he knew the answer. Purdy, Bennett, none of these oafs could be trusted to make sure the Irish wench was killed. If he wanted something done right, it was best to do it himself. He couldn't remain in the background any longer, trusting to scum. He was going to have to take charge, lead these men. It was a risk for him, but having that woman dead was worth it. To Purdy he said, "I'll get the livery—and guns. Those we may need, too. I'll lead you there. And, Mr. Purdy, make no mistake. I'm in charge. You'll do exactly as I say."

The big man shrugged. "As long as I get my money, I don't care what you do."

"Fine." Winslow now smiled broadly. "And since you're so cooperative, I have a bonus for you. The Morgan woman is quite good looking, very beautiful indeed. I suspect you might have some fun with her before you. . . ." He drew his finger across his throat to signify his meaning and saw Purdy's yellow smile broaden as he did so.

30

The supply of quinine from the jungle had long since been exhausted, so Jessie, acting on instructions from the doctor, applied cool towels to Glenna's body until her fever came down. But it did not disappear entirely and Glenna remained very weak. She was also a difficult patient.

"I got to get up, Jessie. I got to go—now."

"Yes, Miss Glenna, we go, but not now. Tomorrow. You're still too weak to go anywhere." She enforced the words by pushing her mistress down into bed and pulling the covers high against her chin. "You listen to Jessie, Miss Glenna. You got to get well."

"But we have to hurry. There's no time to lose."

"I know, Miss Glenna, but tomorrow will be fine."

Glenna closed her eyes, then abruptly opened them. "Have you packed my things? Are you and Joe ready?"

"Yes, Miss Glenna. Now you just rest."

"It'll be a long trip, but don't take too much."

"Yes, Miss Glenna."

She had packed nothing, nor had Joe. He had eavesdropped on Glenna's conversation with Peggy Eaton and Lord Penwood and had tried to explain the problem to Jessie as best he understood it.

"It's bad trouble, Jes, real bad. Seems the missy told the fat old Englishman about what happened to her in Africa, being in the jungle and all. He told somebody else and now all Washington is saying she is a bad woman. They say she even sleep with me."

Jessie was aghast. "They ought to have their tongues cut out for saying such a thing."

"Taint her fault what happened. She couldn't help it."

"I know that and you know that. Mr. Daniel knows that, too. Then why does she want to leave so bad?"

"She thinks she brought shame to Mister Morgan. If she goes away, it be better for him."

Jessie shook her head. "That's silly. We're just going to have to find a way to keep her here till Mr. Daniel gets home. Everything be all right then."

"It won't be easy."

"I know, but you just let me handle Miss Glenna. She's not going nowhere."

And it wasn't easy. Glenna even got out of bed, berated Jessie for not starting the packing, and began it herself. But she tired quickly and allowed Jessie to put her back in bed while Jessie promised to get on with the packing.

With Glenna ill, the house had been particularly empty and quiet, which gave Joe an uneasy feeling. He could not identify what was wrong, but increasingly he sensed that something was. "I got this feeling, Jes. I don't like it."

"What feeling?"

"I dunno. Something's not right. Trouble's comin', maybe."

"We already got trouble."

"I know. Maybe that's it, but there's something more. I can just tell. Maybe we ought to pack up the missy and take her away somewhere."

Jessie scoffed. "Don't be silly. Mr. Daniel would kill us if we did."

But Joe's uneasy feeling would not go away. It caused him to be wary, careful, always on guard. He found himself unable to sleep much. Frequently he got up at night and prowled the house to see if everything was all right. Thus, he saw in the early morning hours, the flicker of lights far down the road. He watched them grow nearer. Torches. That's what they were, torches. In a moment he realized they were being carried by men on horseback. He couldn't see the men or horses, but the speed of the approach could only mean that. From his third floor window he watched a moment longer and calculated from the light that they were passing the Kingston place. They could only be coming here.

Quickly he ran to awaken Jessie. "Men coming on horses. Bad trouble. You get Missy and get her dressed. I'm getting the horses."

"But—"

"No argue, Jes. Do as I say—*now*."

He ran back to his room, pulled on his trousers. Shirttail flapping, he ran out of the house toward the stable. As quickly as he could, he saddled three horses, including Glenna's mare Cork. He led them to the back of the house and tethered them by the kitchen door. Then he ran around to the side of the house where the road was visible. The riders were now much closer. He could see the flicker of the torches and hear the rumble of hoofs against the packed dirt of the road. Many horses, being ridden hard.

Fear rose in him, but he did not panic. Rather, the coolness and cunning he had possessed in the jungle returned to him. He knew what had to be done without thinking. He had to save Glenna, as he had in the jungle.

He ran behind the house and into the kitchen. The other servants, awakened by Jessie, were there, and he was greeted by a hubbub of questions. In the near darkness, lit only by the small flames from the banked fireplace, he raised his hands. As he spoke his newly improved English deserted him. "Men come on horses. Bad trouble. Make no light, no sound. Go wake men in cabins. All go woods. All safe there."

"But we'll fight them."

"No. Do as I say—and hurry."

"What about Miss Glenna?"

"Jessie and I take her away. She be safe. Now go, hurry." As punctuation he dashed up the back stairs three at a time.

Jessie did not yet have Glenna fully dressed, mostly because Glenna, half awake, feverish and confused, was of little help to her. She seemed rather to be fighting Jessie.

"Oh, Joe, there you are. Maybe you can tell me what's going on."

"Men come, hard on horses."

"What men?"

"No know, missy. But we go—quick."

Glenna stamped her foot. "I'm not going anywhere until I know—"

"Please, Missy, no argue. Come quick."

She looked at him sharply then. He had the same wary eyes, the same pattern of speech. He had reverted to the jungle, where once he had saved her. "I'm sorry, Joe, I'm coming." She snatched up her cloak and threw it around her shoulders as she followed her two servants toward the door.

They went down the main staircase, hearing horses on the front lawn as they descended. At the landing, they stopped as rocks crashed through the main windows of the drawing room and parlor facing the front. She heard the shattering of glass and the thud of rocks against a wall, then a voice shouting, "Burn 'em out, men. Burn out the nigger-loving whore."

She recognized the voice, its upperclass refinement not entirely lost amid the high pitched shouting. "My God, it's Winslow," she said.

"Quick, missy."

As Joe pulled at her, she saw a flash of brightness through the open doorway to the drawing room. She gasped at the realization Winslow was setting fire to her beloved Aurial, but she did not hold back as Joe pulled her through the kitchen and out the door to the horses. As he helped her mount Cork, he whispered, "Real quiet, Missy. Make no sound."

As Joe helped Jessie, not at all a horsewoman, mount and then climbed into his own saddle, Glenna heard Winslow's voice from the front of the house. "Some of you men get to the rear. No one gets away, you hear."

Joe turned his mount and began to lead the women, the horses at a walk, toward the grounds at the rear. "Hey, somebody's getting away." Glenna looked back to see dim shadows of men at the side of the house, pointing at them. Fortunately, they were on foot, a thought which entered her mind as she, Jessie and Joe spurred their horses to a full gallop.

They sped across the fields, Jessie holding on for dear life as the trio of horses leaped fences and raced across recently plowed tobacco fields. The horses at full speed, they plunged on for several minutes, leaving Aurial far behind. Then Glenna, whose Cork was the larger, faster animal and thus in the lead, reined to a stop. The others did the same, Jessie almost falling from the saddle in the lurching stop.

Panting, Glenna said, "Where will we go, Joe?"

In the darkness she heard him say, "No know, Missy."

"We can't go to Washington. There's no safety there. We must go north, toward Baltimore." She looked to the heavens to orient herself. The stars were still bright, but the first graying of day was beginning in the southeast. As she found the North Star and turned Cork's head to face it, she thought of Jessie. "Are you going to be all right?" she said to her. "It'll be a long, hard ride."

"If the horse can make it, I can hold on."

"Quiet, Missy."

And Glenna was quiet as she had been long ago in the jungle. She knew Joe was straining to listen and she did, too.

"They come, Missy. I hear."

"We have one advantage. We know the country and they don't."

"It'll be light soon, Missy."

Glenna was a good horsewoman, but the cross country gallop, over fences, across streams and through woods thick with underbrush, quickly sapped her small store of strength. Still feverish, she felt herself go dizzy in the saddle. More and more she had to hold to the pommel to maintain herself. But she kept Cork at as fast a pace as the terrain permitted. She would not allow herself to even think of stopping. This determination was enforced by occasional glances at Jessie, who was truly suffering in the unfamiliar saddle, yet went on gamely. She also knew Winslow was following and would never give up. She had told Penwood. She had ruined Winslow. He would never stop till he had vengeance. She should have realized that before and fled Aurial. Certainly, she knew it now.

Theirs was only a scant lead. As daylight spread over the Maryland countryside, they reined atop a slight ridge to look back. The sight was not comforting. There were forty, at least, perhaps fifty pursuers, their horses at full gallop. She calculated the distance between them at not much over a mile, certainly less than two miles.

She dug her heels into Cork and they sped on toward the north. As the wind swept against her face bent low behind the horse's neck, she tried to control her mounting anxiety about the men who were following. The thought nagged at her that she would not get away. Their horses would soon tire and how much longer could she force herself to stay in the saddle? But she thrust these thoughts aside. Poor Daniel. His beloved Aurial in flames. What she had done to him. He would never forgive her.

They lost a precious minute when Jessie was knocked from the saddle by a tree branch. She lay on the ground, her face distorted with pain from a twisted ankle. Joe dismounted and helped her back into the saddle. She smiled bravely at Glenna as they again raced northward.

Another mile, then a second, a third they galloped

under a bright but cool March morning sun. Glenna tried to calculate. They must have come twenty miles at least. Baltimore couldn't be more than ten miles further. Would the horses make it? And what would they do when they got there?

Then disaster came and Glenna recognized it. Cork threw her right front shoe. The mare ran on bravely, but Glenna knew it wouldn't last long. Winslow had as good as caught them.

Cork was courageous. She ran for as long as she could, standing as much pain as she could, but finally she slowed and then stopped, coming up lame. Glenna prodded the animal to go a few steps further into a shallow stretch of concealing woods, now just beginning to bud and leaf out. From atop a shallow rise, she turned in the saddle to look back. Winslow and his men were closing fast. She could see him in his black coat and hat riding easily at the front. She could hear the hoofs pounding through the grassy meadow. Her spirits sank. All was lost.

"Missy, you hear that?"

"Yes, I hear them."

"What is that sound?"

She started to say it was the horses, then she heard a different sound, a sharp, clear, piercing ping of metal. Her mind closed out the sound of hoofs, the wind in the trees, even her own breathing and heartbeat to concentrate on the new, strange noise. Ping. Ping. Again. Again. A regular sound.

"What is it, Miss Glenna?"

"I don't know, Jessie."

Quickly as she could, the others following, she forced the lame horse through the trees and up to the top of the rise. There, perhaps three or four hundred yards away at the bottom of the hill, was some type of encampment. She saw an array of tents, some sort of squarish four-wheeled wagons standing in a row, large workhorses and men. Some carried black rectangular pieces of wood, while others struggled to lift long, shiny rails. Still others swung heavy hammers against something in the ground. A fraction of a second after the hammer fell, she heard the clang of metal against metal. Then she knew what it was. "It's the new railroad."

"There they are. We got them now."

Without looking back, Joe nudged his horse next to Glenna's and pulled at her arm. "Come, Missy, my horse." In one leaping, turning motion she jumped to the back of his horse and the three fugitives, now on two horses, raced down the hill, Cork limping behind them as best she could.

31

Sean O'Mahoney was the first to see them. He had stopped to rest a moment, leaning against the handle of his sledgehammer and wiping his brow. As he turned to his left, his first view was almost a still life picture, the distance seeming to stop the action. He saw a pair of horses racing down the slope toward him, a third horse limping along behind, then a troop of mounted men bursting out of the woods in pursuit.

The whole scene seemed to stand suspended in time, then he realized the people on the two horses were being chased by the mounted troop. His instinct for the underdog made him choose up sides at once. Without realizing it, he began to cheer. There are few things an Irishman likes better than a good horse race.

In a few moments, when the horses were nearer, he realized the riders were two black people, one a woman holding on for dear life. Then quickly came the realization the lead horse bore two riders. By God, it was a white woman. His cheers grew louder and were joined by the other workers.

The first horses jumped the newly laid tracks and were reined to a halt. O'Mahoney, joined by other workers, ran up to them and helped pull the white woman from the saddle. He saw instantly that she was young, very pretty, almost out of breath and nearly ready to drop from fatigue. He lifted her down from the horse and held her as she sagged against him.

The pursuing horses stopped a few feet away, creating a cloud of dust. O'Mahoney saw there were perhaps fifty of them on lathered animals. They looked like rough types, but the leader, wearing black, seemed well dressed. "Who's in charge here?" he said.

Ben Drake stepped forward. He was of medium height, but so rail thin he seemed taller. His graying hair and spectacles gave him the look of a professional clerk, which he had been until the Baltimore & Ohio Railroad put him in charge of constructing the line from Relay, Maryland, west of Baltimore, to Washington, D.C. Laying track, which no one hardly knew how to do, keeping a schedule set down by the company officers, and dealing with these hotheaded Irish workers made it the hardest job he had ever tried. His entire reaction to the sudden appearance of the riders was annoyance. The last thing he needed was another interruption to put him further behind schedule.

"I am," he said.

Still mounted, Winslow spoke. "This woman and these two niggers are fugitives. We've been chasing them for miles."

None of this had much meaning to Drake, except that it was wasting time. "So?"

"I demand you turn them over to me." Winslow realized he sounded a bit too imperious. He tried to force a smile. "Then I'll thank you and we'll be on our way."

"That's all I want to hear. We got a railroad to build."

Winslow smiled, then motioned to Purdy and two of his men to get Glenna. In a second they had dismounted.

O'Mahoney was not buying it, not yet he wasn't. He had heard Winslow's accent and instantly bristled. A Goddamned English he was. He tightened his arm around Glenna. He saw the fear in her eye as she looked up at the mounted men. "Hold on a minute," he said. "What's this little lady a fugitive from?"

Purdy answered. "That's none of your business. Just hand her over."

Quickly O'Mahoney sized him up. A big one, but he was hardly a runt himself. He'd taken on lots of big guys. "This little lady don't look like she could do anything very wrong." To Glenna, he said, "What they want you for?"

"O'Mahoney, give them the girl and let's go back to work."

He had pronounced O'Mahoney's name as most Americans did, the accent on the wrong syllable, "O'MaHONcy. This was an annoyance which the Irishman found difficult to get used to. A man's name should be pronounced right. "Nothin's going to happen here until we hear from this little lady. You just catch your breath, honey, then speak your piece."

Despite her fever, fatigue and fright, Glenna had a sense of safety, of being home. This man, this big wonderful man with the black beard and deep blue eyes was Irish and from the sound of him a Cork man. She drew a breath and said, "Mr. O'Mahoney—"

She pronounced it the Irish way as O'MAhoney. A big grin spread across the Irishman's face and he turned Glenna to face him, holding her shoulders at arm's length. "Don't tell me you is from the sod?"

And Glenna smiled broadly. "I am that. Born in

County Dublin, raised in County Cork, where you're from I'll bet." As she spoke, she deliberately reverted to a Cork dialect, speaking rapidly, running the words all together. Her speech was unintelligible to the Americans and Winslow, but music to the ears of Sean O'Mahoney.

"You hear that O'Driscoll," O'Mahoney shouted. "She's one of us."

Still speaking in Cork dialect, Glenna told them, "My father was Brian O'Reilly. This man is Lord Winslow, and he shot him down in cold blood, then beat me with a whip. I escaped and he has followed me to kill me. He burned my husband's house. You can't let him have me and my servants, please."

"By God, they never shall," O'Mahoney shouted. "Right, lads?"

Their cheers voiced their agreement. All were Irish, most from counties Cork and Kerry, recruited to build the railroad as a result of Daniel Morgan's efforts.

"Ferriners, that's what they is. Papists stealin' our jobs." It was Stacey Bennett, still on horseback behind Winslow.

"I don't care what they are." Purdy strode forward and reached for Glenna. O'Mahoney stepped in front of her and swung his big fist. The fight was on. With a roar the Irish surged forward, pulling men from their horses into the dust, swinging fists. It was a grand brawl. O'Mahoney had not had such a good time in weeks.

Winslow had turned his horse sharply as the men approached, and thus he remained mounted. He looked down at the melee in disgust, then tried to find Glenna. He saw her a little to the rear, the two blacks holding on to her. He'd get her himself. Spurring his horse, he reached her quickly and bent down to grab her, but felt the sting of a blow from the black man.

"Let her be, damn your hide." It was O'Mahoney running toward them.

Winslow knew he was no match for the big Irishman.

He turned his horse to face him, drawing his pistol as he did so.

In horror, Glenna saw the weapon, the barrel being lowered. It seemed to freeze there a moment, then she heard the loud report and saw the puff of smoke. She saw O'Mahoney stumble, then drop to his knees, his hand reaching to cover a spot of blood on his shoulder.

"Retreat men," Winslow shouted. "We got guns. We'll shoot them out."

Within an hour, the situation in the rolling hills southwest of Baltimore became bizarre and then nearly hopeless for the Irish workmen and the girl they were trying to protect. The Irish were on foot and armed only with their fists and what they could pick up to swing or throw. Winslow and his men were on horseback and armed with guns, not a lot of them, but enough to make it a most unequal battle. The Irishmen overturned the box cars to create a makeshift stockade around themselves. The cars made a barrier which prevented the horsemen from reaching Glenna. But it did not stop the riders from picking them off one by one. Singly and in twos and threes, Winslow would dispatch his men to ride up close to the barrier and fire off a shot from their pistols and rifles. Four of the workers were killed and five wounded, including O'Mahoney. There seemed to be no way to prevent the attacks. It was a hopeless situation and Glenna knew it.

"Sean," she said to the wounded O'Mahoney, "you're all going to be killed. I can't let it happen."

He lay on the ground propped up against the underside of an overturned car, its wheels offering a little protection. In his pain he still managed a grin. "Never you mind, colleen. We'll get out o' this. This is no trouble atall for an Irishman."

But Glenna knew better. She couldn't let these brave men die for her. Then she heard racing hoofs. She turned to see the face of the rider above the barrier, the musket aimed. She heard the report, then the cry of pain from a man not a dozen feet from her. With his weapon fired, the workers jumped up and unleashed a hail of rocks toward the horseman, but it was a puny defense against mounted men with guns.

"Come Jessie," she cried and ran to the wounded man. But there was nothing to do. He was dead, shot through the heart.

"I can't let this go on, Jessie. I can't."

"What can we do, Miss Glenna?"

"I can give myself up. It's better than having these good men die one by one."

"No, Miss Glenna, no. I won't let you."

She stood up and looked out the space between the overturned cars. There, perhaps fifty yards away was Winslow, a figure in black sitting his horse. She could sense his confidence. He was winning. And why not? She saw him motion with his arm for more riders to attack. It was hopeless. Only more killing. She had to stop it.

"No, Miss Glenna, no." Jessie grabbed her arm, but Glenna shook it free.

"I must. There's nothing else to do."

"Joe, help me."

"No. Both of you stay here. They don't want you—only me."

Purposefully, she strode through the barrier and stood in front of it. She was aware of Jessie crying behind her, Joe calling to her, but she could not hear what either said as she placed one foot in front of the other, walking toward Winslow. She saw him raise his hand to halt his men. He was going to let her walk right up to him. How like him.

In a few paces she could see the smile on his face. Why not? He had won. He could afford to smile. He would have her again. And that was just as well. She had disgraced Daniel. Aurial was in ashes. Everything was in ruins, her whole life was a ruin. So many were dead. It was best that she be, too. Then she thought of her child, Daniel's child she was carrying. She was sorry he would not live to know his father, his wonderful father, her beloved Daniel. Unfelt tears began rolling down her cheeks. Oh, Daniel, I did love you so.

The space gradually closed, thirty, twenty-five, twenty. She could see the triumph shining in Winslow's eyes. She felt numb, almost disembodied, disassociated from the world and what was happening. Yet, she was aware of the men behind Winslow turning their horses and pointing off to her right. Still she marched on, uncaring. She heard words, shouts. Something about cavalry. She didn't understand. She saw only Winslow, atop his horse, looking at his left, then at her. She saw his heels dig into the flanks of his horse. It bolted forward and he leaned low in the saddle and extended his arm. She felt the arm strike her midsection, knocking her off her feet, then herself being lifted into the air.

She saw the ground racing below her feet, then in the distance the diminishing barricade of boxcars, now with men on top of them waving their arms and shouting. Then she saw men, a lot of men riding toward her. They wore some kind of uniforms with broad strips across the front, like an X. Then she saw a man in front, riding harder and faster than the others. He wore a dark coat and his black hair was naked to the wind. It was Daniel. Oh, it was Daniel. How well he rode, how handsome he looked. She felt Winslow turn his head, and she heard him swear. Then she hit the ground hard, rolling over and over, feet over head. She felt the cool ground against her face before she blacked out.

In the distance she heard voices. "Somebody get some water. If anything's happened to her, I'll die."

She knew the voice. Daniel's. How wonderful to hear it. She opened her eyes. Yes, it was Daniel, kneeling beside her, holding her head. How beautiful he looked.

"Oh, darlin', are you all right?"

She managed a smile. "I think so."

"Nothing is broken?"

She wiggled her toes, felt her hand. "No, I'm all

right." Then she remembered everything and bolted to a sitting position, staring at him. "How did you get here?"

"The President contacted me by special courier, ordering me home immediately. I came by the fastest ship I could find, arriving in Washington last night. He told me everything that had happened, about you, Lord Penwood, Winslow. He had just learned about Winslow stirring up a mob against you and he feared the worst. Immediately, he ordered a troop of cavalry to ride with me to Aurial. I arrived too late, but I followed you as fast as I could. Oh, God, I was almost too late. I almost didn't make it." He buried his face against her throat, holding her head against his chest, rocking her back and forth like a baby. "When he dropped you and you hit the ground and lay so still, I thought you were dead."

Glenna pushed him away. "I'm all right, Daniel, but that doesn't change anything." Tears welled into her eyes again. "I disobeyed you. I told Lord Penwood. I've disgraced you. Everyone is talking about me. You'll never r—"

"Hush, darlin', hush. Let their tongues wag. Who cares what anyone says?"

"—regain your reputation and all because of me."

"Hush, hush. You're safe and I love you and that's all that matters."

She felt his strong arms pulling her head against his chest, the beat of his heart against her cheek, and for the first time in weeks, a feeling of peace and contentment came to her. Yes, he loved her and she him and that was indeed all that mattered.

BOOK TWO
Moira

32

The gown had been worn once, precisely a year and two months previously at President Zachary Taylor's inaugural ball in March, 1849. Daniel Morgan had suggested Glenna buy it or one very much like it. As a United States Senator from Maryland and a militant abolitionist, he had long since discovered the political advantages of his wife's beauty and somewhat scandalous reputation. On the stump, as well as in the halls of Congress, it tended to make him a marked man, envied, talked about. It was valuable to be noticed and when he rose to speak eyes turned to him and his words were heard.

After almost twenty years, tongues still wagged about Glenna, her mysterious adventures greatly magnified by time and perpetual retelling. Glenna had aged well, her skin softening, her breasts swelling, the wrinkles appearing to add character to her beauty. This fueled the gossip, as did her appearance in the inaugural gown. It was made of blue satin of a shade which deepened and magnified her eyes, worn off the shoulder and so deeply cut it had barely covered her areolae.

When he had seen her in it, Daniel had been most pleased. "That'll get me at least twenty invitations to speak."

Glenna had understood her husband's use of her and never opposed it. Rather, it amused her. Smiling up at him, she had said, "Don't you think it a bit ridiculous for an old married woman with two nearly grown children."

"Indeed," he had said.

And the blue gown had its desired effect, scandalizing Washington for weeks afterward.

Now the gown, snitched from her mother's closet, adorned another body. But on Moira Townsend Morgan, still three months from her eighteenth birthday, the gown had a much different effect. Glenna was more fragile than her daughter, more a classic beauty with delicate features. Her snowy complexion, her maturity and natural reserve, her entire bearing and manner lent a cast of demureness that made her a lady despite the revealing nature of the gown. On her daughter, the gown was shocking, severely daring, edging perilously close to wantonness. This came, in part, from Moira's youth. The dress was really designed for an older, more sophisticated woman. But in largest measure the wantonness of the gown stemmed from Moira's natural appearance.

The sharp dissimilarities in the beauty of mother and daughter were noticed by nearly everyone. The most obvious difference was Moira's mass of red Irish hair inherited from her maternal grandfather. It seemed to contain every shade of red from deep oxblood to bright orange, and it was thick and rich, full of waves and curls, reaching below her shoulders. It was like a beacon. Anyone could recognize Moira Morgan even from a distance. Closer up, an observer was ensnared first by her eyes, large, set wide apart beneath heavy black brows and double lashes. The pupils were— what? Bright green, certainly, the color of a deep pool of spring water, with a border of rich hazel. But they could also edge toward blue, as they did now as she wore her mother's dress. After her eyes, a person noticed her mouth, full, turned out with a depression in the center of the lower lip and extremely smooth without a line or wrinkle.

Moira had inherited the brows and lashes from her mother, but little else. She simply did not have the delicate features of her mother, but rather her eyes were bolder, her lips fuller, the nose broader, as if to balance the more rounded face, the wider cheekbones, the squarer chin. Nor did she inherit her mother's complexion. Probably, she had her father's ruddiness, but it looked for all the world as if the red had washed out of her hair and into her body. There was vibrant rosiness to her skin that increased when she was excited, as now. The red brightened her lips until no rouge was needed, and lent a definite pinkish cast to her finger and toe nails. Barely concealed beneath her mother's gown, her nipples flowered almost as brightly as oleander.

As she stood before the mirror, fussing with her hair, the total effect was of wildness, impulsiveness, yes, wantonness. Her appearance passed beyond the startling to the shocking. She was anything but demure. She stopped combing and lowered her arms, looking at her reflection in the mirror. She bent over slightly and raised her head so she could see the image, inspecting the pink mounds leaping toward her. She had worried that the dress might not fit. It did and that knowledge made her smile in triumph. She was as developed as her mother, maybe more so. She stood up straight, revolving slowly as she turned her head first to the right, then the left, to see herself. As she again faced the image, she said aloud, "At last the butterfly has left the cocoon."

"Good land, child. What are you wearing?"

Moira turned to see Jessie in the doorway of her room, an expression of surprised disapproval on her face. Moira was tempted to scold Jessie for entering without knocking, but thought better of it. Jessie only became angrier if she thought she was being sassed. Instead she smiled and turned to face the servant. "What I'm wearing to the Kingston's party."

Jessie strode toward her. She was still a handsome

woman, although a good bit thicker in the waist and hips. Years of contented marriage to Joe had done that. And years of running the large household and looking after Moira and her brother Andrew Jackson Morgan had added maturity and authority to her manner and her voice. "Oh no you're not. That's your mama's dress."

"So what if it is? Mother's never going to wear it. All she's going to do is mope around her room and cry her eyes out for father."

Daniel had been killed on Thanksgiving Day, just before the turkey was to be served. He had been riding his new horse, a spirited stallion which Glenna had feared and urged him not to ride. Daniel had scoffed at her fears and ridden off. The horse, frightened by a rabbit which skittered in front of it, had reared and thrown Daniel. He had died instantly, his neck broken in the fall. Joe had ridden in to tell Glenna. Virtually her last deliberate act had been to send for the rifle and shoot the horse. But the light went out of her life. Through Christmas, New Years, all winter, even now, she had hardly left her room. She remained a figure dressed in black, sitting by the window as though waiting for her husband to come back from his ride. She barely ate or drank and ignored all Jessie's entreaties to come downstairs. Thus, the burden of maintaining the estate and running the household had fallen squarely on the shoulders of Joe and Jessie.

"Hush your mouth, child," Jessie scolded, grabbing Moira's wrist. "You will not talk that way about your mama, and you will not wear that dress and you will not go to any party."

Moira pulled her hand free. "Oh, yes, I will. I loved father every bit as much as she did. But I'll not spend the rest of my life grieving for him. He's dead and there's nothing I can do about it. I'm going to the party tonight, and I'm going to have some fun for a change. I've stayed in this dreary morgue of a house all I'm going to."

Jessie glared at her and saw the defiance in the girl's face. Her own spirit sank, although she tried not to show it. Glenna's daughter had always been difficult and Jessie felt the impossibility of trying to control her. If only Mr. Daniel were alive. If only Miss Glenna would come out of her room and deal with her children. Moira and Andrew were both heading straight for trouble. She knew it. She wanted to stop it, but she didn't know how. She just couldn't cope with either of them.

Her trouble was she understood this child. She had helped to deliver her. She had seen her grow up, indeed helped to raise her. She had seen the trouble start, then slowly grow, powerless to stop it, as the clash between mother and daughter mounted. Now, an avalanche of defiance, it was thundering down. Who would be the victim? Mother? Daughter? Both?

The problem had always been there, yet it seemed to Jessie it had worsened immeasurably within the last year. Now, seemingly overnight, there were two beautiful women in this house, one older, one younger, one mature and self-confident, the other so terribly young and dangerously impulsive. The problem was easy for Jessie to see. Moira was torn between her love for her mother, her admiration, even awe of her, and her own consuming jealousy. She had adored her father, clinging to him, doing everything to please him. She knew his love of horses and had become an expert equestrian, winning prizes as a young girl. She had been a tomboy, going in the fields with her father, playing games with him, sensitive to his every wish and thought. And she had won his love. Daniel Morgan adored his daughter. She was the apple of his eye. But for Moira it had been an impossibility. Nothing she could ever do could even in the smallest way supplant his love for Glenna. He loved his wife, as Jessie knew he should, to a degree seen in few marriages. There was a closeness, a devotion between the two, which forever left Moira second in his affections.

The competition with her mother was hopeless for Moira. To have a young and celebrated mother who grew more beautiful and talked about each day became a curse to Moira. Jessie had overheard her say to a girlfriend, "If I hear one more time how she crossed that damn desert, I think I'll scream." The night of the inaugural when Glenna had worn this very gown and a proud, enraptured Daniel had gotten his children to exclaim how beautiful their mother was, Jessie had seen the look in Moira's eye when her mother turned to leave, not hatred certainly, but something perhaps more dangerous, envy mixed with determination.

While Daniel Morgan had lived, the problem had merely boiled beneath the surface. He gave his daughter undiluted love. His doting on her, indeed his spoiling of her, his incessant compliments to her beauty and ability, had maintained, perhaps even inflated Moira's wounded ego. He certainly kept his daughter and her jealousy under control. Never was she going to risk letting her father know of her real feelings about her mother.

Daniel's death had been a monstrous tragedy for Glenna and for her children. The rudder went out of Moira's life and Glenna in her grief was powerless to give her new direction. So the child had just drifted, arriving at this night. Jessie loved Glenna almost more than she loved herself. Her devotion to Glenna Morgan was boundless. She would brook no criticism of her. Indeed, she would easily lay down her life for her. That notwithstanding, Jessie knew Glenna was not a very good mother to Moira and she grieved for her failure. She understood. She made excuses for her. But that did not alter the fact of Glenna's failure. Oh, the daughter did not want for attention. She was fussed over and petted and admonished and bought for—bought for too much in Jessie's view. But she did not receive what she really needed from her mother.

Glenna had not known her own mother. She had been raised by her father, then cast adrift at a young age. Glenna had no example of motherhood and didn't really understand what was required of her as a mother of a daughter. She had made her way alone, survived somehow from her own inner resources. She truly had no understanding of the help a child, particularly a girl child needs from her mother. Nor was Glenna's own girlhood of much help. She had grown up in an isolated existence with her father, largely without a friend, in a land an ocean away, radically different in culture. Glenna had known only poverty. Now she was rearing her children amid wealth, plenty and privilege. Glenna Morgan, who was sensitive to every nuance of her husband's desire, thoughts and behavior, who was inordinately thoughtful and considerate of her, Joe and others, was strangely, even inexplicably insensitive to the real feelings of her only daughter and not much better with her son. There were times when Jessie bit her lip to keep from sharp words as her beloved Glenna insisted on crinolines and bows for her daughter. When she tried to suggest how grown up Moira was becoming, Glenna would reply, "Why she's still a little girl." Was her mistress blind?

Jessie had tried to cover for Glenna, doting on Moira, telling her how beautiful she was, how womanly she had become. She spent as much time as she could with Moira, fixing her hair, admiring her experiments with makeup, listening to her girlish fantasies about romance, giggling and hugging her. But Jessie knew she was no substitute for her mother, whose attention had been non-existent since Daniel Morgan's death seven months ago.

All these thoughts welled into Jessie's mind as she saw this beautiful, impetuous child dressed for a party in her mother's shocking gown. She found herself saying, "Just ask yourself, child, would your father allow you to wear a dress like this?" It had been the one weapon Jessie had used most effectively of late in the increasingly difficult task of restraining Moira.

"My father is not here." Despite herself tears shone

in her eyes. "Will no one in this house accept the fact he is dead? He is not ever going to see me again. I am going to wear what I want, when I want, where I want. I'm wearing this. This is 1850 and I'm almost eighteen years old. I'm not going to the Kingstons looking like a child."

The thought passed through Jessie's mind: if only Glenna had bought her some proper clothes. But different, harsher words came out her mouth. "Moira Morgan, you look like a hussy in that." Instantly, she saw Moira react as though she had been slapped, and Jessie bit her lips, wishing she could take back the words. "Oh no, child, forgive me. It's not so. You look so lovely. It's just—"

"After tonight, there are no justs. Is it so hard for me to be grown up?"

Jessie tried a new tack. "And the Kingstons. He's a slaveholder, one of the biggest in Calvert County. You know how much your father hated that. You shouldn't dishonor his memory by going there."

Moira shook her head. "It won't work, Jessie. You've used my father's memory too many times already. I'm so sick of hearing about slavery. It's all anybody talks about—that and gold in California. I just wish all the damn niggers would—" She stopped, realizing what she had said, "Oh Jessie, forgive me. You know I didn't mean that." She threw her arms around the black woman who had so often meant more to her than her own mother. "I wouldn't hurt you for anything."

"I know, child, I know. It just came out—like what I said did. Neither of us wants to hurt the other."

Moira pulled away from Jessie, her hands on her shoulders, looking at her intently. "Oh Jess, can't you be *with* me? Can't you tell me how beautiful I am? Can't you send me off with your blessing?"

Jessie smiled at her, the glint of a gold tooth showing at the corner of her mouth. "You're just like Miss Glenna. She always wanted me to tell her how beautiful she was, never knew for herself."

"Really?" The statement surprised Moira. Her mother always seemed so assured and poised.

"You don't really know your mama, child. Why the night she wore this dress I had to tell her over and over how beautiful she was and how right she was to wear this dress. But she wouldn't believe me till she saw that certain look, that look of pride in your father's eye."

"Oh Jessie, I do wish father could see me."

"Oh, no you don't. You'd get a scolding and be made to change—and right this instant."

Moira smiled. "Yes, I know you're right. But—"

"You needn't tell me again. I'm not your father and I'm not your mother. I'm the old housekeeper who's going to tell you how beautiful you look, absolutely stunning. You'll knock 'em dead." She saw the beaming smile on Moira's face and knew she had said the right thing. She had been so tempted to say the dress wasn't right for her, that it belonged on an older woman, but as she watched Moira dance away from her, making her skirt swirl and her hair whip wildly around her face, she knew the words were better left unsaid. All they would do would undermine her confidence, make her unsure of herself, spoil her evening which she was determined to have.

"Oh, yes, Jessie, I do feel so beautiful. Such an evening it's going to be, the best party of the year. 'King' Kingston's going to be there. He's come straight in from New York. Oh, the things they say about him."

"Now you listen to me, Miss Moira. I don't want you to have a thing to do with him."

Moira smiled coquettishly at her reflection in the mirror. "Of course I won't. He'll not even notice the little neighbor girl."

"Miss Moira, you just better be careful."

Moira heard, not the warning, but the appellation "Miss Moira."

She had grown up. She was no longer "child."

When she accompanied Moira downstairs, Jessie saw the look of disapproval in Joe's eyes and saw him open his mouth to speak. Jessie stopped him with a withering look. "Our Miss Moira is going to a party. Doesn't she look grand?"

Joe, little aged in twenty years and still a quick learner, shut his mouth, then opened it to smile broadly, bow and say, "My goodness, I'll say she looks grand."

As her husband escorted Moira out to the carriage, Jessie stood there looking after them, her smile fading. Suddenly she felt cold.

33

If ever the nickname "King" seemed to suit a man it was Bradford Kingston III, oldest son of the man whose name he bore. He was thirty-two years old and at the absolute peak of his prowess. There was command and self-assurance written into his slightest movement. And the appearance was only the measure of the man.

Two days home from the bright lights and a successful run at the gaming tables of New York City, he exuded the polish and sophistication that success in the big city can bring. His boots bore a high sheen. His black suit with the ruffled shirt was expertly tailored to accentuate his small waist, slender hips and broad shoulders. All had cost a fortune, not that he had given it much thought. He was tall, a good two inches over six feet, and handsome by any standards, with straight black hair combed back above his ears, eyes so dark brown they looked black from a few feet away, and a carefully trimmed black mustache which filled most of his upper lip. His face was squarish with a bold chin, graced by the deep Kingston cleft inherited from his father and grandfather.

There were times when he struggled to shave and snip the hairs out of that cleft that he cursed it, yet he knew it was his trademark, which distinguished him from other handsome men. When the shaving was finished and he had bathed his face in scented water, he could smile approvingly at the face in the mirror. On occasion he would even utter aloud, "The face that launched a thousand girls."

King's assurance was rooted in two capacities. He was an adroit womanizer. He simply had not yet met the woman he couldn't get into bed if he wanted to. Nor had he met the woman whom he hadn't been able to satisfy—at least for the evening. His feats of bedmanship were legendary and he neither said nor did anything to dispel the lore which wafted around him. His second capacity was gambling. He had met his match at the tables, but he had never been bested. He earned his living gambling. Although he was chronically short of funds, he never had the slightest doubt of his ability to come up with more.

At the moment, standing before the fire in his father's study, he was irritable and trying a little not to show it. He was already sorry he had given in to his father's entreaties to return home for a visit. He knew the reason for the requests—the annual rites of spring, a party designed to hopefully, desperately marry him off to one of the local belles. He'd been to them almost every year, ghastly, tiresome bores filled with silly, giggling females. Would his father never give up? The old man had no idea what a real woman was.

He swirled his brandy again, so sharply some spilled over the rim, then corrected the problem by draining the glass quickly. Setting it on the mantle, he said, "Is there no way I can get out of this?"

Except for the cleft in his chin, Bradford Kingston

bore scant resemblance to his son. He was a half head shorter, with thin, largely gray hair, and a significant paunch. His pride in life as his name, this estate named Kingston, and his eldest son. Right now pride was not enough to offset his annoyance with him. "I don't understand your objections. I've invited the finest young ladies."

"And that's why I object—because you invited them. I don't want to get married. When I do, I'll select my own bed partner."

"Fine. Pick one of these."

King sighed. "I don't—oh, what's the use? Father, don't you understand. I've met all these ladies and their scheming mothers, last year and the year before and the year before that. I didn't like them last year and the year before that and I won't like them now."

Bradford Kingston smiled. "But I think you're in for some surprises. The Morgan girl, for example."

King reached for his snifter and in disgust poured it half full. "The Morgan girl," he said, mimicking his father. "That scrawny kid. You must be desperate, father."

"You're in for a surprise, King, a real surprise. I want you to pay her special attention. Her father died last fall, you know, and with a little luck, who knows, maybe that Morgan land will—"

"For God's sake, father, can't you ever give up on getting the Morgan property?"

"No, and I never will. Kingston will not be complete till that river front is mine. This house belongs there, on the bluff, not back here in the backwater."

King had heard it a million times. His father's passion for another man's property was silly to him.

"I've waited for that girl to grow up. She has and quite nicely. I want you to court her. It's time you settled down. Heavens knows you've sowed enough wild oats for ten men. I want you to marry that girl and help your father obtain the one thing he's ever wanted in his life."

King saw the flush in his father's face and heard the intensity in his voice. He was tempted to ridicule his father, then thought better of it. Instead, he said, "If it's Aurial you want so bad, maybe I should court the Widow Morgan. She was always a helluva good looking woman."

The father was shocked. "Don't be silly. She's too old for you. The girl is the one."

"Not for me. I'm no cradle robber. Marry her off to Ned. She's more his age."

"I'll arrange things for your brother in due time. Right now I'd appreciate it if for once you did as your father asked."

King said no more, merely shaking his head in disbelief and looking down at the swirl of brandy in his hand. To forget the unpleasantness, he concentrated on the gleam from his diamond pinky ring as it reflected through the amber fluid.

"I hear our guests arriving. We should go now."

King sighed, set down his glass and stood up. He went to the French doors which opened out on the garden. He took a couple of deep breaths of the fragrant air, then resignedly followed his father to the drawing room. He refused to stand in a receiving line, but managed to be civil and courteous, smiling at the inanities and pure drivel mouthed by the mothers and proud fathers as they asked him if he remembered Gertrude or Hazel or Marybelle. He did remember and he asked the appropriate questions and said how good it was to see them again and how divine they looked. But from long experience he kept moving, circulating to keep from being ensnared by anyone.

Thus, it was with only minimal difficulty that he found his way to the bar to stand next to his brother Ned. At twenty-one, eleven years younger than King, Nathaniel Kingston had been an afterthought, a bedroom accident conceived at an age when his parents had almost ceased conjugal activities. His mother, Louise Kingston, had been in her forties when he was born, an act which claimed her life. An afterthought of conception and birth, Ned Kingston was an afterthought in his father's regard. He was also the antithesis of his older brother, quiet, shy, nearly diffident. He was not handsome, possessing unruly brown hair, brown eyes and no hint of a cleft in his chin. He favored his mother in fact. He had never had an actual date, did not wager on anything, and found his greatest pleasures in working his father's fields getting his hands dirty. He was already winning the respect of the overseer, as well as auctioneers and buyers, for his knowledge of tobacco.

Ned knew it was mostly the land and the tobacco which kept him there. His relations with his father were minimal and non-existent with his brother. He knew of his father's constant envy of the Morgan property next door, and he shared it—but for radically different reasons. His father cared almost nothing for farming. It was only the ownership of Aurial he wanted, the possession, the location. Ned envied Aurial because it was so much more prosperous and grew much better tobacco. It was not the fertility of the land which did this, Ned knew, but the difference between free labor and slave. He knew Kingston would prosper more as a free plantation, but to suggest that to his father and brother was to be scoffed at. He maintained his silence, but knew that if his chance ever came, he would know what to do.

Ned's interest in Aurial had another cause, the face and form of Moira Morgan. They had grown up together. He would see her at school, occasionally meet her as she rode her horse Hickory. In fact, he had become pretty good at figuring out her schedule so as to make the meeting less accidental. And, since her brother was near his age, reasons could always be found to ride over to Aurial to discuss some matter with Andrew. He and Andrew really didn't get along, but what did that matter.

Yet, for all his connivance, his love for Moira

Morgan was entirely unrequited. She had no real interest in him, he knew, except to tease him and make him blush. These wounds not withstanding, he continued to think about her, spinning dreams of what might someday be, and contrive to see her to gather a new wound. He did this despite the fact that in the last year the mere sight of her hurt him greatly. She seemed to have changed so much. Just yesterday he had seen her riding Hickory in the warm spring afternoon. He had seen her breasts rising and falling with the motion of the horse. Last night, as many previous nights, had been torture for him as he lay in bed trying to sleep.

"Having a good time, little brother?"

Characteristically, Ned shrugged. He never seemed to know what to say to his brother.

"The annual mating rites of spring. I promise you this will be the last of these I'll attend." King turned to hand his glass to the slave who ran the bar. He accepted a fresh glass of whiskey, paying no more attention to the black servant than he would to a piece of furniture. He turned to face the dancers, sipping his whiskey as he leaned against the bar. The Virginia Reel, no less. Didn't these yokels know any modern dances?

Then the music stopped and the floor cleared. Across it, just entering the doorway, he saw a girl with brilliant red hair. He saw her stand a moment, her chin high, her eyes sweeping the room. He saw the blue sheen of her dress, then his eyes fixed on the pink roundness of her breasts. My, my, my. The party is picking up, he thought. Aloud, he uttered, "Little brother, who's that girl over there, the redhead?"

Ned Kingston gasped in astonishment, barely able to say, "Why that's Moira Morgan."

As was both the custom and necessary following a ride in an open carriage, Moira had gone first to the powder room. There were perhaps half a dozen mothers and daughters fussing with their hair, powdering their noses, chatting softly. Moira knew one of the young women. Charlene Baughman had been a couple of classes ahead of her in school and Moira had always envied her in a rather friendly fashion.

"Hi, Moira. What a pretty blue dress."

"Thanks, Charlene. You look lovely as always."

Mrs. Baughman, a large woman with massive breasts now covered in gray crepe designed to be formless, butted in. "Oh, yes, you're the little Morgan girl, aren't you?"

Moira bristled at the word "little" but smiled sweetly and said, "Yes," as she reached up to untie the short matching cape to her gown.

Mrs. Baughman had just opened her mouth to inquire about the health of Glenna Morgan, when she saw Moira's costume. Her tongue stopped in mid-movement and she gasped, "Why I never!" She stared at Moira's decolletage a moment longer, then grabbed her daughter's wrist and pulled her. "Come with me this instant, Charlene."

Moira turned to see the other women, a shocked expression on their faces, leave the room abruptly. Before the door closed she heard one of the women say, "I never. What a hussy."

Moira had stood there looking at her reflection in the mirror, feeling herself flush all over. Suddenly, the gown which had been so pretty and exciting when she was alone in her room, now seemed lewd and obvious. She looked at the mounds of exposed flesh. How could she have? Inwardly she shrank. What could she do? The cape. She would wear the cape. She picked it up and swept it around her shoulders. But as she started to tie it at her throat, she hesitated. Her mother had worn this dress. She remembered her own envy that evening and the pride in her father's eyes. "If she can wear it, so can I," she whispered. She pursed her lips in determination.

When Moira stood at the entrance to the drawing room, however, her courage fled again. She mistakenly thought the musicians had stopped playing when they saw her. The silence seemed to stun her, as she saw everyone staring at her, many with mouths open or silly grins on their faces. She had dreamed of making an entrance, but now that it was happening, it was unpleasant. She didn't know what to do. She was alone and nowhere did she see a friendly face. She tried to smile, but it came out nervously. There simply was no place to hide.

34

Bradford Kingston the elder roused himself to remember his manners. He came quickly to Moira, extending his hand. "My dear Miss Morgan. How nice of you to come."

She saw him, fat, bald and wrinkled, but at that moment he looked like an angel. She smiled, certainly more in relief at his greeting than from pleasure from being there. "You were so kind to invite me, Mr. Kingston." She saw his gaze dwell upon her bosom, then rise to meet her eyes.

"You are lovely, Miss Morgan, just lovely. Your dear mother couldn't come?"

Glenna now heard the buzz in the room. She knew they were talking about her. "She was not feeling well. She sends her regrets."

Again his broad smile—and something else, a look in his eyes she couldn't decipher. "Oh, well, at least we have one beautiful member of the Morgan family with us." He took her hand. "Come. You remember my son King. I know he'll want to see you again."

He led her across the ballroom and she heard the drone of voices increase. Expressions such as "Would you believe?" and "How disgusting" reached her ears. But there was no time to react. She saw Ned first, an expression of astonishment on his face, then beside him the handsomest man she had ever seen. She saw black hair and mustache, the deep cleft in his chin, a flash of white teeth. She took his extended hand and saw him bow to kiss her fingers.

As she came toward him, he made a quick appraisal of her and his reactions to her, both based upon long experience. Young, very young. Doubt if she's eighteen. Much too young. And scared stiff. Wearing her mother's dress. He'd wager a fortune on that. Masses of red hair, the most glorious he'd ever seen. Extraordinary eyes, green and blue and hazel. Most remarkable. And such lips, dewy red, hungry for kisses. He saw her breasts coming toward him. Gutty kid. That dress would be a sensation in New York. Here, it was unbelievable. But she was too young for it. Such a body, such glowing skin. God, she was ripe, ripe for plucking. There was something wild, untamed, almost animalistic about her. Simultaneous with these thoughts came an awareness of a rising in his loins, a slightly faster heartbeat in anticipation of the chase. She would be so easy, so very easy. If only she weren't so young.

"Of course I remember Miss Morgan. At least I remember some skinny kid who lived down the road." His smile broadened. "I wonder whatever happened to her."

Moira laughed lightly, suddenly charmed and a trifle more relaxed under his attention. "I have an idea she's around here somewhere, Mr. Kingston."

"I don't see a sign of her anywhere. And please call me King. Everyone does."

She felt drawn to those black eyes, that handsome

face. It was as though she were being viewed closely under a magnifying glass, so undiluted was his attention. And she felt a new sensation. Her fear and timidity of a moment before was being replaced by a strange flutteriness and excitement. King Kingston, the handsomest, most desirable man in Calvert County, the man everyone talked about, was looking at *her*, smiling at *her*. Unbelievable.

"Father," she heard him say, "see if you can get those overpaid musicians of yours to play something more spirited and modern, a waltz perhaps. We need to liven up this party." His penetrating gaze again returned to her. "And you want some punch, don't you, Moira?" Again the flash of teeth. "I may call you Moira?"

Somehow it wasn't a question, more a command. It felt almost as if he were taking charge of her. "Yes," she said, smiling back at him, "to both your questions."

Ordinarily King would have dispatched his little brother or a servant to fetch punch. On this occasion he went himself. It was customary to serve two punches, one of fruit juices for the ladies, another of seriously spiked fruit juices for the men. It was the latter he went for. As two cups were filled he had for the first and last time that night a tussle with his conscience. Had it been a physical fray, an observer would scarcely have noticed anything more than a nudge or shove, so slight was the battle. She was too young, said his conscience. If she's old enough to wear that gown she's old enough to have it come off. Issue settled.

"How could you Moira?"

She turned her gaze from the handsome figure in black at the punch table to meet Ned Kingston's gaze squarely. She saw his emotions written there, astonishment still, wonder, even awe, disapproval and, yes, desire. She had always known his attraction for her. She had found a certain usefulness in teasing him. He was good practice. "How could I what?"

"That dress. How can you wear it?"

"And why not? What's wrong with it?" She saw him glance at her bosom. "It looks to me as though you like it." She saw him blush.

"I do—I mean. It's—oh, you know what I mean."

Inwardly she laughed at him, but she kept her mien serious. "I have no idea what you mean. Your brother seems to like it."

She felt a hand on her arm, turning her away from Ned to face the dance floor. The coolness of the hand, the firmness of the touch, sent an involuntary shiver down her spine. She looked up at King and smiled, accepting the cup of punch.

"Do you waltz?"

She did not. The waltz was a new dance and considered rather scandalous, for the partners held each other in their arms, their bodies touching at least occasionally. She panicked a moment, then wisely saw no point in lying. "I'm afraid the new dances are rather slow to reach here."

He looked out at the floor. "Perhaps, but I see one or two couples doing it."

"If you'll give me a moment to watch, I think I'll be able to pick it up."

"Of course. It's really very simple, just one, two, three with the music. You watch and we'll drink our punch, then I'll show you the rest." He clicked her cup with his. "To the prettiest girl at the annual spring rites."

"And what does that mean?"

His eyes seemed to envelop her. "It means I find you enchanting. Drink up."

Dutifully she sipped the punch. She knew it was heavily spiked.

"I said drink up—all of it. You need to relax and enjoy the party."

She smiled over the rim. "You're a hard man to resist," she said and tilted the cup deeply to her lips.

The waltz absolutely thrilled her. When he took her into his arms, she again felt sensation arc through her from his hand holding hers. Then she realized his right hand was in the middle of her back. It seemed to catch her shivers and hold them in that one spot. He was a marvelous dancer and she was able to follow him instantly as they swirled in circles within larger circles around the floor, her skirt billowing, her hair flying. The music seemed too wild and fast and insistent. Despite herself she laughed with pleasure.

He smiled broadly at her. "You like the waltz?"

"Oh, yes, but it makes me dizzy."

"You'll get used to it."

The punch, the swirling movements did make her dizzy, but she didn't care. This was to her pure happiness, to be dancing, swinging effortlessly in the arms of a handsome man while the world was filled with joyous music. Such fun, such excitement. The music stopped and she rested a moment, her chest heaving for air. "I can't catch my breath," she panted.

He looked down at her. So ripe, so very ripe. "That's half the fun."

The music started again and once more she was swept up in the excitement of the dance. As she was whirled around the dance floor, the whole universe seemed to shrink to just this moment and this man. Other forms in the room, indeed the room itself, seemed to disappear and she closed her eyes, enjoying the thrill, yes, the passion of the dance. She felt his hands, his arm at her shoulder as he guided her in circle upon circle, his knee against her knee, his thigh against her thigh. As he turned her, she felt her breast crushed against his chest. Heavenly. Her whole body seemed to be coursing with warm and strange, compelling sensations. She opened her eyes. He was looking at her, a half smile on his face, his eyes bright with excitement. And something else. She knew. Desire. He wanted her.

The dance seemed to go on interminably and when the music finally stopped she was so dizzy she had to hold on to him. She heard him chuckle. "Focus on one thing. It'll go away." The whole room seemed to be spinning. In vain at first she saw a face and forced her attention upon it. It worked. Gradually, the spinning stopped and she recognized Ned Kingston, looking sad, disturbed about something. But she had no time to think. "Fresh air is what you need," she heard him say, then he had her elbow and was leading her out to the terrace. "Isn't this better?"

The soft, warm May air caressed her skin. She smelled the delicious fragrance of flowers. She ought to learn more about flowers. She felt his arm around her waist and felt him guide her off the terrace and down into the garden.

"How about that moon?"

She looked up and saw the moon, full and pristine in a starless blue-gray sky and felt the enchantment of the night, the pearly light, the long dark shadows of trees and shrubs. Again she looked up at the moon.

Then she felt his lips at her throat, and sweet sensation coursed through her. "You're so lovely. I can't resist you," he whispered, then she was in his arms, crushed against him, his lips open and moist devouring hers. Her knees buckled under the onslaught of sensation and she would have fallen had he not held her. Indeed, she sagged weakly against him, almost unable to bear what was happening to her. It was her first real kiss and with the moonlight and the alcohol coursing through her veins, it was rapture. And when his tongue entered her lips and found her tongue, she felt an eruption of sensation that seemed to melt her.

In a moment he stood away from her, but only long enough to pull her into a shadow. Then he was at her again, his lips and tongue devouring what was aching to be devoured. Somewhere in the onslaught, she lost all restraint, all resistance. It was as though she had been magnetized by sensation to constantly seek it out, wanting more and more. Thus, as he arched his body away from her, their mouths still joined, she found herself thrusting toward him. Then she felt his hand at her breast, on, over, around, deep in the valley

between them. He tore his lips from hers, and with his
hands lifted her breasts up and out of her bodice.
"God, you're beautiful," he said, and bending to her
wreaked a havoc upon her. She was lost, gone, helpless
to do more than lean against the trunk of the tree as she
felt herself sink into a well of desire.

She felt him stand. "Come," he said, and taking her
hand led her through the garden and inside a doorway.
She had an impression of a masculine room, shelves of
books, a desk. a leather couch. He left her standing in
the open doorway, her gown still disarrayed, and
quickly went to douse the candles on a table. In quick
strides he went to a door opposite her, and she heard
the turn of a key in a lock. In the flickering light from
the fireplace, she saw him come back to her, removing
his suitcoat and tossing it aside, close the outside door
and lock it. Then she was in his arms, sinking again into
a sea of sensation made stormy by his mouth and his
hand at her breasts. It didn't last long and she felt
herself pulled across the room and pushed down on the
couch. As her skirts were lifted up she heard music.
One last shred of restraint remained. "The party.
People'll—"

"Hang the party. You'll be back in ten minutes
anyway."

His voice was urgent, yet there was a matter-of-
factness to it, no, a hard sound, almost cruelty. She felt
his hand at her waist, then a sharp tug and the sound of
tearing fabric as he ripped away her pantaloons. "God
awful garment," she heard him say. "Why do women
wear them."

Fortunately for Moira, King was no insensitive brute.
He wanted his women responsive and knew how to
make them that way. This one was no problem at all.
Kneeling beside her, he caressed her thighs and heard
her moan. He parted them and felt her dampness. She
was almost ready. He reached up and stroked her
nipples with his left hand as he intensified the motions
of his right.

Moira had a sense of floating. She seemed to be dizzy, unable to rise, indeed to move at all. Far away she knew what was happening. She knew she was being violated, yet she seemed powerless even to protest, as his fingers with each movement shot excruciating sensation through her. Oh, she wanted him. She knew what he was going to do and she ached for it. Never had she known such desire. When would he come to her? When would he smash this mountain of need inside her. When, oh when. She was in his hands. She could do nothing but moan.

When he took his hand away, she had such a feeling of loss, even of pain. She opened her eyes and in the dim light saw him fumbling with his trousers, then something long and white in his hands. She felt her thighs being spread, his body over her. She felt his lips reaching for her and she turned to scoop them into her open mouth, her teeth clawing at his mustache, wanting to bite him, gnash him, anything to end this terrible need which was devouring her. Then she felt a hard rod pushing at her, once, again, then she felt something almost spread her apart. She gasped. It was too big. It wasn't possible. She was bursting. It came out, then back again. It was too big, hurting her. "No," she moaned.

"Yes."

Then, all at one moment, she felt his full weight crash down upon her, a burst of sharp pain which made her shriek against his mouth, and a rapturous sensation of fullness. She felt him rise up and plunge down into her again. Once more she cried out and tried to bite him. She clawed at his shirt, feeling the fabric rip under her fingernails, as he plunged again and again into her, propelling her, making the ache inside her rise until it was unbearable. Then, as she could stand no more, she felt a cataclysmic eruption, which left her writhing, shuddering, shivering, gasping and moaning. It seemed to go on for the longest time, finally ending as she heard him moan and gasp against her ear.

She felt him come off her, but not much else, as she lay there spent, exhausted. In a moment she heard him speak, his voice strangely normal, almost lighthearted. And he was lighthearted. He had broken his record. She was the quickest conquest he had ever made. "You were fantastic, honey."

She heard the words. She had been fantastic.

"But you better get up and get back to the party."

The party. Oh, yes, the party. She felt him pull her to her feet. She seemed too weak, too dizzy to stand. She felt him tugging at her dress, adjusting the bodice, smoothing down her skirt.

"You okay, honey?"

She heard herself say, "I guess so, a little weak and dizzy."

"The punch." She heard him chuckle. "Another dram will fix you right up." He led her to the door, unlocked and opened it. She felt him brush her cheek with his lips. "When we get inside, you go fix yourself up. I'll get us some punch."

Alone in the powder room, she saw her reflection in the mirror. There were a few wrinkles in her skirt. Her hair was tousled and her lips strangely red. Otherwise she looked the same. But she knew she wasn't. Underneath the shining satin skirt, she was naked and she could feel a trickle down her leg. More sober now, she felt a mixture of emotions, shame, but also pride. King Kingston, the most sought after man in Calvert County, the man who had dozens of women in Philadelphia, New York and God knows where else, had wanted her, had her, and declared her fantastic. As she combed her hair, she smiled at the reflection in the mirror. Yes, she had been fantastic.

She reentered the ballroom, conscious again of eyes and voices, but caring much less this time. She went right to King, smiled at him, accepted the cup of loaded punch and drank. She leaned forward to whisper conspiratorially, "Was I really fantastic?"

"Yes, and you will be again in a little while."

She smiled, feeling a sense of triumph. He had to be the handsomest man in the world. Her eyes bright, she looked up at that rugged face and felt drawn to it, almost magnetized by his attentions. Imagine, King Kingston smiling at her, talking to her, touching her arm. She was thrilled. Oh, she was aware they stood alone. She had noticed the shocked expressions on the faces of others, Ned's sullen avoidance of her and his brother. But she didn't care. She had captured King Kingston and nothing, but nothing would alter that.

She drank a cup of the strong punch and then another. She felt its effects, but somehow it didn't make her giddy, but rather made her feel slow, heavy, and when he waltzed with her she had to struggle against nausea. She smiled and laughed, but it took effort to do so.

She was grateful when the dance ended and he led her out into the garden. She looked up at the gorgeous moon and breathed deeply, feeling her riling stomach calm a little.

"You all right?"

She smiled her best at him. "Of course."

"Then come on."

She had expected it to be as before, rapturous kisses in the moonlight, thrilling desire, mounting need. Instead he led her directly to the darkened study and locked the door. She stood there afraid, trembling. It was all happening so quickly.

"You are some girl, Moira."

The coquette in her surfaced. "Am I?"

"Yes. I'm about to prove there are no doubts."

She was swept into his arms. His lips smothered hers, his hands found her breasts. She felt breathless, then thrilled that this was happening to her with him, and the first beginnings of desire. Then he stood away and pulled her to the couch. Too suddenly to protest, she was in a familiar position, on her back, being kissed, nipples stroked, skirt up, his hand between her thighs.

Again she felt irrepressible streams of sensation, then that too quickly stopped and he was in her, roughly, insistently. It was painful. She felt dry, not ready. She felt cold and knew she was not enjoying or wanting this. She was merely enduring his demanding thrusts into her. It seemed to go on and on. She felt his repeated movements inside her. She found herself concentrating on the sensations he caused, the strange wonder of it all. Then, suddenly, unbelievably, she was propelled into a climax. It had come out of nowhere, quickly, viciously, shatteringly.

More pleasant than her physical sensations was her sense of triumph as a woman, as she heard and felt his shuddering, gasping eruption within her. When she held him tightly in her arms, it was not so much in passion as in victorious delight which knew no bounds as she heard him say, "You are something else."

"Am I?"

"Yes, most young girls would—"

"I'm not most young girls."

He laughed. "I should say not. You know, if we didn't have all these clothes. . . ." Despite his satiation, he could still view with lust the possibilities with this girl. "Tomorrow night. I know a place we can go. We'll have some dinner and—"

Her dress now thoroughly wrinkled and not unstained, she walked back through the garden toward the terrace, holding his arm quite openly. The music was still playing, but the guests, dismayed enough for one night, had all left.

He laughed. "I'm afraid you're making some tongues wag."

She smiled. "I guess it runs in the family." She said it with a sense of triumph and yet—something else.

"You want to spend the night here?"

"No. I better go home. Tomorrow night will be soon enough."

As he walked her through the garden and out to her carriage, helping her in and kissing her goodnight, neither was aware of a solitary figure in the shadows who watched them sorrowfully.

35

Moira was not the only member of the Morgan household to have an adventure that night. Her brother, Andrew Jackson Morgan, saddled his horse and rode off somewhat earlier than she in a state of excitement and anticipation not dissimilar to hers. He was bound for Washington and a return to the silken arms he had dreamed about.

There was no doubt Andrew Morgan physically favored his mother. His hair was almost as black as hers, although its natural curliness undoubtedly came from his father. Andrew had inherited her sapphire eyes almost uncannily, her pale skin tone and her delicate features. Andrew was just about six feet tall, small boned and very slender. In fact, his build, his coloring, his delicate facial bones gave him somewhat of a feminine appearance. Even his fingers were long and tapering, more like a woman's. He had some native talent for drawing. With his shyness and obvious sensitivity, he might have pursued a career as an artist. But this was unthinkable for the heir to Aurial. Indeed, no one thought of it, including Andrew.

There was no escaping the fact Andrew was a disappointment to Daniel. Father and son had not really fought. Son had done as best he could all that the father had required, but it had been as a duty. This Daniel recognized. His son simply did not have the love of the land, the sense of place and history, the compulsion for adventure of his father. Politics, the free for all in the pits of government, held no lure for the son. All this disappointed Daniel and might, had not their love been so strong, become a wedge between he and Glenna, for she instinctively defended her son. "Why he's just young," she would say. "Give him a chance to grow up. He'll be just like his father one day." Daniel hoped so, but kept his doubt to himself.

Daniel's untimely death had made Andrew at age nineteen the man of the house. His mother had said so, then retreated to mourn her husband in her room. Andrew tried in fits and spurts to operate the thriving estate, but he had no taste for it. Increasingly, he left the operations to Joe, although he rather arrogantly asserted himself from time to time.

This night, Andrew cantered his horse through the nation's capital to the more plush village of George-town, which was already being encircled and swallowed by the city of Washington. He stopped before what looked like a commodius three-story private home, dismounted and tethered his horse, all in barely restrained excitement. He could feel his heart pounding and his breath quickening in anticipation. But he deliberately slowed his movements in a conscious effort not to appear young and eager. His only sign of outward nervousness was to feel inside his vest pocket to make certain for the twentieth time the small gold key was there.

With deliberate strides, he entered the gate of what was known in Washington simply as Lila's Place, although no nameplate identified it as such. Lila's Place was unique in Washington and had its real nature been known, it probably would have been closed. It might best have been described as an emporium of relaxation, for it was a place for congressmen, senators, diplomats, cabinet officials, politicians and other important and well-to-do men of Washington to take their ease. There were bars where a proper drink was served, a dining room for a tasty meal, other rooms for a few games of chance. If a gentleman wished some female companionship, some of the more elegant whores in the city were available. Or, if he preferred to bring a ladyfriend of his own for a discreet tryst, there were quiet, comfortable rooms all with outside entrances. It was a place where no questions were asked. Above all, indiscriminate talk of Lila's Place was simply not engaged in by its clientele. All understood it was far too useful ever to be closed up.

Entrance to Lila's Place was gained by a gold key. Most widely dispersed was the key to the front door. Other gold keys were issued for the private rooms to clients who had reserved and paid for them, the key being left in the room at the end of a hopefully satisfying evening. Andrew had in his pocket the most valuable key of all. He knew it as he walked up the front walk, then along the right side of the building to the back. He mounted stairs to the third floor and stopped on a small enclosed landing. He removed the key from his vest and, his fingers trembling despite himself, inserted it into the door of Lila's private apartment.

Pushing aside a beaded curtain, he entered a room which was to him dimly and seductively lit. It was a high ceilinged room of significant size, opulently decorated. The walls were papered in a deep wine color. The curtain, the cushions were of a soft, rosy pink color that had been perfectly selected for contrast. All this color was extensively reflected and enlarged in an abundance of mirrors. Just standing there, he saw himself reflected from three angles in the cleverly arranged mirrors. The centerpiece of the room was a four poster bed on a dias. It, too, had a pink coverlet and was enshrouded in soft folds of transparent pink curtains.

He stood there a moment, uncertain in the silent

room, then heard the click of a beaded curtain.
Standing there to his right was Lila. She wore a gown, a
negligee actually, of the same pink shade as the room.
It was not a sheer gown. Her body was modestly
covered, yet the sight of her made Andrew shake with
excitement.

"You're right on time, Mr. Morgan. Promptness is a
virtue."

If Lila had a last name, no one knew it. To one and
all, including Andrew Morgan, she was simply Lila.
Any more of a name didn't matter. What did matter to
him was that she was the most desirable female he had
ever known, and he had indeed known her. Lila had
beauty, no doubt of that. But far more powerful was
the mystery which surrounded her. No one knew much
about her. She simply existed, and for Andrew as for
many others, that was enough.

Among slaves, which Lila had been born, mothers
considered it a curse for a daughter to have beauty.
Comely daughters were fair game to be raped or
otherwise seduced by white men, most usually the
master, his sons and the overseers. Lila must have
sprung from a succession of beautiful daughters, for her
Negroid blood had been diluted to a remarkable result.
She had straight black hair which fell softly to her
shoulders, curving out at the ends, deep, rich brown
eyes, sloe and sultry, a small ridged nose and delicious
lips, full and puffy with flesh, now painted pink to
match her gown. She was tiny, perhaps not even
five-two, with a small, delicate face and seemingly
fragile bones. She was extremely lithe with not a speck
of fat anywhere. Beneath the gown she was small of
breast and hips, tiny of waist. When she moved, as she
did toward him now, there was an effortless grace to
her which Andrew could only think of as feline.

Yet none of this was what made her attractive. Her
beauty stemmed from her skin color. The confluence of
races in her blood seemed to have almost created a new
race. The most common description of her was as

"dusky." Her coloring was sometimes said to be that of smokey crystal. Her skin was a shining gray, tinged with brown and bearing a hint of pink. The latter she accentuated with her careful choice of pink in her attire. Her skin which Andrew had caressed and never forgotten, was smooth and flawless, soft, cool and yielding to the touch, and shining in the proper light, such as in this room.

Lila had been born a slave, which neither Andrew or anyone else knew, in Haiti. Her mother, also fair skinned, had somewhat of a local reputation as a witch, expert in various voodoo arts. Lila had absorbed some of this knowledge, but her experiences had taught her to depend more on her body and her cunning than on any potions and incantations. She had been raped by an overseer at age twelve. At fifteen she was a servant in the house of her French master, regularly seduced by him. At eighteen, this master, much taken by her talents, had set her up as his elegant mistress in a house in Port au Prince. She surreptitiously entertained wealthy planters and military officers on the side until at twenty she was one of the best known whores in all of Haiti. This she kept from her master, conniving always to get from him the one thing she truly wanted, her emancipation papers. The day after she finally obtained them, she fled, taking the first boat she could find. She was twenty-two, although her petiteness made her look younger.

She landed in Baltimore. Knowing she needed to hide, she learned that Daniel Morgan ran a free plantation. She had applied for a job as a maid and because she spoke French, which appealed to Glenna, and with the help of a tearful lie, she was hired. During her fifteen-month employment at Aurial, Lila had quickly discovered that Daniel Morgan, quite remarkably, was not seduceable. He was too damn interested in his wife to pay any attention to her. Lila chose the next best alternative, and Andrew Morgan had been easy. A seventeen year old boy was a toy in the hands of a greatly experienced twenty-four year old woman, and at night in his room, she drove him manic with passion.

For her, the repeated seductions of Andrew Morgan were just a means to an uncertain end. She derived no pleasure out of him, other than relief from the stupefying boredom of Aurial, and the satisfaction of turning on a white boy and seeing him squirm and beg for her skin and her expert touch. She was just beginning to see some possibilities in this dalliance when Joe discovered what she was doing and abruptly sent her away. Within a year, she had opened this place, becoming the secret talk of Washington males. Talk centered on her and the mystery surrounding her. The latter was greatly deepened because no one had the slightest idea who had set her up in this remarkable establishment.

As she approached Andrew, he smelled her musky perfume, dark and secret to him, and felt the allure of her remembered skin, her curved body beneath the gown. "Why have you refused to see me?" he asked, his voice cracking under his intensity.

She took his hat and held it, slowly turning the brim through her fingers. She smiled at him, a ledge of white teeth showing. "What am I doing now? You *are* Andrew Morgan."

"I mean before tonight. I've tried to see you for over a year."

She reached up and patted his cheek. "Does it matter? We're together now."

Quickly he grabbed her hand and held it against his cheek, savoring its cool smoothness, the turmoil even her slightest touch could cause him. "But why so long? I thought we promised each other we'd—"

She pulled her hand away. "We did, and I meant every word of it. But this—" She made a sweeping gesture. "It took time. I've been very busy."

"Too busy for me."

She smiled and a low laugh came from deep in her throat. "Don't be silly. I'll not let you spoil our evening. C'mon, you need a drink." She took his hand

and led him to a small table near the bed. She unstoppered a decanter of brandy and poured them each a glass. Raising it to her lips she said, "To us, to old times, to new times to be."

"Oh, Lila, I want you so." He set the unwanted brandy down and in one motion took her in his arms, sinking his mouth into those soft lips he found so irresistible. She responded for a moment, standing as she had been, her arm outstretched holding the wine. Then she pulled away from him. "My, you still are the impetuous one."

"I can't help it, Lila. There is no one like you." Quickly he undid her gown and opened it. She made no effort to resist as he removed it from her shoulders. Indeed, she transferred the glass to her other hand to help him free her from it entirely. Nor did she feel any embarrassment as she stood there naked. Rather she raised the glass to her lips and over the rim saw the heat in his eyes as he gazed at her.

"There's no skin like yours Lila."

She sipped her brandy, its wetness making her lips glisten. She let his passion build a moment longer, then she said, "Hadn't you better get out of those clothes?"

She knew all the secret places to touch him, all the seductive, teasing motions of her body. With ease, she had him squirming on the bed with passion and impatience. She teased him without mercy, taking him inside, then ejecting him to inflict some new torment of skin and hand upon him. When she finally accepted him, it was with quick, hard, pouncing movements of a cat, which left him spent and panting beneath the pink curtains.

She arose and left the room to wash and douche herself, then returned to put on her discarded robe. "C'mon," she said. "Better get dressed now."

He raised himself on one elbow to look at her. "Why? I thought—"

"Don't be silly. We can't do it all the time. There'll be plenty of time later. I thought right now you might like some other diversion."

"Like what?"

"Oh, some of the men are having a little game downstairs. I thought you might like to sit in."

"Gambling? I don't know. I'm not very good and—"

"It's just small stakes. C'mon, get dressed. You'll enjoy it." She smiled in a slow, sultry fashion. "And you'll be ready for later."

"Was I good, Lila?"

He had done nothing for her, never had. "Very. I can tell you've been practicing with too many other girls."

36

Andrew had long suffered the uncertainties and insecurities of youth. This night had changed that. He had felt Lila's writhing movements and heard her moan and gasp and knew he had done well, far better than when she had sneaked into his room at Aurial. And he could tell she had been pleasured by the way she fussed over him afterwards, helping him dress, laughing and flirting with him.

She had taken his arm, crushing her breast against his elbow, and escorted him to the gaming table, introducing him to the others. She brought drinks and lit cigars, but mostly she stood behind him, her hands on his shoulders, bending over frequently to whisper encouragement in his ear, her breath and lips sending shivers through him. Yes, he had grown up this night. Everything was going his way.

That included the cards. The game was draw poker, a rather simple game which he had played and understood. Five cards were dealt and bets, quite small ones really, were made. Then one, two or three cards were discarded and new ones drawn to make the best possible hand, which was bet on again. All cards were concealed and a good player could still bluff and win, even without the luck.

Andrew had fantastic luck. To be sure, he lost an occasional hand, but even then it had taken a truly exceptional hand, three of a kind, even a full house to beat him. His luck was phenomenal. If he needed a card for a straight, there it was more often than not. Cards for a second pair or three of a kind seemed to appear magically. He won a lot and when it was suggested the stakes be raised, he did not object and indeed continued to win.

Nor was it just luck. He sensed his skill. Twice he won with bluffs, causing others to fold with better hands than his. After the second time, he heard Lila whisper in his ear, "My, but you're good at everything tonight." He felt her lips brush his ear lobe, and he shivered with delight.

He studied his opponents. The principal one, who did most of the betting and losing was a fat, baldheaded man named Ed Daugherty. His age was difficult to determine, perhaps in his forties. He had a pink flabby face and small, sharp brown eyes. His short, stubby fingers seemed to extend almost out of his immense belly, shrouded in a black suit. Andrew saw the long expanse of gold chain across his vest and was glad he wasn't fat. Daugherty handled the cards well enough, indeed more expertly than Andrew, but he seemed a poor player, talking too much and too openly, and making rather poor bets. There was a man named Wagner, a small nervous individual who said he worked at the War Department. He played extremely cautiously, constantly guarding his losses. Andrew thought him easy to bluff. The fourth man was named Fitzgibbons.

He ran a dry goods store where Andrew had once shopped. He was a positively stupid player, who bet heavily and almost always lost. He soon ran out of chips and left.

Andrew never could get a look at the face of the remaining player. He wore a wide brimmed hat and the overhead lamp left his face in shadows most of the time. For the most part, Andrew saw only his hands, soft and white with long fingers, and an occasional glimpse of his chin and thin line of a mouth. He said his name was Smith, then almost nothing else, except such necessary words as "open," "raise" and "call." Andrew could not tell much about Smith's play, but he seemed to stay with nearly every hand, although he played in bad luck. He was seldom a winner.

In another time and another place, indeed in what seemed to him a whole different era, Smith had been James Charles Winslow. It was still his name, but he had recently adopted the name Smith. His mystery and silence were genuine, however, for in his bitterness and hatred he spoke no more than necessary. He wore black always and was never seen without the wide brimmed hat shielding his face. He avoided crowds and was almost never seen in public. His appearance at this game occurred only because he was perpetrating a long awaited, carefully planned act of vengeance against the woman who had destroyed him.

Winslow had returned to England not long after his narrow escape from Morgan and the troops. As he had feared, Penwood had ruined his reputation, and Winslow had been socially ostracized. He had not even been invited to the coronation of the young Queen Victoria in 1837. He had remained in England a few years, growing more alone, mean and embittered, then traveled to Egypt and India. But his reputation preceded him there. He tried his hand at several schemes, but all his investments seemed to turn sour. As the years passed, he seemed forever dogged by bad luck, which only fueled his relentless, smoldering hatred for that Irish wench, as he continued to think of Glenna.

He had again returned to England to try to regain the social and governmental acceptance his title deserved. But it had remained hopeless. Lord James Charles Winslow was simply unacceptable to the English peerage. Finally, in 1845, he had sold his estate and other property to his eager brother and returned to America. He had lived in New York, investing in a corrupt company that sold rotten food to troops fighting the Mexican War. He had made a little money at that, but with the end of the war that had blown up in his face. He remained largely friendless, for in his bitterness he was truly unlikable. Thus, alone, he fed on his hatred. A newspaper article about Senator Daniel Morgan, leading abolitionist, would send him into fits of rage, particularly if a reference were made to his "beautiful wife." He saw her one time, from the back of a hall where Morgan was speaking. She sat on the dias, young, demure, smiling proudly at her husband's idiotic words. Again he vowed to make her pay and pay and pay for what she had done to him.

A plan gradually came to him by which he hoped to ruin Morgan, and thus his wife. Secretly he came to Washington and with the last of his fortune purchased a large building in Georgetown in 1848. He had a clear conception of the type of place it was to be. But he had no one to run it for him. It took several weeks, but eventually he found Lila, recognized her talent and induced her to run it for him. Her terms were harsh. She wanted a third of the gross before expenses, and she wanted a free hand to run it. Above all, he was not ever to try to lay one finger on her. She loathed him. Thus Winslow, as Smith, remained Lila's mysterious backer. He lived in an upper floor apartment and was rarely seen.

His plan, concocted and relished in fine detail, was to

ruin Daniel Morgan by enticing him to Lila's Place. Scandal, blackmail would follow quickly. Winslow had been delighted beyond reason, actually dancing a little jig, when he learned that Lila had worked in the Morgan household. It figured to be easy to lure Morgan to indiscretion. But it wasn't. To Winslow's fury, Morgan never came near Lila's place. Then he was killed. Winslow cursed his luck and despaired, until Lila suggested perhaps she could renew her friendship with son, Andrew. He pressed her for details and quickly evolved the plan he was now executing.

Lila was to stop spurning the lovestruck Morgan boy, and entice him to Lila's Place and into a card game. Winslow knew he could not do it himself, so he employed Ed Daugherty, one of the shrewdest gamblers in the East, to con Andrew into a high stakes game. Winslow's deal with his cohorts was that Lila and Daugherty could split the money won, but Winslow wanted a slip of paper—the deed to Aurial.

Andrew was having a splendid time, watching his pile of chips grow. When the stakes were raised until there were sometimes hundreds of dollars in a pot, he continued to win. Such a good time he was having, he did not mind when about midnight Lila whispered in his ear, "I got to attend to something, sugar. Be back in a little bit."

"Where you going?"

"I'll be back in a few minutes. You just have fun."

"But you're my luck."

She had smiled and kissed his cheek, careful to press her breasts against his neck. "You don't need any."

What she had to attend to was a surprise visit from Bradford Kingston III. He had been taken to her apartment and was waiting for her in the red and pink room. He smiled at her and said, "He must be awfully good to hold you up like this."

"He's lousy, just a rich kid. We got him in a game. He doesn't know it yet, but he'll be lucky to get out with the shirt off his back."

"Can anyone play?"

"No, most especially not you. The kid's a mark and I don't want you messing it up."

He smiled broadly. "Whatever you say. Who's playing?"

"Ed Daugherty."

King whistled under his breath. "I already feel sorry for the kid, whoever he is."

"Don't. He deserves it."

She smiled at him. King was more than welcome to her. He had come regularly last spring, then again at Christmas time. She enjoyed him. He was one of the few men who could turn her on and really do it to her. There was something animalistic about him, and he made love with command and authority. He didn't settle for any fake moans, but made her feel like a real woman. After this Morgan kid he could be a welcome change.

"What brings you here, King?"

He smiled back at her, reading her meaning. He didn't pick up though. "I need your best room for tomorrow night."

"Oh, anyone I know?"

"Not hardly. Young kid, too young for me, really. Showed up at father's annual spring mating ritual. But Lord has she got a body. And now that I've broken her in, she's—"

"Good, uh?"

"Maybe. In the right hands."

She laughed. "And you're the right hands."

"You ought to know."

"Yeah, I know." Then she smiled again. "Sounds like your annual spring rites have a sacrificial lamb."

"Not on your life. There's no way any woman will get me."

She looked at him for just a moment, the edge of a

mocking smile on her lips. He attracted her, no doubt of that. It was not so much his handsomeness, as his assurance and masculinity. He knew just who and what he was and made no apologies for it. She had the thought, as she had each time she was with him, that they would make a perfect pair. Both used their wits for money. Both were realists about themselves. Yes, they belonged together—only she was black and he was a slaveholder. That was a twain that never would meet. Too bad. She smiled broadly. "Of course, you can have a room." She went to a bureau and brought him a gold key.

"Your young mark couldn't get along without you for a while, could he.?"

"I thought you'd been with your gorgeous body tonight."

"I was—twice."

She saw the grin on his face. A wicked man. Just like her. There were never any games with him. He was flat on the table always. "Well, don't just stand there," she said, opening her gown. "I don't have all night."

When he was naked in bed beside her, she was aware of skin color, gray molded against white. "What's a slaver like you doing in bed with a nigger woman, changing your luck?"

There was mockery in her voice, but he ignored it. "Hell, no," he said just before he reached her luscious lips, "my luck is running too good right now."

When Andrew felt her hands on his shoulders again, he sighed with relief. He had been wondering where she was and worrying. The distraction had caused him to lose a couple of hands.

"Where you been?"

"Sorry to be so long, but I'm here now."

He looked up at her. She seemed to be smiling particularly radiantly.

"How's it going? Still winning?"

"I'm doing okay, I guess."

"From that pile it looks like more than okay to me."

They played till close to two a.m., then Daugherty moved his chair back, stood up, yawned and stretched. "It's late and you've cleaned me out, son. You're good, but I just know I can beat you. Wanna give me a chance to get even tomorrow night?"

Andrew glanced at Lila and saw a tiny, knowing smile on her lips. She nodded almost imperceptibly to him. He turned to Daugherty. "Sure, I can play."

The gambler gave an expansive grin. "Fine. How about you other gentlemen? Mr. Smith, can we count on you?"

The man in the black hat was still seated at the table. He nodded his assent. Deep shadow under the brim, he was smiling.

37

For Moira awakening was a continuation of falling asleep. She had lain awake a long time the night before reliving the evening. Now, in mid-morning, the same ecstatic sense of triumph came to her. She and King Kingston. Half the girls in Calvert County had been at that party. Women had come from as far away as Washington, even Baltimore. And he had selected her, *her*, little Moira Morgan who had grown up next to him. She laughed from the pure pleasure of it.

She remembered everything about the evening, the

moonlight, the garden an enchanting fairyland of flowers and fragrance, and his passion as he kissed her. And she remembered her gown, her mother's gown really, the sensation it had caused and the look in King's eyes when she first came up to him. And the waltz. How wonderful it had been, a dizzying swirl of ecstatic movement, held in his arms, the whole room whirling, utterly dependent on him to keep from falling. Her thoughts returned to the garden again and she relived his kisses, such kisses, and his wondrous words, "God, you're beautiful" as he exposed her breasts. Yes, she had been beautiful. She was beautiful. And he had wanted her. He could have any woman and he wanted *her*.

Lastly, she remembered the study. It was somehow strangely difficult for her to think of it. What had happened there was not like the moonlight. It was not romantic at all, rather powerful, too urgent, in some way animalistic, even painful. But she did remember and involuntarily moved her hands under the covers. She was tender, a little sore. There was a dull ache in her hips and thighs. He had been too strong, too powerful, too demanding. How he had wanted her, unable to resist her. But she had been unable to cope with him. It all just seemed to happen. She had been powerless.

She closed her eyes, then opened them. Her room was the same, chintz curtains at the window, her dolls on shelves in the corner, the blue gown tossed carelessly on the back of a chair. Everything was the same. She raised the coverlet and looked down at her body. She was the same, too, except for the first time in her life she had slept without a nightgown. Why had she done that? But she was not the same, never could be again. She was now a woman, yes, a whole woman. Accept it. She had done it, not wanting to have it happened. Or had she? It had to happen, sooner or later. And wasn't she lucky to have it be with such a handsome man, such a good lover.

Full on, not shrinking from the reality, she remembered her own lust, her own aching need. She remembered how her body had demanded him and the eruption within herself as he relieved her. Yes, she had been made into a whole woman. She hadn't wanted it to happen, but it had. Again, her basic honesty asserted itself. Or had she? She faced the only really painful memory of the night, her return to the study with him the second time. There had been nothing romantic about it at all. They had passed quickly through the moonlight, directly to the booklined room. He had kissed her very little, but had gone to her breasts and thighs. She was not cold there in bed, yet she shivered a little.

Why had she gone with him to the study the second time? A new glass of strong punch? A new whirl of dizzying waltzes? No, she had known what these would bring. She had known what he was doing. Was she powerless against him? Perhaps, even yes. But, lying there in her bed on a late morning in May, 1850, she knew she had wanted to go with him. She had wanted to feel the passion of King Kingston. She had wanted to feel his hunger and need. She had wanted the triumph of getting him, whatever it took. She smiled. And she had. Had she ever! And she knew it would happen again tonight. He would come for her, take her to a fine restaurant, then where? She didn't know, but somewhere alone, private. There would be no encumbrances of clothes. He would see her body and she would look at the secrets of his. Yes. There would be no pretense of being swept off her feet. She would go, knowing what would happen. Yes, she would go—because she wanted to, because she was no longer a little girl content with kisses in the moonlight. She was a woman who wanted to be made love to by the handsomest man in the world. That ache in her loins told her so.

She could see him, so handsome, so devilishly handsome, so insistent. He would be courtly, attentive.

His eyes would speak of how lovely she was. Lovely? Good Lord, what would she wear? She sat up in bed, the coverlet falling away from her. She saw the blue gown. She couldn't wear that again. He'd think it all she owned. What could she wear? She had only crinolines and calico and modest little girl's dresses. Damn! He was a wordly, sophisticated man. He wouldn't want to be seen with a child. He wanted a woman, an exciting woman. He had liked her in that dress last night. He would expect as much. But what? She thought of her mother's overflowing wardrobe. She would have something. But which gown? Her first theft had been difficult enough—Jessie was everywhere—but she had gotten away with it because she knew exactly the gown she wanted and snitched it quickly. Suddenly she couldn't remember any specific gown of her mother's. And there would be no time to stand there, pull them out of the closet, hold them up and make a choice. Damn!

Quickly she jumped out of bed and quite naked ran to her closet. Frantically, she whipped through her dresses, pushing hangers right and left. Nothing. Nothing at all. Damn! Then she remembered, the blouse father had bought her. He had been away on a speaking trip to New York and Boston. As always, he returned with gifts, a splendid mink cape for mother, a fine riding crop for Andrew. He had brought her an elegant Parisian blouse of the sheerest white silk with delicate Flemish lace at the yoke and cuffs. She had been thrilled with it, but her mother had said, "It's lovely, dear, but a little mature for you, I'm afraid. You save it until you're a little older, and always remember it as your father's." She had seen her father's glance and read the dismay in it. But he said, "Whatever you think best, dear." Now she leaped to a bureau drawer. "Save it until you're a little older." She certainly was that.

She was standing at her mirror holding the blouse in

front of her when there was a gentle tap at the door. Jessie entered unbidden. "Good morning, sleepy-head," she said.

"Good morning, Jessie."

"What're you doing?"

Moira looked at the blouse in the mirror. "Oh, just trying on some old clothes."

"It doesn't look very old to me."

"Oh, father gave it to me a long time ago. I've never worn it."

"It is lovely—but it would look better if you put some clothes on. My land, child."

Moira laughed. "I guess maybe I better." She went to her closet and put on a soft robe. As she turned back to face Jessie, she saw the Negro housekeeper holding the blue gown. There was a look of shock and sorrow in her eyes.

"What have you done to your mother's gown?"

Guilt and fear gripped Moira. "Oh, that. I must have spilled some punch. How clumsy of me?"

"It don't look like no punch to me. And these wrinkles. They'll never press out. You must have—" Then the truth dawned on Jessie. "Child, you didn't?"

Caught, cornered, Moira fought back. "So, it's to be child again."

"You didn't let that no good rake touch you, child."

She raised her voice. "I will not be called child."

"All right, *Miss Moira.*" The word was a mockery. "I needn't ask. I can see what you did."

Defiance was Moira's only recourse. "So what if I did."

The Negro shook her head sadly. "Oh, child, child . . ."

"And I'm going out with him again tonight. There's nothing you can do to stop me."

Jessie looked at her in sorrowful horror. "No, I can't stop you. But you can stop yourself. Don't you realize he's no good, a gambler, a-a womanizer, a slaver?"

"I don't care. He's the most wonderful, the hand-somest and gentlest man I've ever known, and he loves me, *me*, do you hear ME!"

"Loves, huh?" Again the mockery. "I'll bet he loves you a whole lot. Miss Moira, you're a fool, a plain, ordinary fool. And so is your brother. He didn't come home last night. God knows, what *he* was doing."

Moira's anger flared, so much she was unable to speak.

"I'll bet you think you grew up last night. Well, let me tell you, you didn't. You grew *down*." With that Jessie turned and stomped out of the room. In her anger, Moira could do no more than slam the door behind her.

Seething, Moira dressed in her riding habit. Whip-ping her boot with her crop, she marched downstairs and out to the stables to saddle Hickory. Who was she to talk to her that way? Time she learned her place. And what did she know about being a woman? Married to Joe. That must be something. Why they didn't even have children.

She rode Hickory hard through the fields for a mile or two, then stopped to give him a breather. She saw a horse approaching her at a canter and recognized the rider long before he reined beside her. He wore work clothes and his hands were dirty. She spoke in a mock drawl, more deeply southern than Marylanders nor-mally use. "I do declare, Mr. Kingston. I seem to run into you almost every day while riding. It can't be all coincidence."

"No. I rode out here hoping to see you."

Still the mocking accent. "I do declare. What on earth for, since you just saw little ol' me only last night?"

He ignored her teasing. His voice seemed different, lower, firmer. Indeed, she could see he was angry. There was more determination to him, less of his usual sullenness when she mocked him.

"Yes, I saw you last night. I was embarrassed for you. How could you have worn that dress? How could you have made such a fool of yourself?"

Moira's anger flared, but she maintained her foolish accent, believing it her best defense. "Is that what you think, Mr. Kingston? Some people thought I was most attractive. You wouldn't be jealous, would you?"

"Damn right I'm jealous. I'm also sad you let my brother use you."

"What on earth are you talking about?"

"You know what I'm talking about. He never has been worth anything and never will be. Oh, he's handsome, but there's nothing underneath it. He only knows how to use people for his own pleasure."

"Is that so?"

"Yes. And you let him. You let yourself join a long line of conquests by Bradford Kingston III. If you think you were anything but a conquest, if you think he's going to marry you—well, I feel sorry for you. I'd thought you a better person."

Her anger blazed into rage. All her pretense dissolved. "I'll not be talked to this way, Ned Kingston, by you or anyone."

"Looks to me like you need to be."

She struck at him with her riding crop, the blow narrowly missing his face, landing on his shoulder. He caught her wrist and held it firmly.

Moira struggled with him a moment, then relaxed her arm. Forcing a smile and returning to her mock drawl, she said, "I do declare. I thought you a gentleman, Mr. Kingston. I never thought you'd accuse girls falsely of things you know nothing about."

"Perhaps you're right," he said, his voice as cold as his eyes. "But you inadvertantly left one of your belongings at our house. I thought it best to return it to you." Reaching into his saddle bags, he handed her the torn pantaloons. Abruptly he turned and spurred his horse.

Moira sat her horse, watching him ride off. She felt

the torn fabric in her hand and felt a flush rise to her face. Then she, too, rode off, kicking Hickory to a full gallop.

By the time Moira returned to the house, groomed the lathered horse, bathed and dressed, her anger had cooled off. Ned was just jealous. He had always liked her, she knew, but what did she want with a kid with dirty fingernails? So what if he knew. So what if everyone knew. She had captured King Kingston and that was all that mattered.

There was a tapping at her bedroom door.

"If you're going to scold me, Jessie, you can just stay out."

"No, it's me, Morrie."

"Oh, Andy. Come in." He entered still wearing the dark suit of the night before, somewhat wrinkled now. He was smiling at her.

There existed a remarkable closeness between brother and sister. Their fondness for each other resided perhaps in their genes, but certainly in the manner of their upbringing. They were children of a prominent politician who was away too much and of an outstanding beauty who did not neglect them so much as she failed to understand them and their approaching maturity. Andy and Morrie, as they called each other, had been thrown together a lot, left alone evenings, even whole days as Glenna accompanied Daniel on his trips. There had grown a closeness, an acceptance, even an intimacy between the siblings.

"And what are you being scolded about, little sister?"

Moira's smile was rueful. "I guess because I'm not so little any more."

"You haven't been for a long time." He smiled and gestured with his hands in front of himself, drawing the outline of her figure. "So what'd you do?"

"I went to the Kingston's party. I couldn't stand being cooped up here another evening."

"So? What's wrong with that?"

"I wore mother's dress. You know, the one she wore to the inaugural."

Andrew made his eyes revolve in a circle. "You didn't. I'll bet you were a shocker in it."

Moira smiled, feeling pride in herself again. "Yeah, I was that all right. You should have seen the eyes pop. You could practically step on them."

"I'll bet."

"But King liked the dress, liked me a whole lot."

"Wow! He's pretty fast company."

"Is he ever!"

Andrew hesitated, but only a moment. "Morrie, you didn't?"

"Yes. He took me to his father's study. I was scared, Andy. But he was so masterful. It hurt at first, but then—oh, Andy, it was so wonderful and I was so good. He liked me, I know he did." She saw the pensive look on her brother's face. "You aren't going to be angry with me, are you?"

He looked at her a moment, then smiled. "No little *grown up* sister. It had to happen sometime. I'm glad it was nice for you. It isn't always, you know."

"Oh, Andy, thank you." Her eyes moistened. "I need you to understand so."

"What's a brother for?"

"And you're the best brother in the world." She leaned across the bed and kissed him on the lips. "You were out all night I hear."

"Was I ever. I went to Washington to Lila's Place."

Moira was genuinely surprised. "Really? I thought—"

"I know, forbidden fruit. But I can't help it. Lord, she's exciting. I spent the whole night with her. The things she does to me."

"What does she do? I want to know everything."

Andrew smiled, but not at her so much as from his memories. "Oh, it's hard to explain. She's like a cat, so quick, hard to hold on to. She's all over me. She takes me inside and then pulls away and is at another part of me. Drives me wild. I think I can't stand it sometimes."

Just seeing him and listening, Moira felt her own desire mount.

"Wow, Andy. Are you in love with her?"

"No, but she sure is exciting."

"Did you do it all night?"

He laughed. "Hardly. I got into a poker game, won a lot of money." He pulled a large roll of bills from his pocket.

"Good heavens, Andy. You won all that?"

"Sure, it was easy. Nothing to it. I'm going back tonight and win that much more."

"Are you sure? Maybe you—"

"Don't be silly. I'm good at it. Why I bluffed those suckers right out of their pants."

She laughed and clapped her hands with pleasure. "Oh, I'm so happy for you, Andy. Such an exciting thing to be a man."

"It does seem to be getting better, doesn't it?"

She looked at the money in his hand. "Andy, could you let me have a little. I got to buy some proper clothes."

He hesitated. He knew he might need this for tonight's game. But he smiled. "Why not, big little sister. We're in this together, as always." He peeled off a significant stack of large denomination bills. "That ought to be enough to buy out the whole store."

"Oh, thank you, Andy." And she hugged and kissed him. "Have good luck tonight."

"No problem. I'm a born winner. But I better get changed." At the door he paused. "What're you doing tonight?"

"Going out with King."

He looked at her. "Can I tell you to be careful?"

"You can and I will. Don't worry."

His smile was pure affection. "I won't—and you have a good time."

He left her then and busied himself with various affairs. Before leaving that evening, he went to his father's study and opened the safe. He intended to replace only the money he'd given Moira, but on impulse he stuffed all the money into his pocket. One never could tell what might happen.

38

Both Morgan children were in Lila's Place that evening, but neither knew it. Andrew had no knowledge his sister was being taken there. Yet, as he enjoyed the gray-tawny flesh of Lila, Moira was in the next apartment sipping champagne poured by Kingston. Moira, of course, knew Andrew was going to Lila's Place, but she did not know that was where she was. She had expected to go to a fine restaurant, and had been disappointed to be led up a dark stairway and into an empty room, however plush it was. She did not ask where she was, nor did King mention it.

Cheered by her talk with Andrew, Moira had dressed for her evening in a state of high excitement. She had brushed and brushed her hair till it sparkled with highlights, bathed again and powdered and perfumed her body. She had dressed with enthusiasm, so much so she even giggled in delight. Father's blouse was heavenly, puffy billows of sheer silk, yet so prim with its high collar and lace at the throat and cuffs. She adored it and smiled knowingly at her reflection as she thought of King's reaction. She wore the blouse with her favorite skirt and cape. It was linen and of a shade of green that enlarged and deepened her eyes. She was stunning and knew it.

King picked her up at dusk. He boldly went to the door and calmly endured Jessie's slings and arrows aimed at him. His manners were impeccable. He flattered Moira, saying how lovely she looked, then helped her into the buggy. He then climbed in beside her and flicked the reins to begin the journey to Washington.

Beneath his smiles and compliments, he was perturbed. The girl was pretty, no doubt of that, but in this outfit she looked about sixteen and this was making him uncomfortable. He was glad not to be seen in public with her. Lila's Place would do just fine. And he would make a short evening of it, get this child home to her mother early. The truth was, and he knew it, he was rather satiated from his exertions with her and Lila the night before. Right now, he felt more like the company of men, then squiring a young kid around. A good, high stakes poker game would be perfect. Perhaps after he took this Morgan kid home . . .

He had wanted to stand her up and had thought seriously about it. But father, blast him, had made that impossible. The old man had been ecstatic about the party. Gleefully, he'd boasted, "See, didn't I tell you? A fine looking girl. I knew you'd fall for her."

The elder Kingston had been waiting for him in the foyer as he returned from putting Moira in her carriage. King had lit a long panatella of Maryland tobacco, grown and made on this very estate. He exhaled the smoke as a sigh. "I fell for no one, father."

"Oh-h yes you did. Locking my study from the inside. Damn clever, son."

"I wonder sometimes, father, if you're a gentleman."

He laughed. "'Course I'm not a gentleman—and you're a chip off the old block. When you seeing her again?"

Another smokey sigh. "Tomorrow night."

"Splendid, splendid. You know, son, I don't think it would be too soon to pop the question. Oh, you won't get married right away, but—"

"For crissake, father." King was so annoyed he was speechless.

"Look, this is the best chance I've had to get hold of that Morgan property. I intend to pursue it. And you could do a lot worse than Moira Morgan. She's a very handsome young woman. That dress she wore, that figure. She could do a man proud. Why, if I were younger, I'd—"

King had walked away from him. By morning, he had made up his mind. He'd take the girl out tonight, just to please his father, then he'd hightail it back to New York.

Moira's excited anticipation had quickly melted under the reality of the evening with Kingston. She felt isolated, uncomfortable all during the ride to Washington. He seemed attentive only to the matched team of bays, all but ignoring her. There were no magnetic smiles or knowing glances and he spoke hardly at all. Suddenly she realized she really didn't know what to talk to him about. She said it was a nice evening, but he only grunted agreement.

"That sure was a grand party last night, wasn't it?"

He turned to look at her, his smile knowing, quite wicked. "You had a good time, didn't you?"

She had felt a flush in her face and looked away, unable to answer.

"Didn't you?"

She blushed more. Flustered, she answered softly, "Yes." Then immediately she bit her lip. She shouldn't have said that. She should have laughed, said she really wouldn't know, teased, flirted. But the time for that had passed. Why was she so nervous, flustered? Nothing was going at all well.

Her mood worsened abruptly as she entered the trysting place. She felt dampened, defeated, strangely afraid. The room depressed her. It was done in blues, very ornately with a great deal of velvet. Really quite nice, she supposed, except she knew what it was, a place of assignation. There could be no doubt. The centerpiece of the room, right in front of her eyes, was a bed. It stood on a raised platform and was covered with curtains, much like her own at home, to insure intimacy and privacy. Why had he brought her to a place like this? All these mirrors. Heavens, there was even one over the bed. Then she saw the painting, a nude Negress with strange gray skin in a disgusting pose. Moira was appalled. It was the first nude painting she had ever seen. Why had he brought her here? What kind of a girl did he think she was? Her mood plummeted as she realized the answer.

"I knew you'd like this place. We'll have a quiet dinner, just the two of us. Here, let me take your cape."

Instinctively, she reached to her throat to hold it. "No. I'm fine, thank you."

"As you wish." He turned. What a disaster this evening was going to be. "Champagne. That's what we need." While she stood there rigid, he busied himself opening a bottle and pouring two glasses. He brought it to her and smiled. "Those remarkable green eyes of yours look large enough to make a lawn. How about drinking up and not being so scared? I'm not the bogeyman."

She tried to smile.

He clicked her glass. "To a lovely evening. C'mon, drink up." She did as she was told. "All of it. That's better," he said, then refilled her glass. "Bubbly is the greatest relaxant there is." He said and did the right things, but inwardly he was cursing. The last thing he felt like was a seduction. For two cents he'd take her home right now and forget it.

Moira was not unacquainted with alcohol. She had drunk champagne at parties. Wine was frequently served with meals. But having slept late and then taken the long horseback ride, she had not eaten a bite all day. In only a minute or two the champagne was affecting her. She shook her head.

"Is something wrong?"

"I suddenly realize I haven't eaten all day. I'm really feeling the wine."

King smiled, but thought, God, what a child. He was a cradle robber. "It'll go away in a moment. Just have a little more." He swallowed half of his and watched her take a tentative sip of hers. "Besides, I think you're only too warm." He set down his glass and removed his jacket, placing it on the back of a chair. In his shirt sleeves he approached her. "Why don't you take off that silly cape?"

She clutched the cape to her throat. "No."

"For crissake, Moira, you're acting like a kid. And a kid is what you are. I feel like a cradle robber. I'm taking you home."

His words stung her and she felt hot tears in her eyes as she watched him stalk to the chair and snap the coat from it. She had no conscious thought, only the pain of hurt and humiliation. Slowly she pulled the tie to the cape and slid it from her shoulders, watching him slip quickly into his coat and snug it to his shoulders. As he turned back to her, she saw surprise, then delight on his face.

She had worn nothing underneath the sheer silk. As she had dressed, it had seemed merely bold, daring, wickedly enticing. Now she felt shamed and embarrassed. And she remembered from her mirror what he was looking at, her breasts barely concealed, her nipples rosy red beneath the fabric. She closed her eyes in an effort to blot out the horridness of what was happening.

King felt excitement surge through him. It was not her near nakedness, although her breasts were compelling, it was the whole idea of such a garment. More than anything else, he was stimulated by boldness, by risk taking and daring. It was why he adored gambling, risking everything on the turn of a card. To him, a great gamble was far more sensuous than any woman. Suddenly, he was thrilled by this girl's boldness. What a remarkably shocking thing to wear. What a magnificent woman she could be for a man like him, if only she could pull it off.

Her eyelids closed, she heard him say, his voice soft, even husky, "You are right now perhaps the most remarkable woman I've ever seen."

"No."

"Yes you are, believe me."

She opened her eyes. He was smiling. She heard him say, "You know, my dear, you have a most becoming streak of daring in you. I like it. I like it a lot. It's what attracted me to you last night—even more than your obvious attractions. That was a bold dress you wore and you did it with—the French have better words for it—panache, élan. You were remarkable and very exciting. I think you can do as well tonight, if you try."

Tears scalded her eyes. "I'm so ashamed. I feel like a tramp."

He laughed. "What on earth for? You're stunning. C'mon, hold that chin up. That's the girl. Now smile."

She tried, but the smile was a pathetic imitation of one.

Again he laughed at her. "You've got to know how lovely you are. You wanted to excite and entice me, and so you have. Indeed, boldness is the one thing that will excite me. But you're ruining it with your tears and shame." He moved toward her.

"No, please. I can't. This place, I can't bear it."

"This place? It's one of the most elegant in town. I reserved it especially. What displeases you about it?"

"Everything. That picture. It's horrid."

He turned to look at the painting, recognizing it as Lila's little joke. "It is a bit gross, isn't it? Can't have her watching us." Quickly he strode to it and turned its face to the wall. "There, that's better. What else?"

Despite herself, Moira smiled. Then she laughed. It

was suddenly quite funny to her. But she held on to the dregs of her depression. "All these mirrors."

Again King pretended to look around. "'Fraid I can't do much about those. Beside, I like them. You're so lovely, I get to look at you again and again, everywhere I turn. See?" He turned slowly in a full circle. "There you are over there and there, magnificent in all."

She decided the multiple reflections were fascinationg. If only she had worn . . .

He came to her and slowly began to unfasten the tiny buttons of her blouse. She wanted to stop him, at least part of her did, but her hands seemed unable to move from her side. In a moment, he pulled the garment back from her shoulders. "Lord, Moira, you're lovely. There may be more beautiful breasts in the world, but it has been my misfortune not to see them. And I mean every word of that." He touched her with both hands, gently, his caress as a whisper. "Such remarkable skin, so soft, like a rose petal." His fingers found her nipples. "And you are a flower. No rose was more beautiful."

She stood there, truly unable to move as the sensations of his hands mingled with the champagne. He kissed her, gently, his lips barely touching her lightly parted lips. Sensations tickled through her, quickly followed by an inundation of feeling as he pulled her lower lip into his mouth and pressed it, his tongue like cold fire against it. She felt desire exploding within her. How could he do this to her?

Abruptly, he stopped and stood back to look at her. He saw passion welling in her eyes. It seemed to suffuse her whole body. Huskily, he said, "I think you're ready now."

She blinked and heard herself say, "Yes, oh yes."

He laughed. "I don't mean that—at least not yet. I'm taking you out to dinner as I promised. You're about to set the nation's capital on its collective ear."

Dismayed, she exclaimed, "I can't. Not like this."

Suddenly he guffawed, slapping his knee in laughter.

"You could," he said, "but we'd both get arrested."
Still chuckling, he pulled the blouse back on her
shoulders and began to button it. "What makes this
outfit work, you know, is that this blouse is so demure,
high neck, all this lace and ruffles, while beneath. . . .
My dear, you are a clever, clever girl."

"I can't wear this in public."

"Why not? You had planned to."

"I was going to wear the cape. I intended this only
for you."

"Well, it'll be for me. I expect to have the time of my
life."

"I'll be a spectacle."

"That's exactly right."

He finished buttoning the blouse, then undid her
skirt to tuck in the tail. In a moment he gasped. "You
never cease to amaze me. And you do what I want. I
said I didn't like those awful pantaloons and you wore
none." Unable to resist, he stroked her brilliantly hued
down. "Lord, you're lovely." Then he sighed, thinking
of later, and refastened her skirt. "Now, you continue
to do as I say and everything will be fine tonight."

He took her to the Claridge, the finest restaurant in
Washington. It was crowded with officials, diplomats
and their wives. Many eyes turned as they entered,
attracted by the girl with the flaming hair.

She heard him say, "Your cape, my dear. Let me
help you." She shrank from his hands moving toward
her. "Yes." There was firmness, command in the word.
As the cape slid from her shoulders, she heard, "Just
hold your chin up and follow the maitre d'."

She did as she was told, hearing a hush come over the
room. She felt her whole body being scalded by burning
eyes, but she kept her gaze fixed on the back of the
maitre d's neck. He seated her. Then the quiet was
broken by a babble of voices around her. "Ignore
them," she heard, "and smile at me, just at me all
evening. Don't look around. Fine. Beautiful. Now your
napkin."

He ordered champagne, then, as they clicked glasses he said, "Lord, but you're exciting. I'm having the time of my life."

"Why?" she said. "I don't understand."

"Smile. Look like you're having fun, which I promise you will have. Because I'm excited by daring, risk, boldness and the person with panache to pull it off. You have tremendous verve, my dear."

Again she smiled. "I'm scared to death."

"Of course you are. That's part of the risk, much of the excitement." He sipped his champagne and watched her do the same. "You're doing splendidly. Shall we order, then dance?"

Again it was the waltz, the exciting, stirring rhythms, the swirling skirt. She realized they were soon alone on the dance floor, and suddenly she didn't care. She laughed, tilting her hair back so it flew around her. She *was* having fun, the most ever in her life. She arched her back, so her hair swung straight down as he moved her in circles within circles. She knew everyone was staring at her and she didn't care. More, she was suddenly glad, more than glad, thrilled to be the center of attention and in the arms of this handsomest of men.

When they returned to the table, both of them panting, he said, "Didn't I tell you? You are right at this moment the most exciting woman in the world."

She saw the desire shining in his eyes. Again she felt triumph at the effect she was having on the famous King Kingston. She tossed her head in her instinctive, coquettish gesture. "Am I?"

She heard his voice suddenly husky. "Yes." He paused, then said, "My father wants me to marry you. Right now, it seems an appealing idea. We might make a magnificent pair."

His words shocked her. "Good heavens, I don't know what to say."

He laughed. "You're supposed to say you're not sure you want me."

Again the flirt surfaced. "That's true. I'm not."

"I'll do my best in a little while to undermine your doubts."

He was already thinking of later and had been all evening. Excitement roiled his loins and he had a sense of his overwhelming power. What a luscious body. She was so young, so virginal—well, not virginal, and he smiled at the thought, but inexperienced, so ripe to be taught, to be used. Even now his fingers could feel the soft curves and mounds of her flesh, and he remembered her pliant passion as he had merely touched and kissed her earlier. He laughed. It was going to be a remarkable night, quite splendid really, one to remember.

They ate, danced, drained the bottle of champagne. It was well after midnight when, carrying more champagne, they returned to the reserved room. She felt giddy from the champagne and the excitement of the evening, yet once again the room depressed her. It was so obvious, it's purpose so apparent. Suddenly she remembered her feelings of the night before, the second time he'd taken her to the study. The first time there had been moonlight, enchantment, enraptured kisses. The second time . .

Without realizing it, her hand clutched the cape at her throat. She looked at him and of a sudden the room was full of him. There seemed to be three, six, a dozen images of him in the mirrors, all of them taking off their jackets and putting them on the back of chairs, loosening their ties, unbuttoning their shirts.

"Don't just stand there, darling, get undressed."

She couldn't move. She felt transfixed by the multiple images of a man removing his shirt, raising one leg then another to take off his boots, fumbling with trousers. Then all the men disappeared and there was just one stepping toward her. She had never seen a man naked before. She saw his smiling face. Why wasn't he as embarrassed as she was? She had an impression of white skin, very white skin, masses of dark, curly hair on his chest that seemed to arrange itself into a V down his flat stomach, a pointer, pointing. . . .

"You've never seen a man naked before?"

He was standing in front of her. She looked at his smiling mouth, avoiding his eyes. "No." Her voice sounded strange, hoarse, husky to her.

The smiling mouth said, "It's time you did."

She sensed him step closer to her and her hands being taken by his. They seemed disembodied from her wrists, her arms, as he lifted them from their place at her throat and bore them outward and downward through space until her fingers touched unfamiliar hairiness, then were filled with soft, pundulous warmth. She had a sensation of heavy, wrinkled aliveness.

She was conscious of his laughter. "You are the strangest combination of boldness and timidity I've ever seen."

He was leaning his face toward hers. She saw and heard the mouth speak. "That, my love, is what's going to bring you such pleasure." His lips kissed her eyelids closed, hot, moist against them, then brushed her forehead, the tip of her nose, her cheek. There was a pause. She opened her eyes to see his eyes close to hers, straining her vision, then felt his lips touch hers, softly, barely making contact, brushing against her lips, then gently moving, nibbling her lips apart, pressing each in turn between his, caressing the inner surfaces with his tongue. The sensation seemed to buffet her like a physical blow and she felt herself shaking all over, almost unable to stand. Her trembling hands were quickly filled with a hard, throbbing, pulsating mass as his lips devoured hers, his tongue suddenly filling the ravenous cavern between them. She began to tremble uncontrollably as his hands slid the cape from her shoulders. Her hands gripped him tightly, almost to hold on against the sensations his mouth produced in hers, as she felt him slowly unbuttoning her blouse. It seemed to take forever before it was undone, pulled back from her shoulders and she felt his hands at her breasts, kneeding, crushing, pulling, his fingers delivering quick, hard, painful pinches to her nipples which made her gasp and jump and, without realizing it, squeeze and twist his throbbing organ until he gasped and jerked in responsive pain. She felt his fingers fumbling at her waist, then the fabric of her skirt slide from her thighs. The torment at her breasts was joined by new, excruciating sensations as his hand reached between her thighs and reduced her to paroxysms of shaking.

She felt assaulted with sensation, hardly able to stand under the havoc he performed at her mouth, breasts and pelvis. Then a sharp stab of pain tore through her from below and she knew he had pinched her hard. In shock, she tore her mouth from his and saw his wet, smiling lips. "You like this, don't you?" Then he pinched her hard again between the legs as his mouth found hers again. She felt the stab of pain then the convolutions of pleasure-pain-need which followed. She had to bite. She clawed at his mouth with her teeth, trying to bite him, but he moved his mouth and tongue always to escape her. She knew she was maddened, crying out, moaning. And suddenly his hands were on her shoulders, pushing down hard. His mouth followed her for a distance, then left hers and she was on her knees, her head tight in his hands, her mouth filled with hot, hard, saltiness. She recoiled, shaking with revulsion, then, so quickly she was unaware of it happening, he seized her shoulders and rolled her sideways and over until she was on her back and he was kneeling above her, his hands reaching between her thighs, spreading, lifting, encircling her legs with his arms. Her hands free, she tried to push him away, then all the strength went out of her as she felt his mouth and tongue at her. She felt swept by sensation that quickly built until he levied a convulsive climax upon her that seemed to make her flesh fall away from her bones.

When he was apart from her, she raised herself, spitting and gagging. "How could you?" she screamed and lunged at him, hitting at him with her fists. "How *could* you?"

But he only laughed, hard, uproariously, ducking her blows. "You liked it. You know you did." Still he laughed, even as he grabbed her wrists and pinioned her back to the floor. "Maybe you'll like this better." He pounded on top of her.

She looked up at his laughing face. "Let me go."

"I'll let you go all right, " he said and lunged into her so hard she cried out.

She was helpless, his weight atop her, her arms immobile under his outstretched arms. She felt her whole insides filled up with him.

"What a magnificent girl you are."

She looked up at his smiling face. His laughter had given way to a sort of softness and wonder.

"Let me go—please." She tried to twist away from him, although she knew it was futile.

"Go ahead, fight all you want." Then he began to move against her.

Despite herself, Moira felt the rise of sensation, then desire and need. Faster and harder he moved and she felt borne along, only dimly aware of her moans of pleasure, the release of her hands, his mouth on hers, her arms clutching him, her cries of pleasure. She knew only the tension building within her, leading inevitably to an eruption joining with his.

She lay there a long time, spent, almost too exhausted to be helped to her feet and hold the glass of champagne he offered her. She heard him command her to drink. She tried, but seemed unable to raise the glass to her lips. Something pulled at her arm. Then she heard him laugh. She looked in the mirror. Her blouse, father's blouse, was still around her back, the lace cuffs still buttoned at her wrists. Suddenly it seemed terribly important to remove them, but she didn't know what to do with the glass of champagne. She heard him laugh harder, then suddenly it seemed very funny to her and she heard herself laughing, too, and saying, "Will somebody please help me?"

He came to her, unbuttoned the cuffs and threw the garment aside. "What a woman you are, Moira Morgan."

She looked at him, her eyes questioning.

"Yes, you are. Look at yourself."

She followed his fingers and saw multiple reflections in the mirrors of a girl with tousled hair and bright red lips, a stemmed glass in her outstretched hand, moving it toward her mouth. Again she saw the naked girl, multiply reflected in the mirrors, hands playing over her breasts, waist, hips, thighs, derriere, between her legs. It struck her the girl was a stranger with red hair, a not very nice girl to allow such things to be done to her, and, still looking, she could see the wantonness in the girl, the open mouth, the quickening breath of desire. Then the girl in the mirror was gone, and she was aware of being led to the bed. She heard the rustle of curtains and felt the soft mattress beneath her and there was the girl again, above her, looking down at her lasciviously, a man kneeling over her, hands on her body.

Then the image was gone. She was pulled to a sitting position. Her glass was filled and she was ordered to drink. A handsome, smiling, black haired man, lust shining in his eyes, took her in his arms. Again she felt the welling of desire. She had the awareness that there was apparently no end to it with him. She seemed unable to prevent him from doing anything he wanted. She felt herself being turned, lifted up until she was on her hands and knees. She felt his hands caress her back, reach under her, kneed her pendulous breasts. What was he going to do now? It didn't matter. She'd do anything with him.

By dawn when he took her home, he had in a single night introduced her to the bizarre methods and exotic perversions he had learned in a lifetime. When she finally fell drunk and exhausted into her bed, the early rays of the sun streaked her window and she was madly, hopelessly in love with him.

39

The whole evening went splendidly for Andrew, at least to that point where he lost his inheritance and impoverished his mother and sister. And that happened with an abruptness, with such speed, he could do nothing but stand there, dismayed, disbelieving, unable to comprehend the monstrous thing he had done.

Lila welcomed him with open arms. To his delight, she was for the first time eager to see him. "It's been the longest day of my life," she whispered. "I don't know how I've waited for you to get here." And she proved her passion with her lips and her willing body. She seemed unable to get enough of him. Even after he reminded her he had promised to join the game, she begged for one more time and had astounded and thrilled him with her quick, lascivious movements. Even after they had dressed and he joined the game, she stood behind him, holding his shoulders, stroking his hair, pinching his ear lobes and whispering encouragement. Once or twice when he won a particularly big hand, she was so thrilled, she impulsively kissed him openly and deeply in front of the others.

Thus, Andrew played poker in an almost exalted state, the most desirable woman he knew at his shoulder virtually panting with desire for him, the cards falling for him like magic. He could not believe his luck. Oh, he lost a hand or two, but his luck would return, pairs, straights, flushes, full houses, even fours of a kind seemed to pop into his hand at will. He bet and bluffed extravagantly, but he could do no wrong.

Then his luck seemed to turn. He lost a succession of hands. His chips disappeared, won mostly by Daugherty and Smith. His money won the night before disappeared. Reluctantly he dipped into the reservoir of funds taken from his father's safe. Again and again, he reached into it, fear and panic rising within him.

Then he heard Lila say, "I think you gentlemen need a break. Why don't we recess for ten minutes?" There was some grumbling, but she grabbed Andrew's hand and pulled him after her.

He was taken into a small office, her office obviously. It was plain, utilitarian, obviously not much used. Lila was hardly the type for orderly business practices. She poured from a decanter. "Here, have some brandy."

"I think I've had too much already."

"No you haven't. Do what mama says and drink."

As he obeyed, she spoke to him, authority in her voice. "Now you listen to me. You're playing right into their hands. You've lost a little and you think your luck is gone. You're down. You think you're a loser. If you keep that up you will be a loser."

"I can't seem to help it."

"But you can. Luck isn't in the cards. Luck is in the head. If you believe you're a winner, you'll win. If you believe you're a winner, you can actually will the card you want. You've been doing this for two nights, up till now, and didn't even know it. Now you go out there, full of confidence, and you'll beat 'em. I guarantee it."

Suddenly, he knew she was right. He was playing to lose. "You're right—and thanks. I'll be all right now."

She came close to him, smiling as she removed the glass from his hand. "I know you will. And I'm the one who would thank you. You know what I am. There have been lots of men, far more than I want. But there's never been one like you. No one does to me what you do." Deftly she unbuttoned his trousers and reached inside, gripping him tightly. "There's no one like you. You're a tiger. I want you so bad right now I can hardly stand it." Still gripping him, she pulled his head down and kissed him, her soft lips seemingly feverish with passion. He felt desire race through him and strike hard at his loins. "Hurry up and get this game over," she said. "I can't wait." She took him back to the table. As the first cards were dealt, she whispered in his ear, "Go get 'em, tiger."

Incredibly, his luck did change and with a vengeance. He couldn't lose. Quickly he drove Wagner and Fitzgibbons from the game. Daugherty was reduced to only occasional play. He folded frequently, nursing his small stack of chips in hopes of a big hand which never came. Smith was the big plunger, raising and raising against Andrew. And Smith had good hands, but Andrew's seemed to be always a little better, a pair of queens to beat jacks, three fours to exceed three deuces. It was uncanny. He heard Smith cursing under his breath as he went down time after time. He saw the older man in the black hat reach into pocket after pocket for rolls of bills. The money was not even changed into chips.

Then came the hand, the most remarkable of his lifetime. Daugherty was dealing. Smith opened with a heavy bet. Andrew looked at his hand, deuce of hearts, seven of clubs, nine of diamonds, jack and ace of spades. It certainly wasn't promising. Quickly, he showed it to Lila, shrugging his shoulders beneath her hands. He met the opening bet. Daugherty raised and Smith raised again. Andrew was about to fold. He had nothing.

Then he heard Smith say the most words he'd heard from him in two nights. His voice was acid. "As soon as I get a hand you're going to fold. Is that it?"

Andrew smiled. "No, I came to play poker. I seem to be doing quite well at it."

He met the raises and stayed in. When the time came to discard, he kept the two spades and asked for three cards. He watched his opponents. There was a slight twitch near Daugherty's left eye. Andrew knew he had not done well. Beneath the shadow of Smith's hat brim, he saw a tightening of his thin lips. He had improved his hand. Slowly, concentrating on a poker face, Andrew picked up his cards, one at a time. When the third one was revealed, he felt Lila digging her nails into his shoulders. He still did not move a muscle.

Daugherty dropped out, but Smith bet heavily. Andrew raised. Smith met that and raised again. There were in all three rounds of raises. Finally, it was Smith's turn. Andrew watched the mouth. It seemed to express determination, but something more, a savage internal glee that was barely suppressed. A minute or two passed, although it seemed longer. Smith seemed uncertain. Finally, he shoved his stack of money into the center of the table. "That is five thousand dollars. It is all the cash I have left in this world. If you can beat my hand, it is yours."

The size of the bet did not bother Andrew. He had that much and more. All he had to do was raise the bet and he would drive Smith under. Should he? For reasons he would later not understand, he said, "Call" and counted his money into the center of the table. Gleefully, Smith laid down four eights and instantly reached for the pot.

Andrew felt Lila's nails digging into his shoulders. "Just a moment, Mr. Smith. I called, remember." Slowly, his face still a mask, he laid down his cards. "There are five spades in a row. I believe it is called a royal flush."

Smith's chair fell backwards to the floor as he slowly rose to his feet. For the first time, Andrew saw his face, wrinkled, pasty white with a wild, tormented look to his strange gray eyes. He looked at Andrew in disbelief.

Slowly, his voice little above a whisper he said, "Not many people know it, but I am owner of this establishment. Lila, who seems to adore you so much, is my employee. You, Mr. Morgan, have beaten me at my own game in my own house. All right, so be it. I propose a wager to you. I will bet this property, which is of far greater value, against all the money you have won this night. If you win, you will have everything I own in the world—including this black piece of trash behind you."

Andrew heard her gasp. His anger flared. "That, sir, is no way to speak of Miss Lila."

"Cut it out, Morgan. I'll speak anyway I want to her, unless you accept my wager. If you win you can call her whatever you want."

Andrew stood up, ready to swing at Smith, but Lila held his arm. "It's all right, Andrew. Pay him no mind. He doesn't own me." Andrew did not raise his hand, but he continued to glare at his adversary.

"Is it a bet or isn't it?"

Andrew felt instinctive dislike for this man. He would love to see him crawl on the floor. But bet all he had won? He turned to look at Lila. She was smiling at him, her eyes shining with excitement. "What'll I do?" he asked.

Her smile broadened. "Whatever you want—Tiger."

He sat back down. "I think Lila is about to get a new and better employer. What game will it be?"

Smith sat down, too. "Showdown, five cards, all up, best hand the winner. As an impartial observer, Mr. Daugherty can deal."

"Okay, fine with me."

The cards were carefully shuffled. The fat dealer suggested Lila cut, which she did. Slowly, one after the other, the cards were dealt, Smith first, called out by Daugherty and looked at. "A queen of hearts for Mr. Smith . . . a seven of clubs for Mr. Morgan . . . A four of spades to go with a queen . . . a pair of sevens for you, Morgan. . . . A ten of diamonds for Mr. Smith, still queen high . . . a king of spades for Mr. Morgan, still with a pair of sevens. . . . Fourth card is another queen for Mr. Smith, pair of queens showing . . . a lucky seven, three sevens for Mr. Morgan."

Andrew could barely restrain his glee. Three sevens in five card showdown was a virtually guaranteed winner.

". . . a queen for Mr. Smith, three queens showing . . ."

As Andrew's last card, an ace, was called, the words were lost in Smith's gleeful shout. He jumped to his feet, screaming and waving his arms.

Andrew was dumbfounded. "It can't be," he said. "You can't take with a single card everything I've won all evening."

Smith seemed to be cackling as he raked the huge pile of money and chips toward himself. "But I have, I have."

Andrew was on his feet. "But you can't. I demand another chance."

Suddenly, Smith stopped raking in his money. "All right. What do you want to bet."

Andrew reached in his pocket for the last of the money taken from his father's safe. "I'll bet this."

Smith smiled. "That seems a rather paltry amount after our recent wagers."

"It's all I have."

"I doubt that, Mr. Morgan. You are a very rich man. And you have talent for this game. Unfortunately, you lack the spirit of the true gambler. You are unwilling to wager all on a gamble. You lack the courage for great risk."

"What do you mean?"

"I mean I was willing to gamble all—my money, this property, even the services of my beautiful and faithful employee behind you. I did that because I know great courage is what it takes to win in adverse times. You will learn that one day." He bent to pull in more of the money.

Andrew could feel the sting, the condescension. Angrily, he said. "I'll do that. I'll wager Aurial. It is worth more than all that money and this establishment."

Smith looked up at him and smiled. "No, Mr. Morgan. I don't think that would be wise of you."

"But I insist. I demand the wager."

Again Smith smiled. "Do you have the deed with you?"

"No one carries such a thing around."

"Well, then. Perhaps another day."

"I insist on the wager, sir. I am a gentleman, a man of my word. If I lose you shall have the signed deed to Aurial back here within two hours."

Again the thin smile from Smith, followed by a resigned shrug. "Since you have suggested the wager, you may select the game."

"A single cut of the cards. High card wins."

"Really, Mr. Morgan. Are you sure?"

"Yes. Let's get it over with quickly."

Again Smith shrugged. "Will you do us the honor of shuffling, Mr. Daugherty?" That was done, slowly and expertly by the fat gambler. Smith said, "Do you wish Lila to cut for luck, Mr. Morgan?"

Andrew looked at her and smiled. Suddenly he knew he was going to win. He was certain of it. He said to her, "Cut 'em good, Tiger." He saw her try to smile at him, but it was a most forced effort. "Don't worry, Lila, I'm going to win."

"You first, Morgan."

Quickly, calmly, Andrew reached into the deck and turned over. He gasped his pleasure, then said calmly, "I have a king of spades."

He saw Smith look at the card, then up at him, his eyes squinting. "And so you have. Now it is my turn."

He reached for the pack. His hand seemed to hesitate over it, then he turned over his card.

When Andrew saw the ace of diamonds in Smith's hand, the blood drained from his face. He looked at the card a moment, then at the triumphant face of Smith. "My word is my bond, sir," he said hoarsely. "I will return within two hours with the deed."

He walked on weakened legs out of the room. When he reached the street and mounted his horse, it was already eight o'clock of a sunny new day.

40

During the ride back to Aurial, Andrew did not engage in self-recriminations. Nor was he ensnared by panic and fear. He simply had a cold, numbing realization of the magnitude of the calamity which he had wrought. In a single foolish moment, he had created ruin for himself, his mother, his sister and all who lived under the grace of Aurial. Like most humans faced with true disaster, Andrew could find no place in his mind for such petty emotions as guilt and fear. There was no looking back. He had brought disaster and there was no changing it.

He rode rapidly and purposefully toward home, and when Aurial came into view in the distance, he felt no emotion. Indeed, he hardly noticed the beauty of the estate, although he had many times in the past. He tethered his horse out front, entered the house and went straight to his father's study. He opened the safe and took out the deed, not even looking at it. He gathered up some other papers, then went to his mother's room.

His mother sat in a rocker before a window, staring out into—what? Andrew visited her almost daily, and she always seemed to be in this position. What was she looking at? The view was of the fields across which his father had ridden that last day. Was she sitting there, gently rocking, waiting for his return? Or was she seeing only some private vision? Many times he hoped it was a happy vision of happy times with her husband, his father. He wondered, many times, if his mother had gone mad with grief.

She wore black, only the ghostly pallor of her hands and face showing out of the shroud. Her hair was pulled back from her face in a bun, never a becoming style for her. It seemed to him she had aged a million years. Although she was not yet forty, she resembled a little old woman waiting for death.

"Good morning, mother."

He saw her turn to look at him. She spoke. "How nice to see you, my son." But there was little life in any of it. Her voice was flat, dry, her blue eyes, once so alive and sparkling, now dull and empty.

He thought of asking her how she felt, but that was a futile exercise. A fool could see how she felt. "I'm afraid I must bother you to sign some papers again."

She looked up at him with her faded blue eyes, seeming to have difficulty comprehending. Then she dutifully arose and walked to her desk in the corner. Andrew was startled to see how thin and frail she looked. There seemed to be no evidence of the once glorious figure.

She sat down on the edge of a stiff chair, took up a steel pen and dipped it in ink. He placed the first paper before her. As she began to scrawl her signature, now strangely small, crowded and squiggly, he said, "These are just some bills and receipts, mother." She did not reply, but bent to her task as he placed paper after paper in front of her, holding them, telling her where to sign.

The deed was last. For a moment, a twinge of fear

tugged at him. What if she saw what it was? Asked him about it? He knew he had not the courage to look her in the eye and tell her what had happened. He would be dishonored first. Slowly, he covered the deed with the other bills. Only the line for her to impoverish herself was showing. "This is the last one," he said, his voice hoarse, and held it on the desk before her, his knuckles pressed white against the fatal paper. She dipped the pen in the glass inkwell, then applied the tip to the paper and signed.

When she was finished, she sighed, put the pen in its stand, covered the inkwell and stood up. She looked at him. "You are doing such a good job with Aurial, Andrew. I don't know what I would do without you."

Her words stabbed at him. Guilt and grief flooded him like blood from an open wound. His mouth opened, wanting to pour out his terrible secrets. Instead, he turned and walked away from her. At the door he stopped and looked back. She was already back in her chair, staring at the window. He knew pure agony looking at her. Tears in his eyes, his voice breaking, he said, "Mother, whatever happens, please know I've always loved you."

The silence stretched on. He wasn't sure she'd heard. Then the single word, barely audible, was said, "Yes."

Everyone knew him as Joe. Indeed, most people did not know he had any other name. But, as a free man he needed a last name for legal purposes. At Glenna's suggestion, he had long ago taken the incongruous Irish name of O'Reilly. She explained it was her father's name and he would do it proud.

Joe O'Reilly told people he was thirty-five, although he still didn't know how true that was. In any event, he looked much younger, indeed, not a great deal older than when he had rescued Glenna. He was still coal black, thin as a sapling and as protective of Glenna as any lion of her cubs. In nearly twenty years, a dozen of them married to Jessie, he had become thoroughly

Americanized. He was the perfect servant, overseeing Aurial with a professionalism which made the Morgans envied by their neighbors.

Despite appearances, however, the jungle had not left Joe. Thus, it was with wary eyes from behind the stairs that he watched Andrew descend and enter his father's study. By methods he could not begin to understand, Joe sensed danger. He smelled it. It prickled his skin. He had no idea how he knew, but there was menace about.

The jungle had taught Joe to wait for trouble to arrive, not seek it out. Danger was to be avoided, if at all possible, never confronted. So it was, he remained a long time, over a quarter of an hour, staring at the door of the study. But the feeling of menace grew within him, rising sharply, until he was driven to the uncharacteristic action of seeking it out. -

He opened the door to the study and in one glance saw the door to the safe open, the strong box empty, Andrew sitting at the desk, Glenna's jewels piled in front of him, a sheet of paper half-covered with writing.

His voice low, steely, Joe said, "What has happened, Mr. Andrew?"

Andrew looked up. Joe saw the surprise in his eyes—and much more, fear, hostility, guilt, panic.

"Get out of here, Joe. I want to be alone." His voice was strained, high pitched.

"What is wrong?"

"Nothing I tell you. Just get out of here."

Joe hesitated. He had learned not to butt into family affairs. The children were the province of their parents. Whatever he might think, he stayed out of it. He had warned Jessie to do the same many times. But now, his sense of danger overrode this restraint.

"No. You have made trouble for the Missy."

"Who?"

Joe realized he had used his long ago name for Glenna. "Your mother. There is bad trouble. I know it."

"There is no trouble. Get out."

Joe saw the lie in his eyes. "Young master, you will not lie. There is bad trouble for missy. You will tell me."

He saw Andrew open his mouth to speak, but no words would come out.

The steel in Joe's voice hardened. "Young master, you will speak—this instant."

Then the words came tumbling out of Andrew's mouth. "I have lost everything gambling, all our money, even this house, all of Aurial. I was a fool, but it can't be helped. I've tricked mother into signing the deed. I must deliver it in Washington within the hour."

Joe was emotionless, his face impassive. The nature of the danger was of no importance. Escaping it was all that mattered. "Who you lose it to?"

"It doesn't matter. It's all gone, everything is gone. I thought about killing myself, but what good would that do? I'm going away. There's gold in California, mountains of gold. I'm going to find it. I'll buy Aurial back. You'll see, I will, I promise. I'll remove this stain on my honor."

None of these words, although he heard and understood them, had any importance to Joe. At this moment, he didn't care about Aurial, its loss, its possible recovery, gold in California or anything else. He didn't even care about Andrew, what he had done, or anything he might do. His focus was entirely on the danger to Glenna. "This man. Who?"

Andrew had never seen Joe this way. There was something almost savage about him and he felt frightened.

"Who is he?"

"His name is Smith. He own's Lila's place in Washington. I was in a game with him and—"

Joe tuned out his words. He didn't care about the game. He recognized the name Lila and knew of her place in Washington, but he didn't care about that either. "Who is Smith?"

"I don't know. Nobody knows anything about him."

"How he look? Tell me."

Andrew raised his hands in a gesture of futility. "God, I don't know. He doesn't look like anybody—medium height, pasty face, thin lips."

"How old?"

"God, I don't know. In his fifties."

"Eyes?"

"What does it matter?"

"Tell. Now."

"He has funny eyes, very strange. They're gray, I suppose, but so pale it is almost as if he has no color in them."

An image flitted through Joe's mind. He had seen Winslow close up only once, nineteen years before, at the railroad construction site. He had been on horseback, demanding Glenna be turned over to him. Joe had seen those strange gray eyes.

He heard Andrew speaking, though little of it registered on him. "I'm sorry, Joe. I've been a fool. But I'll go. I'll earn Aurial back. Tell mother I'm sorry to steal her jewels, but I've got to have money to get to California. She'll understand. You'll make her understand."

"Yes," the black man said, but his mind was racing. The man's name had been Winslow. He had tried to kill Missy before. She was in great danger.

"Tell her I'm sorry. I've tried to write it, but it's no good. Please tell her and Moira I'm sorry. I'll make it up to them."

Coldly, his mind elsewhere, Joe looked at him. "Yes. Now you go. Quick."

"Joe, I'm sorry. Will you look after—"

"Yes. Now go."

Joe truly gave no thought to Andrew, that he was going away, that he might never be seen again. His mind was entirely on Winslow and the menace he posed for Glenna. He saw, but did not register the meaning, as Andrew stuffed his mother's jewels in his pocket, took one of his father's pistols from the case, and left the house. Joe followed him to the door to watch him ride away, then he turned, closed the door and entered the house. Jessie must be told. Together they would do what was necessary to save Glenna.

Lila was terribly tired. She had been up all night and as midmorning passed, she still had not had any rest. More than physical fatigue, she felt she had been through an emotional wringer. The entire charade left her drained, the phony passions with Andrew, the endless game and tricking of him, the elation at the success of their scheme. When the mark rode away to bring back the lease, the trio had embraced and danced around the room heady with jubilation. They had counted the money, thousands of dollars, and divided it between Daugherty and herself.

As she heard Daugherty and Winslow brag of each card, each nuance of their con of Andrew Morgan, Lila had succumbed to an overwhelming fatigue and then an unexpected depression. She was finding, suddenly, no joy in their accomplishment. What had they done that was so marvelous? A well-known gambler and card cheat, an unscrupulous and vengeful man and a vastly experienced whore had taken advantage of a boy not yet twenty years old. Such a triumph. Slowly she shook her head in dismay. She wasn't feeling very good about herself. So it had been easy. And why not? He was just a boy. And what had he ever done to her really? She was angry at Joe, spiteful for his sending her away. But, truly, what had the Morgans ever done to her? They had taken her in and given her employment when she needed it. Now she had repaid a dead man, his wife, daughter and son by taking away their home and leaving them penniless. Wasn't she proud of herself?

"The two hours are past and he's not here. I knew it, I knew it. He'll renege. I knew he would."

Slowly, Lila turned to look at Winslow. He was

pacing the room in a high state of agitation. "He'll be here. I know he will." And she did. Andrew may have been played for a foolish sucker, but he had handled himself like a man, no tears, no whining, no begging. He had accepted the loss like a man. He had walked out proudly. If he said he would pay his debt, he would. His sense of honor was obvious. Her depression deepened as these thoughts came to her.

"Well, he better. And you two don't get that money unless I get that deed."

God, the skinflint. What a horrid man. And she had helped him skin a decent boy who had never done her any wrong. Her self-loathing was almost more than she could bear.

In a few minutes Andrew Morgan entered. He looked ghastly, deep lines of fatigue and sorrow in his face. She saw the droop of his shoulders. But when he stood before Winslow, he squared his shoulders. She saw him look Winslow squarely in the eye. His hands were steady as he reached inside the breast pocket of his coat and laid the folded piece of paper on the desk. "My debt, sir." He uttered not another word as he turned on his heel and stalked out.

"Wait," she called and ran after him. "I have to talk to you." She pulled him back into her office. He stood there, not speaking, unsmiling. She looked at him, not knowing what to say herself. She longed to tell him he had been tricked, by her, by a gambler to please a man whose quarrel was not even with him. It had something to do with his mother. She wanted to blurt it out, to relieve the pain he must be feeling, to have him know it wasn't his fault. But she couldn't. There would be a duel, at least. Andrew would surely be killed. And she would be ruined, probably arrested. There was no way she could tell him the truth. But she had to tell him something, anything.

"I'm sorry, Andrew."

He looked at her. She couldn't read his expression—then she could. Pride. That was all he had left.

"I know. And I'm sorry. I have hurt innocent people terribly."

"It wasn't your fault, Andrew. It couldn't be helped."

His tiny smile was wan. "Oh, yes, dame fortune."

"They'll be other times Andrew."

"Not for me. I'll never play cards again. As long as I live, I won't."

His stubbornness, his pride in adversity, his determination tugged at her. "What'll you do?"

"I'm going to buy back my estate if it's the last thing I do."

"But how?"

"I'm leaving immediately for California. There's gold there. I intend to find it."

The infernal gold rush. Everyone off to find a fortune in California. She had thought it so stupid. Now she said, "I believe you will, Andrew."

He looked at her. She detected a slight softening of his expression. "Thank you for that."

"Andrew—" She hesitated. "—I did mean what I said about you and me. Truly I did." It was all a lie, but she had told so many lies. Why not one that made her feel better?

He looked at her, a softness intermingling with pride. For just a second he was a little boy on the verge of tears. Then he turned and left her without saying a word.

She remained standing there several moments, trying to quell the ache in her throat, then she slowly left the office. She saw Winslow rushing out, the precious paper clutched in his hand. She heard him shout, "Now I'll have her. By God, now I'll have her."

Slowly Lila climbed the stairs to her apartment. She disrobed and climbed between the sheets. She knew she wouldn't be able to sleep, but she was so tired. She lay there, eyes open, thinking of Andrew and this remarkable night. The loser somehow seemed the winner.

She heard a gentle tapping. A maid came in. "I'm sorry, Miss Lila, but there's a gentleman to see you. He insists I call you."

Lila sighed. "Who is it?"

"Mr. Kingston."

Lord, what did he want? She almost said to have him brought up, then changed her mind. She was in no shape to entertain him, if that's what he wanted. "Tell him I'll be there in a moment."

Five minutes later she confronted King downstairs. She reacted with disbelief to his words.

"I forgot to leave the key last night. I knew I'd better return it."

She sighed in exasperation. "Really, King. You called me down for this. I've not been to bed all night. You could have left it with anyone."

He smiled. "May I say you look it?"

"No, you may not. Now I *am* going to sleep."

"Actually there was something else. As I rode up I saw the Morgan boy come out. He looked like a ghost. Putting two and two together, let me ask if he was your mark."

"It is none of your business."

"I think perhaps it might be. It was his sister I entertained here last night. She is a tasty morsel and I went a bit overboard. I fear she has gotten ideas about me. Let's just say they are going to have to be discouraged. Let me ask again. Was her brother Daugherty's mark?"

She sighed. "Yes."

"What did you do to him?"

"Everything. He is penniless. He lost everything, including his property."

King whistled through his teeth. "Why all that? What's Fat Ed want with an estate in Maryland?"

"He doesn't. He got the money. Win—I mean Smith got the estate."

Slowly a smile began to break up King's face, then a chuckle, finally loud laughter. He was consumed by it.

"I'm afraid I don't see anything funny."

King laughed a moment longer, then was able to tell her. "No, you wouldn't. It's a private joke. You see my father has wanted Aurial all his life. It's been his passion. He's been after me to bed and wed the Morgan girl to help him get hold of it." Again he laughed. "Now somebody else has it. Funny how things work out in this life."

"Yes, isn't it. Good night, I mean good afternoon, Mr. Kingston." She left him and started back upstairs.

41

Moira first felt the insistent shaking of her shoulder, then an urgent voice saying something she didn't understand. She moaned and rolled over on her side. When the shaking became more vigorous, she rolled to her stomach and tried to bury her face in the pillow.

But the shaking only worsened. She recognized the voice. Jessie. Jessie was shaking her and saying something. "Get up, child, now, this instant." She felt hands trying to turn her over and pull her out of bed. It was unbearable. "Leave me alone," she moaned.

"I got to get you up, child."

There was a particularly hard shake. "Stop it, I say."

"Then get up. You got to, Miss Moira."

Angrily, Moira sat up in bed, opened her eyes and knew what she suspected was true. She had never had such a headache in her life. Her whole head throbbed and her eyes were dry and aching. She felt like her scalp was ready to split open.

Through the pain, she saw Jessie and heard her talking frantically, something about getting dressed, packing, leaving and hurry, hurry, hurry. It made no sense to her, none at all.

Then she heard, "I got to go help Miss Glenna. Can you manage?"

That made sense. Anything to get rid of Jessie. "Yes, yes, I'm fine." When she saw Jessie leave, she tried a moment to focus on what she had been saying, but she couldn't. Her only reality was her pounding head. "Oh-h," she said, and slowly sank back into the pillow. "Oh, God, my head."

Then she remembered. The champagne. She'd drunk lots of wine. Hungover, that's what she was. She'd heard of it, but God, she never thought it would be like this. Then in an instant she remembered the evening before, all of it, and a flush pervaded her body, father's blouse, dining and dancing at Claridge's, returning to—Her flush deepened. The things they had done! How could he have? How could *she* have? Under the coverlet she ran her hands down her waist to her pelvis. The things he had done to her. The things she had done to him. Quickly she reached up and touched her face. She had never dreamed. It wasn't decent. Then she smiled. But so thrilling. She had wanted to. And she would want to again. She would do anything with King. "Oh, my darling," she whispered, "I love you so." In her happiness she gently fell back asleep.

Her second awakening a half hour later was ruder and more determined. Jessie ripped back the covers and pulled her nude body out of bed. Despite the shock of it, Moira realized her head was somewhat improved as she heard a torrent of scolding from Jessie.

"Stop it, Jessie," she screamed. "I don't understand a word you're saying. Try to make some sense."

Her outburst silenced Jessie. Moira saw the acute

agitation on her face, the tears running down her cheeks. "Try to tell me calmly, Jessie."

"We got to run, Miss Moira. There's terrible danger. Miss Glenna is ready. You got to come, too."

Moira shook her head. "I still don't understand. What danger? Please tell me from the beginning."

Jessie breathed deeply and swallowed, trying to get hold of herself. "Mr. Andrew . He did a terrible thing. He went to that awful Lila's Place last night. He got into a card game. He lost. He lost everything, all the money, this house, the land, everything. We got to run, Miss Moira."

She still didn't understand. "Where is Andrew?"

"He's gone to California. He stole Miss Glenna's jewels and has run to find gold in California. We got to go, too, quick."

"Andrew? Gone to California?"

"We got to hurry, child. Please get dressed."

"Why do we have to go?"

"'Cause he lost Aurial to that bad man."

"What bad man?"

"That man Winslow."

"Who is Winslow?" There was a hint of exasperation in her voice

"That bad man who whipped Miss Glenna and tried to hurt her."

Then Moira remembered her mother's stories, the garret in Ireland, the burning of Aurial long ago. "He's alive? He owns Aurial?"

"Yes, yes. And he'll come. We got to get your mama away."

Moira tried to think calmly. "How do you know all this is true?"

"Mr. Andrew. He told Joe. He left a note."

Moira asked where the note was, then quickly flung on a robe and dashed downstairs to her father's study. In a moment she was reading the hastily scrawled words:

"Dearest Mother and Moira: I cannot ask you to

ever forgive me. What I've done is too horrible for that. I've gambled away everything. Aurial is lost, all our money, everything. It is all my fault. I've thought of suicide, but I am not even man enough for that. I'm going to California. If it is the last thing I do I shall buy back— "

She read the words a second time. All was true. Oh, Andrew, Andrew. A wave of compassion for her brother swept over her. Gone to California. Oh, he mustn't.

Jessie had followed her. "Please, Miss Moira, come. We got to hurry."

Moira felt strangely calm. The whole situation was suddenly clear to her and she began to cope with it. "Where are you taking mother?"

"Joe says to go to my Aunt Beulah's in Baltimore. She'll be safe there."

Moira remembered Aunt Beulah, a big fat woman with a gold tooth and a ponderous bosom. She had visited her house once with Jessie. She lived in the Negro section of Baltimore. Moira remembered sitting in the kitchen eating cookies and milk. "Yes," she said. "That's the place to take her."

"Please hurry, child. We all gotta go."

A plan was forming in Moira's mind, but she knew she had to think. "No. You and Joe go ahead with mother. I'll come later."

"But—"

"No buts, Jessie. I know what I'm doing. I'll pack a few things and come later on Hickory. Now you go with mother. She's the one in greatest danger."

Jessie stood there, as though rooted.

"Do as I say, Jessie. I know what I'm doing." She pushed the older woman out into the foyer and saw Joe coming down the stairs, suitcases and grips under both arms. "Joe, make your wife listen to me. I want you to take mother safely away. I'll come later on Hickory."

She saw the strange look in Joe's eyes, fear, wariness, command. He was looking in her direction, yet it was almost as though he were not seeing her, his mind elsewhere. "Yes," he said. "Jessie fetch the Missy."

Moira went back to her room and began to pull some dresses from her closet. She saw figures pass her doorway and went to the door to watch. Her mother, shrouded in black, being led, as though lifeless, down the steps by Jessie, slowly, painfully. She saw Joe enter the open front door, put his arm protectively around her mother and lead her out to the carriage. It was like a tableau, and Moira felt a sudden ache for her mother, that pathetic figure. Oh, mother. Would she never see her again? Then the door to Aurial closed behind her.

Fighting back tears, Moira turned back into her room. Think. She had to think. But she couldn't. The house seemed so quiet, so empty, and the knowledge she was alone for the first time in her life preyed on her. And her mind seemed empty, too. The mechanical action of taking dresses from her closet and piling them on her bed seemed all she was able to do.

Then from downstairs she heard the treble chimes of a clock. She had lived with that sound all her life, yet she thought she was hearing it for the first time. She stopped in mid-stride listening to the sixteen musical notes, separated into sets of four for each quarter hour. Then she heard the hour struck. Four o'clock. Oh why hadn't they awakened her earlier?

The clock returned her to reality. Andrew, oh Andrew, gone to California. She had to find him. She had to find her brother. Somehow they had to stay together. Everything would work out if only they did it together. How had he gone? By ship or overland? How could she find him if she didn't know how he went? Then she remembered King. How could she have forgotten him? He'd know what to do. He'd help her. Oh King, blessed King, so strong. He loved her. And right then she knew that more than anything she needed to be loved. She could almost feel his strong arms around her, comforting her, telling her what to do.

Quickly, she dressed for riding, boots, black skirt, white blouse and jacket. She snatched up a few garments and other possessions, ran to the stables and filled saddle bags. Then she saddled Hickory and rode toward the Kingston estate.

King had awakened at midmorning with a bad taste in his mouth, and it was not entirely from the champagne. He had let himself get carried away, and that, he felt sure, was an uncharacteristic action. The girl, her beauty, that ripe young body, her eagerness and her bold flouting of convention had all ensnared him. But that was last night. In the sober light of a new day, he knew he had a problem. The girl was in love with him. He had to find a way to let her down easy. Ordinarily this would be no problem. He had done it many times. But there was the old man and his stupid machinations. He wouldn't be just getting rid of a lovestruck girl, he would be disappointing his father. If the old man sided with her, there could be real problems.

Unable to sleep, he had ridden into Washington to return the key to Lila. There he had learned of Andrew Morgan's escapade and the impoverishment of the Morgans. That would make his problem easier. Father wouldn't give a damn anymore. Such a disappointment for the old man. But it made getting rid of Moira more difficult. It wasn't just ending a romance, it was kicking a girl when she was down. He swore several times, both under his breath and audibly. By the time he saw her ride up he was in a very sour mood.

His problem of how to greet her was solved when she ran up to him and into his arms, burying her face against his chest. "Oh, King, I have to talk to you."

They were standing in the foyer. "Anytime, honey. Let's go to the study where it's more private."

The door was hardly closed, when she began to blurt out everything. "Andrew went to Lila's Place last night. He got into a poker game and lost everything, our money, Aurial, everything."

"I know."

She looked at him in surprise. "How do you know?"

"I went to Lila's to return the key to the apartment we used last night. I found out then."

"Lila's Place? Is that where we were last night?"

"Yes. I thought you knew."

"No. How would I know? Oh, I wish I had. I could have stopped Andrew."

"I doubt that very much. He was set up, a mark—"

"What are you talking about?"

He was very uncomfortable. A feeling of guilt tugged at him, although he didn't know how it could be his fault. "I had been to Lila's the day before yesterday. I knew they had a mark, a sucker they were fleecing. They'd brought in Big Ed Daugherty. I know him. He looks fat and jolly, but underneath he's an unscrupulous card shark. When you play him, you have to watch his hands all the time."

"Why didn't you stop him?" Moira's voice was high pitched, almost a shriek.

"It was none of my affair. I didn't know who the mark was. If I'd dreamed it was your brother, I would have stopped it—or tried to. But how was I to know?"

His words seemed to deflate her. "I suppose you couldn't. But I wish you had. I wish—"

"So do I, Moira. I'd give anything to have known. He went to the table and poured himself a large brandy. "Do you want some?" he said.

"No, I don't want anything." Her mind seemed elsewhere, as she struggled to understand what she had learned. Then she seemed to. "Well, that settles it. More than ever I've got to find Andrew. I've got to tell him it wasn't his fault. He was cheated. Maybe he can bring legal action against them."

King swallowed half his brandy. "It's possible. Where is Andrew?"

"That's just it, I don't know. He left a note saying he was going to California. He can't have gone far. But I don't know which way he went—by sea or overland."

"If it is any help to you, most people go overland. It is longest and hardest, I'm told, but cheaper. Most people don't have money for ship passage. Did Andrew have any money?"

"He took mother's jewels. I have no idea of their worth."

King thought a moment. "A forced sale, probably not much. It would seem most likely he'd head for Independence, Missouri. That's the jumping off place for the California Trail—either there or St. Joseph's, a little further north. My guess would be Independence."

"You're right. That's where I'll find him."

King opened his mouth to speak. He knew he should tell her the terminal to the California Trail was no place for a young girl alone. But no words would come out. Intent only on finding her brother, she had made no mention of last night and what they had done. Perhaps it meant less to her than he thought. Rather than words, he filled his mouth with brandy and poured another glass.

King was not to be so fortunate. Moira broke the awkward silence by saying, "I thought perhaps, after last night, you'd urge me to stay."

She saw him hesitate, pursing his lips as though words had a bad taste.

"Of course you should stay. You belong with your mother."

Her Irish anger flared. "My mother! I doubt if she even knows what's going on. She's been hidden among blacks in Baltimore. Is that what you want me to do?"

Again she saw his hesitation, his difficulty in speaking, and heard, "No, of course not."

She was having difficulty comprehending him, then as she began to understand, believing it. For the first time, she realized she was in the room of two nights previously. In daylight, it looked much different, but behind him was the couch where they had lain. "This is the place you brought me, isnt it? What was it that happened here?" She saw him looking at her, his mouth firm, an expression in his eyes—of what? He looked like a guilty puppy. "And last night? What was that?"

Then she saw him smile, the handsome, glittering smile she thought so devilish. "It was great fun, wasn't it?"

"Fun!" She shouted the word, her anger flooding over her. "Fun! You don't remember what you did? I do. You did disgusting things to me, vile things. I would never have, only I thought—"

"Did I ever say I loved you?"

"Not in so many words, maybe, but you talked of marriage."

"I did not."

"You said we'd make a great pair."

Again the rakish smile. "And so we did. You were magnificent."

She couldn't believe what she was hearing. "My God! It can't be true. You put your thing in—"

"You didn't seem to mind."

"Damn you, King. I minded. But I thought you loved me. If you didn't, how could you do those things to me?"

He tried to laugh, but it was a trifle forced. "Don't make so much of it, Moira. People do it. I thought you needed to learn. The experience was good for you."

"Learn! Experience! Who are you to decide what I need to learn? Who gave you the right to play with other people's lives?"

Her words stung him. She saw it in his face.

"If I'd known, if I'd thought for a moment, I'd—"

"Oh, you know all right. And you thought. Did you ever think of Bradford Kingston III? Oh, what a fool I've been." She stamped her foot in her rage.

"Oh, come on, Moira. Grow up. You're making too much of it."

"Grow up! Thanks to you I have. Have I ever." She stood there a moment, eyes wide in disbelief and anger, then said, "I just hope I never see you again. If I ever meet a man like you I'll know what to do. Goodbye, *Mister* Kingston." She turned toward the door.

"Where are you going?"

She stopped, her hand on the doorknob and turned to face him. "Does it matter to you?"

"Believe it or not, it does."

"Well I'm going to find my brother."

"I wish you wouldn't."

"And I wish you hadn't."

Her anger arced across the silence to him and he had to look away. His boots were of sudden interest to him. "I'd like to give you some money."

A bitter smile spread her lips. "Now it's money. You don't leave a girl any pride, do you?"

"I didn't mean that." He blurted the words. "I do care what happens to you. I just thought—"

"Thinking again. Let me tell you, King, you've already given me too much—way too much, and I didn't want any of it."

She left him standing there, ran outside, mounted Hickory and in anger, humiliation and determination rode north to the nearest train station. From the sale of her beloved horse, as well as the money she had obtained from Andrew, she financed her trip west.

Throughout her visit, Ned Kingston had stood in the garden listening through the open doorway to every word spoken inside the study. His instant reaction was to be deeply hurt by new knowledge of sexual relations between Moira and his brother. So that was the kind of girl she was? She deserved everything that happened to her. Good riddance. How lucky he was to have her gone.

His jealousy and pain consumed him for several days, then, almost despite himself, these feelings gradually gave way to concern then open worry about her. She had gone to Missouri to begin the long trek by wagon train to the gold fields in California. He had heard stories of the hardships of the journey. Many people died of disease, starvation. He had even heard of people going mad on the way. For a girl alone it was impossible. For a girl like Moira, so young, so sheltered, why she didn't stand a chance. Accompanying his worry was guilt. How could he have let her go? He should have stopped her. But, no, all he could think of was himself and his damnable jealousy. Moira was out West, God knows where, suffering horribly, and he was doing what?

The days, more than two weeks of them, went by in this fashion for Ned. Increasingly, he became upset, irritable, dissatisfied with the life he had once enjoyed. Then came the day when he realized he loved her. It was not just physical desire for her, a pining for the girl next door, but deep and genuine love. He was worried sick about her. He would never be able to live with himself if anything happened to her. Suddenly he knew he didn't care what she'd done with King. He had to find the girl he loved.

The next morning he took what money he'd saved, packed a few things into saddle bags, mounted his horse and rode west in search of Moira. This was the seventeenth day after she left, and he was beginning his search for her far behind.

From Aurial, Andrew Morgan had gone to New York and with much of the money from Glenna's jewels, purchased a passage to Panama. It was the shortest and quickest route to California, but in many ways the hardest. After landing at the village of Cruces on the east coast, he had gone up the Chagres River by canoe, then hiked for five days over mountains and through jungle along a narrow, sometimes nearly impassable trail. He had suffered from heat, drenching rains, and swarms of mosquitos and insects. Dysentery and fever greatly weakened him.

When he arrived at Panama City on the west coast, he found a hellhole, crowded with thousands of men just like himself with bad food, bad water, and no place to sleep. He remained there for weeks, suffering terribly, his money disappearing rapidly. In the end, he was lucky, managing passage on a ship to California. He was one of the few to get on board, while hundreds of others rioted on the wharf in frustration. There were, it seems, far fewer ships stopping on the west coast of Panama than bringing Forty Niners to the east coast. Andrew landed at San Francisco, spent the last of his money for mining gear, and struck out for the gold fields near Sacramento.

Part II

42

Moira Morgan arrived at Independence, Missouri, on June 12, 1850, having traveled by train, stagecoach and riverboat to reach there. She was already a considerably changed young lady. Her first night on the train had taught her the perils for an attractive young woman traveling alone. Many men eyed her suggestively, several made frank, open and indecent invitations, and one, quite drunk, had grabbed her as she made her way to the women's room. She managed to scream, bringing two chivalrous middle aged men to her rescue. One of those sat with her for a few miles, indicating quite plainly that his chivalry was temporary and his motive ulterior.

Moira had learned her lesson. As soon as she could, she discarded her rather formfitting riding costume for a loosefitting, quite demure dress, and tied her flame-colored locks inside a poke bonnet. The effect was to make her look much younger. Ignoring everyone, remaining by herself while reading or pretending to read, she made the remainder of the trip to Missouri without being accosted further.

Her transformation was not limited to her physical appearance. She had a great deal of time to think about King and her affair with him. Beneath her bonnet, her face flushed as she remembered the acts they had performed together. Over and over she asked how he could have done such things? To have then jilted her, to have thrown her over like a used toy, proved that he was a cad. She obviously was just another conquest, and that knowledge was bitter humiliation to her.

She also castigated herself. She had led him on. She had deliberately enticed him. How could she have gone off to a party alone wearing her mother's dress? And father's blouse. What had possessed her to wear it with no chemise? In the pain of self-recrimination she asked herself if it wasn't as much her fault as King's. Hadn't she wanted what had happened? Hadn't she been a willing partner? Wasn't she the kind of girl King had expected? But as the miles melted behind her, she was able to answer: no, she wasn't. She had been foolish. She had made terrible mistakes. But she was not bad. It was not too late to become virtuous again, not too late to start over, sadder and wiser. She resolved to find Andrew, help him recover Aurial, and lead a decent life from then on. Silently she prayed to the Blessed Virgin for forgiveness of her sins and strength to recover her virtue.

Independence, like St. Joseph, Missouri, and Council Bluffs, Iowa, further to the north were small Mississippi river towns which had suddenly become boom towns as jumping off places for the Forty Niners striking out over the California Trail. In the spring, Independence had been swollen by an influx of tens of thousands of pioneers, all bent on gold in California. They had overflowed every available campsite, milled by the thousands outside the post office and filled the streets of the once sleepy river town. Independence had been a sea of wagons and contained uncounted thousands of oxen, mules, horses and cattle, all primed for the trip west. Merchants of the town, as well as many who came to bilk the pioneers, made fortunes selling the vast array of supplies needed for the long trip. At its peak, Independence had resembled few places on earth, a huge campground, an immense open air market, filled with people of all races, creeds, nationalities, ages and descriptions. The lure of gold had spread around the world, helping to converge many of its people on these three Mississippi River towns, as well as San Francisco in the West. The great migration of Americans, the tremendous influx of nationalities, changed the face of a continent and forged a great nation. There was precious little gold in California, perhaps no more than $600 apiece for the hundred thousand or so miners who sought it. But the gold, or rather the pilgrimage to find it, forever changed America.

When Moira arrived in Independence in mid-June, however, the town was not nearly so busy. Had she been a little older, a little wiser, she might have recognized that fact and taken note of it. The overland trip to California was 2,100 miles long. It required a minimum of four months, more commonly five, of the most back-breaking labor and extreme hardship. Those who made the trip—or tried to—left in April or early May. A major departure day was May 1, when the wagon trains stretched beyond the horizons in both directions. The spring departure meant the pioneers would reach California in September or early October at the latest. It would mean travel over prairies still green from spring rains. There would be forage for the mules, oxen and cattle.

Most of all, the early departure meant the wagon trains would be over the Sierra Nevada mountains in eastern California before the winter snows came. Everyone knew, or should have, the fate of the Donner party in '46. Long before the Gold Rush they had set out, leaving in April actually. But the Donner party had sought a shortcut, become lost and wasted precious time and even more precious food. They had become trapped by snows in the Sierras in October, snows which reached thirty feet in depth. Members of the group died daily from cold, hunger and disease, and their bodies had been eaten by the survivors, only a few of whom were found alive when rescued the following spring. The specter of cannibalism was the goad which forced the pioneers to endure the cold and chill at starting time to avoid the greater cold of winter. It also forced them to drive themselves past human endurance to make all possible speed on the trail.

To leave in mid-June meant blistering heat in the plains, short dried stubble for forage and a nearly hopeless race with winter snows. Even if the trip could be made in four months, late starters would have to pray the snows were late in the mountains. Experienced people warned everyone not to set out so late, calling those who ignored the advice damned fools. There were damned fools that June in Independence and Moira found them.

She had been inquiring through the remnants of the camps and stores if anyone had seen her brother Andrew Morgan. She had no success. The name was meaningless among so many thousands of names and her description of him was so vague it could fit hundreds of young men. But enough people, wanting to help so distressed a young girl, had said, "Yeah, seems I did see somebody like that a while back," that she assumed he was ahead of her on an earlier wagon train. She heard the warnings not to go, but ignored them in her eagerness to catch up to Andrew. For a day or two she panicked that no more wagon trains would leave, then she heard about one of the damned fools preparing to set out.

It was a small train of eight wagons, poised across the river at the "line" to Indian territory, ready to set out the next morning. It seemed tiny to her, compared to the vast plain stretching out ahead. She wandered around the wagons, trying to find a friendly face to approach. At first she saw no one, then near the fourth wagon she saw a boy, at least she thought of him as a boy. Maybe he would know who was in charge.

Determined to have a beginning, she went up to him. "Hi, I'm Moira Morgan."

He had been lifting sacks of flour into the wagon. Now he stopped and looked at her unsmiling. He was rather tall, perhaps six feet, and thin, but big hands and broad shoulders indicated he would one day fill out to considerable size. He had long blond hair, lighter in color than straw, tied at his shoulders beneath a wide brimmed black hat. She saw pale blue eyes, set wide apart, and a young beardless face with fair skin. He looked about fourteen or fifteen. Actually, he was only two months younger than she. But such was the difference between a seventeen year old girl born to wealth on a Maryland plantation and a dirt poor Ohio farm boy; the two months made a void of years.

Toby was shy and awkward at best. Now he was tongue tied. He had never seen a girl close up who was so beautiful.

Moira tried again, smiling her best. "I said my name is Moira Morgan. Do you have a name?"

"Toby, Miss. Toby Hamilton."

His voice was so low and deep in his throat she could hear only his first name. She settled for that. Again she smiled, and as she did so, she untied her bonnet and let her hair fall out. She saw his gaze dart to it and remain there. "I was hoping perhaps I could hitch a ride west." He seemed dumbfounded to see her red hair. "Do you suppose I could?"

He seemed to catch himself. "With us, Miss?"

"Yes, if that's possible."

He looked at the wagon and shook his head. "I dunno. We're awful full. I don't know where I'm going to put the last of this stuff as it is."

Moira was annoyed with him. He seemed so ridiculously dumb and uncooperative, a waste of her time. But she smiled again, "You don't suppose any of the others would have room for me, do you?"

He shrugged. "I dunno."

This was getting nowhere. She'd try elsewhere. "Well, thank you very much, Toby."

As she turned to leave, she heard him say, "You

could ask Brother Quacker. We're all sort of travelin' together—come from the same church in Ohio—and he's the leader."

"Where do I find this Reverend Quacker?"

Again a shrug. "I dunno. He's in town someplace."

Another dead end. "Thank you again, Toby. I'll just have to come back later." Again she turned to leave.

"Miss, you'd be better off talkin' to Mrs. Quacker. She's—well, more understandin'. The reverend is . . . sorta severe, know what I mean?"

Moira had no idea what he meant, but again thanked him.

"That's her comin' over there, the lady in gray with the packages."

Moira looked to where his finger pointed, and saw a heavy set woman all in gray. "Wonderful. I'll go talk to her now."

"Wait, Miss."

"Yes?"

He hesitated, then stammered, "Maybe—maybe you should, well, put your hair back in your bonnet."

"Why should I do that?"

For the first time he smiled, a slow, shy grin. "I like it myself. Your hair is so purty. Never saw anythin' like it myself. But the elders, they don't approve of hair on women. They think hair is sinful." She looked at him so directly, he blushed and looked down at his feet.

Quickly she began tucking her hair back inside her bonnet. "Thank you, Toby. You're a good friend."

Bess Quacker, closer up, had a round, fleshy face with soft brown eyes, deepset under eyebrows so thin and light in color she appeared from a short distance to have none at all. Her mouth was soft with lips turned out near the center but not the sides. The effect was a small looking mouth, as if it had been crowded together by her cheeks. Moira had the impression that she had once been pretty, but something had gone wrong. The pinched mouth, deep wrinkles around her eyes, and indeed the uncertainty and, yes, fear in her eyes had sucked the beauty from her. Bess Quacker was only forty-one, but looked at least ten years older.

"Mrs. Quacker, my name is Moira Morgan. That boy Toby over there told me to ask you if I could go to California with you."

The woman looked at her only fleetingly, then said, "I don't think so, child."

Desperation rose in Moira. This was her last chance. "Oh, please, Mrs. Quacker, you have to help me. I've nowhere else to go. We've lost our home, everything we own. My brother, whom I love, is out there somewhere on his way to California. I have to find him. I've nowhere else to turn." Tears welled in her eyes and she pressed her hands against Mrs. Quacker's which were clutching a sack of groceries against her bosom. "Please, ma'm, you got to help me."

Mrs. Quacker looked at her now, fully, her soft eyes intent. Involuntarily, she shifted the heavy load in her arms.

"Here, let me help you," Moira said, quickly lifting the sack from her arms.

"Thank you, child, but I don't know."

"I can pay, Mrs. Quacker. And I can work. I'm young and strong. I'll be a big help, you'll see I will."

Again Moira saw the woman's intent gaze on her. Did she detect a slight softening of it?

"I have no doubt you'd do your share. But that's not the problem. We are, you see—" She seemed uncertain in expressing herself. "We are traveling together. We are all members of one congregation. My husband is the preacher. He—he says it is God's will that we make this journey. I believe him, of course, but—" Her hesitation, the lack of conviction she expressed, gave way to a small smile. "My husband decides everything for us. You'll have to ask him."

"Oh, thank you, Ma'm, thank you." Moira threw her arms around the preacher's wife.

"In our society, sister, we are all brothers and sisters, the children of God. We call each other that. I'm Sister Bess."

"And I am Sister Moira then."

"We will have to see what my husband says, my dear. He'll be along shortly."

The Reverend Isaiah Quacker was a tall man in a black suit which accentuated his long, bony legs. Under a wide-brimmed black hat, he had the longest, thinnest, most angular face Moira had ever seen. The nose was long and beaked over a lipless line of a mouth, the corners of which turned down sharply. He looked at her with cold brown eyes. Moira thought it the most gaunt and grim face she had ever seen. He was empty handed except for a worn Bible clutched against his chest.

"Isaiah, this is Sister Moira. She has no home and must get to her brother in California. She begs permission to travel with us."

Quacker continued to stare at her with piercing eyes. Moira felt herself shriveling and going cold.

"She is willing to pay her way and to work hard at God's will."

Still, she felt his merciless gaze upon her, his eyes strangely unblinking. Nor could she see any movement in his pupils. He might have been looking through her, not at her.

"Please, Reverend Quacker. You must take me." She dropped to her knees in the dirt before him, raising her hands in supplication. "Oh, please, I beg you. I must find my brother."

He stood there unmoved. The breeze whipping at his coattails provided his only movement. Then he spoke in extremely low, mellifluous tones. "I am the new Isaiah, the Messenger of God's will. We are few in number, but our power is mighty, for we are chosen by God Himself to stamp out sin and evil on this earth. Do you hear me, child?"

"Yes," Moira said, almost inaudibly.

"We have no room for sin in our midst. And you are a sinner. I can tell you have sinned greatly. You are wicked. Hellfire and damnation will be your reward."

For the first time he looked away from her. It was an act of dismissing evil. Moira knew she had lost.

Then a sudden gust of wind blew her bonnet back from her head. In her haste to talk to Mrs. Quacker, she had not tied it tight enough. She saw him look at her in astonishment, then gasp.

"You *are* Satan's child. Look at that hair. A child of Satan sent here to test me." Suddenly he dropped to his knees and turned his face upward to the heavens. "Thank you, Lord. I knew you'd send me a test. Satan's child, sent by Thee oh Lord to test my will, my strength. I will not fail thee Lord. Mine is the strength of iron."

He arose to tower over the kneeling Moira. In one movement he untied her bonnet and pulled it from her. When Moira's hair fell free he cried out, "Satan himself in the form of a woman. Hair like hellfire itself. The Lord has given me a mighty test."

"Are you certain, Isaiah? She is just a child."

"Silence, woman. Evil has many disguises." He reached down and lifted up Moira's hair. "Fetch the scissors, Bess. I will cut off Satan's power."

"No, please," Moira gasped. She tried to pull her head away from him, but he held her fast. In a moment she saw the scissors in his hand. Again, her eyes wide with fear, she begged him, then closed her eyes as she saw the scissors move toward her.

She felt nothing, then opened her eyes. He was standing above her, the unused scissors in his hand.

"No," he intoned, "I cannot remove God's test. Hell's fire shall remain, a symbol to us all of Satan's power and of God's test of us all." He threw down the scissors and placed his hand flat atop her head. The Bible clutched tightly in his left hand, he said over her, "Satan, thy power is great, but the Lord is mightier. As God's Messenger, I shall destroy thy power." To her he said, "Sister Moira, as Satan wants you to be known, I shall destroy the evil in you. I will conquer Satan. Sin shall not exist in you. Your flesh shall be purified. I will make thee the Lamb of God."

Moira could think of nothing to say. The man was obviously mad, but she was willing to do anything to find Andrew. Privately, she said a prayer of thanks to the Virgin for helping her find her brother.

43

Brother Isaiah Quacker may have considered himself an instrument of God's will, but he was not above planning for the trip. God may have told him to lead his flock to California at this late date, but he took sensible precautions in entering the race against the inexorable clock of winter.

He had heard and listened to all the tales of foolish pioneers. In their madness for gold, they had in 1849 and even the spring of 1850 set out in a bewildering variety of ridiculous conveyances, carriages, farm wagons, even handcarts. Some had lumbered forth in Conestoga wagons,* and none of these were proper conveyances for the journey.

Quacker purchased sturdy wagons of seasoned lumber that had been braced with metal and caulked so they were as watertight as any ship. The wagons had

---

*Contrary to the movies and television, the Forty Niners did not use the Conestoga wagon or "prairie schooner." It was simply too big and heavy to go over the mountains to California.

heavy springs and large axles to support the weight and permit the bed of the wagon to be raised for fording rivers. The wheels were sturdy and the spokes bolted to the rims so they could be tightened and held firm along the way. A bucket of grease was carried to lubricate the moving parts. Harness for the mules was as strong as money could buy, and along with the cattle, extra mules were driven westward as spares.

In their stampede for gold, many of the Forty Niners carried their most prized possessions, chairs, tables, four poster beds, heirloom china, shelves of books, even an occasional piano. Such items added greatly to the weight, slowing the passage and wearing the teams of animals. Nearly as much extra baggage was discarded until, as hundreds of thousands moved westward, the California trail resembled a junkyard strewn with the heirlooms of civilization and the broken dreams of myriad lifetimes.

Invoking the Will of God, Quacker forbade any such foolishness. His wagons were stripped as light as possible. Personal possessions were limited to little more than a change of clothing, tents, blankets and cooking utensils. Space in the wagons was for food, sensible food, useful on the way. And there was even room to carry some feed for the mules. By Quacker's orders, each person's ration for the trip was a hundred twenty-five pounds of flour, fifty pounds of cured ham, fifty pounds of smoked side bacon, thirty pounds of sugar, six pounds of ground coffee, one pound of tea, a pound and a half of cream of tartar, two pounds of soda, three pounds of salt, a bushel of dried fruit, one sixth bushel of beans, twenty-five pounds of rice, sixteen and a half pounds of hard or "pilot" bread, and small amounts of pepper, ginger, citric acid and tartaric acid. The very afternoon she was accepted as Satan's child, Moira was sent off to make these purchases, as well as a small tent, blankets and cutlery. After she gave Quacker two hundred dollars for her passage, she was virtually penniless.

A few minutes after dawn on June 14, 1850, the tiny

train of wagons headed west. To lighten the loads, all but a driver, the elderly Mrs. Cohl, and eventually the sick walked. Moira's task, along with Toby and his little sister Jane, was to drive the cattle and extra mules alongside the slow moving wagons. She soon found it tiring, running after the cattle to whack them forward with a stick, then exhausting as the prairie sun rose hot under a nearly cloudless sky.

Most of the trains went only a short distance the first day. This gave the drivers time to get used to the mules. If problems developed with the wagons or harness, these could be repaired. If necessary items were forgotten, it was not too late to return to civilization to obtain them. Quacker would have none of it. He drove on mercilessly all day. Most wagon trains stopped for two hours or more at midday to rest during the hottest part of the day. Quacker pushed on, crossing Indian Creek in the early afternoon. Most wagon trains thought it good to go twenty or twenty-two miles a day on the prairie. Quacker pushed on almost to dark, reaching Bull Creek, where the trail branched off to the south toward Santa Fe. This was more than thirty miles from Independence.

For Moira it was an endless day of numbing fatigue, searing heat and choking dust. she tended the cattle and other animals with particular diligence, for Quacker had given her a motive of fear that morning. "If one of this herd is lost, child of Satan, you shall know the wrath of God." She thought him mad, a demon himself, but she let no cow, horse or mule escape her.

At times she felt the lonely band had been swallowed up in the endless plain. It seemed to stretch to the horizon in every direction with hardly a tree or other feature to break the monotony. She observed, however, that the land was not really flat, but an endless series of tiny swells. As the midday sun dizzied her, the land itself seemed to undulate around her.

They were traversing a trail where many thousands had gone before. It was not a path, but a wide swath through the prairie. The wagons had not gone single file, but in columns three and four abreast, the hoofs of the animals tearing up the dry and dying grass to create a makeshift roadway from which clouds of dust arose. At points the trail was deeply rutted by wagons caught in rainstorms and mired. In other places the trail was almost invisible, all traces of passage blown away by the wind.

When they camped after crossing Bull Creek, Moira felt too tired even to move, yet her work was not done. She was sent by Quacker to fetch firewood from the scrub brush along the creek bank. But so many thousands had camped at the site, she had to walk nearly a mile to find any wood at all. She was further delayed because she was unable to resist the water. She was afraid to really bathe, but she removed her shoes and stockings and dived headlong into the creek. For a few heavenly minutes, she enjoyed the coolness and paradise of washing the dust and sweat from her body and hair.

When she arrived back, staggering under a load of sticks and brush, it was deep dusk. Quacker was waiting for her. He saw her limp hair, her dress clinging to her body. "Child of Satan," he screamed, "sinful idler, evil wastrel." He beat her hard with a stick. Worse than the pain of the blows was the public humiliation in front of the others.

She helped with the fire and the cooking, then took her plate of food off to eat by herself. She was too weary even to rage at Quacker for what he had done to her. She could rouse only the resolution that he would somehow pay for what he had done. Mostly she resigned herself to enduring whatever was necessary to find Andrew in California.

She did not pitch a tent, but rather spread her blankets on the gound to sleep under the stars. She had lain down, although not yet fallen asleep, when she felt rather than saw a form towering over her. She saw it was Quacker a moment before he dragged her to her feet and forward, stumbling, to the campfire. Most

Forty Niners amused themselves on the long westward trek by singing around the campfire to the accompaniment of a banjo or guitar. It was the only pleasant part of the long day's toil. To Quacker, music, fun and laughter were sins. He began a prayer meeting, then waxed into a long exhortation, haranguing his parishioners about evil, sin, Satan and hell. He held Moira by the arm, citing her over and over as Satan's daughter, the personification of evil he was determined to drive from the earth. Moira was too tired to do more than endure. She truly thought him mad and wondered where he got the strength to carry on so.

It ended with her being forced to kneel before him, confess her sins and beg for God's mercy. Finally, she was allowed to stagger back to her blanket. But in her anger, humiliation and deep weariness, she was unable to fall asleep right away. In the tent nearby, she heard Quacker still praying with his wife. Then, beneath his sonorous denouncements of sin, she heard other sounds, moans, grunts and rustling sounds, the slap of skin against skin. She knew what he was doing. And she also knew the root of the fatigue and pain which showed in Bess Quacker's face. Memories of King flooded her mind, and she knew she was blushing in the darkness.

The wagon train arose at dawn and after a quick breakfast, set out for another endless day, crossing the Wakarusa River, where most who had preceded them had camped, then pushing on to make as much distance as possible. Because of Quacker's religious harangue, Moira had not had enough rest. Her body ached as she set out for a new day. But she forced herself on. For a time the cattle and mules trudged along peacefully, and she was able to walk beside Toby.

"Is he always like that?" she asked.

"Pretty much, Miss. He's powerful against sin."

But she had seen a hint of a smile on his face. "He is that—and please call me Moira." She heard him tentatively say her name. "Do you believe all that, Toby." She saw him look at her out of the corner of his eye, wary, uncertain. She smiled. "You can trust me, Toby. I won't tell."

"Promise."

She smiled, but her words belied it. "The only thing I'll tell him is to go to hell—where I'm sure he's headed anyway."

Toby was surprised to hear such language from her, but it drove him closer to her. "Hah, I don't believe none of it."

"Then why are you here?"

"Same as you, I guess. Got no choice. Gotta go with my folks." He waved his stick at a cow that was lagging behind. "When I get to California, I'll leave, go find gold on my own."

Moira smiled her pleasure at finding a confederate. "I'll bet you will."

"Yeah, can hardly wait."

They walked along a few steps. "Who is he, Toby? Where's he come from?"

"I dunno where he's from. All I know is he was the preacher back in Ohio where we lived. Little place called Gamble's Mills. Just a tiny place. He was a regular preacher in the Baptist church. Then one day he claimed God had come to him. Began all that stuff about being Isaiah the second, the new Isaiah. Said he was the messenger from God sent to wipe out sin. Most folks didn't believe him. They drove him out of town with just a few people who believed him. My folks had to be among those who did." For punctuation he kicked a stone, which nicked the flank of a cow, making it trot a few steps before settling down. "I'm sorry he beat you, Moira."

"It's all right. Didn't hurt too bad."

"Never saw him do that before. Seems like he's been wild ever since you joined us."

"He doesn't like red hair, I guess."

"Sure is purty, Moira. I like it—a lot, a whole lot."

Smiling, she thanked him. "A girl can use compliments out here." She laughed. "I suspect I do look like the devil."

"Oh, no, miss—I mean Moira. You're real purty, the purtiest girl I ever seen."

She was touched by him, his simple words, his directness. How different from the smooth elegance of King, yet in many ways even nicer. "How old are you Toby?"

"Me? I'll be eighteen in October."

"Really?" Her surprise was genuine. "And I'll be eighteen in August. We're almost the same age."

"Yes."

He didn't seem to know what to say after that, and the conversation dwindled out for awhile. She would have loved to know what he was thinking. Instead, she said, "Can I tell you something, just between us?"

"Sure, I can keep a secret, too."

"I heard him last night in his tent. He was praying and praying, but I heard what else he was doing to her. Is that an awful thing for me to say?"

"Nah. I've heard it, too. Everybody's heard it."

"He's really an awful man, Toby. That's an awful way to do it to a woman, especially his wife."

Now he really was aghast at her. "How you know? Have you—"

Quickly she interrupted him, hiding her embarrassment behind a laugh and hoping she wasn't blushing. "No, of course not. My mother told me."

"Is your mother living?"

Moira sighed. "Yes—sort of. It's a long story. Maybe I'll tell you sometime."

"Where's your home?"

"Maryland."

"I heard o' that. Is it nice?"

"The nicest, I think. We lived in a big house on the river called Aurial. The loveliest spot on earth. I loved it, but it's gone now."

"Do you miss home, Moira?"

Without realizing it, she turned to look back over her shoulder. She had been doing it often and she had seen others doing it. Everyone, except Quacker probably, was longing for the homes they'd left and the journey was only just started. "Yes, I miss it terribly. I never thought I could miss home and family so much."

"Me, too, Moira."

And then as they walked along, she truly did know what he was thinking. Her thoughts were much the same, Aurial, her father and mother, dear Andrew, faithful Joe and scolding Jessie. She smiled. Yes, she missed them. Almost reluctantly, she thought of King. Did she miss him? Not hardly. Yet, despite the heat she felt herself shiver. The things he had done to her. Memories of that last night, his impassioned lovemaking, her crumbled resistance swept her mind. She had been like an animal. Again she shivered and forced the thought from her mind. She did not miss Bradford Kingston. He was good riddance. All he had been was a highly regrettable episode. All she missed about him was the glamour. It had been exciting to dress up and be beautiful. Out here in the wilderness anyone would miss that.

That night she was more tired than she had ever been in her life. Quacker held another prayer meeting, finding somehow the energy to denounce sin at length, but he did not make a particular spectacle of her, for which she was grateful. When at last she climbed into her blanket, she again had trouble falling asleep. The pain in her feet and ankles, the aches throughout her body, kept sleep from coming for a little while. She lie there, looking up at the stars. To think here she was, out in the wilderness sleeping under the stars. It seemed only yesterday she had slept in her own wonderful bed, secure, happy, loved. Loved. Thoughts of King flitted across her mind. What a fool she had been. Sleep dragged at her and she closed her eyes.

She did not really hear anything, but on the edge of sleep she had been snapped awake by—what? She opened her eyes. Towering over her she saw the tall, gaunt figure of Quacker looking down at her. She was about to cry out, when he turned and walked to his own tent.

The next day dawned the hottest, sultriest yet. She

and Toby struggled all day with the herd. The animals seemed particularly nervous and unruly. Moira ran and ran and ran after cows to force them back into the herd. In late afternoon, storm clouds began to appear from the north, menacing, the color of charcoal. But Quacker did not stop. The wagons rolled on as the clouds blotted out the sun. The air was deathly still, oppressive, and Moira knew it was to be a bad storm.

When the wind struck, it almost knocked her off her feet. As she tried to lurch forward against it, a few large drops of rain pelted against her. Then came a burst of hail such as she had never seen. The smallest were the size of marbles, but the largest were as big as hen's eggs. The balls of ice tore into her, ripping her dress. One huge hail struck her head, almost knocking her out. She screamed, but the sound was lost in the wind. Frantically, she tried to run, seeking someplace to hide from the pelting fury of the heavens. But there was none. She stumbled and fell face down in the mud. At that instant she felt an arm around her shoulders, a body covering hers. Dimly she heard Toby's voice telling her to lie still.

The hail was over in a minute or two, then followed torrents of rain, great sheets of it stretching across the plain. Toby crawled off her and helped her to her feet. In an instant she was drenched to the skin. She turned her back against the rain and saw the wagon train stopped in the distance.

She felt Toby, still holding her hand, pull her toward the wagons. She ran a few steps, then stopped. "Wait, Toby. The cows." A few were in sight, but most weren't, and all had scattered to escape the stinging hail.

"Oh, God, no!"

"We got to find them," she screamed and began to run after them through the drenching downpour. She ran as hard and fast as she could, and one by one brought the cows back to a central place. She lost sight of Toby, but each time she returned the number of recovered animals had grown. Finally, with the rain diminishing a little, they stopped to count the herd.

"One missing," Toby said.

"Oh, God, no. Count again."

He did and with the same result. "You stay here. I'll find the stray."

"No, I'll help. It could be anywhere."

Taking a deep breath to fill her starved lungs, she began to run again, away from Toby, her soaked dress clawing at her legs, weighing her down. She ran as long as she could, then stumbled to a halt. After resting a moment to catch her breath, she began to walk, calling frequently for the missing beast. More tired than she had ever thought possible, she stumbled along. The rain decreased to a drizzle, but she hardly noticed. The cow was nowhere in sight. But fear drove her on. She did not want to find out what Quacker meant by the wrath of God.

She lost track of time and distance. With the sun obscured by clouds, she lost all sense of direction. Only as the light began to diminish did she realize she had to get back, cow or no cow. Then suddenly she knew she was lost. Which way to the wagons? She turned in a circle, seeing nothing in the dusk but the gentle swells of the plain. Oh God, where was she? She had no idea which way to go. She was lost in this immense wilderness.

Fatigue rescued her. Despair, adding to exhaustion, made her crumple to the mud. She could go no further. She pulled her legs up, clasped them with her arms and laid her head against her knees and slept. For how long she had no idea. But when she awoke it was dark. When she stood up, she saw in the distance the glow of the campfire diffused by the intermittent drizzle. It was the opposite of where she thought it was. She had gone in a semicircle around the camp.

Grateful for the fire to act as a beacon, she began to trudge slowly toward it. It seemed forever that she walked. For a long time the glow never got any larger, but at last she was able to distinguish the actual flames. Slowly, painfully, hardly able to put one foot in front of the other, she labored on, wondering from time to time if Toby had found his way back or was he lost, too.

When at last she reached the campsite and lurched between two wagons toward the fire, it was to be greeted by an enraged Quacker. "So you lost a cow, did you, you child of Satan." She felt him grab her arm and pull her toward the fire, a stick in his right hand.

With energy she didn't know she had, she screamed at him. "Leave me alone. Don't touch me." She jerked her arm away from him, but the reaction to the effort made her fall to the ground. He pounced upon her, dragging her to her feet.

"Satan is in you. I'll beat him—"

"No, God no," she screamed and struggled against him with the last of her strength. He had her caught in his long arm, pulling her aginst his body. She screamed and kicked and fought, but she was powerless as she saw the stick raised in his arm. She let out a scream and involuntarily closed her eyes.

The blow did not fall. She opened her eyes to see Toby, as drenched and worn out as she was, standing there, holding Quacker's wrist to stop its downward thrust. Through clenched teeth he said, "Leave her alone. Don't you ever hit her again."

They seemed to struggle a moment, but Toby's strength was too great for Quacker. He dropped the stick and Toby released his wrist.

His wild eyes grabbing the light from the fire, Quacker shouted, "So Satan has ensnared you, too?"

His voice firm, Toby said, "I don't care what you have to say. Just don't hit her again." He then turned and walked away.

And Moira fled, too, back to the wagon. As quick as she could she put up her tent and crawled inside, huddling beneath the blanket.

In time she heard, "Moira, I brought you some food." The tent flap opened and Bess Quacker thrust a plate and cup toward her. "You must be starved."

"Yes."

"Well, eat, then sleep." She hesitated a moment, her face peeking into the tent. "He won't bother you no more now." Then she was gone.

Moira devoured her food, then lay down, pulling the blanket around her for warmth. Her clothes were soaked and the ground was wet, but she was too weary to change. Just before she fell asleep, she remembered the demented Quacker ripping her dress and the feel of his clammy hand against her breast as she had struggled with him. She shivered just before she fell asleep.

44

Day after day, week upon week, Quacker's wagon train wound its way west, then more sharply northwest across the wide Kansas River, Red Vermillion Creek and Black Vermillion Creek and the Big Blue River into what would some day become Nebraska.

From there the trail wound north by northwest along the Little Blue River and, after crossing Thirty-Two Mile creek, joined a day later the shallow, languid waters of the Platte River, by mid-July reduced from its spring width of a mile or more to a modest stream bordered by broad reaches of mud flats. This foul smelling, insect infested river was followed for days more until it divided into the North and South Platte rivers.

Under the lash of Quacker's tongue, whip and will,

the wagons made surprisingly good time, routinely twenty-five or thirty, occasionally under favorable circumstances forty miles a day. Being last across the plains had an advantage. They did not get held up at rivers. In the spring, during the major migration, wagons would pile up at the major crossings, such as the Kansas River. Days were lost waiting to get across. Being so late and the rivers lower in summer, Quacker's train negotiated these pitfalls relatively easily. Good time was being made.

Occasionally they passed wagons, mostly in ones and twos, coming eastward. The occupants had surrendered the notion of gold in California for a return to the joys of home and civilization. In his antipathy to all "sinners," Quacker refused hospitality to these travelers or even to talk to them. But the haunted look in their eyes and their warning cries testified to the horrors they had fled from.

And horrors Quacker's party did begin to find. The worst, without doubt, was the homesickness, the feeling of being lost in an endless wilderness, far from home and comfort. More and more, Moira found herself looking back from whence they had come. She missed home terribly and realized she had lived in truly incredible luxury. Her antipathy toward her mother had long since melted away, and it was not without guilt that she regretted not going to see her one more time before she left. At least she would have the comfort of knowing where her daughter was. So, Moira looked back many times a day. She told herself it was homesickness, an expression of regret, a means to keep from looking ahead, which she was viewing with increasing dread. But there was something more. She couldn't escape the feeling of being followed, that someone would come for her and take her away from this nightmare. But always, as the thought came to her she dismissed it as wishful thinking.

The trail became increasingly littered until it began to resemble a dumping ground, the whitening bones of dead animals, some still in their yokes and harness, broken wagons, the spokes often smashed in so no one following could use them, the weighty possessions of a lifetime, dishes, beds, books, and a piano which someone's child would never play again. There was something tragic, futile and ugly in all this jetsam of civilization, most depressing to Moira. It told more than words ever could the hardships of the journey and the desperation of those who had gone before. Too much of it showed their meanness, the broken wheels, the mutilated harness, the deliberately poisoned sacks of flour and other foods. In their eagerness to get to the gold first, many of the Forty Niners would give no aid to those who followed by leaving anything usable behind. Indeed, there were instances of men, so greedy for gold, they raced ahead of wagon trains to set fire to the prairie so there would be no forage for those who followed. Some even threw dead animals into springs to poison them.

Yet, Moira also saw goodness and humanity along the way. Every rock or flat place bore initials or names of those who had passed. The trail was strewn with hastily scrawled messages bearing warnings of what lay ahead or tips on where water and forage could be found. Humanity, as well as hardship, also began to show up in trailside graves, marked by piles of rocks and pathetic signs. The California Trail was obviously extracting a high price in human lives. Singly, in pairs, even whole families, were being wiped out in the passage.

Hardwork, accident and exhaustion took some, and doubtlessly homesickness and the maddening monotony of the prairie others. But the principal cause of death was disease. There were many illnesses which ravaged the wagon trains, including malaria, smallpox, typhoid fever, diptheria, but the pioneers had a single word to cover them all: "cholera." It seemed to strike with ruthless suddenness. A person could be healthy in the morning and in his grave by nightfall, ravaged by fever, his life fluids drained from him by vomiting and savage diarrhea. And the travelers knew of no prevention or cure.

The dread cholera was a particular enemy of the Quacker train. It was the unrealized but special penalty for being last on the trail. All those who had gone before had made the trail, particularly the shallow rivers and streams into a human cesspool from which flies, mosquitoes and ticks rose in clouds. The members of the Quacker party were drinking badly polluted water, and there was nothing they could do about it, even if they had realized it.

Mrs. Cohl died first, then the Wassermanns, both in their late fifties. Their supplies were divvied up; the rest, including the wagon, ruined by Quacker so no "sinners" could make use of it. Beside the Platte, a second wagon was lost to the scourge. It became so bad that sometimes Moira felt she, Toby and Quacker were the only ones well. Along with tending cattle—frequently alone now, for Toby often had to drive one of the wagons—she cared for the sick as best she could. It seemed to her that almost daily she helped dig a grave and said a prayer as a member of the tiny party was laid into it, Toby's sister Jane, then his mother, Alexander Pritchard, Benjamin Nelson, so many names. Bess Quacker lingered for a long time, perhaps because Moira gave her special attention, forcing liquids into her until she, too, finally, mercifully succumbed. Moira grieved for her especially, yet she knew it was a blessing. The ravages of the illness were over, as was her miserable life with Quacker.

Moira had dysentery and suffered for three or four days. She was certain her life was going to end in some unmarked grave, swept by the winds and flooded by the quick torrents of rain. But to her surprise, she recovered. In truth, she was stronger and healthier than she had been in her life. Most days she was tired, on some of them so weary she didn't think she could get through the day, yet the open air, her miles of running after cattle each day, her heavy labors of cooking, serving, tending the sick, helping to hitch wagons, and the sometimes frantic pushing of vehicles mired in the mud, gave her health and strength she never knew was possible. Her weariness persisted because she did more, but actually her endurance and capacity for effort increased greatly. She was thin, but her muscles were honed to a fine tone. In fact, she was more beautiful than ever. She didn't realize it, but this fact was noticed by others, especially Toby and Quacker.

For the Messenger of God, the disease which ravaged his flock was for a time easily discernible as the work of Satan and his daughter in their midst. But after a while, this certain knowledge began to crumble as Moira tended the sick, going even to those so diseased no one else would approach them. His antipathy ended as Moira extended herself in a vain effort to keep his wife alive. He seemed to stand helplessly, too shocked even to pray over her, as Bess Quacker slowly succumbed to her disease. Moira took her into her own tent at night to be able to cool her fevered skin and try to pour liquids into her. Moira had learned from her own illness that drinking seemed to be best in treating cholera.

Of necessity, Moira was thrown more with Quacker than she would have liked. She fixed his meals and gave reports about his wife's condition, but spoke to him only briefly and icily. She hardly ever looked at him. Yet, even in her dislike for him, she had to admit his grief for his wife was sincere. She told herself he only missed his meal ticket and bedmate, but he did seem lonelier, less militant. He tried once to thank her for helping his wife, but she spurned him with an icy glare.

When at last Bess Quacker was placed in a shallow grave beside the Platte River and Quacker knelt to pray over her, she saw tears in his eyes. She had not thought him capable, but realized things happen between husband and wife of which she had no knowledge. When at last his prayers ended and he arose from his knees, Moria was moved to say, "I'm sorry. I tried to save her."

He reached out and took her hand. It felt clammy and cold, repulsive to her, but she endured.

"'Tis God's will," he said. "You did all you could and I thank thee."

She pulled her hand away, saying nothing. She felt more comfortable with him when they were inimical.

The trail continued along the Platte for nearly a hundred miles of that wide, shallow mudflat of a river. Pioneers called it "the river that runs upside down," an apt description of the mud and bogs separated into channels by a large number of islands. The going got harder for the train. There was not only the stench of the mudflats and the infestations of insects, but heavy sand into which the wagon wheels dug deeply. Just before the river forked into the South and North Plattes, they came to an area of large sand dunes, which sapped their strength as they pushed and pulled the wagons through weird sand formations. Despite their efforts, wagons became stuck axle deep, the mules unable to pull them out. Wagons were unhitched and double teamed before progress could be made. It was an exhausting day for Moira.

The so-called California Crossing of the South Platte made another difficult day. The wagons had to be snaked through a mile and a half of mud, swamps and quicksand of the river bed. With so few able bodied men to help, Moira ran from wagon to wagon, pushing and shoving and dragging at the weary mules. The narrow stretches of river were never more than three feet deep, but the current was strong. Moira would have been swept downstream, except that a last desperate lunge enabled her to grab a wheel and save herself.

A day later they came to Ash Hollow and the most hazardous experience yet. Ash Hollow lay near the North Platte. At first it was a welcome sight to Moira, a lovely dell of trees, some of ash, for which it was named, but also cedars, hickory and others. The dell abounded with wild berries. But the lovely sight lay five hundred feet below, and they had to take the wagons down a steep incline through narrow rutted trails much used by those who had passed before them. Since the wagons had no brakes, it was hard labor trying to hold back the wagons and lead the mules slowly down the grade. Time after time it was a losing battle, ending in a mad flight to level ground below. One wagon overturned and was wrecked. Two mules broke their legs and had to be shot.

It was now the second week in July, blisteringly hot, the ground parched and yellow. The animals were nearly as tired as the humans, but Quacker pressed relentlessly onward. The train followed the North Platte through increasingly rough country, sandy, barren hostile. They began to encounter herds of buffalo, so vast they seemed to reach to the horizon and take hours to pass in front of them. Moira saw evidence of the mindless slaughter of these noble beasts, dozens of rotting carcasses, some shot for the pure pleasure of it. Others had been "butchered" and maybe only a tongue removed or a kidney. The waste appalled her. She saw more of it than the others, for it was her task to collect "buffalo chips" to start the fires. It made an acceptable alternative to wood, of which there was none, but so many travelers had passed along this route, she sometimes had to walk two or three miles before collecting enough for that evening's fire.

To Moira's pleasure, the country began to change, evidence of the approaching mountains. Strange, even exotic features began to rise out of the plains, huge rocks and bluffs. In the distance, these bluffs, notably one called Scott's Bluffs, took on the shape of castles, pyramids, domes, even whole towns. Moira did not know if these distant shapes actually resembled what she saw or whether it was her imagination and longing for home deceiving her eyes. A particularly enchanting sight was Chimney Rock, a high square spire looking for all the world like a chimney atop a conical rock.

The trail left the river near Scott's Bluffs, passing across an eight mile level plain to the south of a huge outcropping of stone. As the ground rose, they were able to see their first glimpse of the Rocky Mountains more than a hundred miles to the west. The rocky peaks, some snow covered, filled Moira with both excitement and dread. The trail wound back closer to the river, but clearly they were leaving the plains behind them. In the near distance were the Black Hills, so named for the dark pines which covered them. The terrain was getting rougher.

Unchanged, however, was Quacker's antipathy towards all persons encountered on the way. He was thoroughly democratic about this, offering unrelenting hostility toward all, the occasional pioneers stranded or returning on the trail, a few trappers and traders they met, and all Indians. They were passing through the lands of the Pawnee, Sioux, Arapahoe, and Moira was intensely interested to see and learn more of them. For the most part the Indians gave them a wide berth, passing in the distance, small parties on horseback and afoot. Once or twice small war parties of braves approached the wagons. Moira had been fascinated by their half naked bodies, feathers and other paraphernalia. She observed they were as interested in her as she was in them. It occurred to her that it was she and the others who were the strangely dressed intruders in the Indian lands, and this thought amused her.

None of the Indian parties seemed particularly warlike. They were not yet hostile toward the white intruders. Rather they were accustomed to trading with white men, usually skins and furs for food, cattle, liquor and, most valuable of all, guns and powder. They thought this was what white men did, and it was with some dismay that they encountered Isaiah Quacker. Most of the pioneers on the trail west knew the Indians, armed with bows, arrows, spears and only a few guns, would not dare attack heavily armed wagon trains. But they could be a nuisance by stealing cattle. Most trains solved the problem by simply giving the Indians a few trinkets, odd pieces of apparel, a sack of flour, even an occasional cow. It would be stolen anyway. Indian attacks on wagon trains in gold rush days were a rarity.

Quacker lacked such wisdom, however. To him the half-naked savages were heathen, not to be recognized or dealt with in any way. When Indian parties approached, he frightened them off by firing a shot or brandishing his whip and shouting fiercely at them. The tiny train paid a price in loss of cattle, spirited away in the night. Quacker railed at this in undisguised rage, but it did little to stop it.

Moira had no fear of the occasional Indians they encountered. She merely thought Quacker stupid for not giving them something, try to trade or at least act civilized toward them. But her irritation over this was minor compared to her anger when he refused to stop at the occasional trading posts. There had been one at the bottom of Ash Hollow. He went on by it, not even glancing at the astonished men who called to them. Worse was his refusal to stop at Fort Laramie, nestled beneath the Black Hills. It was not a military station, but a facility of the American Fur Trading Company maintained to foster trade with the Indians and trappers who acted as intermediaries. Most pioneers stopped there to buy needed supplies, shod mules, repair wagons and rest for the difficult passage through the Rockies. Quacker passed Fort Laramie as though he didn't even see it. Moira knew they had to make all possible speed, but this was ridiculous. Her rage availed her nothing, however.

Moira's situation in regard to the wagon train had changed—in ways both beneficial and ominous. She had long since been accepted socially by the austere group. The incidence of cholera had largely subsided with the discovery of clearer waters in the foothills, but her efforts for the sick and dying were remembered by all. The pioneers, once numbering almost fifty, had dwindled to twenty-nine and many of them were widows and widowers, some with young children. Her efforts to help with the youngsters, as well as her hard work with the wagons at the river crossings and at Ash Hollow made her a respected and accepted member of the community.

Her tasks with the herd had also become easier through attrition. Most of the animals had simply been used up, injured and killed, or stolen by Indians. The few cows and mules that remained were often tethered to the back of wagons, leaving her free to walk along beside or to help push through mud and sand. So lightened were the loads that she was sometimes invited to ride. She rode beside various drivers, but most enjoyed the quiet company of Toby. All of this was beneficial, giving her both rest and a feeling of belonging.

More ominous was the changed attitude of Quacker. With his wife in her grave, he began, to Moira's dismay, to show signs of viewing her as his woman. After all, he had taken her on as the third member of his party, and now there were only two of them. Moira saw the signs early on and sought to discourage them, his feeble attempts to smile at her, his efforts at idle conversation, his frequent invitations for her to sit beside him as he drove the team. These she could ignore or refuse. More difficult was his exaggerated praise of the meal she had to cook for him and his touching of her hand as she brought him his plate. She had begun to pitch her tent further from his and closer to that of Toby Hamilton and his father. Quacker thwarted these efforts by pitching her tent for her while she searched for buffalo chips. He erected it right next to his. She slept out in the open that night and for several subsequent nights. She remained wary of Quacker and worried about his amorous intentions. There was no way she would ever let him touch her.

Quacker's failure to stop at Fort Laramie had unnerved Moira. There had been friendly faces there, people willing to help them, but he had refused to stop. It had depressed her more than usual, and she had avoided him as much as possible all that evening.

The day after Fort Laramie they were following the dry bed of a fork of Bitter Cottonwood Creek when a party of a dozen Indian braves rode up. From their gestures, it was apparent to Moira they wanted gifts. The leader obviously coveted the rifle which Quacker held primed and cocked in his hands. As he had before, Quacker refused all dealings. Rather, he brandished his rifle in a threatening manner.

The Indians seemed unafraid. Mostly they were curious about the wagons, the contents, and the small band of pioneers. Two Indians poking around a wagon pulled a lady's bonnet from it. When he put it on his head, it brought excited laughter from his companions. Another Indian approached the Hamilton wagon, motioning to Toby for a drink. When offered a dipper of water, the Indian took a swallow and spit it out. He wanted whiskey and there was none of that anywhere in the Quacker train. One Indian rode directly up to Moira. She stood her ground, feeling surprisingly unafraid, even when he raised his rifle and pushed back her bonnet with the barrel. She saw him gape at her red hair. She smiled at him.

Quacker was in a rage at the inspection of his wagons. He shouted at them, "Heathen," "Blackguards" and brandished his rifle in an effort to scare them away.

"For God's sake," Moira called up to him, "give them something and they'll go away."

"It is for God's sake that I will not deal with heathens," he screamed. Then he fired his rifle, fortunately into the air.

The Indians were startled by the noise. They clustered together, staring back at Quacker, then rode off, disappearing quickly over a hillside.

"You should have given them something," the elder Hamilton shouted at Quacker. "I have a feeling they'll be back."

"If they do, I won't miss the next time."

The train moved on for an hour or more, climbing a high ridge, then descending the river bed precipitously to Horseshoe Creek, a lovely stream of clear, cool water. There they made camp.

Moira had a nagging worry about the Indians all that evening, but at bedtime, this concern gave way to a far more serious problem. She was returning from her necessary trip into the darkness outside the tiny perimeter of wagons, when she felt Quacker grab her wrist. She had not seen or heard him in the darkness, and he surprised her. She was on the edge of a scream when he said, "It's only me, Isaiah."

"I know who it is." She felt her heart thumping. "What d'you want?"

"I feel the need to talk to you."

"About what?" She made her voice as cold and impersonal as possible, and pulled her wrist away from him.

He hesitated, then the deep voice, little more than a whisper, came out of the darkness. "Can't you like me a little? I truly am sorry for the things I said and did to you."

"Not half as sorry as I am. Now I'm going to bed—quite alone."

She took one stop forward when he grabbed her again, this time with his arm around her shoulder. "Give me a chance to show you how sorry I am."

"No! And let go of me or I'll scream."

She tried to twist away from him, but couldn't.

"Oh, Moira, I'm so lonely and you're so young and beautiful." Then he pulled her to him, both arms around her, thrusting his face toward her, trying to find her mouth. She felt his hot breath panting over her and the rasp of his stubble against her cheek and lips. She tried to struggle, but to no avail, as he pushed his body hard against her. She felt his bony knees holding her legs as in a vise and as she tried to scream his hand over her mouth. He held her thus, with his legs and the elbow of his left arm hooked over her shoulder. With his right he tore at her dress trying to reach her breasts. She struggled, but he was too tall, too strong for her to get free of him.

Trapped, desperate, she did the only thing left to

her. She relaxed, as though yielding to him. She heard his hoarse voice. "That's the girl. I knew you wanted it." She felt him forcing her to the ground. But this act forced him to free her arm. Quickly she reached out toward the face above her and raked it as hard as she could with her nails. She heard him gasp in surprise and felt his weight come off of her. Twisting, she tried to crawl away from him. She felt herself free of him. She was just pushing herself up to run, when he grabbed her ankle and pulled her back. She tried to scream, but it seemed to her little sound came out. The ripping of her skirt was both heard and felt, then his weight on her again. His hand found her mouth and muffled her further screams.

Moira knew what he was doing. She felt the cool breeze on her naked thighs. She struggled but she was helpless against him. In terror she waited for what she knew would happen next.

But it didn't. Quacker's weight was suddenly pulled off of her. She heard no voice at first, just a sound she didn't recognize. Then she did, the sound of a fist striking bone, followed by running footsteps. In the darkness she heard, "Are you all right, Moira?"

She knew it was Toby's voice and that he had saved her, but her panic overrode that knowledge. She jumped to her feet and ran into the darkness, away from the wagon train. She had no idea how long or how far she ran, scrambling up a hillside, then down, through the creek and up another hillside. Spent, she stopped finally, panting for breath.

"Are you all right, Moira? Where are you?"

Toby had followed her. "Yes, I'm all right. Up here."

In a moment he had climbed up to sit beside her. She leaned against his shoulder inside his arm and suddenly realized she was sobbing.

"Did he hurt you, Moira?"

In a moment she was able to say, "No, I guess not. I'm not going back there. I can't."

He said nothing for a time. Finally, he broke the silence. "We have to go back. We can't go on alone."

"Well, I'm not going back there tonight."

"All right. We'll go in the morning."

He held her for a time, then they lay back, side by side and slept on the warm hillside under a starry sky, her head in the crook of his arm. Without the hard-driving Quacker to awaken them, both slept past the dawn. Even then it was not the light which aroused them, but the sounds. It was Toby who first heard the strange cries and shrieks. When he sat up, it awakened Moira and both sat up. From their hilltop, they could see over Horseshoe Creek, even over the first hill she had climbed. In the distance the cluster of wagons was visible. It was from there the shrieks came.

"What's going on?" she said.

"I don't know. What's all that dust around it?"

Then she knew. "God, Toby, it's Indians. They're attacking the wagons." She jumped up to run toward the scene, but he grabbed her wrist.

"No, wait. There's nothing we can do."

They stood there watching, but it seemed to be over so quickly. The popping sounds of the distant gunfire didn't last long. Through the dust she saw the circling Indians turn in on the wagons and overrun them. They watched as Indians jumped from their horses and ran through the wagons. Moments later, she saw clouds of black smoke begin to rise. "God, they're burning the wagons." As the smoke thickened, she saw Indians, some carrying things, jump back on their horses. They seemed to ride off, away from them, in groups of twos and threes. Soon the last rider was gone.

They remained on the hilltop a long time, close to an hour, watching the smoke and flames before coming down the hillside toward the wagons which had been their home for weeks. As they neared the burning vehicles, both began to call out the names of those they knew, but there was no answer.

The scene sickened Moira and she turned away in horror. All the members of the Quacker party were not only dead, but scalped. "Oh God, Toby, it's so terrible. "

He put his arm around her and led her a short distance from the burning wagons. "Don't look back," he said. "There's nothing to see."

"But we have to do something. We have to bury them at least."

"We can't. We got to get out of here. That Indian saw your hair. When he doesn't have you or your scalp, he'll come lookin' for you. We got to get out of here and quick."

"But we're alone, on foot. What'll we do? Where'll we go?"

"Where we started, I guess, California. We walked most of this way already. I guess we can make it the rest o' the way."

Instinctively, both looked to the west. Over the foothills, the Rockies towered stark and forbidding. The sun was warm, but she couldn't help shivering.

45

Jessie wondered if a person could die of a broken heart. It seemed to her she was witnessing it, as each day Glenna Morgan deteriorated a little more. The hasty departure from Aurial had deepened her depression. She had wanted to know where she was being taken and why, but her protests had been feeble and her resignation complete when Joe explained it to her. She had asked about Andrew and Moira. When told they both had gone to California, Glenna seemed to tilt over the edge and begin a long slide into the pit.

Jessie tried everything she could. She arranged with Aunt Beulah for Glenna to have the best room in the small house. It was not much compared to Aurial, whitewashed walls, a threadbare carpet on creaking floor, a vintage bed and mattress, a few pieces of furniture long ago discarded from Aurial. But the room had sunlight and Jessie, who believed in the healing properties of the sun, hoped this would cheer Glenna. It didn't. Nothing did, not Jessie's cheerful prattle, not her reading to her, not her frequent entreaties to go out for a walk or at least join them at the dinner table. Nothing she did had any effect on Glenna. She simply sat in the rocker brought from Aurial, stared out the window at the dusty street, spoke little and ate almost nothing.

"She's going to die. I know she's going to die." These were almost daily words Jessie spoke to Joe, this time in an evening early in July. "And why not? She's lost everything, her husband, her children, her home. She's not yet forty, but she's already a penniless woman with a broken heart waiting for death."

As usual, Joe infuriated her. He sat in a chair in the parlor reading the newspaper, showing no reaction to his wife's words.

"Don't you care what happens to Miss Glenna?"

The accusation was so ridiculous to Joe he would not honor it with a reply.

"Won't you do anything to at least try to help her?"

He turned another page of the paper, seemingly studying it intently. But he said, "I am helping her—by waiting patiently. Miss Glenna will be all right."

"Oh-h!" Jessie was appalled by him. "The man sits and reads the paper and says he's helping that poor woman. Joe O'Reilly, there are times when I think you're—" She stomped away.

Learning to read was Joe's proudest achievement. He had been too proud to be taught, so he had forced himself to learn, slowly, painfully. He still did not read rapidly. He sounded out every word, often moving his lips as he read. His dictionary was tattered from looking up so many words. His speaking vocabulary was often larded with strange words like "enthusiasm" and "paradoxical," which he did not always use correctly.

In reading the paper carefully, as he had done every evening since leaving Aurial, Joe was indeed helping Glenna. He knew exactly what he was looking for and when he found the news item, he would know what to do. Three days later the item appeared and a smile brightened his face. He said nothing, wanting to surprise Jessie.

The next morning he left the house, purposely aggravating Jessie by not telling her where he was going, and went to downtown Baltimore, all the way downtown, following Calvert Street to its end at the inner harbor, guarded by Federal Hill across the water. Then he walked along the crowded quay past several ships until he found the one who's name he had seen in the paper the evening before. He walked a short way along the wharf, then up the gangplank to the ship, entering a cabin. Perhaps twenty minutes later, Joe emerged from the cabin with a companion. Together they left the ship and returned to the quay. Rather than walking, they hired a cab. Joe made his surprise complete by knocking at the front door of Aunt Beulah's house, rather than simply entering.

Jessie was indeed surprised. When she opened the door, the pupils of her eyes went wide with delighted surprise. She stood there a moment, then said, "Lord o' Mercy, Cap'n Mac." She threw her arms around him. "Thank God you're here." When she had welcomed the returning ship captain into the house she turned on Joe to scold him. "You nasty nigger. Why didn't you tell me?"

"Because of your tongue, woman. You thought I wasn't doing anything for Miss Glenna."

"How is she?" Captain Ian MacDoul was if anything a more imposing figure. Now fifty-three, his red beard had patches of white around his chin, and his waist and barrel chest had thickened. But his eyes were still bright, his voice a profound basso, his step firm. He seemed indeed in the prime of life at a time men his age were heading for an unwelcome grave. Age merely added to his stature, and he was a widely known and respected sea captain.

"Oh, Cap'n Mac, it's terrible. Her heart is broken and why not? Mr. Daniel, her children, Aurial, everything she knew and loved is gone. She has nothing to live for and doesn't want to."

"That hardly sounds like the lassie I know."

"It's true. You won't know her Cap'n Mac."

He shook his head sadly. "Well, take me to her, then leave us alone."

Jessie had hardly prepared him for the sight of Glenna. She was a shrunken figure in black huddled in a rocking chair, looking out the window. Her face looked glassy white and so deeply lined, she looked ten years older. Her hair was tied back from her head in a bun, and he saw the first streaks of gray in it. When he said her name and she slowly turned to look at him, he saw the blue in her eyes, once so vivid, was now listless, the life gone from them.

"Glenna," he repeated, then went to kneel in front of her, his hands encircling her frail upper arms.

Recognition seemed to come slowly to her. She looked at him unblinkingly for a moment. Her mouth opened, but no sound came out of the pale lips. Slowly she raised her hands and cupped his bearded face. Finally she said, "Mac, is it really you?"

He smiled. "Aye, lassie, it is no one but the wanderer come home."

It cannot be said who took whom in their arms, but her head was against his broad shoulders and they hugged each other close. Tears smarted his eyes and he patted her back as though she were a child. "I loved him like a brother, lassie—more than a brother. I miss his not being here more than I can say."

"Yes, Mac, yes."

"He was the finest man I ever knew or expect to know, Dan'l was. I am only sorry I was not here when he died. We, you and I, could have helped each other."

It was a strange, incongruous thing to say, the handsome, towering master of the sea being helped by a frail widow in grief. She pulled herself away to look at him. "Help you?"

"Aye," he said soberly. "Grief is a bitter medicine that comes to us all. It is no respecter of persons or stations."

Her hands were down in her lap now and she looked down at them. "Yes, and I know you loved him."

"Aye, I did that."

He pulled up a straight chair and sat opposite her, crossing his heavy legs and placing his hat on his knee. "I'm told by those that love ya that you got a sea o' troubles, lassie. That blackguard Winslow has come back, has he? I shoulda gone ashore at Cork when I first thought of it and done him in then."

He sat there waiting, but she did not reply. She did not even look at him. He saw her retreating from him. The fight was gone from her. She had been defeated and given up. What should he do? He thought about scolding her, making her angry at him, putting the fight back in her, but he knew he couldn't do that to her.

"Why don't you tell me all these troubles, lassie? Maybe we can think of something together."

She said nothing for a time, then sighed, "I know you mean well, Mac, but it's no use."

"Perhaps. But I been at sea for over a year. I at least deserve the telling of what has happened." He knew full well, having been briefed by Joe, but he had to get her talking somehow.

She raised her head slowly, looking at him or perhaps through him. "Daniel went riding. It was last Thanksgiving Day. I had never liked the horse. It threw him.

His neck was broken. He was dead when I reached him."

He said nothing for a brief time, then softly said, "I have seen many good men die, lassie. It is never easy, but a quick death is better than sufferin'."

"I suppose."

Another hesitation. "And you figure your life ended at that moment." When she did not reply, he went on. "At sea these many years I've seen some mighty storms, lassie, some you wouldn't believe possible. You are buffeted by the wind. Like to tear your arms from their sockets. And what the wind doesn't do, the waves try to finish. You think this surely is the end, but it never is—at least not yet, not for me. And the storm blows itself out. The wind goes, the seas grow calm and the sun comes out. Soon you forget how awful the storm was—until the next one comes along."

He waited for her to say something, but she didn't. "I seem to remember you bein' in a storm once. I seem to remember a young lassie workin' the pumps and helpin' the injured till she nearly dropped. That lassie sound familiar to you?"

To her hands she said, "But he was with me then."

"Was he with you in that heathen desert and jungle?"

"But he was alive. I knew he loved me. There was hope."

"That's true, lassie, quite true." He lifted his hat and recrossed his legs. "Tell me how that scoundrel Winslow got hold of Aurial."

She looked at him, then back down at her hands. "I didn't know he was anywhere around, but apparently he was. He got Andrew into some sort of game and won everything from him."

"And Andrew had no idea who he was or what he was up to."

"Andrew wasn't a very good card player."

"Aye, but I've no doubt there was a lot of thievin' and cheatin' went on. Then what happened?"

"Joe and Jessie brought me here. I seem to be always escaping Winslow."

"Thank the Lord for that. But I'm talkin' about young Andrew and pretty little Moira."

She sighed. "Andrew went to find gold in California, hoping to buy back Aurial. Moira has run after him."

"That gold has created a madness. If there was enough gold to finance all the dreams of wealth, the whole continent would have to be one big, shining nugget."

She looked at him, resignation in her eyes. "Everything is gone, Mac, everything I love, Daniel, the children, Aurial, everything."

He smiled. "Gone, you say. I rather doubt that. I'm not a prayin' man, although I've been known to utter a few words from time to time. But I believe there is a great reward someplace. I believe you and I will see Daniel again—but in due time, in due time. And what a grand reunion it'll be. I promise you that. Andrew and Moira are gone but only to California. They're alive out there someplace, Praise the Lord. We can find them. And Aurial is hardly gone. It stands there, beautiful and serene on the river. It merely needs a new owner. Am I gettin' through to you at all, lassie?"

Her sigh was the deepest yet. "What can I do? Don't you understand, I'm penniless? I have no money. Andrew took my jewels. There's nothing at all for me to do."

"Wrong again, lassie. If you'll be so kind as to put on your hat and fix yourself up however you ladies do that, I've got somethin' to show you."

She protested, but he insisted, calling Jessie to make her ready. A few minutes later he led her out of the house and into the waiting cab. They rode downtown, along the quay to the inner harbor, past the ship MacDoul had sailed into Baltimore, then turned east toward the Chesapeake Bay. The cabby led the horse over a cobblestone street for perhaps ten minutes, then on MacDoul's instructions halted. He climbed out, then guided Glenna under a sign which read: "Benson and McCarthy, Shipbuilders."

They walked together into the yard, passing ships in various stages of construction, stopping finally before the most beautiful ship either of them had ever seen.

"There she is," MacDoul said proudly, "the dream of a lifetime, the finest, fastest ship ever built. I'm sure o' that."

Glenna had indeed never seen such a ship. It had a long, sleek, extremely pointed bow. The entire hull was narrow, like a greyhound, built for racing. The bottom was copper, the hull black with a gold ribbon at the deck level, terminating at each end in flowing scroll-work. Polished brass capped the bulwark from end to end. There were three masts, stretching it seemed to heaven, surely as high as the ship was long, and a mass of rigging which the workmen were even then putting in place.

"Do you remember my dream, Glenna, that one day ships would sail like the wind?"

"Yes, I do."

"And there she is, 190 feet from stem to stern, a mere twenty-seven and a half in width, from keel to deck only eighteen and a half feet. Small as ships go, a mere 770 tons, but she will fly, Glenna, fly as a bird. The wind will have to howl to keep up with her. She will make twenty knots for sure, maybe twenty-one, even twenty-two if the wind is right. She is a ship for records, for destiny."

He ran on, telling her how the prow was made to cut through the waves, not ride on them, and how the masts were stepped back toward the stern, and how the vessel would raise enough sail, courses, studdings, topsails, topgallants, royals and skysails and more to fly with the wind. "She'll be like a cloud, effortless, the best and most beautiful ship that ever sailed."

His excitement was contagious. "It's beautiful, Mac. I've never seen such a ship."

"I have, but only once or twice, the *Sea Witch*

mostly. They are new and being built in America. Most men call them clipper ships. They seem to clip through the water, rather than wallow. They are built for speed. They don't carry much cargo and it must be light. But are they ever fast! This ship will sail from here to San Francisco around Cape Horn in a hundred days, maybe less. Think of it. It will sail to China and around the world, carrying tea, in mere months. Think of it, lassie, twenty knots. Men will fly as the birds."

She listened to him in growing confusion. "It's a fine ship, Mac, but I thought it had something to do with me."

He laughed excitedly. "It does, lassie. It has everything to do with you."

"I don't understand."

"You will, you will. Come." He led her forward toward the bow of the sleek vessel, then pointed upward toward the hull. "There, the gold letters. What do you see, lassie?"

Glenna looked up, squinting against the sun and saw the lettering. Her vision was suddenly swimming as she read: GLENNA MORGAN. "Oh Mac, oh Mac." And she burst into tears. Leaning against the Scotsman's shoulder, she had the first real cry since Daniel Morgan's death.

"It bears more than just your name, lassie. It truly is your ship. It was to be a surprise. Dan'l never told you. He believed in this ship as much as I did. He wanted me to have my life's dream, and he put up half the money for this vessel, asking only that it be named after you. Not that I minded. I can't think of a better name for her. The last year has been the hardest o' my life, being away when this ship was built. I wanted to be here, handle every stick o' wood, every fitting, see everything was done right. But I had to earn my half. And so I have. Everything is fine, perfect. I know it is. And I'll soon walk her pitching deck on her sea trials."

Glenna tried to say something through her tears, but he couldn't understand her.

"Don't you see, lassie? You're not penniless. You own half this ship and everything she earns. We'll sail her to California and she'll more than pay for herself on that one trip. The *Glenna Morgan* will earn a fortune. You're rich, lassie, richer than you ever dreamed."

"To California?"

"Aye, lassie. We'll sail her to San Francisco, you and I. You can find your children there. You'll make so much money you can buy Aurial back with small change."

She looked at him through tearing, red-rimmed eyes, disbelieving, still unable to comprehend. "We'll go to California? Find Andrew and Moira?"

"That's right, Glenna. The storm has passed. Smooth sailing ahead."

Suddenly, impulsively she threw her arms around him, burying her lips in his beard, then smothering his mouth.

"Aye," he said at last, " 'tis a happy day all around."

"A ship named after me? I still can't believe it."

"Not just any ship, but the finest, fastest ship in the world. There's no better name for her."

Smiling, ecstatically happy, she took his arm and again looked at the clipper. "She truly is beautiful, Mac. Can I go aboard?"

"No."

She turned to look at him. "Why not? It is nearly finished."

He was suddenly somber. "It would be bad luck."

"Bad luck? That's silly. I thought I was to sail with you."

"You will, but I don't want you aboard today. You see, this vessel was named for the most beautiful and radiant, the bravest and most daring woman I ever knew. I fear some of the crew might be aboard. I would not want them to see the real Glenna Morgan in widow's weeds, wan, pale, defeated by the storms of life."

She looked at him, her eyes wide.

"I want my men to meet the real woman for whom

this ship was named." He paused, looking at her intently. "I'm sorry, lassie, but that's the way I feel."

She looked away from him toward the ship, biting her lips as she did so.

"I truly am sorry, lassie. You know I wouldn't hurt you for the world."

She looked back at him, smiling ruefully. "The truth does hurt, but you are right to speak it. I have it coming." Her smile broadened. "I'll have to hunt around to find the real Glenna Morgan."

"T'won't be hard, lassie. Just a visit to a dress shop might do it."

"Whatever it takes, we'll find her." She took his arm and together they began to walk toward the cab. "Since it is confession time, I think I should say something else. Mac, earlier when you spoke of your grief over Daniel's death, remember? You spoke of our shared grief."

"Yes."

"A thought came to me at that moment, but I brushed it aside like nearly everything else these past months." She paused there in the busy shipyard and looked up at MacDoul. "I realize now, thanks to you, that I have been selfish. For all these months, I've thought only of myself and my grief. I've not thought at all of the others who knew and loved Daniel and grieve for his untimely death. I certainly never gave any thought to how you, his best friend, must feel. Worse, I never thought of the grief of Andrew and Moira. *My* love for him, *my* loss was all I thought about. The children must have suffered, their father gone and, yes, their mother, too. I have failed them terribly. Mac, I want more than anything I've ever wanted to find my children and somehow try to make it up to them."

He smiled down at her. "You will, darlin', you will. I promise you that."

She looked up at him startled. "Daniel always called me that—darlin'."

"He was a most sensible man, Dan'l was."

When the ship was ready to set sail for Cape Horn

and California in September, so was Glenna. She rented a row house for two months and moved into it with Joe and Jessie. She busied herself with homemaking, incessant shopping, and packing and repacking for the sea voyage and a new life in San Francisco. She took an abundance and diversity of possessions, for MacDoul explained to her that anything and everything was of great value in San Francisco. Prices paid there were not to be believed.

While he took the *Glenna Morgan* on its shakedown cruise, returning in three weeks to declare excitedly that it was the wonder of the seven seas, she continued to plan and prepare for her trip. To Jessie's delight, she quickly returned to her old self, adding weight and color, discovering her own glamour, enthusiasm and at least some of her gaity. Except for the shakedown cruise, MacDoul visited her almost every evening, taking her out to dinner or dining quietly with her. With the ship, the voyage, their plans for new lives, there never was a shortage of conversation. She felt friendship for him, affection and something more. Could it be?

They set sail September 15, heading out of Baltimore, down the majestic Chesapeake Bay into the open sea with a diversified cargo selected to bring highest prices in San Francisco, powder and shot, rifles, shovels and pickaxes for mining, bolts of cloth, spices and salt, coffee and such. It was not the lightest cargo and no record would be set on this voyage, but a great deal of money would be made. MacDoul explained that perhaps more money could be made carrying passengers at a thousand dollars a head. But he didn't want them messing up his new ship, and he didn't want the headache they would entail. He wanted to study and learn his new vessel on her first voyage. Privately, he knew he wanted Glenna's company to himself. Joe and Jessie, the mates and crew would be enough people around.

When she boarded the ship, Glenna was thrilled by

the unveiling of the new figurehead, a carved likeness of a woman with white skin, daring blue eyes, and long black hair streaming behind her in the wind. An ample bosom was encased in gold leaf. She clapped her hands in glee when she saw it, but also blushed a little. When she boarded the vessel for the first time, it was to applause from the crew. First Mate George Emerson was most gallant. "You do us great honor, madam. But the figurehead doesn't do you justice."

They sailed south through warm Caribbean nights, blessed by a full moon. Ian MacDoul had never been happier and part of his happiness was knowing Glenna Morgan seemed happy, too. He was in love with her, he knew. Probably, he had always loved her, but she had been his friend's lassie, then his wife. But Daniel Morgan was gone. Could there be any hope for him? Could she ever love him, even a fraction as much as her husband?

He thought, but he did nothing, although his eyes, his attentiveness revealed his feelings. Glenna saw and knew, but had no conception of her own feelings. She loved Ian MacDoul as her husband's oldest friend. She was grateful for his devotion, for his saving her from her own selfish grief, for giving her this new chance at life. But what else did she feel? She could never love another as Daniel, she knew, but what did she feel toward this kindly, jolly, very dear Scotsman.

Late one night as they were drenched in moonlight, the masses of sails rising above them like a cloud, the wind whipping at them as the ship rendered its incredible speed, he kissed her, quickly and impulsively, then immediately stammered apologies. "I had no right," he said.

"No—I mean, yes, you had every right. I know you love me, Mac."

"Aye, Glenna. I cannot help myself."

"And I am honored to have your love. I—I just don't know what I feel."

"I cannot take his place, lassie. I know that. I don't

want to try. But life goes on. The storms pass and there are beautiful nights like this, enough to enchant the devil, it is."

"Yes." She stood up on tiptoe to kiss him. She felt his strong arms around her, his chest so much more massive than Daniel's against hers. But the kiss was not without passion. She felt a stirring within herself.

"In time, Glenna, when you are ready, perhaps—"

She kissed him again, or perhaps he her, and she felt the surge of desire within herself, like an old welcome friend she thought she would never know again.

"I am uncertain, Captain MacDoul," she whispered against his ear. "If you will allow me to change my mind, even to fail, and not hold it against me, I will try now, this enchanted night. I do want you, Mac."

She did not fail. He was loving and patient, understanding as usual. He was not Daniel Morgan. She did not feel the love and passion she had so often with him. But she did rediscover and relish the pleasures her body could bring her. More than ever, as this graceful bird of a ship flew southward, Glenna realized a whole new chapter was beginning in her life. She would never be the same again.

As the *Glenna Morgan* crossed the equator and passed the coast of Brazil, three others were boarding passenger vessels bound for California. Leaving New York was Bradford Kingston III. His father had urged him to stay in Maryland. King had tried for two days, but he felt restless and unhappy, feelings he attributed to boredom. He returned to New York to resume his former activities at gaming tables, enjoying the company of various accomplished women. Yet, his unhappiness lingered. This he attributed to the fact more and more of his gambling friends were heading for the gold fields. King sometimes felt he was the only person he knew for whom gold mining had no allure. The idea of grubbing in the mud with a pan and living in a mining camp appalled him. Yet, as the weeks drifted by, he found himself more and more alone in the metropolis. Finally, he accepted the inevitable. California was where the real action was. He didn't have to mine the gold, but he could win it at the gaming tables from those who had. Thus, nearly four months after returning to New York, he booked passage on a ship sailing around the Horn to California.

Lord James Charles Winslow was also unhappy, although that was a more normal mental attitude for him. The accursed Irish wench had escaped him again. He tried every way he knew to find her, but to no avail. The search, however, kept him at Aurial. He tried to find pleasure in once again owning a baronial estate. He even threw a grand party for his new neighbors, but few came and those who did were hostile to him. He tried to get interested in tobacco and in operating the plantation, but such activities bored him as they always had. He was soon reduced to prowling Aurial like a caged and very grumpy animal.

His interest rose when he learned that Glenna was being seen in the company of a ship's captain in Baltimore. His brain spun with plans to capture her. It was not easy, but he hired some thugs who were to attack her on the street at night, kill the captain if necessary, and return her to him at Aurial. In excited anticipation he awaited the deed, relishing the thought of her standing helpless before him. Again his hopes were denied. When he heard that she had slipped away aboard a clipper ship for California, he broke up two rooms in Aurial in his rage.

There was nothing for him to do but go to California. He had given his life to hatred for this woman. There was nothing to do but follow her to the ends of the earth. Again he schemed. He could not arrive openly in California. She might attack him as easily as he her. Doubtlessly she would have an ally in the ship captain. There might be other friends. He would need a front to hide behind while he awaited his moment to strike. It was not hard, however, for him to form a plan. He sold Aurial at a sacrifice price to a delighted Kingston, then sold Lila's Place in Washington. With a considerable amount of money to make a new start, he set sail for California from Baltimore with a reluctant Lila as his companion.

46

"You stay here, Moira. I'll see if I can find some things we'll need.",

"No. I'll help. We're in this together."

She had to steel herself to walk back into the burning wagons. As best she could, she avoided looking at the mutilated bodies. All of the wagons were burning and much of what they had contained was either looted or ruined, but working separately the two young people scavanged and laid aside a quantity of materials they figured they might need. Toby found a canteen for water and to his delight an old musket and full powder horn which had been hidden deep in his father's wagon. He also found a knife and axe and some usable pieces of rope.

Moira gathered some flour, cornmeal, beans and coffee, as well as a skillet, two pewter cups and plates, knives and forks. The pile of stuff outside the ring of wagons was growing.

"Blankets, Moira. We'll need those."

Each found one, smoky and a little scorched, but serviceable.

"What about my tent?" she said, pointing. It had been collapsed, but otherwise unharmed.

"Yes, we'll need some shelter."

All collected, it was far too much to carry, but Toby, using pieces of harness, rope and unburned sections of canvas fashioned a pair of makeshift back packs, the larger one for him, a smaller one for her. When they packed them and lifted them to their shoulders, making adjustments in the straps, they were reasonably outfitted for camping. Moira even managed a smile. "I guess we're as ready as we're going to get."

His face flushed. "There's one thing. Your dress, Moira."

For the first time Moira looked down at herself. She was half naked. Quacker had ripped her bodice open. Her skirt exposed her legs. Instinctively, she pulled her bodice closed with her hand. "I'll see what I can do."

She ran back to the wagons and rummaged through them, but the clothing had held a particular fascination for the Indians. There was virtually nothing that was usable. As best she could she tied her bodice together with bits of rawhide and with pieces of unburned fabric fashioned a sort of skirt for herself. "It's the best I can do, Toby."

"You're fine, but we better hurry. That Indian may come back looking for you."

"There's one more thing, Toby." She found a piece of paper from a half burned Bible and, using a sliver of burnt wood as a pen, began to write.

"No one'll ever find it, Moira."

"I know, but I got to, Toby. I got to leave some word that we're alive and where we've gone."

She wrote quickly, then looked for a place to leave the note. There was no tree, no post to nail it.

"I know, here," Toby said. He threw water on the side of the least burned of the wagons, then nailed the note to the side. "If anyone comes along, maybe they'll find it."

They lifted their packs to their backs and headed directly west across the foothills, avoiding the trail.

Both knew the Indians, if they did return, would be looking for them there.

Moira and Toby soon discovered the going far harder and slower than they had on the plains. Walking under their heavy packs and up and down the ever larger foothills quickly sapped their strength. They had to rest more frequently and by late afternoon Toby was often helping her up the last of a grade before they fell to the ground to rest. They built a fire and ate meagerly, then slept out under the stars. It was this way for two full days and part of a third, tiring, but possible.

For Moira, her initial euphoria at the outset of their adventure, quickly gave way with her weariness to apprehension. If she had often felt how small the wagon train was in the plains, she now felt like an insignificant speck in an endless wilderness. She said nothing to Toby, but her terrible feeling of loneliness and emptiness grew inside her. And, as the forbidding massif of the Rockies loomed ever closer, apprehension gave way to open dread. How could they ever get through those peaks? How would they survive?

On the afternoon of the third day, the warm, sunny skies surrendered to a savage storm. It was as if the whole repertoire of the heavens were unleashed against them, thunder, lightning, hail, and torrents of rain, driven by a chill wind. They struggled forward against the elements until nearly nightfall, soaked to the skin, everything in their packs wet through. They pitched their tent under a steady rain and climbed inside. There was no possibility of a fire and thus they had no food. All they could do was lie on the soaked ground under damp blankets.

Through chattering teeth, Moira moaned, "Lord, but I'm cold. I've never been so cold and wet in my life." She felt his arm around her shoulders, and they nestled together seeking warmth from each other's bodies.

Still she shivered, almost uncontrollably, her teeth chattering. She endured it a few minutes more, then sat up. "M-maybe, if we g-get out of these w-wet c-clothes." Quickly, she pulled off her dress and lay back down. "C'mon, Toby, we got to get warm."

He obeyed her finally and lay down beside her. Without the wet clothes to draw off the heat, their bodies were soon warmed. Her teeth stopped their clicking and she began to shiver less. Suddenly heat suffused her body and against his ear she said, "Oh, it's heavenly." Suddenly, he was kissing her, his lips hard against hers. She did not protest or try to resist, but rather enjoyed both the sensation and the heat which swept through her body. She felt his hand, trembling as it clasped her breast, then his fingers inexpertly at her nipples. Despite herself, she felt desire mix with the heavenly heat suffusing her body. Then he stopped and she felt him move to climb atop her. "No," she said softly. "Not yet. I'll tell you when." He lay back down beside her.

She was his first she knew, and something in that knowledge reached out to her. Her promises of virtue were remembered, but discarded in the need for comfort in this nightmare of a night. She showed him how to soften his mouth when he kissed her and how to be gentle when he caressed her. There was something about the warmth of his body, his incessant trembling—she knew it was not from the cold—his excited passion which stirred her greatly. His delight in her body and his own exploration of it filled her with wondrous womanly feelings, and when at last she told him she was ready, he obeyed her when she told him how to position himself and to go slowly, waiting for her.

All in all, it was a highly successful effort and they lay back warm in each other's arms, so warm, steam arose from the damp blanket in the darkness.

"I'm sorry, Moira," he said softly. "I know I shouldn't have done it."

"It wasn't just you. I wanted it, too. It may not have been right, but it felt so good on this miserable night."

Holding her, he was silent for a time. Then, his voice barely above a whisper, he said hoarsely, "It was not the first time for you, was it?"

"No."

He said nothing for a time. She heard only his rather rapid breathing and the steady drone of the rain on the tent.

"Was he. . . ."

He seemed unable to formulate a question, but she knew what he wanted to say. "He was no one you know. It was long ago—oh, not really long, but certainly far away. He was an older man. He took advantage of me."

"Was he better . . ."

She lay there remembering King. It seemed almost impossible to believe it had happened. What a fool she had been. "He was more experienced. Oh, he was all right. But better? No." She couldn't put into words what she felt. With King it had been more exciting, far more thrilling. Lust had made it so, she imagined. With Toby it had been—what? Gentler, more natural, more a product of need, an act of giving, sharing.

In the darkness, she could not see him smiling, yet she knew he was. His words surprised her, though.

"I love you, Moira."

She didn't know what to say at first, then she found the words. "Oh, Toby, I am so fortunate. But I cannot say it is love I feel for you. I am terribly fond of you and more than grateful. Is that enough for now?"

"Yes, more than enough."

She felt him turn to face her once more, his hand again at her breasts.

"You are so beautiful, Moira."

She laughed lightly. "Out here that is the finest compliment in the world."

"I mean it. There is no one like you."

She felt his hand move at her breast as she had showed him, then heard him ask if they could do it again.

"You needn't have asked," she said softly.

In the light of morning, however, he turned shy, rolling out of the blankets to dress quickly. "I'll leave so you can get dressed," he said and bolted out of the tent. His sudden modesty amused her.

The storm had passed and the day was again bright and warm, but Moira knew there could not be many more. August was passing rapidly. What would they do when it turned cold, as it had to? They had not a thread of winter clothing.

Within a few days more they were in the mountains. Moira was fascinated by their beauty but alarmed at how they would get through them. As far as she could see there was jagged peaks and sheer rock cliffs, the tops all swept bare of earth, the surfaces sculptured into strange, bold shapes by wind and water. They tried to stick to valleys and low lying areas, walking through primevil forests so dense nearly all sunlight was kept out. Often she shivered from cold in the shade.

They did not want for fresh, clear water or for food. There was much game and even one deer was far more than they could eat. They began to carry strips of meat across the top of their packs, hoping to dry some for the future.

They meandered through canyons, wasting days getting lost and winding up in dead-end after dead-end. "We can't get through," Toby said. "We'll just have to go over." Moira nodded, fear clutching at her.

They began to climb, taking hours, sometimes a whole day of torturous effort to reach a small summit, only to see an endless range of summits ahead of them. They fell often, scraping skin from their legs and bodies. Moira's hands and arms bled frequently. Toby slung a rope between them to help prevent, he hoped, a serious fall.

But the terrain and their tired, bleeding bodies were not their worst problem. As they climbed the eastern slopes of the Continental Divide, the cold numbed them. They clutched each other at night for warmth and shivered during the day. The most savage storms they had ever known flailed at them, creating noise that almost deafened them as the thunder echoed through the mountains, joined by the crack of splitting rocks and the roar of cascading water and trees felled by lightning.

By early September both knew winter was coming. Storms were more frequent and devasting. The air, even on a sunny day, had a nip to it and the nights produced frost and even thin ice on the banks of quiet streams. Both had taken to wearing blankets around themselves for warmth, but it was a stopgap they knew. If they didn't get help, they knew they would perish in these mountains.

For all their fears and discomfort, they still saw panoramas of unparalleled beauty, vistas of mountains, lakes, white water rivers that provoked feelings of majesty and grandeur. They walked beneath trees so large they must have been there since time began and beside streams choking with fish. Game was plentiful, deer, antelope, elk, moose. They even caught glimpses of mountain lions. There were birds and fowl of great variety, and an abundance of beaver, muskrat, weasels and other small animals. Overhead eagles soared. Had they been better prepared for the wilderness, both young people would have enjoyed these mountains as a paradise.

As it was they found what pleasures they could. They made love frequently at night, and during the day, at least on easier terrain, they walked hand in hand. Toby showed his love for her in innumerable ways, an arm to support her, a handful of wild flowers, a choicer cut of meat roasted by an open fire. It seemed to Moira, and it was indeed true, he was maturing rapidly, becoming stronger physically, more aggressive and decisive about which direction to go. The challenge of the wilderness and his love for her seemed to bring out the masculine quality of protectiveness in him. Yet, he remained frequently shy, modest and inarticulate.

Thus, when she impulsively suggested a bath, he blushed and stammered. They had come across a particularly lovely glen beneath a high rock face. A waterfall created a small pool of clear water admist a stand of pines. It was a warmer day than they had been having and the idea of bathing appealed to Moira.

"Oh, come on, Toby. You've seen me naked before."

He held back. "I don't know."

She laughed. "You are silly. I'm going whether you do or not."

As she began to remove her dress, he said, "What if someone—"

"There are no someones, Toby. We haven't seen a soul in these mountains and we've been here for weeks."

She dove in the water. "It's cool, but heavenly, Toby."

Unable to resist any longer he, too, disrobed and jumped in after her. The water was clear, but too shallow for swimming, but they sat in it and laid in it, letting the water lave their scratched and bruised skin. In a minute, they were standing under the waterfall, squealing as the frigid water cascaded over them, then frolicking through the pool, splashing each other amid squeals and laughter.

So absorbed was Moira in the pure pleasure that it was some time before she saw the figure standing on the bank looking at them, a smile on his face. She screamed and immediately dove into the water for what covering it could provide her nakedness.

The man on the bank laughed, a big booming laugh. "Don't be afraid, li'l darlin'. I was jus' standing here figgerin' I must be dead and lookin' at paradise."

"You get out of here," Toby shouted and immediately began marching toward the mountain man.

"Hold 'er there now, newt," he said. "I'm not goin' to harm ya."

Toby kept advancing. "You'll not spy on us— you . . ."

"I'm sorry for that, lad. But one hardly expects to see a lovely young thing bathin' deep in these here woods." He laughed. "You can unnerstan' that, I hope."

Toby stood near him now, his fists clinched for a fight. "You just get out of here and leave us alone."

Despite his efforts, the naked Toby was simply not very menacing to the intruder, as his laugh revealed. "Tell ya what, lad. I'll turn me back, even close me eyes, while you and the li'l lady get your clothes on. I hope thas a good deal, 'cause it's the bes' I can do."

Toby agreed reluctantly. After the mountaineer turned his back, an embarrassed Moira quickly jumped into her clothes.

"Is it all right now, li'l lady?"

"Yes, I'm dressed, but I never—"

He turned, looked at her and laughed. "And I never did either. I never did see a woman as purty as you and thas a fact."

His name was Clay Bancroft, and even after she was dressed, Moria's reaction to him was fear. He was huge, nearly a giant, with a long and straggily brown beard, wild hair and that booming voice. He was dressed in cowhide and moccasins and looked for all the world like a savage. Yet, for all his size and appearance, he did not seem to intend them harm, and Moira's fear quickly dissipated.

"What you youngin' doin' here?"

They told him.

He looked them up and down, then slowly shook his head. "You'da been better off with the Indians. You ain't gotta chance in these mountains. It'll be snowin' soon. And you ain't never seen snow like in these here mountains."

Just his words, affirming her fears, made Moira shudder.

"Well, we'll jus' have to see what we can do for you two. Follow me."

He led them downstream from the waterfall to a sort of shack, actually a lean-to built against the rock face of a mountain. It was fashioned of heavy logs and sturdy poles and made watertight with heavy thicknesses of pine boughs. "Taint much," he said, "but it's home."

Moira and Toby stayed with Clay Bancroft for ten days, learning a great deal that might enable them to get through the winter. "You ain't goin' to get through these mountains afore winter comes. No way you gonna do that. And you ain't gonna live a week unless you learn how to. So you better listen and listen good."

He taught them how to build a lean-to and where. "The wind is somethin' fierce. Howls like a banshee she does—but always from the west. So you wanna find a spot, facing east, with yer back against a mountain. An' make 'er strong, 'cause you ain't never seen snow like there is 'ere. Yer gonna get buried in snow, but as long as ya gotta pole to knock out an air hole, ya ain't gonna freeze. Why snow is warm. Dogs and other beasts bury under the snow to keep warm. You can do the same."

He taught them how to dry and store fish and meat for the winter, and how to make and lay traps. They learned how to skin beaver and mink, and how to prepare the skins, even how to fashion them into clothing and footwear. "I be a damn fool, but I give you these pelts. You won't have enough time to catch yer own before winter. But come spring, you come back this way and repay me. Is that a deal?" Moira and Toby assured him they would. A couple days later both were attired in warm moccasins and leggings, heavy fur jackets, even fur hats.

"It be too warm fer now, but come winter you'll be grateful to old Clay Bancroft."

Moira smiled. "I am already."

They asked him if he was the only one living in the mountains. "Nah. There's more mountain men up here than you might think—too many to suit me. Whole place is gettin' crowded. It's nice havin' visitors—specially a purty girl. But not fer too long. Wouldn't work out. Thas why I'se sendin' you off. Better you make it on yer own. Know what I mean?"

"Yes," Toby said. "And we'll make it—thanks to you."

He drew a rough map and suggested a spot in the

next valley. "It'll do fine for you, some shelter, plenny water, lotsa beaver. 'Course, somebody else may a latched onto it. If so, there's always another spot. Jus' stick to yerselves, use yer heads and be careful. You'll be fine." A smile split his beard. "An' if you get stuck, you can always come back here, hollerin' for help."

As they prepared to leave, Bancroft gave them some parting advice. "Chances are nobody'll bother ya, but if ya see anyone, I suggest the li'l lady make herself scarce. Mos' mountain men is decent enough, but come winter, some would sell their souls to have a woman. Believe me, I thought about it myself—only I'se too old for such foolishness."

Moira smiled at him. "You're not too old. What you are is too decent."

"Maybe yer right, li'l lady, but there's those who'll do anythin' fer a li'l lady like you. Ol' Jack Knight-fer one. Meanest sonagun who ever lived. But I don't think he's in these parts no more. But if he do come around, there ain't nothin' to do but shoot him quick."

"I'll look after her, Mr. Bancroft," Toby said.

"See that ya do, youngin'."

47

They found the valley described by Bancroft and it was unoccupied. Moira, whose spirits had risen with the hope engendered by the mountain man, squealed with delight when she saw the small valley nestled among the mountain peaks. There was a small, swift stream of cool water that led down to a small pond created by the dams fashioned by beaver. There were fish in the stream and among the stand of pines evidence of plentiful game.

"Oh, it's wonderful, Toby. We'll make it through the winter here, won't we?"

"Yes, but we'll have to hurry."

With both energy and excitement, they began their tasks, first building a snug lean-to as Bancroft had showed them. As they piled it high with pine boughs and brought others in to make a snug bed by the open fire, Moira realized she was truly happy. She was as healthy and strong as she had ever been in her life and pleased with herself and Toby that they were surviving in the wilderness alone with little more than their own resources. Over and over she said to herself, and frequently aloud to him, that they were making it. This knowledge gave her such confidence and pleasure.

This pleasure and her good health increasingly demonstrated itself in her lovemaking with Toby. More and more she gave herself to him without restraint, even abandonment, enjoying her own body and the pleasure she gave Toby. She often noticed how strong and self-assured he was becoming. Young he might be, but he was in many ways more of a man than King. How could she have been such a fool? Yet, she could not quite forget her first love. The memory of the moonlight, that first kiss and of all they had done together often came back to her, and she could feel the flush rise in her face. And she thought of her mother. What had happened to her? And of Andrew. Was he alive in California? Would he still be there when she and Toby arrived next year? She even thought of Ned Kingston. He was, she now knew, much like Toby, simple, shy, both men of the land. How she must have hurt him. How could she have flouted her romance with King in front of him?

She and Toby shared the labors equally. They built

the lean-to jointly. While he hunted, she fished. While he built and laid out traps and snares, she felled trees and cut a huge store of wood for the winter. Her hands became blistered, then heavily calloused, but she didn't care. She was far from civilization and enjoying every minute of it. While he skinned the animals and made hides and furs, she dried fish and meat for the winter. Their flour and coffee was nearly gone, but she accumulated a hoard of berries, dried fruit and edible greens to vary their diet for the winter. When the snows came and the stream began to freeze, she packed fish and meat away, as Bancroft had taught them. In the evening, she and Toby worked together to fashion a table and two chairs. With skins and hides, a bouquet of dried flowers, she felt the first real home she had ever made was positively cosy. When the first heavy storm of winter came, dumping two feet of snow over their domain, they greeted it with excitement, declaring it a wonderland of beauty. For more than twenty-four hours they remained snug and happy in their lean-to, twice steaming it with their energetic lovemaking.

"You are happy, aren't you, Moira?"

"Yes, I truly am. And that surprises me. I was not a city girl. I probably wouldn't be alive today if I had been. But I lived in luxury. I never wanted for anything. I certainly did nothing like I've done these past months. I know now I was selfish and spoiled. I can only view it with shame now, and know I am a lucky girl."

"I'm the one who's lucky," he said, his eyes shining with love, "to be here with you."

She smiled at him. "We're both lucky in that, Toby."

"Moira, do you—" His shy stammering had surfaced again. "do you think of that other man?"

"Sometimes. Not very often."

"Have you—you come to . . . love me a little?"

She kissed him lightly on the lips. "I don't know if it is love or what, Toby." She boldly clasped him in a

most private place. "But I've never been happier. I like
you, your body, what you do to me." She smiled. "I
will hate leaving here, leaving you. I just may stay here
forever. If that is love, so be it."

As he bent to her, he said, "I think maybe it is love."

When the storm passed, Moira and Toby dug out the
door to their lean-to and made paths to the woodpile,
food storage locker and creek. Then Toby donned
makeshift snowshoes and headed off to tend his trap
lines, leaving Moira to do housekeeping chores and
prepare supper. She was bent over the table preparing
a stew for cooking when she heard the door open and
felt a blast of frigid air. "You can't be back already,"
she said, and turned.

To her astonishment, it was not Toby, but a man she
had not seen before. He was not a big man, indeed, he
was rather small and wiry. But there was an evil look
about him which made Moira shiver. He had a heavy
black beard, long unkempt black hair beneath his fur
hat and cold black eyes. She saw the edge of a livid scar
amid the beard on his left cheek. He wore a rough
jacket made of bearskin. The odor of it, of him,
assaulted her.

"What d'you want?" she said.

He flashed broken, yellowish teeth. "Only the
hospitality of the mountains, Miss."

She hesitated, then said, "Of course. My husband
will be back in a few minutes."

His laugh was low and gutteral. "He ain't yer
husband, miss—and he won't be back in no few
minutes. I been keepin' my eye on you two love birds.
He jus' went off to tend his traps. He won't be back fer
a long time." He pulled a chair over and sat down on it
backwards. "There's plenny o' time fer us to get
acquainted." He smiled up at her wickedly. "My
moniker be Jack Knight. Whas yours?"

With a start she remembered the name and Clay
Bancroft's warning to shoot him if he ever came

around. But Toby had taken the rifle. She had no weapon other than the kitchen knife in her hand. Slowly she tightened her grip on it.

"I asked what yer name be."

"Moira—Moira Morgan."

Again his smile. "Real purty that be."

Moira looked away from him. Her fear had turned to alarm and she could feel it shrieking inside her. What could she do? Oh, if only Toby hadn't left.

"Would you like some coffee, Mr. Knight?"

"If thas the best ya got to offer," he said, leering at her.

"If you mean whiskey, I'm afraid we don't have any."

"Thas too bad, but I got whiskey at my place." He stood up. "I was talkin' 'bout somethin' else."

She shrank back as he stepped toward her. "No, please."

"Like I say, Miss, I been awatching you fer some time. You sure is a purty thing. That young pup don't disserve you all to hisself. Why you is the purtiest thing I ever did see, or my name ain't Jack Knight."

She retreated as far as she could into a corner.

"Ol' Jack wont hurt you none. Fact is, I be a lot better than that young whelp."

"No," she said and raised the knife in her right hand.

He laughed. "Goodness, you'd use that mean ol' knife on li'l ol' Jack here. Why I never. Well, if thas the way you're gonna be . . ."

She saw him turn, as if to leave her alone and instantly she bolted toward the door and escape. But with a cry, he grabbed her.

"Gotcha. Now let me have that plaything."

In an instant the knife was torn from her grasp. He held her by both wrists, pulling her against him. She felt his foul breath and his rough beard as he tried to kiss her. But she turned her head and struggled and kicked, screaming for him to stop.

"A wildcat you sure is. But ol' Jack, he knows what to do about that."

She barely saw the fist that knocked her out. When consciousness swam back to her, it was an awareness of pain and pressure. Her head and jaw ached, but there was other pain. Then she knew. She was half naked and he was atop her thrusting into her, his foul mouth on hers. She tried to push him away, but managed to twist her mouth from his.

"You is a good one, you is," he grunted, and redoubled his thrusts into her, and Moira felt herself sinking again into unconsciousness. This she did not fight.

Then came a blast of cold air and a cry of rage. She felt a new weight pounce on top of her, then Jack Knight being pulled away. Opening her eyes she saw Knight on the floor, Toby towering over him in a rage. She saw Toby pick up his rifle and aim it at Knight.

"Hold on there. I don't mean no harm."

"I was told to kill you, now I am."

Knight rolled away from the aimed rifle and got to his feet, pulling up his leggings as he did so. "You ain't gonna shoot ol' Jack, you young whelp. You ain't got the nerve."

It was true. Toby had no capacity to shoot a man in cold blood, even in the rage he felt. But he kept the cocked rifle aimed at Knight.

"I'll jus' be on my way and we'll forget the whole thing. All right?" Cringing, he slowly inched his way around the rifle toward the door. He picked up his fur hat and placed it lopsided on his head. Then, still eyeing Toby's rifle, picked up his own rifle from beside the door. "Like I say, no harm intended."

"I ought to kill you—and I will if I ever see you near here again."

Knight smiled his relief to be escaping unharmed. "Sure, sure, you'll never have any trouble from me again, no sirree." In the doorway, he said, "Jus' put that piece down, son, 'for it goes off and hurts some-body."

As Toby began to lower his rifle, Knight raised his and at short range blasted Toby full in the chest. A look of surprise on his face, he slowly slumped to the floor, instantly dead.

Moira screamed, "Toby! Toby!"

Through the acrid biting gunsmoke which filled the room, she heard Knight say, "That won't do you no good. He ain't ever gonna hear nobody." Like a rag doll, he pulled her off him and threw her on the bed. "Now les you and me finish what we started."

She screamed and fought to no avail. He slapped her hard twice, then lunged into her. When it was over, he stood up. "You sure is a sweet one, you is. This is gonna be the bes' winter ever." He refastened his clothes and picked up his rifle. "Now you get yerself dressed. You's movin' in with ol' Jack here."

Moira's winter of happiness became her season of hell. Because she tried to run from him, he bound her wrists in leading her back to his filthy, smelly log cabin in the woods. He immediately raped her again, hitting her because she resisted. This became a daily, some-times multi-daily occurrence. He beat her regularly and frequently because he did not like the food or she moved too slow or was not quick enough to get out of her clothes or often just for the pleasure of it. He hit her with his fists until her eyes were blackened and her face so sore she could hardly open her jaw to swallow. Her body, particularly her breasts, were a mass of bruises. He even pelted her from time to time with a rawhide whip.

He kept her bound hand and foot much of the time and then tethered her like an animal while she prepared his meals. Her only respite from him came when, having raped her, he fell into a drunken stupor. Even then he was careful to tie her to the bed so there was no escape.

Under the onslaught of brutality, her spirit wilted

like the flowers of autumn. She was rendered passive, trying only to please him in a vain effort to stop him from beating her. In moments both of respite and of torment, she wished for death.

48

It was July 4, 1850 when Ned Kingston arrived in Independence, Missouri, on horseback in his quest for Moira Morgan. He was just in time for a drunken, riotous four-day celebration of the nation's birth. As befitted its name, Independence traditionally gave its all to observance of the event. Ned was reasonably patriotic, but chafed because the celebration made it impossibly difficult for him to find out anything about Moira.

In his search for her, Ned used her most obvious feature, her red hair, in describing her. It became almost like a beacon for him to follow. But Moira had deliberately worn the concealing bonnet, and Ned could find no one who had seen a young girl with brilliant, flaming hair. He had just about despaired. She must not have come to Independence after all. Perhaps she had gone to St. Joe or Council Bluffs. Then he heard about the Quacker train of "damned fools" which had left so late and finally found a livery owner who had helped outfit that train. It seemed to him, yes, a girl had joined the train late. Maybe she had red hair. He couldn't be sure. Then Ned met a party who had given up on the trip west and returned. One of them remembered seeing a girl with red hair driving cattle on the last train.

By the time Ned confirmed that Moira had gone west with the Quacker train it was July 11. It took another three days for him to outfit himself for the trip. He was impatient to be gone, yet he outfitted himself sensibly for both the journey and the winter. He bought an extra horse and used it as a pack animal, carrying sufficient food, clothing, ammunition and other essentials for survival in the wilderness in the winter. At dawn on the fourteenth, he set out on the California Trail alone, a month behind Moira.

The trail was not hard to follow and he made excellent time, although he was careful not to wear out his mounts. He made forty and fifty miles a day, once close to a hundred, yet there were times when he was slowed by heavy rains and mud through which the horses labored. He had a poncho and a wide brimmed hat which kept him a little dry. Still he often shivered through the damp nights when he was unable to build a fire. Worse was the loneliness and the emptiness of the plains which he was crossing.

He gave no thought of giving up his search. He had set his mind to finding Moira, and he would not deviate from that quest as long as there was breath in his body. There were lonely nights when he asked himself why. She surely had not encouraged him. Quite the contrary, she had ridiculed and spurned him in favor of his brother. But he knew he loved her. And as he lay under his blanket at night, his saddle for a pillow, he fell asleep to visions of her riding across the fields of Calvert County. Just before sleep came, he would frequently hear her angry words as his brother jilted her. Something more than his love and determination drove him onward, however. He had the strongest sense that she needed him. He believed he knew the signs of an early and terrible winter. She was in danger. She needed him. Increasingly, he was sure of that.

Ned had hoped to catch up to the Quacker train and

was disappointed that he did not. Barring that, he was sure he'd hear word of a red-haired girl. Toward that end, he lost time asking about her at the ferry crossing, the trading posts and from occasional pioneers he encountered. None of this was to any avail. No one had seen any girl resembling Moira. Rather, at the trading post at Ash Hollow he received warnings of Indians. A wagon train had been attacked.

This information stabbed at him, and he hurried on, arriving at Fort Laramie on August eighteenth. Surely, the Quacker train had stopped there. Every train going west refitted and repaired there. No. But someone remembered a small train that had passed without stopping awhile back. It figured to be the one the Indians had gotten.

In desperation, fear gripping him, he rode out, and the next morning found the charred remains of the Quacker train. But there was nothing to identify it. The bodies had been buried, the remnants of possessions stolen. All that was left were the charred and broken wagons. He looked at the site in desolation. Had it all come to this? Was his beautiful Moira lying in one of those graves? Then he got control of himself. He hadn't come all this way to give up. He would not give up until he knew for certain Moira was either dead or alive. Why she might not have been on this train at all. He had to find out for certain. Thus determined, he returned to Fort Laramie.

From the barkeep and traders he learned that it had indeed been the Quacker train. Quacker himself had been killed and scalped. He was identified from his Bible. Everyone had been scalped by the bloody savages—either that or captured, a worse fate surely. A sickening feeling grew in the pit of Ned's stomach as he listened to exaggerated and hair raising tales of Indian atrocities from the men in the bar. This had gone on for some time before someone mentioned that there had been two survivors. Eventually, Ned held in his hand the note scrawled by Moira. Trembling with excitement, he read the hasty words:

"All dead, Indians. Going west through mountains" With excitement and relief he read the penned names: Toby Hamilton and Moira Morgan. Again and again he read the note. She was alive. Thank God, she was alive. He would find her.

The next day he rode out, more rapidly now, reaching the burned out wagons at nightfall. He camped near there, then the next morning he headed directly west, away from the trail, toward the mountains. He slowed his progress, repeatedly circling a wide area in hopes of finding some trail. There was none. Any footprints had been swept away by rain and wind.

It was the sixth of September by the time he reached the mountains. For another week, he struggled through them, getting lost in the maze of canyons, finally beginning to climb as Moira and Toby had done a month before. Already the wind was cold and the storms which battered him told of the approaching winter. He would not give up. Moira and someone named Toby Hamilton had entered this vast chain of mountains. He would find them—or their bodies, if that is what it was to be. Yet, he knew that he himself had to survive. Reluctantly, he returned to Fort Laramie to purchase supplies and gear that would keep him and his horses alive through the winter. Men at the fort told him he was a damned fool to try it, but gave him advice which ultimately saved his life.

The nights were bitter cold when he returned to the mountains in late September and soon snow was falling in the higher passes. But he struggled on, to where he didn't know. He had to search. That's all he knew to do, that and follow the only evidence he had, the direction west. When the first heavy blizzard came, he survived it by following the advice given at the fort. He built a temporary shelter of pine boughs. With a small fire and the heat from the horses which he brought inside the shelter, he waited out the storm. After two days, he struck out again, but with painful slowness. He managed in the snow shoes he had purchased, but the horses had to struggle through the deep snow.

That first October snow melted some, but the savage storms kept coming with terrifying regularity. Thus, it was January when he stumbled on the lean-to of Clay Bancroft, who cured the painful frostbite in his finger and toes, and February when he found the frozen body of Toby Hamilton. But where was Moira? As another blizzard swept in, he remained in the lean-to she had helped to build, feeling encouraged that he was at last close to her.

For Andrew, it was not snow which was the enemy, but mud, seas of muck, slides of ooze in the interminable rains of Northern California. In the area northwest of Sacramento more than a hundred inches of rain falls a year, creating magnificent forests. For those such as Andrew searching for gold, it meant the hardship of wet, cold, damp, mildew and omnipresent mud.

The gold fields lay due west of San Francisco Bay and stretched for hundreds of miles along the western slopes of the Sierra Nevada Mountains where they met the valleys of the San Joaquin, Feather and Sacramento Rivers. These rivers were fed by scores of westward running rivers and streams bringing melted snow from the Sierras. These rivers bore such names as Mariposa, Mercer, Tuohumne, Stanislaus, Calaveras, Consumers, Yuba and, of course, the most famous of all, the American. It was this which yielded the first gold near Fort Sutter, just outside Sacramento.

It was surely the rarity of gold that made it so valuable and led hundreds of thousands of young men like Andrew to endure unimaginable hardships to obtain it. But gold held other fascinations than its preciousness. Gold is one of a very few metals, along with silver, platinum, copper and tungsten, which can be found in its pure or nearly pure state. No heating or smelting or refining is necessary to develop gold. A person can kick over a rock or pull up a weed and there it is, shining, shimmering with an inner warmth. Indeed, both these events happened in California. These and scores of other incredible stories of lucky finds swept through the mining camps and fueled the search for gold.

The metal has other fascinating properties. It is extremely heavy, ten times heavier than clay. A block of gold measuring five by five by six inches weighs a hundred pounds. Gold is also impervious to air and water. It does not tarnish or rust. It is insoluble in water and is never worn away by it. Nor does gold pulverize when crushed. It is a soft metal, extremely malleable by hand. It can, for example, be flattened with the edge of a knife. An ounce of it can be spread so thin that it can cover 250 square feet as gold leaf. When heated it melts easily into a liquid.

All these properties of gold created the special character of the California fields where Andrew began his search. There were a few veins of gold, but this was not the rule. Most of the gold was in the form of placers. For centuries, water washed over a gold vein in a mountainside. The gold was eroded from the vein by the water, but still remained the shiny yellow metal as it was washed downstream. Being heavier, the gold dropped to the bottom of the stream, mixing with sand and clay. Other metals, iron for example, were rusted away, making the gold purer and purer. More sand and gravel washed over the gold, eventually covering it.

Most of the gold in California was found in and near rivers and streams, borne there by the heavy rains and melting snows. But not always. Perhaps there had been an earth tremor or an avalanche. The course of a stream changed, leaving the most precious of metals high and dry far from water. All this gave the gold in California its character, fields of gold. If enough earth was dug and sifted, gold could be found. The young Forty Niners undertook to do just that.

Since there was no mountain of gold to be dug, a pick and shovel were of less use than the simplest of man's inventions, a shallow pan, a wash basin. Andrew quickly learned how to pan for gold. A pan was filled nearly full of gravel and sand and placed just under still water. One hand held the pan steady, while the other stirred the contents until all the clods and lumps had been broken up. As the water became muddy, the pan was tipped to drain off the mud and take on fresh water. The larger stones were tossed out. Then the pan, still under water, was shaken vigorously with both hands, a process that allowed the heavier gold particles to sink to the bottom. The pan was removed from the water and tilted so the lighter sands floated out. That left only heavy sand and hopefully some specks of gold in the bottom. This sludge was dried in the sun or over a fire, then the sand blown away to leave only gold.

Panning for gold thus meant standing and working in cold water. Andrew discovered that if he worked constantly from dawn to dusk, he could pan perhaps two tons of earth a day. It was cold, hard, backbreaking work of stultifying boredom to produce a few flecks of yellow.

Some miners were lucky and found nuggets of some size. The largest Andrew had found was the size of grains of wheat and only one of those. Mostly he found dust, and it took a lot of dust to make an ounce of gold worth perhaps fifteen dollars. At that, he was fortunate, for many of the hundreds of thousands of miners who descended on California never found any or certainly enough to pay their expenses.

Like other greenhorns, Andrew went to the American River where the original gold had been found. Almost immediately, he saw the folly in that. The area was a rabbit warren of miners. Tens of thousands of men had descended on the place. Every inch of riverbank had been staked out and worked over.

He headed north, up the Feather River, past Marysville and Otoville, finally finding a reasonably isolated area high in the mountains near the Butte River and a mining camp called Rich Ba. He wanted to be by himself. The raucous miners with their whiskey and drunken roistering, their brawls and foolish squandering offended him. Mining for gold was serious business to him. If he was going to be cold, wet, bored, tired and lonely, it was all for the purpose of buying back Aurial. He was not going to squander his specks of gold dredged from the stream bank on rotgut whiskey at ten dollars a bottle.

He quickly saw that those who made money in the goldfields were not the miners, but the merchants who leeched the precious mineral from those who found it. Molasses and vinegar sold at a dollar a bottle, melons up to five dollars apiece. Flour sold at a dollar a pound and the same sum bought a single potato or onion. A single candle often cost more than a dollar, the cheapest pair of boots sixteen dollars. As fast as gold was found, it went for the necessities of life.

To avoid this, Andrew lived like a hermit. He was quite alone in a tiny shack he slapped together himself. He ate meagerly. In fact he was hungry so much of the time, it became a constant sensation. Wryly, he told himself that hunger was pleasant. He felt sure that when he got thin enough, his niggardly diet of flour, a few bites of salt pork, augmented with an occasional fish, a few berries and greens he gathered, would keep him alive.

He worked alone. There were times when he envied his fellow miners banded together in threes, fours and larger groups. With more hands, a real mining operation was possible. One device used was the "rocker," an open box with holes in the bottom which could be shaken over a trough. It allowed the sediment with the gold dust to be filtered out in a continuous operation. Also used for faster panning was the "Long Tom," a trough or sluice into which dirt could be shoveled steadily. As water was added, the dirt ran down the shoot, the gold settling out at the bottom much as happened naturally in stream beds.

Andrew was tempted to take in partners. He would have welcomed the companionship, and he knew those continuous operations produced more gold faster and with less individual effort than he could. But he also knew the gold had to be split among the partners. Moreover, he knew that partners would force him to spend more for food, whiskey and entertainment than he wanted to.

So, he panned for gold alone. He made up for the slowness of this method by persistence, panning steadily from dawn to dusk, his determination to buy back Aurial propelling him through the fatigue and boredom of his task. He worked at his search through sun and wind and storm, through his own weariness and not infrequent colds, flu and fevers. He was a driven young man. Indeed, there were times when he wondered if he were not going mad.

At night after a meager meal, not uncommonly a cold one because he was too tired to build a fire, he fell into the lice infested straw he called a bed. He would think of Aurial, his happiness there, and of his mother and sister. His eyes would smart with longing. Sometimes, too, he thought of Lila and her silken arms and impassioned kisses. But that memory was too tied in with his disgrace at gambling for him to think of her often.

Andrew found gold, speck by speck, ounce by ounce. By spending as little of it as possible, while hoarding it in small leather pouches, he knew his cache was growing. He had a hundred, then thousands of dollars accumulated, hidden for safekeeping. With the gold was the last of his mother's jewels, a large sapphire cut from a necklace given her by his father. He had held on to the gem for he wanted to return it to his mother. If he could just do that, he knew at least some of his guilt would be assuaged. His most common dream was of

returning to Maryland to triumphantly present his
mother with a hoard of gold to buy back Aurial and the
sapphire given her by his father. The dream always
ended with her embracing him in forgiveness.

49

The evidence was unmistakable to Ned
Kingston. Someone had come into this lean-to. There
had been a struggle, then Toby Hamilton—he was sure
that's who it was—had been shot in the chest, probably
from the open doorway. Whoever had committed the
murder, had taken Moira away.

Fear nagged at him that maybe he was wrong. But he
could find no sign of a second shot being fired and
abundant evidence that Moira had left precipitously,
the bed in disarray, the half finished stew. What he
feared was that Moira had run out alone into the snow
in an effort to escape. Would the spring thaw reveal the
frozen body of a red-haired girl? He told himself over
and over it was unlikely. Whoever had burst in here to
commit murder would not let her get away.

Another, traitorous thought came to Ned. Suppose
there had been no intruder? Suppose Moira had
murdered Hamilton herself and then fled. It was
possible. Hamilton looked like a young, innocent kid,
unable even to grow a beard. But he could have been
mean. She could have killed him to get away from him.
But to where? Or maybe when the intruder came and
killed Hamilton, she had been grateful and gone away

with him willingly. Remembrances of Moira giving herself willingly to his brother tore at Ned. Anything was possible with Moira. The thought of her in the arms of another man filled him with jealousy, leaving him to struggle to suppress such morbid thoughts.

Thus, he waited out the February storms in a mire of conflicting thoughts and fears. All he could decide was that she was somewhere nearby and one way or another he would find her and settle this issue.

Nature did not cooperate with his determination. Storms raged almost continuously through February and well into March. About the time he'd dug out from one and prepared to commence a search for Moira, a new storm bore down on him. Fretfully, he spent the days in the lean-to with the horses. His only comfort was the knowledge that Moira had lived here, slept where he slept, helped cut the wood he burned and prepared the food he ate.

When at last he was able to begin his search for her, he had no idea where to look. He wasted almost two weeks struggling through the snow and over mountains in a futile search for the girl he loved. It was the twentieth of March when, having traveled nearly a full day to the southwest, he spotted a tiny log cabin in the woods, a tuft of smoke rising from the roof.

He longed to go boldly up to the door and find out if Moira was there. Such an action would be entirely appropriate in these woods. Shelter and food were offered freely. But he held back. If Moira was in that cabin, it was with a murderer. If he had killed once for Moira, he would again. Caution made him huddle down in a snowbank to spend a frigid night in the open.

The next morning, the sun was bright, although the air remained well below freezing. Spring came hard in the mountains. By nine o'clock the sun was high enough in the sky to rise above the mountains and flood the front of the cabin with sunlight. The smoke from the roof increased, so he knew the cabin was occupied. By whom? Was Moira in there? He was about to despair of anyone ever showing themselves when the door of the cabin opened and a figure came out.

His heart thumped in anticipation of its being Moira, but it was a man with a black beard dressed in a bear skin. The man stood in front of the door, a rifle in his hands. He looked up at the blue sky, then stretched and pounded his chest with his free hand. He then began slowly to walk around the area. Ned remained motionless in the woods perhaps fifty yards from the cabin. He hoped the man would leave, perhaps to tend a trap line. If he did, Ned could approach the cabin in his absence. But if this was to be, it wasn't happening very rapidly. The man tromped around outside to no purpose other than to test the solidness of the snow and perhaps breathe fresh air. After a bit he went back inside. Ned waited well into the afternoon and no one emerged from the cabin. Reluctantly, Ned accepted the fact he had no alternative but to approach the cabin directly.

After carefully reloading his rifle and cocking it, Ned walked toward the cabin as if he had just come out of the woods. He felt extremely alone and exposed. With each step, he expected a shot to explode from the cabin, ending his life right there. But there was none and in a few minutes, he was outside the door. No one had seen him. He pondered what to do for a moment, knock or walk in? He'd just open the door and enter. Why give up his element of surprise? He reached for the latch and pulled, but the door didn't budge. Locked from the inside. There was nothing to do but knock. He pounded on the door. No answer. He pounded more and louder.

"Who's there?" It was a male voice.

"A friend."

"Taint got no friends. Go way."

"I need help," Ned called out, then pounded on the door some more.

"Stop that infernal poundin' afore I blast ya."

That thought had already occurred to Ned, and he had moved to the side of the door where the logs would protect him from a rifle shot. He had also moved behind the door, so if anyone came, they would have to step outside to see him. "Please," he shouted. "I'm lost."

He stopped pounding to listen.

"All right. Just a goddamned minute."

The black bearded man he had seen before emerged from the cabin. Ned saw his scar beneath the beard and the evil black eyes. He was smaller than Ned, but carried his rifle at the ready.

"I tol' you to git, now git."

"I'm lost."

"Nah, you ain't lost. Just go back the way you come."

"But—"

"There ain't no place to get to anyway. So git, afore I blast ya."

Ned tried a new tack. He had to get inside. "I'm out of food. Haven't eaten in two days."

"Too bad, greenhorn. Taint nothin' here. Now git."

Ned hesitated, eyeing the man. But glaring at him was of no use, for he had his cocked rifle aimed right at his midsection.

Then he heard sounds from inside, moaning, squealing sounds.

"What's that noise?"

"Taint no noise. Just the wind."

"Sounded like a woman to me."

Jack Knight's face parted into a yellow smile. "Oh that. Just my squaw woman. You came at the wrong time and she wants me back. Now you git."

Ned glared at him a moment longer, then shrugged. Gripping his rifle, he slowly began to walk away from the cabin. But he did so at such an angle he could still see Knight on the far periphery of his vision. Five, then perhaps twenty steps he moved, being careful to make it look as though he was leaving, until he saw Knight lower his rifle and turn to re-enter the cabin.

Instantly, Ned whirled and placed the defenseless

Knight under the sights of his rifle. "I think I'd like to meet your squaw woman," he said, and began to advance back toward the cabin.

Knight eyed him a moment, then shrugged and showed his flash of yellow teeth. "Suit yourself."

Ned saw him open the door, step inside, then immediately dart to the right of the door. Instinctively, Ned ran the remaining steps and dove low through the door, feeling the heat of the musket as it blasted above him. Ned's dive carried him into the cabin and he crashed into a table and chair, knocking them over as he rolled forward to gain his feet. Quickly, too quickly, he fired at a figure seen dimly through the smoke. He missed and neither man now had a gun to fire.

As Knight lunged at him out of the smoke, Ned tried to swing his musket at him, but Knight ducked under the blow and leaped at him, knife in hand. Ned raised his left arm to turn aside the knife and felt a stab of pain in his shoulder. He rolled from the blow, drawing his own knife. Over and over they rolled on the dirt floor, cursing as they flailed with their arms. Then Ned felt his knife sink into something soft and heard a gasp and cry. Twice more he raised the knife, feeling it crunch into bone. Then he struggled to his feet, panting, to look down at the startled expression in Jack Knight's eyes as he died.

For a moment longer, Ned stood over the body, his fear and rage mingling with his sense of horror that he had killed a man in a knife fight. Then he remembered what he had killed for. Frantically, he looked around the cabin. For a moment he saw nothing, then he saw her on a filthy bed in the corner, tied hand and foot to stakes in the ground and gagged with a rag through her mouth. He would never have known it was Moira except for her red hair.

As quickly as he could, he cut her bonds with the bloody knife, then slit the gag away from her, helping her to her feet. Except for her hair, now a tangled matted mass, he saw nothing to recognize. Her whole face was blackened and swollen, one eye nearly shut from a livid bruise. Her left cheek was so puffed, her mouth was swollen into a lopsided, macabre grin of cut and scabbed lips.

"My God, Moira. What has he done to you?"

She had stood there, looking at him with the one open eye. He saw the fright in it, just before she began to scream. He took her by her bony shoulders and shouted, "It's me, Moira, Ned Kingston." Still she screamed. "It's me, Ned Kingston," he repeated. "Thank God I found you."

Finally she stopped screaming and stared at him in shock and disbelief, then slowly collapsed into his arms.

He wanted to carry her away from the horrid place, but knew she was in no condition to be moved. Instead, he laid her on the filthy bed, found a cloth, wet it and applied it to her face. Next, he dragged Knight's body outside and buried it out of sight in a snowdrift. Back inside, he built up the fire and and straightened the overturned table and chairs before returning to change the cloth on her face.

She was awake, looking at him. Her voice was weak and distorted through her swollen, misshapen mouth, as she said, "Is it really you?"

"Yes," he said. "Thank God I found you."

He almost didn't hear her next words, but on the edge of asking her to repeat, he understood. She had said, "You don't look like you."

He smiled and, remembering, touched his face. "My beard. I'd forgotten it. I'll shave it off."

"How did you get here?"

"It's a long story. I'll tell you later, after you're stronger."

He made her some food, such as it was, a thin gruel of flour and cornmeal to which he added some dried meat. But when he tried to raise her head to eat it, he saw her wince from a sharp pain. "Where do you hurt, Moira?"

"My ribs," she moaned. "He hit me."

She did not protest as he unfastened her torn and filthy shirt and skirt. How often he'd dreamed of seeing her naked, but now he gasped in dismay. She was little more than skin and bones and a mass of bruises and lacerations. "The beast," he said. "Thank God, he's dead and gone to hell."

He could see the ugly bruise on her left ribs where he'd hit her. Gently he touched the outline of the bones. "I don't think they're broken. Maybe just cracked." Using her skirt as a bandage, he quickly bound her ribs to give her some relief from the pain, then covered her with a blanket. "As soon as you've eaten, we've got to get you clean."

He built the fire as hot as he could, then brought in snow to melt for water. While it heated, he moved her to a chair, then carried her whole filthy bed outside and replaced it with clean pine boughs. Finally, he began to bathe her while she sat in the chair.

"Don't look at me, Ned."

"I have to, if I'm to wash you."

He saw a tear rising in her eye. "I'm so ugly."

"You'll always be lovely to me, Moira. And soon you'll be as good as new. I promise you that."

For nearly a week, he fussed over her, feeding and bathing her, cleaning out the cabin and even doing laundry. She watched him in wonder, never dreaming that an angel of mercy could be a man. She felt the swelling go down in her face and eye, though it remained grotesquely discolored.

She asked him how he'd found her and heard him say, honestly and without guile, "After you left Kingston, I first hated you. I was jealous of your choice of my brother." She tried to speak, but he raised his hand to silence her. "Let me finish. I also came to realize I loved you. I wanted you and I could not imagine life without you." He hesitated. "That left me no choice but to go and find you. I followed you everywhere you went, first to Independence, then along the California Trail. When I found the burned-out wagons, I thought I'd really lost you. Then at Fort Laramie I saw the note you left and knew there was hope. I wandered all over these mountains in the cold and snow. Luckily, I stumbled on your Clay Bancroft and he told me where you were. I found your friend's body, Toby Hamilton, and stayed in your lean-to nearly a month. My horses are still there. You know the rest."

Tears were in her eyes as she said, "I always had the feeling someone was following. I don't know how or why, but—"

"I just wish I'd been closer and could have spared you all this."

"You're here now." She knew she ought to say something more, but couldn't seem to find the right words. Finally, she said, "I'll always be grateful to you, Ned."

They were not at all the words he wanted to hear and inwardly he was stung. Smiling he said, "Oh, I'd have done it for anyone." That night he regretted saying that. He should be glad for gratitude. How could he hope for more from her?

On the sixth day he said he just had to be back to the horses. She'd be all right for a night and he'd be back the next day.

She looked at him in horror. "Don't leave me, Ned. I couldn't bear it. Let me go with you. I know I can make it."

He protested, but in the end gave in, bundling her up in furs for the trip back to the lean-to. He went slowly, helping her constantly, carrying her through the worst drifts. They left at the first graying of day and arrived just as dusk became night.

In ensuing days, he enlarged the lean-to to hold the horses, so they could have more room. He built a separate bed for himself, not failing to notice there had been only one bed when she shared this habitation with Toby Hamilton. He cared for her unceasingly, taking pleasure in seeing her bruises turn from black and blue to sickly yellow then gradually disappear. With her natural color came greater strength, as her weight began to return to normal.

They talked a great deal. She told him of her trip across the plains, of Quacker and his attack upon her, of surviving the Indian attack because she had run off to escape him. She told him of Toby, speaking of him with great fondness.

"Did you love him?"

"I don't know—no, I don't think so. Like you, he was fine, courageous, extraordinarily good to me." She saw the wound in his eyes. "Oh God, Ned, why do I always say the wrong thing to you? I don't want to hurt you."

"It is never the wrong thing, when you say what you feel."

Then she truly didn't know what to say. She could only shake her head and wish she could bite off her tongue.

In truth, she was again in a quandary. For the second time, a gentle, kindly man was caring for her, helping her. She was grateful. She was full of tender feelings, but was it love? She didn't know. And did it matter? She had given her body to Toby, willingly, an act of pleasure, of gratitude, of sharing, a gift of affection in a hostile wilderness. As her health returned more toward normal, she knew she would do the same with Ned, indeed even wanted to. But he remained physically aloof from her, sleeping on his bed of boughs across the lean-to. She felt she could not, should not invite him to hers, so the gulf between them physically at night stretched into a spiritual separation by day. None of this was translated into antipathy or even unfriendliness. Yet, there remained a formality between them which made her uncomfortable. She knew it made Ned far more than uncomfortable. He deserved far more from her. Smiles, thank yous, and tender words could not give him what he needed and surely deserved. Try as she would, she could do no more.

It was mid-April before the snows melted enough for them to recommence the journey to California.

Part III

50

The *Glenna Morgan* made the trip from New York to San Francisco in ninety-seven days, four hours. Ultimately, the *Flying Cloud* would set a record of eighty-nine days, eight hours on the run, but MacDoul was nonetheless delighted with the speed and handling of his much prized clipper.

The flesh-and-blood Glenna Morgan aboard the ship became a different person during the voyage. There was something about the ship, the wind and salt spray, the feeling of isolation on an endless expanse of sea and sky, plus good food and ample rest cleared the cobwebs from her brain and caused her to think sensibly about herself and her future.

Ian MacDoul, the jolly, considerate Cap'n Mac, had more than a little to do with it, she knew. Glenna had never willingly given herself to a man other than Daniel Morgan, nor even thought of wanting to. Her misadventures as a maiden, while remembered, had been dulled by time. Aided by Daniel's tolerant understanding, she had never felt a shred of guilt, except perhaps for her unbelievable depravity with the pasha in Fez while under the influence of drugs. It had always worried her a trifle that perhaps those aphrodisiacs had brought out some secret person in her that she didn't know or like.

She made love with Mac, not every night, but frequently during the voyage. The first time, she had approached it with desire, yet also with guilt. She was being unfaithful to Daniel; if not the man, his memory, and with his best friend. But under Mac's considerate and skillful hands, she had been led, a little to her surprise, to the blessed relief of consummation.

That night before she fell asleep and the next day with the tropical breeze playing with her hair, she had talked to Daniel, explaining her feelings and how it had happened. She was drenched in the most exquisite love for him. Never, she thought, had she loved her husband so much. No one could ever take his place. But with that feeling came the awareness that she was still a woman, still attractive, still with a body capable of all the sensations and pleasures a woman was born to feel. She was alive. The saltiness on her lips told her that. And as long as she was alive, she should be all the woman she could be until the time came for her to rejoin Daniel. She would never remarry. She was certain of that. But she would enjoy being a woman and feel no guilt about it. As she stood near the bow of the ship, just behind that outlandish figurehead of her, she made the decision effortlessly and decisively and thereby knew she had changed.

That night she gave herself to MacDoul with abandon. Almost clinically she thought of the differences between him and her late husband. Daniel Morgan was a more passionate man, more romantic by far, tenderer. When he made love to her, it had been almost as though he were making an offering to some diety of love. Nothing in her whole life would thrill her as much as Daniel Morgan's love making. Ian MacDoul was not so passionate, nor so serious about it. He was hearty and vigorous and very masculine, no doubt of that. He was a more muscular and a heavier man than Daniel, which brought a whole range of new sensations, making her feel smaller, more helpless with him. And his organ was larger, too, which created its own delights. But mostly the difference was in attitude. He was more lewd in his demands upon her. He approached the bed as rollicking good fun. He was far more boisterous and they laughed together far more than she had ever dreamed possible while making love. To all this she responded, and the differences between these two men in her life helped any lingering guilt disappear.

The style of Ian MacDoul changed her. She found herself laughing more boisterously during the day, indeed wanting to laugh more. Because he so enjoyed her body, she found herself dressing more provocatively. Indeed, she surprised herself by the lascivious suggestions and lewd remarks she uttered to him, not uncommonly at inopportune times. "I think you are making me into a wanton, Captain MacDoul," she said. "I used to be more of a lady."

"You're still a lady, lassie-the most desirable lady in the world."

Once he asked her if she was having fun. Parodying his Scots brogue, she replied, "Aye, that I am—more than I myself ever thought possible—thanks to you." After he had kissed her, she said, "Tell me again, Mr. MacDoul, exactly what it is the proper Scotsman wears under his kilt."

Nothing had prepared Glenna for San Francisco. When the *Glenna Morgan* sailed into the bay through the narrow inlet already becoming known as the "golden gate," she thought it the most beautiful sight she had ever seen. She had long considered the Chesapeake Bay, particularly at the mouth of the Severn River at Annapolis, the most beautiful place on earth. Now, as the clipper sailed majestically between the green hills and into the splendid bay, she was witnessing a rare sight of awesome beauty.

The harbor at San Francisco was also lovely with its hills and islands, or would have been except the huge, natural harbor was clogged with abandoned ships. Upon arrival at the gateway to the gold, whole crews, including captains and mates, jumped ships to run off in search of their fortunes. MacDoul tried to thwart this by being generous with the crew and offering a bonus for staying with the ship. He was aided in this effort by the fact that in December, 1850, common sense was beginning to cure gold fever. Tales of the hardships of the miners and their failure to find much in the way of riches were beginning to override the lust for wealth. MacDoul lost some of his crew, but managed to pick up enough others to have a full crew by the time he left.

If Glenna thought the California scenery thrilling, she had the opposite reaction to the city of San Francisco. In her ignorance, she had expected to find a metropolis, a thriving, established city like Baltimore. To her dismay, San Francisco was a shantytown clustered at the water's edge. There was no structure over two stories high and nearly every building was a slap-bang affair of roughcut lumber erected in a great hurry and liable to fall down or burn down just as quickly.

There was not a shred of sanitation, creating a hellish stench. Rats were everywhere, having left the abandoned ships for better pickings on shore. There were no sidewalks and the "streets" were mudholes, some so deep as to be impassable. Boxes, cases, trunks, logs, all kinds of debris were thrown into these holes in a usually fruitless effort to fill them. Signs were erected near the worst of them, reading "Through Passage to China," "Head of Navigation, No Bottom," "Horse and Dray Lost, Look out for the Soundings" and "Office to Let in the Basement." For Glenna, the only way to get across the street was to be carried by MacDoul.

The city was a mass of miners, some just arriving dazed and forlorn, others back from the fields, either disgruntled or joyfully squandering their swag of gold dust on women, incredibly bad whiskey or games of chance. The whole city seemed to have one purpose— to fleece the miners and would-be miners. In an inconceivable array of shops and outdoor stalls, mining supplies, foodstuffs and nearly everything else was huckstered at truly fantastic prices to miners who, if they were not unwitting, had no choice anyhow. Items that sold for a dollar in the east brought twenty-five and fifty dollars in San Francisco. It was a raw, untamed, raucous, not entirely safe city, a meeting place for the nationalities and races of the world. Glenna saw Indians, Chinese, Mexicans in great numbers, plus blacks, French, English, Canadians, Swedes, Germans, Italians, even Arabs. The lure of gold both baffled and astounded her.

Glenna had somehow expected Andrew and Moira to be standing on the dock to greet her. When they were not and she entered the city to search for them, she was disheartened by first the magnitude, then the impossibility of the task.

"Face it, lassie," MacDoul said after days of searching, "they are not here. They may be in California somewhere, but they are not in this city at this time."

Glenna would not give up. "They have to be here. Where else can they be?"

"Andrew came to find gold. I assume he is in the gold fields. Moira came to find Andrew. I assume she is with him."

"Then we'll go there."

"Think, lassie, think. Miners are looking for gold over thousands of square miles of land along scores of streams and rivers. They move around constantly. You could spend a lifetime searching for your youngin' and still miss 'em. It is better, Glenna, believe me, if you stay here in one spot. They'll have to come to San Francisco sooner or later. Let them find you. Tis better, really it is."

Glenna spent another discouraging week, finding neither her children nor a clue to their whereabouts. Besides, she was highly uncomfortable. It was now January and a cold rain fell almost constantly. The city was a quagmire and she was beginning to catch a cold. Reluctantly, she accepted the truth of MacDoul's advice and remained on the ship.

One reason she trusted his advice was because she knew it was hard for him to give it. MacDoul thirsted to quit San Francisco Bay and take his ship to Shanghai. There he could load a cargo of tea and sail it westward, around Africa to London, selling it for an immense profit. Another cargo could be sold in New York or Baltimore. He would have circumnavigated the earth. The clipper ships were designed expressly for such a voyage, carrying a light, profitable cargo faster than mankind had ever known. MacDoul itched to be part of it, she knew.

She also knew he wanted her to sail with him. Another time, she might have thrilled at the prospect of seeing the exotic lands of the Orient, but now her thoughts rested only with finding her children and uniting her family. With considerable honesty, she admitted to herself that she had failed her children. She wanted a new chance to be a better mother. More than occasionally, she prayed to the Virgin that she be given the opportunity.

She would remain in San Francisco to let her children find her. But doing what? She couldn't just live in one of those shacks waiting for them to knock on her door. How would either Andrew or Moira know she was there? They would not expect her and hardly be looking for her. Wandering the streets looking at faces hardly seemed sensible. No, she needed to be visible. She had to be the candle attracting the moth, the magnet who would draw her children back to her.

The decision of what to do came easily to her, and she discussed it immediately with MacDoul. "What would you say if I opened a saloon?"

"A saloon?"

"Yes, one of those taverns all the prospectors go to. I thought of calling it Morgan Manor or some such.

Andrew or Moira would see the name. They would at least drop in. I'd find them that way."

"But Glenna, you don't know anything about operating such a place. Besides, there are a million of them already."

"True, but they're such small, dirty, horrid places. Everyone spits on the floor and there are fist fights every five minutes. I had in mind a larger, more elegant establishment, fixed up really nice, with good drinks and good food, some gambling of course, but also some dancing and maybe some entertainment, singers, that sort of thing. There's nothing like it here now. Do you think it would work?"

MacDoul looked at her soberly for a minute, then broke into a smile. "I find it difficult somehow to think of Glenna Morgan, the elegant wife of a United States senator, running a dance hall and gambling den."

She laughed lightly. "It is even more difficult for me. But I've changed, Mac. I'm either the wife of a former senator or the former wife of a senator, I don't know which. My life has changed radically. Did I ever expect to be in this Godforsaken town? You've changed me, too, Mac. Somehow it seems right to me to try this new thing."

He took her in his arms and kissed her. "And here I thought I was the one who was different, done in by love for the most beautiful woman in the world. My lassie, I have an idea you'll be merely fantastic as proprietress of Morgan Manor."

Next she spoke to Joe and Jessie about it. "Do you think we can do it?" she asked.

"I don't know about *we*," Joe said, "but if you set your mind to it, I've no doubt you will."

"But I can't do it alone. There is so much to do. Joe, I want you to be my assistant, my general manager. I'll make the final decisions, of course, but I want you to be in charge of the whole public part of the operation, the bar, the dance hall, the gambling tables, everything.

And Jessie, you're in charge of all the housekeeping, the supplies, the kitchen, everything."

Joe looked baffled and Jessie spoke for them both. "What do we know about anything like this, Miss Glenna? We'll do all we can but—"

"I don't know anything either—less than you in fact. But we'll all learn together and hopefully not make too many mistakes.

Still they looked uncertain.

"Look. You two ran a great estate in Maryland. How much different can this be?"

It was a great deal different. Glenna had never in her life had any involvement in business affairs, nor even dreamed of it. She had always left these matters to Daniel and instinctively she sought to do it now with MacDoul. But in considerable wisdom, he refused to become involved. He knew that when he left for China, she would be on her own. She might as well learn to sink or swim at the outset. "I'm a ship captain, madam. I know nothing about taverns. I will happily taste the wares. Oh, and yes, I'll volunteer to personally select the dancing girls."

"Don't you dare."

So, Glenna was cast into a strange milieu of land speculators, real estate agents and lawyers; contractors, carpenters and suppliers of the bewildering variety of goods and equipment her place would need; painters, upholsterers and decorators; barmen, piano players, prostitutes masquerading as dancing girls, and professional gamblers. All were eager and adept at parting her from her money, and she was first awestruck, then bilked, and finally inundated with work and decisions. Her first reactions were fright, panic, an overwhelming desire to forget the whole thing, anger at MacDoul for not helping her more, and not a few tears.

But she came to grips with herself within a few days much to MacDoul's pride and relief. If she was going to find her children, this was the way it had to be done. She buttoned up her courage, began to say no, learned to apply her native tastes and standards in making decisions, and above all found the knack for bargaining down the charlatans and sharpies who swooped down on her like vultures. She developed a demeanor which was both natural to her and highly effective. She took great pains to be always splendidly coiffed and elegantly dressed, if somewhat provocatively, in dresses and gowns of no small amount of decolletage, accenting her figure and complexion.

Thus attired, she was always the lady, sweet, considerate and a wee bit frail. She had no head for business, she let it be known, but was merely a poor bereaved widow trying to make her way in a big, bad world of men. So many people took advantage of her, and she was sure whoever she was dealing with was not such a person. If the occasion demanded, which was several times a day, she was not above a sniffle or two, a few tears, a sudden attack of the vapors as a means to get her own way. And when the stunned merchant realized he had just made a very bad bargain, she made it up to him with smiles and mildly flirtatious glances which suggested his personal attractiveness to her and a coming of nirvana when her bereavement ended.

Once she got the knack of it, Glenna became a superb business woman. Merchants who ordinarily would have refused to deal with such a skinflint and Shylock came away dazzled. Later, they would be in admiration of her acumen. Seemingly overnight, she became the talk of San Francisco, a situation she did nothing to discourage.

As all other structures in the gold capital of the western world, Morgan Manor went up with amazing rapidity. San Franciscans were accustomed to seeing a whole house built in a single day. Morgan Manor, being so large, took a while longer, but amazingly, it was under roof in mid-February and ready for business two weeks later. It was far from finished. Glenna could add to it and redecorate incessantly, but the sign was nailed up on the first of March and the first customers served March 5, 1851. The following day MacDoul, feeling she was all right, indeed more than all right, eagerly set sail for Shanghai.

51

Morgan Manor was the first large, elegant dance hall built in San Francisco, the prototype for many to follow. It was a two-story frame building, painted white, with a porch overhanging a wooden sidewalk along Sutter Street. The second floor was given over to a suite on the left front corner for Glenna, and MacDoul when he returned, an apartment for Joe and Jessie, and rooms reserved for Moira and Andrew when they were found.

The downstairs was a huge, columned room measuring approximately one hundred feet by one hundred twenty five, with the kitchen, laundry and supply rooms to the rear. The customer entering the swinging doors could go to the bar on the extreme right. It was a hundred feet long and built of the finest walnut Glenna could find. Ten, or if they were busy, as many as fifteen bartenders and bar maids worked it. There were round tables to the front of the bar where drinks were served. Gambling tables were to the front and left as a person entered. Dining was in the left rear on tables covered with red linen cloths. The center of the room was a dance floor and behind it a piano, orchestra and a small

stage. A wide staircase swept to the upstairs from the
right of the dance floor.

While offering something for everyone, Glenna did
her best to apply her own standards of quality. She
insisted on good or at least tolerable whiskey, wine and
ale. More than a few kegs of vile, rotgut were thrown
out or returned. She didn't want her customers poisoned. They couldn't spend money if sick or dead. The
food was simple, mostly steak and eggs, but reasonably
good and fairly priced.

Glenna had always intended to offer female companionship to her clientele, but when it came down to it,
this part of her business offered a difficult problem. In
the end, she solved it by personally selecting every girl
on the basis of attractiveness and cleanliness. A good
many of them were Irish girls who seemed to flock to
San Francisco in large numbers. They were to serve
drinks, mix with customers and dance with them,
usually the lively hurdy-gurdy. For this they were paid
well and expected to dress well. There would be no
slovenliness in Morgan Manor. A few of the more
talented girls were. paid extra if they sang a few
numbers or joined the can-can line on the stage.

All this was reasonably easy. It was the solicitation
for prostitution that bothered Glenna. She solved it by
deciding what she didn't know didn't hurt her. What
the girls did on their own time was their affair. If they
went home with a "gentleman" or had "gentlemen
callers" after work that was their business. But such
activities were not to interfere with their work. Above
all there was to be no solicitation on the premises.
There were no assignation rooms in Morgan Manor.
There was a frequent turnover among the girls. Marriage, venereal disease, drunkenness, unlady-like conduct, and simple inability to abide by simple rules led to
a good bit of firing and hiring. It consumed a large
amount of Glenna's time. But in the main she kept a
core of girls who knew a good thing when they found it:
good money, relative safety, and a chance to make a

few dollars on the side without splitting with a pimp or madame. If anyone wanted to get Glenna's Irish up, it was to suggest that she ran a house of prostitution. Prostitution may have gone on, but she wasn't running it. She simply closed her eyes to it.

Glenna was there constantly, never missing an evening, even when she became royally sick of the whole atmosphere and longed desperately for a quiet evening alone. She was omnipresent in part because she was constantly watching for Andrew and Moira to walk through the door. She also knew her presence had a profound affect on how well the place ran and on the customers. For a dance hall proprietress, she was really rather prudish. She had made a major investment in seventy-five brass cuspidors, and she expected her customers to use them. Spitting on the floor led to a nod from Glenna. Joe immediately arrived with his duo of strapping bouncers and the offender was led out. If he resisted, he was thrown out into the mud amid roars from the spittoon-using customers.

Foul language, at least of the excessive kind, met the same fate, as did quarreling, cheating at cards, or too much familiarity with the female employees. If a miner, somewhat in his cups, risked a pinch of an attractive behind, he had better hope she didn't squeal too loud or protest to Glenna or Joe.

Thus, Morgan Manor became a place to have fun, eat, drink, dance and gamble, get quietly drunk and make a lot of appropriate noise. Indeed, the din from the place could be deafening, with several hundred patrons jammed inside. If the customer spent a lot of money and staggered out drunk and broke, he could always say he had a helluva good time doing it. He even got a smile and a kind word from Glenna Morgan, the most beautiful, elegant and sexiest looking woman in the whole damn territory of California. She quickly became well known, famous, then a legend.

The biggest and stubbornest problem for Glenna was the gambling operation. She disapproved of gambling. Hadn't it impoverished her and sent her children away from her? But she knew she had to have it if the business was to succeed. Indeed, gambling made the most revenue in Morgan Manor. But it was not going well, and she was powerless to do anything about it. She didn't gamble herself, so she didn't understand what was going on. She insisted on honest games with absolutely no cheating, but she had no ability to enforce the rule. Disputes over cards, faro, three card monte, roulette and dice, led to most of the fights in the place. And it wasn't just the players cheating each other. She knew her own dealers were cheating both the customers and her. She wasn't getting the revenue she should be, but even her most careful observation, as well as that of Joe, failed to detect the shenanigans. What she called the "gambling problem" consumed a great deal of her time and caused much worry.

A solution began to develop during the second week of April when a voice from behind her said as she talked to patrons at the bar, "Do you greet old neighbors, too?"

She turned and for a moment she was perplexed. She had been so busy for the last three months she had hardly given a thought to home. Besides, she hardly knew Bradford Kingston III, having met him only once or twice. Then she was able to smile. "Good heavens, if it isn't Bradford Kingston."

He smiled back at her. "That's my father's name and I never liked it. Call me King, please."

"What brings you to San Francisco?"

"I should imagine much the same things as brought you—the lure of all that gold in them thar hills."

She hesitated. "My situation was a bit more complicated."

His smiled faded. "I know. I deeply regret your loss of Aurial. And I mean that. It was a beautiful place."

"Yes, and thank you." She brightened. "I fear I'm not giving you a very warm greeting." She extended her hand and smiled in amusement as he bent to kiss it. "How long have you been in our fair city, as they say?"

"This is my third day. And it seems all I hear talked

about is the beautiful Glenna Morgan and the splendid emporium she runs. I told myself it couldn't be the same Glenna Morgan I knew back home, but I had to come and see for myself. It is indeed a splendid place you have, and you are, again indeed, a remarkably beautiful woman. The talk is inferior to the fact."

She smiled warmly and despite herself blushed a little. "Goodness, such gallantry will be wasted out here in the rough and ready west, but I thank you for it, nonetheless."

He hesitated. "And how is Moira?" Then as an afterthought, he added, "And Andrew, of course."

"I haven't found them. Neither is here and I'm beginning to be very worried. You see, all this—" she waved her hand in an encompassing motion. —"is just a device to make sure they find me. I can only hope it works, although I have people searching for them everywhere."

"You'll find them. I'm certain of that."

There was an awkward silence, finally broken by Glenna. "King, I have several things to attend to now, but I usually have a small supper in my rooms at eleven. I'd be honored if you'd join me. We have much to talk about."

King accepted with a bow and his usual impeccable manners.

The food was served by Jessie. She gave King a glare which would have withered a rock. He ignored it, assuming it was her normal behavior. Glenna was puzzled and later asked Jessie what that was all about. She sullenly replied, "Nothin'." It was not her place to tell Glenna about Moira, but as far as she was concerned Bradford Kingston III was nothing but bad news.

King had said he would be "charmed" to have supper with Glenna, and he was. He calculated she was seven or eight years older than he, but, Lord, she was a good looking woman. He remembered his long ago joke about marrying the widowed mother rather than the daughter. He hadn't realized how much sense that made, although the idea of marriage was absurd. But there was no doubt this creature across the table from him was one helluva woman. She wore a gown of startling green and blue, matched to perfection. As he stared into those sapphire eyes and witnessed her dewy lips and those thrusting mounds of snowy skin, he knew why all San Fráncisco was talking about the elegant and daring Mrs. Morgan. He also knew he had been on too long a sea voyage. Lord, did he need a woman, this woman.

As she sipped her aperitif, Glenna sensed all that and was not offended. Rather, it excited her to know she was having such an effect on such a handsome, younger man. Besides, it was useful to attract him. She knew of his reputation as a gambler. Perhaps he could be induced to solve her problem.

"My late husband always said how much your father wanted Aurial. It must be a disappointment to him to have it fall into other hands."

King laughed quite loudly. "If I know father, he's quite enraged by such a development."

"No more than I." There was a touch of bitterness in her voice. "How did you learn of my loss?"

"Oh, from general talk." Then he hesitated, looking into her eyes. "No, that's not quite true. I should be more honest. I learned from—can we just say a friend of mine——that your son was tricked into a game with a professional card cheat. I know him and he is a good one. Your son had no chance. In effect, your property was stolen from you."

Glenna did not react. "I knew, or at least suspected as much. And I know who did it. It is a very long story, but I have a bitter enemy, going back many years. He would do anything to destroy me. He has almost succeeded several times." She smiled. "But only almost."

He raised his glass. "May I toast the almosts that has left such a beautiful woman for me to supper with."

She accepted the toast, her eyes bright under the

compliment, then said, "But I do want to thank you for your honesty in telling me. My only wish is to find Andrew and tell him. His guilt at losing Aurial must be more than he can bear." She set down her glass. "But enough of such sadness. May I serve you? I believe this is stroganoff. I've been fortunate to find a French chef who was unsuccessful as a prospector and needs to earn his passage home."

As they were eating, he said, "I am devastated."

"You don't like the stroganoff?"

"No, no," he laughed. "It is fabulous. And it's all part of what I mean. Here I am, dining alone on this superb meal with the most beautiful and elegantly gowned woman I've ever seen—"

She laughed. "Really, King, this is too much."

"No, let me finish. A stunning woman who travels to the western extremity of the civilized world, then opens and operates a dance hall and emporium that is the talk of the whole territory. Is there no end to your talents?"

Again she laughed. "And is there no end to your compliments?"

"As far as you're concerned, there is not."

She laughed a moment longer. "May I test you? I have a serious problem which I cannot resolve. I abhor gambling, for reasons you must surely understand."

"Yes."

"But I must have it here. I will do so only if the games are honest. I will not have cheating. Yet, I know it is going on. Players are cheating each other and fights resulting. Dealers are cheating both the patrons and me. I know it, but I am powerless to catch them at it." She smiled. "I was hoping I might induce you to supervise these gambling operations for me. Could I?"

"Perhaps, possibly. It would depend upon the arrangements."

"Of course. I had thought perhaps of a quarter of the gambling profits."

"It occurs to me that a third might be a better thought."

Her eyes softened and she looked down at her plate. "Mr. King, I am but a poor widow alone." She looked up, saw the amusement in his eyes, then burst out laughing herself. "I think I should agree to a third before I give away all my secrets."

And together they laughed.

"When would you be able to start?"

"I could have a look tonight. Perhaps I might spot one or two little irregularities."

"Indeed you might."

She saw him hesitate, then with a deadpan face say, "Perhaps I could return here after closing to give you a confidential report."

She met his gaze, smiling mostly with her eyes. "That is a suggestion with a certain appeal."

Later, she spoke to him several times, standing beside him for a time as he observed the games. "What do you think?"

She saw the tinge of wickedness in his smile. "I think I'll have quite a report to make to you later."

She already regretted her coquettish remark made earlier. She knew what he had in mind, and she was not about to indulge it. Her relationship with Mac might be a little confused, but she was quite determined to be faithful to him. "I think you misunderstood," she said, smiling, trying to be as gentle as possible to her new business partner. "I imagine one of the younger ladies will be much the better for your needs."

He smiled. "I fancy myself a connoisseur, Glenna, of find wines and superior women. Both require a little aging for the proper flavor."

"I fear I can offer only wine."

He laughed. "And I can offer only my report."

He came a little before three. She dallied in her room, not wanting to change her dress or offer any encouragement to seduction. He was an attractive man, no question of that, but she had quite made up her mind. But damn him. Why was he not coming up? She should never have suggested he could.

He came, bearing chilled champagne and two glasses.

"I did promise you wine," she said. "I quite forgot."

"As you see, I did not." He deftly opened the bottle and poured two glasses. Giving her one, he toasted her. "To the most beautiful and desirable woman in San Francisco."

"Heavens!"

He laughed. "Forgive me, I should not have placed such a limit on you. Drink up."

She merely sipped, avoiding his eyes.

"You know my desires, Glenna. Are they so awful? Need I ask your forgiveness?"

His boldness flustered her, and she stammered. "Of—of course not. A-a woman always enjoys the—the attentions of a—a younger man. It is most flattering."

"It is not flattery and you are hardly Methuselah."

She smiled. "I hardly thought I was. Besides, he was a man, I believe."

He laughed and looked boldly at her decolletage. "And you most definitely are a woman."

She met his gaze when it returned to her eyes. She recognized her own excitement. He was a most magnetic man. She felt his powerful presence, so much so she was unable to move as, still holding his champagne, he touched her waist with his left hand and kissed her. It was soft, gentle, but she felt a surge of sensation.

"Please," she said. "I can't."

"But you are a widow, as you say, a poor widow alone in the world."

Again he kissed her, longer, more insistently, his arm further around her, pulling her hard against him. Desire raced through her and out her lips.

In a moment he stood away from her and took the wine glass from her hand, setting hers beside his on a table.

"No, please, I—"

She felt his lips, scalding, demanding. She tried to resist, even pushing at his shoulders, but it was a weak and futile effort, and her arms went around his neck and she surrendered to the impassioned demands of his kisses, even as she felt his fingers at the buttons at the back of her dress. She heard him speak. "Lord, but you're lovely." She felt his hands, talented, commanding. Her resistence remained for a time, but it was a feeble thing, quite inadequate to the demands of her own flesh. Finally, she surrendered, wholly, hungrily to his polished, adept, highly demanding and in the end exhausting lovemaking. Repeatedly she tried to rise from the bed, catch her breath, stop his lewd and lascivious actions, nurture her sense of offense and revulsion at her ravishment, but her efforts failed until he was at last finished and lay spent beside her. "I fear," she was able to say, "I am not going to be up to this on any sort of regular basis."

He laughed. "Nor I. I'm afraid you were a victim of a long sea voyage."

The next morning, having awakened strangely early, she remembered her reply, "I'm not sure victim is the correct word." How could she have said that? What was happening to her? She had done acts to and with him that she would have sworn she could have performed only with Daniel. Not even Mac at his lustiest had so bent and used her body. A wave of shame and revulsion came over her as she remembered. How could she have. And with a man she hardly knew? She couldn't have wanted it. She couldn't have enjoyed it. God, those things he did. But, looking down at his naked body in bed beside her, she knew she may have not wanted or intended it, but she had enjoyed it. Yes, damn it, she had. She was forty years old. To have a younger, virile, attractive man find her still so desirable and command such responses out of her body. . . . A statue could not have resisted him. Memories of the young pasha in the sultan's harem flecked through her mind. Was there some streak of wantonness in her? With Daniel gone, was she destined to pass from man to man, unable to resist a succession of hands and mouths and bodies? She shuddered at the thought.

Again she looked down at him. He was sleeping soundly, flat on his back, his organ, so powerful only hours ago, drooped sadly between his legs. He had liked her. And he had wanted her, so urgently, demanding more and more, insatiably, in strange, obscene ways. What would life be like with a man like him? Should she awaken him, tease him awake so he could ravish her again? That's what it had been: ravishment. And it was that she had enjoyed, being so used up and filled to overflowing, constantly spent and then aroused when she thought no arousal was possible. Yes, that was the appeal of it. She had been ravished. But, as that thought came to her, she knew she had not been loved. She had made love like that with Daniel, many times. But Daniel had loved her, oh how he had loved her. This man, this King, hardly knew her and certainly did not love her. All that had transpired between them was only of the flesh. Like the pasha, it was a night of passion. As in the harem, she had been used for pleasure. Her receiving pleasure from it was only a device to increase his pleasure.

Abruptly, she arose from bed, washed and dressed hurriedly, and left the room. At the doorway, she looked down on the sleeping figure. She knew she was not angry with him. She had indeed been pleasured. If there was something of the harem girl in her, it might happen again. She would not attempt to swear it would not. But she would not become romantically involved with King. She was not a fool.

Another who slept very little that night was Jessie. She lay awake beside a snoring Joe much of the night. That man was in there making love to Glenna, having previously made love to her daughter. The possibilities of the situation filled her with horror. Should she tell Miss Glenna? She couldn't. She just couldn't. All she was capable of was lying awake consumed with fear and worry.

Lord James Charles Winslow had no difficulty finding Glenna. When he heard the talk about her and walked down the street at night to stare at her establishment, he reacted with rage. The bloody woman had more lives than a cat. He destroyed her on one coast and here she was three thousand miles away, rich, successful, on top of the world. It was more than he could bear. With advancing years, he had become more physical in his anger, as the restraints of his noble upbringing gave way. Lacking any other outlet for his rage, he stood in his hotel room and tore his suit jacket to pieces.

But, with the dissipation of his frustration came a quiet determination to get her once and for all. Again he would bide his time. He would have to remain carefully hidden. But his chance would come. He would make it happen.

To support himself, he financed a sort of Lila's Place West. It was not as elegant and genteel as in Washington. No little gold keys were passed around. Nonetheless, under Lila's sensitive administration, the new place became the finest bordello in San Francisco. A man could get a good drink, play for high stakes, and enjoy the company of some of the finer prostitutes in the West. As before, Winslow lived secretly in an upstairs apartment, out of sight, all but unknown. He took the name of James Hackett.

For Lila, the new place was a come-down, poorer, seedier, less respectable. She was perfectly willing to be a whore and run a brothel, but she preferred that it look like something else. This new place—despite her attempts at a name, quickly became known as Lila's Place again—was an out-and-out bordello with little pretense at being anything else. She envied Glenna her dance hall. It was more open, respectable and fun. Why if she had that place, she'd make a fortune.

Lila was also bothered by the clientele. She was not about to do tricks with dirty, filthy miners. There would be no muddy boots under her bed. She reserved herself for the better citizens of San Francisco, merchants, bankers, professional men. But even these seemed to lack the class of Washington. More and more she wished she had not agreed to come out here to the end of the earth.

Such unhappiness took a turn for the better, however, when Bradford Kingston showed up at her door. Perhaps there was some future out here after all.

52

Moira and Ned traveled slowly through some of the most majestic country in the world, mountains reaching to the sky, virgin forests, lakes of the purest water. They were not unappreciative, but the hardship of their journey understandably dampened their enthusiasm for scenery.

Many times Ned thought and occasionally said, "If only we had a guide." Being perpetually lost was the greatest hardship for him. He never knew which stream to follow, which valley actually led somewhere, when the long way around a lake was really the quickest route, when a short climb now would save a harder climb later. His only guide was the direction west. But it was a torturous, meandering course they followed.

He helped her constantly, taking her hand to pull her

up a slope, pushing her uphill when she faltered, making her rest frequently. "There's no hurry, Moira. We don't have to push. The weather will only get better now." Some days they made only a few miles and others none at all as he insisted on sitting out bad storms. "We've got to save the horses," he told her, "and we've got to preserve ourselves. We've a long way to go."

"Will we ever get out of these mountains? Do they go all the way to the coast?"

He laughed. "I understand there is a desert beyond the mountains. I've an idea we may be wishing for this shade and fresh water before we're through."

Moira felt security with Ned she had not with Toby. She had a near absence of fear and a certainty that Ned would keep any real harm from her. She rode or climbed beside him. She did everything he did. She helped with the camping and cooking. They were companions in this sense. Yet, she knew he was the leader. He selected the route ahead, sometimes not even consulting her. Ned Kingston was simply a more mature and assured person than Toby Hamilton.

The days were pleasant. If they had the breath and something to say, they talked, particularly around the fire at night. Frequently they spoke of home.

"Do you miss Maryland, Moira?"

"Uh-uh. Sometimes a great deal."

"What do you think about?"

She laughed. "A roof over my head, a great warm soft bed to sleep in, crabcakes, fried chicken and biscuits, a warm bath and a pretty dress to put on. I guess I'm a frivolous person."

"Hardly. I miss those things, too—but not the dress."

"No, I really think I was frivolous—quite silly really. All this has taught me that. I've changed. I like to think I've grown up, but who knows? What do you think about?"

He paused, poking at the burning fire as he thought.

"The land mostly. I love the feel of the warm earth crumbling in my fingers. I miss the tobacco, I really do, planting, watching it grow, the silky softness of the leaves in my fingers, the delicious odors from the drying sheds. I'm just a farmer at heart, I guess. I worry about Kingston, and I guess I feel a little guilty for leaving it. Father'll never run it right. He insists on slaves. No man can work well if he has to be driven, whipped. Your father was right to hire free labor. That's why Aurial is so much better than Kingston." He looked at her, saw her smiling, encouraging him to go on, but he felt he'd said enough about home. "All this out here is grand. Lord, it is so beautiful sometimes I get all choked up looking at it. You ever feel that?"

"Yes. Today when we looked down at this lake."

"It is so raw and unspoiled. It's like it's original, just as God created it. I enjoy seeing it. I like the feeling of being the first person ever to see it, though I don't suppose we are."

"I doubt if many have. Indians, mostly."

"I imagine I'll brag about this the rest of my life, but I'll be back in settled Maryland when I do it, up to my waist in tobacco plants. This is all the adventure I'll ever want." He laughed, suddenly embarrassed. "See what a dull clod I am."

He amazed her in a way. He could be confident, even commanding during the day as they inched their way forward. But in moments like this he reverted to—what? Shyness? No, not exactly shyness, but a certain social dis-ease, an inherent lack of confidence in himself and his acceptance by others. Somewhere he had missed out on his self-esteem. Unsmiling she said, "No, I don't see that at all."

They were silent for a time, each with their own thoughts, then Ned spoke. "What do you want out of life, Moira?"

Her silence continued a bit longer, then she said with a sigh, "I don't know. Wish I did."

"What sort of person do you see yourself as becoming?"

"I can't answer that either. I just don't know. I could say I'll be a wife and mother, but the truth is I can't visualize that. I can't imagine settling down. When I said I was frivolous, maybe that was the truth. I know I'm too young, too impulsive to make any real decision beyond today, this minute. All I really know is that I want to find Andrew. What'll happen after that is—a mystery."

For all their togetherness, shared hardship and occasional honest soul searching, there was a reserve between them. He took her hand to help her, put his arm around her to bolster her when she was tired, but there was a total absence of physical intimacy between them. It was as if there was a wall between them. They slept in separate tents, and when they went to bed there was an unavoidable formality to the "good nights" each said.

This side of their relationship bothered Moira. And it bothered her that it *did* bother her. Why did she think about the physical separation between them? Why was she somehow hurt because he did not come to her? Why did she feel less a woman because he left her alone? What was wrong with her that she expected to have physical intimacy with a man she was alone with? What kind of a girl was she? She should be grateful to be left alone. Why wasn't she? Worse was her puzzlement. He loved her. He had said so and in myriad ways she knew it was true. Then why in God's name didn't he do something about it? Perhaps if he kissed her, held her, caressed her . . . Perhaps a feeling for him would grow. It had happened with Toby and they had started with less. Oh Lord, was she a tramp? What kind of a girl was she? Then she remembered Jack Knight. Perhaps that was it. Ned wouldn't want her after him. But why did he love her?

This conflict of feelings was an almost nightly occurrence for Moira, expectations and desires mixed with self-castigation for having them. Then came the night she heard him outside her tent, his tread on the ground, pacing back and forth slowly. He was trying to make up his mind. She nearly held her breath in anticipation. She heard the crackle of pine needles near her tent, silence, then the rustle of the tent flap. A sliver of the waning moonlight flashed across her blanket.

Then she screamed. It was a bear. God, it was a bear. The animal seemed surprised, then confused by her screams. It stood upright, pulling the tent out of the ground. She lay there rigid with fear a moment, looking up at the animal towering over her, flailing its paws to free itself from the tent. Then she rolled away. As she got to her feet, she saw Ned emerging from his tent, rifle in his hand. He fired into the air, then picked up a flaming stick from the fire and ran toward the bear, brandishing it. The animal grunted, then slowly turned and padded back into the woods.

"You all right, Moira?"

She ran to him and he took her in his arms. "God, I was so scared."

He patted her back. "It's all right, everything is all right. He'll not come back. He was just hungry. I was afraid to fire at him for fear of hitting you."

She scarcely heard what he said for she was sobbing, her head against his chest, as he patted her and uttered soothing words.

In a few moments, her sobs passed, and she raised her head to look at him, her eyes wet and wide. Then a new sensation tore at her as they suddenly embraced, his mouth on hers, soft, moist and salty from her tears, devouring, compelling in its urgency. She felt herself go weak and she sagged against him in surrender.

"No." He tore his lips away from her and held her at arm's length. "I can't."

He left her and went to repair her tent.

"Why, Ned? You have to tell me that."

He said nothing, but worked savagely at erecting the tent.

"Is it because of King . . . and Toby . . . and that beast Jack Knight?"

He had straightened out the tent and raised the ridge pole.

"Is that it? Am I not good enough for you anymore?"

He had started pushing the stakes back into the ground, but with those words he stopped, arose and came to her. She saw him shudder as he looked at her.

He did not understand his own actions. These weeks of cohabitation, being near her, yet so faraway were agony for him. He wanted her so badly he could hardly bear to look at her. Yet he did not touch her and that he did not understand, except that deep beneath his longing, he knew that he would never win Moira if he competed with King. However difficult, he must fight on his own terms, not his brother's. That is not what he said, however.

"Oh, you're good enough all right. Don't ever think that. It's just that I love you. I've always loved you, always wanted you. I can hardly bear being close to you and not touch you. But I must. You see, I know I'm not going to have you. You'll never come to love me. These days in the wilderness are the only real time I'll ever have with you. That's all there'll ever be for me in my whole life. I know that. I know I'll be forced to get over loving you. But I'll never be able to if I kiss you anymore or make love to you. Good night, Moira."

She stood there, her hand at her mouth staring at his back as he left her. Then she slowly turned and went to her own tent.

The next morning was crisp and frosty, but blue skies and bright sun promised a warmer day. They had been silent, except for the usual "good mornings," until camp was broken.

"I thank you for last night."

"Oh, I think the poor bear was more scared than you were."

"I'm talking about what you said. It does make a girl feel good to know someone feels that way about her."

Unsmiling, he squinted down at her against the glare of the sun in his face. "I wouldn't call it a good feeling."

"How do you know I'll never love you? I just might, you know."

He turned, picked up the reins and prepared to mount. "We'll see." He swung into the saddle. "Let's go."

When she was in the saddle, she turned to him and smiled. "Anyway, that was some kiss."

Two evenings later by the fire, they again spoke of the subject. It began with his asking her what she was thinking.

"Of you, me, my mother."

"Your mother?"

"Yes. I find myself thinking of her a lot lately. I wonder where she is and how she is. I know Jessie was very worried about her. I doubt if mother will ever get over the loss of my father. She'll just sit there in that rocker and grieve, grow old quickly and die. I think she wants to die to be with father. And it will be such a shame. She was beautiful, you know, really special. I've always envied her, her beauty, her poise, that special magnetic quality she had. And I sure envied her that skin. Like fine, silky powder it was, and so white."

"You're more beautiful."

She laughed. "Thanks, but I already know your judgment is not to be trusted. Anyway, that's not what I was thinking. When mother was young, she had these incredible adventures, pirates, Arab pashas, jungle natives. Went across deserts, mountains, God knows what. I used to hear these stories. Over and over I'd hear about what a wonderful, courageous woman she was. And I grew to hate them—and I guess her for being the way she was."

She grew silent a moment. "What I'm trying to say, I

guess, is that history has repeated itself, sort of. Oh, I haven't met any pirates or romantic Arabs, but I've done pretty well—or bad, depending on the point of view. That beast in that cabin was no—"

"There's no point in remembering that."

She sighed. "You're right. When mother had all her adventures, she'd already met father. They weren't married, but they were terribly in love and separated. Mother said that love for father was the only thing that kept her going." She paused. "I haven't had that kind of love to keep me going. Being jilted by your brother hardly qualifies as undying affection."

He said nothing.

"Does that hurt for me to speak of him? You already know the truth."

"It's okay, Moira. I understand, I really do."

Strangely she felt annoyed at him. "What on earth do you think you understand?"

"I understand how it happened. You say you envied your mother. Well, I can understand that, too. I'm the same way about King. Damn it, I hate his use of that name. The king, emperor of the boudoir, first in the hearts of his countrymen—especially my father." His voice was rising. "Yes, I'm jealous all right. I'm jealous of that cleft in his chin, of his damnable handsomeness, of his all conquering attitude, of his always winning, of his having you when I wanted you. You didn't stand a chance with him—not when you showed up in that dress. You were a babe in the woods with him." Then he stopped and took a deep breath, trying to cool off. "Face it, I am jealous of him. If he were here right now instead of me, I can assure you we wouldn't be talking. He wouldn't be lying alone in his tent—oh, what the hell, Moira."

She knew there was something she ought to say, something she should want to say, but no words would come out. They sat that way a long time.

"I guess we should get some sleep," he said and stood up.

"There's another part of my mother's story I didn't tell you." She looked up at him. "My father loved her and wouldn't give up. He looked a long time and finally found her in Africa."

"So?"

"They lived happily ever after." She stood up beside him. "I just thought that ending might encourage you. Maybe mother and daughter aren't so different after all."

"Don't Moira. The mere fact you felt the need to say that proves you don't love me and never will."

It was the second week of May when the mountains seemed to end abruptly, and there below stretched a great, sandy plain. In the distance they could see the Great Salt Lake and the thriving Mormon town beside it. "No wonder Brigham Young called it the Promised Land," Ned said.

They spent three days in the town, resting, buying supplies for the rest of the trip. Moira had a warm bath and both enjoyed a good home cooked meal in a restaurant. Because of the skyhigh prices charged to wayfarers, Ned did not have enough money to splurge on a hotel room. Instead, he bought her a present.

"Go on, open it."

Her fingers trembling with excitement, she tore open the box, then stared, gasped her astonishment and burst into tears.

"Don't you like it?"

"Of course, I like it, silly," she said, wiping her eyes. "It's the most beautiful dress I've ever seen." It was hardly that, just a plain blue calico with a line of pink ribbon at the throat. But not having any dress for a long time, Moira indeed did think it the loveliest she had ever owned. "You shouldn't have, Ned."

"Yes, I should have. You don't know how tired I am of seeing you look like you just shot a grizzly. Go on. See if it fits."

She went into her tent and quickly slipped into it. If anything it was a shade too small, especially in the bodice, but there was no thought of her even wanting to try to exchange it. She emerged to stand before him. She saw the expression in his eyes, but asked anyway, "How do I look?"

He was almost sorry he bought it, for he knew the sight of her womanly shape would only increase his torment. "Like a girl," he said.

The Great Basin which separates the high Rockies from the Sierra Nevadas of California was usually a horror for pioneers. After crossing the plains and struggling through the mountains at South Pass, they somehow figured the worst was over. It was only beginning. Ahead lay hundreds of miles of sand, salt and alkaline wastes under blistering heat. It was in the passage along the Humboldt River and the great Humboldt Sink in Nevada that the spirit of the pioneers was broken. Of those who did not die of heat and thirst and kept their animals from certain death by plunging in to drink the alkaline waters, many went mad from the loneliness, the vista of graves and rotting carcasses and the sheer magnitude of the Nevada desert.

Replenished at Salt Lake City, Moira and Ned made the trip with relative ease on horseback, mostly by traveling at night and resting in the heat of the day. They came out of the desert at the town of Reno and soon entered the Sierra Nevadas. After the peaks they had passed through, these were positively diminutive and the California Trail which they were again following afforded easy passage. Their descent through Truckee Pass was hardly more than started when they entered the sprawling gold fields. Moira was instantly excited at the prospect of finding Andrew.

Moira had an image of the California gold being lodged in a mine or mines, rather central in location. She had envisioned her brother, grimy perhaps, working with a pick to knock golden nuggets out of a wall of stone in a shaft. The reality stunned her, mountain sides and valleys sprawling with shanties and wooden sluices, piles of dirt and mud, mud, mud everywhere. The living conditions were pure squalor and the miners to a man dirty, stinking and scraggly, grubbing away in the mud and water for a few specks of gold. The thought of her brother living like this appalled her. These were the most pathetic creatures she had ever seen.

Everywhere she went, men stopped working and ran long distances just to gather around her. At first she was alarmed.

"We won't hurt you, little lady. It's just been so long since we see a purty girl—We just gotta look at ya."

Another raggedy man held up a leather pouch. "I'll give ya this here gold dust, mam, if ya jus' lemme touch yer hair. I never see red hair like that."

Her eyes misting over, Moira said, "No, please, I can't."

Andrew was at that moment well to the north of her, working his claim beside a small, nameless stream leading into the Butte River. Had she seen him, the compassion she had already felt would have been greatly magnified, for he was skinny, filthy dirty and far from well.

The winter and spring of 1850–51 were an unspeakable hardship for him. To say he suffered is not an exaggeration. He suffered from the cold, the nearly incessant rains which turned the earth into a quagmire, the dampness, sores, illness, hunger, bone weariness, boredom and excruciating loneliness. He worried a great deal about his sanity and took pains to maintain it. He developed games designed to provide some touch with reality which so frequently seemed to slip away from him. One game was to decide which of his discomforts was the worst. One day he would decide it was the sores on his feet from standing in water and mud. Another day he was sure it was hunger or his lightheadedness. On days when his scurvy sores broke out or his fever scorched him, his decision was easy.

Another game was to remember some facet of home which he had not thought of previously, some nook in the house, a board in the stable, a snatch of words spoken by his mother or Moira. He carried his remembrances back so far he believed he could remember being in the cradle. Still another game was to think of all the reasons he could for quitting this immeasurable folly of mining for gold. He developed quite a long list, headed by the fact he could make more money doing almost anything else. Having come to the rational conclusion that he was a fool, he then shoveled more dirt into his pan and went on.

All these devices were necessary to combat his loneliness. In nearly a year Andrew never once left his claim. There was nowhere he wanted to go, except home. He was not about to spend a single grain of gold dust he didn't have to to keep himself alive. And he was terrified of claim jumpers. He kept himself armed constantly with his father's revolver, even sleeping with it beside him. In his fear of being robbed or run off his claim, he spurned all overtures of friendship with other miners. The four men who worked a claim on the hillside across the stream from him had tried to be friendly. One named Duckworth had even brought whiskey and tried to talk to him. But Andrew offered only monosyllabic grunts. Most of the time he was desperate for companionship, but this need never once overcame his fear of being robbed, driven off his claim, or killed. Andrew developed a reputation among the other miners as a loner, a hermit and misanthrope. Because he lived so frugally, it was assumed he was doing poorly in his search for gold and was exceedingly dumb to continue on the site.

This was not the case. Andrew never produced any significant amount of gold at one time, but he was consistent. A high percentage of his pans rendered at least a few flecks of the heavy yellow metal. It was this consistency, this knowledge he was finding something, however little, that kept him grubbing away day after endless day. He stored the gold away in pouches at the end of the day. He never looked at it or attempted to weigh or measure it. He knew he would go raving mad if he did. The idea of being a miser, of carrying about gold itself, revolted him. The yellow dust was simply money, he insisted, the means to buy back Aurial and his honor.

The winter snows gave way to bitter cold rains which went on as if the heavens were inexhaustible. He had panned the whole river front of his hundred foot claim, sifting the bottom and the shores. As he moved further from the water, the work became harder, for he had to both dig the earth and carry it to the water to be panned. He toiled on in a state of physical numbness, only his games maintaining what little sanity he possessed.

Almost without realizing it, he learned a lot about finding gold. The heaviness of the metal amazed him. It seemed to sink to a degree he wouldn't have thought possible. It seemed to sink through mud, sand and clay till it reached bedrock. Thus, he discovered that by digging down he could occasionally find greater quantities of gold resting in the crevices of rocks well below the surface.

More and more, he came to associate gold with rock as well as water. There came to be some sense to the search. His claim was consistent in yielding gold, suggesting to him that at some time in the past there must have been a vein of gold somewhere above him in the mountains. It had washed down to where he was working. Frequently, he would stand at the stream bank and look upward, but there was no crevice or gulley which carried water down from the mountains. How had his gold gotten to where he found it?

Every miner, including Andrew, hoped for luck, some incredibly fortunate occurrence, a shining nugget in a shovelful of earth, the overturned rock revealing a motherlode. Andrew had long since had such hopes ground out of him. His luck did come, but in such a form it took him a long time to recognize it. The heavy rains of winter and early spring gave way to an unusual dry spell in May and June. Andrew considered himself fortunate to have the warm sun and chance to dry his clothes. But he thought little of it in terms of finding gold until perhaps two weeks had passed and he noticed he was still working in mud. On part of his claim, the earth had dried and become firm underfoot. But in the more westerly area, the ground remained soft, mushy and muddy.

He thought nothing of it for a time, attributing the mud to shade from nearby trees. But as the lucky dry spell continued, he began to consider the mud more seriously. There had to be an underground source of water, a spring perhaps which created the mud. Looking aloft, he saw that the trees beside the mud had greater size. He decided to dig into the mud in hopes of finding a spring. His one acknowledgement of hope was to reduce the amount of panning he did in favor of digging. He began to throw the dirt into piles rising above him. They could be panned at a later time.

Moira remained in the gold fields for a futile week of searching, then listened to Ned. "We don't know if he's here at all. It's been almost a year since you've seen him. Chances are he isn't here at all. He's probably made his swag and gone on to San Francisco. He might even be back home by now. We'll have to go there to find out."

So they pushed on, through chaotic Hangtown, the informal capital of the goldfields, the San Joaquin Valley, Stockton, finally reaching the city by the bay. Nothing ever surprised Moira so much as when she and Ned rode down a muddy street in a mid-afternoon in June and saw a sign reading MORGAN MANOR. "It can't be," she said. "It just can't be." Then she saw a figure standing in the doorway. Her mouth came open and her hand instinctively covered it, "My God, my God, that's Joe."

53

It was a reunion to remember, with Joe gaping in stupefaction, then shouting for Jessie who squealed with joy and shrieked for Glenna to come downstairs. There were running footsteps and cries of dismay, delight and disbelief and hugs and kisses, and looking and fondling, followed by more hugs and kisses, and tears of joy and damp hankies, and an immense outpouring of words, mostly incoherent and unintelligible with dozens of questions asked and none answered. And yet the most important answers of all were given through embraces and tears and a great outpouring of love.

The reunion went on all that afternoon and evening in a torrent of telling and retelling, then continued for days more. Actually, it never did stop, for it was not so much a rejoining of those who had been separated and in danger, as it was a discovery of a whole new quite wonderful relationship between mother and daughter. The old tensions, Glenna's smothering mother love, which was really neglect, and Moira's envy and competitiveness, surfaced briefly, almost unrecognized, within both of them, then quickly wilted and died in the brightness of their affection and their newfound candor.

It was Jessie who got mother and daughter to stop

talking at once. "You'll never find out nothing if one of you isn't quiet."

Both laughed, said "of course," and stopped talking, then giggled, their arms entwined, at the silence.

Jessie laughed, too. "Miss Moira, we all know what happened to us. What we want to know is what happened to you."

Standing downstairs in the middle of the dance floor, Moira told them briefly of going to Independence, the wagon train, the Indians, running away into the mountains, Toby, her capture by Knight, her rescue by— She had forgotten Ned. "Oh, Ned," she said, going to him. "Forgive me. How could I be so thoughtless?"

He had been standing back a few steps from the happy foursome, smiling from his own happiness at Moira's happiness. But he became embarrassed as Moira took his arm and pulled him forward.

"He saved my life, mother. He followed me all the way from Maryland. He found me when I had nothing left. I wouldn't be here except for him."

Glenna looked at them both, trying to guess at their relationship, then went to Ned and kissed him warmly. "I'll never be able to thank you enough."

His embarrassment was acute, but he managed to say, "Moira's happiness and yours is all the thanks I need."

Glenna looked at him in amazement, then tears began to fill her eyes. "How remarkable you are," she said. "How like her father." Then she smiled and took his arm. "Come, both of you, tell us all about everything."

Moira and Ned, Glenna, Jessie and Joe spent that afternoon around a table downstairs telling and listening. Perhaps more than other mothers, Glenna heard with a particular ear and reacted with greater feelings because of her own youthful experiences. She could almost visualize Quacker and she sensed the real relationship between her daughter and Toby Hamilton. Moira spoke only of Jack Knight holding her prisoner, but Ned added to it an entirely too vivid description of the condition he found her in. Hearing, Glenna wept, for she could actually feel, not just imagine, the pain her daughter had known. She wept, too, because she knew what had happened to Moira sexually, visions of the herdsman outside Marrakesh sparking from her memory. Moira was about the same age she had been. She knew how she had felt and the effects of the rape upon her. Moira had grown up, but why did it have to be that way?

Her weeping almost got away from her, but she fought for and won control of herself. Drying her eyes, she said, "I do so hate weepy women." Then a moment later she asked, "What made you follow her, Ned?"

Instantly she saw him flush, but again his words belied it. "I guess I was just the neighbor kid to you, Mrs. Morgan, but Moira was not just a neighbor to me. I had to try to find her."

As he spoke, Glenna looked at her daughter, trying to figure her reaction, but she was unsure. "Thank God you did, Ned."

"He reminds you of someone else, doesn't he, mother?"

"Yes, very much so."

"Oh, God, how could I forget. Is Andrew here?"

"No. We haven't seen him."

"No! I was so sure he'd be in San Francisco. We looked everywhere for him in the gold fields. We decided he just had to be here."

Glenna shook her head sadly. "I'm sorry. He hasn't come yet."

"Could you have missed him? Could he have gone home already?"

"No. I've checked all the shipping companies, the post offices and banks. He came through San Francisco, but he has not returned."

"Oh, mother . . ."

"I know, darling, I'm as worried as you are. All we

can do is be patient—'' She smiled. ''—and not let our worry spoil your homecoming.''

Glenna offered to let Ned use Andrew's room, but he insisted on going to a hotel. ''I think it's better if you two are alone.''

And they were. Glenna took her upstairs to her suite, ordered a steaming bath and food and wine and fussed over her, scrubbing her back and brushing her hair till it shone and talking and talking. But there was a signal difference both in the content of what was said and the manner of saying it that began a new relationship between them. The door to her room was hardly closed when Glenna embraced her. ''I'm so glad you're here. I was so worried, so afraid I'd never see you again, so fearful I'd never get a chance to be a better mother to you.''

''Oh, mother—''

''No, it's true, Moira. I was so selfish. All I cared about was your father when he was alive. And when he died, all I cared about was myself. I was so selfish. I thought only of my loss, my grief, not at all of yours and Andrew's. Is it too late for me to make it up to you?''

Moira's eyes were moist with happiness as she listened. ''No, no, you have nothing to make up. It was me. I was so envious of you, I almost hated you some times.''

''Really?''

''I know it's awful, but it's true. You were so beautiful, so lovely, so poised and perfect, so loved by father, I thought I couldn't bear it.''

''If only I'd realized.''

''Oh, I'm glad you didn't.'' She smiled. ''And you're still so beautiful. You look absolutely radiant.''

''Please don't hate me for it.''

''Oh no, mother, never again. But I'll just have to try to keep up with you.''

Glenna laughed. ''You won't have any problem. A bath, a proper dress and no one will notice me.''

During her bath, Glenna told her, in answer to innumerable questions, about MacDoul, calling him Cap'n Mac as the children did, the splendid clipper ship named for her, and how she had become mentally well on the voyage to California. And she spoke with an intimacy and candor she had never used with her daughter before, indeed with anyone save Daniel Morgan.

"I owe everything to Mac. He taught me that I am still a woman, still attractive, capable of the joys and pleasures a woman feels, still able to enjoy love and give love."

Perhaps it was Moira's nakedness in the wooden tub that aided the intimacy. "Then you love him, mother?"

She sighed. "I don't know. I certainly don't love him as your father. That will never be possible for me. But he is so good to me—and good *for* me."

"Will you marry him?"

"No. I cannot remarry. I'm sure of that. But I have lived with Mac, shared his bed, and I will again when he returns. Does that shock you? Does it make you think ill of me?"

Moira looked at her, compassion welling up inside her. "No, not at all. In fact, I'm glad for you. I can certainly understand why you look so radiant."

Glenna opened her mouth to tell her of her relationship with King, but hesitated, then couldn't. An affair with an old family friend who loved her was one thing. Intimacy with a younger man on a basis of pure physical lust was quite another thing to confess.

Instead she asked, "And Ned? What is with you and him?"

"Oh, mother, I so need to talk to you. I'm so confused and upset. He loves me. He loves me very much, and he is the kindest, sweetest person, very much like father really, although he's more shy."

"Only younger, dear. But you don't love him, is that it?"

"I don't know. That's the problem, I just don't

know. I want to, I think. I'm certainly grateful to him. The last thing I want to do is hurt him, and I do, constantly, because I can't say I love him and mean it."

She sighed. "I certainly can see it's a problem all right." She hesitated. "Have you? . . ."

"No, and it's not of my doing. I thought if it happened, maybe I'd know what I feel. But he won't touch me. He says he knows I'll never love him. It will be too painful for him, he says, if we've . . ."

"How extraordinary. What a remarkable young man."

There was a break in the conversation. Moira wanted her back scrubbed again and Glenna happily obliged.

"There's more, mother, and I might as well tell it to you. It was just before I—I left. Jessie tried to stop me from going, but I wouldn't listen. There was a party at the Kingstons. I went. I-I snitched your dress and wore it, your inaugural gown."

Glenna was shocked. "You didn't. I should have helped you, stopped you."

"It doesn't matter, mother. I wouldn't have listened to you anyway. So I went to the party, shocking everybody to death—everybody except Ned's brother, King. We danced. I got a bit, oh, more than a bit tipsy on punch he gave me. He took me out in the moonlight and we kissed. Then he took me into his father's study, locked the door and . . ."

Glenna's head whirled. King and Moira? It couldn't be. No wonder Jessie acted so strangely. She must know. And she was sleeping with her daughter's lover. Lord, no. It couldn't be.

"And that's not all. I went out with him the next night—the same night Andrew lost Aurial. But I didn't know that. I went dancing with him—then . . . then I spent the night with him."

"Then it's King you love?"

Moira protested vigorously. "No. Oh God, I don't know. I don't think so. I thought I loved him. I wouldn't have done—let him—if I didn't think I did.

All I know is I went to him as a lovestruck girl. And he jilted me. Aurial was gone and that's all he wanted."

"Actually it was his father who wanted it." Glenna hesitated, her mind still unable to comprehend all these developments and her role in the situation. Her affair with King had been casual, entirely physical. But she had felt guilt about it. She was being unfaithful to Mac. And she did not like herself for accepting another partner. It made her a type of woman she had no desire to be. Now, hearing of Moira's involvement with the same man, she was dismayed. But again her newfound love for her daughter came through. She had instant understanding and compassion for Moira. King Kingston was an expert and impassioned lovemaker. She had been unsuccessful in breaking off the relationship. His effect on a virginal young girl would be devastating.

"There's more, mother. I haven't told it all. Ned knows of my affair with King. I can't bear to tell you how he knows, but believe me he does. And that's why he won't touch me. All his life he has been second to his older brother. King was the favorite, the handsomest, the ablest, the best at everything, irresistible to women. Ned feels he can't compete with him for me. He thinks he can't win."

"Can he?"

"I think in time I'll forget King and learn to love Ned."

"It won't be that easy, Moira. King is here, in San Francisco. I imagine he's downstairs at this very moment."

He was, and in the process of destroying Ned Kingston's happiness in six words, "Well, if it isn't little brother."

Even as the reunions were occurring in San Francisco, another form of discovery was occurring near the banks of the Butte River northeast of Sacramento. It was surprisingly easy, so much so Andrew had difficulty believing it. He merely dug straight down six or seven feet until he struck rock covered by free standing water. Then he began to dig a trench toward the spring which was the source of the water.

To his surprise, Andrew was strangely unexcited. He felt absolutely certain he was approaching the source of the gold in his claim, so certain he didn't rush to get there. Rather he became more concerned about how his digging must look to the quartet of miners on the hillside opposite him. In his fear of being robbed, he went to great pains to conceal the fact that there was anything to steal. For two days he did nothing but pan for gold, moving his piles of earth to the bank of the stream, much as he always did. The difference, which he went to great lengths not to reveal, was that the bottom of his pan contained much greater amounts of gold.

He decided the best way to conceal his true activity was to make it look, if anyone were watching, as though he were simply moving the site of his operations. He spent another couple of days carefully digging a trench from the river to his underground pool, angling the trench so as to make it look as though he was creating an artificial pool of still water for panning gold. When it was finished, he indeed did pan gold there. Only a small part of these days was spent actually digging toward the spring.

Thus, more than a week elapsed before he dug back, perhaps 30 feet from the stream, to reach the underground spring. When cleared of earth, the spring bubbled with considerable force, the clear water from some source high in the mountains running freely over some sizeable rocks to the bedrock below. Andrew took one look at what lay in the crevices between the rocks and quickly shoveled dirt over it. Then, he made his way back down his trench and proceeded to pan for gold at his artificial pool the rest of the daylight hours. Thus, his joy was an inner one. He was too conscious of being watched to do other than appear perfectly normal. But as he knelt and bent over to swirl the muddy water in his pan, his eyes smarted with tears.

Over and over he said to himself, Thank God, thank God, at last he could buy back Aurial.

Near nightfall, as always, he went into his cabin and fixed his meager meal. To anyone watching, it would have appeared he soon went to bed. He did not. In the wee hours of the morning, he crept outside and by the light of a waning moon, he dug the gleaming metal from between the rocks.

Andrew had no idea how much gold he now had, but he knew it was enough. He was not greedy. He suspected more gold could be found by digging back along the source of the spring. He was not about to. He wanted to leave, go home, find his mother, hand the money to her, along with the sapphire he had saved all this time. But he suspected it was not wise to leave too abruptly. Someone might become suspicious and way-lay him. He decided, as hard as it was, to remain a few days more, fill in his trench and make it look as though he had abandoned the claim.

54

"You've had a long trip, Moira. I think you should rest a few days, then when you're—"

"No, I want to see King now. I want to find out what I feel for him."

Glenna thought a moment, then smiled. "Goodness, such a girl I raised. All right, we'll just have to find something for you to wear."

Moira pushed herself from the water and began to towel herself. "I think I'm more like you than I ever dreamed."

"Maybe, maybe not. For one thing, I never had a figure as good as yours."

"Ridiculous. I happen to know your clothes fit me perfectly." She laughed. "And I'm still jealous of you."

Glenna joined her laughter, saying, "You won't be for long." Then she became more serious. "I think I know one way in which we're different. I never had any doubt if I loved or who I loved. That changed everything for me."

"Which is another reason I'm envious."

A few minutes later after combing and powdering, Glenna brought out a dress. "This is a new one I haven't worn. If it fits, it's yours. And tomorrow we'll start getting you a wardrobe."

"Why it's gorgeous."

"Let's see how it looks on you."

The gown was of copper-colored silk and absolutely magnificent with Moira's blue-green eyes and her mane of red hair, darkening it a little as it brought out the deeper tones. The bodice was deeply cut, providing only minimal covering for the forward curve of her breasts.

Glenna pulled and tugged at the fabric, smoothing and adjusting. "It's good for business for me to appear in gowns like this. After tonight, business will double."

Moira looked at herself in the mirror, both delighted and aghast. The gown was almost as daring as the inaugural dress. "Should I wear this mother?"

Glenna smiled. "You did before."

"And look at the trouble I got into."

Glenna stood back to look at her. "Goodness. Not very long ago you were a little girl in crinolines."

"And I hated you for that."

"I can see now why you did."

Moira was puzzled, uncertain. "Should I really wear this?"

Glenna hesitated, then gave a slow smile. "There are a number of gentlemen downstairs who know of my long search for my daughter. Doubtlessly they have already heard of your arrival in San Francisco. I will be proud to introduce them to my beautiful daughter." Her smile widened. "And if it so happens that one of the gentlemen—and I use that word not entirely advisedly—seems familiar to you, I suspect you will want to make the proper impression. After all, you are a woman of the world now, not some blushing young girl in the moonlight."

Moira's eyes filled with tears. "Oh, Mother, I love you so. I knew you'd know what I should do."

"No, I don't know," she said, shaking her head. "I've never been in a situation such as this. I have the strongest sensation of your father being here. I just know he would have you wear a dress like this. He had a fine eye for feminine charms and their uses."

"He never."

"Oh, yes. Your father was a very handsome man. I never once forgot it—or the need to keep his eye strictly on me." She laughed. "Now you let me change and we'll make an entrance this town will not soon forget."

Minutes later, Glenna was dressed in a gown of her favorite shade of blue cut similarly to Moira's. Together they looked at each other in the mirror and laughed, partly from mutual embarrassment. "If your father could only see us now." She saw a pensive look enter Moira's eyes. "Does it hurt you when I speak of your father?"

"No."

"He's very much alive to me. I speak to him often."

"That's not it, mother. I'd like to ask you something, but I don't know how to."

"There is always one little word after another until it is said."

"All right. When I told you about King and I—I saw—you. . . . Mother; have you and King? . . ."

Glenna bit her lip and closed her eyes against the pain. "Yes," she said, finally, her voice barely audible. "And I am so sorry for it, so ashamed. But I didn't know—I had no thought—"

Somehow, Moira wasn't surprised. She'd known. And, strangely, she had no feelings of jealousy. Her feelings were more of compassion towards her mother in her acute discomfort. "I know," she said, touching her arm. "You couldn't have known, unless Jessie—"

"I knew something was bothering her, but she never said anything."

Moira hesitated. She suddenly realized the awful possibilities of the situation. "What happens with us now? Do you love him?"

Glenna laughed, but mostly to ease her embarrassment. "Love? Bradford Kingston? Don't be silly. He is a devilishly handsome rake who happens to be a superb bed partner. I wish so much I didn't know that, but I do and I do understand, believe me, your attraction for him. But he also happens to be a nearly worthless human being. He would make the world's worst husband, as I'm hoping you will find out starting tonight."

"Then you don't love him?"

"Heavens no, darling. He's all yours—although I pray you don't want him. His value to me, other than a little highly regrettable pleasure, is running my gambling operations. That he does well."

"I won't want him mother."

"We'll see."

Glenna was tempted to give Moira detailed instructions on how to act, but thought better of it—most wisely, as she soon found out. They swept down the stairs beside the dance floor, as the small orchestra played the customary fanfare for Glenna's entrance. It had begun some weeks earlier as a joke, then became a ritual signal that the fun of the evening had begun. As they descended a smattering of applause was heard. A few steps from the bottom, Glenna stopped and raised her hands for silence. "Ladies and gentlemen, may I present my long lost daughter whom God has blessedly returned to me, Miss Moira Morgan." When the applause died down, she added, "And isn't she lovely?" which led to an eruption of cheering.

Glenna had deliberately not told Moira of her intention of so introducing her, and she was pleased to see Moira handle it well, waving and smiling. As they descended to mingle with the crowd, Glenna watched her daughter with pleasure and pride. It was not easy, she knew, to greet this crush of strangers, mostly males, and act natural and pleased as they ogled her. But she did, displaying wit and repartee in her rejoinders to the sometimes clumsy remarks. Moira was just fine and optimism grew within Glenna that she would be able to take care of herself.

Moira was grateful for the presentation and the attention she received. She had wanted to avoid looking for King, but was far from certain of her ability to do that. The crowd of well-wishers, eager to meet her, shake her hand and welcome her, distracted her. Once, out of the periphery of her vision she saw King and knew he was looking at her. Despite herself that knowledge excited her, but she studiously avoided his gaze and tried to forget him in the fuss being made over her. In truth, she was having a good time. She knew being a "lost" daughter and having just come west through the mountains was not the only reason for the attention she received. She knew she was beautiful and, thanks to her mother, most provocative. She glowed with pride in herself and in her new found ability to be gay and witty. How far she had come in crossing a continent.

It was perhaps an hour later that King approached her. "I always said you were not only the loveliest, but the most exciting woman I've ever met."

Her back was to him and he surprised her. Was it the surprise, his words or him that made her heartbeat jump? She deliberately did not turn to him for a moment, struggling to control herself. When she did turn, she did not smile. "Hello, King. I heard you were here." She tried to say the words matter-of-factly, as though greatly disinterested in him.

But he smiled at her. "And I heard you were here, too. I thought I'd never get a chance to speak to you. You are truly lovely, very special."

Again Moira felt a flutter of excitement. She wanted to be aloof with him, cold and formal, but that handsome face, the aura of familiarity, even intimacy he conveyed weakened her. How could he do this to her? Still, she tried. "More lovely than my mother?"

Again a smile. "Such a trap you lay. Can I say you are both extraordinary women—but in much different ways."

"You should know."

He laughed at her, quite boisterously. "My dear, if you are trying to embarrass me or make me feel guilty, I am sorry to disappoint you. Yes, I have enjoyed the society of both you and your mother. I consider myself doubtlessly the most fortunate man on earth."

Moira was truly shocked. "Really, King!"

His laughter flooded over her. "And why not? If there are two more desirable women on earth, I don't know where. The saints in heaven could not blame me."

He had rendered her speechless.

"C'mon." He took her arm. "You have talked enough. You need to dance."

She did not protest as he led her toward the music, but as he put his arm around her, she said, "Haven't you forgotten the spiked punch?"

Again he laughed. "If that will accomplish my purpose quicker, I'll go get some."

Again all she could say was, "Really, King!"

Her resolve quickly crumbled. She felt a return, then a surge of the old excitement, his arm around her, the tingling of her flesh under his slightest touch, the welling then gushering of her desires pent up over the last months. Memories of their previous lovemaking flooded her mind. As hard as she could, she tried to keep him from knowing this, however.

She sought help from her mother later in the evening. "Tell me what to do."

Glenna took her arm and together they sat in a quiet corner. "It's bad, huh?"

Moira bit her lip. "Is there something wrong with me? I know what he is. I hate him for it. Yet I want him." She looked at her mother, sadness, desperation in her eyes. "I can hardly stand the wanting. What kind of person am I?"

Glenna patted her hand. "Normal, I imagine. Most women are just luckier. They are in love with and married to the man they want. Either that or the fellow they feel that way about can't see them for dirt."

"Tell me what to do."

"I can't, honey. I don't know myself. I'd hoped that when you had all that fuss made over you, he'd just be another guy. I hoped you'd find out your flame for him had gone out. I guess it wasn't a very good idea on my part."

"It's not your fault."

"I know. He is a very attractive man, no mistaking that. When he goes after a woman she's in trouble— how well I know." She thought a few moments. "Look, I couldn't have said this a year ago. Then, I'd have driven him away from you, killed him if necessary. I'd have sent you away, done I don't know what to keep you virginal. But it's too late for that now, isn't it?"

"Yes, I'm afraid so."

"All right. I-I—" The words were difficult for Glenna to say, and she struggled with them. "All I can say now is—oh, Moira, whatever you do, I'll love you. You'll never again be able to do anything wrong in my eyes."

"Oh, Mother, I love you, too. I'm so glad we've found each other—I mean *really* found each other."

"What do I know? So he's not the greatest guy in the

world—but there are worse, I should imagine. He was your first love and first loves are special. I do know that. Maybe you'll never get over him. Maybe he's to be the man in your life. Maybe it's destiny. Maybe he's in love with you. Maybe you'll reform him into a man like your father."

"And maybe the sun will fall into the sea and never rise again."

Glenna laughed. "True, but you see my point. I don't know what'll happen and neither do you. Moira, do what you have to do. And whatever happens, just don't feel guilty about it. I do believe there are times in life when a person just has to sit back and watch what happens. This may be one of them."

"I could kiss you."

"I'm not giving a blessing, Moira."

"I know. I wouldn't want you to." She stood up, then bent over and kissed her mother on the cheek. They held each other a moment. "I just want to get over him. Maybe this is the way."

"I hope for your sake it is."

It was not the way. Oh, she tried to resist. She kept telling herself no, no, no, that he was no good for her, that all he wanted was her body, that none of it was for real, but her only reality was her own ache for him. She left him, speaking to her mother and to others, but this separation led only to a feeling of emptiness and aroused desire. Her resolve was failing and she knew it. All she accomplished was to delay their entry into her room till close to two o'clock.

When they were alone and she heard him say, "I've missed you, Moira, more than I ever thought possible," tears scalded her eyes and ran down her cheeks. She couldn't help it. She knew now she had wanted him, only him, all these aching months, and he had wanted her, too. She knew she was silly, childish to cry over it, but she couldn't help it.

He kissed her, touched her, disrobed her in familiar ways, while she stood there, spasms of desire shaking her. It all seemed to happen in slow motion, his undressing and standing before her, looking at her as she faced him, eyes tearing, body trembling. When he slowly bent forward, cupped her chin and raised her lips to his, she was able for a moment or two to withstand the shockwaves of passion which drove through her, then a moan escaped her lips and she ferociously bit at his mouth and grabbed his distended organ, clawing at it.

Some animal came alive in her that night, a wild thing of lust, which rendered her both helpless and insatiable. It was not really pleasure, she knew, which compelled her repeatedly to probe the outer limits of sensation and endurance, but a wild, impulsive addiction of the flesh which left her both gorged and ravenous at the same time. Her partner was as stunned as she, then swept along by the most amazing woman he had ever encountered.

55

It was a difficult night for Glenna. She had hoped King would emerge rather soon from Moira's room. These matters did not take very long, she knew, and King frequently enjoyed gambling late at night when the place was quieter. When he remained in her room through the night, Glenna found it impossible to sleep.

There were moments that night when Glenna found

the situation almost unbearable. She wondered if any mother in the world had ever been in this situation, for she knew, indeed could almost feel what was happening to her daughter. No imagination was required. She knew this man, knew him well, too well, his body, his movements, his approach to lovemaking and his every expert action. He was a passionate man and extremely capable of arousing passion. This she knew. But there was more. More than Daniel or Mac, King made love with confidence, authority, command that left even a strong willed woman helpless. He was exceedingly bold, even lewd, yet in her experiences with him she had been unable to resist. There was no sharing, only taking, and even her consummations had been his triumphs, his pleasure. There was no shred of tenderness, affection, or respect in his lovemaking. It was lust for lust's sake, lust enshrined, that left a woman feeling supremely ravished, but devoid of pride. At least that's the way she felt. She could not imagine it being different for Moira.

About 4 a.m. she arose and padded down the hall, standing outside the doorway to their room, listening for sounds from within. Good heavens, they were still at it. In the darkness, she felt a rush of heat to her face. Mother of God, was she jealous? She hurried back to her room and silently closed the door. Was she jealous? Of her own daughter? She couldn't be. Even the idea of jealousy was so foreign to her—with Daniel she had never felt anything but beautiful, desired and loved— that she tried to analyze her feelings, knowing what was transpiring in that room. She decided she was not jealous. She had no feelings for King. He had been a diversion, little more than a pleasant toy. But she did care about her daughter. She was not jealous, but extremely worried.

Not too long after that she fell asleep to be awakened much too early by a very noisy Jessie. Glenna could see by her stomping and banging and flinging as she opened and aired her bedroom that Jessie was angry. "All right, Jessie, what is it?" She saw and heard the servant muttering to herself as she put away the gown Glenna had worn last night. "It will be better for both of us if you speak."

Jessie turned on her, eyes flashing. "How could you let her do it?"

Glenna sat up in bed, a little angry herself. "Let her? How could I stop her?"

"Oh, you could have, you know you could."

"Yes, I suppose I could have. But she's a big girl, a woman, Jessie. Not long ago you were scolding me for not recognizing that."

"But this man. Are you just going to lie there and let him ruin her? He's still in there you know."

"How would I know that? And I'm not going to let him ruin anybody—not if I can help it. He didn't ruin me. He won't ruin her."

"I'm not so sure." The words came out angrily, without thought. "I'm beginning to wonder just what kind of woman you are."

That hit close to the mark and hurt. Glenna could only stare at her friend.

Jessie also stared, disbelieving her own words. "Oh, Lord, what have I said? Forgive me, Miss Glenna. I had no right—"

"You had the right."

"It's not true what I said. I'm just so worried about Miss Moira I can't think straight."

"I am, too, Jessie."

"What are we gonna do?"

"We're going to help her, you and I. Neither one of us, most especially you, Jessie, is going to scold her. He takes away a woman's pride. Believe me, I know. We're not going to add to that. We're going to let her know in every way we can how beautiful and special she is and how much we love her. No scolding. No faultfinding, no suspicion. Do you understand?"

Jessie looked puzzled, but her words belied it. "I think so."

"I mean it, Jessie. It's most important."

"If you say so, Miss Glenna, I'll surely try. But I don't understand. If he makes you feel so bad, how come you do it?"

Glenna smiled. "It is not that he is bad, but too good. He does things to you, makes you do things, makes you feel things you never thought possible. It is wonderful while you're doing it, but later you feel used, somehow dirty. Oh, it's hard to explain. You want him, yet you hate him."

"He sounds bad to me."

Glenna laughed. "Maybe you should try him, then you'd understand."

"No thanks. Joe is plenty of man for me."

Glenna dressed, tended to some affairs for Morgan Manor, then shortly after noon went out in search of Ned Kingston. She found him an hour later in the Gold Nugget saloon. He was not drunk, but then not entirely sober either.

"I missed your coming in last night," she said.

"Thank you, Mrs. Morgan, but I'm sure you were the only one."

She watched him drain his glass, make a face as he swallowed the fiery fluid, then pour another glass from the bottle. "I dislike standing at a bar, Ned. Would you mind sitting at a table with me?"

"Sure. Anything for a lady." He picked up the bottle and his glass and accompanied her to a round table nearby. Glenna saw him weave a little during the passage.

"Sorry. You want a drink?"

"No, thank you. A little early for me." She saw him gulp down another glass. If she was going to talk to him, it had better be soon. "Ned, she needs your help."

His laugh was mostly a snort and entirely humorless. "Help? I'm sure she's getting all the help she wants from my brother."

"You're wrong. She needs you as much now as she did back in that cabin in the mountains."

"I doubt that, Mrs. Morgan. I'm sure my dear brother has done or will do essentially the same things that bastard Knight did, but he's cleaner and more suave. I don't know, of course, but I doubt if he'll hit her or beat her." He was sarcastic. His effort to smile came out a twisted leer. "Maybe if she wants him to, he'll go in for the rough stuff. Maybe she likes that. How would I know?"

Deliberately, Glenna ignored his bitterness. "You know what I mean, Ned. She needs your love more than ever."

"Does she really?"

"Scoff if you like, but you know I'm right."

"I'm afraid I know nothing of the kind, Mrs. Morgan."

"Did you cross a whole continent, save her, only to abandon her?" She saw she had gotten to him. "Are you a coward? Are you unwilling to fight for the woman you love?"

He laughed. "What do you have in mind, Mrs. Morgan? Do you want me to drag her off by the hair to my cave and ravish her?"

"Don't be silly."

"That's my dear brother's act. Maybe not the hair, but I'm sure he is an excellent ravisher. I watched the two of them, you know. He met her, he danced with her a couple of times, he took her into the garden, then into the study. The whole thing didn't take much over a half hour. I found her ripped undergarments the next morning."

"I'm sorry, Ned, sorry for her, sorry for you."

Again his leering grin. "I'm sure you mean that, Mrs. Morgan. You've always been a fine lady. But I'm also sure Moira isn't a bit sorry. Tell me honestly, Mrs. Morgan. Did my brother sleep alone last night?"

"No." Her voice was very small as she said the word. She felt the blood drain from her face.

He filled his shot glass again and drained it in a single swallow, banging the glass on the table when he had finished. "This is a rather foolish conversation, don't you think?"

"You forgave her once and followed her. Is it so hard again?"

"It is, Mrs. Morgan, indeed it is. Much too hard. She was young and silly in Maryland. She didn't know what my brother was. I don't believe any of those circumstances apply now."

"You hate your brother, don't you?"

"Hate dear King, emperor of the boudoir? Heaven's no, I don't hate him. I also don't envy him. I consider him foolish, empty, vain, arrogant and—" He spat the next word. "—pathetic. His accomplishments like solely in the bed and at the gaming tables. I feel sorry for him."

"Then why won't you try to save Moira from him?"

"Does she really want to be saved, Mrs. Morgan—or need to be? I may not think there is much right about my brother, but there is not much that is wrong, either. He is handsome, dashing, elegant, very romantic and most adept, I should imagine, in bed. He is very good at gambling and never wants for money. Life with him would probably be most exciting, fulfillment of every girl's dream. What do I have to offer her? I am none of the things he is. I am a farmer, Mrs. Morgan. I love the land and I miss it. There is nothing here for me—including your daughter. There is a ship leaving for New York tomorrow. If I can get on it, I'm returning to where I belong."

"I wish you would reconsider."

"I'm sorry, I cannot."

She saw his hurt, his stubborn pride, and she could neither fail to understand it or blame him. Yet, she felt there must be some way to reach him. She must. But how?

"I think I would like that drink now."

He leaped at the change of subject. "What would you like? Some sherry? Cognac?"

"This'll be fine." She detested whiskey, but impulsively reached out for his glass and drained it. She saw him smile at her.

"You surprise me."

"I surprise myself. I've been doing that a lot lately. Ned, I understand your feeling about land. I admire you for it. But there is plenty of land here in California."

"I saw it. The valley of the San Joaquin we passed through. Rich land. It will be worth far more than all the gold in California. But it is not tobacco land, and tobacco is what I know. Besides, I already have an estate. My father preferred King, but he would not be so foolish as to entrust the ancestral estate to him. Kingston will be mine. I'm sure of that."

Glenna tried a new tack. "Need you leave so soon? Couldn't you wait a few days at least?"

"Perhaps I'll be forced to. I don't know if I can book passage. But I'll leave as soon as I can."

She sat there a moment. There had to be some way. "May I?" she said and poured and drank another shot, again seeing his amusement.

"You are a surprisingly wise young man, Ned. I like you a lot, as I believe Moira does."

"Like is not love."

"True, nor is it love between Moira and your brother. Your evaluation of him is quite correct. He is highly romantic and most exciting. And yes, he is quite something as a lover. I know, because I slept with him, several times. He was quite devastating." She saw the surprise register in his face. "Does it shock you that I tell you?"

"Yes."

"It shocks me, too, almost as much as having done it. You spoke of him as an excellent ravisher. That is a good description. I was quite swept off my feet, and I am an older woman and a widow. I'm more than a little experienced in these matters. If I felt this way, I can only imagine the situation is—well, very difficult for Moira." She hesitated, watching his face, seeing that she was at last being effective with him. "You suggest she will have an exciting life with King. Again, probably true, but much too exciting. I have no doubt that King would sleep with me again, if I so much as expressed an interest or even if he merely thought he could make me interested. And it will not just be with me. There will be many others. I would not like my daughter to waste herself on a faithless, unloving man."

She stood up. "I must go, Ned, but I cannot resist telling you how disappointed I am in our conversation. Oh, not that you are hurt, angry, jealous. That is surely understandable. What disappoints me is your inability to understand Moira. She was brutalized out there in that cabin. She needs desperately to know she was not ruined, that she is still desirable, still a woman in every sense. Believe me, I've been through it. I know exactly how she feels. You may have saved her body out in the woods, but you did not save what is most precious to a woman."

56

Moira awoke a few minutes before two in the afternoon, feeling tired, sore and aching all over, as well as mentally depressed. She remembered the night, not as particular, but as a whole. It was not with pleasure, either. She started to form the thought *never again*, then quickly abandoned it. She had no confidence she would be able to keep such a vow. Amid her weariness and emptiness there was, she knew, a core of longing.

Jessie came in to bring her breakfast. She was exceedingly cheerful, to Moira insufferably so, as she opened curtains and windows, put away clothes and straightened the room. She was even humming and singing a little.

"I'd feel more comfortable, Jessie, if you scolded me."

"No, Miss Moira. I'm so glad to have you home safe, I'm never going to raise my tongue against you again."

"I think I'd like to be scolded."

"Then you'll just have to do it yourself."

Moira asked for and enjoyed a hot bath. She was dressed and downstairs when her mother swept in from the street carrying packages. Her "good morning" was positively musical.

"Good morning, Mother."

Glenna sat her packages on the bar, told the barman it was a new supply of playing cards, and asked him to put them away. She came over to Moira who was sitting at a table near by. Smiling, she said, "I gather you don't feel so well."

"Oh, Mother, why is everyone so insufferably cheerful. I feel ghastly."

"You don't look ghastly—maybe just a little tired, but—"

"You know what I mean. How could I? He makes me feel—"

"I know, believe me I know. But at the time . . ." She smiled conspiratorially. "It's something else, isn't it?"

"What am I going to do?"

"That's easy. You're going to put a smile on your face and go shopping for clothes as we agreed. There's nothing like shopping to cure the dumps."

"Oh, I couldn't."

"You can and you will. C'mon."

They spent the afternoon, mother and daughter,

shopping. They bought several dresses as well as other purchases, and ordered several gowns from a dressmaker. They stopped at a tea room operated by a Chinese. All in all it was a companionable afternoon with much time to chat. Moira tried, but except for brief periods was unable to shake her depression.

Over tea and oriental cakes, Glenna said, "I guess you haven't, but I've had such fun. Every mother dreams of times just like this with her daughter."

"I'm sorry, Mother. I really am having a good time. It's just—oh, you know how I feel. I'm so ashamed. Over and over I keep asking myself, how could I, How could I?"

Glenna laughed. "Maybe I should buy you a little whip."

"It's not funny. I feel terrible, physically, mentally. I feel positively rotten about Ned. He didn't even come last night. I guess I should be grateful for that."

Her mother smiled. "That's quite a long list. Could we take it one at a time? Of course you feel bad physically. I should imagine you're tired and with good reason. He's a bit demanding, isn't he?"

"Lord, Mother, that's what I mean. How could I? He makes me feel depraved, like some kind of wild animal."

"Yes, I know. It was exactly how I felt, although I didn't put it as well." She smiled. "Does some sympathy and tea help at all?"

"Yes, yes. I don't think I could bear it if I couldn't talk about it to someone. I must say you're the last person I would ever have thought it would be with."

"I'm a little surprised myself. But it has made me the happiest woman on earth to discover we can be close. Maybe it is a dividend from the suffering we've both had."

"Yes."

Glenna quietly sipped her tea. "Did it ever occur to you that King *has* to make you and me feel that way? I never thought about it till just this minute, but do you suppose under all that handsomeness and self-assurance lies a man who is afraid?"

"King? Afraid?"

"Oh, I don't mean real danger. It's hard to explain, but it occurs to me that he has to make a woman want him to prove to himself that he is attractive and irresistible. You said he made you wild and depraved. I should imagine he's rather pleased with himself today."

"He ought to be ashamed."

"Don't hope for that, dear. Guilt, as least as far as women are concerned, is hard to find in him. No, I think he's probably preening himself, bursting with pride at this very moment. His self-assurance is doubtlessly at floodtide—having fed on yours."

Moira tried to visualize King as her mother described. "Maybe. But what good does it do me?"

Glenna smiled. "Good question, and I'm not sure I know the answer."

"Well, how did it make you feel?"

"Like you, I can understand how you feel. But I'm older, several years older than he actually, a widow. I'm not so guilty as you."

"But how did you feel?"

Glenna hesitated, then smiled. "It's hard for me to speak of, but then I wanted a frank talk with my daughter. All right, I felt like I received one stupendous loving. I felt totally used, expended. More, it meant an awful lot to me, more than I can express, to know at my age I had so excited a younger, virile, very handsome and desirable man. It was a tremendous boost for my ego. Is that so terrible for me to admit?" She looked at Moira, her intensity showing in her face. "I know it's not the same for you. Being so young and at the peak of your beauty, you probably have no idea what I mean."

"I do, yes, I do."

"And I never had any romantic involvement with King. He means nothing to me—except what I said. But you are *involved* with him. You love him or think maybe you do. Ned is all mixed up in it. It cannot be the same for you or as easy. Does this make any sense?"

"Yes, a great deal."

They were silent for several minutes. Moira's thoughts were a turmoil: amazement at her mother, pleasure at their being able to speak together this way, a glimmering of understanding of what her mother was saying, confusion, doubt, her own heartache and depression.

"You're talking about pride in being a woman, aren't you?"

"I don't know. I guess so. He stayed the whole night. You must have been very good for him."

"Yes. I was."

"Maybe it's not much, but it's something, isn't it?"

For the first time that day, Moira genuinely smiled. "Yes, it is something." She looked down at the new dress she'd worn out of the shop a few minutes before. "I like my new dress, Mother."

"That shade of green is perfect for you."

"When you suggested this dress, I didn't like it. I didn't want to wear anything like this. I wanted to go hide. I wanted to be old and flat and ugly."

"And now?"

"You already know. You deal in pride, don't you?"

"Sometimes it's all there is. I lost mine when your father died. Having been helped to regain it by Mac, I know how precious it is."

"Mother, I love you, so very much."

Both their hands reached out to touch each other, and they squeezed their knuckles white, trying to press into each other's flesh the affection which consumed them.

In a few moments, Glenna spoke. "I saw Ned today. He says he's going back home."

"Oh, no, Mother, and all because of me."

"I suspect he thinks so. He's hurt, he's jealous. He knows leaving will hurt you the most."

"Lord, mother, that's awful. I've got to see him, talk to him. Where is he?"

"Remember what I said last night about being a spectator on life sometimes? Could I urge you to be that way with Ned?"

"Not go to see him?"

"Most definitely *not* go to see him."

Glenna was doing anything but following her advice to her daughter. A spectator she most definitely was not. She had arisen that morning determined to speak to Jessie, Ned and Moira. All had gone rather well, she believed. She had been ecstatic over her conversation with Moira. She had seen her transformed from the mousey, defeated girl of midday to the radiant, confident beauty who descended the staircase with her to applause.

Glenna sought two faces in the crowd, but saw only one. There was admiration in it and some pride. She watched as he held back for awhile, then came forward, took Moira's arm and led her away to sit by themselves at a table. After a bit, Glenna approached them. "I would have thought you two weary of each other by now."

King replied, "I fear that will never be the case."

Glenna smiled at Moira. "I hope you don't believe a word of it. Just in case you do, may I steal him away a moment. The labors of a businesswoman are never done."

She had thought of a pretext. It looked legitimate enough and he did not question it. "That man at table six is winning a great deal. Is he cheating?"

From a distance King watched a couple hands being played. "No. He's all right. Just a lucky streak."

"Good." She smiled at him. "You can go back to her now. I imagine I shall be thoroughly neglected from now on."

"I see no reason for that."

"Really? I would think a choice mandatory in this instance."

He laughed. "How can I choose between two of the most desirable women I know."

"I imagine you could if you tried."

"Why should I try?" He laughed again. "Oh, I know you think me terribly wicked. Perhaps I am, but you are both fascinating—really quite different, you know."

"We are? A brunette and a redhead, is that it?"

"There's far more than that. You, my lovely Glenna, are the consummate lady, discreet, a little reserved, perfectly poised even when you're enjoying yourself the most. Most fascinating and delicious."

"My daughter?"

"Quite the most exciting woman I've met in a long time. It may be her coloring, but she is wild, impulsive, daring, quite splendidly demanding."

She looked at his wicked smile. These were truly outrageous things he was saying. He knew this and that was why he said them. "It sounds like you have made your choice."

"Do I have to?"

Very seriously she said, "I'm afraid you do." She saw in his eyes that she had been effective. "If it will do any good, I ask that you not hurt her."

The disarming smile returned. "I'm a bit surprised, but I suppose this attack of protective motherhood is to be expected. I can only repeat that she is the most exciting girl I have met in a long time. As I've told her, it is her boldness that attracts me most. I think we're a most interesting combination. It should not be dull."

"I'm sure of that."

She watched as he returned to Moira and led her to the dance floor. They made a handsome couple, absolutely no doubt of that, and she was able to understand Moira's attraction for him, his rugged handsomeness, his self-assurance, his sense of himself. Ned had said it best. If there wasn't much right about him, there wasn't much wrong either. He made no pretense of being other than he was. And there was a most refreshing honesty about him. If a woman accepted him as he was and loved him enough to live with the way he was, some happiness might be possible. As he said, it would not be dull.

Such thoughts, however, were just a rationalization, a search for a silver lining in the cloud of despair that engulfed her as the evening wore on. Ned had not come and she had been so sure he would. She felt certain her words had reached him. But as the night wore on and he did not appear, her confidence shrank, then disappeared. She remained smiling, the perfect hostess in her establishment, but inwardly she railed at herself for not letting Moira go to him when she wanted to. It was by just such misplaced overconfidence that young lives are ruined.

When she saw him enter shortly after midnight, it was all she could do to restrain herself from shouting with joy and forced herself to go up to him naturally. "I'm so glad you came, Ned—truly."

He smiled back at her. "I guess I had to."

"Is it to say goodbye? Are you leaving tomorrow?"

"No."

Her smile was never broader or more genuine in her life. "Thank God."

"No, Mrs. Morgan, it is thank *you*. I will try, but it is not very easy for me, as you can imagine."

"Nothing we really want comes easy, does it? She's over there."

"I see her. If I could find her in the middle of the Rocky Mountains, I can find her here."

Glenna leaned forward and brushed his cheek with her lips. "Good luck. For what it's worth, I'm rooting for you."

A little embarrassed, as he frequently was in public, he said, "I hope it's worth a lot."

Moira had her back to him and didn't see him enter. King had begun a poker game, and she stood behind him "for luck," her hands resting lightly on his shoulders. She was feeling vaguely uneasy, attributing it to tiredness and boredom with the game. When Ned appeared to her right and spoke, it surprised her. Instinctively, she jerked her hands from King's shoulders. "Oh, Ned, it's so good to see you," she said.

King looked up. "Hi there, little brother."

"King." It was more a statement of recognition than a greeting, cool but not unfriendly. He improved on it, however. "How's the game?"

"Good, little brother, and improving—with my girl here for luck."

"Then you might be good for a small loan."

"Sure. Help yourself."

Ned reached to the table and lifted off a bill. "I'll pay you back soon."

"That won't buy anything." Quickly King picked up a stack of bills and put them in his brother's hand. "And it's not a loan. It's in the family." Generosity, real or genuine, was a pronounced trait of King's.

"Thank you." To Moira he said, "Now I can buy you a drink."

"Hey, what's this? You borrow money from me then use it to steal my girl." But he was smiling as he said it.

Moira accompanied him to a relatively quiet table near the end of the bar. She felt uneasy and nervous, yet she was glad Ned had come.

"What'll you have? Champagne?"

She saw his nervousness, too. "No. Just a cup of tea."

"Really?"

"You know I hardly drink. I didn't think you did, either."

He smiled sheepishly. "I'm afraid I overdid it a bit earlier today." He ordered a bottle and a glass. "Hair of the dog, you know."

She almost asked if it had been over her, then thought better of it. "I'm glad to see you, Ned. I missed you last night."

And he almost said: did you really? Instead he lied, "I was bushed. Fell asleep early."

The tea and the bottle were brought, but it did nothing to alleviate the awkward silence between them. Moira finally spoke. "Mother said she saw you today. Are you leaving?"

"No." He swallowed part of a whiskey, obviously more in restraint than that morning.

"I'm glad. Why not?"

He smiled, a little shyly. "Oh, there are many lovely things to see out here. I shouldn't rush away."

"Yes. San Francisco is beautiful."

"San Francisco is an ugly, rat infested mudhole. You're the lovely thing I'm talking about." When he saw her blush a little and smile, he burst out laughing. "See, my brother isn't the only one with a talent for elaborate compliments."

And she laughed, too, and the ice between them was broken. "I thought you didn't like me to wear dresses like this."

He met her gaze for a moment, then looked rather boldy at her decolletage. He smiled at her. "That was over a year ago and a continent away. We've both changed. Right now you're merely devastating. No wonder that bear wanted in your tent."

She laughed, but her words were serious. "Thank you, Ned. I find myself in need of your approval."

Suddenly, he was embarrassed and shy again, making another awkward moment between them. He filled it by finishing his whiskey and pouring another. "He calls you his girl. Are you?"

"No." The word came quickly, but was said very softly.

"He always has had a tendency to appropriate whatever he admires." Again he felt nervous, and again turned to the whiskey.

"You shouldn't drink so much."

"I know." He pushed the glass and bottle away. "I'm just nervous, I guess."

"Me, too, and we shouldn't be. We're hardly strangers."

He smiled. "You're right. Say, I saw a poster today. It appears some civilizing influences are coming to San Francisco. A theatrical group is putting on *The Drunkard* tomorrow night. It would probably be a good influence on me. Would you like to see that it is?"

"Oh, yes. This is my second night in this place and I'm already sick of it. I'd love to go, Ned."

They talked awhile longer and he left. She urged him to stay, but he refused. "You may be able to take this nightlife, but I really am tired."

"I am, too. I won't be up long regardless of how much mother thinks she needs me."

"I'll see you tomorrow evening. You'll be the most beautiful girl at the show."

She smiled. "With such a handsome escort, I'll have to make a special effort."

She did go to bed not too long after he left, leaving King enmeshed in his game. She fell asleep rather quickly, but not until she tried to decipher her feelings. She had been glad to see Ned, and she was pleased to have been asked out. But how could he? He must know? What sort of person was he? He really ought to be angry with her. Was he just trying to make her feel guilty for being so shabby to him?

It was after two a.m. when King's game broke up. In all his years as a gambler he had never had such luck as the last two nights. He had won big and repeatedly against skilled players. Several times he had bet to his last penny, then won with hands, four of a kind once, a royal flush another time, such as he seldom saw. Two of his opponents had been miners, sticking when they shouldn't and losing their bags of gold dust, but two others had been skilled. Winning left King exhilarated. More, as always high stakes gambling had an aphrodisiac effect upon him. He wanted a woman and as he looked around for her, he realized he wanted Moira Morgan. That wild, insatiable vixen was made to order for a night like this.

He went to the bar, picked up a bottle of champagne and two glasses, and mounted the stairs two and three at a time. So she was asleep. He'd awaken her all right, and he'd also explain to her how it was with him so she'd be available for early morning celebrations.

To his surprise the door to her room was locked. He turned the handle hard and pushed, but the door wouldn't budge. Angrily, he thought of breaking down the door. He'd show her not to close him out. But he quickly changed his mind. He had a good deal with Glenna, and if he was too rough he'd lose it. He looked down the hall and saw a light under Glenna's door. She wasn't asleep yet. What the hell? Any port in a storm. Smiling, he made two strides down the hall, then stopped. She had played the chaste, protective mother earlier. He wanted a woman, not an argument.

His indecision lasted only a moment and he smiled, having made up his mind where to go.

57

Lila knew she was looking at a mad man. The colorless eyes of Winslow-Smith-Hackett had always made her uncomfortable, but lately there was a wildness, a feverishness to them which she could only associate with lunacy.

She had gone to him for money. The whole establishment was to her extremely minimal. Its decrepit, seedy furnishings depressed her, and she knew that an investment in posh furnishings and a semblance of elegance would only increase profits. But Winslow had not wanted to talk about it. He never did. She couldn't even be sure he heard her pleas and arguments. All he did was rant.

"That Irish wench, that she-bitch. I'll destroy her. Do you hear? I'll destroy her. She has tried to destroy me. Has she ever! She has followed me to the ends of the earth, spreading lies about me. But she shall not win! I'll never let her. I'll never give up. Her hideous lies. I'll destroy her for them. She thinks she's so high and mighty now. The talk of San Francisco, so elegant in her fine gowns. But I'll fix her. She thinks that putrid dance hall offers her protection. I'll fix her. I'll get her. You'll see I will. She'll not escape me this time."

Lila watched him. Mad, that's what he was, pacing the floor, waving his arms, his eyes shining. Mad, truly mad. "Why do you hate her so, Mr. Winslow?"

He stopped in mid-stride and turned on her. "Don't you call me that—ever! My name is Hackett, do you hear, Hackett."

"All right, Mr. Hackett, I'm sorry. But I still don't understand why you care about her so much. She seems like a nice enough woman. Her place is run well—a lot better than this one I might say."

"You don't know her. She's a bitch, the evilest woman on the face of the earth. I'll destroy her."

"You already tried that, and all you did was destroy an innocent boy." She still harbored guilt over what she had helped to do to Andrew Morgan.

"That whelp! Anything that came out of her body is evil, too."

Lila shook her head in disgust. Absolute madness.

"But I'll get her this time. That bloody sea captain saved her the last time, but he's not here now. And I'll get her. You'll see." He turned to face her. "I've got a plan, a foolproof plan. There'll be no escape for her. She'll burn this time. Will she ever burn!"

Lila knew it was useless to talk to him and stood up. "I'll see you tomorrow."

"What did you want to talk to me about?"

She saw the confusion in his demented eyes. He hadn't heard a word she'd said. "Nothing, Hackett. Good night."

As she left the room, she knew she'd made up her mind. It had been a huge mistake for her to come out here with him. He'd gone over the edge and now she was stuck with a crazy man and a sleazy bordello. God, what a fool she was. But it wasn't too late. She was just going to have to look out for herself and try to salvage something out of a hopeless situation. She wasn't going to spend her life turning tricks. She could see the end of the road, disease, poverty, a horrible, slow death. It just wasn't going to be. She hadn't escaped slavery in Haiti to have that happen.

Filled with anger and determination, she arrived back in her own suite to be handed a card. She read it and smiled, a plan already forming in her mind. "Yes, send him up."

As soon as King walked in the door she saw he was lusty, full of himself. That knowledge stirred her, for he was still the only man who was any good for her. "Well, if the lost haven't returned," she said.

He immediately reached for her. "Who's lost?"

She found herself being pulled against him, his arms around her, his lips seeking hers. She turned her face away. "Your luck is bad? You need it changed?"

"My luck is just fine."

Again she turned a cheek to him. "So I hear. The Morgan girl. She shut you off tonight?"

"Just shut up."

As his lips found hers, she felt the passion of him and that aroused her. He could be so good when he was like this. And she needed him. Yes, she did. He was like a cleansing agent, washing all the phony sex and fraudulent passion out of her. He made her feel like a real woman. She felt her breath quicken in genuine response.

"There are no lips like yours, Lila. Just the greatest."

As she saw him start to undress, she was tempted to tease him, deny him, send him back to the Morgan girl, even demand money first. No. If she could handle him right, King could be her ticket out of this dump.

His passion was towering, quite a challenge, and she used all her practiced moves to drive him wild, pouncing on and over and around him until at last she allowed herself to be caught and overcome. And she indeed felt overcome, shattered by her own quite genuine orgasms. God, what a man he was. How right he was for her. If only there were some way. . . .

When at last he was spent and lay back on the pillow beside her, she said, "If you'll stay awake, I'll tell you something."

"I'm awake. What?"

"You're the only one who can really do it to me."

He laughed. "You don't have to be the businesswoman with me."

"It's the truth, King. I've never faked it with you. If I had, you'd know the difference, believe me. You make me feel good—a real woman." She raised herself to look at him and smile. "Now wasn't that worth staying awake for?"

He smiled back. "Yeah. And I like doing it with you. That's why I keep coming back. If only—"

"If only I wasn't the wrong color."

Again he grinned. "It sure would help. But that's not what I meant."

"The Morgan girl. You like her."

"Yeah. She gets to me a little. Something about her and I'm not sure what. Got a fantastic body." He made a motion with his hands to indicate her breasts. "But I'm not a kid. It's more than that. There's a wildness to her, a boldness that's exciting. And she really likes it when she get's going. I'm not sure I can keep up sometimes. It's a challenge. Know what I mean?"

His words, the far away look in his eyes stung her,

and her anger flared. But only briefly. At least he was talking to her, more honestly about his real feelings than he ever had before. She was getting a glimpse of the real King, and she was not about to shut him off. "Yes, I know. She's not the only one you have that effect upon."

He seemed not to have heard her. "And she has a way about her. Wears clothes well. When she walks into a room, it's like she's the only one there. The red hair, I suppose." He seemed lost for a moment in his private vision. "Sometimes I think maybe I ought to change my ways, settle down more."

"You mean marriage?"

He laughed. "I doubt if I'm ready for that. No, I was just thinking—instead of moving from game to game, I ought to, well, settle down. I make money, sure, but I spend it as fast as I get it. I ought to try to save some, get my own place, let the money come to me. I ought to be in my own home, be a man of substance."

"Sounds like marriage to me." She laughed as she said it.

"No, I don't think so. I'll never be *that* settled. I just can't see myself with a squawling brat on each knee. I'm talking about my own establishment, run right, earning money even when my luck is bad. I got a deal like this now at the Morgan place, but a third isn't a whole, know what I mean?"

"Yes. I've been thinking the same thing."

"Really?"

"Sure. That's about all I think about anymore. This guy—Hackett he calls himself now—is crazy, absolutely mad. He scares me. I gotta get away from him."

"Is he after you?"

"No, not that way. He's just so mad, unpredictable. I got to get away from here, get my own place, look out for myself. As you say, a third isn't a whole."

"Then why don't you?"

"For the same reason you don't. It takes money, a

lot more than I got. And I don't want another place like this. A whorehouse is all this is. I want a real place. Face it, I want something like your girlfriend has."

"You mean her mother."

"It's all in the family, isn't it?"

He was silent for a few moments. "What're you suggesting?"

"I'm not suggesting anything. It just occurs to me—"

He laughed. "—that two people who want the same thing ought to work together."

And she joined his laughter. "The thought had occurred to me."

"Along with what other idea?"

She raised herself on her left elbow and looked at him. She was very serious, so much so that when he began to toy with her breast, she took his hand away.

"Win—I mean Hackett, has money. How much I don't know, but a lot more than you and I have. He's mad, I tell you, ready for the lunatic asylum. There is no telling what he's going to do. My guess is the end result will be he'll lose all his money. That seems a shame to me." She smiled. "I think you and I could find better uses for it."

King laughed. "I gather he gambles."

"Yes, and very poorly."

"I see." He was silent for a moment. "And you have in mind?"

"Call it a mutual building fund. We could both get what we want."

"Partners, is that it? But a half's not a whole."

"It's more than a third."

"Your arithmetic is excellent. See if you can arrange a little late night game for our benefactor."

"Don't rush it. Don't do it all at one time. Take him slowly, over a period of time, almost like he doesn't know it's happening."

"I know. Leave it to me."

She smiled at him, then ran a hand over his chest,

curling the hairs around a finger. "Anything else I should leave to you?"

He bent his head toward her inviting lips. "Then can I sleep?"

58

Moira couldn't make up her mind. She twice changed her dress, then surrendered to her indecision and consulted her mother. "Which should I wear?" she asked and held up two gowns, one low cut, the other a more modest afternoon dress.

"Either one is appropriate for the theater, dear, and you're lovely in both." Glenna saw the disappointment in Moira's eyes and laughed. "I see I'm to make the decision. All right, I've always said if you can't make up your mind on which dress, don't wear either of them. When you're wearing the right thing, you'll know it. You won't have to ask. Consider that a little motherly advice."

"Then what?"

"Let's see." Glenna went to her own closet, moving various gowns aside. Then she smiled. "Here. I wore it once, but Ned won't have seen it."

When her mother pulled it out of the closet, Moira gasped, both in admiration and consternation. It was of soft, white silk, empire style, with a tiny bodice set with sequins. "It's so lovely, mother, but I'll be practically naked in it. I don't know."

"You don't know what? If Ned will like it?"

"Yes, he's—"

Glenna laughed. "He's flesh and blood male, isn't he?"

"Yes, but—"

"There isn't a man alive who doesn't want his girl to look as desirable as possible."

"He'll be embarrassed."

"And also proud. C'mon, try it on."

Moira's feelings of delight and doubt continued as she surveyed herself in the mirror. The doubt won out as Glenna, pulling and tugging at the shoulders settled the neckline even lower on her pink mounds.

"I wore a dress very much like this on my first date with your father."

"I can't, mother. I'm a spectacle."

"That's exactly what I said. And your father said I sure was and made me wear it."

"But Ned isn't father. He's shy for one thing."

"He is, isn't he? You'll have to help him get over that."

"I can't mother. I'll be uncomfortable all evening."

Glenna smiled. "We'll have to think of something. Oh yes, I know." She went to a drawer and returned with a stole of fine white silk. "Try this." As Moira draped it around her shoulders and across her bosom, she laughed. "That ought to protect your modesty enough. And if you wish not to, you can always be a little careless."

Moira tried the stole in various positions. "Well . . ."

"Ned may be shy, darling, but he'll adore you. You've never looked lovelier and there isn't a man alive who doesn't react to a special dress and a special effort."

When Moira saw the warm, adoring expression in Ned's eyes, she knew her mother had been right. He led her outside and lifted her bodily into an open buggy he had rented. "Thank God we're riding," she said. "Any girl who wears white on the streets of this town is foolish."

"Not really. Didn't you know all this mud is deliberate? It allows a fellow to pick up the girl and carry her."

"How clever. I never would have thought of it."

The theater was little more than a shanty, then typical of San Francisco. There was a small, largely bare stage. The props and scenery were modest, leaving much to the imagination. The audience sat in plain wooden chairs. The play turned out to be ghastly, so much so the audience hooted and howled and stomped their feet in disapproval, turning what had been intended as high drama on the evils of drink into a hilarious parody. Seated near the front, Ned and Moira joined the fun, having a better time than the original show had promised. Moira kept fussing with her stole, for when she applauded the silk tended to slip from her shoulders.

It was a little after ten when they left the theater. As he lifted her back into the buggy, he said, "Are you as starved as I?"

"Yes."

"I promise you it will be worth the wait."

He drove out of the city and perhaps half an hour south into the country along *El Camino Real*, the royal road built along the California coast by the Spanish to link the series of missions. It was a lovely, fresh summer night, but Moira was puzzled. "Where we going?"

"To my place."

"You live out here?"

"Yes, just today. I thought since I'm in California, I might as well find out how the real Californians live. I think you'll like it." He drove on a while longer, then turned into a lane. "This is La Paloma, the hacienda of Señor Raoul Ramirez. He lives very well. Acres and acres of vineyards."

"Mexican?"

"Yes. They are the real Californians, although the Indians might dispute that. I really can't bear San Francisco. There's nothing there for me—except you.

So I came out here. I expect to learn about grapes and wine making. And I think you'll like Señora Ramirez and her daughters."

As they approached La Paloma, Moira was enchanted. In the light from lanterns and torches, she could make out a large, sprawling house of white stucco. They drove into a walled courtyard filled with flowers and trees and the delicious scents of bougainvillea and oleander. "It's heavenly," she exclaimed.

He helped her from the carriage. They both stood a moment enjoying the *jardin*, then he touched the brass knocker on a heavy door of dark wood and wrought iron. In a moment it was opened by a shy girl of perhaps eight or ten with dark hair in pigtails. She let them in and stared at them with luminous brown eyes a moment, then ran.

"That was Maria Carmen, I believe. The youngest."

He led her to the right of the foyer and into a large room so beautiful it made Moira gasp. It was paneled in walnut and had a high ceiling with exposed beams, also of walnut. At the end opposite them was a large stone fireplace in which a small fire burned to relieve the chill from even a summer evening in the Bay area. The room was furnished with large, heavy wooden pieces, yet lightened with silver and brass and brightly colored carpets, drapes and upholstery. Moira had never seen a room like it, so warm and cheerful, yet elegant.

"It's lovely, Ned."

"Yes. The Mexicans are a fine people who have known how to live well for a long time. I thought you'd like it."

He led her across the room to the fire. Above the mantle was a portrait of a fierce looking gentleman with a gray drooping mustache. "Señor Ramirez' grandfather, I believe. He fought with General Augustin Iturbide in the Mexican War of Independence in 1821. Quite fierce looking, isn't he?"

"And proud."

He looked down at her smiling. "Not as much as I

am," he said, reaching to remove her stole. Instinctively she held on to it. "I've been trying to get that away from you all evening."

"I'm not sure, Ned. Your friends—"

"I am."

When he slid the silk from her shoulders, she tried to measure the expression in his eyes. "It's mother's," she said, a little apologetically. "She insisted you'd like it."

The white satin picked up and reflected the light from the candles, and her skin seemed to glow more pink from the fire. His voice was a little hoarse as he said, "You should always listen to your mother."

Señora Ramirez entered with her daughters. She was in her forties, rather short and heavy, with fair skin and bright black eyes. Her brown hair was tied severely in a bun, but her generous mouth was smiling as she gave Moira a Spanish *embrazo*, kissing both her cheeks. Then she stood back, *"Monísima, muy hermosa."* To Ned, she said, "Beautiful, yet?"

She spoke almost no English, but somehow it didn't matter. Moira basked in the warmth of her personality. Her admiration for her and her dress was both open and affectionate. Again and again she exclaimed over the gown touching it, saying words that obviously praised her figure and complexion, and again and again touching her hair, exclaiming to her daughters, *"Pelo rojo! Fabuloso!"*

The mother's name was Maria Louisa and her oldest daughter Maria Elena, a stunningly beautiful girl with her mother's coloring. Moira guessed her age was near her own, but because of her slight, slender figure and extreme shyness, she seemed younger. The father entered carrying a bottle of wine and glasses on a tray, which he set down on a table before greeting them. He was a rather short, slender man with hair turning gray above brown eyes. Moira thought he had great dignity and an in-born pride. Whatever he said was lost in another stream of excited Spanish from his wife.

In a moment, he shushed her and said in slow, halting English. "*La Señora*—my wife says you are most beautiful and I agree."

Moira's murmured "thank you" was lost in more unintelligible words from Maria Louisa.

"And she says Señor Ned here is a most fortunate man. I agree with that, *también*." He smiled. "My English not good, but I must learn. My vino, it is better."

Red wine was quickly served all around, even to the youngest daughter, and drunk and admired. "And your home is so lovely, Mrs. Ramirez, and your family. Your daughter may be the most beautiful girl I've ever seen."

That was translated among sounds of pleased deprecation. Maria Elena blushed when the flattering words were understood.

Perhaps the wine encouraged it, but Moira felt immersed in the warmth and happiness of the family. She was given a tour of the house and garden by Señora Ramirez and her daughters. Moira did not understand a word of the woman's incessant chatter, but it did not matter. She understood fully that this was a warm, lovely woman who lived well and took immense pride in her family and her home. Moira's smiles and compliments were thoroughly genuine. When they returned to the men still with their wine by the fire, she saw Señora Ramirez hug Ned and then felt her extend her warm embrace to her.

"My wife thinks you will both be happy together."

Moira saw Ned's embarrassment and felt her own. There was nothing to do but say, "Thank you."

They were taken to the dining room. It had an immense table with high backed chairs for a dozen, but places had been set opposite each other at one end for two with a crystal candelabra and flowers between them. They were served Mexican dishes, then left alone behind a discreetly closed door. "These are called enchiladas, I believe," Ned said. "You can see why lots of wine is served with them."

She smiled and made a gesture of fanning her breath. "And I can see why people speak of hot-blooded Mexicans."

"Yes." He hesitated, unsure what to say. "I'm sorry. I didn't tell them you were my girl."

"I know. She just assumed. Anyway, I'm glad you brought me here. And I'm glad you chose to live here."

"Yes. They don't take in boarders, but I told them I wanted to learn about vineyards—which is true."

"This really is you, isn't it?"

"I suppose. Not here, of course. I'd never get the hang of growing grapes, making wine." He hesitated. "But I wanted to remind you, as best I could, of where we came from, Kingston, Aurial, the good life. I know it is where I belong. Do you?"

She looked at him for a time, unblinking, then down at her plate. "I don't know, Ned."

"I'll try to be patient." Then his voice brightened. "Would you like to see the garden again?"

"Yes."

As he stood up and came around to hold back her chair, there were smiles, then shy glances, an overpowering feeling of heat and closeness, then she was crushed in his arms, his lips soft and hungry upon hers, and she felt a surge of passion through her as she responded to him. Then she was swept by desire as she felt his trembling hand reach between their bodies, down, down, between her breasts and inside her dress. She felt her body go weak.

But it ended too soon. He stood back from her, shuddering, a little flustered. "I'm sorry. You shouldn't wear a dress like that around me."

She heard herself say, quite breathlessly, "Maybe that's why I wore it."

Then she was back in his arms. "Oh, Ned," she said before his mouth devoured all further sounds than her involuntary, unheard moans. She felt her body trembling, as his hand again found her breasts. And again he tore his lips from her and stood a moment looking down at her, the tormented passion in his eyes matching hers. Then he reached out, slid the white silk from her shoulders and on his knees before her inhaled the hard, rosy orbs, first one and then the other, her flesh immersing his face, leaving her so wracked with sensation she had to hold on to both his head and the back of the chair behind which she stood. "Oh, Ned, Ned," she moaned from behind closed eyelids. "I want you. I've wanted you for so long."

She felt him leave her abruptly. She opened her eyes to see him on his hands and knees before her, his whole body shaking and shuddering. In a moment he stood before her, his face tormented. He looked at her breasts a moment, his mouth involuntarily opened, then with shaking hands reached out and pulled up her dress to cover her breasts. From deep in his throat came the husky words, "I can't, Moira. I won't. I want you, all of you, not just your body."

She stared at him in disbelief.

"Can't you understand?"

Embarrassment and humiliation flooded over her, and her passion instantly turned to anger. "I'm flesh and blood, Ned."

"I know that."

"I can't help it. It's the way I am."

"I know, I—"

"You don't know anything—except how to make me feel ashamed, dirty, some kind of tramp."

"Moira—"

"What's the matter with you? You say you love me. Well you don't. You're in love with some dream, some angel, some girl on a pedestal. I got knocked off a long time ago. I'm me, Moira Morgan, flesh and blood girl and very real."

"Moira, I—"

"And I want a real man, a flesh and blood man, who'll love *me*, the real me, not crawl on the floor like a dog saying he can't."

Her words stung and his anger flared. "Then my brother's the one for you."

"You better believe it. If you'll take me home I'll prove it."

She seethed with anger all during the drive back to town. How could he? How could he make her feel like—yes, like a whore, a tavern trollop, not good enough for him. He started it. If he couldn't finish it, someone else could. In her rage, she almost snarled aloud. Why had she bothered with little brother? She wanted a man, a real man.

At the door to Morgan Manor, he reached out and took her arm.

"I can help myself. You needn't bother."

"I'm just trying to say I'm sorry. I shouldn't have—"

"You're damn right you shouldn't have. Now leave me alone."

Again his anger flared. "You better believe I'll leave you alone."

As she stepped out of the carriage she said, "See that you do," and swept inside her mother's dance hall.

Typically, Ned's anger did not last long, leaving him with a miserable night of self-recrimination. He'd gotten carried away. Unable to resist her, he'd made a terrible mistake. He'd lost her. There was nothing to do but forget her, or try to.

Glenna saw Moira enter and quickly read the emotions written on her face. "I gather it was not a good evening," she said.

"The worst, Mother. The positive worst."

"What happened?"

"Nothing—that's just it. Oh, I don't want to talk about it."

"All right. You don't have to."

A bit of Moira's anger melted. "Oh, I'm sorry. It's not your fault and I shouldn't take it out on you. He kissed me, he started—then he declared he couldn't, it wasn't right. How do you suppose that makes me feel?"

"Terrible, I should imagine. Why would he do that?"

"Who knows anything about Ned? All I know is I've made up my mind. I'm me, a real person with real feelings. I want a real man and I'm not ashamed of it."

"Of course not, dear." She hesitated. "Then it's King?"

"Yes." She looked around the big room. "If I can find him."

Glenna pointed toward a poker table. "He's right over there."

As Moira walked away from her toward King, Glenna felt a sinking emptiness. What could have possessed Ned? Had he no sense? She remembered her own romance with Daniel. They had discovered and cemented their love in physical intimacy. How could Ned be so stupid?

Moira came up to King from the rear, put her arms around his head and bent low to kiss his cheek. The delight in his smile was genuine.

"The wanderer has returned?"

"You better believe it. Can I talk to you?"

"As soon as this hand is finished."

He played the hand, won with three sixes, then asked to be counted out for a couple of hands. He took Moira's arm and led her to an isolated table. "So how was the night out with little brother? Not the greatest, I gather."

"I don't want to talk about it."

"Well I do. I want to know if you found out anything."

She felt flustered, a bit like a little girl caught in a naughty act by an angry parent. "I don't know what you mean?"

"I mean this." He reached out and quickly snatched the silk scarf from her shoulders. "What in the world is a girl like you doing with little brother? Look at yourself, just look at yourself."

REAP THE WILD HARVEST

She was so confused, she stammered. "I-I don't know what you m-mean."

"Oh yes you do. Does he know what to do with a girl like you? What'd he do, hold your hand and buy you a lollipop?"

With relief, she understood and smiled, "Well, almost."

"For crissake, don't be a sap. You're a magnificent, exciting woman, the best I've ever seen. It's a ridiculous waste, your being out with him."

"I know."

"I'm glad you do, 'cause if you're going to be a kid, I'm not going to bother with you."

"I'm not a child, King, you know that."

He smiled. "How well I do. When this game is over I'll let you prove it again."

Just those words produced a surge of excitement in her. "How long will you be?"

"As long as I am. Now bring me a brandy and watch while I help these miners lose their swags."

She did as she was told and stood behind him, hands on his shoulders, for the next two hours, moving only to fetch another drink, light his cigars and encourage him with secret caresses. She felt—what? She did not try to analyze her feelings in any particular depth, yet she was aware of a strange sense of relief. She had made a decision. King was the man for her. And why not? He was the handsomest, more virile and exciting man she had ever known. He was a real man, sure of himself, what he was doing and who he wanted. And she now knew he wanted her. How could she ever have considered Ned? King was right. He wasn't for her. She had mistaken gratitude for love. She was grateful to him, truly so, and would remain his friend for life. But she could not love him. King was the man for her.

In considerable contentment, but with more than a little impatient anticipation, she waited for King to finish his game. When they went upstairs to her room, she responded to him with as much passion as she had ever known.

Glenna watched her daughter with King and without being told knew what was going to happen. She reacted with a genteel shrug and resignation. She had done all she could. Moira had made her decision. Perhaps it was the right one.

Suddenly she felt strangely depressed. The music and boisterous laughter and noise from the dance hall seemed too raucous to her. She could hardly bear it. And she was tired, very tired. She asked Joe to close up and went to bed.

59

In his desperation, Silas Duckworth, known to his many friends and admirers as "Ducky," was being forced to do something highly uncharacteristic of him—make a decision and carry out a course of action. All his twenty-seven years, he had just sort of drifted, taking advantage of the opportunities that came along. He was most comfortable with the spur-of-the-moment, very uneasy with the sort of premeditated action he was now contemplating.

Uneasy or no, Duckworth was determined to go ahead with his scheme. Unless he did something, he was condemned to shovel dirt in these gold fields the rest of his life. He simply was not cut out to be a gold miner. Grubbing in the mud for a few yellow flecks struck him as dumb. His idea of sensible activity was a bottle of whiskey, a few hands of cards and a warm and naked body.

Duckworth recognized that these sensible pleasures and his own impulsiveness in enjoying them, especially the warm body, had gotten him into this fix in the first place. Back in New Haven, Connecticut, the warmest body he knew belonged to Molly Pringle, just sixteen, ripe and ready. His loins ached just thinking of those smooth white thighs opening up like the gates to paradise. And it was paradise he offered, and she couldn't get enough of it. Only trouble was her father, Otis Pringle, figured she was a virtuous girl, or ought to be. When she had the misfortune to become pregnant, Pringle developed the old-fashioned notion of marriage. To escape the shotgun, Ducky had, like many others, felt the lure of gold in California.

He had come overland, in the process striking up a friendship with three other lads. They had arrived the previous fall and tried a couple of sites further south with only small success. Shortly after the first of the year, the four of them had come north and set up camp on this godforsaken stream near the Butte River. Whatever appeal mining had, which had never been much for him, was quickly lost in the cold, torrential rains and ankle deep mud. Many the time he railed at himself for ever agreeing to dig for gold. He should have gone on to San Francisco. Hell, he could make more in a single night at the gaming table than he had here in nearly six months. Now he was stuck. He'd spent his last nickel on camping gear. Unless he found some gold, a lot of it, he didn't have a prayer of getting back to civilization.

His desperation to escape was fueled by the knowledge of what was happening to him. His hands had turned into a mass of callouses. He could not believe what he saw in the cracked mirror, a grubby character with matted hair and scraggly beard. He had once been considered the best-looking guy in New Haven. The girls loved his honey blond hair and hazel eyes. Christ, if they could see him now. He squared back his shoulders. Hell, he must have lost twenty pounds. If he didn't get out of this mess of mud, he'd waste away to nothin' and go crazy in the process.

Yet, there had been no recourse for him for a long time except to shovel dirt into the rocker in the endless search for gold. He had it calculated pretty well to do just enough to avoid too many complaints from his companions, but not one shovelful more than necessary. They found some gold all right, but by the time it was split four ways, it was hardly enough to finance a night in the camp at Rich Ba and a little whiskey. He knew he was getting nowhere and by June this knowledge was making him increasingly desperate. Was he doomed to spend his days shoveling dirt?

The idea of robbing Morgan on the other side of the stream had occurred to Ducky a long time previously, but robbery really didn't appeal to him. He knew he was short on courage. If he wasn't, he would have stood up to Otis Pringle and never gotten into this fix in the first place. He had made a serious effort to buddy up to Morgan, even making a social call with a bottle of whiskey. That had gotten nowhere. Morgan was about as friendly as a rattlesnake. About all Ducky learned from his visit was that Morgan carried a revolver and had the personality to use it. That drove thoughts of robbery from Ducky for a long time.

Desperation to get out of these mine fields put the notion back in his head. Particularly when he was drunk, a nearly nightly occurrence, he felt so driven to have some money that he began to think Andrew Morgan and his revolver far less formidable. He struggled with the problem for some time, weighing his fears against his greed. He tried to tell himself that Morgan wasn't worth the risk. There had to be better and easier pickings. But then Morgan had been on that claim a long time. If he only got a pinch of gold each day, he must have a swag hidden somewhere.

Despite his monumental hatred for gold mining, Duckworth found himself more than slightly interested in Morgan's strange new diggings, his hole and trenches. What the hell was he up to? Then he saw him panning as before. A strange duck, that's what he was.

As it must for all men, Ducky found his luck. It came quite unexpectedly when he wasn't looking for it, which is how luck usually occurs. He had gotten drunk early. Claiming to be sick, he had quit work in mid-afternoon to "lie down." He had, with a bottle, and quickly got unhappily drunk and passed out in his bed. He snored away through supper and until long after his companions had gone to bed.

Duckworth had no idea what time it was when the liquor wore off and he awoke. All he knew was that he had a throbbing head and a powerful thirst. Not unquietly, he staggered over to the water barrel and stuck his pounding head in it, gulping down water as he did so. He stood up and held his head. Lord, but he felt awful. Maybe some air would help. He opened the door of the shack and stepped out to the ground, sitting down and resting his aching head on his arms crossed atop his knees.

He remained that way a few moments, pondering the evils of drink, then raised his head. Might as well go back to bed. Trouble was he knew he wasn't sleepy. Maybe a drink. No, he had finished the damn bottle. Lord, what a place to be stuck with no whiskey. What a fine mess he'd gotten himself into. He was about to put his head back on his knees when he saw a figure walk across the hillside on the opposite side of the river. What was Morgan doing up at this hour?

He watched him go to his dig and drop into his trench. What a funny thing to do in the middle of the night. He shrugged. Hell, Morgan was crazy anyway you looked at him. Duckworth did then resettle his head on his knees. But not for long. Morgan intrigued him. He raised his head and peered at Morgan's place across the stream. In the pale moonlight he could catch no glimpse of Morgan in his trench. Had he imagined seeing him go there? Ducky was about to conclude he must have been seeing things, when he saw Morgan climb out of his trench and head back to his shack. To Ducky, he looked for all the world like he was carrying something heavy.

Duckworth never did sleep any more that night. He sat outside for a time, then lay in his straw bed, his mind consumed with thoughts of Andrew Morgan, what he had found in his dig and how he might be relieved of it. The next day, much to the surprise of his companions, Duckworth actually worked at mining with some vigor. But as he shoveled dirt into the rocker, his eyes were watching Morgan across the way. He saw him filling in his trench and then panning for gold. What was he up to?

It was reasonably easy for Duckworth to decide to rob Morgan, but figuring out how to do it was a problem which nagged him all that day and well into the next. He would be most adept, he knew, at somehow tricking Morgan out of his swag. A card game, a little drunken rowdiness would be easiest. He felt he could easily concoct some phony scheme, a partnership, a business venture of some kind that would relieve Morgan of his gold, however much he had. Duckworth spent a lot of time concocting various schemes of this type, but discarded each one as quickly as he thought of it. There was simply no way he was going to get that unfriendly cuss drunk, into a card game, or even into a social conversation. He had already tried that and failed. Duckworth smiled as he thought how awful it was for Morgan to be so suspicious of everyone.

By early morning of the second day following Morgan's moonlight visit to his dig, Duckworth had made up his mind. He would get the gold from Morgan anyway he could, even kill him if necessary. He had no great confidence in his ability to commit cold-blooded murder, but his desire for gold and escape from this hellhole encouraged him to believe he could do anything if he had to. Do what? He thought about Morgan's revolver, which grew larger and more deadly in his mind. He always carried it. Probably slept with it. There had to be some way to get to Morgan when he didn't have the gun on him.

At midday the idea came to Duckworth. He actually laughed out loud in appreciation of how good it was. It was so simple, so easy, so natural for him, he wondered why it had taken him so long to think of it.

Duckworth waited impatiently for the sun to go down and darkness to come. Barely able to conceal his excitement, he had forced himself to eat supper, chat with his fellow miners, then appear to go to bed early. Perhaps the hardest part was feigning sleep until he heard the others were asleep, then waiting till past midnight when the moon arose in its later phase. It took so long, he began to think something had gone wrong with the heavens and the moon never would rise.

But the heavens were regular and the moon did rise, a yellow half melon in the summer sky. Duckworth quietly got out of bed, picked up his boots and went outside. By the time he had put on his boots and buttoned up his resolve, he could see Morgan's cabin across the way, bathed in the palest of moonlight.

Duckworth hesitated, his courage fleeing, but he whispered aloud to himself, "It's either this or you rot here." Then he was able to stride quietly, but purposefully down the hillside, through the shallow creek, and up the bank toward the shack of Andrew Morgan.

Outside the door he stopped and listened, trying to pick out amid the music of the water and the rustle of the trees some sound from inside the cabin. He could hear nothing. For a moment, he was tempted to try the door. Maybe it was unlocked and everything would be much easier. But Duckworth had already told himself that Morgan would never fail to lock himself in. He thought of Morgan in there, waiting, gun in hand. Duckworth felt his courage waning, then he commanded himself, *Stop thinking. Stop worrying. Do it.*

He reached to his waist and pulled his knife from its sheath. Holding it in his hand and folding his arms across his middle, he bent over and moaned very much like a man with a terrible pain in his belly. He moaned again, a little louder, then said in a hoarse voice, "Morgan, help me, I'm hurt."

He listened and heard no sound from the cabin, then reached up and rattled the door insistently. He moaned more loudly and said in a louder voice, although it still sounded like that of a man in mortal pain. "Morgan, Morgan, help me, please. I'm hurt—real bad."

Finally he heard a sound from inside. "Who's there?"

"It's me—Duckworth from across the way. I'm hurt bad. You gotta help me."

"What's wrong with you?"

"We had a-a fight. I got—" He moaned most convincingly. "—stabbed in the gut. I'm bleeding—" Again a moan. "—real bad. You can't let me die out here."

His moans and entreaties were rewarded with a crack of light under the door. Morgan had gotten up and lit a candle. Duckworth heard the rasp of heavy bar being lifted and the rattle of the latch as the door came open. Bent nearly double over his hands, he looked up toward Morgan, hoping he was registering a proper degree of agony. He saw the revolver in Morgan's hand. Damn!

Duckworth lurched forward and fell, still bent over, face down into the shack. "God, it hurts, Morgan. You gotta help me."

"Okay. Let me get you to the bed."

Duckworth felt a hand on his shoulder, trying to lift him. He resisted any movement. "God, I don't think I can make it."

Then he felt a second hand trying to lift him. Morgan had put down the gun. He permitted himself to be helped to his feet, even staggered a step or two toward the bed, then raising himself and swinging his arm back in the same motion, he saw an expression of surprise in Morgan's eyes a second before he plunged the knife as hard as he could underhand into his midsection. "It's not me who's stabbed, Morgan. It's you," he said and swung the knife into him a second time.

The impact threw Andrew back onto his bed. He had terrible wounds in his stomach and chest, but he was alive. Despite the searing pain, he was able to keep from making any sound. He knew this man would finish him off if he thought him still alive. So he lay there, sucking in his breath, watching through a crack beneath his eyelids as Duckworth searched for his gold.

It was not hard to find in the heavy wooden box under the bed. He slid it out, then used his bloody knife to pry off the hinges. It only took a moment. Andrew heard him gasp, "Good God, there's a ton of it here."

In her depression and weariness, Glenna had gone immediately to sleep and slept soundly. Suddenly—she had no idea of the hour—she bolted upright in bed, clutching at a pain in her chest. "Andrew," she said. "Something's happened to Andrew." Almost immediately she began to scream for Jessie.

60

Moira was awake, indeed in the throes of a thrilling fulfillment, when she heard her mother's scream, but the demands of her passion overrode the sound. It was not until the second scream that her conscious mind registered who was screaming and that there was trouble. She tried to get up, but King's weight was atop her. She struggled a moment, movements quite misinterpreted by him, until, her desperation mounting, she felt his most powerful movement and heard him grunt out his pleasure.

"Something's wrong with mother," she said. "I gotta go." As she pushed him and squirmed out from under him she heard him swear. She scrambled into a robe, fastening it as she ran to her mother's room, and arrived moments after Jessie. Her mother was sitting in bed, a look of horror on her face. Moira had never seen her look so frightened. "What's wrong, Mother?"

"It's Andrew. Something's happened to Andrew."

"What're you talking about?"

"Andrew. I was asleep. Suddenly I felt this terrible pain in my chest. It's Andrew. Something's wrong with Andrew."

Moira sat beside her mother on the bed and put her arm around her shoulder. "It's just a bad dream, Mother."

"No, it wasn't a dream. It was Andrew. I know it was."

"Don't be silly. You've just had a nightmare." She patted her as though she were a child. "You're awake now. We're here. Everything will be all right."

"No, it *won't*, Moira. Something's happened to Andrew. He's hurt, maybe dead. I could feel it."

"There, there."

"Why won't you believe me?"

"Because you're here, in your own bed, and no one knows where Andrew is. You've just had a bad dream."

"No I *haven't*, Moira. Andrew's in trouble. I know it. I feel it. I've got to go to him."

Moira had never seen her so upset. She had not even been this way when father was killed. There had been shock and grief then. This was pure fright. "Jessie, fetch some hot tea. That'll calm mother. And bring the brandy."

Glenna twisted away from her and slid out of bed. "No, Jessie, I don't want any tea. I want you to begin packing immediately. I'm going to Andrew. He needs me. I know he does." She went to her closet and opened it.

Moira couldn't believe the way her mother was acting. "It's the middle of the night. You can't go anywhere."

"I don't care when it is. I'm going to Andrew."

"You don't know where he is. Ned and I couldn't find him."

"I'll find my son. I know I will."

Moira watched her pull one garment after another out of the closet, tossing them on the bed to be packed. She heard her giving instructions to Jessie as to what bags to use and what else she would need.

Moira watched her in frustration, knowing there was no reasoning with her. But she tried. "Why can't you accept it as a bad dream. Nobody has premonitions like this."

Glenna turned to her. "I did. I know you don't believe me. I know you think I'm silly. But I know what I must do. I'm going to Andrew."

"But you don't know what you're doing. You're too upset. Those gold fields. I've seen them. It's no place for you and you'll never find Andrew."

"I'll find him. I know I will."

Moira sighed. "Then I'll go. I at least know where I've already looked."

"No, Moira. I know you love Andrew as much as I do. But he is my son. I am his mother. He needs me."

"But—"

"You stay here and run Morgan Manor. I'll try not to be gone long."

"Oh, Mother. Why won't you listen? It is no place for a woman alone."

"She won't be alone. I go, too." It was Joe, standing in the doorway, unmindful that Glenna was still in her nightdress. "I have never left your side, Missy. I will not do so now."

Glenna clutched one of her dresses to her front to

cover herself. She looked at Joe, seeing the determination in his face. "Moira will need you, Joe."

"No, Missy. I go with you. Jessie stay with Moira."

Glenna looked at him a moment, his old instinctive trust, born in the jungle, asserting itself. "Yes, Joe. I'll need you."

"You people are ab-so-lute-ly *crazy*," Moira shouted, and stalked out of the room. In her own room, she hurriedly slipped out of her robe and began to dress. She was not angry with her mother, but concerned. She repeated to herself that her mother didn't know what she was getting into. She just couldn't ride off and hope to find Andrew. She had to be stopped from going. Why wouldn't she listen to her? Then, as she buttoned her dress, a new thought came to her. Yes. It was the only way. In a moment she went back to her mother's room and announced, "I'm going out for a bit."

"Out? Where?"

"I haven't time to explain. Just don't try to leave till I return."

She heard her mother shouting after her as she ran down the stairs.

Forty minutes later she was rapping frantically on the great front door of the Ramirez hacienda. When Señora Ramirez came to the door, her hair in braids, swathed in a voluminous robe, Moira managed to convey to her that she had to talk to Ned. The Mexican woman left her, and Moira waited impatiently until Ned appeared.

He rushed into the room, a little breathless. He had pulled on his boots and trousers, but was still buttoning his shirt. His hair was still uncombed. "What's the matter, Moira? Are you in trouble?"

"No—I mean, yes. Oh Ned, it's mother."

"What's wrong with your mother?"

She told him. "I can't stop her. She won't listen to me."

Ned listened, relieved to know Moira was not hurt and that her mother's trouble seemed so inconsequential. Yet he was confused as to why Moira was there. And, some of the anger and frustration from their earlier quarrel still lingered in him.

"Oh, Ned, I know I have no right to ask it. I know it's too much to expect. But I have no where else to turn. I—"

"What Moira? Just say it."

"She insists on going. She has no idea what those gold fields are like. She'll never find Andrew. Joe is going with her, but he'll be no help. I'm so scared for her. She'll—"

He put his hands on her shoulders to silence her. "What is it you want me to do, Moira?"

"Go with her Ned, please. She needs someone to look after her. She needs help. You were in the gold fields with me. You know where we looked. Please, Ned. I know it's a lot, but. . . ."

He felt her shoulders trembling under his hands. He saw the fear in her eyes, her desperate reaching out for his help. "Of course I'll go with her." Then he felt her in his arms, hugging him, her face against his shoulder.

"Oh, Ned, thank you, thank you."

He felt awkward, embarrassed, unsure of himself. "When does she want to go?"

She pulled away from him. "Immediately. It was all I could do to get her to wait till I get back—if she did. We have to hurry."

"All right. Give me a minute to pack a couple things."

She spent the next few minutes futilely trying to explain to Señora Ramirez what the problem was. When Ned appeared he was dressed for the saddle, heavy boots, buckskin britches and vest, wide brimmed hat. He carried full saddlebags and his rifle. A pistol was strapped to his hip. Moira recognized him as the man she had traveled through the mountains with and that gave her a feeling of security.

Hurriedly she kissed Señora Ramirez on the cheek and murmured her thanks. She and Ned hurried toward the stable amid cries of "vaya con dios" and "buen viaje." It was not until they were riding full speed back toward town that she realized she had not given a thought to King since her mother had screamed.

Glenna was ready when they arrived at Morgan Manor. Her luggage had been put into a small buggy rented from livery. Joe was already holding the reins while Glenna waited impatiently at the door. With surprise she said, "Ned."

"He's going with you, Mother."

"Yes," he said. "I can help you find him quicker."

Impulsively Glenna hugged him. "Oh yes, thank you. We'll find him together." Her hug was brief. "We must go. It's almost light already." She went quickly and climbed into the carriage beside Joe.

Ned stood in the doorway a moment, looking at Moira. Both seemed to want to say something, but there was no time to form thoughts into words.

"I'll take care of her," Ned was able to say finally. "And we'll find Andrew."

Her voice was little more than audible as she answered, "Yes, I know that."

"And you take care of yourself."

She never replied, merely watched him mount his horse, tip his hat to her and ride off behind the carriage already rolling down the street, now less muddy because of the dry spell. She saw him turn and wave, then they were gone.

She watched a moment longer, then slowly turned inside. She put her arm around the waiting Jessie. "Looks like you and I are in the dance hall business."

The Negro servant managed a small laugh. "And may God be our partner."

Suddenly very tired from a sleepless night, Moira slowly walked to her room, thinking she might lie down a bit. She couldn't. King was sound asleep astraddle the bed. He lay on his stomach snoring. She looked at him a moment, then turned and went downstairs to begin the day's work.

61

The next few days passed slowly for Moira, but exceedingly rapidly for Glenna, Ned and Joe. They felt at times as though the sun had hardly risen on a day of searching for Andrew before it was already beginning to set.

Glenna's anxiety fo find Andrew turned to consternation that first afternoon when they reached Stockton, the first town on the edge of the gold fields. At Ned's insistence, they went to the newspaper office seeking help and advice. Editor Frank Bidwell, much impressed to see such a handsome woman in town, was polite to Glenna, but in the end he showered Glenna with hopelessness.

"You have only a name, madame? No camp where he is? No idea at all?"

"No."

He smiled at her, rather in the manner of a banker turning down a loan. "I'm sorry, madame, truly I am. I would like to be of help to you, but you seek the impossible."

"Don't you understand? I must find my son."

"I understand that, madame, but you don't understand the size of these gold fields. They cover the whole western slope of the Sierra Nevada mountains for a distance of at least three hundred miles as the crow flies. That is from north to south. From east to west, again following the crow, the fields stretch perhaps a hundred miles. We are speaking of perhaps thirty *thousand* square miles of largely mountainous terrain. There are at least a hundred, perhaps two hundred thousand miners out here, scattered along the banks of scores, no, hundreds of rivers, streams and gullies. Do you begin to grasp the magnitude of the task you have undertaken?"

Glenna felt as though she had been slapped. Her eyes filled with tears.

Ned spoke up. "But, Mr. Bidwell, is there no central register of claims?"

The editor's smile became condescending. "I fear you are used to the more civilized east, young man. You must understand that to all intents and purposes there is no government at all out here."

"But the claims. Miners must have some legal right to them. There must be some registry."

"My dear young man, there is no legal right but possession. A man comes, he picks a piece of likely looking ground and he says it is his. He may not even bother to put up stakes making a boundary. As long as he can defend it and work it, it's his."

"You mean a man can just steal land?"

"No, no, no. You don't understand. The miner—this good lady's son, for example, does not *own* the land. He just assumes the right to look for gold on it. If he finds gold, good for him. It is his by right of finding it. But he is in no way a landowner."

"Then who does own the land?"

"Good heavens, I don't know. The government, I suppose, maybe the Indians. But it doesn't matter." Bidwell looked at Glenna, his expression softening. "I am truly sorry, madame, but what I tell you about the difficulties is the simple truth. It would not be a kindness for me to suggest otherwise."

Ned saw her growing panic and tried to avert it. "If you were us, Mr. Bidwell, how would you try to find Mrs. Morgan's son?"

The editor sighed. "There are a few towns, Sacramento is a major center, then there is Marysville, Otoville, Placerville, sometimes known as Hangtown. There are many camps—Poker Flat, Whiskey Flat, Sonora, Dutch Flat, many of them. All I can do is tell you to go to these places and inquire for this Andrew Morgan in saloons, from various merchants, from everyone you meet. You will, I believe, find the miners friendly, more than willing to help so beautiful and distressed a lady. I can only wish you luck."

Ned looked at Glenna. She seemed to be physically melting, her hopes of finding Andrew dashed. Hurriedly he thanked Bidwell, and with Joe led her out of the newspaper office and down the street to the nearest saloon. He sat Glenna and her servant at a table while he went to the bar, returning in a moment with three glasses and a bottle of whiskey. He poured a shot for Glenna and told her to drink.

"No, I-I—"

"Drink."

She looked at him, then acquiesced, downing the whiskey, making a face as she did so. He poured a second shot and ordered her to drink that, which she did.

"I'm sorry, Mrs. Morgan. I don't wish to be unkind, but if you fall apart, it will be no help in finding Andrew. I realize your agitation. You are worried about Andrew, what with your dream and all. But agitation and panic will not find him. Believe me, Mrs. Morgan, I know I'm right."

The whiskey warming her stomach, Glenna looked at him, her eyes wide. "How remarkable you are," she said at last. "How very much like Daniel. You are right, of course. I am the one to be sorry." She looked at Joe. "I wasn't such a ninny in the jungle, was I?"

Joe smiled. "You fine then, Missy. You fine now."

"I will try. Ned, tell us what to do."

"I'll try. Only a little while ago, Moira and I came through this area looking for Andrew. We came over Truckee Pass from Nevada, stopped at Placerville, Sutter's Sawmill and the other camps in this area. No one knew anything about Andrew. I think we can assume he is not in this central area of the gold fields. That leaves us two choices. We can look for him either north or south of here. Which direction do you want to go, Mrs. Morgan?"

Luck sometimes reveals itself in a single word. Glenna wavered a moment, then declared, "North. I believe north."

Moira was surprised to discover how much work her mother did. There seemed to be an endless number of responsibilities, getting the place cleaned properly, buying what seemed to her a huge amount of liquor and food, handling employees so Morgan Manor was properly staffed. Just counting the money, banking it and paying the bills—tasks normally done by Joe—took her a couple of hours. Moira quickly realized she didn't know anything about the business. Making decisions as her mother would was extremely difficult for her.

She discovered that afternoon that the handsome man she had chosen never worried about anything other than whether his shirt was clean and his suit pressed. He came downstairs well rested, declared himself starved and asked for a steak. Grateful for a little rest, Moira sat with him while he ate. She told him what had happened.

"Oh, yes, I remember hearing the scream. Wondered what was up."

"She was so frightened, King, so convinced Andrew was hurt. I almost tend to believe it myself. Can something like that happen? Can a mother—"

"Nah. She's just being silly and female. She's been worrying about Andrew. She just worked out an excuse to go find him."

"Then there's nothing to it."

He inserted another bite of steak into his mouth and talked through it. "Of course not. She'll find Andrew. He'll be as healthy as I am. Stop worrying."

She smiled, basking in his confidence. "I won't be

able to stop completely, but I do feel better having Ned with her."

"Little brother? What good'll he do?"

Moira opened her mouth to protest, to defend Ned, but never got a chance to speak.

"Well, he'll be company for her anyway. Besides, I'm glad to have him gone. I can have you all to myself now."

"Don't be jealous of Ned."

"Jealous? Are you kidding? I just want you to get over the stupid notion you owe him something."

She started to say she did, now more than ever, but the words wouldn't come out. It wasn't something King wanted to hear.

"And there's another reason I'm glad he's gone. You and I can have this place to ourselves." He had finished his steak. After swallowing his coffee and wiping his mouth with the napkin, he spoke again. "I've been thinking about you and me. We should have a place like this someday. Maybe right here in San Francisco. God knows it's an awful mudhole right now. But it won't always be so. I imagine a real city will be built here and in the not too distant future. There's gonna be a lot of money made and spent in this country. I think we should get our share, don't you?"

"I suppose. I hadn't thought about it."

"Well think about it." He laughed. "On the other hand, leave the thinking to me. I've got a little deal going. Should make me some money, a lot of money. Oh, I'll blow some of it. Want to take you to London, Paris—"

"Paris?" Her voice registered her surprise.

"Sure, why not. Rome, too. You'll set Europe on its ear. I want to show my beautiful wife around and—"

"Wife?"

He laughed. "Don't tell me you're surprised? You know how I feel about you."

"But-but, you hadn't said marriage."

Again he laughed. "Well I am now. We'll spend a few months in Europe. Lots of money to be made there. That's where there's real gambling. When we've made our pile, we'll come back here and open a place like this—only bigger and better. How's that sound?"

Her head felt like it was whirling. It was all so sudden, so unexpected. "I don't know, King. I have to think."

"What's to think about? You either want me or you don't."

"Of course I want you."

"Then it's settled."

She looked at him somberly. He was so handsome, so sure of himself. She felt a wave of confidence in him and smiled. "Yes, I guess it is settled. When does all this take place?"

"My deal will only take a couple of days, I imagine. As soon as your mother gets back with Andrew, it'll be off to London with us. Why wait?"

"That soon?"

"Sure. When I make up my mind, I like to move fast. I'll see about tickets today."

King's stunning announcement, the promise for marriage and a trip to the fabulous places of Europe, buoyed Moira all evening. Mrs. Bradford Kingston III. Moira Kingston. The name did have a certain ring to it. How exciting, how absolutely thrilling.

Even Jessie noticed the difference in her. "You gotta be as tired as I am, Miss Moira. You didn't get much sleep either. Yet you look as bright and sparkling as a new baby."

"That's about the way I feel. King has asked me to marry him."

Jessie felt like she had been stabbed, but struggled not to show it. "Why . . . why that's wonderful, Miss Moira."

Moira hugged her. "Yes. He's so handsome, so . . . oh, you know what I mean."

Jessie laughed. "I fear I don't, but as long as you know."

"Oh, I know all right. I can hardly wait for Mother to get back to tell her. She'll be so surprised."

Against the shoulder of the girl she'd helped to raise, Jessie said, "I'm sure of that."

It took more than euphoria, however, to keep Moira going that evening. Her lack of sleep, the pressure of running Morgan Manor, the incessant greeting of customers left her wilted with fatigue, but unable to allow herself to show it to others. As long as King was there, she was all right. But when he left about eleven for his "deal," she felt terribly alone, vulnerable and a little afraid. She knew her mother was much more adept than she at diffusing the arguments and incipient fights which seemed to break out all the time. It seemed to her everyone, employees as well as clientele, tried to take more advantage of her. There were no real problems, but with both her mother and Joe away she felt much more taxed to handle the throng in Morgan Manor. Because she was younger and alone, she felt men leered at her more. She was sure she had to fend off more indecent remarks, even open proposals than her mother did. Two men in particular stared at her so long she felt extremely uncomfortable, even afraid. Why couldn't King have stayed to help her?

He had told her to wait up for him. She did, but in a state of weariness she had seldom known. Several times she nodded off as she waited. When he returned close to three o'clock, she saw that he was vastly excited and extremely amorous. All she wanted in the world was to fall into her bed and sleep, but she forced herself to drink champagne with him and listen to his recounting of the marvelous hands of cards he'd held that night. When at last they went up to bed, she tried to give herself to him with enthusiasm, hoping he did not realize how very tired she was.

Lord James Charles Winslow, alias James Hackett, was also in a state of euphoria. He had worked out a foolproof plan to eliminate the Irish wench once and for all. She would not escape him this time. He would make her pay and pay for what she had done to him. She would suffer as she made him suffer. He laughed with glee as he realized there simply was no way for her to avoid the fate he was preparing for her. Everything had come full circle. His patience was about to be rewarded, and there was no Morgan, no sea captain to protect her this time. Glenna O'Reilly, the witch of the universe, would get her just deserts.

To add to his euphoria, Lila told him she had come up with a mark, a rich fool named Kingston. He liked to play poker, thought he was good, but wasn't. With Lila's help, they'd take him. Even as he lost the first two nights, Winslow cackled with glee. Not only was he going to rid himself of the Irish wench, he was going to end up richer than ever. This Kingston, so suave, so confident, was a lamb for the slaughter, just like Glenna O'Reilly.

62

"Ducky" Duckworth was already experiencing the joys of sudden wealth. After finding gold—he almost immediately began to think of it as *his* gold, dug out of the ground by himself rather than stolen—he made his way to the camp at Rich Ba. Early that morning he used the first of it to buy a horse, then he rode hard all day through Otoville, Marysville, arriving at Sacramento less than twenty-four hours after his "lucky strike." He was motivated to put as much distance between himself and Morgan as possible, but also to reach civilization as soon as he could.

He didn't even stop to weigh the gold he had found,

but all during his flight southward along the banks of the Feather River, he told himself it was a lot. "I'm rich, I'm rich," he said, sometimes aloud, until the words matched the rhythm of the horse's hoofs.

He checked into a hotel in Sacramento. After languishing in a hot bath and relishing every second of it, he examined his strike. He had no scale, but the amount of it staggered him. Joyfully, he let the shiny golden dust sift through his fingers. Heaven on earth, that's what it was. Tenderly he picked up the nuggets, some almost a half inch across, and fragile pieces of gold leaf, all scraped by Andrew from the crevices of the rocks beside the underground spring. God, there must be forty thousand dollars here, maybe fifty or sixty. What a find!

The shiny blue stone—a sapphire he guessed—set with tiny diamonds, both puzzled and thrilled him. What was a gem like this doing in a bag of gold dust? But who cared where it came from? What a bonus. He let out another whoop of pure joy.

He put the gold back into the pouches and hid the swag in his saddle bags, then he went out, ate the biggest steak he could find—the hell with the prices—and got roaring drunk. The next day he slept it off, then treated himself to a shave and haircut, and bought the best suit of clothes he could find in Sacramento. He would do better in San Francisco—hell, New York, London and Paris—a helluva lot better than shoveling dirt into a rocker beside that goddamned stream. If old Otis Pringle could see him now. He sure as hell would want his quick-assed daughter to marry him. Well, he'd do a lot better than Mollie Pringle. Indeed, he would—starting tonight.

That evening he prowled the saloons of Sacramento, enjoying the best drink he could find while keeping his eye open for the best looking woman. That turned out to be a disappointment, for there were damn few women at all in the town of ten thousand and none of them had much appeal to a suddenly wealthy young man determined to enjoy the finer things of life. He had just about made up his mind to forego a woman till he got to San Francisco and instead have a go at a little poker, when in the Placer Saloon he saw a real woman. She had some years on her, but the black, shining hair, blue eyes and rising bodice suggested there was still plenty of life in her. Best, she had class. He could tell from her clothes, the way she held herself and acted. That was the kind of woman he had in mind. Too bad she wasn't a little younger, but one can't have everything.

He watched her for a bit. She was sitting at a table with a nigger and a young dude. Probably her son. No sign of papa. He waited awhile for her to be alone. He was suddenly encouraged when the young fellow got up and came over to the bar. Duckworth hesitated a moment, then muttered, "What to lose?" As casually as he could, he went up to Ned Kingston.

"Hi, there. Buy you a drink?"

Ned turned toward the voice, seeing a handsome blond fellow not much older than himself. He wore an obviously new suit. "Thanks, but I'm with a party," he said.

"I noticed. She's a fine looking woman. You don't see a real lady like her in these parts too often."

Ned looked at him intently. He saw that the guy was half drunk and probably didn't know what he was doing. He decided to avoid any trouble. "Yes. I'll tell her you said so."

"Well, I do appreciate that, my friend. Maybe I could tell her myself."

Ned had been fending off advances toward Glenna all day. "No, I don't think so. We gotta be going."

"Wel-l, that's too bad. Like to buy you and the lady a drink. What brings you to these parts?" He smiled. "Going to pan for gold?"

"No. Mrs. Morgan is looking for her son. Maybe you know him. Name's Andrew Morgan."

The name struck Duckworth like a blow to his belly.

He sucked in his breath. Off guard, unable to think, he said, "Morgan. Seems to me like I heard that name." Suddenly, he felt a hand on his arm, propelling him toward the table where the woman sat.

Glenna had not wanted to spend a full day in Sacramento. They had arrived in the town late the previous afternoon. That evening they had made the rounds of saloons inquiring about Andrew. She had found it most difficult to enter most of the places, but had made herself do it. Anything that might help find Andrew.

They spent the night in a hotel and that day had visited the newspaper office, banks, livery stable and merchants, trying in vain to find someone who had heard of Andrew. By mid-afternoon, she had wanted to push on toward Marysville, but reluctantly gave in to Ned's insistence it wasn't safe. They should stay another night in Sacramento, then start out early in the morning. Rather than waste the evening, they had returned to some of the saloons in hopes of learning some scrap of information about Andrew. But there was nothing to learn. It took all her willpower to hold herself together. Ned was right. If she panicked, she would be no help to anyone. But so much time was going by so fast. She had to find Andrew before it was too late. Her persistent feeling that Andrew was in danger had not diminished, but grown.

"Mrs. Morgan, this guy says he knows Andrew."

She heard the excitement in Ned's voice, then looked at the young, blond man with him. He seemed ill-at-ease, even worried. She saw him smile nervously.

"I didn't say I knew him. I said maybe I heard the name."

"Good God, man, tell us where you heard it."

Glenna saw him hesitating. He seemed terribly unsure of himself, almost afraid. Despite her agitation at this first shred of hope, she instinctively reached out to calm the blond man. Smiling, she said, "Please do sit down, Mr. . . ."

"Duckworth, ma'm. Silas Duckworth. My friends call me Ducky." He smiled nervously.

Glenna motioned to a seat which he took. "Mr. Duckworth, my name is Glenna Morgan. My son Andrew is somewhere in these gold fields. I'm trying to find him. Will you help me if you can?"

Ducky felt trapped. What had possessed him to even talk to this guy, let alone mention that he knew Morgan? "I don't know, ma'm. You hear lots of names."

She saw Ned opening his mouth to speak. Both the expression in her eyes and the motion of her hand told him to be silent. Turning to Duckworth, she said, "I'm sure that's so. Tell me, Mr. Duckworth, where were you when you thought you might have heard the name?" She saw his nervousness and hesitation. Despite the pounding of her own heart, she tried to smile sweetly and reassuringly to him. "Surely you know where you were, Mr. Duckworth."

"Oh sure, I know that. I struck rich up off the Butte River near a camp called Rich Ba."

"Where is this Rich Ba, exactly?"

"Rich Ba? Oh, It's north of here."

"How far?"

"Oh, a good day's ride north of here. But I wouldn't bother if I were you, ma'm. It's no place for a lady like you. Besides, the more I think of it, the more I'm sure I never heard the name Morgan before tonight." He stood up. "In fact, I'm positive of it. Now, if you'll excuse me, ma'm, I really gotta be going."

"Of course, Mr. Duckworth, and thank you."

"Don't thank me, ma'm. I tell you I'm sure I never heard of your son."

As quickly as he could, he left the table, the saloon, the hotel and even Sacramento.

It was all Glenna could do to wait for dawn. She tried to tell herself that it was so tenuous a lead that she shouldn't get her hopes up, but she couldn't help it. At last there was something to go on, some place to look.

They rode hard all the next day, stopping only to rest and feed the horses. It was late afternoon when they arrived at Rich Ba, a squalid camp of tents and makeshift shacks. Glenna had no trouble attracting attention, so long had it been since any woman, let alone one who looked like her, had appeared there. As soon as she alighted from the carriage, scraggly men ran up to her to stare, many of them speechless with admiration.

"Do any of you know a young man named Andrew Morgan," she said. "He's my son. I must find him." She stared at the unwashed, unshaven figures, most pathetically thin, all staring at her, their mouths open. "Please. Do any of you know Andrew Morgan. I heard he was here."

Finally a voice said, "Ma'm, you is the purtiest woman I ever did see."

Glenna sighed to mask her exasperation. "Thank you, but my son. I'm trying to find him. His name is Andrew Morgan."

She received many compliments, but no word of Andrew.

"I'll tell you what, ma'm. If you just stand there and this Morgan fellow is hereabouts, somebody'll come who's seen him."

"But I can't just stand here being stared at. I've got to find my son. Please, can't someone help me?"

Ned again sensed her mounting panic. "There's a saloon over here, Mrs. Morgan. Perhaps if we waited there."

As promised, the news of her arrival traveled fast, and the shack of a saloon soon became crowded with miners who came just to stare at her. Over and over she asked if anyone knew her son. For a long time no one did. Then, after nightfall, a voice said, "Yes, I know Andrew Morgan—only he ain't here."

She leaped to her feet and turned to the voice. She saw a tall, extremely lanky man with a heavy brown beard and pale blue eyes. "You know Andrew?" She almost screamed the words.

"Sure, I knew a guy named Morgan. He had a dig across the creek. But he ain't there now."

"Where is he?" Hysteria was creeping into Glenna's voice.

"I don't know where he is, ma'm. He left—same day as Duckworth."

"Duckworth!" Ned and Glenna said the name at the same time. Glenna's voice prevailed. "He's the man who said he thought he knew him."

"He knew Morgan all right. None of us knew him well. He wasn't too friendly. Kept to hisself mostly. But that was his name—Morgan."

Ned saw Glenna shaking and took her arm to steady her. "Can you take us to where Morgan lived?"

"Sure, I can take you there. Be glad for the ride."

Glenna couldn't stop trembling during the ride through the dark. It seemed to go on interminably, but actually it wasn't much more than a half hour till the carriage stopped. She could see nothing in the darkness, but heard the sounds of a running stream nearby.

"His shack is just up the slope there, ma'm. I'll take the lantern and show you the way."

Glenna was not even able to murmur thanks. All she could think of was Andrew. She could not even form a coherent thought about him. She felt herself helped down from the carriage and a light being held for her to find her way upward over rough ground. "Go on, hurry," she said. "I'm coming."

At last she could see the outline of a shack, then saw it under the light of the lantern. She heard the creak of a door opening. "Here you is, ma'm. Morgan lived here."

She was now able to murmur her thanks as the door was held open for her. She entered, feeling boards under her feet. "The light. Let me have the light," she said. When it was in her hand and she held it aloft, she saw nothing in the small space except an overturned table and chair. She took a step further inside and raised the lantern. There in the corner on a bed of straw, covered with blackened blood lay a figure. "My God, my God, it's Andrew," she screamed.

She rushed to him, saying his name over and over. But there was no response. "He's dead. Oh, my God, he's dead."

Ned pushed her aside and bent over Andrew. He put his ear to his chest. "No, he's still alive—but barely." Suddenly very calm, he turned to the miner who had brought them there. "Is there a doctor around here?"

"There's a barber in Rich Ba. He does some healin'."

"Take the carriage and get him. We'll make it worth your while."

63

Moira could think of several reasons why she wanted to see her mother. She was extremely worried about where she was, if she was all right and if she'd found Andrew. Moira was unable to imagine her elegant mother out in the grubby gold fields going from one squalid camp to another inquiring for Andrew. She'd never find him. And how long would she continue to search? Maybe Ned would talk some sense into her mother as he had once to her. Lord, she wished she hadn't gone. Telling herself she was being silly and childish did nothing to alter the wish.

Operating this whole place, virtually alone was getting to her. Morgan Manor was falling down around her ears, and she felt powerless to prevent it. Last night there had been two fights, one of them involving a pair of hostesses quarreling over a man. She was sure at least one and maybe even two of the bartenders were shortchanging the house. This sort of thing hadn't happened when her mother was here. Moira was upset both that the problems were occurring and that she was unable to cope with them.

More than anything, though, she wanted to talk to her mother about King. Her relationship with him was deteriorating and she seemed powerless to stop that, too. She was angry with him because he wasn't helping her. He kept saying he would, but he didn't. Actually, he was doing less to run the place than when her mother had been here. He was going off before midnight every night and leaving the gambling operation to run itself, and she knew absolutely nothing about gambling. When he was there, she felt a measure of protection. With him gone, she felt at the mercy of men trying to get her to go upstairs with them. She had fended off trouble so far, but she found it exhausting to laugh, flirtatiously turn off really offensive proposals, and somehow maintain both her own safety and the good will of the clientele. Yet, she knew men were looking at her, sometimes even touching her in ways that had not occurred with her mother. Glenna had a way of making people treat her like a lady which Moira knew she did not possess.

Last night, as her problems mounted, she had become increasingly angry at King. Why wasn't he staying there to help her? Couldn't his big deal wait a few days? What sort of a man was he? At closing time, she had been so exhausted she had gone up to bed. She couldn't wait for him to decide to return. And in her anger she had locked her door. He was leaving her to fend for herself all day, then he could fend for himself at night. She didn't want to be touched. She had pretended passion the last couple of nights, so tired she couldn't arouse any real feelings. He had no right to come back from God knows where and then demand that his "needs" be met. Had he no consideration for her?

These thoughts had filled her mind as she lay in bed behind the locked door. Then, when she had least expected it, sleep had come to her, and she had slept soundly, not even hearing him try the door. Now, having her tea, she faced a new day as proprietress of Morgan Manor. God, how she hated the place. If King expected her to run a dance hall after they were married, he had another think coming. She couldn't imagine doing this for the rest of her life. King. Where was he? Where had he gone for the night? Was he angry with her? She tried to tell herself she had behaved badly, like a child. She shouldn't have locked him out. She should have been more understanding of him. After all, he said he was working on their future. But the simple fact was that these thoughts carried no particular conviction. She was still angry with him, grossly disappointed in him for neglecting her. It came as a surprise to her to realize she really didn't care very much how King felt toward her.

"Miss Moira, I have a suggestion."

"Good morning, Jessie." She smiled. "If there's anything I need today it's a good suggestion."

"Why don't we close for a few days till your mama returns?"

"Close?"

"Yes. This place is too much for you—me, too. If Miss Glenna and Joe were here—but they aren't. Miss Glenna won't mind if we close. She'll understand. She wouldn't want to see you so tired and upset."

"No, Jessie, I'm all right."

"No you're not, Miss Moira. I've known you since

you were a baby. You're not all right. You're tired, beside yourself with worry. The responsibility is—"

"No, Jessie. I'm fine. Let's not talk about closing."

Jessie couldn't resist, nor did she try very hard. "If only Mr. King would help you more."

Moira looked at her, trying to read the expression in her face. "And that's another subject I don't want to talk about. Shall we get started on the cash box?"

Moira was busy all day, but not too busy to notice that King never showed up. This told her more clearly than any words just how annoyed he was with her. He was a man who didn't like to be crossed, especially by a woman. Moira did not consider herself a domineering person. She was perfectly willing to let a man run things, but what was King doing? He was hardly running Morgan Manor. When he had not shown up by early evening, she knew she would have to make some effort to pacify him. After all, he was the man she was going to marry. She had been childish, really too cruel to him. She began to anticipate his coming, even his anger. When he didn't show up by nightfall, her anticipation began to turn to worry.

She needn't have. King was doing quite well. He had spent the previous evening in the most remarkable poker game. Lila had said Hackett was crazy and King had come to believe it. There was a sort of demented look about those strange gray eyes. He seemed distracted, as though he wasn't there, indeed, like he were off somewhere else in his mind. He certainly played poker like he wasn't present. King liked poker. He liked the concentration, the battle of wits, the risk and gamble. There was none of it with Hackett. He was wild in his betting, sticking with hands that any fool would have known couldn't win. He made stupid bets and seemed unconcerned by his losses. King knew he would have become bored with the game and dropped out, except that he was winning so much money.

He said as much to Lila midway through the game

when Hackett left for a half hour or so. "He's crazy. I've never seen a man lose like this." He laughed. "Almost makes me feel guilty."

"Well, don't. Just keep winning."

"It isn't hard." He swallowed a brandy and refilled his glass. "Where's he gone now? To get more money to lose."

"There are a couple of guys to see him."

"What's that about?"

"I wouldn't know and I don't care. He's been all excited about something lately, some crazy project he's got cooking. I don't know what it is. All I care about is getting as much money out of him as I can. Then I'm leaving." She draped her arms around his neck. "It is sort of fun to get rich, isn't it?"

"Sure. I just wish it was a better game."

"You'll have plenty of better games. And speaking of better—what are you doing tonight, afterwards?"

He kissed her quickly, marveling at what really soft lips she had. "I think your boss better not find us this way, my dear," he said and pulled her arms away.

As the game wore on, King did indeed forget his dissatisfactions with the quality of the poker in his enjoyment of winning. He had no idea how much money Hackett had, but he sure was losing a lot of it.

When King left, he had been greatly tempted by Lila's obvious desire for him to spend the night. But his concern for the feelings of his fiancée won out. When he returned to Morgan Manor and found Moira's door locked, he was only slightly annoyed. So she was playing goody-goody. Let her. She hadn't been worth a damn the last couple nights anyhow. Abruptly he returned to Lila. Again he marveled at the softness of her lips, the catlike movements of her lovemaking. He had never seen her so passionate. It had to be all that money, which together they counted between bouts in bed. It was near dawn when he finally fell asleep beside her. He slept late the next day, then went to his own room for a bath and change. He studiously avoided going to Morgan Manor. That little miss should be taught a lesson.

"Ducky" Duckworth would never have gone to Morgan Manor had he not been drunk. Just the name of the place would have kept him away, so unnerved had he been by the encounter with Glenna in Sacramento. But his arrival in San Francisco was grounds for a celebration, and in his new clothes he made the rounds of saloons, buying drinks like a drunken miner, which is exactly what he was by the time he arrived in Morgan Manor. He didn't even notice the name of the place.

Ducky's thought processes had been reduced to a single notion. He was going to sleep with the most beautiful woman in San Francisco. Indeed, he was well along in his search. He had almost chosen a blonde in the Gold Nugget and certainly had her in mind to go back to when he saw Moira. Her flaming hair, the pink mounds rising above her dress made his decision for him. This was the most gorgeous girl he had ever seen.

He stood the bar to a drink, including her, and told the bartender he wanted to speak to her. When she came over, he was even more convinced he had made the right choice. Such gorgeous eyes and that mouth, the pink skin. God, she had to be something in bed.

"Struck it rich, did you?"

He was weaving a bit as he pulled himself to his full height beside her, and his smile was a bit crooked, but he was aware of neither. "Silas Duckworth's the name, miss, but my friends call me Ducky. You're my friend, aren't you?" A slight belch punctuated his words.

"Everyone's a friend here, Mr. Duckworth. Just enjoy yourself."

He reached out and grabbed her arm. "Hey, don't go."

"I'm sorry I must."

"I didn't tell you about my strike. Found the mother lode, I did. I got more gold than you ever saw."

"Really?" That single word reflected Moira's total disinterest.

"You don't believe me, do you? It's the truth. I got so much gold I haven't had time to count it all."

"That's wonderful. You spend as much of it here as you want. Now I must—"

"What's the hurry? I wanna buy you a drink. Wanna buy everybody a drink." He signaled to the bartender with a sweeping motion to indicate the whole bar. "You think I haven't got gold? Well, I do. I'll show you." With only minimal difficulty, he reached inside his coat and extracted a significant pouch of gold dust, dumping it on the counter. "That enough?"

"I'm sure it's more than enough."

He spread out the mound of dust with his hand. "An' I got plenty more where this come from."

It was precisely situations like this which Moira found so difficult. Ordinarily, she would have had nothing to do with such a drunken lout. At Aurial she had never even seen anyone who acted like this. Now they were a nightly occurrence. And they were customers. She had to smile at them and encourage them to spend their money. The problem was to be nice to them, yet get away from them. Somehow she didn't feel she handled it as well as her mother. If King thought she was going to do this for the rest of her life . . .

She smiled her best and tried again to get away. "I'm happy you found gold, Mr. Duckworth. Now you just have a good time."

"You're the purtiest gal I ever saw."

Those words were as predictable to Moira as his hiccup which accompanied them.

"Never did see hair as red as yours. Why it's like fire."

"Thank you, Mr. Duckworth. Now you—"

"How about you and me goin' somewhere and havin' a real good time."

She told herself she ought to be getting used to it. "There's a good time to be had here. Now you just enjoy yourself."

She saw him look down at her decolletage, then back into her eyes, leering. "You know what kind of time I mean. And I'm just the guy to show you the best time you ever had."

"I'm sure of it, Mr. Duckworth." She made an encompassing gesture. "But I've all these customers. I really must attend to them."

"I'm not good enough for you, is that it?"

Moira sighed. Why did it have to be this way? "Of course you are, Mr. Duckworth. It's just that—"

"I got lots of gold, tons of it." He picked up a pinch of dust from the bar and dropped it down the crevice between her breasts.

"Really, Mr. Duckworth, I—"

He raised both hands, palms toward her in a gesture of mock apology. "You're right. Gold ain't good enough for you. I got something better." He reached into his vest pocket. "Something just perfect for a lady like you."

Moira saw the large sapphire surrounded by diamonds and gasped, for she recognized it instantly. Her mother had worn it dozens of times. "Where'd you *get* that?"

Duckworth misunderstood her surprise as delight. "You like, eh?"

Moira knew the gem was her mother's and could only have come from Andrew. Almost screaming she said, "Where did you get that sapphire?" She reached for it.

He closed his hand over it and chuckled. "It don't matter where I got it. What matters is how *you* can get it."

Moira was on the verge of screaming that it was her mother's and he had stolen it from Andrew, when she was able to check herself. This man had to know something about Andrew. He had seen him. He had either bought or stolen the stone from her brother. She had to find out.

Forcing back her excitement, she smiled flirtatiously. "Let me see that again." When his hand opened, she bent closer to look carefully at the stone. There was no doubt it was her mother's sapphire. It had been the center stone of the necklace father had given her. It had been her greatest pride. "That sure is beautiful. Aren't you going to tell me where you got it?"

"There's only one way you'll find out about this."

Moira's mind raced. She had to find out where he got the stone. "Did you find it? Did somebody give it to you?"

He laughed. "Oh no, you're not gonna find out that way. You just come with me and I'll tell you all about it."

Moira saw his leering face and was repulsed by it. But she had to find out about Andrew. She forced a smile. "I'd love to, Mr. Duckworth. I'd love to find out all about you. You're so—so fascinating. But I can't now. I'm just a poor working girl."

"Nah, I'll give you more than you'll earn here."

"Oh, I'm sure of that, Mr. Duckworth, but—"

"Ducky."

"Yes, I forgot, Ducky, but I'm in charge here tonight. I can't get away now. You do understand."

"Later?"

She smiled as she had seen the other girls in Morgan Manor do dozens of times. "Of course. Why don't I come to your place?"

"I'll hang around."

"Whatever you say. But just in case anything goes wrong, where can I find you?" She smiled. "I have to leave the word where I'm spending the night." She saw his delighted reaction to the suggestion.

"Oh, sure, the Mission Hotel."

"The Mission. That's very nice." Again she smiled and patted the hand containing the sapphire. "Now you just hold on to that while I attend to a few things."

Moira was so excited she had difficulty telling Jessie a coherent story. Her first efforts produced only a stream of questions from the housekeeper. "What are you talking about? What sapphire? Who's got it? What about Andrew?"

Moira tried to calm herself and try again. "All right.

There's a man at the bar. He's got a sapphire. I'm sure it was mother's. You remember, the center stone from the necklace?"

"Sure, I know the one you mean."

"This fellow has it."

"Where'd he get it?"

"That's just it, I don't know. He had to have gotten it from Andrew, which means he must have seen Andrew."

"Didn't you ask him?"

"Of course I asked—but he won't say. He won't say anything unless I sleep with him. I'm going over later to the Mission Hotel and—"

Jessie was aghast. "Oh no you're not! Over my dead body!"

"Don't be silly, Jessie. Of course I'm not going to bed with him. But I've got to find out."

"It's too dangerous. I won't let you."

"He's so drunk now he can hardly stand up. A couple more drinks and he'll tell me anything."

"Then talk to him here. I won't let you go to no hotel, Miss Moira. I mean it."

She smiled at her. "Perhaps you're right. Maybe I can find out here."

Moira went back to Duckworth and tried her best, encouraging him to drink more and more. It didn't work. Duckworth had a solitary idea, get her in bed. He understood her curiosity about the sapphire was the way to do it.

Moira was also frustrated in her efforts to get him to pass out from whiskey. He seemed to have an unlimited capacity to remain on his feet and at least somewhat coherent. As the night wore on, she grew vehemently determined to get the gem and find out about Andrew. She would do whatever was required and told Jessie as much. "If only King were here. He could help me."

"That man wouldn't help his mother cross the street. Now you listen to me, Miss Moira. You're not going to that hotel with that man. We know where he is and we'll find out about him tomorrow."

Moira knew she was right. She would not be able to handle Duckworth alone. If only King were there. He could go with her. He could force this drunken miner to tell what he knew about Andrew. In vain she hoped to see King enter. Where was he?

As two o'clock came and passed and Duckworth became more impatient for her to leave with him, plans raced through Moira's mind. Maybe she could take one of Joe's bouncers with her. When she was alone in the hotel room with Duckworth, he could break in, save her. No, that would never work. Why wasn't King here? She just had to find out about Andrew.

Thus, Moira was in a state of high agitation when a short man with rust colored hair whom she had seen in the bar on earlier nights came up to her and handed her a note.

The note was the brainstorm of Ollie Spooner. When he and Little Red Dickson contracted with Hackett to abduct the Morgan girl and bring her to him, Spooner figured it would be the easiest five hundred dollars he ever made. The old geezer was obviously looney, but what the hell, he couldn't be blamed for wanting the Morgan girl. He wanted her himself. Indeed, he was sorely tempted to have a little fun with her first. But the thought of possibly losing the two fifty he would get upon delivering the girl forced him to embrace at least a little of his virtue and abandon his lust.

It had seemed so easy when he and Little Red contracted for the job. Just abduct the girl off the street. Trouble was she never went out after dark. She stayed in the dance hall every night and then went up to bed, usually with that gambler, Kingston. What had seemed so easy had become difficult and Hackett was getting impatient and mad. Just that evening, he and Red had gone to see him and promised faithfully to bring the girl that night. Christ, the old geezer had been so happy. Well, he couldn't be blamed for that.

Spooner had just about concluded the only thing to do was to break into the place after closing and steal her out of her bed, when his big idea came to him. He heard her asking if anyone had seen Kingston. Spooner laughed. He'd help her find him. He sure would. Smiling at his own cleverness, he borrowed a pen and paper from the barkeep. Standing at the end of the bar in Morgan Manor, he wrote out the note which Little Red delivered to Moira shortly after two-thirty.

I'SE AT THE GOLD NUGGET. NEED HELP. COME QUICK. KINGSTON

If Moira had been less agitated or had taken time to show the note to Jessie, she would have seen the poor spelling, the use of "Kingston" rather than "King," and known the note was fraudulent. But in her anxiety, she merely said, "Can you take me to him?" Little Red said he sure could.

Grabbing a scarf, she ran outside after the little man with red hair. She had gone halfway through the next block when she felt a strong arm grab her from behind and sweep her into an alley. She wanted to scream, but the hand clasped over her mouth prevented it.

64

The thought kept occurring to Glenna that after all the worrying and searching, it wasn't fair to find Andrew and have him die. But each time the thought occurred, she forced it aside, praying to the Blessed Virgin to save her son. While Andrew hovered on the edge of death was not the time to argue with God and challenge His fairness.

When the "doctor" had come, he had done little

more than shrug and say there was nothing he could do. "I don't know how he's stayed alive this long." But Glenna was determined. She bent all her energies to maintaining the spark of life in Andrew. She bathed him, the first time since he'd been a baby, and cleaned and dressed his wounds. She had Joe cut fresh pine boughs to make a new bed for him. Then she cleaned the whole cabin and opened it up to try to disinfect it.

Through it all, she prayed constantly and with a fervor she felt she had never known. "Mother of God, don't let him die. He's so young. He's suffered so much. He needs his chance for life. Please, oh Blessed Mother, I'll do anything you ask." Over and over she would say, "As a mother, you must know how I feel. Please save our son."

Besides prayer, there was little Glenna could do for Andrew. She was appalled at his condition. He seemed little more than skin and bones and so filthy she could not believe it. She knew that if he were not so wasted physically, he might have some chance against his terrible wounds. But all he could do was hold on to some flicker of life. She sent Joe back into Rich Ba to buy what food he could find. She made some broth and tried to force it down the throat of the unconscious Andrew, but it seemed to do no good. If only she had found him sooner.

"He'll live, won't he Joe?"

"Yes, Missy. He'll live. Be as good as new soon."

But both of them knew, however unwilling they were to admit it, that Andrew's condition was hopeless. His bleeding had mostly stopped, but he had lost too much blood already. The wounds did not look well. There was an angry redness spreading from them and a sickening odor which could only mean that infection had set in. Tiny bubbles and a hissing sound came from the wound in his chest, indicating a lung had been punctured. Still, Glenna could do little more than make him as comfortable as possible, wait, hope and pray.

It was in the evening of the second day, nearly twenty-four hours after she found him that Andrew regained consciousness. She had raised his head to try to spoon some broth into him, when he suddenly coughed and opened his eyes. She saw the vacant expression in them and feared for a moment he was dead. Then she heard him rasp, nearly inaudibly, "Mother?"

"Yes, yes, Andrew. It's mother." Quickly, she put down the bowl and spoon and kissed his face. "Oh, Andrew, Andrew, I'm so glad I found you." She saw a thin smile on his face and realized he was trying to say something.

Bending her ear near his mouth, she heard, "Is it really you? I'm not dreaming?"

"No, no. I'm here Andrew. You're going to get well. I'll see that you get well."

He closed his eyes and she thought he had lapsed into unconsciousness again. Then she felt a movement under the blanket. He was trying to touch her. Quickly she reached under and pulled out his hand and held it in both of hers. "I'm here, darling. I won't leave. You just rest and get well."

He remained immobile for several moments, eyes closed, a tiny smile on his lips that revealed his inner happiness. When he opened his eyes, however, it was with a troubled look. His voice a little stronger, he said, "I'm sorry. I—"

"It wasn't your fault, Andrew. You were tricked by Lord Winslow. He was trying to get at me, and he tricked you into that poker game. It wasn't your fault. You're not to blame. You must never think you were."

He seemed to be trying to say something, but it took more strength than he had. "Tell me . . . everything."

And Glenna did. She told of leaving Aurial, hiding in Baltimore, Captain Mac and his clipper ship, coming to California to find him, Morgan Manor. "Then I had a dream. I woke up screaming in the night. I had a terrible pain in my chest and I just knew you'd been hurt. I came here to find you. Oh, Andrew, you must get well. you must."

"Moira?"

And Glenna told him about Moïra, too, her coming overland to find him, her arrival in San Francisco, their reunion. "Oh, she's so beautiful, Andrew, so lovely, so strong. I love her so much. And I love you so much, Andrew. I was such a terrible mother, but now I want—"

"No, Mother, no. Moïra . . . here?"

"She's coming, Andrew. She'll be here soon."

That seemed to please him. She saw the smile on his face and felt his grip tighten on her hand. She closed his eyelids with her hand. "Sleep, Andrew. You need rest to get well."

But he was not finished. "I found . . . gold . . . lots of gold. Enough for . . . Aurial . . . buy back . . ."

"It doesn't matter, Andrew. All that matters is for you—"

"Duckworth came . . . stole . . . stabbed . . ."

"Yes, yes. It doesn't matter. Just rest, get well, darling."

She felt his grip tighten on her hands. Oh, Mother of God, watch over him, help him get well.

She continued to hold his hand and pray for him, her appeals for the Virgin's help coming incessantly and with her greatest fervor. She had no idea how long she prayed, kneeling beside Andrew, gripping his hand and looking at his sleeping face. Then she felt his grip tighten on her hand. His eyes opened and he looked at her, a beautiful smile on his face.

His eyes held her several moments, soft, tender, a strange expression of happiness in them. His voice was surprisingly clear as he said his final words, "I love you, Mother. And I'll be good."

Her own heart and breath stopped and she squeezed his hand till her knuckles ached from the effort. But there was no way to hold the life in him. Tears scalding her eyes, she sobbed, "And I love you, my son." But she knew he could not hear her.

Moïra was relieved to at last have the filthy sack

removed from her head. She knew she had been carried, slung over someone's back for only a few minutes. She also knew she had been taken into a building and carried up some stairs. But when the sack came off and her eyes had adjusted to the candlelight, she didn't know where she was. It seemed to be a small room, devoid of any kind of furnishing. Her head pounding with rage and fear, she saw the two men who had abducted her. The one was the small redhaired man who had brought her the note. The other, taller with a full brown beard, was the one who must have carried her. She remembered seeing him in the bar the last couple of nights, but didn't know his name. What did they want with her?

"Are we supposed to leave her gagged?"

The taller one answered. "He didn't say nothin' 'bout a gag."

"What if she screams."

With that Moira did try to scream, but managed to produce only sharp squealing sounds.

"Maybe we ought to leave it on, Ollie."

"Yeah, if he wants to hear her scream, he can do it hisself."

She looked at them in horror. Why were they doing this? Who were they?

The shorter one seemed nervous and in a hurry to leave. "I don't like any of this, Ollie. Let's get our money and go."

"Wait. He said she was to have her hands tied behind her and—"

She saw the sudden leer in his eyes.

"—and no clothes on. That oughta be fun."

As he moved toward her, grinning, she tried to move away from him, squealing her protests. But she was soon trapped in the corner. In terror she saw him raise both his hands, reach out to her and grab the front of her dress. In one quick motion he ripped the gown off of her, then her undergarments.

"Lordamighty, ain't she somethin'?"

Both men stared at her nakedness, mouths open in wonder and lust. "I can sure see why he wants her."

"She sure is a ripe'n."

"Yeah. You don't suppose . . ."

She saw them hesitate, staring at her body. Cringing, she saw the big one called Ollie make a move toward her.

Little Red held him back. "Better not, Ollie. Let's go."

"But what's he want with one like this? She's a beaut. Too good fer the likes o' him."

Little Red was insistent. "That's his business, Ollie. Let's get our money and go."

With relief, she saw Ollie be persuaded. He turned from her reluctantly, picked up the candle and went out of the room behind Little Red. As she was plunged into darkness, she heard a bolt rattle in the door.

God, where was she? What was going to happen to her? She was gagged, unable to scream for help. Her hands were tied behind her and she was absolutely naked. What was going on? Panic welled in her, but she fought against it. There had to be some way to get out. In the darkness, she slid along the wall to the door, turning her back, and tried to push against it. It wouldn't budge, as she'd known it wouldn't. There had been nothing in the room, she remembered. Nothing to break down the door. Nothing to defend herself with. Oh, God, what was going to happen to her? It was so dark in there. Not a shred of light. Then above her she saw stars shining. There must be a window high above her. Maybe she could. . . . But as the thought came to her, she knew it was hopeless. She had no way to reach the window, nothing to throw to break it.

In despair, she walked back across the room till she bumped into the wall, then slid down to a sitting position. Who were these men? Ollie was the big man and Little Red. What did they want with her? What had she ever done to them? Then she remembered. They talked about collecting money. They had been hired to bring her here. By whom? Why? What did anyone want with her? Then she remembered King. Was he part of it? Was it some kind of joke? Then she visualized the note from him. It hadn't been from King at all. She had been kidnapped. Someone wanted ransom. But why had she been undressed? What on earth was going to happen to her? Trembling with fear and chill, she sat there waiting for whatever was to happen. In time she fell fitfully asleep.

65

The frequent comments by Lila and King that Lord Winslow, alias James Hackett, was mad was the measure of the fact. Somewhere in a lifetime of hatred, his mind had slipped over the brink, and he was frequently unable to tell the real from the unreal. As he planned his final vengeance against Glenna O'Reilly, his perception of reality became almost entirely distorted. To him the girl waiting in the upstairs room was not Moira Morgan. He had never heard of Moira Morgan. To him the girl, now his captive, was her mother, Glenna O'Reilly. This was not a case of mistaken identity to him, but rather firm belief. His reaction to Spooner's report that the Morgan girl was upstairs was one of supreme elation. At last he had her and she would not escape this time.

In their eagerness for their money, Spooner and Dickson had entered the small room where Winslow was deep in his poker game with King. Certain of the news they brought, Winslow jumped up immediately and went with them to another room. He actually danced a jig of joy when Spooner said, "She's upstairs, Mr. Hackett, jus' like you said."

Winslow said nothing. The delight on his face spoke for him.

"You pay us now, Mr. Hackett?"

"Surely my good man. You've more than earned it." He reached into his pocket for a pouch of gold long since weighed for just this purpose. "You'll find more than enough there as a reward for your excellent work."

Spooner licked his lips as his fingers clasped the gold. "Thankee, Mr. Hackett. You're a real gentleman."

Winslow laughed, his excited anticipation turning it more into a cackle. "You don't know how true that is."

Spooner and Dickson wanted to leave, but felt the need to say something further to honor what had now become a social visit.

"I see you got yerself a poker game, Mr. Hackett."

"Yes, yes, a mark I'm about to fleece."

Spooner was surprised by that. "Not him, sir. He's a well-known gambler."

Winslow was stunned to speechlessness.

"Didn't you know, Mr. Hackett? He's the Morgan girl's man. Hangs out there all the time."

In his madness, Winslow may have lost the ability to recognize fact from fancy, but that did not in any way diminish his ability to plan. Of Spooner's words, he heard only "Morgan" and "man." Of course. He should have recognized him. The Irish wench had sent him over here to trick him out of his money. Well, he'd show her. His gray eyes took on a wild, shining look as his mind quickly concocted a plan. "I've another purse of equal size, gentlemen, if you will do another little task for me."

A few minutes later, Winslow returned to the poker game. With barely restrained excitement, he played a few more hands, losing heavily. Finally, unable to suppress a smile of triumph that was utterly incongruous to King and Lila, he said, "I fear you have cleaned me out, sir. If you'll accompany me upstairs to my safe, I'll pay you what I owe you."

"Yes. I think we should call it a night." King arose, put on his suit jacket and quickly stuffed his pockets with his considerable winnings. Turning to Winslow, he smiled his best. That was not hard to do, for he now knew he was a rich man. "If you'll lead the way, Mr. Hackett, I'll follow."

As he followed his victim up the stairs, King tried to imagine how much money he'd won. Many thousands of dollars, certainly. But he knew better than to gloat. "I'm sure you'll have better luck next time, Mr. Hackett."

"There will be no next time, Mr. Morgan. I fear you've—"

"Morgan? My name's Kingston, Bradford Kingston."

Winslow chuckled. "Oh, yes, I quite forgot." He stopped at the landing and opened a door for King to enter. "After you, sir."

Smiling, King stepped into the room. He registered the fact it looked like a man's bedroom just before the blow to the back of his head turned it black.

"All right, quickly men. Get him into that chair and tie him up."

The binding and gagging of the unconscious King took several minutes, while Winslow watched in unrestrained glee. It had never occurred to him that he would get the chance to repay Morgan, too. How sweet it would be. He even went to King and pulled up his head by the hair. Yes, it was Daniel Morgan all right. It was that mustache which had fooled him. Well, he wasn't going to be fooled anymore.

Winslow gave another purse to Spooner and Dickson and dispatched them out the back stairway. Then, still smiling, he returned downstairs.

"Where's King?" Lila asked. She had been waiting in barely suppressed excitement, anticipating a big celebration with King in her room.

"You mean your poker playing friend?" The words dripped with sarcasm, but Lila didn't catch it. "He left by the back stairs. Said he'd see you at his place." He saw the surprise in her face. "You do know where he lives, don't you?"

"Yes."

"Then why don't you go there now. There's nothing to do here tonight, and I'm sure he wants to see you."

Lila looked at the smiling face of her employer. She saw the wildness and craziness in it, but that had been an ordinary thing of late. All she really wanted was to get away from him forever. Now she could. "Yes, I believe I will."

He held her coat for her and hurried her out the door. Then he ran from room to room, rousting out the prostitutes and their clients, telling them the place was closing and to leave instantly. In less than a half hour, the whole house was empty and locked, leaving Lord James Charles Winslow alone with Glenna and Daniel Morgan and his vengeance. She would be first. Oh, how he'd waited for this moment. How long had it been? Didn't matter. His time had come at last. Giggling as he mounted the stairs, he said aloud, "All things come to those who sit and wait."

Moira was awakened by the rasp of the bolt against the door and in her fear instinctively pushed herself erect against the wall. In the darkness of the cell she looked around futilely for some way to escape and saw the first graying of the sky through the window high above her.

In horror she watched the door open slowly. She was blinded by the candle carried into the room. It was not until it had been set on the floor that she was able to see the figure who carried it. He was more apparition than man, and Moira gasped against her gag. He wore boots rising above his knees, a loin cloth, a short vest open at the front and long gloves, all of some kind of shiny brown leather. On his face was some kind of mask, also of leather, which made him resemble an animal. She heard a voice, high pitched with hysteria, say, "So we meet again, Mrs. Morgan. How nice to have you as my guest."

Moira could not take her eyes off his hideous mask and the short, thonged whip he held in his hand. She was rigid with fear, yet she was still able to wonder who this was and what he wanted.

"You will not escape me this time. You know that, don't you?"

She heard him giggle insanely, then saw his hand raised. Almost as she registered what he was doing she felt the hot streaks of fire across her shoulder and chest. Even as she looked to see the bloody welts rising on her skin, she both felt and saw new ones appear. Against her gag she screamed in pain, but produced only moans and squeals.

"How thoughtless of me. You're still gagged. And I do so like to hear you scream."

As he moved toward her, she shrank along the wall until she was trapped in the corner.

"As before, my dear, there is no escape." He reached up and snapped the gag from her face. "Now you may scream."

And she did, as loud as she could, both from terror and the pain he had inflicted on her body.

"You know, my dear, you are as lovely as ever. The years have been good to you. And the red hair is so becoming on you. You thought I wouldn't know you, didn't you? Well, you can't fool me." He accented the word "fool" by raking her savagely with the whip, creating streaks across her breast.

As a scream split her throat, she heard him laugh. "Yes, do scream. There is no one to hear you—except your dear friend Morgan. And he isn't going to save you this time. No one is going to save you."

Twice more he brought the whip across her flesh, tearing the skin of her hips and thighs. Moira tried to run from him, but was forced back into her corner by the flailing whip. "There's no escape," he shouted. "None for you—you Irish wench."

Screaming in agony such as she had never known, Moira sank to the floor and hid her burning breasts and midsection behind her knees.

"Oh, yes, you did that the last time."

She felt herself being pulled to her feet.

He ran his hand over her breasts, smearing the rising blood. "You always were so lovely. In a way, I hate to do this to you." Then he pinched her nipple hard. "But you lost your chance long ago to be nice to me. Remember? I did want you. But I'll not defile my body with an Irish whore like you."

Against her horror and pain, Moira managed to say, "Who are you?"

She saw and heard him laugh. "Don't tell me you don't remember? Maybe this will help?" And he whipped her repeatedly, savagely, driving her down behind her knees again. "You remember me all right."

Far back in her mind, Moira knew there was something to remember, but neither thought nor words could be formed, only screams as he brought the lash down upon her again and again. He grabbed her foot with one hand and flailed at her with the whip. In her struggles to twist away from him, the leather strips bit into her back. Blow after blow came down on her, ripping, searing, taking her breath away. In a moment she could struggle no more against the pain. She was only momentarily aware of lying there helpless before she passed out.

Consciousness came slowly to King, first as an awareness of terrible pain in his head, then that he was bound hand and foot to a chair. It took some moments for memory of where he was to come to him. He had been playing poker with Hackett. He had gone upstairs to get money. Someone must have knocked him on the head and tied him up.

He struggled against his bonds for a few moments,

but it was no use. What was going on? Then he remembered the money. He had been robbed. He looked down. No, his pockets still bulged with his poker winnings. Not robbed. Then what was going on? In the name of God, what was happening?

His head pounding, his hands and feet numb, he tried to think. But no reason, no explanation would come to him, except that Hackett must have done this. He was as mad as Lila said. What did the madman want with him? Then he began to hear screams, shrill shrieks of intense pain. Again and again the high pitched screams stabbed at his ears. A woman screaming. Who could it be? It sounded like Moira, but it couldn't be, just couldn't be.

66

Ned knew it was futile. Andrew could not live long, perhaps only hours, even minutes. Yet, when Glenna begged him to bring Moira to see her brother before he died, Ned did not argue. He rode as hard as he could, changing horses at every opportunity, and arrived at Morgan Manor just before dawn. He had been in the saddle for twenty hours and was so tired he could barely walk through the swinging doors.

He found Jessie in a state of agitated surprise, running toward him. "Oh, Mr. Ned, Mr. Ned," she said, "thank God you're here." She stopped just short of him. "Miss Glenna? She's—"

"Mrs. Morgan is fine, Joe, too. We found Andrew.

He's been stabbed. He's near death, if not dead already. Mrs. Morgan wants me to bring Moira as soon as possible." He was aware of Jessie trying to speak over his words, but he plunged on. "Where's Moira? Asleep?"

"Listen to me, Mr. Ned, please. I'm trying to tell you. Moira's not here."

Finally he understood. "What'd you mean? Where is she?"

"That's just it, I don't know."

Ned had discovered with Glenna the need to remain calm himself to help her cope with crises. He took the same stance now with Jessie. "All right, don't get excited. Tell me what happened." When she blurted out another stream of words, he said, "Slowly, Jessie, calmly."

Jessie knew he was right. "Yes," she said, "I'll try." She took a deep breath and forced herself to use it slowly. "Some man came into the bar tonight. He had a jewel, a big sapphire belonging to Miss Glenna, one of those Andrew stole—least that's what Miss Moira claimed. She was determined to get the jewel back from him and find out what he knew about Andrew. I tried to stop her, but I know she went off with him. I know something terrible has happened to her, Mr. Ned."

"What'd this fellow look like? Did you see him?"

"No, I didn't see him, Mr. Ned. I was in the kitchen all—"

"Did you learn a name? Where he was staying, anything?"

"Yes. He was staying at the Mission Hotel. She did say a name. Duck something, Duckman maybe."

"Duckworth?"

"Yes, that was it."

"Stay here. Don't go anywhere."

Ned was running at full speed by the time he hit the swinging doors. He raced three blocks to the Mission Hotel and shook the sleeping desk clerk awake. "Duckworth. What's his room?"

The frightened clerk blurted, "Two fourteen" and Ned mounted the stairs three at a time.

Duckworth had left the door unlocked in hopes Moira would show up to keep her "date" with him. Asleep in his clothes, even his boots, across the bed, he was still in a drunken stupor and no match for the enraged Ned Kingston.

Ned grabbed his shirtfront and pulled the sleeping figure off the bed. He recognized him as the blond man from Sacramento only a fraction of a second before he propelled his fist as hard as he could into his mouth. Ned felt the satisfying sensation of teeth breaking under his knuckles and saw a spurt of blood from Duckworth's mouth. "Where is she?" he shouted. "What have you done with her?"

The blow and the pain shocked Duckworth sober, but he was powerless to stop the second blow which crashed into his nose, breaking it. Duckworth fell back on to the bed, doubled up, his hands covering his mutilated face.

"Where is she?" Ned shrieked as he pulled Duckworth's hands from his face and cocked his fist to deliver another blow. But even in his rage, he knew there was no point in hitting the helpless man again. "What have you done with her?"

Spitting bits of teeth from his bleeding lips, Duckworth screamed, "Don't hit me. Don't hit me."

"Then where is she?"

"Who, for crissake? What are you talking about?"

"Moira. Moira Morgan."

Duckworth, while cringing, was still trying to examine the state of his broken teeth. "I don't know anybody by that name." When he saw the fist cocked again, he screamed, "Don't hit me. I don't know I tell you."

The blow fell, hard, cracking into his cheekbone under his left eye. Duckworth shrieked in pain and tried to cover his face against the bed.

"Don't lie, Duckworth. You were with her last night. You showed her the sapphire."

"Why didn't you say so?" He turned to face his abuser. "The redhead?"

"Yes, Moira Morgan. What have you done with her?"

"I don't know nothin' about her."

Again a blow fell. "Don't lie, Goddamn you. I'll kill you."

"Oh, God," Duckworth screamed. Then he began to cry, holding his head. "I tell you I don't. She was supposed to come with me. But she didn't." He looked up and saw the fist raised again. "Please, for God's sake, don't hit me. I'd tell you if I knew."

Suddenly Ned knew he was telling the truth. "She didn't come here with you?"

"No, dammit, I told you. I waited for her, but she left on her own. Some guy with red hair showed her a note and she ran out. I waited for her, but she never came back. I don't know nothin' about her."

Ned kept his fist ready, but knew there was no sense in hitting him. "Where's that jewel and the gold you stole from Andrew Morgan?" When Duckworth hesitated, Ned raised his fist more menacingly.

"All right, all right. There, in my saddle bags."

Ned jumped to the saddle bags and turned out the contents on the bed, then he stuffed the bags of gold back into the bags and threw them over his shoulder. "The jewel. Give it here."

Reluctantly, Duckworth reached into his vest pocket and tossed it to Ned.

His voice icy, Ned said, "You deserve to hang for murdering Andrew Morgan and you will one day. The only thing that's saving you now is I have to find his sister. You better run Duckworth—as far and as fast as you can."

Ned sped back to Jessie at Morgan Manor. "She's not there, Jessie. He hasn't seen her," he said panting.

"He's lying, Mr. Ned, I know he is."

"I believe that's what she said, but that's not where she went."

"Mr. Ned. She said as plain as day she was—"

"No, Jessie. Believe me. She's not there."

Jessie remained unconvinced. "How you know?"

"Because he knew I was ready to kill him." He held out his fist. "He won't eat any steak for a long time as it is."

Jessie saw his cut and bleeding knuckles. "Mr. Ned, your hand."

"It's all right." He remembered the saddle bags. "Here's Andrew's gold and Mrs. Morgan's jewel. Duckworth killed Andrew and robbed him." He dropped the heavy saddlebags on the table and plopped down in a chair, suddenly very tired. "Save this stuff for Mrs. Morgan."

"Yes, Mr. Ned, but what about Moira?"

"I wish I knew. Duckworth said something about a note. He was waiting for her, he said, when she got a note and ran out. He said something about a redhaired man giving her the note. Mean anything to you?"

"No, sir. I never saw no note. She never said anything to me."

"Think, Jessie. Who could have written her a note?"

The black woman went through the motions of trying to think, but it was clearly hopeless. "It's no help, Mr. Ned. Means nothing."

Ned suddenly knew he was more tired than he had ever been in his life. And, he was aware his frustration about Moira added to it. "There's got to be some explanation. We've got to think. Maybe if I had some coffee."

"I'll get some right away."

When she returned he was sitting at the table, a bottle of whiskey and a half emptied glass in front of him. With disapproval she said, "Is that gonna help us think about Miss Moira?"

"Probably not, but what is there to think of anyway."

"Try coffee." She poured him a cup from the pot and sat down opposite him.

Then he saw her sit upright in her chair and bristle as

she looked over his shoulder, past him toward the door. Her words came out as a hiss. "What you doin' here, you black hussy?"

Ned turned to see a young black woman in a fine pink dress standing in the doorway.

"You no account hussy. Don't you dare come around here."

"Jessie, please."

"Don't you please me. You're nothing but a common whore. You don't belong in a decent place."

Ned saw the mulatto woman with the strange gray skin advance toward them. "Call me anything you want, Jessie. I just want to know if you've seen King."

Jessie's anger and tongue were at floodtide. "He's another no good. I've not seen him and I hope I never do."

Ned shushed her. "Be quiet, Jessie." To Lila he said, "Where is my brother?"

"Are you his brother?"

"Yes, I'm his brother Ned. Where is he?"

"That's just it, I don't know. He was supposed to meet me at his room. I waited there and he never showed up. I thought he might be here with with Miss Morgan."

"He's a skunk, that's what he is. He never turned a finger—"

"Be quiet, Jessie. Moira's not here. Could she be with King?"

"I don't know. He might have come back here."

"That skunk hasn't set foot in here in over a day. Why he's—"

"What's your name, Miss?"

"Her name's Lila and she's a common whore, plain and simple."

"Jessie, please. Miss Lila—"

"She's not a Miss anybody. She's just plain Lila, a whore."

"Goddamn it Jessie, stop it. Miss Lila where did you last see King?"

"At my place. He was in a poker game with Winslow—I mean Hackett and—"

Jessie reacted as though struck. "God Almighty, did you say Winslow?"

"Yes. That's his real name, but he goes by Hackett now."

"Does he have gray eyes, like there's no color in them at all?"

"Yes."

Jessie let out a wail. Over and over she moaned, "Oh, my God, my God. . . ."

"What's the matter now, Jessie?"

"Oh, Mr. Ned, Winslow is the man sworn to kill Miss Glenna all these years. He's an awful man, Mr. Ned. He'd do anything to hurt Miss Glenna." Suddenly her eyes went wide and she slowly rose to her feet. "Oh God, I bet he took Miss Moira. I'll bet he did. He'd do anything to hurt Miss Glenna."

"Don't be silly. Why would he do that?"

"You don't know him, Mr. Ned. He'd do anything. He's the one who stole Aurial in the poker game from Mr. Andrew. He's—"

"That's right. He did that."

Ned looked at Lila. "But why would he take Moira? What'd she do to him?"

Lila's voice was calm but there was an edge of panic to it. "I don't know, but he's crazy, so crazy he'd do anything. He lost a lot of money to King. It was an honest game, but Winslow lost heavily. I think he's got King over there."

"Where?"

"C'mon, I'll show you."

It was long past sun up when Ned and Lila arrived at the brothel to find the door locked. No amount of knocking and rattling would raise anyone. "Winslow's in there. I know he is. He's always there."

"Only one way to find out." Ned rammed his shoulder into the door, but it wouldn't budge. He tried a second time.

"The window. Break the window."

In a moment, Ned found a large rock and hurled it through a window to the left of the door. With his pistol, he broke out the remains of the glass and climbed inside. As he darted toward the front door to let Lila inside, he both heard the report of a gun and the splatter of a bullet into the wall near his head. Ned dropped to the floor and rolled, turning, gun in hand, in time to see a figure dart from view up the staircase. Ned scampered to his feet and followed up the enclosed stairs. As he reached the top, he halted, hiding behind the wall. Whoever was up there still had a gun.

Slowly, he removed his hat and held it forward into the hallway. A shot punctured the brim. Ned jerked the hat back, transferred it to his left hand. Holding the hat above him to draw another shot, he dove into the hall, firing his own gun as he hit the floor. His shot missed, but he again saw a figure, half naked in some outlandish costume, dart away at the other end of the hall.

Ned climbed to his feet and ran after him. But the hallway was too long. By the time he arrived at the other end, Winslow had sped down the outside stairway and was running down the street. Ned fired a shot wildly after him but did not chase him. Instead, he turned back down the hall toward the voices he heard. The doorway was open to a room at the head of the stairway. Lila, who had climbed in the window, was leaning over King, clutching him, weeping.

She had untied his gag and was smothering his face with kisses.

"Dammit, Lila, untie my hands."

"Oh, yes, yes, thank God, you're all right."

Then King saw Ned. "Well, if it isn't little brother."

"Where's Moira?"

"I don't know, but I kept hearing a woman screaming."

It took less than a minute for Ned to find her. He broke down the door without even bothering to unbolt it. The huddled, bleeding form on the floor stopped him dead in his tracks. "My God," he said. "What has he done to her?"

When he touched her, she screamed. "It's me, Moira, Ned. Everything's all right now."

Her mouth was still open, her eyes wide with fright, but she did not scream again. "Ned?"

"Yes, darling, yes. What has he done to you?"

"Oh, Ned, is it really you?"

"Yes. I'm getting you out of here." He dashed out of the cell and across the hall, returning with a blanket.

As he covered her mutilated body and bent to pick her up, she said, "He whipped me, Ned. Oh God, how he whipped me."

He was standing erect with her now, her body cradled in his arms. "In God's name, why, Moira?"

"I don't know. I just don't know."

As he carried her out of the room and down the hallway toward the outside staircase, she looked back to see King standing there with Lila. They had their arms around each other.

67

As he carried her through the front door of Morgan Manor, Ned silenced Jessie's wails. "He whipped her. We got to get her to bed."

"Yes, Mr. Ned."

As she started to run up the stairs ahead of him, he barked, "I know where to take her. You bring hot water and clean towels."

As he laid her gently on her bed and removed the blanket, he saw she was a mass of welts and streaks, some filled with dried blood. There was no pattern to her stripes. Her whole body was crisscrossed with them, one overlaid atop the other in maddened fury. "Oh God, Moira. How could he do this?"

"Is it really you, Ned? How did you get here?"

"We found Andrew. He's badly wounded, stabbed by that scoundrel Duckworth. Your mother sent me to bring you before he died." Looking at her body, he swore. "If only I'd come sooner."

"You're here. That's all that matters."

Jessie came with the water and soft towels and with Ned began to bath her tormented body. As Moira winced and uttered small cries of pain, Ned said, "I'm sorry, darling. I'm being as gentle as I can."

"I know. It's all right."

Jessie kept making soft sounds that were a mixture of dismay and outrage. She kept calling Winslow a "beast" and "madman."

"Why would he do this?"

"Oh, Mr. Ned, he's an evil man, the evilest man ever. He did this once to Miss Glenna. Tied her up and whipped her real bad. He'd have killed her, except Mr. Daniel found her and rescued her."

"But why Moira?"

Wincing with pain, Moira said, "I-I think he thought I was—was mother. He ke-kept calling me an Irish wen-wench and telling me I re-remembered him."

"He's mad. Just plain mad. I wish I'd shot him."

The bathing removed the caked and blackened smears of blood, but also revealed the mass of welts on her pink skin, some so deep they were still shining with fresh blood. "God, darling, you need a doctor."

"I'll be all right."

"Oh no you won't. I'm going for a doctor."

"Don't, Ned. Please stay."

He would have listened to her had he known a figure dressed in a ridiculous leather costume, his gray eyes crazed with frustrated rage, was lurking at the rear of the building. But Ned did not, and he quickly hustled out of Moira's room, down the stairs and out into the street.

Doctors were scarce in San Francisco in 1851 and Ned did not know the city very well. It took him several minutes to find a doctor's office. It was not yet open and Ned ran in search of the physician at his home. Thus, nearly a half hour had elapsed before Ned, standing on the steps of the doctor's house halfway up the slope of Nob Hill, turned and saw the smoke rising from below. He was transfixed by it for a moment. No real conscious thought came to him. He already knew where the fire was. Only the magnitude of the horror immobilized him. Then he ran down the hill, fear giving his legs greater speed.

Fire was a constant menace in San Francisco, almost a way of life. Hardly a day elapsed without a building or two going up in flames. Large portions of the town were burned out more or less regularly. The sharp winds from the ocean and Bay would whip the flames furiously and the wood shacks and buildings offered ample fuel. Despite the fire danger, San Francisco as yet had no fire equipment. In a sense, everyone was a fireman, running with a bucket as each blaze broke out. Since there was little hope of saving any structure once on fire, most efforts went toward saving nearby buildings to keep the fire from becoming a conflagration.

Ned could see and hear the fire as he ran toward Morgan Manor, and then could feel the heat of it. There was a large crowd in the street and a great deal of shouting and screaming as a bucket brigade tried to save adjacent structures. Ned ferociously pushed his way through the crowd, knocking down two men as he struggled toward the front door.

Someone grabbed him and held on. "You can't go in there. It's suicide."

Ned turned to see King. "Where's Moira?"

"I don't know, but you can't go in there."

Ned jerked away from him and ran into the building. Winslow had started the blaze in the rear, using hot coals from the kitchen to spread the fire. The front of Morgan Manor was as yet largely untouched by flames, though filled with dense smoke. The rear, however, was a mass of flames. They consumed the walls and were spreading over the first floor walls and ceiling. The stairway was a flaming pathway to the second floor.

It was there Ned ran. Covering his mouth with his neckerchief, he bounded up the flaming stairs three and four at a time. The walls and ceiling were already burning as he ran down the hall calling for Moira. The whole upstairs was so filled with smoke, his lungs so pained for air, he felt disoriented for a moment. Then he found her room. For a second he thought it empty, just a mass of gray, yellowish smoke against a background of creeping flames.

"Moira! Moira!"

Against the cracking and roar of the fire he heard a single word, "Ned."

He lurched forward through the smoke, bumped against the bed, then groped for Moira's body. She lay crosswise, having tried to get up to escape. As he bent over to pick her up, he was sent sprawling atop her by a hard blow between his shoulder blades.

"Die! You'll all die!"

He rolled off of Moira and saw a shadowy form above him. Jessie was struggling with Winslow, clawing at him. He was pushing her away with one hand and trying to strike again at Ned with the other.

"Burn! Burn! All of you burn." His voice was maniacal.

Ned struck out with his feet, his closest weapon. Jessie fell to the floor and Winslow staggered backwards, then rushed toward Ned again. But that was long enough for Ned to get to his feet. He met the leaping Winslow with his own arcing fist and felt him crumble to the floor.

Ned bent and picked up Moira and started for the door. "Jessie," he called. And again, "Jessie." There was no reply. At the doorway he bumped into a figure.

"King, I got Moira. Bring Jessie. She's on the floor."

It seemed to Ned the stairway was giving way as he carried Moira down it. The first floor, when he reached it, was rapidly being consumed with flames, but he marched through them with relative safety and carried Moira outside. He handed her to waiting arms and ran back inside.

Again he mounted the stairs, knowing they could not last long, and ran down the hall, meeting King struggling with the heavy weight of Jessie. He pulled and led them forward to the top of the stairs, now a solid mass of flames. "How fast can you move, big brother?"

"Fast enough."

Carrying Jessie between them, they raced down the stairs, jumping the last few feet as the stairs collapsed beneath them.

Moira, wrapped in a blanket, was coming around as they arrived with Jessie and soon both women, as well as Ned and King were coughing the smoke from their lungs.

"Is everyone out now?"

Ned turned toward the voice and amid his coughing said, "All but the man who started it."

Morgan Manor was consumed quickly, putting off such heat the would-be firefighters, as well as the survivors were forced to stand across the street and simply watch it burn.

"What a shame," Ned said. "It was a nice place."

"Think nothing of it," King said. "In San Francisco it'll be rebuilt almost as quickly as it burned down."

"By whom?"

"That remains to be seen."

"Andrew's gold is in there someplace."

King laughed. "Fire won't hurt gold. Just make a great big nugget." He turned his blackened, seared face toward his brother. "Say, did I move fast enough for you, Ned?"

Ned looked at him in amazement. "You know, I believe that's the first time you ever called me anything but little brother."

68

Glenna returned from the gold fields the second day after the fire and immediately diluted her grief over Andrew's death by taking full charge of Moira's recovery. She rented a suitable home and acted for all the world like a combination doctor, nurse and mother hen. The daughter basked in a superabundance of mother love. Her wounds mended quickly.

Glenna and Moira talked a great deal, at times as though words were going out of style and they had to be used up quickly. Glenna told her every detail of her trip to Rich Ba, the finding of Andrew, and again and again, tears running down her cheeks, of his death.

"He had suffered so much Moira, so needlessly. But when he died, he had such a smile on his face, the most benign smile. I know he'd already been with God. He had to have been to smile that way. And when he spoke, his voice was so clear and strong. I know he came back for just a moment to tell me he loved me."

"Oh, Mother."

"And he loved you, dear. He asked for you. I'm so sorry you weren't there to see him."

"It's all right. It couldn't be helped. I'm just glad you found him."

"Oh yes, Moira. If he'd died without ever knowing I

loved him. . . . If he'd never known I'd forgiven him, that none of what happened was his fault. . . . Oh, I couldn't have lived knowing that." She wiped away tears. "Oh, Moira, you do believe he's with God, don't you?"

Daughter smiled at mother. "I'm as sure of it as you are."

Glenna told of burying him under a giant tree on a grassy knoll above his shack. "It really is a lovely spot to rest. I-I couldn't take him to Aurial. It wasn't possible."

Moira held her in her arms and comforted her with gentle pats to her shoulder. "I know, I know. We'll put up a stone marker at Aurial, next to father."

"Yes, that's what we should do." Glenna wept against her daughter's shoulder. "It was a nice service, I think. Just Joe and I, but I said the Twenty-Third Psalm and many prayers—yes, many prayers."

"They were heard, Mother. Believe me they were."

Together mother and daughter cried out their emotion for a few moments. Then Glenna pulled away from her and spread her wet cheeks in a smile. "Enough of tears. I learned my lesson about crying over the past. We have the future, our future. Oh, Moira, I'm so glad I have you."

"Yes, Mother, yes."

They talked of Winslow and Moira listened, now able to understand and appreciate the old tales of Three Oaks in Ireland and her father's rescue of her mother.

"Why did he hate you so, Mother?"

"I don't know, really. Oh sure, I knew later. I had escaped him. I was a threat because I knew what kind of a man he really was. When I told Lord Penwood about him, I destroyed him. But I've never understood why he hated me in the beginning. He was an English nobleman. Surely there was little harm an Irish girl could do him. I can only conclude there is so much hate in the world—and hate always causes trouble."

"For the haters especially."

"It certainly ruined Lord Winslow's life."

"He was mad, Mother—absolutely crazy. I saw it in his eyes."

"Yes. Perhaps he was always mad. Maybe that explains the whole thing. I should have pitied him more, I suppose."

"As one pities a viper. You never harmed him, Mother—no more than he deserved. You only tried to escape him—and thank God you did." She hugged her mother to prove the statement.

"You, too, darling. He's gone at last. Let's forget Lord James Charles Winslow."

Mostly they spoke of their future.

"Are you going to rebuild Morgan Manor?"

"No, never. It was never the life for me. I hated it."

"Me, too. I only ran the place a few days. It was enough to find out it wasn't me. I can't be that."

"Then you don't want it?"

"Heavens no. There's nothing to have anyway, except ashes."

Glenna hesitated, then decided to speak. "King wants to rebuild. He has Winslow's money. I told him to go ahead. Is that all right?"

"Fine. It's the life for him. It's what he wants."

"Then . . . you and he . . ."

"It's over, Mother," she said, and received the biggest hug of her life from her mother.

She told King the same, although more tactfully when he came to visit her.

"So how's the maiden in distress?"

When she looked at him, it seemed to her she was seeing him for the first time. He was so incredibly handsome, that dark hair and mustache, that devilish smile, that remarkable cleft in his chin. His suit was impeccable and his self-assured manner so appealing. It was not hard for her to understand her attraction for him.

"Fine, King. I'm going to be as good as new."

He sat down on the bed beside her. "And that's awfully good, you know."

She smiled her pleasure at his compliment. He did know how to make a woman feel good. "I hear you're rebuilding Morgan Manor."

"Yes, bigger and better. Going to be the finest place in the West—maybe the East, too."

"I'm glad for you, King."

He smiled. "What d'you mean, me? It's for us. We'll—"

"No, King. It's no life for me. Those days I was in charge were monstrous. I can't."

"Okay, then we'll get a manager—"

"Lila?"

He hesitated, obviously embarrassed. "Yes, sure, why not? She'd be very good at it. Excellent suggestion."

She laughed at him. "As if you hadn't already thought of it."

His embarrassment deepened. "Of course I'd thought of it, but I didn't know how—how you'd feel."

"I think it's the perfect thing for you to do."

"Splendid. She can get the place going while we're off to Paris."

She looked down at her hands. "No, King," she said softly, then looked up at him. "You must know as well as I."

"Know what?"

"I'm not the girl for you. I'm not what you need. I can never be the girl you want."

"Don't be silly."

"I'm not being silly. I'm being sensible. Nothing like knowing you may be going to die to make you sensible."

He seemed genuinely distressed. "But you and I. All we did together, all—"

"It was wonderful, wasn't it? I'll always think of you as the handsomest, most dashing—" She started to say "man," but didn't. "—the most exciting lover in the world. But it takes more than excitement, doesn't it? You have to come down off the mountain top sometime."

"But Moira . . ."

"Stop protesting. You know I'm right."

"I know no such thing." His voice had raised. "Is it because Ned rescued you?"

She laughed. "He does make a habit of it, doesn't he?"

"It could have been me just as well."

"Of course. King, isn't it enough that I'm grateful to you? You made me a real woman. With you I felt like the most beautiful and exciting woman in the world."

"You were. You are."

Again she laughed. "I did learn a lot and I think I'm blushing."

He looked at her intently. "You don't love me?"

She took his hand in hers. "I've come down from the mountain, King, that exciting mountain you live on. I'm not for you. Lila is."

"A black woman!"

Moira's laughter flooded over him. "And why not? That was her picture that time in Washington, wasn't it?"

"Yes."

"She's beautiful, King. Really remarkable skin. And she's used to the sort of life you lead. And she loves you."

"What're you talking about?"

"I saw you and her together. You may fool yourself, but not me."

"I'll never give you up."

Again she laughed. "My, but you're wonderful. Every woman should have some handsome man in her life who is pining away for her."

And so he became.

Captain Ian MacDoul returned, proudly sailing his clipper ship into San Francisco Bay. When Moira first saw her mother and him together, it bothered her a little. It was so strange. Her mother looked so tiny snuggled against Cap'n Mac's massive shoulder, his great arm around her. It didn't look right. It wasn't right. He was different from her father, so big, a red beard, so jolly and hearty and loud. She felt pangs of grief for her father nearly as great as when he had been killed.

But such feelings were only fleeting, swept away by Glenna's happiness.

"Is it all right, Moira?"

"Oh yes, Mother, yes, yes. He loves you so much."

"And I love him. Not as your father, Moira. I can never hope to replace him, but—"

"I do understand, Mother. It is so right, so very right." She kissed her. "Just be happy."

Cap'n Mac brought news which Moira knew she needed to tell Ned. Thus, it was a bright, warm afternoon in early August, 1851, that she flicked the reins and spurred the horse to greater speed along *El Camino Real*. She looked particularly lovely, in her new yellow dress trimmed with white lace and ribbons. She wore a matching sun hat with a wide brim. Beside her on the seat of the buggy was a small parasol, matching her dress.

It had been several days since she had seen Ned. So much had happened. She was so eager to see him and tell him. At last she approached La Paloma and turned the buggy into the lane to the Ramirez hacienda. Señora Ramirez had seen her coming and met her in the courtyard as she drove up. There was an abundance of hugs and kisses and repetitions of *"monísima"* and *"muy bonita."*

Rather than go inside, Moira waited in the garden, sitting on a bench under a flowering mimosa tree. The yellow blossoms matched her gown and she was a vision to Ned when he approached. He wore work clothes, and his hands were dirty, his boots dusty.

"I'm sorry to keep you waiting," he said, "I was—"
Then he looked at himself and became embarrassed. "I guess I'm a sight."

She laughed. "For sore eyes."

He had stopped perhaps half a dozen steps in front of her. "You're a vision, Moira. I like you in yellow."

"Thank you, sir. Come sit in the shade."

"Yes," he said. As he sat, he started to take her hands in his, then stopped because his own were dirty.

Again she laughed at him and clasped his hands in hers. "Honest dirt never soiled anyone."

"Oh, Moira, it's so good to see you."

"You *have* been staying away."

"Not intentionally. I figured you were in good hands with your mother. You must have lots to talk about."

"Oh yes, and I'm bursting to tell you. Cap'n Mac has come. He sailed the *Glenna Morgan* into the bay. I went on it with mother. It's the most beautiful ship in the world. He sailed it around the world, setting a record on the Shanghai-London leg. And that's not the best part."

Smiling at her happiness, he teased her. "There can't be more?"

"Yes, yes, Mother and Mac are going to be married."

"Married?"

"Yes, actually married by a priest and everything. I'm so happy for her."

"What about Morgan Manor?"

"Oh, she never wanted it. I asked her. She said, 'It's never been the life for me. I only had it to find my children'."

"Then she's going to be a sea captain's wife?"

Excitement seemed to bubble out of her. "Yes, yes. And she's going to sail with him, seeing the world at his side. I think it's so thrilling."

"What about Aurial? I thought you were going to buy it back with Andrew's gold."

The mention of Aurial triggered her memory. "Lord,

Ned, I forgot the real reason I came to see you. Oh God, how could I?"

He saw her change of mood and sought to avert it. "And here I thought you came to see me."

"I'm serious, Ned. Cap'n Mac brought awful news. He stopped at Baltimore. Ned—your father—he's dead."

She saw him sit there a moment, unmoving, then stand up and turn his back to her. "I'm sorry, Ned. He was always kind to me." She didn't know what else to say.

After a time he spoke. "Well, I guess I'm not surprised. He was of that age."

His back to her, she heard him sniffle, and saw him raise his arm to wipe his nose with the back of his hand. When he turned to her his eyes were moist.

"Does King know?"

"Yes." She didn't know what else to say but that single word, nor did he ask for more information. She felt awkward, unable to console him properly. Suddenly she realized she did not understand his relationship with his father. She knew her own heartbreak at her father's death. Was that what Ned was feeling?

"That wasn't much to say about him, was it?"

"What?"

"He was of that age. I'm sorry he's gone. I'd always hoped there might be more between us some day, but it's too late now."

"There's a letter." She reached into her purse and handed it to him. "It's from a law firm in Baltimore."

He held it in his hand, reading the address. "It's for both King and me. He's the eldest. Shouldn't he read it first?"

"Does it matter so much? Open it."

He ripped the seal with a stained finger. She watched as he pulled out a heavy sheath of folded paper.

"It's his will."

"I thought as much." She saw him reading. It was a moment or two before she realized he was crying. Not until a tear appeared as a drop in his eyes, hanging a minute before dropping, did she know how hard he was struggling to choke back his sobs.

He handed her the papers and sat beside her. Brusquely he said, "There's a letter. You read it."

She glanced at the handwriting. "Is it from your father?"

"Yes."

"Shall I read it aloud?" She saw him nod assent. She read for a moment to herself, then began in a soft, clear voice, as though reciting in class:

My Dear Sons:

All my life I coveted my neighbor's property. I felt it belonged to me—or rightfully ought to—and I hated my neighbor for his good fortune in owning it. I schemed for years to own Aurial. When the opportunity came I thought I was very happy. I bought Aurial for a song from that scoundrel Winslow. I live here now. I can overlook the river even as I write this. It is a life's dream. Or is it? I walk these rooms and these grounds surrounded by beauty. Yet there is none for me. I am alone with no one to share my triumph. Such a hollow one it is. My Rachel is in her grave these many years. I have two sons, but I've no idea where either one is.

If this letter ever reaches either of you, believe the sadness of an old man alone. Triumph is disaster. I gave my life to coveting and scheming what was another man's. Such a wasted life is mine. I neglected my wife. I neglected my sons, most especially you, Ned. I apologize to you both. Please forgive me.

Father

Moira was barely able to read the last swimming words aloud, and when she finished she saw and heard Ned crying openly. His voice distorted, he asked, "How did he die?"

"Don't ask," she sobbed and buried her face and

hands against his shoulder. "I'm so sorry, Ned, so terribly sorry."

They wept in each other's arms for a bit, then separated. There were moments for embarrassment, wan smiles, and the blowing of noses into respective hankies.

To fill the void in conversation, Ned took the papers from her and read the accompanying will. "He's left the whole estate to me. King is to receive bonds and shares in railroads." He read a moment more, then folded the papers and put them in his pocket. "Since the estate is mine, I'm returning Aurial to you."

She gasped, "No."

"Yes, it rightfully belongs to you and Mrs. Morgan."

"Mother doesn't want it. She's going to sea, remember?"

"Then it's yours. I insist on it." He had expected happiness. Instead he saw her frowning. "What's the matter? Don't you want it?"

"I don't want to live there alone anymore than your father did."

"Then you don't want it?"

"I said alone, silly." Now she smiled at him. "You asked me once what kind of life I wanted. I said I didn't know. I—"

"And you do now?"

She laughed lightly. "Lately, I find myself thinking a great deal about the wonderful smell of curing tobacco. Besides, with you rescuing me all the time, I ought to stay close to make it easier for you."

"What about your great romance with brother King?"

"It seems he won all of Winslow's money playing poker. He's already rebuilding Morgan Manor, although he'll call it something else—probably Lila's Place."

"Lila?"

"Yes. They're partners." She laughed. "And in more ways than one."

"I still find it hard to believe."

"I did at first, but they really are much alike. I talked to her. She's really not a bad person. She wants to get out of—has for a long time. She's right for King. I'm sure of it."

"It's still hard to believe." He laughed for a moment, but when it ended, there was an awkward silence. "That leaves you and me, doesn't it?"

She looked at him intently. "Do you know what's been hardest for me in all this?"

He smiled. "There are several excellent choices."

"I'm serious. The hardest thing for me was back there in the mountains when—"

"I can understand. Jack Knight was—"

"I'm not talking about him. I'm talking about you and me. The hardest thing for me was not being able to say I loved you when you wanted me to." She looked intently at his somber face. "Is it too late for me to say it now and truly mean it. I love you Ned Kingston—with all my heart."

Under the mimosa tree in the garden, watched by bright brown eyes from inside the hacienda, they kissed, long and deeply and passionately.

"God, Moira, I want you. Let's get married right away."

She was breathless from her passion, but still could tease him. "I thought you wanted to wait till we got to Aurial."

"Hang Aurial. I can't wait any longer for you."

She jumped up. "Let's see if Señora Ramirez knows a padre. I want to be married in Spanish."

"What about your mother?"

"She and Mac can be married in Spanish, too."

Unable to resist, he scooped her in his arms and kissed her again. But she broke away. "There is one problem, though. Jessie insists on returning to Aurial with me and Joe says he can never leave mother's side."

"Heavens. There's no end to problems in this life," he said, bending his mouth again to hers.